D0065512

WITHDRAWN

10×5-10 (2-11)
14×6-13 (10-13)
17×(7/15)10/16

Dear Reader,

I couldn't be happier that *The Wind Dancer* and *Storm Winds* are being released in one volume. They are two of my favorite books of all time. When I first got the idea for these two historicals, I knew they'd be special to me. The concept of moving a mystical statue joined with the history of a family through centuries was intriguing. The research was mesmerizing. But once begun, everything else soon took second place to the characters. I *love* these characters. They came alive for me and wrote the books themselves.

From the moment I finished *The Wind Dancer* and *Storm Winds*, I wanted to share them with everyone. I wanted everyone to love Lionello, Sanchia, Jean Marc, Caterina, and all the rest of them as much as I did. And Lorenzo. How could I not mention him, when he was so fascinating to me? You'll understand after you finish *The Wind Dancer*.

Do you get the impression that I'm a little enthusiastic? Even after all these years I still feel all the emotion, the love, the laughter, and the tears that I felt when I first wrote these books.

Join me. Come into the Wind Dancer world. You won't be sorry.

Happy reading!

Iris

SAN CARLOS BRANCH LIBRARY
7265 JACKSON DR
SAN DIEGO, CA 92119

SEP 2 5 2008

BOOKS BY IRIS JOHANSEN

P9-DXM-841

The Wind Dancer

——

Storm Winds

IRIS JOHANSEN

SAN DIEGO PUBLIC LIBRARY
SAN CARLOS BRANCH

BANTAM BOOKS

SEP 2 5 2008

THE WIND DANCER/STORM WINDS
A Bantam Book / February 2008

Published by
Bantam Dell
A Division of Random House, Inc.
New York, New York

These are works of fiction. Names, characters, places, and incidents either
are the product of the author's imagination or are used fictitiously. Any
resemblance to actual persons, living or dead, events, or locales is
entirely coincidental.

All rights reserved
The Wind Dancer copyright © 1991 by Iris Johansen
Storm Winds copyright © 1991 by Iris Johansen
Cover art by Alan Ayers

These titles were originally published individually by Bantam Dell.

Bantam Books and the rooster colophon are registered trademarks of
Random House, Inc.

ISBN 978-0-553-38572-4

Printed in the United States of America
Published simultaneously in Canada

www.bantamdell.com

OPM   10 9 8 7 6 5 4 3 2 1

The Wind Dancer

The Wind Dancer was born of a
    white-hot bolt of lightning.
So legend has it.

The Wind Dancer's worth was beyond price;
    its beauty beyond belief.
So legend has it.

The Wind Dancer could punish the evil,
    could reward the good.
So legend has it.

The Wind Dancer wielded the power
    to alter the destinies of men and nations.
So legend has it.

But legend, like history, can be distorted by time,
    robbed of truth by cynicism—
        yet be gifted with splendor by imagination.

One

Stop, thief! Stop her! I've been robbed!"

Sanchia tore across the Mercato Vecchio, raced past the church and on down the street, jumping over an emaciated brown-and-white mongrel that devoured garbage scattered over the flagstones. She ducked under the outstretched arm of a leather-aproned cobbler, but his large hand caught the coarse woolen shawl covering her head. She jerked it from his grasp and kept running.

The merchant chasing her was plump, but still he was closing the distance between them, and Sanchia's heart slammed against her ribcage in a delirium of panic.

She was going to be caught.

Her hands would be chopped off at the wrists.

She would be thrown in the Stinche to be eaten by the rats.

Hot, agonizing pain shot through her left side. A stitch. She had to keep running.

What would Piero do? she wondered wildly. The others were older; they would find a way to survive. But Piero was only six. So many things could happen to so young a child. . . .

"Grab her, you fools. The slut stole my purse!"

Dio, Sanchia thought, he sounded close. How could he run so fast with all those rolls of fat hanging around his middle? She dodged around a wheelbarrow filled with fish, turned the corner of the Canto di Vaccereccia, then bolted down an alley yawning between a goldsmith's shop and an apothecary.

Darkness. Twilight lay over the city but full darkness reined in the alley.

Bright eyes glittered in the deep shadows at the base of the small buildings.

Rats. Dozens of them!

She stopped short, involuntarily recoiling.

The stones beneath the thin soles of her shoes were greasy from the garbage thrown out there by shopkeepers. She need have no fear of the rats, though, while they were feasting on the garbage.

The smell of rotting food in the closeness of the alley was overpowering. She swallowed, trying to fight down the nausea caused as much from terror as the stench.

"Which way did she go?"

The merchant's voice was wheezing and sounded a little farther away. Had she lost him when she darted into the alley? She shrank back into the densely clotted shadows of the goldsmith's shop, her palms pressed flat against the stone wall. Her breath was coming in harsh, painful gasps. Could he hear her? She tried to hold her breath, but there was no breath to hold. *Cristo*, what if he had heard her?

The cold, wet slime-covered wall chilled her back as it penetrated the wool of her gown. Her muscles felt leaden, the blood frozen in her veins. She was suddenly acutely conscious of the sharp, rough texture of the stone wall against her palms, but the sensation was almost pleasurable. Touch. What would she do without her hands? How could she live? How would all of them live?

"This way, you stupid blunderer."

She stiffened. The voice was not that of the fat merchant but one with which she was bitterly familiar. Her heart gave a wild leap of hope. The alley door of the apothecary shop had opened, and even in the darkness she recognized Caprino's slight, foppishly dressed silhouette.

She darted the few yards separating them and almost fell through the doorway into the shop. Her gaze flew to the front of the store, but the apprentice behind the small counter was scrupulously avoiding looking in her direction.

"He's safe," Caprino said. "He does work for me."

Poison, Sanchia thought with a shiver, or perhaps the strange white powders Caprino gave his whores.

Caprino slammed the door and held out his hand. "The purse."

She fumbled beneath her shawl for the soft leather pouch and then dropped it into his palm. She leaned back against the door, her knees shaking so badly she could barely stand upright.

"You were clumsy," Caprino said harshly. "I should have let that fat fool catch you. Next time I will."

She had to wait until she could speak without panting. "There won't be a next time. I'm never going to do it again."

"You will," Caprino said coolly. "You're frightened now, but it will pass. You'll forget the fear and remember only the money that buys bread. You're not usually this clumsy. You may not come this close to being caught for the next ten lifts."

"I'll find another way." Sanchia's hands clenched at her sides. "There has to be another way."

"You didn't think so when you came to me." Caprino opened the door. "I have no more time for you. I have important business at Giulia's. Stay here for another few minutes before you go back to Giovanni's." The door swung shut behind him.

He hadn't given Sanchia her share of the purse, she realized dully. Trust Caprino to try to steal even the smallest purse, if given the opportunity. She would have to seek him out tomorrow and demand her portion. She had mouths to feed and Caprino was right about hunger being a sharp dagger that might goad even a saint into thieving.

But was hunger worth the risk of having her hands chopped off?

Fresh panic clutched at her as a chilling memory returned. Two months before she had seen a thief thrown out of Stinche Prison into the streets, his arms ending in bleeding stumps. Since then the fear of that punishment had lived with her during the day and invaded her dreams at night, She had tried and tried to think of another way to earn money to feed them, all the while fearing her frantic scheming would come to nought. There was no other way.

As there would be no other way the next time or the time after that. She would have to steal again just as Caprino had predicted. But he was wrong about the terror holding her in helpless thrall; it wasn't a thing of the moment.

She knew the fear would never go away again.

"Good evening, noble messeres, I have the honor to present to you my greetings. I am Guido Caprino." Caprino stood in the doorway and smiled ingratiatingly at the two men sitting at the polished table across the chamber. "The enchanting Madonna Giulia assured me I could be of some slight service to you."

He carefully kept a bland expression on his face as he appraised the two men. The older had to be Lorenzo Vasaro, he decided. His high cheekbones and deepset eyes matched the description Giulia had given him of the man—and besides, Caprino's own instincts responded to the shadowy aura of menace surrounding him. The man was lean, faultlessly elegant in his fashionably slashed black doublet, and clearly more dangerous than his companion. He gazed at the other man and felt a ripple of distaste. He was so *male*. Lionello Andreas might stand well over six feet, Caprino surmised, and he was too big-boned to lay claim to elegance no matter how richly he was garbed. Now, dressed only in gray hose and a loose white shirt, he appeared to be exactly what Caprino had expected: a barbarian warrior with more brawn than brains, he was not wearing a weapon, not even a dagger. Andreas might be the lord of Mandara, but Caprino would wager it was Vasaro who was the shrewd power behind the scenes there.

"Come in, Messer Caprino." Andreas picked up the silver goblet on the table in front of him and waved it at a cushioned chair beside the window before raising it to his lips. "Be seated."

The arrogant bastard hadn't bothered to stand up to greet him properly, Caprino thought as he smiled politely and crossed the room to take the seat indicated. No doubt Andreas did not think him worthy of respect. He would soon learn differently.

Lorenzo Vasaro rose and moved with silent grace to lean against the wall to the left of the window. He folded his arms across his chest and gazed blandly at Caprino.

A good move. Caprino's respect for Vasaro rose even higher. His action had placed Caprino between Vasaro and Andreas. Caprino was tempted to address Vasaro as the worthier of the two but turned instead to Andreas. "I am always overjoyed to accommodate any friends of Madonna Giulia. What is your pleasure?"

"I need a thief." Andreas leaned back in his chair and studied Caprino with narrowed eyes.

Caprino met his eyes and continued to smile politely. "It will be my pleasure to provide you with the finest thief in all of Florence, Your Magnificence. Only a thief, or must he possess other talents? An assassin, perhaps? I have a few associates who have talents in that direction, but no one with the extraordinary skills of Messer Vasaro."

Andreas stiffened. "You know of Vasaro?"

"How could I not?" Caprino remained sitting forward in his chair, one graceful hand resting with seeming casualness on the jeweled hilt of his dagger. "He shines in the firmament like a bright star, dazzling all who see him. Is it any wonder I should recognize him?"

"Not at all." Andreas cast an amused glance at Vasaro, who was still gazing at Caprino with no expression. "Do you hear that, Lorenzo? A star, by all that's holy. Aren't you going to thank the kind gentleman?"

Lorenzo inclined his head in acknowledgment.

"No thanks are needed," Caprino said quickly. "I merely gave homage where homage was due. It was foolish of me to suggest you might need an assassin when Messer Vasaro is in your service. Why should you need any—"

"As you say, I need no assassin," Andreas interrupted with sudden impatience. "I need a thief with hands as swift and sure as an arrow drawn by a master bowman and a touch as delicate as the kiss of a butterfly."

"There are many thieves in Florence," Caprino said thoughtfully. "I myself have trained an honored few."

"So I've been informed." Andreas's lips twisted in a cynical smile. "No doubt you've also tutored many individuals in my friend Lorenzo's former profession."

Caprino shrugged. "One or two. But to be an assassin requires a certain fortitude not found in every man. A thief is different. Easier. Not as profitable but . . ." He trailed off. "How long would you need this thief, my lord Andreas?"

Andreas went still. "You know me also?" His voice was dangerously soft. "Does my name, too, shine in the firmament?"

Caprino's hand tightened on the hilt of his dagger. He could feel a bead of moisture dampen his temple as he realized his mistake. He had judged Vasaro to be the threat. A stupid error. In his experience most soldiers, even condottieri, had none of the skill and subtlety Caprino admired. But he shouldn't have let his contempt for the profession overshadow his judgment of the man. No, that was not entirely true, Caprino admitted reluctantly. His instinctive revulsion at Andreas's overpowering virility had also contributed to the blunder by keeping him from a serious study of the man.

Now he discerned the intelligence, as well as cynicism, in Andreas's brilliant dark eyes which were fully as merciless as those of Vasaro. Caprino moistened his lower lip with his tongue. "Your fame has spread over all Italy, my lord. An illustrious condottiere such as yourself must expect to be recognized and—" Caprino broke off. "I had no idea your visit to our city was in secret. If you wish to go unrecognized, then it goes without saying that I never have seen your face, never heard the sound of your voice, never even heard your name pronounced."

"And who did pronounce my name to you?" Andreas asked silkily. "And on what subject? I asked Giulia to tell no one I was in Florence."

"You know how careless women can be, *Magnifico*. When Madonna Giulia summoned me here, she mentioned your name but nothing else. I swear this, my lord Andreas. Would the Madonna have sent for me if I wasn't a man of discretion and honor?"

"Lorenzo?" Andreas's gaze never left Caprino's face.

Vasaro's voice was hoarse and scratchy as a wooden coffin pulled over flagstones. "He will betray you for a price high enough. Shall I dispose of him?" Lorenzo asked as casually as if he'd inquired about throwing out the dregs of the wine in Andreas's cup.

Caprino leaned forward in his chair, prepared to spring, his dagger at the ready for a—

"I think not," Andreas said. "He doesn't know enough to hurt me, and I'd find it inconvenient to search out another procurer."

"A wise decision." Caprino's grasp on his dagger relaxed. "A man should always keep the long view in mind. Now about this thief?"

"Just this moment I have thought of a quality he must possess," Andreas said, looking down at his heavy leather gauntlets on the table. "I must own him."

"Own?"

Andreas's long, broad index finger rubbed at the brass riveting of the gauntlet. "He must be mine body and soul. I'll not have him running back to you with tales you can sell to the highest bidder." Andreas smiled. "Of course, I could have him removed after he finishes his task, but I dislike rewarding good work in that fashion. Not an intelligent way to proceed."

"I can see that." Caprino's uneasy gaze darted to Vasaro. Rumor had it that Vasaro had accepted service with Andreas when the condottiere was a boy of seventeen. How had Andreas managed to hold such a skilled assassin all these years? Did he own *him* body and soul as he wished to own the thief? It was something to ponder, for who but Satan was capable of possessing a demon? "Such men aren't easy to find. How could I—"

"You must know ways." Andreas pulled a purse from his belt and tossed it on the table to Caprino. "Greed, revenge, a woman. We both know the weapons to bind a man. Use them."

Caprino opened the pouch and counted the ducats. "A fair price."

"A princely sum for one insignificant thief, as well you know, but a small price for the soul of a human being."

Caprino smiled. "I'm sure you'll discover shortly whether or not that is so." He paused. "I'm to keep this?" he asked as he tucked the purse inside his belt. "I'm honored by your trust."

"I can afford to trust you, Caprino. I know where to find you, if you disappoint me. When can I expect you to send me the thief I've paid for?"

"I'm not sure." Caprino stood up and edged toward the door. "I must consider and de—"

"Tomorrow." Andreas's tone had not changed, but his smile held the gleam of a feral creature. "No later than three. I'm an impatient man." His gaze searched Caprino's face. "You already have someone in mind. Bring him to me."

Caprino was startled. "But, Your Magnificence, I must study and think upon . . ." He stopped. How had that whoreson Andreas managed to read him so easily? "I do have someone in mind who might meet your requirements, but there are difficulties."

"Overcome them."

"I may need many more ducats than this pouch holds in order to do so."

Andreas's lips tightened. "I have an aversion to being preyed upon by the greedy. It would be wise to remember that."

Caprino lowered his lids to veil his eyes. "I'll not be beggared to obtain what you want. I'm worthy of my hire."

"If I slip a dagger between his ribs tonight, tomorrow there will be another Caprino in the streets of Florence," Vasaro said with little inflection. "Perhaps a man less greedy to deal with, Lion."

Caprino felt a chill quiver through him but carefully kept himself under control. He nodded. "Tomorrow or the next day or the day after that. I'm not so foolish as to think I'm irreplaceable. But Your Magnificence is impatient, and I'm the man who can help you today."

Andreas was silent for a moment during which Caprino tasted the sourness of fear.

Then Andreas made an impatient gesture. "I must see the skill of your light-fingered villian." He paused. "Tomorrow."

"But it's too soon. I can't—" Caprino stopped. He had gained a valuable concession, and it would be best not to push too hard at this juncture. "As Your Excellency bids me, I will move heaven and earth to do as you wish."

"I'll be at the Piazza of San Michele tomorrow at two with another purse containing an equal number of ducats," Andreas said. "If your thief can claim it from my person, the purse is yours. If not . . ." He shrugged. "Then I will be most unhappy with you. So unhappy they may end up fishing you out of the Arno." He waved a hand of dismissal. "Good night, Caprino. Why don't you see the gentleman to his home, Lorenzo?"

"It isn't far. I have a house near the piazza." Caprino moved quickly toward the door. "Good evening, my lords. Until tomorrow."

Andreas smiled mockingly. "Do accompany him, Lorenzo. The streets are so dangerous for a man with a purse full of ducats."

Andreas was toying with him, Caprino realized with a surge of rage. He turned at the door and smiled through clenched teeth. "You test whether I'm afraid of Messer Lorenzo? Well, I do fear him. I'm not a brave man, but it's not courage that's made me what I am. You might consider who has called the tune this night." His index finger tapped his left temple. "Up here. That's what counts." He bowed. "As you shall see tomorrow. "

The door swung shut behind him, and the breath immediately rushed from Caprino's lungs in a soft explosion of sound as the tension eased from him. He straightened his short scarlet cape, meticulously adjusted his velvet cap at the angle he preferred, and started down the stairs. He gazed appraisingly at the painting of Venus in all her naked glory on the wall beside the stairs. The painting was new and exceptionally well executed, but the Venus was not overly beautiful, a circumstance which did not surprise him. Giulia would never permit anything or anyone to overshadow her own charms in her own *casa*.

"Buona sera, Caprino." Giulia Marzo met him at the bottom of the stairs. She smiled sweetly. "All is well?"

Caprino shifted his cloak to reveal the purse.

She held out her hand palm upward. "A joy to work with you, Caprino."

"Tomorrow," he said as he tried to edge past her.

"Now." Her smile never wavered. "Or I'll tell my lord Andreas you have no intention of fulfilling your promise to find his thief and even now are hurrying toward the city gates. I doubt you would ever reach that splendid house paid for by the ducats stolen from your whores and thieves."

He stopped short and turned to look at her. He should have known Giulia would have been listening to everything taking place in Andreas's chamber. It was not only the slut's golden beauty that had caused her to rise from one of his own brothels to own this fine *casa*. He reluctantly opened the pouch and pressed five ducats into her palm. "Someday, when I lose patience with you, I'll have you brought back to me," he said softly. "And I'll strip you naked and stake you out in an alley and sell that sweet-smelling flesh to every man who walks by.

How do you think your fine lords will like you after a few weeks of such use?"

"You don't frighten me." She shrugged. "You cannot hurt me, Caprino. I have the protection of many powerful men here in Florence."

"Like that bastard up there?" Caprino jerked his head in the direction of the door at the top of the stairs. "Andreas has no power here in Florence. He rules only in Mandara."

"At present." Giulia's gaze lifted to look at the door he'd indicated. "Lion could rule anywhere. Men such as he are rare."

Caprino's gaze narrowed on her face. "Do I detect a trace of lust, *madonna mia*? Be careful, or you'll lose your one weapon in Cupid's battle. A whore must never lust; she must only be lusted after."

"He *does* lust after me," she said fiercely. "For two years he has come to my *casa*. Never has he asked for any of the other women, only me." Then as she met Caprino's satisfied gaze she tried to shrug unconcernedly. "Not that it matters."

"I think it does matter to you." He studied her. "I wonder why? You have the most peculiar tastes. I find him quite ugly."

"How would you know? I've provided you with too many pretty young boys and wretched-looking men not to know how peculiar are *your* tastes, Caprino."

He tucked the purse into his belt and said mockingly, "He's far too rough for my refined taste. Soldiers can be so crude. But there's another five ducats for you if you find out why our brave condottiere wishes the services of a thief."

Giulia's gaze returned to the door at the top of the stairs. "I'll consider it. But he's not a man who babbles to a woman."

"Not even to *la bella* Giulia?" He turned away. "Seven ducats."

He opened the door and strode out into the street.

It had been a good evening's work, he thought contentedly. The stakes Andreas was hoping to win must be very high to make him yield to Caprino's demands with so little argument. If he was clever he might be able to milk this situation until it rained even more gold into his coffers.

He turned at the next corner and instead of proceeding to his own house off the piazza, he started in the direction of the Via Calimala and the print shop of Giovanni Ballano.

"You gave in too easily," Lorenzo said as the door closed behind Caprino. "I could have persuaded him to take less."

Lion lifted the goblet to his lips. "If Caprino brings me what I want, it will be worth the price."

Lorenzo shrugged. "If you believe it to be so."

"I do." Lion propped his feet on the table, crossing his legs at the ankles. "We leave the day after tomorrow for Solinari."

"If Caprino's thief succeeds in your little test."

"He'd better, or I'll let you have Caprino to persuade as you deem fitting."

The faintest smile lifted Lorenzo's lips. "No, you won't."

Lion lifted a black brow. "You think I'm too kind to condemn Caprino to your tender care?"

"I think you would take pleasure in punishing Caprino yourself, but you'd not give him to me." His gaze met Lion's. "Why do you persist in trying to save my soul when I lost it long ago? When I was a child of eleven, to be precise. That was when I killed my first man. What were you doing when you were eleven, Lion?"

"Following my father's banner, watching his men pillage and rape cities. I killed my first man when I was thirteen." He paused. "And I don't consider my soul lost."

"Ah, but your killing was bathed in glory and honor," Lorenzo said softly. "There's no glory in the world of an assassin."

"Killing is killing."

"If you thought that was true, you'd let me go after Caprino."

Lion smiled. "Perhaps I will."

"No, you won't. To do it, you'd have to live in Caprino's world. My world."

"It's not your world. Your world is Mandara now."

"Because you say it is?"

"Because you earned a place there thirteen years ago."

"With an assassin's knife."

"Which saved my life and avenged my father."

"Glory and honor." Lorenzo's gravelly voice was mocking. "You see how your mind works? I fear you have a grievous fault, Lion. Somehow you've managed to acquire the instincts of a bygone age. Chivalry will never prevail in a land where men like me can grow rich."

"Chivalry? My God, you're demented, Lorenzo. No one is more of a realist than I. If you want chivalry, I'm afraid you'll have to apply to Marco."

"I agree your brother is sickeningly pure and honorable, but I suspect you're infected with a less virulent form of the same disease." As Lion started to speak, Lorenzo held up his hand. "Perhaps you don't adhere to the philosophy, my friend, but the instinct is certainly there. Look how you've insisted on trying to keep me by your side so I wouldn't return to cutting the throats of the illustrious noblemen of Naples."

"Most of them needed killing."

"But I never inquired whether they did or not." Lorenzo smiled faintly. "Killing is killing."

"By all that's holy, Lorenzo, will you stop turning my words against me? Why will you not admit that you're no longer what you were?"

"Because I am what I am and what I was and what I will be."

"Cristo!" Lion drew an exasperated breath. "And what are you then, damn your cryptic soul?"

A sudden smile lit Lorenzo's narrow face. "I told you I had no soul. I am many things but I can think of only one that has merit."

"And what is that?"

"I'm the friend of Lionello Andreas," Lorenzo said softly.

Lion gazed at him suspiciously. "I have the uneasy feeling you're making mock of me again."

Lorenzo raised his brows. "But of course," he said blandly. "How can a man who has no soul know friendship? I'm glad you're so perceptive. It shows I've trained you well in these last thirteen years."

Lion swore softly beneath his breath. "Lorenzo, someday I'll—"

"My lord, the hour grows late." Giulia Marzo was standing in the doorway smiling at them. "If you please, I'll show Messer Vasaro to his chamber. Does he wish a companion? I have a sweet little Sicilian girl who could show him much pleasure."

"Lorenzo?" Lion glanced at Vasaro.

Lorenzo shook his head. "Not tonight."

"Nor any night of late." Lion gazed at him speculatively. "I fear you're beginning to have the tastes of a monk. It was not always so."

"I'm an old man of forty-four. Perhaps I've lost my virility," Lorenzo said lightly as he turned and moved toward the door. "I find my books more stimulating than these fair flowers at present. But pray don't let me stop you from frolicking in Venus's garden."

"I won't." Lion's lingering gaze ran over Giulia's bare shoulders and then down to the fullness of her breasts. "I promise you."

When Giulia returned minutes later, Lion was still sitting in the same position, his feet propped on the table, his gaze fixed thoughtfully on his wine goblet.

"Vasaro is a strange man." Giulia closed the door and leaned back against it. "Are you not afraid to call him your friend? Caprino says Vasaro is—"

"No worse than any of us," Lion interrupted. "We live in violent times, and a man must be violent to survive and hold what is his."

"Or take what is another's?" Giulia asked, amused. "Is that why you need a thief?"

His gaze narrowed on her face. "I have no liking for questions, Giulia." He smiled. "In fact, I consider the forming of words a sinful waste from lips that are so accomplished at other occupations. Take off your clothes, *cara*."

Giulia felt the muscles of her stomach clench as she looked at him. She was breathless and trembling—but not surprised for it had been this way with Lion, since his first visit over two years before. Caprino was right in judging Lion as not handsome. Some might even call him ugly as Caprino had done. His features looked as though they'd been carved from stone by the bold stroke of an ax instead of the delicate chisel of an artist. His cheekbones were too broad, his black brows straight slashes over eyes that were night dark and seldom held any emotion save wariness and cynicism. His lips were well shaped but they, too, held a hint of both sensuality and cruelty. His dark hair was still as closely barbered as the days when he had worn a soldier's helmet, and his body, though lithe, held none of the slim grace of the courtier. Even as he reclined in an indolent position now, his loose white shirt gave hint of the power of his massive shoulders, and the gray hose revealed the might of trunklike thighs and muscular calves.

Power, Giulia realized with a start of surprise. Not only did Lion Andreas possess physical strength and power, but also an inner strength and power far beyond those of other men . . . certainly beyond those of any man she had ever met. His curiosity about life, about what was going on around him was more intense, his potential for good or evil more extreme, his appetites stronger, than in anyone of her experience.

"I'm growing impatient, *cara*. Must I beg?"

"You never beg." She started across the room toward him, unfastening the rope of pearls binding her fair hair. "You take." She dropped the pearls onto a table beside him. "And take." Her palm caressed his thigh and she felt the muscles harden beneath her touch. "Until I cannot even lift one little finger."

"How cruel." He lifted her hand from his thigh and pressed the palm to his lips. "I wonder that you still receive me when I so misuse you." His tongue stroked the sensitive flesh of her palm. "You always smell of roses. When I'm away from you I always remember the scent . . ."

"When you're between the thighs of one of your other whores? You come to Florence only two or three times a year. Who pleasures you when you leave me?"

He glanced up, his dark eyes twinkling. "Perhaps, like Lorenzo, I find solace in Plutarch and Aristotle."

She smiled reluctantly. "Not you. There's too much hunger in you. I doubt you could last a week without a woman. Do you keep a strumpet at Mandara to service you? I know that—" She broke off as she felt the sharp edge of his teeth on her palm exerting just enough pressure to send a thrill of lust, not pain, through her.

Lion's large hand reached up to caress her throat. "Does it matter that there are other women?" His fingers gently stroked the hollow where her heart was pounding wildly. "Why? I never ask you how many men you service when I'm not here." He pulled down the square neckline of her gown to bare her breasts, one callused palm moving to the left. He spread his fingers over her breast and watched the nipple tauten in response. "It's what we are together that concerns me." He leaned forward and his lips closed on her now distended nipple, and she felt his warm tongue tease and caress the distended tip.

"Lion . . ." She swayed toward him, her fingers tangling in his hair. "I could come with you to Mandara."

His head quickly lifted and his eyes became shuttered. "No."

How stupid to make such an offer. It had tumbled out before she'd thought it through, and, she knew, it was generated by sheer jealousy of those other women in his life. Lion would never take her to Mandara. He would not even talk to her about his life away from her. "I was only joking," she said quickly, rubbing her swollen breast teasingly against his lips. "Why should I give up my fine life here in Florence? I have everything I want.

Money, beautiful jewels, and one man is much like another."

"True." Lion's tension eased. "But there's only one Giulia," he said lightly. "Giulia, the divine." He stood up and pulled her toward the bed across the room. "Giulia, the generous."

She could see the hunger growing in him, his manhood pressing hard and bold against the material of his hose. Lust speared through her. "Generous?"

"I'm in the mood to test your kindness tonight." He smiled as he sat down on the bed, spread his legs, and pulled her down on her knees before him. He took her palm and brought it to his lips before lowering it to cover his rigid manhood. "And you are going to be generous to me tonight, aren't you, *cara?*"

Tonight, tomorrow, for a few days. It would never be more than that with Lion. But what did it matter? Her hand moved slowly, teasingly on his body as she gazed up at him through her long lashes. He was aroused, hurting, feeling with an intensity that made her heady with power. She was filled with breathless excitement. Lion would be wild, strong and lustful as a satyr, insatiable as he always was when aroused. *More.* "Yes," she whispered. "I'm going to be very generous, *amo mio.*"

"You don't seem to understand, my enchanting Sanchia," Caprino said mildly. "You have no choice. You will go to the piazza and relieve the gentleman of his purse. Then you'll bring the purse to me and I'll see that you're suitably rewarded. You will do this or you will never lift another purse in Florence ever again."

"Why me?" Sanchia asked fiercely. "I told you earlier today that I didn't want—"

"This is a special task."

"It's too soon. I can't—" She broke off as she realized her voice was rising. She cast an anxious glance at the door of the shop set in the alcove behind her. Giovanni mustn't know she was out here with Caprino. It was only because Giovanni had started on his third jug of wine of the evening and was unlikely to notice her absence that she had dared to slip out when Caprino had appeared a few minutes before. "You know I can't leave the shop in the middle of the day. Giovanni will ask questions."

"And you will lie." Caprino shrugged. "It's not as if you haven't lied to him before."

"Not often." Lies were sometimes necessary to survive, but Sanchia had found that an occasional lie surrounded by the truth was much more likely to be believed. "And not unless it was important."

"But this is important. It was you who came to me three years ago and asked to be trained. Out of the goodness of my heart I made you one of the finest thieves in all of Florence and what did I ask in return? Nothing."

"Two thirds of every purse I stole is far from nothing."

"I could have asked for all but a few ducats."

And gotten it, Sanchia thought wearily. She would have had no choice but to give in to his demands. Caprino got his share or there were no thefts, whoring, or killings in Florence. "I've never tried to cheat you of your share, Caprino."

"I know. Such a virtuous child. It warms my heart." He took a step closer. "How are your three little friends? I hear Bartolomeo is becoming quite as skilled as you as Giovanni's helper in the shop. How old is he now?"

"Ten," she said warily.

"And Elizabet? I saw her a few days ago. Such a lovely maid, all golden hair and soft pale skin. She must be fifteen by now."

Sanchia stiffened. "Fourteen."

"Old enough," Caprino said. "When are you going to send her to me? There are easier ways for a pretty pullet to make her way in the world than the one you've chosen for her."

Sanchia's initial surge of panic was quickly washed away by anger. "Stay away from her, Caprino."

"Ah, now that's what I like to see. A little fire." He studied Sanchia objectively. "You're really not bad-looking. A little color in your cheeks and a few pounds on those skinny bones, and I might be able to use you too." He brought his lace-trimmed kerchief to his nose with a moue of distaste. "After a dozen scented baths and a thorough perfuming."

"You do use me." Her lashes lowered to veil her eyes. "I steal for you."

"Only enough to feed that brood you hold so dear."

"It will have to satisfy you."

"But I'm never satisfied. I'm a very greedy man. Haven't you realized that yet, Sanchia?" He smiled faintly. "Give me Elizabet and I'll share the ducats I get for her. I might even be able to persuade Giulia Marzo to take her. Your Elizabet could become the courtesan of a rich and powerful lord. Fine food, pretty gowns—"

"No!" Sanchia saw the frown forming on Caprino's face and instantly began to placate him. "Not yet. Perhaps in another year."

"Why not now?" Caprino's voice lowered to a silky threat. "I'm desolate you're not returning the kindness I've shown to you. Ingratitude make me very unhappy. First you refuse to do me a small favor in the piazza tomorrow, and now you're hoarding that sweet child from me and telling me—"

"I'll steal the purse," Sanchia interrupted. Then, as she saw the flicker of satisfaction on Caprino's face, she realized with frustration that he'd gotten exactly what he wanted from her. He had used the threat to Elizabet to force Sanchia to steal again. Why had she expected anything else? Caprino always got what he wanted through guile or cunning or force. Still, it had been only a threat this time, she thought with relief. "Why do you want that particular purse? If I see an easier—" She stopped.

Caprino was shaking his head. "It has to be the man I point out to you. And why I want it is no concern of yours." He turned to go. "The piazza at two. Don't be late." He glanced back over his shoulder. "If I don't get that purse, I'll have to seek . . . compensation. You understand, Sanchia?"

"I understand." A shiver ran through her as she met his gaze. "You'll have your purse."

"Good. Such a sweet child." A moment later he had

faded into the darkness, and the breath Sanchia had not realized she had been holding came out in a rush.

Dio, she had been frightened. She had known it was only a matter of time until Caprino realized Elizabet's potential value to him. Nothing and no one escaped Caprino's notice for long if it meant money flowing into his purse, but perhaps she had staved him off for a little while.

She stood gazing at the darkness into which Caprino had disappeared. Something would have to be done soon about Elizabet, who was becoming too comely for Sanchia to protect. She had caught Giovanni gazing often at Elizabet of late. His eyes held the same lust he had had for Sanchia's mother. Soon he would attempt Elizabet, if Caprino hadn't already forced the girl into one of his brothels. One solution to Elizabet's problem had occurred to Sanchia, but it would take more ducats than she could manage to salvage from her share of the purses she snatched for Caprino. Perhaps if she could find a way to get away from the shop more often—

She jumped as a crash of splintering pottery sounded in the shop behind her. The sound was immediately followed by Giovanni's loud cursing. "Sanchia! Where the devil are you?"

She consciously braced herself and turned to open the door. "I was just getting some air. It's so—" She gazed in horror at the disaster across the room. A pottery jug lay broken on the scribe table, and Giovanni was making futile dabs with a cloth at the rich red wine spreading on the two leaves of parchment in front of him.

"No!" Sanchia hurried across the room to stand looking down at the first leaf. It was ruined, the ink running over the parchment. She carefully lifted it away from the one beneath. The second leaf was still legible, but the liquid had soaked through and it would also have to be recopied. "You've ruined it."

"You can fix it," Giovanni mumbled, shaking his shaggy graying head. "I don't have to deliver the work until noon tomorrow." He turned and walked unsteadily toward the room at the back of the shop. "Sleepy . . . You can fix it."

Yes, she could fix it, Sanchia thought in weary exasperation, but it would take all night and most of tomorrow. Thank the saints Bartolomeo had put the rest of the folio neatly away in the cabinet as soon as he had finished setting the type for each leaf, or this accident could have been a true catastrophe. He had only left these last two leaves out to have them in readiness to set the type early tomorrow morning. Though this disaster was certainly bad enough. Messer Rudolfo was a scholar as well as a merchant, and he would have been furious to have his original *Convivio* destroyed. He might have yielded to the current fashion of having copies of books in his library printed on the modern marvel of a printing press, but he still had a fondness for the beauty of the originals as well as a merchant's appreciation for their intrinsic worth. She would have not only to replace Rudolfo's original leaves with two of equally fine script but to start setting the type herself tonight. She and Bartolomeo had judged it would take both of them working at high speed from the first light of dawn tomorrow to print those last two leaves and finish on time. Now that Bartolomeo would be forced to do the printing alone while she did the hand copying, some of the typesetting must be done tonight.

"I'll clean off the table."

Sanchia turned to see Piero at the door leading to the small storage room. He was rubbing his eyes with the backs of his hands and looked endearingly tousled and warm, even younger than his six years. She felt a rush of affection and suddenly the world didn't seem such a grim place. Life had its ugly patches but it wasn't all ugly. There were children like Piero and beautiful words on parchment and probably hundreds of other wonderful things she couldn't recall or still had to learn about. "Go back to your pallet," she said gently. "I can do this myself."

He shook his head as he came over to the table and began to clean up the shards of pottery. His small, sturdy body was swaying a little and he was almost asleep on his feet, she thought tenderly. Yet she knew he would stubbornly continue to try to help her. Yes, there were many wonderful things that men like Caprino and Giovanni couldn't besmirch, and companionship and love were two of them.

"I'll get Bartolomeo up." Piero carried the pottery shards to the big straw basket across the room. "He can set the type."

Sanchia shook her head. "Bartolomeo went to sleep only an hour ago."

"You haven't slept at all," Piero answered. "I'll get Bartolomeo up." He disappeared into the room where the four of them slept.

A moment later Sanchia heard the grumbling protests of a very sleepy Bartolomeo and then Piero's determined voice. "No, I won't let you go back to sleep. Sanchia needs us."

Sanchia smiled. Young as he was, Piero could never be deterred once he had decided something must be done. Her smile faded when she remembered it was only his stubbornness that had kept him alive when his mother had abandoned him to the streets and gone into one of Caprino's brothels. Piero had been like a fierce young animal for weeks after Sanchia had found him in an alley off the Piazza della Signoria two years before.

Bartolomeo was yawning as he appeared in the doorway. "Sanchia, I don't—" He stopped, suddenly awake, and shouted, "*Dio!* Can you save anything?"

Sanchia shook her head. "They'll both have to be recopied."

Bartolomeo glowered at the door leading to the room where Giovanni lay snoring. "It's the third time this month. Soon no one will come to him. Messer Arcolo does much better work and doesn't drink like a swilling pig." His gaze went with possessive pride to the printing press crouching like a giant wooden grasshopper across the room. "Giovanni doesn't deserve such a fine instrument. It's wasted on him."

"But not on you," Sanchia said affectionately. "I don't know if you are mother to that press or it is mother to you."

Piero was tugging at Bartolomeo's wool shirt. "Set the type."

"*Dio*, give me a minute." Bartolomeo frowned down at Piero. "Will you at least let me wash the sleep from my eyes?"

Piero shook his head. "Sanchia needs you. She's tired and wants to go to bed."

Sanchia made a face. "There'll be no sleep for me tonight." She handed Bartolomeo the leaf that could still be read. "If you can get this now, I'll try to have the other leaf recopied by morning."

Bartolomeo nodded briskly as he glanced down at the page. His drowsiness had completely vanished, and Sanchia could see the familiar eagerness light his face as he imagined changing the elegant script to his beloved block print. "I can do it." His tone was already abstracted as he crossed the room. "It will only take . . ." He trailed off as his fingers began sorting through the letter blocks.

Piero finished cleaning off the table and then began moving about the room putting things in order.

Sanchia went to the cabinet, drew out a leaf of Giovanni's finest parchment, crossed back to the scribe table, and seated herself. She glanced at the ruined document and quickly set it aside. No help there; the letters had run together until they were completely indistinguishable. Thank the saints she had read the entire work earlier in the week, as she almost always did when Giovanni received a new commission. It was the third *Convivio* the print shop had copied this year, but there were several tiny differences she had noted in this version. Rudolfo's folio had been obtained from the monks of a Franciscan monastery, and the holy man who had copied Dante's work had arrogantly deleted a number of sentences and added others. It would be futile to hope that a scholar like Messer Rudolfo had not pored over these leaves until he had memorized them to the last stroke of the pen.

Piero dropped onto the floor beside her chair and leaned his head against her knee. She absently stroked his fair hair as she tried to clear her mind of weariness.

She felt a sudden rush of panic. What if she couldn't do it this time? What if she couldn't remember? She took a deep breath and tried to steady herself. There was no reason why she shouldn't remember. Since she was a small child she had been able to remember everything she had seen down to the tiniest detail. Surely she hadn't lost the ability now that she needed it so desperately. God was not always kind, but he couldn't be so cruel as to take away this gift.

She closed her eyes and tried to relax, willing memory to return to her.

And it did!

The leaf was suddenly before her with all its willful inaccuracies. Sweet Mary be praised, Sanchia thought with relief.

Her lids flicked open and she quickly reached for the quill.

Two

"You're late." Caprino jerked Sanchia into the shadows of the arcade surrounding the piazza. "I told you two o'clock."

"It couldn't be helped," Sanchia said breathlessly. "There was an accident . . . and we didn't get finished until an hour . . . ago . . . and then I had to wait until Giovanni left to take the—"

Caprino silenced the flow of words with an impatient motion of his hand. "There he is." He nodded across the crowded piazza. "The big man in the wine-colored velvet cape listening to the storyteller."

Sanchia's gaze followed Caprino's to the man standing in front of the platform. He was more than big, he was a giant, she thought gloomily. The careless arrogance in the man's stance bespoke perfect confidence in his ability to deal with any circumstances and, if he caught her, he'd probably use his strong hands to crush her head like a walnut. Well, she was too tired to worry about that right now. It had been over thirty hours since she had slept. Perhaps it was just as well she was almost too exhausted to care what happened to her. Fear must not make her as clumsy as she had been yesterday. She was at least glad the giant appeared able to afford to lose a few ducats. The richness of his clothing indicated he must either be a great lord or a prosperous merchant.

"Go." Caprino gave her a little push out onto the piazza. "Now."

She pulled her shawl over her head to shadow her face and hurried toward the platform where Luca Brezal was telling his story, accompanying himself on the lyre. She had heard Luca many times before and didn't consider him overly talented. She wished the storyteller were Pico Fallone. Pico could hold an audience spellbound and would have made it much easier for her to ease close enough to snatch the giant's purse.

A drop of rain struck her face, and she glanced up at the suddenly dark skies. Not yet, she thought with exasperation. If it started to rain in earnest the people crowding the piazza would run for shelter and she would have to follow the velvet-clad giant until he put himself into a situation that allowed her to make the snatch.

Another drop splashed her hand, and her anxious gaze flew to the giant. His attention was still fixed on the storyteller, but only the saints knew how long he would remain. Her pace quickened as she flowed like a shadow into the crowd surrounding the platform.

Garlic, Lion thought, as the odor assaulted his nostrils. Garlic, spoiled fish, and some other stench that smelled even fouler. He glanced around the crowd trying to identify the source of the smell. The people surrounding the platform were the same ones he had studied moments before, trying to search out Caprino's thief. The only new arrival was a thin woman dressed in a shabby gray gown, an equally ragged woolen shawl covering her head. She moved away from the edge of the crowd and started to hurry across the piazza. The stench faded with her departure and Lion drew a deep breath. *Dio*, luck was with him in this, at least. He was not at all pleased at being forced to stand in the rain waiting for Caprino to produce his master thief.

"It's done," Lorenzo muttered, suddenly at Lion's side. He had been watching from the far side of the crowd. Now he said more loudly, "As sweet a snatch as I've ever seen."

"What?" Frowning, Lion gazed at him. "There was no—" He broke off as he glanced down at his belt. The pouch was gone; only the severed cords remained in his belt. "Sweet Jesus." His gaze flew around the piazza. "Who?"

"The sweet madonna who looked like a beggarmaid and smelled like a decaying corpse." Lorenzo nodded toward the arched arcade. "She disappeared behind that column, and I'll wager you'll find Caprino lurking there with her, counting your ducats."

Lion started toward the column. "A woman," he murmured. "I didn't expect a woman. How good is she?"

Lorenzo fell into step with him. "Very good."

"A woman . . . offers interesting possibilities. The guards at the Palazzo wouldn't be expecting a female."

"Especially not when the woman smells like spoiled trout. I doubt if even a fishmonger would find her alluring."

"That problem seems easy enough to sol—" Lion broke off as Caprino stepped from behind the column and started toward them.

A smug smile on his lips, Caprino held up Lion's purse. "You are satisfied? A lift as graceful as the steps of a pavane."

"Where's the woman?" Lion squinted into the shadowed arcade.

"Gone. I let Sanchia go back to the shop until I learned your decision. There was no point to involving her further, if you found a woman unsuitable for your purpose."

"She may be adequate," Lion said slowly. "If she proves pliable."

Caprino's lids lowered to veil the sudden glitter in his eyes. "A woman you can own is always pliable. Did you think I'd forgotten your second requirement? Sanchia is a slave as her mother was before her. You can buy her and command her to do whatever you wish her to do." He smiled faintly. "And she would never dare betray you by running back to tell me or anyone else of your concerns."

"A slave," Lion repeated. Slavery was not allowed in his own city-state of Mandara, but there were many slaves in other parts of Italy brought from Turkey, Spain, and the Balkans. "In your service?"

Caprino shook his head. "She belongs to Giovanni Ballano who owns a print shop on the Via Calimala."

"Who sends her out to steal for him?"

Caprino shook his head. "He doesn't know about it. Giovanni is a drunkard and a fool who will soon lose his shop and everything he owns. He needs Sanchia's help, but hand him a jug of good wine and a few ducats and he'll be persuaded to give her up to you."

"More gold?" Lion asked dryly. "This thief is costing me dearly."

"I found what you wanted," Caprino protested. "You can't expect me to impoverish myself by buying her for you." A thoughtful frown suddenly wrinkled his brow. "However, out of the goodness of my heart, I'll return half of this purse to you if you decide to buy Sanchia."

Lion's gaze narrowed. "Indeed? Now why is it you're so eager for me to accept your little slave girl?"

"It suits me to have her removed from Florence. I have my secrets also, my lord. Is it agreed?"

Lion gazed at him for a long moment before nodding slowly. "If Ballano can be persuaded to sell her, I'll accept your lady thief." He took the pouch from Caprino's hand. "Come to Giulia's tomorrow morning, and I'll return half the gold in the purse."

"You do not trust me?"

Lion's lips twisted in a mirthless smile. "Trust?" He turned and strode across the piazza.

Lorenzo strolled beside him. "You're going to see Ballano now?"

Lion nodded. "We've wasted too much time. I want to be at Solinari by Thursday."

"You think Camari may move the statue?"

"Who knows what that whoreson will do? He seldom does anything without a reason."

"He hates you," Lorenzo observed. "To keep you from getting something you want may be reason enough."

"Well, he won't succeed." Lion's lips tightened. "The Wind Dancer is mine, and I'll not let anyone take what belongs to me."

Lorenzo stopped as they reached a table near the door of a *trattoria* beneath the arcade on the south side of the piazza. "I'll wait for you here." He dropped onto a chair at the table and drew a slim volume from beneath his cloak. "You're being depressingly grim about this matter, and I have no interest in your petty haggling."

"By all means," Lion agreed ironically. "Heaven forbid you should be bored."

"My thought exactly." Lorenzo opened the book. "Though heaven gave up any interest in me a long time ago. Run along and conduct your business."

Lion shook his head, a faint smile on his lips. "As you command." He turned and strode away in the direction of the Via Calimala.

The rain was falling hard when Sanchia arrived at the print shop; a worried frown marred the serene beauty of Elizabet's face as she met Sanchia at the door. "Giovanni isn't back yet." She pulled Sanchia into the shop. "You're soaked. You're sure to catch a chill. Come and have some wine to warm you."

Sanchia shook her head. "Not now. I have to sleep." She moved heavily across the shop to the storage room and sank to her knees on her pallet. Sighing with weariness, she stretched out and pulled the worn quilt up to cover her chin. "Wake me when Giovanni comes back. Where are Piero and Bartolomeo?"

"Giovanni sent them to the wine shop to get a fresh jug for him." Elizabet leaned down to tuck the quilt more closely around Sanchia's thin body. "Sleep. I'll try to keep Giovanni from waking you."

Sanchia's lids felt as if they were weighted, and she could hold them open no longer. She had to sleep, if only for a little while. It probably would be for a mere few precious moments. She knew Elizabet would try to protect her, but the girl was too gentle-natured and free from guile to keep Giovanni from doing anything he wanted to do. If Messer Rudolfo was pleased with their work, Giovanni would quite likely bring back another commission and want them to start on it at once.

And Messer Rudolfo would be pleased, she thought with a glimmer of pride. She and Bartolomeo had done excellent work on the *Convivio*. Really excellent work . . .

"No, you can't wake her! What do you want with Sanchia?" The note of panic in Elizabet's voice pierced the heavy clouds of sleep beginning to surround Sanchia. Something was wrong, she thought drowsily. She had to force her eyes open. No, it was too difficult. Finally, she managed to awaken herself enough to stare sleepily at the man standing in the doorway.

Brilliant dark eyes looked at her from a face as stone hard as the statue of Lorenzo de'Medici in the piazza. Piazza! Shock cleared the last vestiges of sleep from her mind. This was the man in the piazza!

She sat bolt upright, her heart pounding wildly as she gazed up at him. The giant's massive body completely filled the doorway, and the tiny storeroom seemed to grow smaller by the second as if he were draining it of dimension in some magical way. Like Zeus drawing power from the heavens to loose his thunderbolts, she thought dazedly.

He smiled grimly. "I see you recognize me. It seems the theft of my purse didn't weigh on your conscience. You were sleeping as soundly as an infant in its mother's arms. Do you always nap after your thefts?"

Elizabet, somewhere beyond the giant's broad shoulders, gasped. Sanchia was too frightened to gasp, too frightened to speak, to frightened to do anything but stare at him.

He frowned. "Answer me."

"I don't . . ." She stopped and swallowed hard. "Are you going to imprison me?"

"Isn't that what should happen to thieves?"

Elizabet sobbed brokenly. "Sanchia, I told him not to come in. I told him . . ."

The man was ignoring Elizabet, his gaze fixed intently on Sanchia's face. "Isn't the Stinche where you belong?" he repeated.

"Yes, that's where thieves belong." She forced herself to meet his gaze. "But I no longer have your purse, and if you imprison me, you'll never get your gold back. They'll just cut off my hands and—" She had to stop as terror dried her throat. The bloody vision danced before her eyes and it was a moment before she could continue, "If you let me go free, I'll find a way to pay you back. I promise, my lord."

"The promise of a thief."

"I keep my word."

"A thief but not a liar?"

"I do lie," she said honestly. "Well . . . only when I must. Sometimes it's better to lie than have bad things happen to people. But I don't break my promises."

"Don't hurt her," Elizabet sobbed. "Please don't hurt her."

"Stop weeping," he said impatiently over his shoulder. "She's the one who should be crying."

"Sanchia never cries," Elizabet said.

"Sanchia what?" He turned back to Sanchia. "What's your full name?"

"Just Sanchia." She moistened her lips with her tongue. "I have no other."

He bowed mockingly. "Lionello Andreas, my illustrious lady thief. I think we're destined to become very well acquainted. Stand up and let me look at you."

She scrambled to her feet, hugging her shawl close

to her body to try to stop the shivering that attacked every limb.

"Come here."

She took one hesitant step toward him, then another.

"Stop." He held up his hand and grimaced distastefully. "Do you never bathe?"

"I bathe, my lord." Her eyes were enormous in her thin face as she gazed up at him. "Please, my lord, trust me. I'll return the money."

"I trust only a very few people in this world and none of them is a thief." His gaze ran over her. He scowled. "*Dio*, you're scrawny as a starved cat. Does Ballano never feed you?"

She stiffened. "You know Giovanni?"

"I haven't as yet had that pleasure. Where is he?"

"He'll be back soon," Elizabet wailed. "Couldn't you go before he returns?"

"Elizabet . . ." Sanchia drew a deep breath and tried to subdue her impatience. "Why don't you stand by the door and watch for Giovanni while I talk to his excellency?"

"Yes, Sanchia." Elizabet gave Andreas an uncertain glance and hurried from the room.

"She has the brain of a chicken," Lion said bluntly. "God, how I hate a whining woman."

"She's only fourteen," Sanchia said defensively. "And she's not stupid. You frighten her."

Lion's gaze narrowed on her face. "But not you?"

She nodded. "Me, too." She swallowed. "But being afraid won't save me. As you indicated, weeping and wailing only make men angry."

"Has that been your experience?" he asked, his expression intent.

"Men don't like tears. It makes them impatient, just as it did you, my lord." She stood very straight, gazing at him. "What can I do to keep you from taking me to prison?"

"What would you do?" he asked curiously.

"Anything," she whispered. "I can't leave them. They have no one but me."

"Who are 'they'?" His words were abstracted as his gaze ran over her. By the saints, the woman truly looked the scrawny feline he had named her, he thought with a flash of unreasonable irritation. Sanchia appeared to be little older than the sobbing child across the room; she was as tiny and fine-boned as a kitten. Her triangular face was oddly catlike, too, with its high cheekbones, olive skin, and slightly slanted eyes. Those eyes were strange—gold-amber in color and utterly appealing, even filled with terror as they were now. Her chestnut-colored hair looked as if it had been carelessly chopped and hacked until it was even shorter than his page Nicolo's. Now it was so rain dampened it clung in sodden curls about her thin face. "Who are you so concerned about?"

"Piero and Bartolomeo and Eliza—"

"He's coming," Elizabet cried frantically. "Sanchia, do something."

Sanchia paled. "Please go away. I beg you, my lord."

"You're afraid of this Giovanni?"

"Not for myself. He needs me, so he'll probably only beat me. But if he becomes very angry, he may decide to send them all away and he mustn't do that. I couldn't—"

"A thousand apologies for keeping you waiting, my lord." It was Giovanni's voice booming from the doorway. "How may I serve you?"

Sanchia held her breath, her gaze clinging to Lion's in desperation. She could detect no softening of his expression, only that strange, searching appraisal.

Then Andreas abruptly turned away from her to face Giovanni. "Signor Ballano, I am Lionello Andreas, and I've come to make you an offer."

"A commission?" Giovanni brushed by Elizabet and entered the shop. "I copy by hand or print. My work is known throughout Florence." Giovanni waved a hand at the printing press across the room. "It's the best machine in all Italy and I—"

"I want nothing copied," Lion interrupted. "I need a servant, and I heard you have a slave that may meet my requirements." He stepped aside and indicated

Sanchia standing in shocked immobility behind him. "I'll give you twenty-five ducats for her."

"Sanchia?" Giovanni's bloodshot eyes widened in surprise. "You want to buy Sanchia?"

"Why not? She's young and appears strong and healthy. She has many years of service left in her. That's why I'm willing to make so generous an offer. You should be able to replace her with no trouble."

"Twenty-five ducats," Giovanni repeated. He shook his head, trying to comprehend. "For Sanchia?"

"Is it a bargain?" Lion asked. "Do you have her papers?"

"In my chest in the other room. A bill of sale for the mother and her." Suddenly Giovanni's bewildered expression was replaced by craftiness. "It's not enough. How would I conduct my business? I've spent many years teaching her the skills of copying and running the press. Now you think to take her away from me for a mere twenty-five ducats?"

Cristo, the man was as greedy as Caprino, Lion thought in disgust. "Twenty-five ducats is more than fair."

"For an ordinary slave, perhaps, but Sanchia is not only skilled, she has a talent." Giovanni paused impressively. "She remembers everything. She has only to look at a leaf of script and she can recite it back to you."

"A pretty trick but of no value to me," Lion said impatiently. "Will you sell her or not?"

Giovanni was thinking quickly. "She's young enough to bear you children. That should be worth something."

"I'm not buying her to occupy my bed. She's hardly appetizing enough to interest me in that fashion."

Giovanni looked at Sanchia and reluctantly agreed. "True, but a woman is a woman when a man's blood runs hot. Perhaps you could—"

"I'm weary of this haggling." Lion reached in his belt and drew out his purse. "Fifty ducats. No more. Agreed?"

Giovanni's gaze fastened hungrily on the purse. "It's still too little. She works hard and . . ." He stopped as his glance met Lion's and took an involuntary step back. "Agreed, my lord."

"No!" Sanchia had been enveloped in a nightmare of shock and bewilderment, unable to believe this was happening until Giovanni's final words of assent jarred her from her stupor. She rushed toward Giovanni. "You can't do this. I can't go—"

"Quiet! Do you know how long it would take me to earn fifty ducats?"

"I won't leave them." She clutched at his arm. "You can't do this. How will they—"

She broke off as Giovanni's hand cracked against her cheek and sent her reeling away from him.

"Sanchia." Elizabet started toward her, tears running down her cheeks. "Oh, Sanchia."

Giovanni turned swiftly back to Lion. "She's not usually so unruly. A good beating now and then keeps her in order."

Lion's face hardened as he gazed at the livid mark appearing on Sanchia's cheek. "Don't touch her again. She's mine now and I'll discipline her as I see fit."

"I *won't* go with him." Sanchia's eyes were suddenly blazing. "This is wrong. I've served you well, you stupid fool."

Giovanni took three steps toward her. "Be silent or I'll—"

"Don't touch her." Lion's voice held steely menace. "Or by the saints, you'll regret it, Ballano."

Giovanni stopped and took a deep breath. "She'll be more obedient when she's away from those three strays. I should never have let her persuade me to take them in."

"They cost you nothing." Sanchia's voice was fierce. "I saw that they were fed. I took care of them."

"Sanchia, don't," Elizabet whispered.

"Why not?" Sanchia's eyes glittered with a recklessness born of desperation. "What can he do to me that he hasn't already done? He's a greedy fool who cares for nothing but his *vino*."

"Her papers and a bill of sale," Lion said quickly. The terrified kitten had suddenly grown claws, he

noticed with exasperation. In another minute she would
have Ballano so enraged he would refuse to sell her just
to have the pleasure of beating her senseless. "I have no
more time."

Giovanni cast a furious glance at Sanchia, then
strode over to the scribe table and scrawled a few lines
on the parchment lying on it. "There's your bill of sale.
She's yours now." He turned and strode to the door
leading to his quarters. "I'll get her papers from my
chest."

Elizabet was weeping softly, and Sanchia instinctively turned to comfort her. "It will be all right. I'll find
a way to take care of you."

"But Sanchia, what can you do?"

Lion studied Sanchia. The fury illuminating Sanchia's face was suddenly gone, and it gave him food for
thought. If he had allowed her defiance of Ballano to
continue, the sale might well have fallen through. Had
the girl's anger only been a pretense directed toward
that aim? "Yes, Sanchia, what can you do?" he ask silkily.
"I'm beginning to wonder who was the slave all these
years you've been with Ballano."

She turned to look at him. "There was no question
who was the slave," she said bitterly.

"But you don't deny you were pretending anger just
now to get what you wanted."

She shook her head. "No pretense. I was angry, but
I wouldn't have let it run free if I hadn't thought it might
keep Giovanni from selling me."

"A dangerous device. He might have hurt you
badly."

"I would have healed. He wouldn't have killed me
while I still have value to him. He's a fool, not a
madman."

"You appear to know him well. But you don't know
me at all. I'm not a fool, Sanchia."

Sanchia shivered. "I did not think you a fool. I
wouldn't make that mistake."

"Here it is." Giovanni hurried toward them, a
frayed leather folder in his hands. He handed the folder
to Lion and received the purse of ducats in return. "I

bought them both from a Spaniard who assured me they came of good strong stock. You've made a fine purchase."

"An interesting one at any rate." Lion was abruptly filled with disgust and an overwhelming urgency to be done with the man. "Go get your things, Sanchia. We're leaving this place."

Giovanni said quickly, "There's nothing for her to get. Slaves don't have possessions, my lord."

Sanchia lifted shaking fingers to her throbbing temple, trying to think. "I can't leave yet. There's Elizabet."

Giovanni's gaze shifted to Elizabet. "Elizabet is no longer your concern. However, I may be able to use her. She keeps the shop clean and I'll need someone to—"

"No," Sanchia said flatly. "She isn't going to stay here."

"And where else would she go?" Giovanni asked. "I'll give her a roof over her head and food for her belly. She can't expect more. I may take Bartolomeo, too, but Piero will have to go. He's too young to be of any help."

"You'll not keep any of them." Sanchia turned to Elizabet. "Go find Bartolomeo and Piero and meet me in the piazza."

Elizabet gazed at her in confusion.

"Hurry!" Sanchia gave her a little push. "All will be well."

"Stay," Giovanni ordered. "Obey me, Elizabet."

Elizabet gave him a frightened glance and fled from the shop.

Giovanni began to curse vehemently and obscenely as he turned to Sanchia. "They'll starve in the streets. You'll see, you arrogant bitch."

"No, they won't. I'll not let them starve." She gave him a level look over her shoulder as she moved toward the door. "And I'll not let them be used by you either. I know what you'd do to them if I weren't here. Bartolomeo would soon be as much a slave to you as I was and Elizabet would become your whore. I'll see you burn in hell before I let that happen." She turned to Lion. "We can go now."

"Thank you." Heavy irony laced Lion's tone. "May I remind you that it's you who belongs to me and not I to you?" He followed her from the shop into the street.

"No reminder is necessary." She drew her shawl closer to ward off the chill that came as much from the emotions storming through her as the coolness following the rain. She had to plan, she thought dully, but she was so exhausted and dazed it was difficult to think. "Why did you buy me?"

"Because it suited me, a whim perhaps."

She shook her head. "You're not an impulsive man. I don't think you'd do anything without a reason."

"You find me so easy to read?" Lion asked softly. "You'd be more clever to hide that ability."

"I *have* to understand you." She turned to look at him, desperation threading her voice. "I have to try to see what you are and what you want so that I can give it to you. So that I can find a way . . ." She stopped and drew a shaky breath. "Are you angry with me for stealing from you? Did you buy me so that you could torture me at your leisure?"

His lips tightened. "It doesn't amuse me to torture children."

"I'm not a child. I've reached my sixteenth year."

A sudden glint of humor appeared in his eyes. "In that case, perhaps I'll change my mind. I'll have to see if I can't rummage up a few instruments in the dungeon with which to torment you when we arrive at Mandara."

"We're leaving Florence?" She frowned. "That may present a problem."

"My profound apologies. You must be sure to inform me if my plans further inconvenience you." His sarcastic expression was quickly replaced by a grim look of warning. "We're leaving Florence tomorrow, and I'd advise you not to defy me as you did your former master."

"You're not like Giovanni." Her answer was as abstracted as her gaze. "But I have to know what you want from me."

"It's very simple. I want a slave who'll obey my every

demand without question. Why else would I have bought you?"

"I won't kill for you."

He lifted a brow. "If that's your only reservation, I believe I can accept it."

She braced herself and then said in a little rush, "I'll make a bargain with you."

"Everyone in Florence appears to want to bargain with me," he said dryly. "I can see why it's known as a city of merchants. But I feel bound to draw attention to the fact that I've no need to bargain with you. I've just paid fifty ducats for the doubtful privilege of owning you."

"And you wouldn't want to lose your money, would you?" She moistened her lips with her tongue. "If you'll let me have seventy-five ducats, I'll promise I won't run away from you and I'll serve you in any way you choose with complete loyalty. No matter what you ask of me."

Lion went still. "A threat? Do you know the punishment for a runaway slave?"

"Yes." Her voice was uneven. "But I'd still have to do it. I couldn't leave Elizabet and the others here unprotected. They belong to me."

He gazed at her a long moment and she could feel the perspiration bead on the back of her neck. *Dio*, she was taking a chance. She had known from the moment she had seen him in the piazza he was a dangerous man.

"What do you want to do with the money?" he asked.

"Ten ducats for Bartolomeo so he can apprentice for Messer Arcolo in his print shop. Arcolo is fair, and he has no sons to carry on the business. He'll give Bartolomeo a chance to be more than an apprentice once he realizes what a hard worker he is. Fifty ducats for Elizabet. Alessandro Benedetto, the baker's son, would take her to wife, but his father won't permit it unless she has at least a token dowry."

"She has a fondness for the boy?"

Sanchia shrugged. "Elizabet has a very gentle nature. She likes Alessandro well enough and would grow to love him in time. At least, she'd be safe from Giovanni and Caprino."

Lion's gaze became intent. "Caprino?"

"Caprino wants to use her in one of his brothels. I won't let that happen, but Caprino will have her if I'm not here to prevent it."

"I see." Lion's lips tightened. "A very cunning man, Caprino."

"You know him?"

"I'm beginning to know him better as time goes on."

"He mustn't get Elizabet. She wouldn't live more than a year in a brothel. She's too—" She stopped and then went on. "Fifteen ducats for Piero. Elizabet would take care of him, but I couldn't expect Alessandro's family to accept him without compensation."

"A dowry for Piero, too?" Lion murmured. "I'm beginning to feel like a matchmaker."

"It is not much money for a rich man," she said urgently. "And it would mean they'd all be safe and cared for."

"And give you no reason to run back here."

She nodded earnestly. "I told you I keep my promises. I'll be whatever you want me to be, if you'll only help them."

His gaze searched her face. "Complete obedience without question?"

She nodded.

"Absolute loyalty to me for as long as I own you?"

"Yes."

A crooked smile touched his lips. "Seventy-five ducats. So that's the price for the purchase of a soul these days."

She was bewildered. "What?"

"Never mind." He shifted his gaze from her face to the piazza a short distance away. "You shall have your seventy-five ducats."

Sanchia felt dizzy with relief. "Now?"

"Why not?" He nodded at a slim, elegant man seated at table beneath the arcade. "I'm sure my friend Lorenzo will be overjoyed to go with you to settle your flock in their new havens. He has such a sweet nature."

Sanchia's eyes widened. "You're jesting." She was sure there was nothing sweet about the man sitting at the table gazing down at the open book on the table in front of him. Neither a sweet temperament nor good looks, she thought as she stared at him. His dark brown hair was frosted with silver at the temples, his nose was too long and his complexion swarthy. The hollowed planes of his face and his deepset eyes reminded her vaguely of Fra Savonarola, who had been burned in the Piazza della Signoria when she was a child. Then he suddenly glanced up and Sanchia tensed. The man's gray eyes did not burn with a fanatical fervor as had the monk's but were as remote from human emotion as the stars on a winter night.

He closed the book and, as they approached, his gaze ran over Sanchia in cool appraisal. "She's younger than I thought. Will she be adequate?"

"She'd better be." Lion grimaced. "She's becoming a very expensive acquisition. If we don't get out of Florence soon, I may have to sell Mandara to pay for her."

Lorenzo stood up and bowed mockingly. "Lorenzo Vasaro, at your service, Madonna Sanchia."

A hint of mischief crossed Lion's face. "As a matter of fact, there is a service you can do her. How kind of you to offer."

"There they are." Sanchia had spied Elizabet, Bartolomeo, and Piero across the piazza. "I'll go get them and explain . . ." Her words trailed away as she started off at a run toward the children.

Lorenzo's gaze followed Sanchia across the wide piazza. She reached the children and began speaking quickly and with great urgency. "You haven't, by any chance, bought those other waifs, too?"

"Not exactly. But it appears our Sanchia has a very motherly nature and wishes to get her brood settled before she leaves the city. Go with her and spend what you need to make sure the children are safe." He frowned. "And get her something to eat. She looks half starved."

"*Our* Sanchia?"

Lion shrugged. "My Sanchia, then. It seems reasonable to set her mind at rest before taking her to Solinari."

"Very reasonable," Lorenzo said solemnly. "I can see

that you'd never want your slave to suffer the distresses of worry."

"You find it amusing?" Lion asked. "Gold doesn't always buy what we want, and I need her loyalty."

"And you think settling these three children will purchase what you want from her?"

Lion's gaze flew to Sanchia. She was kneeling on the flagstones beside the smallest child, speaking persuasively, her features illuminated with such a loving radiance that Lion found himself unable to look away from her. "Yes," he said slowly. "This will buy me what I want."

Three

Where are you taking me?" Sanchia asked as she hurried to keep up with Lorenzo's long strides.

"The *casa* of Giulia Marzo," Lorenzo answered. "We're staying there while we're in Florence."

"I've heard of her. She's a famous courtesan and has many rich lovers. Is my lord Andreas rich? I guess he must be or he wouldn't have been able to pay so much for me. He mentioned a place called Mandara. Is that where we're going when we leave Florence? I've never been away from Florence since we came here when I was three. That's when I was sold to Giovanni and—"

"Enough!" Lorenzo sighed. "Don't you ever stop talking? You've chattered unceasingly since we left the baker's house."

"I always talk when I'm frightened."

Sanchia smiled tremulously. "And I'm very frightened right now. I feel . . . strange."

"You didn't appear frightened when you were arguing with that baker about your pretty Elizabet's dowry."

"That was different. Messer Benedetto had to be made to realize what a bargain he was getting in Elizabet. He has a very prosperous shop and could make a much better match for Alessandro. I was worried that if he wasn't totally satisfied with Elizabet he wouldn't accept Piero." She turned to look at him. "Thank the saints you were there. You helped to settle it far more quickly than I'd hoped."

"Me?" He lifted a brow. "I said nothing."

"I know, but that didn't matter. You made him feel uneasy and he wanted you gone. I think you must make most people uneasy."

"I don't appear to intimidate you," he said dryly. "Did no one ever tell you that it's not wise to be so frank? Many men wouldn't like to be told their presence makes one uneasy."

She looked at him in surprise. "But you don't mind. You've lived with it so long it's become a part of you."

"You're very perceptive." He studied her face. "You read people well. I noticed that with Messer Arcolo and then again with Benedetto. You sought out their desires and motives and then used them to suit yourself."

"It was necessary," she said simply. "Sometimes our wits are the only weapons we have. Haven't you found that to be true, Messer Lorenzo?"

"Yes." He was silent a moment. "But I wouldn't attempt to manipulate Lion as you did the good baker. It might prove dangerous."

"I wouldn't do that. I've given him my pledge." She tried to smile. "But it would make me feel better if you'd tell me something about Lord Andreas. I've never belonged to anyone but Giovanni and that wasn't like being a slave at all."

"Indeed? Because he was so kind to you?"

She shook her head. "Oh no, Giovanni is too selfish to be kind to anyone. It's too much trouble for him.

When I was a child I resented him, but when I came to realize what a stupid man he is it was easier." She shrugged. "All I had to do was give him what made him comfortable and he would leave me alone."

"Manipulation again," Vasaro murmured. "Taking in three children off the street doesn't seem the act of a selfish man."

"I had to convince him that it would be a purely selfish thing to do," Sanchia said. "Bartolomeo and Elizabet are brother and sister and lived next door to Giovanni. When their parents died of the fever three years ago they had no relations to help them and I couldn't let them be tossed into the streets. So I told Giovanni how clever everyone would think him if he took them into the shop. It would be as if he had three slaves instead of one—and without having to pay an extra ducat for them. I promised I'd see to it they were no trouble and that I'd share my food with them."

"Evidently you kept your word. You're skin and bones."

She made a face. "It didn't work. There was never enough food to go around. Then when Piero came to live with us, I knew something would have to be done. I was a slave, so I could work for no one but Giovanni, and every time I asked him for extra money he would threaten to throw the children out."

"So you began to steal." Vasaro's tone was expressionless. "That particular bit of charity could have cost you your hands."

She winced. "I know, but it wasn't charity." They started across the Ponte Vecchio, which was lined almost exclusively with the shops of prosperous silk merchants and goldsmiths. Sanchia saw none of them as she gazed into the cloudy waters of the Arno. "They were my family. I was afraid but I'd still do it again. I was so alone before they came."

"And now you're alone again."

"Nothing lasts forever." She added philosophically, "I would have had to do something to protect Elizabet soon anyway. She's too pretty and that's a danger for a woman. And Giovanni was drinking more and more and the business was failing and that meant Bartolomeo would have had to take a position elsewhere."

"And Piero?"

"Piero . . ." Her expression became wistful. "I hoped I could keep Piero for a while." She shook her head and blinked back the tears stinging her eyes. How stupid to cry now when she had managed to stay dry-eyed all through their farewells. Elizabet wept when confronted with any change, and Sanchia had seen tears in Bartolomeo's eyes when they had left him with Messer Arcolo. But Piero hadn't cried. He had only gazed at her with those fierce blue eyes and grasped her hand so tightly it had hurt for several minutes after Sanchia and Lorenzo had left the baker's shop. "But Piero will be safe with Elizabet. She's very loving and—" Her voice broke and she drew a deep breath. "They'll all be much better off than they were with Giovanni."

"And what of you?" Lorenzo's gaze searched her face. "Do you think you're better off too?"

"I don't know." She looked directly at him. "Am I?"

"I, too, do not know the answer." A faint smile touched his lips. "Lion has never had a slave before. It's going to be interesting to watch his reaction to the situation."

"And you'll like that, won't you? I think you must always stand back and watch as if we're all players for your entertainment." She was silent a moment and then asked, "If he doesn't have any other slaves, why did he buy me?"

"I think I'll let him tell you his plans for you."

She grinned coaxingly. "Don't you want to watch my reaction, too? If you tell me, I'll promise you that my response will be very satisfying."

Lorenzo smiled in genuine amusement. "Are you also trying to manipulate me? You must enjoy walking along the edge of a precipice."

"I'm sorry." The vitality in her face faded and she suddenly looked like a weary child. "I suppose it's become second nature. It's not that I mean to . . ." She stopped and then continued haltingly, "I'm afraid. *He* frightens me."

"Lion? You certainly didn't act frightened when you persuaded him to provide a handsome dowry for your little friends. On the contrary, you were exceptionally bold."

"Only because it was something I had to do." She moistened her lips. "He makes me feel . . ." She paused, searching for words. "I feel like I do in that last minute before I steal a fat purse. Scared and trembling but excited too."

"Hmmm. Interesting."

"Help me." Her hand clutching the wool shawl at her breast tightened. "I didn't feel helpless with Giovanni, but I do with Lord Andreas."

"Why should I help you? Lion is my friend and you're nothing to me." He spoke with complete detachment.

Sanchia's hopes plummeted. "I can't think of any reason why you should help me." She paused, considering. "Unless it's because you'd find it more amusing to make things a little easier for me. A scared mouse scurrying around Lord Andreas wouldn't be nearly as entertaining for you."

He suddenly chuckled. "You are anything but a scared mouse." He paused. "Lion's fair. Serve him well and he'll not misuse you."

Sanchia felt a surge of relief as she thought she recognized the slightest break in the wall that Lorenzo Vasaro used to distance himself from everyone around him. "He has the manner of a great lord. Is he very rich?"

He was silent a moment, and she began to think he wasn't going to answer. "He's lord of the city-state of Mandara. He has great wealth but only the one fief. His father was a condottiere and raised Lion to follow after him. Lorenzo de' Medici gave Lion's father Mandara in payment for waging war against one of his less friendly neighbors."

"Where is Mandara?"

"To the south. Between Florence and Pisa."

"And now Lord Andreas is the lord of the city?"

Vasaro nodded. "Since his father died some thirteen years ago. Lion continued as condottiere and maintained his father's armies until he decided to disband them two years ago and return to Mandara." Vasaro gazed at her inquiringly. "Well, have you gouged enough from me to abate your fears?"

"No." She sighed. "I suppose you wouldn't reconsider and tell me why Lord Andreas bought me?"

Vasaro didn't answer.

"I didn't think so."

"Then you shouldn't have wasted—" he broke off and stopped short. "*Santa Maria*, what is that?"

They were crossing the Mercato Nuovo where bankers with ledgers and fat purses sat at their green-covered tables. However, it was not the bankers at whom Vasaro was staring but a plump man surrounded by a crowd of snickering onlookers. "Am I mistaken or is that obese personage peeling down his hose?"

"Oh, that's only a bankrupt," Sanchia said indifferently. "In order to be discharged he has to strike his naked buttocks three times on that black-and-white marble circle that marks the site of the symbolic Chariot of Florence."

"How undignified." Vasaro's lips suddenly began to twitch with amusement as he resumed walking across the *mercato*. "Lion was worried that you might beggar him. I must warn him if he does becomes bankrupt, it most certainly must not happen in this illustrious city."

"I did not ask for so much. It was necessary to—"

"Peace." Lorenzo held up his hand. "I'm not interested in your protests and explanations. Let me have a little blessed silence for a time."

They walked in silence for a short while until Lorenzo finally said, "Giulia's house is around the next corner." He cast a glance at her. "I wonder if she'll let you through her front door. I found Madonna Giulia very particular about all the appointments of her establishment."

She frowned. "I won't steal anything."

"Your larcenous nature wasn't what I was referring to." He wrinkled his nose. "You have a great and profound need for a bath."

"I'm clean. I bathed only this morning. It's the—"
She stopped as they turned the corner, her eyes widening in pleasure as she caught sight of the impressive two-story house. "What a truly splendid *casa*. It looks as grand as a palazzo. You wouldn't think a whore could do this well for herself, would you? It seems strange that men would be foolish enough to pay so much to fornicate with a woman when the pleasure lasts for such a short time."

His lips twitched. "It doesn't seem strange to me. But then I, too, am one of those foolish men."

She turned and looked at him speculatively. His manner was so icy, so remote it was difficult for her to imagine him rutting with one of the strumpets in this splendid house. "Do you really fornic—"

"I think you've asked quite enough questions for the moment," he interrupted as he took her elbow and nudged her toward the elaborately carved door of the front entrance. He didn't look at Sanchia as he opened the door and murmured, "And yes, on occasion, I most certainly do."

"If you want your little slave girl to be permitted to spend the night here, I think you'd better come along and intercede with Giulia." Lorenzo stood leaning on the jamb of the doorway of Lion's chamber. He covered a delicate yawn with his long, slender hand. "I settled Sanchia's flock in their new nests but I refuse to involve myself between two quarreling women."

"Where is she?" Lion stood up and moved quickly toward the door. The glimmer of malicious mischief underlying Lorenzo's pretense of boredom always boded trouble. *Cristo*, what was wrong now? Nothing had gone as he had planned since he had caught sight of Sanchia on the piazza this afternoon.

"In Giulia's chamber." Lorenzo followed him down the hall. "We'd no sooner crossed the threshold than Giulia appeared in the hall and took offense at your little Sanchia's . . ." He paused before continuing euphemistically, "unusual fragrance. She insisted on calling her servants and dragging the child up to her chamber for a bath."

"Which Sanchia clearly needs."

"But which Sanchia clearly doesn't want. When I last saw her she was being forcibly restrained by two of Giulia's maidservants while Giulia herself was undressing her." Lorenzo opened the door of Giulia's chamber. "Ah, I see they have her in the tub. What wonderful progress."

"Why won't you *listen* to me, you stupid woman? I don't need a bath." It was Sanchia's voice, the tone almost as fierce as when she had spoken to Giovanni.

Lion strode into the chamber and then stopped short. "My God, what's happened here?"

Clothing was tossed all over the chamber as if blown by a gale wind, Giulia Marzo's golden hair was hanging loose about her shoulders, the rope of pearls usually binding it had broken and pearls were scattered over the floor. The bodice of her sea blue gown bore a three-cornered rip and torrents of water were splashed on the floor, on Giulia, and on the two servants holding the struggling Sanchia in the hip bath while Giulia attempted to scrub her.

Sanchia's gaze flew to Lion and she suddenly stopped fighting. "They wouldn't listen to me. I tried to tell them that it wouldn't do any good."

"She stinks," Giulia said between her teeth. "Lorenzo tells me this she-devil belongs to you, but I won't have her in my house until I've purged her of this vile odor." Giulia dipped a cloth into the water and then scrubbed vigorously at Sanchia's neck.

"You're hurting me." Sanchia's amber eyes blazed up at Giulia. "And it will do no good. I'm clean!"

She certainly appeared clean, Lion noticed bemusedly. The golden skin on Sanchia's shoulders gleamed above the cloudy water, and she wasn't nearly as thin as he had believed when she had worn that loose gown.

"Tell her to listen to—" Sanchia broke off as she met Lion's gaze. Her eyes widened, and she stared at him as if mesmerized while a delicate pink tinted the gold of her cheeks. Then she swallowed and drew a shaky breath. "Please, my lord, tell her to stop."

Lion gazed at her without speaking.

"*Please*, my lord." Sanchia's amber eyes were enormous in her triangular face.

"I do like a woman who says please."

There was an intensity in his soft voice that caused Giulia to look at him sharply over her shoulder. "Lion, don't interfere. This is necessary."

"Her body looks clean enough to me." He dropped down on the cushioned chair a few yards away from the tub and stretched his legs out before him. His intent gaze returned to Sanchia's pink-tipped breasts which could be glimpsed just below the surface of the water. The god Eros couldn't have created nipples more arousingly pointed and amazingly sensual. "There's no use scraping and reddening that exquisite skin if there's no need, Giulia."

"But the stench is—"

"It's my *hair*," Sanchia broke in with exasperation. "If you'd listened to me, I would have told you. Every morning after my bath I rub a mixture into it. It's my hair that stinks and needs cleansing."

Giulia sat back on her heels and gazed blankly at Sanchia. "You rub something this foul-smelling into your hair?"

Sanchia nodded. "Since I was twelve. Garlic, fish oil, and—"

Giulia quickly held up her hand. "Don't go on. I don't want to know."

"I do," Lorenzo said from the doorway. "Fascinating."

Lion's gaze narrowed on her face. "I'm not as interested in the mixture itself as in her reason for concocting it."

"Giovanni has a very keen sense of smell," Sanchia said simply. "When my mother was alive, every morning he would make her bathe and perfume herself. Then he'd have her kneel naked on the floor of the shop and take her as a dog takes a bitch in the street. After my mother died I knew that soon I'd be old enough for Giovanni to try to use me in the same way."

Lorenzo chuckled. "You chose an exceptionally powerful deterrent."

Lion didn't feel the same amusement. He found he was experiencing a multitude of wild emotions that took him completely off guard. Anger and pity battled with an odd sense of guilt at the mental image that persisted in coming before his eyes. The image of Sanchia kneeling naked on the floor, looking back over her shoulder with those huge amber eyes, her pink tongue moistening her lips with nervousness.

Lust seared him, twisting through his groin in a scalding tide as he realized that the man in his imagination, the man at whom she was gazing, the man she was ready to receive into her body, was not Giovanni Ballano.

It was himself.

He abruptly rose to his feet. "Wash her hair," he muttered as he turned away. "And then bring her to my chamber."

Lorenzo followed Lion from Giulia's room, down the hall, and into Lion's chamber. He strolled to the table across the room and poured a stream of red wine from a silver pitcher into two goblets. "Have a little wine." He turned to hand one of the goblets to Lion, his gaze flicking mockingly to Lion's lower body. "I think you need cooling."

"Is that why you took me to 'intercede'?" Lion sat down in the large chair by the window. "What game are you playing at now, Lorenzo?"

"I don't know what you mean." Lorenzo gazed at him with limpid innocence. "Your little street urchin seemed very concerned about learning what and who you are, and I thought it would be a kindness to throw you both into a situation where revelations would naturally occur." He smiled. "Which they did. I had no idea Sanchia would be so alluring. She has truly exquisite breasts."

"Yes." Lion's hand tightened on the stem of his goblet as the memory of Sanchia clad only in wisps of steam and cloudy water returned to him. "But I didn't buy her to occupy my bed."

"I know. Which makes the possibilities all the more intriguing." Lorenzo dropped onto the embroidered cushions of the chair by the table and raised his goblet to his lips. "I look forward with great anticipation to watching developments between the two of you."

"You mean you look forward to watching us writhe on the stake you're trying to skewer us with," Lion said dryly. "I doubt if we'll furnish you with as much pleasure as you hope. I don't know why you foresee my bedding Sanchia to be in any way unusual when I've had more women than I can count in these last years."

"Ah, but there's one difference. You own Sanchia. She belongs to you." Lorenzo's gaze narrowed with satisfaction on Lion's face. "And no one in this world is more possessive than you, Lion. You can't bear to let anything you own be taken away from you. Look how you're moving heaven and earth to get the Wind Dancer back, and it's only a statue."

Lion's fingers tightened on the stem of the goblet. "It's more than a statue."

"To your family perhaps." Lorenzo shrugged. "To you it's some kind of holy relic you guard and protect. To me it seems more like a beautiful siren luring men to destruction."

"Sanchia isn't the Wind Dancer."

"No, but as your property she's bound to arouse the same instincts." Lorenzo sipped his wine, smiling at Lion over the rim of the goblet. "What do you think will happen when you take her to Mandara?"

"I'm not taking her to Mandara."

Lorenzo lifted a brow. "She said you told her you were taking her there."

"That was before I . . ." Lion trailed off, his dark brows knotting in a fierce frown as he took a long swallow of wine.

"Before you decided to take her to your bed?"

Lion met his gaze. "Yes." The intention that had

been forming since the moment he had seen Sanchia in the hip bath was suddenly made. "Why not? As you say, she belongs to me."

"There's no reason at all why you shouldn't take her." Lorenzo looked down into the ruby depths of his wine. "I thoroughly approve."

"Which should immediately make me wary. Why do you want Sanchia to become my mistress?"

"I admire her."

Lion gazed at him in astonishment. He couldn't remember the last time Lorenzo had indicated he felt anything positive for a stranger. True, admiration wasn't liking, but the confession was still out of the ordinary.

Lorenzo noticed his surprise. "No, it's true. She reminds me of myself when I was growing up in the streets of Naples. She fights with every weapon she has to survive and invents new ones when the old ones don't win the day." He shrugged. "It's a pity she has such a soft heart. It's a weakness that will probably destroy her."

"And because you admire her, you want to put her in my bed."

"It will give her a weapon. She has none against you now. The child has the ridiculous belief that promises must be kept. You'd think she would have learned better leading the life she has."

"She has no need for weapons," Lion said impatiently. "I have no intention of being cruel to her."

"Oh yes, she'll need weapons." Lorenzo's index finger circled the rim of his goblet. "When you take her to Mandara."

Lion stiffened. "I don't take my mistresses to Mandara."

"You'll take Sanchia. Because she belongs to you."

"No, *per Dio*, you know I never—"

"You will this time." Lorenzo cut in, lifting his gaze from the goblet. "I look forward to seeing what will result."

"Because you enjoy watching all our lives thrown into a turmoil for you to savor."

For the first time the mockery faded from Lorenzo's

face. "No, because that foolishness at Mandara has gone on too long. It's time someone changed the course of events."

"Stay out of it, Lorenzo. It's my choice."

The mockery instantly returned to Lorenzo's face. "I don't think I could bear to do that. Our last stay at Mandara offered me no amusement whatsoever. All that sweetness and knightly restraint . . . It made me quite ill."

"How regrettable. I fear you must resign yourself to it. I take no bedmates to Mandara."

"We shall see." Lorenzo drained the last of his wine, set the goblet on the table and stood up. "Now I bid you good night. Do tell me in the morning how you enjoyed your little Sanchia." He moved toward the door. "Do you suppose she's a virgin? The possibility never occurred to me until she told us of her ingenious perfume." His gray eyes gleamed silver in the candlelight as he glanced back over his shoulder. "How splendid for you if she is. Think how tight she'll be around you and how sweet to hear the little cries of wonder and newfound delight." He added softly as he opened the door, "And that would make her all the more yours, wouldn't it?" He started to close the door and then paused. "Ah, Sanchia, how charming you look . . ." He sniffed experimentally. "And smell. Go right in, Lion's expecting you." He threw open the door and stepped aside. "*Buona sera*, ladies."

Sanchia and Giulia entered the room, stopped just inside the door. With a jerky motion of her head Giulia indicated Sanchia. "Well, does she please you?"

Lion's gaze traveled slowly over Sanchia's small form. It was clear to Lion that Giulia was not pleased with the intruder and less with Lion's response to her and had probably given her the most humble garment in all the wardrobes in this house. The simple velvet gown Sanchia wore was of a rich brown shade, but had no elaborate trim or embroidery. The tight sleeves came to her wrists, and the line of the gown was straight and graceful falling from the low square neckline of the bodice. Yet the darkness of the gown made the olive of Sanchia's skin glow golden, and the low square neckline revealed the lovely line of her throat and the swell of her small breasts against the velvet of the bodice.

Lion's gaze lingered on the bare golden flesh of her upper breasts and felt a stirring in his loins so intense it approached pain. "Yes, she pleases me."

"It took three scrubbings to get that stench out of her hair." Giulia's lips tightened as she noticed Lion's gaze was still on Sanchia. "I suppose you'll not want me tonight?"

"No."

Giulia whirled, her blue velvet skirt flying. "You're mad. If you wish a change, I can supply you with ten women who are more beautiful than this . . . this . . . child!"

The door slammed behind her.

"I don't like her," Sanchia said flatly.

"Then I'm sure it won't bother you to know that she has the same feelings toward you." Lion's gaze lifted from the delicate line of Sanchia's throat. "Your hair is still damp."

"I don't know why it should be. She and those two women nearly smothered me toweling it dry."

The color of her hair was not the brownish red he had first thought, Lion realized. The mixture she had put on it must have dulled its color along with its luster. Now, though it was still water-darkened, the candlelight revealed the fiery shimmer of auburn. "Come here and let me look at you."

She hesitated and then walked slowly toward him. She moved with grace, her shoulders back, her spine straight. There was a militance about her stance reminiscent of a soldier marching into battle, he thought suddenly.

She stopped before him. "She's right, you know." Her voice was breathless. "I'm not comely. I'm too skinny, and I don't have that lovely pale skin that Elizabet and Giulia Marzo have. You won't be pleased with me."

Lion leaned back in his chair. "You're wrong. As I told Giulia, I'm very pleased with you." His gaze went again to the smooth flesh of her shoulders. "And I like the shade of your skin. It reminds me of the gold of—" He stopped. He had been going to compare her to the Wind Dancer, he realized with a sense of shock. It must have been Lorenzo's remark that had brought the connection to mind. Possession. The Wind Dancer. Sanchia.

He lifted his goblet to his lips. "You know why you're here?"

"Yes." She moistened her lips with her tongue. "I knew when I saw you looking at me when I was in the bath. It's the same way Giovanni looked at my mother. You want to use my body."

The comparison irritated him. "I'm not Ballano," Lion said harshly.

"You had me bathed. You had me perfumed." She drew a quivering breath. "Do you want me to take off this gown and kneel on the floor now?"

"No!" The explosive rejection surprised him as much as it did her. "There are more pleasurable ways of taking a woman than if she were a bitch in heat."

"Yet the idea excited you," Sanchia said. "I saw that you were—"

"You see too much." A sudden thought struck him. "Are you trying to change my mind by comparing me to Ballano? Lorenzo said you use every weapon you possess."

"But I have no weapons here," she said simply. "I gave you my promise that I'd obey you."

No weapons. Lorenzo had said that, too, Lion recalled with frustration. She belonged to him. It was his right to use her body as he chose, with either tenderness or brutality. She knew this and accepted it. Why, then, was he feeling as if he had to make excuses for bedding her? "It doesn't have to be as it was with Ballano. I'll give you pleasure and—"

"No." Her eyes widened with bewilderment. "Why do you lie to me? It's always the man who has the pleasure. Women are merely vessels who accept them into their bodies and take their seed. Never once did my mother have pleasure."

"Because she was treated like an animal." Lion set

the goblet down on the windowsill with a force that splashed the remaining wine on the polished wood. "I'll show you ways . . ." He stopped as he saw she was looking at him with complete disbelief.

He smiled with sudden recklessness. "Ah, a challenge. Shall I make you a promise, my doubting Sanchia? Suppose I tell you that I'll not use you as my 'vessel' until you beg me to do it. Until you're willing to kneel and let me use you as Giovanni did your mother because you yearn to have me inside you."

She looked at him in wonder. "Why should you make me a promise? You need not consider my feelings. I belong to you. It doesn't matter if I feel nothing when—"

"It matters to me." His tone held exasperation as well as barely concealed violence. "God knows why, but it does." He took her hand and pulled her to her knees before his chair. "And I'll probably regret that promise a thousand times before this is over. Now lift your head and look at me."

She obediently tilted back her head and she caught her breath at what she saw in his face. His eyes held dark, exotic mysteries and the curve of his lips was blatantly sensual.

"What do you see?"

"You want me."

"Yes." His big hands fell heavily on her slender shoulders. "And whenever I look at you from now on I'll be thinking of what I'd like to do to you." One callused hand released her shoulder and began to stroke her throat. Her skin was as velvet-soft as it looked and warm, so warm. . . . He felt hot lust tear through him, adding dimension to his manhood. "I'm going to touch you whenever I like." He slipped the material of the gown off her shoulders. "When it pleases me, I'll bare this pretty flesh and fondle you. No matter where we are. No matter who is watching."

She was gazing at him as if mesmerized, the pulse fluttering wildly in the hollow of her throat.

"Are you a virgin?"

She moistened her lips with her tongue. "Yes."

"Good." He felt a primitive jolt of satisfaction so deep it almost obliterated the memory of Lorenzo's words. "Thank the saints for that obnoxious mixture, whatever it was."

"It was fish oil and garlic and chicken dro—" She broke off as his hand slipped beneath the bodice of the gown and one hard palm touched the nipple of her breast. He could feel the hard pounding of her heart beneath his fingertips. She closed her eyes. "I remember now. You didn't want to know."

"I'd rather know why your breast is swelling so sweetly under my hand."

"Is it? I don't know why. Maybe I'm falling ill. I feel quite peculiar."

"You're not ill." His palm moved back and forth on her breast, stroking it as if it were a favorite kitten. "You'll always respond like this when I touch you." He squeezed her breast gently.

Sanchia's eyes flew open and wild color stained her cheeks. She looked down at his big hand covering her breast. "This gives you pleasure?"

"Oh yes, as much pleasure as it gives you."

"It doesn't give me pleasure. It makes me feel hot and I ache . . ."

Lion squeezed her breast again, running his thumbnail over the rosy tip. "So do I. That's how pleasure starts." His thumb and forefinger began to pull teasingly at her pointed nipple. How would it feel in his mouth when he sucked and teethed it? he wondered. The thought caused his fingers to tighten with unconscious cruelty.

A shudder trembled through her and her gaze flew to his face.

His fingers instantly released her. "That was a mistake. I didn't mean to hurt you."

"You didn't. It just felt . . . odd."

Lion looked down at her. He knew he had gone far enough for now. Not nearly far enough for him, he thought ruefully, but if he didn't leave her at this moment, he wouldn't leave her for the night.

Cristo, why was he leaving her when he was rock

hard and burning to be inside her sweet tightness? So she wasn't ready for him, he would be gentle and— His lips tightened as he realized he was lying to himself. He was too hungry for her and he could never control a hunger such as this if he were between her thighs. He would go wild and drive and plunge in a frenzy of lust until she would think him the same rutting dog as Ballano.

The comparison to Ballano caused him to reluctantly release her breast and draw his hand from the velvet bodice. "Stand up," he said hoarsely.

Bright flags of color burned in her cheeks as she gazed at him in confusion.

"Stand up. It's done." His lips twisted in a smile. "For now."

She scrambled to her feet and took a step back. "You're not going to touch me anymore?"

He stood up and started for the door. "Undress and go to bed."

"Where?"

He gestured to the bed across the room. "Did you think I meant for you to sleep on a blanket on the floor as Ballano did?"

"But that's your bed," she stammered.

"All the more reason for you to occupy it. My bed, my slave. Lorenzo says I have a very possessive nature. If that's true, then I should enjoy seeing you in my bed when I return."

"Where are you going?"

"To Giulia's chamber." Lion's smile held a hint of cruelty. "I need a woman, and Giulia is always accommodating. Unlike you, she knows how to take pleasure as well as give it. She doesn't care what arouses me as long as I pleasure her enough. She'll even be grateful to you."

"I don't think so." Sanchia frowned. "And perhaps she only pretends pleasure. I've heard whores do that."

He looked at her blankly. He had never even considered that possibility. Could Giulia really be . . .

Sanchia started to laugh.

Cristo, the little devil was needling him, he realized

with astonishment. First she had shown the most abject compliance, and now her face was alight with mischievous laughter. A laughter so infectious that a reluctant smile appeared on his own lips. "I'll ask her." His gaze met hers. "If you'll ask yourself if you were pretending."

Her laughter vanished as her long lashes quickly lowered to veil her eyes. "I told you—"

"That it wasn't pleasure," he finished for her. "Think about it when you're lying in bed while I'm gone. I believe you'll discover it was pleasure you felt tonight." His voice lowered to sensual softness. "And as you lie there know that I'm giving Giulia even more pleasure, the pleasure you could have had." He turned to leave. "Sleep well, Sanchia." The door closed with a firm click behind him.

Sanchia gazed wonderingly at the panels of the door. What a strange man he was. He had wanted to take her in the same animal way Giovanni had used her mother. Nothing had been clearer to her as he had sat there watching her while she was in the bath. Why had he not done it? Women were always fair prey to a man whether they were slaves or free women. Sometimes she had thought being a slave was even a little better. At least slaves, as property, were usually provided food and a blanket to cover them. A free woman, if she was comely, as often as not ended up in one of Caprino's brothels. If she was ugly, she might starve in the streets.

When she had awakened to see Lord Andreas standing in the doorway of the storage room, she had been filled with the greatest terror she had ever known. Not only because of her fear of retribution, but because she could not read him. She sensed enormous power and could not guess in which way it might be directed. His motives and actions were an enigma, and that frightened her. She had always believed that to understand was to conquer or at least survive, but without knowledge she was helpless.

She slowly began to unfasten the gown she had so recently donned, her gaze still fixed on the panels of the door. What would he do when he returned? she wondered. His words had been so queer. She had not meant to challenge him, but he appeared to think she had. Was it because she was a virgin? How strange, when remaining untouched had always meant very little to her.

She had known it was inevitable she would lose her virginity, either to Giovanni or to some other man who might catch her unaware on the street. It had almost happened a few months ago when she had been jerked into the alley by a seaman who'd been too wild for a woman to notice the scent of her. She had known better than to waste her breath screaming. Rape happened so often in those back alleys that it provoked no more than a raised eyebrow and a quickening of pace away from the scene. Only luck and a kick in the bastard's private parts had enabled her to get away from him.

Losing her virginity wouldn't have been as important to her as the unfairness of having it taken without her consent. It had always seemed to her that a woman's virginity was greatly overrated. She could see it would be important to ascertain whether a man's son was his own through a wife's purity, but where marriage was not involved it was surely stupid for men to obtain such pleasure from being first with a woman.

Yet Lionello Andreas was not stupid, and his face when he had learned she was a virgin had expressed such intense primitive satisfaction it had given her a queer hot feeling in the pit of her stomach. His hands on her body had evoked the same aching sensation that fell somewhere between pain and hunger.

Hunger? She shook her head as she took off the gown and undershift and laid them carefully on the chair by the table. Why had that word occurred to her? Hunger was for food and rest and for the lovely words in books, not for a man's hands on her body. It must be exhaustion that was making her so sluggish and dimwitted.

She pulled back the velvet spread and slipped beneath it. It was a pity she was too tired to fully appreciate the softness of the mattress and the clean fragrance of pine resin and laurel leaves that clung to the linens. She had never slept in a real bed before and wished she could savor the luxury of the moment. She had always believed moments of pleasure must always be lived to the hilt because the next might never come. During the bad times, she could bring out the memory of a moment of beauty and suddenly the situation would not seem so terrible that she could not get through it.

Sleep beckoned with an irresistible allure. She should really get up and blow out the candle so Lord Andreas would not think she was careless and wasteful. . . .

Four

Cristo, what the hell was the matter with him?

Lion gazed down at Sanchia seething with frustration that almost exceeded the lust hardening every muscle of his body.

Candlelight flickered over the rich auburn of Sanchia's hair and stroked the silky smoothness of her bare shoulders above the coverlet. She was curled on her side, her cheek buried in the pillow, her pink lips slightly parted. Why did he not wake her and tell her she must take him into her body and let him use her to rid himself of his terrible need? She was his property. She had given him her promise that she would obey him in all things. She would yield her body to him without complaint.

Yield. He wished the word had not come to him, for it evoked memories of the many cities that had yielded to his sword. Rape and pillage invariably followed those surrenders.

Looting and raping were the rewards a victorious army expected, his father had taught, and Lion had grown accustomed to both over the years. In spite of Lorenzo's mocking charge he knew well that chivalry was only for fools.

Yet he did not want Sanchia to yield to him because he owned her and she had no choice.

Santa Maria, what was the matter with him? He had been unable to muster any desire for Giulia after he had left Sanchia, and the failure had shocked and outraged him. He had stormed out of her chamber with every intention of satisfying the hunger that Giulia had been unable to appease. A man was a fool to worry about challenges when he needed a woman's body to put out the fires. Since his body was issuing this peculiar demand for Sanchia alone, it was only sensible he should give it what it wanted.

He reached out and drew the coverlet down so he could see Sanchia from the top of her shining hair to her small feet. She was a brilliant butterfly against the stark white linen sheet, all velvet golden flesh and silky wine colored hair. Why did he find her slender loveliness a thousand times more arousing than Giulia's more voluptuous beauty? He had always preferred full-figured women. . . .

Ah, this was better. The blood was pounding in his veins and the quickening in his loins was gaining in intensity until it was almost unbearable. In another moment there would be no question of stopping himself from mounting Sanchia.

He bent closer, his gaze on the pinkness of her distended nipples. Her breasts were truly magnificent. The mere thought of touching them sent his heart slamming against his rib cage. He would have to have gowns made for her that would reveal the beauty of her bosom and—

Sanchia stirred, sighed, and rolled over on her back.

Dio, she was small. She looked like a child except for those erotic breasts and the soft thatch of hair protecting her womanhood.

But she was no child, he quickly reminded himself.

She had said she was sixteen; most women had been wedded and bedded for at least two years by the time they had reached her age. His mother had given birth to him when she was fifteen. He should feel no guilt about Sanchia's age, and not a single compunction because of her helplessness to resist him.

Sanchia murmured in the inarticulateness of sleep.

Lion's gaze flew to her face. Her long lashes cast dark shadows on the curves of her cheeks. But there was another shadow high on her right cheek, he noticed suddenly. Then he realized it was not a shadow but a faint bruise where Giovanni had struck her. He remembered Sanchia's head snapping back with the force of the blow and the fierceness of the anger that had torn through him. He had wanted to kill the whoreson. How dare that bastard touch his property? Couldn't he see how tiny and helpless Sanchia was, how easily she could be bruised and hurt? If that blow had been a little harder, it could have killed her or at least—

No, by God, he wouldn't think how vulnerable she was, but only how much he desired her. He deliberately summoned the image and feelings that had assaulted him when he'd first drawn down the coverlet to reveal her naked body.

A brilliant butterfly. All color and soft velvety textures.

But butterflies were the most fragile of creatures.

Butterflies could be broken and destroyed with only the careless brush of a man's hand.

And he was not Giovanni.

He could wait until she recovered from this exhaustion and felt more secure under his rule.

After all, the woman was vital to him as a thief. She would bring him what he needed and any additional pleasure he took in her would be only secondary.

He straightened and then reluctantly drew the coverlet up to Sanchia's chin. Yes, he could wait.

Perhaps.

He turned away and blew out the flame of the candle.

But he could not stay away from her if he remained

in this bed . . . or even in this room. He moved silently toward the door while considering his options. He couldn't return to Giulia's chamber. She had been most irate when he had left her. Only one solution occurred to him given the lateness of the hour.

He grimaced as he realized he would have to go to Lorenzo's chamber and face his raised brows and faintly malicious amusement.

Oh yes, Lorenzo would take an unholy joy in Lion's predicament.

"Wake up." Giulia's hand on Sanchia's shoulders was less than gentle as she shook her. "Get up. They're waiting for you downstairs."

Sanchia opened drowsy eyes to see Giulia Marzo's flushed face above her. Giulia was angry again, she realized hazily, almost as angry as she had been last night when she had left Sanchia with Lion. "I'm awake." She sat up in bed, and blinked as the early morning sunlight streaming through the window assaulted her with its brilliance. "What time is it?"

"Nearly eight o'clock."

Eight o'clock! Sanchia couldn't remember when she had slept past dawn. She scrambled out of bed, reaching frantically for the clothes she'd laid on the chair the night before. "I didn't mean to sleep this late. Is Lord Andreas displeased with me?"

"You'll have to ask him." Giulia moved toward the door. "He's not a man who likes to be kept waiting." She glanced back over her shoulder as she opened the door. "There's wine and fruit on the table. Eat quickly and join Lord Andreas downstairs in ten minutes."

"Five." Sanchia was dressing hurriedly. "I don't need to eat. Messer Lorenzo bought me bread and fruit yesterday at the baker's. I can—"

"Eat." Giulia's beautiful features were set with a less than attractive hardness. "Lion told me to make sure you broke your fast before you started the journey. He won't be any more displeased with you now than he will be five minutes from now." Giulia smiled with a hint of malice.

"Or perhaps you feel you need to curry favor after last night? I told Lion he'd find no pleasure with you."

Sanchia stared at Giulia in bewilderment. The woman was a wasp trying to sting her with hurtful words, but how could they wound when they made no sense? After all, Lion had spent the night in Giulia's bed. "That's what I told him too. He didn't appear to believe me."

Giulia's hand tightened on the knob of the door. "Insolence."

"No, I didn't mean—"

"You may please him for a few weeks, but he'll grow tired of bedding a child with no more meat on her bones than a scrawny foul." Giulia's blue eyes blazed. "And then he'll come back to Florence and to me. You'll never be able to hold him."

"The question will never arise," Sanchia said quietly. "You forget, I belong to him. *He* holds *me*."

For some reason her answer only seemed to make Giulia more angry. She muttered an obscenity and slammed the door.

Sanchia flinched, then thrust her feet into slippers and finished fastening her gown. She cast a wistful glance at the apple quarters and cup of wine on the silver tray on the table. A real apple. She'd had a taste of one a few years before, but this one certainly looked riper and more juicy. Perhaps she could have just one bite. . . .

She sighed and started for the door. Lion was too much the unknown quantity for her to risk angering him. She could put no store in Giulia's assurance that he would not be irritated if she kept him waiting longer since the woman obviously wished her ill.

Sanchia hesitated at the top of the stairs when she heard voices. Caprino was standing in the hall below talking to Lion. Her hand tightened on the marble bannister. However, her astonishment and wariness were quickly submerged in fierce satisfaction. She had no reason to be afraid of Caprino. He could not touch her; he could not hurt Elizabet. Serenely she now started down the stairs.

Caprino glanced up as she reached the third step from the bottom. "Ah, Sanchia, how charming you look." His gaze traveled appraisingly over her. "I had no idea you'd clean up so well or I might have hesitated about making you a present to the *magnifico*." He held up a leather purse and smiled smugly. "I fear I'll just have to be satisfied with young Elizabet. I believe I'll pay a visit to Giovanni after I bid you good journey."

Sanchia smiled back at him. "I'm sure Giovanni will be happy to see you. I've always thought you had many qualities in common. However, Elizabet is no longer with Giovanni."

Caprino stiffened, his gaze narrowing on her face. "And where is she?"

"With Messer Benedetto and his good wife. As I was forced to leave Elizabet, I thought it wise to have her future settled." Her smile deepened with mockery. "I'm sure you can sympathize with such a decision. I remember you were quite eager to have her settled yourself. She's to marry Alessandro within the month."

"Marriage! But she can't—" Caprino whirled to Lion. "I've been cheated. The money you paid for Sanchia is not enough."

"It was enough two minutes ago." Lion's tone was icy. "The arrangement stands, Caprino."

"But that was when I thought—" Caprino broke off as he met Lion's gaze. He was silent, struggling to subdue his anger. Finally he turned back to Sanchia. "You think you've bested me."

"I didn't try to best you. I intended only to protect Elizabet."

"From me," he snarled.

"From everything and everyone." She gazed at him directly. "But yes, from you most of all."

"You need not worry. Your Elizabet is no longer important to me." Caprino's voice was so soft the underlying malevolence was only barely discernible. "But you and your future are going to be of great interest to me, Sanchia. I don't like to be cheated of something I want."

A chilly finger of fear touched her spine. He couldn't hurt her or Elizabet, she reassured herself, but still she felt his menace. "You won't know my future. I'm leaving Florence."

"I can wait. I'm good at waiting."

"Leave, Caprino." Lion gestured toward the door. "Our business is finished."

"Good day, *Magnifico*." His voice sounded of nothing but politeness now. "I wish you joy in your purchase. May Sanchia bring you what you seek." He opened the door and slanted them a faint smile over his shoulder. "But you'd best hasten in your use of her. Young girls such as she are fragile blossoms that sometimes wither and perish overnight." He gave them no chance to answer as he closed the door behind him.

The tension eased from Sanchia's rigid muscles and she forced herself to release her grip on the bannister. "I'm sorry I overslept, my lord. I'm ready to leave."

Lion's glance shifted from the door to her face. "You do realize he just threatened your life?"

She nodded jerkily as she descended the last steps. "He's an evil man."

"Yet you're paying no more attention to his threat than if he'd just told you he was going to make you a present."

"What can I do about it? He'll try to hurt me and perhaps he'll succeed." She gazed at Lion gravely. "But he'd hurt me much more if I let him poison all my hours and days with worry and fear."

"An interesting philosophy." He gazed at her with an odd intentness. "You advocate living for the present and not the future?"

"All I have is the present. A slave has only the future her master determines."

The intensity of his gaze was making her uneasy and causing a tight stricture in her chest. He was so *big*. He towered above her and his simple apparel of black leather hose and boots and russet suede jerkin served only to emphasize the strength of his massive body.

"Then I agree we must make the most of every single minute," Lion said softly as he drew on his heavy leather gauntlets. "Tell me, did you miss me in your bed last night?"

The tightness in her chest increased until she had trouble drawing breath. "How could I miss you when I've never slept with you? I fell asleep right away and didn't stir until Giulia woke me."

"Remind me to teach you the virtue of flattery. A man has need of pretty lies on occasion." Humor glinted in his dark eyes. "It's an art required of all my slaves."

"But Messer Lorenzo said I'm your only slave."

He airily waved a gloved hand. "Not important. One is enough to set a standard."

He was joking with her, Sanchia realized with amazement. She had seen him in many moods since yesterday afternoon, but they had all been heavy—anger, suspicion, appraisal, lust. Now he appeared light-hearted, charged with energy and good humor. "You're happy today."

"I admit I'm very glad we're on our way. I detest waiting for anything." He touched her cheek. "Remember that, Sanchia."

The hard leather of the gauntlet was rough against the soft flesh of her cheek. She imagined the warmth of his finger beneath the leather and it caused a tingle of heat to spread from her cheek to her throat. She took an involuntary step back. "I'll remember." She moistened her lips with her tongue. "What kept you here in Florence? What were you waiting for?"

"Why, you, Sanchia." He turned to the door. "We were waiting for you."

She gazed at him in bewilderment. "Me? But—" She stopped as the significance of Caprino's presence earlier sank home to her. "Caprino said he sold me to you. The piazza . . ."

"A test of your skill, which proved very impressive." Lion opened the door. "Come along. Lorenzo is waiting outside with the horses. I purchased a few items of clothing for you from one of the women here; they're tied on the back of your horse." He frowned. "I was able to obtain a very gentle mare for you. I assume you've never ridden."

"No." She came toward him, her gaze searching his face. "A thief. That's why you want me." At least she knew now why he'd bought her and felt she was no longer blundering in the dark with him.

"When I bought you from Giovanni, I certainly believed I was getting only a thief." He studied her face. "You seem pleased. I got the impression that taking purses was not to your liking."

"It's not; stealing frightens me. But now that I know what value I have for you I feel better."

"So that you can seek a way to bend me to your will as you did Giovanni?"

Her eyes widened and she gazed up at him helplessly.

"For God's sake, don't look at me like that. I'm not going to beat you." He shrugged wearily, "Sweet Jesus, why shouldn't you try to manage me? I'll do my best to use you in the way I see fit."

"But I promised I would obey you in all things."

No weapons, Lorenzo had said, and she looked poignantly defenseless at this moment, Lion thought. What must it be like to be as helpless as Sanchia, and have to struggle to maintain even a modicum of dignity and independence in an uncertain world? The thought filled him with astonishment. Where did his anger at her situation come from? Why this inexplicable need to comfort? "One theft," he said curtly. "That's all you'll have to do. Once we're finished at Solinari you'll never have to steal again. I'll find some other—"

"Lion, *caro mio*." Giulia was walking down the stairs, a dazzling smile on her face. "Were you not coming to bid me good-bye?"

"I thought we'd said our good-byes last night," Lion replied. "I seem to remember you wished me a swift journey to . . ." He paused and gave her a half mocking bow. "A place with an extremely warm but unpleasant climate."

Giulia shrugged. "I was angry. You know my bad temper is fleeting. Forgive me for attacking you as an apothecary would a barber. *Caro,* I am so sorry for my venomous words. Come, we must part friends." She cast

Sanchia a careless glance. "We had no problem before she came. Do not bring her back and all will be well."

"I don't care for ultimatums, Giulia." Lion's hand encircled Sanchia's wrist and he drew her toward the door. "Nor do I care for viragos. I don't believe I'll be returning to your *casa*."

"But Lion, I didn't mean—" Giulia stopped. The door had closed behind them.

Giulia's hands slowly clenched into fists. She should never have pushed him, she thought. She had known it was a mistake to show her anger the night before, but she hadn't been able to stem the vitrolic words. Jealousy. *Dio,* she was jealous of that bony child. It was just as well that this madness with Lion was at an end. Caprino was right; a woman in her profession had to maintain control. Money was important, not pleasure . . . not the pleasure she had received from Lion, certainly.

She turned away from the door, lifting her skirts as she started up the stairs. Still, she did owe Lion a small debt for giving her so many hours of servicing in the bedchamber. She would repay him by waiting until late this evening to summon Caprino and tell him what she had overheard as she came down to the front hall. Caprino might be delayed as much as a full day before starting whatever it might be he chose to do with the information she would sell him. He'd promised her seven ducats for finding out what Lion wanted Sanchia to steal for him. In this she'd failed, but the name of the place where the theft was to occur should be worth at least five, Giulia thought shrewdly.

Solinari. The name sounded vaguely familiar, she mused. Now in what connection had she heard it?

"Where is Solinari?" Sanchia asked as Lion lifted her onto the saddle of the chestnut mare. She clutched desperately at the reins trying not to think how far she was from the ground.

"It's a palazzo just outside of Pisa."

"What am I supposed to steal there?"

"A kev."

"A key to unlock what?"

"A door." Lion mounted his own black stallion.

"Oh." Sanchia was silent a moment. "What's behind the door?"

She heard a low chuckle from Lorenzo, who was already mounted behind her.

"You're very inquisitive." There was an edge to Lion's tone.

"I'll have to know sometime, won't I?" She asked anxiously, "Do questions displease you?"

"*Cristo,* what do I care? Question away as you please."

Lorenzo chuckled again. "I'm sure she will."

Lion scowled at him over his shoulder. "I never have to worry about you saying what you like, Lorenzo."

"That must be a great comfort to you."

"You'll have to tell me how to please you," Sanchia said quickly. "This is all new to me. I've had no master but Giovanni and he—"

"I don't want to hear any more about that man," Lion said tersely as he turned his stallion, Tabron, toward the south. "I find any comparison between him and me less than flattering."

"And I'm sure Lion will let you know what pleases him," Lorenzo murmured, "when he gains the courage."

Lion's expression was lethal. "It may please me to take a mace to your head in the very near future."

Lorenzo clucked reprovingly. "Such violence. How can you set a fitting example for the young when you are clearly a barbarian?"

"Lorenzo, I'm going to—" Lion stopped abruptly. "Sanchia, you may ask your questions when we stop at the Inn of the Two Swords this evening. I'm in a hurry now." He kicked the stallion into a trot. "Bring her." A moment later he was halfway down the street.

Sanchia frowned. "I made him angry."

Lorenzo shook his head. "The situation makes him angry, but that will change shortly. I'm surprised he's lasted this long." He edged his horse closer and took the reins from Sanchia's hand. "However, perhaps I shouldn't have goaded him so. I believe we can expect to have an extremely hard and fast trip today. Lion grew up on a horse and forgets there are others who prefer traveling on two feet rather than four." He grimaced as he turned his horse and began leading Sanchia's mare in the direction Lion had taken. "*Dio*, how I hate riding these foul-smelling beasts."

The trip was as grueling as Lorenzo had predicted, and Sanchia was near exhaustion when they finally stopped at sunset at the Inn of the Two Swords. A hundred times she had wanted to ask Lion to stop and let them rest, and a hundred times she had bitten her lip and remained silent. It was not her place to complain, and she had little opportunity to speak to him anyway. For most of the journey he rode at least a quarter of a mile ahead of her and Lorenzo.

The interior of the small inn appeared clean and a cheerful fire burned in the stone fireplace in the common room. The delicious aroma of roasting hare drifted to Sanchia's nostrils from the spit that a buxom maid was turning over the fire.

The innkeeper bustled forward, a broad, toothy smile lighting his angular face. "Welcome, my lord, it's a pleasure to have you again under my roof. How long will you be with us?"

"We leave at dawn tomorrow, Antonio." Lion drew off his leather gauntlets and tucked them in his belt. "See that our horses are cared for and water heated for us for washing."

"At once, *Magnifico*. I'll call my son to take your horses to the stable and they'll receive the finest care." The innkeeper snapped his fingers and the maid left the spit and hurried toward them, an eager smile on her lips. "Heat water and bring it to Lord Andreas and his companions at once, Letitia." His gaze went to Sanchia and he frowned. "You remember, we have only the two rooms, my lord. Will the lady—"

"The lady will occupy my bed," Lion interrupted. "Send Letitia with wine at once and with our dinner after we've had an opportunity to wash."

Sanchia caught the flickering expression of disappointment on the servant girl's face before she hurried from the room, trailing the innkeeper.

Lorenzo was already climbing the short flight of stairs. "I'm going to stretch out and rest these aching bones. When the wench brings the food call me." He grimaced as he glanced down at them from the landing. "I don't know why I let you persuade me to mount one of those beasts from hell, Lion."

"Because you're too lazy to walk," Lion said dryly. "And you're afraid you'll miss something if you stay at Mandara."

"Things were much simpler and more comfortable before you decided to save me from my life of iniquity." Lorenzo opened the door at the top of the stairs. "I managed very well in Naples without running from place to place jarring my bones and doing grievous harm to my person." He glanced over his shoulder. "By the way, you'd best care for your urchin. If you weren't avoiding looking at her, you would notice that she may collapse at any moment."

Lion's gaze flew to Sanchia.

"I'm not tired," Sanchia said quickly. "Well, perhaps a little." She tried to keep from swaying. "I've never ridden a horse before and the sun—"

"*Cristo!*" Lion's hand was on her elbow propelling her up the steps. "Why didn't you tell me you needed to stop?"

"You said you were in a hurry."

"So you let me drive you until you were ready to fall off the damned horse? Have you no sense?" Lion threw open the door next to the one through which Lorenzo had disappeared and half pushed her into a small bedchamber. "Lie down until Letitia comes with the wine."

"I don't have to lie down. I'm not ill."

He picked her up and tossed her unceremoniously onto the bed. "And you're not going to be ill. I have no time to be your nursemaid."

A ghost of a smile touched her lips as she thought of Lionello Andreas in a sickroom. He was so big, his energy and vitality so great, she couldn't associate him with illness. "I'll endeavor to ward off all maladies so as not to inconvenience you."

"Are you laughing at me?"

Her lashes fell to veil the glint of mischief in her eyes. "I would not dare, my lord."

"You'd dare." He stood looking down at her for an instant before turning on his heel. "Rest. I'll go next door and let Lorenzo laugh at me awhile. I'm more accustomed to his barbs than yours."

Sanchia raised herself on one elbow. "Barbs, my lord? I merely jested a bit. If you'd rather I wouldn't laugh, you must tell me and I'll—"

He held his hand up. "Must you be so obliging? I'm not so puffed up that I can't laugh at myself." Suddenly a smile lit his harsh features with rare warmth. "And I always get my own back eventually."

The door shut behind him before she could answer.

She gazed at the door for a long time before she settled her cheek on the pillow and closed her eyes. He was difficult to understand, she thought wearily. So many hard, sharp edges and so much brutal driving force and yet his hands had held nothing but rough kindness when they touched her just now.

And his smile had been beautiful. . . .

Five

"Well, if I must face the horrors of mounting that repulsive monster at dawn, I suppose I must bid you good night." Lorenzo pushed back his chair and rose to his feet. A faintly mocking smile was on his lips as his gaze rested on Sanchia sitting on a stool by the hearth. "A *very* good night. Shall I tell Letitia to take away the remains of this sumptuous repast so as not to disturb you . . . later?"

"I'll clear it away." Sanchia jumped to her feet, eager to have something to do to relieve the tension that had been building steadily within her during the meal. "There's no use your troubling yourself, Messer Lorenzo. I'll be glad to—"

"Sit down, Sanchia." Lion's voice was as lazy as the position of his big body sprawled in the chair opposite Lorenzo. "Tell Letitia to come and take care of it, Lorenzo."

"But I can . . ." Sanchia trailed off as

she met Lion's gaze. The room was suddenly close, airless. She quickly sat back down on the stool and looked at the reflection of the firelight in the ruby red wine in her wooden goblet.

Lorenzo nodded as he moved toward the door. "I'll see you at dawn."

The silence in the room after the door closed behind him was broken only by the hiss and crackle of the olive logs burning in the fireplace. Sanchia could feel Lion's gaze on her face but avoided looking up to meet his eyes.

The tension was growing, the tightness in her chest robbing her of breath. Why didn't he speak? Then when he let the silence drag on she realized she must be the one to break it. "You should let me serve you. It is my place."

"I didn't buy you to serve me at the table. Your time will come."

Involuntarily her glance flew to the bed across the room.

He chuckled. "I didn't buy you for that either. It will only be an extra delight for us both."

"Not for—" She broke off. It would be foolish to anger him when he seemed to be more mellow than she had ever seen him. There were answers she must have if she was to understand him. "What lies behind the door, my lord? The one that I'm to steal the key to unlock?"

"Why does it matter to you?"

"It's important for me to try to know about things that have an effect on my life. You're a very rich man. Why should you steal more?"

Lion smiled cynically. "My dear Sanchia, haven't you found there's never enough wealth for some men?"

"Yes." A frown furrowed her brow. "I do not know you very well, but I don't think you're one of those men."

"No, but Francisco Damari is." The wooden chair creaked as Lion leaned back and stretched his legs out before him, his gaze on the fire. "Ruling all the city-states of Italy would only whet Damari's appetite. He thinks to reign over the world." Lion's lips tightened.

"But he'll not use the Wind Dancer to buy him more power."

"The Wind Dancer?"

"A statue belonging to my family." In the firelight Lion's rugged features were softened to real handsomeness in sharp contrast to the bitter tone of his voice. "While I was away in France negotiating the purchase of another shipyard, he bribed one of my servants at Mandara, a man called Giuseppe, to steal it and bring it to him. He's now keeping the statue at his palazzo at Solinari."

"How do you know?"

"Lorenzo and I chased down Giuseppe and asked him a number of pertinent questions. He was delighted to answer . . . eventually."

Sanchia shivered and looked away from the stark brutality of his expression. "If the statue is yours, why don't you just march in and take it? Lorenzo said you were a condottiere."

"It may come to that. However, I disbanded my armies two years ago and it would take a good deal of time to form another condotti. I do not wish to bring Damari, even Borgia perhaps, down on Mandara until I have a chance to refortify. Mandara is well guarded but not strong enough to withstand a thrust by Borgia."

"Borgia?" Her gaze flew back to his face.

"Oh, you've heard of the illustrious Duke Valentino?" Lion's lips twisted. "But of course. All of Italy knows of the great Cesare."

"Yes, I've heard of him." Who in Florence was not familiar with the name? Borgia had been eyeing Florence with greed and speculation for many years and, after his recently completed conquest of the Romagna, every week there had been a new rumor that the duke was on the march to lay siege to the city. "I've heard that he wishes to rule all Italy, but who is this Damari?"

"Damari is a condottiere who is now serving under Borgia's banner. They have similar goals and similar methods for obtaining them."

Sanchia didn't have to ask the nature of those methods. The ruthless slaughter of women and children, the maiming of innocents by the captains serving Borgia had become legend over the years. "Then why do you not let him have the statue? You can buy others."

"There is no other statue like it in the world. It's part of my family history." His voice vibrated with intensity. "We guard it." He paused. "And it guards us."

"I don't understand."

"You don't have to understand. All you have to do is go to the palazzo, steal the key from the officer on guard, and bring it to me."

"It sounds very simple."

Lion's hands closed on the arms of his chair. "We'll make it so. No harm will come to you, I promise."

"I take comfort from your promise. I fear I'd not look forward to facing your Messer Damari. Men such as he don't regard the life of a slave as having any more value than a cool drink of water." She lifted her shoulder and let it drop expressively. "Less, if they have no thirst."

"Just do what I say and you'll not even see Damari. We've laid a path of gold to get into the palazzo and buy the information as to the location of the store house where Damari keeps his treasures."

"And you're sure Damari will have your Wind Dancer there?"

He smiled crookedly. "Oh yes, it will be there. Damari regards the Wind Dancer as the ultimate treasure."

"Why?" Sanchia took a final sip of wine before setting the wooden goblet on the hearth. "You said it was important to your family, but why should it be important to him?"

"Because it belongs to me," Lion said grimly. "And he knows I want it back. He knows I *have* to get it back."

"But why would Borgia let himself be swayed by Damari into protecting it?"

"The pope is a greedy man and dazzled by all things ancient and classical. Pope Alexander's treasury grows daily with the loot Cesare brings to Rome from his conquests. As long as Cesare continues to send him such treasure Alexander will protect his clever son and give him access to the papal monies for his campaigns."

"And the Wind Dancer is ancient?"

Lion smiled curiously. "Oh yes, very ancient. Damari is hoping to dangle the Wind Dancer before Cesare and Alexander and possibly gain a dukedom from the pope."

Sanchia's eyes widened. "But they would surely not give so much?"

"They might. Alexander is superstitious and there are many legends about the Wind Dancer."

"What kind of legends?"

Lion shrugged. "Power. Legend says the Wind Dancer can give any victory to the one who possesses it."

"But you don't believe it."

He was silent a moment. "I don't know. The lives of my family have always been too intertwined with the Wind Dancer for us to look at it objectively. If the statue does possess power, we've never tried to use it."

"Why not?"

"Kinship," Lion said simply. "The Wind Dancer is of our family. We of the Andreas family may not be shy about manipulating others to suit us, but we stand together. We will not use each other."

She shook her head in disbelief. "But a dukedom for a statue . . ."

"What's a dukedom in Italy today? Cesare gathered a parcel of little states into his basket this year alone." His lips twisted. "For that matter, what is Italy today? Genoa and Milan are gone, Naples torn between the French and Spaniards. Florence is licking at the French boots and still out to pluck Pisa. All the rest of the signories are maneuvering to survive and not be swept by the pope and Rome into the empire Cesare is trying to create for himself. While France, Spain, and England have finally become unified and have strong national armies, we still hire mercenaries who have loyalty only to the highest bidder. I don't wonder Borgia considers all of Italy ripe for conquest."

There was an indifference in his tone that surprised her after the passionate intensity with which he'd spoken of his family and the Wind Dancer. "You don't care? It's your country, after all. Is it not important to you?"

He shook his head. "Mandara is my country. I have no interest in what the rest of Italy becomes as long as they leave me and my people out of their petty bickering." He tilted his head to look at her curiously. "Is it important to you?"

She thought about it. "A slave has no country, I suppose." She paused. "But I think I'd like to feel as if I belonged somewhere. It would make me . . . warm."

His gaze narrowed on her face. "You accept being a slave so meekly?"

"I don't remember ever being anything else."

"And yet you have courage. I would have thought . . ."

She looked at him inquiringly.

"I couldn't *stand* it," he said with sudden violence. "I'd want to kill someone or run away to a land where I could be free. Haven't you ever wanted to do that?"

"I've never thought about it. From the time I was a tiny child my mother kept telling me I must accept my station in life and make the best of it." She smiled tremulously. "And I'm not really very brave. Sometimes it was hard just to live from day to day. I have had little time to think about what it might be like to be free."

"But you should have thought about it," he said fiercely. "Giovanni had no right to—*Gran Dio*, what am I saying? In another moment I'll be talking you into running away from *me*." He stood up. "Don't try it. I warn you that I'd find you and be most annoyed. And don't mistake a temporary madness brought on by the warmth of the fire and those huge eyes gazing at me for anything enduring. Your mother was right. Accept that you're mine and will stay mine."

She was bewildered. "But I have accepted— Where are you going?"

"To look to the horses." He was already at the door. "Antonio's son is a cowardly lout. The last time I was here he was too afraid of Tabron to unsaddle him."

"So you're going yourself to see if he's been taken care of?"

"A horse can be the difference between life and death to a man. It doesn't denote softness to see that an animal is well cared for." He scowled. "What are you smiling about?"

She quickly wiped any trace of amusement from her face. "Nothing, my lord."

"No? I'm getting very weary of being thought a weakling," he said with menacing softness. "First Lorenzo and now you. I think I must put an end to it." He paused. "I was stupid not to take what I wanted in the beginning and I'll wait no longer. When I come back I want to see you sitting on that stool wearing nothing but firelight. You understand?"

"Yes." The air in the room was suddenly charged with the same stormy intensity as earlier. She moistened her lips. "I understand, my lord."

"Good." He slammed the door shut behind him.

Sanchia started to speak quickly as soon as Lion entered the room. "Letitia came and took the trenchers and left fresh wine. Was Tabron well?" Her hands were locked together on her lap and she flexed her fingers nervously, her gaze fixed on the fire. "Will we go straight to Solinari tomorrow or must we stop at another—"

"Stand up. I want to look at you."

Sanchia tensed and then rose slowly to her feet. She turned to face Lion, but still would not meet his gaze. "You've seen me before. In the bath. There's nothing more to see."

"I disagree." His gaze ran over her naked body, lingering on the soft thatch guarding her womanhood. "There's always something more to see and . . . appreciate."

A wave of heat tingled through Sanchia that had nothing to do with the fire burning in the hearth. Her nails bit into the flesh of her palms as her hands clenched into fists at her sides. She welcomed the sharp pain; it pierced the rigidity attacking her every muscle. "Shall I kneel on the floor now?"

"No!" The sharpness of his voice caused her gaze to move to his face. Her breath caught in her throat and she felt as if she were suffocating. Lion's dark eyes were fierce, and the flesh drawn tight over the broad planes of his jaws hollowed his cheeks as if he were being consumed by a terrible hunger. "When will you learn I'm not Giovanni?" He took a step forward and she caught the clean scent of hay, soap, and crisp spring night clinging to him. "My name is Lion. Say it."

She could feel the heat his body was emitting though he hadn't touched her yet. The muscles of her limbs felt suddenly heavy, weak, unable to support her weight. "Lion." The name trembled uncertainly from her lips. "My lord."

"Just Lion." He reached out a gloved hand to caress her slender throat.

She inhaled sharply and a shiver ran through her.

He stopped with his hand still encircling her throat to gaze at her searchingly.

"The leather is cold," she said quickly, seizing wildly at the first excuse that came to mind for her moment of revealing weakness.

"Is it?" His smile was purely sensual. "Then we must do something to warm it, for I cannot trust myself to touch you without them right now." He turned to the fire and held out his gloved hands to the flames. "Do you know what I thought when I came through the doorway and saw you sitting naked on your stool?"

Her gaze was fastened in helpless fascination on the heavy, scarred gauntlets he held before the warmth of the fire. They came almost to his elbows, the brass rivets shining in the firelight, each finger now limned in blue-orange flame. "No, my lo-Lion."

"I thought what a stroke of fortune it was that brought me to Giovanni's shop."

"It wasn't fortune; it was Caprino."

"And that I want you to be like this always. I want to think of the fire shimmering on your flesh and shining on your hair while you wait for me to come to you." His gaze remained on the burning logs. "Come into you."

Her heart gave a jerk and then began to pound wildly. Her thoughts were an incoherent jumble and she was only conscious of the raw vulnerability of her own nudity, the dominance of Lion's fully clothed body, the violence she sensed beneath those garments.

And, most of all, the power of his leather-gauntleted hands held out before the flames . . .

"You're very small." His gaze was still on the fire. "It will hurt you the first time."

She didn't answer. She almost wished he would touch her and end the maddening tension between them. She felt as if the next breath she drew would shatter her composure.

"I'll try to proceed slowly but—" He stopped and was silent a moment before continuing haltingly, "My appetites are great. Sometimes it's like a frenzy, a madness. You must not fight me or I might injure you. I don't want that to happen."

"I will not fight you."

Lion's hands closed slowly into fists. "I know. You will yield because I own you." He smiled recklessly as he turned to face her. "And why not? It's the way of the world." His gloved hands reached out to encompass her breasts. "Why do you gasp? The leather is no longer cold. I made sure of that, Sanchia."

The leather *was* warm, almost hot, she thought hazily. The hard, seamed leather was strangely seductive against the smoothness of her flesh.

His hands were cupping her, squeezing her gently while his gaze studied her face. "My hands are even warmer," he said softly. "But I dare not take off these gloves yet. The texture of your skin excites me and if I touch your flesh I will need you at once . . . and I will take you at once. It will go easier for you if I do not." His left hand slid down her abdomen to the thatch of curls surrounding her womanhood and began slowly to rub back and forth. "Such a pretty nest." His voice was hoarser, his nostrils flaring as he looked at her. "I want to move into you and feel those curls brushing against me. Part your limbs now, Sanchia."

She was trembling so badly she wasn't sure she could move. His hand stroking her was igniting a strange burning sensation between her thighs.

"Sanchia." The softness of his tone failed to veil the underlying command.

She obeyed him, her gaze fastened blindly on the lacings of his leather jerkin.

"Wider." Her gaze moved up to his strong brown throat, and she watched in fascination as the pulse in the hollow abruptly accelerated. "Ah, that's right. Now stand very still."

His hand moved down between her thighs and she felt the warmth of his hand through the gauntlet as his palm moved against her, caressing, stroking. Everywhere he touched left a trail of that same moist burning sensation that was close to pain. She closed her eyes, swaying helplessly as sensation after bewildering sensation tore through her. "It . . . hurts."

"No." His palm cupped, squeezed, released. "It's not pain, Sanchia. Hunger." His voice was uneven. "It's hunger."

"I don't think so." She reached out to clutch desperately at his upper arms.

He stiffened. "Don't touch me."

She jerked her hands away. "I'm sorry, my lord, I didn't mean—"

"Lion," he cut in through clenched teeth. "It's too soon for you to touch me. I can't hold off, if you do." He lifted her in his arms and started across the room toward the bed. "There are many kinds of hunger." He laid her down. "This is the best." He parted her thighs, his index finger searching. "And the worst."

He found what he sought and began to gently press and rotate.

Her eyes widened with shock as she gave a little cry.

He was a huge, dark shadow bending over her, his expression intent, his lips parted to take in more air as his massive chest labored with the harshness of his breathing. His face was a devil's mask above her as the glow of the firelight lit only one side of his face leaving the other in darkness.

Darkness. Flame. Hunger.

She bit her lower lip to suppress a moan as the unbelievable ripples of feeling spread from his gloved finger to every part of her body. It *was* hunger, she realized dazedly, a hunger more terrible than any she had ever known. She couldn't bear it. She instinctively tried to close her thighs.

"No!" He stopped her, moving her thighs even farther apart until she felt totally vulnerable, totally exposed. His finger continued to press gently as he gazed down at her. "I want to look at you." His tone was almost guttural. "Beautiful . . ." His other hand moved down and he inserted one finger carefully within her. "*Dio*, you're tight." A second finger joined the first with some difficulty and he paused, his gaze lifting to her face. "Tell me what you're feeling."

The seams of the leather gloves pressing against her, his fingers invading her, the burning hunger increasing every second. She shook her head helplessly. "I . . . can't." She gasped and instinctively arched up against him as he plunged deeper, withdrew and plunged again. "Please, my lord—"

"What do you feel?" he demanded.

Her head thrashed back and forth on the pillow. "Heat." Her nails dug into the coverlet. "Hardness. The leather is . . ." The muscles of her stomach clenched as a third finger slipped into her. "Fullness."

"And hunger?" He moved slowly, then faster, then slowly again. "You want this?"

"Yes." The affirmative was a whisper. She was surprised she could speak.

"It's pleasure?"

"Yes, I think so."

"Good." His fingers left her and he straightened and stepped back away from the bed. "Let's hope you'll soon know so, for I can't wait any longer." He drew off the leather gauntlets and threw them aside. "*Santa Maria*, I want to *feel* you." He touched her breasts, his long fingers light and gentle on her flesh. A shudder ran through him. "I told you," he whispered. "I knew it would be like this." His callused palm cupping her breasts was nearly as hard as the leather of the glove, but it was infinitely different. His flesh was warmer, vibrant with life. "Your skin is like nothing I've ever touched before. It makes me—" He threw back his head, drawing in a great breath as if starved for air. "I'll show you how it makes me." He pulled her to a sitting position on the bed and began to strip off his clothing.

She crouched on her knees on the bed, her arms crossing her breasts in an attempt to still her trembling. "You're undressing too?"

He didn't look at her as he pulled off his boots. "As quickly as possible."

"Giovanni never undressed when he took my moth—" She broke off as he cast her a stormy glance. "I can't help comparing you. He was my master. Now you're my master. My acquaintance is not so large that—" She stopped, her eyes widening as his rampant arousal sprang free when he pulled off his black hose. She swallowed and moistened her lips. He was not like Giovanni at all. Naked now, Lion was all iron muscles and brawny power. The triangle of springy dark hair thatching his chest ended in a V before it reached the flatness of his stomach, but another thatch surrounded his manhood. Where Giovanni was soft and flabby, Lion was taut and muscular. Where Giovanni was small, Lion was—

"You see?" Lion asked softly as his gaze followed her own. "This is what you do to me. Looking at you, touching you . . ."

"I see." She couldn't keep her gaze off him. She stated positively, "You won't fit, you know."

He chuckled. "I'll fit very well. A woman's body is marvelously accommodating. After the first time it won't even hurt."

She had grave doubts his assurances would prove true but, since there was clearly nothing she could do, it would be foolish to worry about possible pain until it happened. Besides, she was still feeling the tingling urgency between her thighs that tempered her fears with curiosity and excitement. "You look very . . . strong."

"I notice you don't call me handsome." He threw the hose aside and stepped forward. "I know well I'm an ugly bastard. But, as you say, I'm strong as a bull and that can be of use in such jousts as this."

"You're not ugly."

He smiled cynically. "You learn the arts of flattery quickly. However, sweet words are futile when I have a mirror to look into each morning."

He didn't believe her, Sanchia realized. "No, truly, I do not—" She broke off as he knelt on the bed facing her. He was so close her nipples brushed the thatch of hair on his chest.

He cupped her face in his hands as he gazed down at her with an expression that hinted at anger. "I don't want this. I have no liking for taking virgins."

"Then don't do it."

"Easy words." His hands moved down to her shoulders and began to knead her flesh with yearning tenderness. "I must do it. From the moment I saw you I knew I must have you like this."

"Not from the first moment. Only when you saw me in the bath and found I wasn't as ugly as you thought."

"*Cristo*, must you always argue with me?" His hands tightened on her shoulders. "I like you better when the only sounds you make are gasps and moans."

Obediently, she kept silent. What was he waiting for? she wondered. She could feel the unbearable tension gripping his body and yet she also sensed reluctance.

"And don't look at me like that." He shook her. "I don't want to hurt you, dammit. It will bring me no pleasure, but I must . . ." He pushed her back on the bed and moved between her thighs. His arousal nudged against the center of her womanhood as he muttered, "One stroke and it will be over." He covered her lips with his palm. "One stroke . . ."

He drew a deep breath and lunged forward.

Pain. White hot. Lightning swift. Her cry was smothered by his hand but her eyes widened with shock and agony as they gazed up at him.

"Close your eyes," he commanded roughly as he eased farther into her tight passage. "Don't look at me."

Her lids fell and she was in darkness. The pain was

fading, and she was conscious only of an exquisite fullness and a sense of something lost that had been found. She could feel the soft prickle of the hair dusting Lion's thighs brushing the smoothness of her own and heard the harsh sound of his breathing above her.

He was still, filling her completely but not moving. "It's done." His palm petted her, smoothing her around him. "*Dio,* you've taken all of me. I wasn't sure you'd be able to do it. You're so tiny . . ." His finger began to press and circle that bewitching place he'd fondled before. A hot shiver ran through her and she could feel the muscles of her stomach clench. A moment before she had felt pinned, staked to Lion's body and content only to accept, but suddenly now she felt the need for something more. "May I . . . move?"

He froze. "I cannot stop." His voice was savage with frustration. "I'll try to hurry but I cannot promise."

"That wasn't what I meant. I wished only—" She broke off as he drew out and then plunged forward. Pleasure streaked through her. This was what Lion had meant, she thought dazedly as he began a wild, pounding rhythm. This must be the pleasure men felt when they fornicated with a woman. She wished Lion hadn't condemned her to darkness. She would have liked to watch his face to see if he was feeling the same pleasure as she.

Yet he must be enjoying her body for he was shuddering, trembling as he moved, his breath coming in sharp gasps that resembled sobs. The intensity of his need filled her with a heady excitement and increased her own hunger tenfold. It was as if he were feeding her his frustrated desire for completion and somehow making it her own.

He was petting her again, his big hands trembling, urgent. "Take me," he muttered. "Help me. I want all of you."

He sounded like a man in agony, she thought with a rush of maternal tenderness. What must it be like to feel desire with such overwhelming intensity? She clenched around him and heard Lion give a low groan.

"Sweet . . . That's right. Hold me. Only a little longer."

She tried to hold him but he was too wild, out of control, almost lifting her from the bed with the force of his thrusts. She was suddenly conscious of something building within her, growing stronger with every movement. Something . . . strange, coiling toward fever heat.

Lion was moving her, shifting her, trying to take more of her. The hotness pouring through her was a clear stream of pure desire. Then the stream merged with Lion's until there was only one river, one entity striving to reach . . . to reach what?

Then she knew!

The knowledge broke over her in a release of rapture that left her gasping and shivering in the shimmering aftermath.

Lion cried out thickly as if strangling on a surfeit of pleasure.

The silence in the room was broken only by the crackle of burning logs in the fireplace and Lion's harsh breathing above her.

"May I open my eyes now?"

She heard his breathing become arrested and then he muttered a low curse beneath his breath. "*Gran Dio.*" Then he was moving off her. "Of course you can open your eyes. Why the hell shouldn't you?"

Her eyes opened to see him striding across the room, the muscles of his tight buttocks rippling as he moved toward the washstand. Slowly she sat up and gave a wistful sigh. He was angry again. She wished she'd been allowed a few moments more to enjoy this odd sweet languor before having to gather herself to try to understand what was troubling him. "Because you told me you didn't want me to look at you."

"That was because I didn't want to see your—" He broke off and kept his gaze averted as he dipped a cloth into the water in the basin and wrung it out. "I didn't mean you had to keep them closed. Have you no sense?"

"I don't know you well enough to always know what you want from me," she said simply. "I thought perhaps it made your pleasure greater if I didn't distract you by looking at you."

"No, it wasn't that." He averted his gaze as he turned and came back to the bed carrying the damp cloth. He sat down on the bed and moved the cool cloth between her legs. His gaze remained fixed on the cloth as he asked in a low voice, "Does it still hurt?"

"There's a little soreness." She shrugged. "I thought it would hurt much more. You're right; a woman's body is very accommodating."

"Yes." His hand moved caressingly and she could feel the warmth of his flesh through the coolness of the cloth. "I've never known a body as sweetly accommodating. You're so small it was like handling a child and yet you're a woman here." He abruptly threw the cloth aside, pushed her back on the bed and stood up. "Sleep. I won't want you again tonight."

She looked at him in surprise. "I didn't think you would. Giovanni never took my mother more than once a day."

"Then I fear your lot will not be as easy as that of your mother." He moved back to the hearth to stare into the depths of the fire. "I told you I was different."

And she was learning those differences, she thought drowsily. He gave pleasure as well as took it and, since she was to become his leman, she was glad it was so. Perhaps after she learned the way of it she could perform this duty as well as she had the tasks she had been given by Giovanni. It was important to have pride in your work.

Sleep persisted in closing in around her, but she forced her lids to remain open to ask, "I did not displease you?"

He was silent a moment, gazing into the fire. When he spoke his voice was muffled. "No, you didn't displease me."

"I'll get better at it." Her eyes closed and she turned and curled up on her side. "I learn quickly. Show me how and I'll find ways to please you. Show me . . ."

She had drifted off to sleep. Lion didn't have to turn his head to know she was no longer with him. His senses were still so acutely attuned to her physical responses that he believed he was aware of the actual second when she slid from the state of wakefulness to the depths of sleep. Why in Hades should this be so when he had never been similarly attuned to any other woman? Yet, in some mysterious fashion, he *had* experienced her pain when he had robbed her of her virginity, he had felt her yielding and then the first stirring of response. It was as if he had somehow absorbed her into himself. Sweet Mary, it was all madness.

Show me, she had said. His lips twisted in a mirthless smile as he remembered the plea. There would be no question he would show her all the ways a man could take a woman. Even now he was stone hard and yearning to be back in the tightness that had cradled him and made him never want to leave. He desperately wished to wake her now and move once more between her thighs. There was no reason he should not do it, he told himself. She wanted to please him. She would not complain if he used her a score of times this night.

She would not complain because she was not free to complain.

She wanted to please him because to please him was to survive.

He whirled and strode back to the bed. He lay down beside Sanchia, stretching out full length, careful not to touch her. He stared straight ahead, his muscles locked, his groin aching and heavy. Perhaps the soreness she was feeling would be gone in the morning.

He would lie beside her and think of all the ways he would take her tomorrow.

For he knew well that he would not sleep tonight.

"Solinari." Caprino's brow furrowed in a thoughtful frown. "You're sure he said Solinari?"

"I'm sure." Giulia turned and lifted the lid of the exquisitely carved ivory box on the table and dropped the five ducats into the velvet-lined interior. "I seldom make mistakes when it means ducats."

"You waited long enough to tell me. I may not even be able to use the information now."

She avoided his gaze as she seated herself beside the table. "I was busy."

"Or soft?" Caprino suggested silkily. "It couldn't be that you wanted your ducats and to give Andreas his chance too?"

"I was busy," she repeated. Her gaze lifted to his face. "You know who is lord of Solinari?"

"Yes, and so do you. Francisco Damari. You should remember the name. We did some business with him some nine months ago."

"Oh, yes, I remember Damari, it was the name of his palazzo I'd forgotten. You handled the negotiations and the transporting." She grimaced. "If I'd known it was Damari, I might not have summoned you at all. You promised me he'd send Laurette back in six weeks. It wasn't easy to replace her."

"Accidents happen." Caprino shrugged. "You knew there was a risk when you let him have her, but he paid enough for his pleasure to persuade you to take that chance."

"I notice you didn't send him one of *your* whores."

"Damari wanted only the best, as is common in these condottieri who raise themselves up from the peasantry. He would have been insulted if I'd sent him one of my women. Besides, I had none so uniquely qualified as your Laurette. Most women are regrettably squeamish about having pain inflicted on them."

"He had no right to kill her. As you say, she was unique." Giulia made an impatient movement with her hand. "But I suppose there's no way to force him to recompense me now. Solinari is where you sent her? I knew I'd heard the name before."

Caprino nodded. "Solinari is his palazzo, but he has lodgings in Pisa as well. The question is where to find him now." He was silent a moment, thinking. "I'll send Santini with a warning to the palazzo first, but if he isn't there, tell him to go to find Damari in Pisa."

She looked at him in surprise. "A warning? When have you ever given a warning that was not paid for?"

"Since you gave me no time to negotiate." A snarl edged Caprino's tone. "I'm not going to forgive you for that, Giulia."

"If you have nothing to gain, why bother to send a messenger?"

"Oh, but I do have something to gain. Damari will be in my debt, and it's always valuable to have a man who is on the rise in the world owe you favors."

Giulia laughed. "You trust Damari to honor a debt?"

"Perhaps." He smiled. "But if he doesn't, I'll still win if he captures little Sanchia. And you'll win, too, Giulia. Rumor has it that you weren't pleased about your hulking lover's acquisition of my little thief. What do you think Damari will do when he lays hands on her?"

Giulia knew very well what a man of Damari's perverse tastes would do to a woman who angered him. For a moment she felt a remote sympathy for Lion's slave. The anger Giulia had felt toward Sanchia had vanished when she had set aside her attachment for Lion. One emotion could not exist without the other, and she would allow neither to get in the way of what was important to her. "You hate her so much?"

"Hate?" He looked astonished. "She's not worthy of my hatred, but she must be made an example. If word got out that she'd bested me, it would cause endless trouble in the streets. I'm not like Damari, who loves punishment for punishment's sake. For me, revenge must have purpose or it's not worthwhile." He turned away. "I bid you a profitless night, Giulia, and may the man to whom you give your favors have the same tastes as Damari. I'm not at all pleased at your delay."

"I'm sorry to disappoint you, but the man who occupies my bed tonight is gentle as an untried boy and trembles at my every frown." She smiled sweetly as she stood up. "And in the morning he will gift me with a jewel that will make you drool like a street mongrel in front of the butcher's shop."

"Very different from Andreas." Caprino opened the door. "How fortunate for you."

He shut the door behind him, and she stood there a moment before moving her shoulders as if shrugging off a burden. Caprino was right—she was very fortunate to be free of Lion Andreas.

She strode briskly to the bellpull and gave it a sharp tug to alert her maid to send Messer Gondolfo to her chamber.

Six

No!" Sanchia sat bolt upright in the bed, her arms flailing wildly. "*Cristo!* No, don't—"

"*Santa Maria*, what in Hades is wrong with you?" Lion raised himself on one elbow, a frown darkening his face. "Are you ill?"

Sanchia gazed hazily around the room. This chamber was firelit and clean, not dark and vermin-infested. She raised her arms and dizzying relief soared through her. "I still have them."

"Have what?"

"My hands." She held her hands out before her, flexing the fingers. "I thought they were gone. I thought they'd caught me stealing and thrown me into the Stinche and chopped them off. But they didn't . . ."

"A dream." Lion's voice was gruff as he lay back down again. "Go back to sleep."

"A dream," she repeated. She obediently lay down, but she didn't want to release the warmth and safety of wakefulness and return to sleep where those hideous nightmares stalked. She lay there, conscious of Lion beside her. How strange to be in bed with a naked man. She supposed she would get accustomed to it in time. If she was given time. Who could know how long Lion would choose to fornicate with her? Nothing stayed the same in this world.

"Do you often dream of having your hands chopped off?" Lion asked in a low voice.

"Yes, I told you I wasn't very brave."

He was silent for such a long time, she thought he'd fallen asleep. "You cannot help your dreams, and it's not cowardly to be afraid of danger. It's intelligent."

She laughed shakily. "Then I must be as wise as a seer. I'm almost always afraid. Ever since I saw a thief thrown out of the Stinche, his poor, bleeding stumps of arms waving as if begging someone to—"

"It will not happen to you."

"I hope not," she whispered.

"It will not. I must have the key, but no harm will come to you."

He was angry. She should try to placate him, but she was suddenly too weary to make the effort. She turned on her side. "I'm sorry I woke you, my lord."

"Lion."

"I forgot." Oh dear, he did sound fiercely impatient. Perhaps it would be better to return to the uncertain threat that lay waiting for her in sleep than face his displeasure. "I'll try to remember. Forgive me . . . Lion."

His only answer was a low imprecation.

She didn't fall asleep for a long time, but as she finally drifted off, she realized Lion still lay rigid and wide awake beside her.

"What are you smiling about?" Lion snapped at Lorenzo as he lifted Sanchia onto her horse.

"Why should I not be smiling?" Lorenzo asked innocently. "It's a bright, clear spring morning and I've had a good night's sleep. You should not be churlish just because you can't say the same. I'm sure you had compensations I didn't enjoy."

Lion didn't answer as he swung onto the saddle and spurred the stallion into a gallop that left the stableyard of the inn behind him in seconds.

Lorenzo sighed. "I foresee a day like yesterday on the horizon. I had hoped for something better after Lion had appeased his lust for you." He kicked his horse into a trot. "Come along, Sanchia, or he'll be half way to Solinari before we catch up with him."

Sanchia nudged her mare into a trot. "How did you—" She stopped. "You must know him very well."

"Well enough to know he'd reached the end of his patience last night when I left you." Lorenzo gazed at her objectively. "Lust can be a strong tie to bind a man, and you'll need that bond to keep you safe at Mandara."

"Safe? Why should I not be safe?"

A faint smile touched his lips. "The situation there is complicated. Lady Caterina will not be amused at your arrival."

Sanchia tensed. "Caterina?"

"The Lady Caterina Andreas, Lion's mother. She's a virago when she's displeased."

"Oh." Sanchia thought about it. "Then I'll have to find a way to please her, won't I?"

He chuckled. "You'll find Lady Caterina a challenge. There are still stories told of the way she defended Mandara when Lion and his father were away fighting in Tuscany. Nicolino, a condottiere who decided Mandara was a rich plum ripe for the picking, laid siege to the city. Lady Caterina rallied her troops to repel the attacking army, then led a foray into the enemy camp, captured Nicolino, and brought him back to Mandara. She stood on the battlements and called down to Nicolino's second in command that if they didn't give up the siege she'd hang Nicolino. Unfortunately, the officer didn't believe she would do it and renewed the siege."

"What happened?"

"She hanged Nicolino. Then she lowered his body by a rope to dangle from the battlements in full view of his condotti. The army retreated at dawn the next morning."

A sinking feeling fluttered in the pit of Sanchia's stomach. It wasn't enough she had to please Lion; now she'd also have his warrior mother to worry about. "She sounds very strong."

"Yes." Lorenzo glanced at her. "But you have your own strength. She'll respect you, if you don't give in and let her ride over you." He smiled. "And if you do give in, you deserve to be trampled and Lion will be well rid of you."

"I won't be trampled." Her brow furrowed as she considered this new factor complicating her life. "For some reason you want me to fight her, don't you? Will you help me?"

"No. I merely position the chess pieces on the board; I don't interfere with the play itself."

"Never?"

He met her gaze. "Never."

Sanchia's hands tightened on the reins. She felt very much alone. "He may not even take me to Mandara. He's angry with me this morning."

"It's not anger. You'll have to learn to read him better." Lorenzo's gaze shifted to Lion's broad back several yards in front of them. "He suffers the same malady that afflicted him last night. It's not a horse he wants to be riding right now."

"You mean—"

"Exactly, my dear Sanchia." Lorenzo's tone was definitely more cheerful as he kicked his horse into a lope. "Which gives me hope that we may stop before we reach Solinari after all."

They halted at noon beside a tiny brook twisting through a forest glade.

One moment Lion was riding several hundred yards ahead of them on the trail, and the next he was wheeling Tabron and galloping back to them. "We'll stop here until the sun is less hot," he said curtly.

"I hadn't noticed that it was the sun that was hot," Lorenzo murmured. "But I'll accept any falsehood, if it will get me off this animal."

Lion ignored him as he dismounted and strode over to Sanchia. "Get down." He reached up, his big hands encircling her waist. "Hurry."

The urgency in his tone surprised her until she saw his face. Her eyes widened and she suddenly lost her breath. Lorenzo was right; it hadn't been anger driving him. The expression on Lion's face held the same intense hunger she'd seen last night.

He almost jerked her from the saddle before setting her down quickly. His hands on her waist kneaded her flesh through the soft fabric of her gown. The heat of his body reached out to her, claiming her. "You wish to—"

"Be quiet." His voice was hoarse as he backed her against the mare. "Don't talk. Just give me what I need." He jerked her gown from her shoulders, baring her breasts.

She gasped and then collapsed back against the mare as his mouth enveloped her left nipple. He sucked avidly, strongly, his teeth pressed against her while his hand cupped her other breast and began to squeeze rhythmically. The same liquid burning she had known last night tingled between her thighs. Her eyes closed as her throat arched back, her head resting against the mare's saddle. "Here? But Messer Lorenzo—"

"Is politely averting his eyes," Lion muttered as he lifted his head. Color flushed the tan of his cheeks, and his nostrils flared with every breath. "And is more than pleased." He grabbed Sanchia's wrist and pulled her away from the horses, striding from the trail and deeper into the forest.

"Where are we going?" She had to run to keep up with him.

"Not far."

He stopped a few yards farther into the forest and pushed her against the bole of a tree.

Rough bark pressing against the soft velvet of her gown, the pungent scent of earth and leaves and the leather of his jerkin . . .

His fingers worked frantically beneath his jerkin at the points of his hose until his aroused shaft sprang free.

"Don't fight me," he ordered as he lifted her skirts and undershift to her waist. "Do as I tell you." His palms were cupping her buttocks, raising her, adjusting her body against his manhood. "Put your legs around my waist."

Her thighs obediently encircled him. "I won't fight—" She broke off as he entered her with one wild, urgent plunge. Her head sank back against the rough bark of the tree as she felt every ridge, every inch of the wild, hot length of him.

He cried out and stopped, flexing within her. His face held a pleasure and relief that was nearly unbearable. "*Dio*! Yes . . . yes." Then he was driving, plunging with a force that rocked through her. Her shoulders were pushed back against the bole of the tree as he took and took and took . . .

She should have been frightened by the violence of his hunger, but she wasn't afraid. She was somehow aware that he didn't want to hurt her but was driven by that voracious appetite of which he had warned her.

"Give . . ." He muttered. "Hurry. Give."

He wanted her to give him not only her body but the response she had shown last night, she realized dimly.

He reached between them and pressed, his thumb and forefinger plucking at her. She cried out and arched up to him.

"Now," he groaned in a guttural tone. "Now." He plunged deep.

She gave him what he wanted, what she was helpless to deny him. She bit her lower lip to keep from screaming as wave after wave of pleasure radiated through her.

"That's right," he gasped, his hot cheek resting against her temple. "That's what I wanted."

She had pleased him, she realized hazily. How fortunate that in pleasing herself she could also please him.

His hand was awkwardly stroking her hair as his other arm held her bound to him, even now refusing to let her escape his possession.

After a moment he slowly stepped back and lifted her off him. "I didn't mean to be rough. I waited too long," he said haltingly. Then, as if regretting the half apology, he added, "But you must get used to my ways, and now is as good a time as later." He quickly tied the points of his hose before straightening her gown. "When I need you, then you must take me into you. There will be many occasions when I won't be able to wait until we find a bed."

"I understand."

"Good." He turned away. "Refresh yourself at the brook and then let's be on our way. I want to be at Solinari well before nightfall."

Lorenzo was reclining lazily beneath a tree beside the path and pulled a face as he saw them coming out of the woods. "Already? You were hotter than I thought, my friend. I was hoping for a longer respite." He rose to his feet, meticulously dusting off his gray velvet jerkin. "But perhaps we'll have another rest later." A ghost of a twinkle glinted in his light eyes. "It's such a very hot day."

"We won't stop. Not until we've reached Solinari." Lion swung onto the stallion and started down the trail.

"*Now* he's angry," Lorenzo said as he lifted Sanchia onto the mare. Then, as her gaze flew down to his face in alarm, he shook his head. "Not with you. With himself. He allowed you to distract him from his quest for the Wind Dancer. Not for long, but he still considers it a weakness in himself that he won't tolerate. Personally, I find it a very good sign for the future."

"Why?"

He gazed at her a moment, as if trying to decide whether to answer. "Because Lion's sense of responsibility has become a form of bondage. He regards himself not only as the guardian of the Wind Dancer but of everything in his particular world. I suppose it's not surprising. I understand his father instilled that belief in him from the time he was hardly more than a babe. In a way, the statue is a symbol of that bondage."

"Bondage? He's a great lord. Responsibility is not bondage."

"In some men it is." Lorenzo shrugged. "So keep

him so aroused he can't think of responsibilities, Sanchia. It's the best thing for both of you."

"I don't know how to keep him wanting me." Sanchia's cheeks felt hot. "And I don't know if I'd want to make him forget his responsibilities. Surely it is only honorable to—"

Lorenzo groaned as he mounted his horse. "*Santa Maria*, another acolyte burning incense at the temple of honor and glory. I thought you had more sense." He shook his head. "Oh well, perhaps that's what draws him to you. Like to like."

Sanchia stared at him incredulously. "We're not at all alike."

"Yes, you are. But you, Sanchia, are also like me. It will be interesting to see which aspect of your character triumphs in the end." He turned to look at her with cool appraisal. "Power can be very heady. It may occur to you that it would be to your advantage to use the passion Lion feels for you to rise in the world. I have nothing against ambition, but I won't have Lion used. If you show signs of doing so, I will have to remove you."

"I have no power over him."

"Continue in that belief and you'll remain in robust health."

"You care about him." The knowledge that a man as chillingly objective as Lorenzo could care for anyone filled her with wonder. "Why?"

"Who knows?" His smile was self-mocking. "Do you wish me to mouth some maudlin drivel about Lion being the man I would have been in other circumstances? Or even the son I might have sired?" He shook his head. "What makes any man feel anything? Life is filled with strange, exotic emotions, with great mysteries. Which is what makes it tolerable." His horse moved forward at a faster clip as he touched his spurs to the animal's sides.

It was late afternoon when they approached a small farmhouse on the edge of a clear blue lake.

"We go no farther," Lion said as he reined in Tabron. "The village is only a short distance from here, and Solinari lies just beyond it. I don't want word of our arrival to be carried to the palazzo, so we'll wait here for Marco to come to us. I'll talk to the owner of this farm and make arrangements for us to stay the night in his house."

"Who is Marco?" Sanchia asked.

"My brother." Lion dismounted and strode across the barnyard and into the small sod farmhouse.

Another surprise. She really knew nothing about Lionello Andreas, she thought. Was this brother as fierce as Lion and the mother who had borne them both? It was more than probable. She experienced a sudden longing for blessedly familiar Florence where every danger was at least known.

"Marco is not at all like Lion." Lorenzo's assurance came as if he had read her thoughts. He dismounted, then helped her to do so too. "You may find him charming. Most women do."

"It's not her place to find him charming." Lion had returned and was standing on the step. "I have no intention of sharing Sanchia with him."

"How ungenerous of you," Lorenzo said. "Not to mention surprising. Why are you so miserly with Sanchia when you're so willing to share—"

"The house looks clean enough," Lion interrupted. "I've paid the farmer for a night's lodging, and he and his wife will go to his father's farm a few miles from here to shelter tonight. The man will walk to the village to seek out word of Marco and give him a message that we're here while the woman heats water for bathing."

"Excellent," Lorenzo said. "And since you're so fond of these four-footed beasts, I know you won't mind taking care of the horses while I rest." He prudently didn't wait for a reply but strode into the farm house.

Lion smiled lopsidedly as he gazed after Lorenzo. "He'd be very disappointed to realize that I don't mind." He took the reins of the horses and led them toward the small barn. "The hut has only one room, and there's going to be little privacy until we leave Solinari." He glanced over his shoulder. "Why are you just standing there? Come with me to the barn."

She finally understood and hurried after him. "You wish me to lie with you again?"

"If we can find a pile of hay or a blanket free of vermin." He opened the door to the small barn, led the horses inside, and tied their reins to an empty stall. "Otherwise we'll have to be content with a post to lean against." He suddenly stopped and turned to face her in the shadowy barn. "It makes no difference. Nothing matters but this." His hands reached out, moving over her shoulders as a great shudder ran through him. His gaze raked the barn with frantic urgency until he saw a small heap of hay beside one of the stalls. "I wanted you again not ten minutes after we left the brook. I ached with it. I ache now." He led her quickly to the pile of hay and pushed her to her knees. "Make it stop." His voice was low, fierce with frustration and anger. "*Santa Maria*, make it stop!"

He pushed up her skirt and took her with even more wildness than he had shown earlier that afternoon and had scarcely reached the peak when he took her a second time, drawing her with him into a vortex of fiery pleasure.

Lion moved off her, lying beside her on the hay, his chest laboring as he tried to catch his breath. She was also panting, still trembling helplessly from the emotional storm through which Lion had swept her.

"I hate this." Lion thrust his arm over his eyes, speaking through clenched teeth. "It won't last, you know."

"I don't know. I don't know anything about this," Sanchia whispered. "But it seems to me that if you hate it, you wouldn't do it." He didn't answer and she continued uncertainly, "Is it any different with me than it is with Giulia Marzo?"

His arm fell away from his face to reveal dark eyes still glittering with resentment. He smiled cruelly. "Of course; she's much better at it. Do you think I'd bother with you if she were here?"

She felt a wrenching pain that took her off guard. "I'm sorry you don't find me adequate. Perhaps if you'd tell me what I'm doing wrong . . ."

"What are you doing wrong?" His voice was suddenly savage as he jumped to his feet and began unsaddling Tabron. "You're too tight around me, your nipples are too rosy and pointed, your skin is too soft." He jerked the saddle from the stallion's back and dropped it to the earthen floor. "And you stare at me as if I were going to devour you until I cannot stop myself from doing it." He stood with his back to her, his head averted. "Take off your clothes."

She gaped in amazement. He surely couldn't want her again already.

"Stand up and take off your clothes!"

She scrambled to her feet and hurriedly pulled off her gown, slippers, and undershift.

"Come here."

She walked toward him, her gaze fixed anxiously on his averted face.

He turned his head and his gaze went over her body searching out every curve and hollow, every secret place. "Mine," he said hoarsely, his nostrils flaring. "Every bit of you is mine for as long as I care to keep you. Do you understand?"

She nodded quickly.

His hands reached out and cupped her breasts. "Mine. No one is to touch you. You will not let anyone lay his hand on you." His hands moved to the tight curls protecting her womanhood. "Never. You will give no other man so much as a smile unless I bid it."

His voice was so fierce she could do nothing but stare up at him helplessly.

"Say it. You belong to me."

"I . . . belong to you."

"No man will ever touch you but me."

"No man will ever touch me but you."

He seemed curiously tormented as he stared down into her face. Then his hands dropped away from her body and he turned away. "Now you can stop looking at me with those big frightened eyes and get out of here. Put on your gown and go to the house."

She stumbled back away from him and swiftly started to dress. "I could help you with the horses."

"Go to the house."

She walked across the earthen floor and glanced back over her shoulder as she reached the door. Lion hadn't moved; his spine was taut with tension. "I'm not really frightened of you any longer. I was at first, but I don't think you mean me harm."

His hands clenched on the mane of the horse. "I must have the Wind Dancer."

"I know you must," she said, puzzled at the sudden change of subject. "I'll get the key. I promised you and I keep my word. When do I have to go to the palazzo?"

"Tonight, if Marco has the information we need."

Shock ran through her. "So soon?"

"Yes." He turned away and began to loosen the cinches of the mare's saddle. "Go and tell Lorenzo to see that you're bathed and freshly gowned before Marco arrives."

Not garbed for Lion's pleasure this time, she thought numbly, but to go to the palazzo.

"Hurry!"

Sanchia whirled and walked quickly across the barnyard toward the house.

Marco Andreas rode into the barnyard just as the last glorious scarlet rays of sunset were caught and mirrored on the still surface of the lake. He stopped a moment gazing at the beauty before him and a smile warmed the chiseled perfection of his features.

"Well, what do you think of him?" Lorenzo murmured to Sanchia as they watched Lion as he walked across the yard to greet his brother.

Sanchia gazed at the handsome man laughing down at Lion and an involuntary smile touched her own lips. "He's one of the shining people."

"The shining people?"

"You know, the ones you see walking along the streets who always seem to be so happy and full of life. They wear the gayest clothing, they play the mandolin and sing serenades to their ladies. They usually paint or have a passion for sculpting or writing poems . . ."

Lorenzo raised a brow. "And what do you think is Marco's particular passion?"

She tried to gaze objectively at Marco Andreas who was now in deep discussion with Lion. Objectivity proved difficult when faced with such comeliness. Marco bore little resemblance to his brother. He was perhaps a few years younger and his features were classically beautiful in the manner of Michaelangelo's statue of David. His shoulder-length hair was not the onyx black of Lion's but a shining acorn brown, and his eyes were not cold, glittering ebony but warm hazel. At last she said, "He paints."

"And how do you come to that conclusion?"

"He was gazing at the sunset and smiling as he rode into the barnyard. A sculptor is usually concerned with solid shapes and probably wouldn't have noticed the sunset. A poet would have been frowning as he tried to transform the beauty he saw into words. Messer Marco accepted what he saw with joy, knowing that he need only copy what was there."

Lorenzo burst into laughter, and Lion and Marco turned to look at him inquiringly.

Lorenzo nodded at Marco, his lips still twitching with amusement. "Good evening, Marco."

Marco smiled easily. "You seem very happy to see me. Have I done something deserving of mirth?"

"Would I dare laugh at one of the shining people?" Lorenzo turned to Sanchia. "He does paint and, though he does not play the mandolin, he has quite a pleasing tenor." He turned back to Marco. "Tell me, have you sung any serenades of late?"

Marco grimaced. "I won't rise to your jabs, Lorenzo. I take it I'm the butt of one of your less than kind jokes?"

"You malign me. I was just verifying Sanchia's estimate of your character. She finds you very pleasing to the eye."

"Does she indeed?" Lion asked softly, his gaze narrowing on Sanchia's face.

"I meant no offense," she said quickly. "Messer Lorenzo merely asked me to— It was like a game, a puzzle."

"A puzzle you wish to solve?" Lion asked, his tone silky. "In what manner, I wonder?"

Marco cast a quick glance at his brother before stepping forward and bowing gravely. "I'm honored you find me of interest, Madonna Sanchia. Knowing Lorenzo, I'm sure his words have no real weight. He takes pleasure in amusing himself by setting us all topsy turvy. Isn't that so, Lion?"

"At times."

"Most of the time." Marco went on quickly, "Lion tells me you're going to aid us in retrieving the Wind Dancer. It's very kind of you to offer your help. When you see how beautiful the statue is, you'll understand why a man like Damari should never be allowed to possess it."

"Kindness has nothing to do with it. She has no choice. Sanchia does as she's told." Lion took the reins of Marco's horse and abruptly turned away. "Go into the house. I'll join you as soon as I've stabled and watered your horse."

"I can do it," Marco protested.

Lion didn't answer as he led the horse across the barnyard.

Marco pursed his lips in a soundless whistle. "Lion appears to be in a less than felicitous temper. I suppose it's to be expected considering this night's work. He'd much rather go after the key himself than have to wait while you bring it to him, Madonna Sanchia."

"Sanchia," she corrected. It was pleasing to be addressed with such unusual respect but it also brought with it a sense of awkwardness. "Call me Sanchia."

Marco smiled gently. "It would be my delight. A lovely name for an exquisite lady. And you must call me Marco." He gestured for her to precede him into the house. "We must make sure nothing happens to you tonight."

The words were spoken with such warmth Sanchia felt as if she had been touched suddenly by sunlight. She smiled back, feeling a surge of optimism. "Lion said I would be safe."

The faintest frown marred Marco's brow. "I hope so. The task won't be easy."

"You have the information?" Lorenzo asked as he followed them into the house.

Marco nodded as he reached beneath his cloak and pulled out a folded parchment from his belt. "I was able to bribe old Vittorio to draw me this map. He was a gardener at the palazzo before Damari bought it, and he greatly dislikes the new master. He was glad to have sufficient ducats so he could retire to the home of his grandson in Genoa, and he very wisely left Solinari this morning while Damari was still in Pisa."

"Damari isn't here?" Lion asked from the doorway.

Marco unfolded the parchment and spread it on the roughhewn table in the center of the room. "He's been in Pisa for two days and isn't expected back until early next week." His gaze lifted from the parchment to meet Lion's. "According to Vittorio, the captain of the guard said he went there to meet with Duke Valentino."

"Borgia?" Lion tensed. "Then we have little time."

Marco shrugged. "Perhaps more than we think. Cesare may not be in a mood to listen to Damari's proposals. He's had his hands full to overflowing with his conquest of the Romagna and, as you know, it was only a few months ago he used his old friend De Lorqua's head to decorate a pike in the piazza at Cesena because of the unrest there."

"Borgia's always in the mood to further his ambitions." Lion strode forward to peer down at the parchment. "What is this?"

"A map of the grounds of the palazzo."

"It's getting too dark to see in here. Someone light a candle."

Sanchia hastened to obey and set a fat tallow candle on the table.

The flickering flame illuminated a crudely drawn map that seemed to consist of a complicated series of dashes. "This doesn't look like a map," she said, puzzled.

Marco made a face. "Vittorio is no mapmaker, but I hope he's accurate." His slim index finger tapped the longest dash at the top of the paper. "This is the palazzo." He traced a complex square of markings near the middle of the parchment. "And this is the maze in the garden." He pointed at a square in the exact center of the maze. "And this is the storehouse where Damari keeps his treasures. The maze has only two entrances, each guarded by two men."

"Very clever." Lorenzo stepped closer to the table. "Even if someone manages to overpower the guards at one entrance the chances are that, without a map, a thief would become lost in the maze either before he reached the storehouse or when he was trying to leave with his loot."

"And Damari would undoubtedly have the guard-posts checked at frequent intervals," Lion said.

"Every thirty minutes," Marco agreed. "Damari usually keeps at least fifty men in the guardroom at the palazzo, but he took an escort of fifteen to Pisa with him."

"Thirty-five men against three," Lion remarked dryly. "Let's hope we can move through the maze fast enough to avoid them."

"Is that where I have to go?" Sanchia touched the square in the middle of the maze. "The storehouse?"

Marco smiled reassuringly. "No, you only have to go as far as the south entrance to the maze. Rodrigo Estaban, the officer guarding the entrance, has the key to the storehouse on a ring at his belt." He reached beneath his cloak and pulled out a large iron key and handed it to Sanchia. "It looks a good deal like this one. Your task is to steal the key to the storehouse and substitute this key in its place on the ring in such a way that Estaban won't realize it's been stolen."

"Are there other keys on the belt?" Sanchia asked.

"Two. One to the dungeon and one to the gates of the high iron fence that surrounds the palazzo and the grounds. There's dense shrubbery bordering the fence that will be useful for cover, and you don't have to worry about the gates. Vittorio gave me his key to unlock them and passed on a bribe to the soldiers who usually stand guard there."

Sanchia gazed blindly down at the iron key in her hand.

"What's wrong?" Lion asked sharply.

"The other keys. I'll not only have to steal the key and put this one on the ring but keep the other keys from clanging together. I'm not sure I can do it."

"You can do it," Lion said. "You have to do it."

"Lion, for God's sake, if she can't do it . . ." Marco frowned. "I didn't consider the noise."

"Ducats clink in a purse, but she lifted mine with not a whisper of noise in the piazza." Lion's expression was unrelenting. "She'll just have to be careful. You can do it, Sanchia."

She swallowed and then nodded jerkily. "I can do it."

A rare smile lit Lion's face. "In a few hours it will all be over and you'll be handing me the key. We've tried to make it as safe for you as possible. We've hired three whores from the village who will distract the guards at the entrance of the maze and try to prevent the watch from making rounds on time."

"Won't they wonder why the whores decided to come to the palazzo?"

"They may wonder, but it won't keep them from availing themselves of their services," Lorenzo said dryly. "Most men don't think with their brains when a pretty whore offers to spread her legs for them."

Lion nodded. "You go in with the women and pretend you're one of them until you manage to get the key."

"Very well," she said faintly.

He frowned. "It will be all right, I tell you."

She tried to smile. "Do you use the key to steal the statue tonight?"

"No, tomorrow night."

"I see." Her hand clenched so tightly around the key that it cut into her palm. "Could we go to the palazzo right away? I don't want to think about it. I just want to do it. Could we go now . . . please?"

A multitude of emotions flickered across Lion's face as he gazed at her. "Yes." He turned abruptly away. "We can leave this instant. Marco can go to the village and get the whores and meet us at the gates of the palazzo in one hour's time." He turned to Lorenzo. "Marco tells me there's a grove about a quarter of a mile from the gates of the palazzo. We'll need you to come with us and wait there with the horses."

"Splendid. I always prefer the passive role. Though I could think of more stimulating companions with whom to spend an evening."

Lion held out his hand to Sanchia, and again the smile that made his strong, brutal features appear almost beautiful lit his face. "Come along, *cara*."

Cara. The word of endearment echoed warmly in her ears. No one had ever used such a word to her before and she was suddenly filled with a glowing eagerness. She took two steps forward and shyly took his outstretched hand. "I'm coming."

His big hand closed tightly around her small one. She was safe. For this moment there was no fear, no threat. Lion had called her *cara*, had sworn she would be safe and was holding her hand as if there was affection between them.

She let him lead her from the house.

Seven

"I didn't realize the Wind Dancer actually existed." Cesare Brogia lifted an ornate goblet to his lips. His gaze was fixed on the muted colors of the tapestry portraying Diana at the hunt on the wall beside the door of the loggia. "I've heard how the Wind Dancer was brought to Italy, but I thought it only an exaggerated tale. You wouldn't be trying to gammon me, would you, friend?"

Borgia's tone was idle, almost playful, but Damari was not lulled into a false sense of security. Cesare's temperament was known to swing abruptly from laughter to violence. "It exists and I have it in my possession."

The faintest flicker of interest crossed Borgia's features. "Here in Pisa?"

Damari shook his head. "In a safe place. You do not hire fools to fight your battles, my lord."

"True." Borgia sipped his wine, his gaze

still on the tapestry. "How do you know the statue to be genuine?"

"There could be no other like it. You will realize when you see it that it's beyond compare." Damari leaned forward in his chair, speaking quickly, persuasively. "Think, my lord. Think of the power it would give you. You know the legend of the Wind Dancer. You've heard the tales—"

"Oh yes, I've heard the tales. That the Holy Grail for which the Knights of the Round Table sought was not a grail but a golden statue, that Alexander the Great kept a golden-winged Pegasus in his tent during his conquest of Persia." Cesare shifted his gaze from the tapestry to Damari's face. "There are a hundred tales about the Wind Dancer and I believe none of them." He smiled. "And neither do you. We don't rely on talismans to bring us what we want when a sword is more certain."

"But your father does believe in talismans," Damari reminded him. "And so does King Louis of France. You don't have to believe in a pawn to use it."

Borgia laughed and for a moment his raddled face held a remnant of its comeliness before he'd been afflicted with the pox. "As you intend to use me."

"No one uses you, my lord duke. Your mind is too quick not to perceive deception."

"Sweet words won't buy you what you want from me. We're too much alike." Borgia set his goblet down on the Venetian carved table next to his gloves. "If Andreas owned the Wind Dancer, why did no one know it? It would have increased his consequence to possess such a treasure."

Damari shrugged. "He is a fool. His family brought the Wind Dancer from Persia over a hundred years ago, and they regard themselves as guardians of the statue. The Wind Dancer was kept in a tower room at the castle in Mandara. Even persons who were very friendly with the family were never invited to see Wind Dancer."

"Then how did you come to know of it?"

"I was born in Mandara and I served as an officer under Lionello and his father before him. I listened, I watched, I planned to form my own condotta, and I knew that when I left Mandara I would take the Wind Dancer from them."

"I detect a lack of affection." Cesare smiled. "Your service with Andreas's condotti was not to your liking?"

Damari swiftly hid the bitterness festering within him. Borgia's eyes were too sharp and he would use any knowledge with lethal skill. "Lionello did not like my methods when I served under him after his father died. He thought me fit to be only a common soldier for the rest of my life. He was wrong. I have known from childhood that I was destined for great things."

"Certainly a mistake in judgment. You are definitely not common." Borgia added, "Though I understand your birth is not of the highest."

Typical of Borgia, Damari thought: a pat and then a sharp jab of the spurs. He quickly smothered the fury surging through him and said, "A man is what he makes himself, Your Magnificence. Look at what you've become since you shrugged off your cardinal's cape. With the Wind Dancer in your hands nothing would be beyond your reach. If His Holiness won't give you the armies you need for conquest, then take the statue to France. Louis likes you well enough. Use the statue to turn his favor into armies to strike at Spain or Florence or Rome."

"Rome?" Borgia's gaze narrowed on Damari's face. "You speak treason. You cannot believe I would attack the papal states and my own father?"

"Yes, if it meant ruling a kingdom as vast as Charlemagne's."

A frown twisted Cesare's face. "You go too far, Damari."

"Men like us can never go too far, my lord. It's beyond the realm of possibility."

Borgia gazed at him a moment and then began to laugh again. "You're right, Damari. There are no limits for a man with the stomach to do anything he must to seize what he wants." He stood up and adjusted the chain bearing the bejeweled insignia of the Order of St. Michael that hung low on his chest. The jewels were set off to great advantage by the black velvet of his jerkin. "I will consider your terms for the Wind Dancer."

Damari rose to his feet. "Do not consider too long."

"By God, you're bold." Borgia's smile faded. "Don't make the mistake of taking the Wind Dancer to another buyer, Damari. It would not be wise."

Damari bowed. "When may I expect to hear from you?"

"Soon. I must write my father for his views on acquiring the Wind Dancer. Who knows? He may not be as mad to have it as you seem to think."

"Perhaps." Damari changed the subject. "Will you sup with me and then try out a little Turkish servant girl I acquired recently? She's very beautiful and has many skills."

"I think not." Borgia started to don the black velvet mask he was seldom seen without in public these days. He paused, a smile twisting his lips as he looked down at the mask in his hands. "Perhaps we're not as alike as I thought, Damari. You are not as vain as I. Our faces are both pitted and far from pretty, but you go uncovered into the world."

"I'm accustomed to my scars, since I had the pox when I was a small child."

"I have the pox still. The French pox." Borgia suddenly threw back his head and laughed. "And I'd wager the little Sicilian wench who gave it to me was far more captivating than the Turkish girl you so kindly offered. The bitch was almost worth it."

"You might say that there was a bitch connected with my pox as well, my lord," Damari said. "So you can see our afflictions make us truly brothers in adversity. Are you sure you won't stay and try Zaria? She's only fourteen and ripe as a plum fresh from the tree."

"Your little beauties have no spirit and often bear marks that spoil their comeliness. I'll find a woman more to my liking elsewhere." Borgia slipped the mask over his face and started for the door, his form supple, manly, and full of grace. "You should learn to practice restraint."

"Why?" Damari smiled. "Have we not just agreed

that men such as we should not be bound by limits? Excess can be very exhilarating."

"You clearly find it so." Borgia paused at the door. "Remember, you will do nothing until you hear from me. *Buona sera*, Damari."

Politeness called for Damari to accompany Borgia to the front entrance, but he had already decided not to accord him that courtesy. Borgia must be made to regard him as an equal from this day forward, not just a lackey trailing at his heels. "*Buona sera*, my lord."

Borgia hesitated and then closed the door behind him with a sharp click.

Damari smiled with supreme satisfaction as he turned and walked across the loggia to gaze out at the night sky. All was going extraordinarily well. Borgia wanted the statue and would crave it even more when Pope Alexander fired him with his own enthusiasm. Perhaps it would be possible to gouge even more than a dukedom from the pope. What a triumvirate the three of them would make! No army or country would be able to withstand them. Of course, a triumvirate could not last forever, and one man always emerged the leader in such an arrangement. Why should it not be he? As he had told Borgia, he had known all his life he had a great destiny. How far he had come already! He possessed a fine palazzo, this small but elegant house in Pisa, and a storehouse of treasures he'd secreted from the pope's greedy hands.

And now he had the Wind Dancer.

"My lord, a messenger from Florence begs to see you."

Damari turned to frown at the lackey standing at the door of the loggia. "By what name?"

"Tommaso Santini."

"I know no Santini."

"He said to tell you the message was from Guido Caprino."

"Caprino," Damari murmured. A sudden memory of soft white skin and frightened blue eyes wavered before him. Laurette. The thought of the whore sent a surge of heat to harden his loins. Perhaps Caprino had another choice bit of merchandise to offer him.

"Send Santini in. I'll see what he has to say."

"I've sent the other whores on into the garden," Marco whispered as soon as Lion and Sanchia reached the gates. "This is Maria. She says Rodrigo has come to the village and used her before. I thought he might more easily be distracted by someone he knew."

The dark-haired woman leaning against the gates smiled confidently. "For enough gold I could distract Satan himself, and Rodrigo has always found me pleasing." She held up the jug of wine she was carrying. "And this will do no harm."

"Make sure he believes you to be Venus incarnate. Your task is to keep him from paying any attention to Sanchia, to keep him so busy she'll be able to leave with no suspicion." Lion turned to Sanchia. "You know where you're to go?"

"The south side of the maze." Sanchia moistened her lips with her tongue as she peered through the tall iron gates. She could clearly discern the tall holly hedge looming fortresslike in the distance. She hadn't expected the maze to be so large, stretching at least three hundred feet in length and ninety feet in width, the hedges themselves rising to a height of more than nine feet. "I suppose I should go now." She cast a glance at Lion but his expression was impassive in the moonlight. She opened the gate. "You'll be here? You won't leave me?"

"We'll be here." Lion's hand clenched on one of the iron bars of the gate.

She drew a deep breath and then turned and followed Maria in the direction of the maze.

Lion stood watching her until she disappeared beyond the corner of shrubbery.

"She has courage," Marco said, his gaze following Lion's.

"Yes."

Marco shifted restlessly. "I have no liking for this

Lion. Sending a woman into danger while we merely stand by—"

"Do you think I do?" Lion's tone was savage. "But she's the only person now who can bring me the key that will give us the Wind Dancer."

Marco fell silent and the minutes stretched on. "It's a great service she does us. How will you reward her if she does bring you the key?"

"What do you mean?"

"You told me she was a slave. Will you free her? It seems a fair—"

"No!"

Surprised at the violence in Lion's response, Marco asked, "Why not? You have no liking for slavery. You refused to have slaves at Mandara. Surely it's—" He stopped as comprehension dawned on him. "You use her in your bed."

"Is that so surprising?"

"No." Marco studied his brother, anxiety growing within him. He was aware that Lion was never celibate when he was away from Mandara, and he had known many of the women Lion had bedded. Without exception they had been knowledgeable in the ways of carnal pleasure and as invulnerable and cynical as Lion himself. Courtesans, bored wives looking for distractions, widows ripe and willing to enjoy the bed sport of which they'd been deprived. Never had there been a woman as vulnerable and young as Sanchia, and never had Lion's response been violent at the idea of parting with a leman. "You're not—" He stopped. *Dio*, he had no right to ask this and yet he felt compelled. He began again, "You're not going to take her to Mandara?"

"No."

Relief poured through Marco, followed immediately by a twinge of guilt. "It's not that I don't wish you to have everything you want, Lion. It's simply—"

"I know." Lion's gaze wearily shifted from the maze to his brother's face. "Don't worry, nothing has changed, Marco."

Marco had an uneasy feeling that a good many things had changed since Lion had gone to Florence to find his thief, but he preferred to accept Lion's words as truth. "Perhaps you could place Sanchia in a fine house in Pisa. Since you've acquired this passion for shipbuilding, you spend more time in Pisa than Mandara anyway. It would be a solution to—"

"Suppose we worry about solutions to other problems after we have the Wind Dancer back," Lion cut in as his gaze returned to the maze. "The Wind Dancer is all that's important right at this moment."

The false key had been exchanged for the key to the storehouse. Now Sanchia had only to return the key ring to Rodrigo's belt.

Only? Panic swept through her at the thought of leaving the comparative safety of the haven in the bushes across from the maze and venturing out once again to complete her task. She had been unusually lucky to be able to quickly, quietly take the key ring and carry it away into the shrubbery to make the switch. Only the fact that Rodrigo had been occupied with pulling the teasing Maria into the maze had made it possible to whisk it from his belt, but it would be madness to believe it would be as easy to replace it.

A shout of laughter followed by a squeal interrupted her thoughts and she turned toward the labyrinth to see the other guard once again mounting the whore with the bronze-dyed hair.

It was senseless to linger in the bushes cowering with fear. Rodrigo was still in the maze. She had no choice but to go after him. She tucked the key ring in her belt and drew her cloak more closely around her shoulders as she stepped boldly from the protection of the shrubbery into the moonlight.

"Ho, there you are." Rodrigo Estaban strolled out of the maze, carrying the jug of wine Maria had given him.

She froze. Had he discovered the keys were gone?

He lifted the jug to his lips and drank deeply before lowering the jug. "You shouldn't have run away. I have enough for both of you. I'm from Spain, where they grow us men as strong as bulls." He gestured toward the maze. "I left your friend so tired she was barely able to swing her hips."

Sanchia quickly lowered her lashes to hide her relief. "I was waiting." She walked toward him. "I didn't want to get in your way."

"I want you in my way. I've always liked redheads." He took a step forward. "Show me your breasts. I want to see how you compare with Maria." He didn't wait for her to show him but grasped the neck of her gown and ripped it downward with one tug, baring her breasts. "Pretty. Not as big, but pretty . . ." His dark head lowered and his wet mouth enveloped her left breast.

Violation. He smelled of garlic and wine and his teeth were hurting her. She felt . . . dirty. Bile rose in Sanchia's throat as she clenched her fists to keep from pushing him away.

She blocked out all thought and feeling. The key ring. She had to return the key ring. Her hands moved with purely automatic skill transferring the key ring back to Rodrigo's belt. He didn't notice. He was grunting, making animallike sounds, whispering vile promises. She should be grateful he was so distracted, she told herself.

She wasn't grateful. She hated it.

The key ring back on his belt, she had to find a way to releasing herself and getting back to Lion with the key. Dear God, where was Maria?

The man's head was lifting, his mouth leaving her breasts. "Come." He grasped her wrist and pulled her toward the maze. "I want you to lie beside that other whore so that I can take turns dipping betw—"

"Rodrigo, where did you go?" Maria emerged from the maze, her bodice still unlaced, her large breasts pale and ripe in the moonlight. A sulky pout pursed her lips. "I close my eyes for a minute and you're off to mount another woman. Send her away."

Rodrigo grinned. "Two is better than one."

Maria flowed toward him, her breasts jiggling as she moved. She stopped before him. "You're wrong. I'm more than enough woman for you." She smiled as she deliberately reached a hand between his legs and squeezed.

He inhaled sharply, his hand releasing Sanchia's wrist.

"You keep telling me what a bull you are. Now show me your *coglios*." Maria backed away teasingly.

"Wait here." Rodrigo tossed over his shoulder as he quickly moved after Maria. "Later I'll have . . ." The rest of the sentence was lost as he followed Maria back into the maze.

Sanchia ran!

The cool wind whipped at her face as she fled across the grass, her lips forming prayers of thankfulness. Only a few yards more.

Lion was opening the gate, his gaze searching her face. Then she was outside the gates, thrusting the key into Lion's hand. "Here," she gasped. "Here is what you wanted."

"No trouble?" Marco asked.

Sanchia drew her cloak more closely around her to hide her torn gown. "No trouble."

Lion's gaze mercilessly raked her features until she felt he must see the imprint of the foul violation she still felt on her flesh. Then, to her relief, he turned away and strode toward the grove where Lorenzo was guarding the horses. "Let's get back to the farmhouse."

During the journey back to the farmhouse, Marco was jubilant and Lorenzo his usual mocking and remote self.

Only Lion was grimly silent.

He knew, Sanchia thought miserably. Somehow he knew she had broken her promise and let herself be touched by another man. She could see it in the way he looked at her, in the tension of his hand grasping the reins, in the tightness of his lips.

When they reached the barnyard Lion dismounted, came around and lifted Sanchia from her horse. His gaze held her own with compelling force. "Who?" he asked softly.

She felt the panic rise within her. "Rodrigo. I couldn't help—"

He was turning away, his hand grasping her wrist with bruising force as he pulled her toward the barn. "Leave the horses in the barnyard," he said in a fierce rasp over his shoulder to Lorenzo and Marco. "I'll tend to them later."

The interior of the barn was dark and frighteningly alive with strange, scurrying sounds. Her heart was pounding so hard she was sure he could hear it.

His powerful body was silhouetted for an instant against the paler darkness of the night sky before he shut the doors. Then there was only blackness.

"Rodrigo?" The harshness of his voice vibrated in the silence. "No other men?"

"No one else." She rushed on frantically, "I couldn't help it. I had to get the keys back and Maria wasn't there and there was no other way to—"

"So you spread your legs and took him into you." His hands fell heavily on her shoulders and he shook her hard. "You let him mount you and—"

"No, he only touched me with his mouth and his hands. He didn't—Maria came and he let me go."

Lion went still. "You're telling me the truth?"

Sanchia nodded frantically, then realized he couldn't see her in the darkness. "I swear, my lord."

"*Cristo!* Then why in hell did you look so guilty?"

"I *was* guilty. You told me I was never to be touched. And he touched me." She shuddered. "I felt befouled. Unclean."

He was silent, his hands still heavy on her shoulders. Abruptly he released her and she heard him moving away.

"My lord?"

"I'm lighting the lantern."

The candle suddenly flared, revealing the grim harshness of his features. He set the lantern on the earthen floor. "Where did he touch you?"

She gestured to her breasts.

He crossed back to her and pushed back her cloak

to reveal the ripped bodice of her gown. His face was hard. "Did he hurt you?"

"Only a little. I'm sorry, my lord."

"My God, why should you beg my pardon? It was by my will you went where that whoreson could get to you." He glanced up and smiled crookedly. "Why are you so surprised? I have my rare moments of fairness. Unfortunately, since I've made your acquaintance my sense of justice appears to have been obscured by my appetites." His palms gently cupped her breasts. "Poor Sanchia, you haven't had an easy time of it since you left Giovanni, have you?"

His voice was almost tender. She held her breath, waiting for more.

There was no more. His hands dropped away from her and he stepped back. "You're not unclean," he said quietly. "You're a clear, sweet river wandering through very muddy banks. But you've reached the sea now and that mud will never touch you again." He gazed gravely into her eyes. "Just as danger will never touch you again. You've done your part to help us and done it well. I'll not ask you to do more."

"You're not angry with me any longer?"

"No." He gazed at her a moment unsmilingly before turning away. "I'm not angry with you." He opened the doors of the barn. "I must get back to the house. Now that we have the key, plans must be made for tomorrow night." He frowned. "I'll have to study the map again. Vittorio's scrawling gave me no idea of the size of the maze. There may be problems." He stepped out into the barnyard. "Tidy yourself and then come to the house. I have no desire to have Marco and Lorenzo gasping at those pretty breasts."

"Lorenzo has seen me unclothed before."

"That's no reason he should do so again. He gets enough enjoyment from tormenting me without your giving him any additional rewards. Things are going to be different."

"Different?"

But he was gone, striding swiftly across the barnyard toward the house.

Sanchia made a futile attempt to adjust the torn gown before finally giving up and drawing her cloak over it. She could do nothing to mend the rip since neither needle nor thread was at hand. Perhaps she could find both when she returned to the farmhouse. Her gaze fixed dreamily on the glowing windows of the house. Different. What had he meant by saying things would be different? Nothing could be more different from her previous life than the hours and days since Lion had purchased her. Yet he must mean there would be still other changes on the horizon.

She had never been afraid of changes before, but now she felt a queer stirring within her that could be fear . . . or the first fragile beginnings of hope.

"Is all well with you?"

Sanchia turned to see Marco standing a few feet away from the door of the barn. "Did Lord Andreas send you to fetch me? There was no need. I was just coming."

Marco shook his head. "Lion is studying the map of the maze. I thought to seize this opportunity to—" He broke off and then added, "I knew he was angry with you."

"No more."

He looked relieved. "I wasn't sure. I cannot always read Lion."

So Marco had come out to the barn to make sure she had met with no harm, Sanchia thought with a rush of warm gratitude. "Yet it's obvious there is a deep affection between you."

"We are brothers." He smiled and shook his head. "No, it's more than that. We don't think alike and seldom act for the same reasons, but the bond is still there."

"It doesn't surprise me that he mystifies you at times. I have no understanding of the way he thinks," Sanchia said. "He has so much. Why should he risk his life for a statue? He says the Wind Dancer is of his family but I cannot see how anyone can think of a piece of metal as if it were flesh and blood." Her gaze lifted to meet his. "As if it were alive."

"But then you've never seen the Wind Dancer," Marco said softly. "The first time I saw it when I was a child I thought it *was* alive. It took away my breath and filled me with wonder." He bent and picked up the lantern from the earthen floor. "Come, we will go back to the house. Lion may need me."

"What does it look like?"

"The Wind Dancer?" Marco took Sanchia's elbow and steered her through the doorway of the barn. "It's not easy to describe it. Let's see, it's a bejeweled golden statue of Pegasus, the winged horse of the gods. It stands only eighteen inches high and is no more than fourteen inches in width. And the wings . . ." His slender left hand made a graceful motion as if caressing the statue. "The clouds on which the Pegasus is running are—"

"Running, not flying?"

Marco nodded. "The horse is running, his wings folded back against his body, the wind braiding his mane. His lips are slightly parted and his eyes are huge almond shaped emeralds. Only his left hind hoof is touching the cloud on the base of the statue so that, unless you look closely, it appears the Wind Dancer is truly sailing through the air."

"It sounds very beautiful."

"Too beautiful. It hurts to look at it."

That was a strange thing to say, and the sadness in his expression was even more strange. "Lion said the statue was very ancient and that there were many legends told of it. How old is it?"

Marco shrugged. "Who knows?"

"Well, how long has your family possessed it?"

The sadness was suddenly gone from Marco's expression and his hazel eyes twinkled with amusement. "You wouldn't believe me if I told you. We're a *very* old family."

Sanchia chuckled. "You go back to Adam and Eve in the garden?"

"Don't we all?"

"No, tell me. You must have some idea when—"

"Back to the ancients of Greece, near the beginning of time. Have you heard of Troy?"

She frowned. "Oh, yes. From a storyteller in the piazza . . . and once in a manuscript brought to Giov—" She stopped. He could have no interest in her former life. "Troy?"

Marco smiled down at her. "According to the stories passed down from generation to generation in my family, it was in Troy where Andros was first given the Wind Dancer."

"Andros." Sanchia repeated thoughtfully. "Andreas."

"Names change through the centuries. We're not sure whether Andros was our ancestor's true name. It is said he was of the Shardana and consequently very tight-lipped about himself."

"I've never heard of a people called the Shardana." She gazed at him uncertainly. "You're jesting with me, are you not? Is this a story you've concocted to punish me for being too curious?"

He shook his head. "I only tell you what I've been told."

"Troy never existed. I have heard of the *Iliad*, but thought it was a myth, a fiction."

"Alexander the Great thought Troy existed, and so did Julius Caesar. Many scholars believe Homer merely repeated what centuries of storytellers before him had handed down through the ages."

"You think the *Iliad* is true?"

"I have no idea. Stories, like names, become twisted through the centuries. The tale I was told certainly didn't agree with Homer's."

"What story were you told?"

"You won't believe that either." He turned to gaze out over the mirrored stillness of the lake. "But I'll tell you anyway, if you like. Andros was a Shardana, one of the sea people. They were great raiders and warriors and very secretive about where they came from. They had reason to be discreet. For centuries they had raided the cities of Greece, Persia, and Egypt, and there had sprung up tales of the splendid city which had been founded from the wealth of their raids. All the cities of that time raided and pillaged but the Shardana were the most successful."

"Corsairs."

Marco nodded. "Andros's ship was storm-wrecked on an island off the coast of Troy, and Andros and his crew were captured. His crew was sacrificed to the god Poseidon, but the Trojans saved Andros to be tortured to try to get him to reveal the location of his homeland." Marco grimaced. "Evidently Troy was quite a raiding power itself and wished to bring home even more treasure and slaves. Andros refused to reveal the location of his city and would have died under the lash if Agamemnon hadn't chosen that time to launch his attack on Troy. The Trojans became distracted."

She frowned. "But the Trojan war went on for years and years, didn't it?"

"That is Homer's story. Our version has it that less than a year passed until Troy fell. Andros was given to Paradignes, the king's brother, to recover his strength until they could once more direct their full attention toward getting the information they wanted from him. The two men became friends over the months of the siege and after Traynor opened the gates they—"

"Wait." Sanchia held up her hand. "Who's Traynor and why would he open the gates?"

"Traynor was a Trojan warrior, and he opened the gates for the oldest reason in the world. He was bribed. He was captured outside the gates in a foray and kept in the Greek encampment for over a week before he supposedly escaped and returned to Troy.

"One night, a few days after he returned, he opened the west gate and the Greeks rushed into the city. They were finally beaten back, but the Trojans lost many warriors and the Greeks managed to set fire to the gate as they left Troy. Traynor had been seen opening the gates and the king ordered that he be hacked to pieces, his remains burned in the square of the city." He paused. "In Traynor's lodgings the king's guards found the Wind Dancer."

"The bribe."

Marco nodded. "The king gave the statue to Paradignes and ordered him to burn it until there was nothing left of the Wind Dancer but molten rubble."

"But he didn't do it."

"He was a lover of beauty and couldn't bring himself to destroy the statue. He didn't want the Greeks to have it either and knew it was only a matter of time until they conquered the city." He smiled at Sanchia. "Can you guess what he did?"

"He gave the statue to Andros?"

"And showed him a way to get out of the city. It seems Troy had been destroyed and rebuilt many times and there was an underground passage that led to a hill far beyond the city. Paradignes showed Andros the entrance to the tunnel and wished both him and Jacinthe well before—"

"Jacinthe?"

"One of the conditions of Andros's release was that he take not only the Wind Dancer but a woman from Troy. Paradignes didn't want the Greeks to have her either."

"Was the woman Paradignes' wife?"

"He had no wife."

Sanchia's eyes widened. "Helen . . ." she whispered.

"There was no mention of a woman called Helen, only Jacinthe." Marco smiled faintly. "But I find it significant that the word *Jacinthe* means 'the beautiful one.'"

"And they both left Troy that night with the Wind Dancer. Where did they go?"

"South. Toward Egypt. The legend says the two of them stood on a hill some distance away from the city and watched it burn."

"So that was the night the Trojans brought in the Greeks' wooden horse?"

Marco chuckled and shook his head. "That's Homer's tale again. There was no great wooden horse. There was only the Wind Dancer."

Only the Wind Dancer. A statue so beautiful that a man would betray his home and his people to possess it. A work of art so exquisite it would inspire tales that would endure for over a thousand years. "Do you believe what you've been told is true?"

"Sometimes. Is it not more reasonable that the gates of Troy would fall because of bribery and betrayal than such a stupid ploy as a wooden horse?"

"I suppose it is," Sanchia said slowly. "Where do you suppose the Greeks got the Wind Dancer?"

"Before he died Traynor said the Greeks told him two shepherds found it in the hills above Mycenae during a great storm and brought it to Agamemnon. They claimed it appeared in a flash of lightning."

"Nonsense."

"Legend. And not nearly as unreasonable as some of the other legends connected with the Wind Dancer through the centuries."

Sanchia was tempted to ask him to tell her those other legends, but suddenly she knew she didn't want to know more about the statue. The Wind Dancer was now looming in her imagination with an odd sentience, taking on a dimension and life of its own. She could almost see the golden statue shimmering in the darkness of the storehouse, waiting patiently for Lion to come for it, uncaring what danger he ran to free it from its prison.

Foolishness. She had never even seen the statue. Her nerves were merely on edge and crying out from the terror and strain she had undergone this evening.

She forced a smile as she turned away from him. "A fantastic tale, but certainly an entertaining one. You're a far better storyteller than Pico Fallone, who entertains in the piazza in Florence." She glanced back over her shoulder. "But, of course, I don't believe any part of it."

A gentle smile lent fresh beauty to Marco's fine features. "Of course not. You're clearly a very sensible woman. Why would you believe such a preposterous legend? I only told you the story because you asked."

"I was merely curious." Sanchia quickly opened the door and stepped inside. "But naturally I realize none of it actually happened."

"It's going to take longer than thirty minutes to make our way through the maze to the storehouse, find the Wind Dancer, and then travel back to the maze entrance again." Lion scowled down at the map. "There's no question that the watch will discover we've entered the maze and have guards waiting for us at both ends."

Marco bent closer. "*Jesú*, you're right. We'll have to stop every few turns and study the map." He made a face. "What a puzzle. That labyrinth looks like a passage through hell."

"Then Damari must feel completely at ease there," Lion said.

"I could go with you and wait in the shrubbery across from the maze to dispose of the watch," Lorenzo offered.

Lion weighed the suggestion. "I don't like having no one to watch the horses, and it would probably give us only another five or ten minutes before someone else was sent to see why the watch hadn't returned. I doubt if that would be long enough."

Lorenzo shrugged. "What other choice do we have?"

She wouldn't answer, Sanchia thought, looking down at her hands clenched tightly together in her lap. They weren't talking to her. She could sit on the stool by the fire and not say a word. Lion had told her she need do no more to reclaim the Wind Dancer. She would be foolish to go back to the palazzo when Lion said she did not have to help them.

"No choice," Lion said.

She would remain silent. Lion had said she need not endanger herself again.

But she had promised him loyalty as well as obedience. Was it loyal not to speak now?

"Then you and Marco go inside the maze and I stay outside and take care of the watch," Lorenzo said. "Marco can carry the lantern and you can try to read the map."

"And hope we don't lose our way among all those damned dashes," Marco said ruefully, "or we'll find ourselves hacking our way through those hedges with a broadsword."

"Those hedges are almost four feet thick. At any

place but the last outer hedge that borders the perimeter it would take the better part of a day to cut our way through." Lion grimaced. "Providing we knew in which direction to cut. We'll just have to—"

"I can lead you through the maze."

The three men turned to look at Sanchia.

Sweet Jesus, why had she spoken? she wondered, slowly unclenching her clammy palms and rubbing them on the skirt of her gown. She stood up. "I can lead you to the storehouse and back to the entrance in less than thirty minutes."

Marco shook his head. "I know you want to help, Sanchia, but this maze is hellish. No one can—"

"I can." She came forward and looked down at the map. "I won't have to stop and check the map every few minutes and I won't lose my way. I'll know exactly where I'm going every minute."

"Astonishing," Lorenzo said. "And unbelievable."

"No, it's true." She closed her eyes and envisioned the map before her. "When you enter the maze you turn right, go past two passages and then turn left, go past another three passages and turn left again, then—"

"Enough," Lion said.

She opened her eyes to see him looking at her with a faint smile on his lips. "It seems Giovanni wasn't trying to raise your price as I suspected."

She shook her head. "I remember everything. From the time I was a small child I had only to see something once to keep it forever in mind."

"Surely a mixed blessing, but in this case a fortunate one for us." He paused. "If you choose to come with us."

"Choose? You do not command me?"

"I told you that you need not go back to the palazzo. I won't break my word."

Lorenzo cupped his hand to his left ear. "Hark, do I hear the glorious peal of trumpets? I don't think I can bear many more of these appallingly honorable moods to which you persist in subjecting me, Lion."

"Be quiet, Lorenzo." Lion's gaze did not leave Sanchia's face. "I won't force you to go back with us."

"But you have need of me."

"Oh yes, we have need of you, Sanchia." He smiled that rare, brilliant smile that always succeeded in touching some mysterious emotion within her that had never been tapped before. A smile was a mere expression, she thought, puzzled. It should not have the power to cause this warm flowering of hope. A smile should not be able to make her do something so foolish as to go back to the palazzo. She should ignore his smile and tell him she would never return to the palazzo again.

"I'll go," she whispered. "I'll lead you through the maze."

Eight

Sanchia shivered as she gazed through the iron bars of the gates at the maze. When she had first seen the tall hedges of the labyrinth last night she had thought they resembled the walls of a fortress, but she had never dreamed she'd actually have to breach them.

"I still don't think we should enter the maze through the south entrance," Marco whispered. "Why don't we try the north entrance, where there's no officer in charge?"

"No." Lion didn't look at him as he opened the gate. "We go through the south entrance."

"But we should—"

"I want Rodrigo," Lion said savagely. "Give me five minutes and then bring Sanchia." He faded into the dense shrubbery bordering the gate.

Her body icy now with foreboding in addition to fear, Sanchia wrapped her cloak closer about her and continued to stare at the maze. Death. Rodrigo Estaban was going to die within minutes at Lion's hand.

"It's time to go." Marco took her elbow and propelled her gently forward. "Quickly, Sanchia."

There was no sign of Rodrigo or the other guard at the south entrance of the maze. Lion came out of the maze and knelt to wipe his sword on the grass before sheathing it. Blood edged his scabbard. Sanchia couldn't seem to tear her gaze from the wet, dark stain on the grass.

"I dragged them both just inside," Lion said tersely. "Be careful not to stumble over them." He turned back into the maze.

Marco lit the lantern as soon as they had joined Lion within the screening confines of the hedges.

Rodrigo Estaban and his fellow guard lay on their backs, their dead eyes staring sightlessly up at the black heavens.

Sanchia swallowed to ease the queasiness in her stomach. She wheeled sharply away from the bodies. "This way." She kept her eyes fastened straight ahead as she moved swiftly down the first passage and turned right.

After several minutes of convoluted, twisting turns, Marco asked doubtfully, "Are you sure you didn't take the wrong path, Sanchia? I think we may be going around in circles."

Sanchia shook her head. "Two more turns and we should reach the storehouse." She had a sudden terrifying thought. "If the map is right." What if Vittorio had drawn the map incorrectly? She took the last turn and felt weak with relief. A small, windowless wooden building lay before them. "There it is!"

"We don't have much time." Lion moved quickly forward and inserted the key in the lock of the door. "It must have taken us at least ten minutes to make our way here." The door swung open. "The lantern, Marco."

Sanchia waited outside as Marco and Lion disappeared within the storeroom. Now that she was alone she was beset with a fear so intense it almost suffocated her. The air seemed to vibrate with a sense of waiting menace.

Marco emerged from the storehouse a few minutes later. "We found it!" His hazel eyes were shining in the lantern light. "It was there, Sanchia."

Lion followed him, carrying a medium-sized wooden chest. "Considering the trouble we've suffered I would have been a little irritated if it wasn't," he said dryly. "Get us out of here, Sanchia."

She nodded eagerly, her gaze on the mahogany chest. The Wind Dancer was in that plain wooden container. How strange that such a small object, an object she had never set eyes upon was important enough to Lion and his family to cause all this effort and fear. But soon the terror would be over, soon they would all be safe.

She turned and began the complicated trek back to the south entrance. She had been foolish, she told herself, to let her own cowardly fear give way to an icy sense of doom. She took a right turn and then a left, her pace increasing. Everything was going well. Lion had his Wind Dancer. They would be back at the entrance before the watch passed.

She turned right, left, right again. The high walls of greenery were pressing in on her in a smothering blur. She was almost running now, the pulse in her temple pounding wildly. "The entrance is right ahead," she called back to Lion and Marco. "One more turn and we'll—"

Drawn swords glittered in the moonlight!

She skidded to a halt, her eyes widening in horror. "No!" The narrow passage ahead was crowded with men in armor dressed in the same yellow-and-white livery Rodrigo and his comrades wore.

Sanchia heard Lion's low voice cursing behind her. "Damari."

"Greetings, Lion." A man at the forefront of the soldiers took a step forward. "What a pleasure it is to see you at my palazzo under such intriguing circumstances. I don't suppose you'd be willing to put down the Wind Dancer and surrender to me?"

"No."

"I didn't think so." Damari took another step forward and the light cast by the lantern in Marco's raised hand fell full on him.

Sanchia was taken aback by the looks of Damari. Barely of medium height with a barrel chest and overdeveloped torso, his muscular legs were round as tree trunks and far too short. He seemed almost grotesquely malproportioned to Sanchia. And when her gaze rose to his tea-colored eyes glittering in the lantern light, she realized his soul was as misshapen as his body. She saw only malevolence in him.

"I hoped you wouldn't give up too easily," Damari said lightly. "Of course, that is why I permitted you to come into the maze and retrieve your property instead of cutting you down as you entered the gates. I knew you'd struggle harder once you had the Wind Dancer in your hands. It's always more difficult to give up once victory is in our grasp."

Lion's expression was impassive. "A trap. You knew we were coming."

Damari nodded. "What a wonderful surprise when I learned you were going to visit me. I hadn't even realized you'd returned from France and discovered my acquisition of your statue until I received a message last night in Pisa that you'd made plans to get it back."

"Then you didn't permit Sanchia to steal the key from Estaban?"

"Oh no. Either your thief is exceptionally skilled or Rodrigo was extraordinarily thick-headed. I wasn't happy with Rodrigo." He shrugged. "And so I assigned him to guard duty tonight."

"In order that I would kill him?"

"A fitting punishment for his stupidity, don't you think?" His gaze shifted to Sanchia. "And this must be your clever little thief. Present me to her, Lion."

"Who sent the message?"

"Guido Caprino." The smile lingered on Damari's lips. "He requested one thing only in return—that I use your little slave in the fashion which will give me the most pleasure."

Marco began to swear softly yet vehemently.

"That distresses you, Marco?" Damari asked. "But then you always did have a soft heart where the ladies were concerned. Lion and I are of a tougher breed. We don't balk at using any means at hand to get what we want." His gaze remained on Sanchia. "Do we, Lion?"

"But I protect what is my own." Lion's grip tightened on the wooden chest. "You should have known I'd never let you take the Wind Dancer."

"But I did take it, just as eventually I'll take everything from you, Lion. After I'm done toying with you, I may even let you live so that you can appreciate your loss."

"And are you toying with me now?"

"Of course." Damari's smile widened as his pale eyes returned to Lion. "Isn't that clear? When are you going to begin wriggling on my hook, so that I can enjoy myself? Perhaps I should detail your predicament. There are ten men blocking this passage and another ten outside the entrance. I've deployed another ten outside the north entrance of the maze." He lifted his gloved hand and slowly closed his fingers into a fist. "The trap is closed. Consequently, either you surrender or you run."

"Run where?" Lion asked warily. "You have a fancy to chase us through this damnable maze?"

"How clever of you to understand. Naturally, it will be to no avail. I know this maze and, even with the map I assume you've managed to bribe from one of my men, you'll soon become hopelessly lost. It's impossible to read a map while you're being pursued. How long do you think you'll be able to avoid capture, Lion? Fifteen minutes? An hour? And every minute you'll know we're right behind you or waiting around the next hedge."

Lion studied Damari's expression. "You've played this game before?"

"Only on a few special occasions. I make it a practice not to indulge myself too frequently or the pleasure loses its bite. Though I admit the maze was the reason I purchased this particular palazzo. I immediately saw its splendid possibilities." He drew his sword from its scabbard. "Now, which shall it be? Surrender or the maze? I do hope you choose the maze. I'll even give you a few minutes' head start as an incentive."

"Then I'd hate to disappoint you." Lion shifted the chest under his right arm and his left hand closed on Sanchia's elbow. "The maze."

He turned and ran down the passage from which they had come, dragging Sanchia behind him.

Marco was right behind them as they made the first turn. "*Cristo*, Lion, what's the use in letting him play with us when we—"

Lion's words cut through his question. "Damari's right; a map is useless in a chase through this maze, but he doesn't know about Sanchia's gift." He turned his head toward her. "Take us to the western perimeter and hurry!"

Sanchia wasted no time in questioning him. She turned and started at a dead run through the maze.

"Your head start is over." Damari's voice rang through the greenery. "Do you hear me, Lion? I'm coming after you!"

Sanchia's heart plunged and she began muttering frantic prayers beneath her breath. What if she became too frightened to remember the way? No, there was the long border hedge directly in front of her.

"This is it." She gasped. "But there's no entrance here. Why do—"

"The south and north entrances are blocked." Lion set the chest down, drew his sword and begun to hack at the hedge. "But Damari didn't say that the entire maze was surrounded. If we can hack our way through this hedge, we have a chance to slip away into the shrubbery that skirts the gate."

Marco drew his sword and joined Lion, slicing away at the branches. "The gate has to be guarded now."

"We'll worry about that when we get out of the maze. *Dio*, it's like cutting through stone."

Sanchia stood watching as the two men attempted to cleave their way through the living wall. It was taking so *long* and she could hear Damari's taunting voice. He was closer.

"Take the lantern and go to the end of the passage, Sanchia." Lion didn't look at her as he gave the hedge another mighty blow. "If you see or hear any sign of Damari run back to us and we'll forget about getting through this wall and try the east hedge."

"Yes, my lord." She snatched up the lantern and ran the several yards to the end of the passage, desperately glad to be able to do something to help.

The whacking of the swords against the hedge branches was ominously loud to her ears. Surely Damari would be able to hear if he drew closer.

And he was very close! Damari's voice carried faintly to her from a distance that could not be farther than two passages over. "Are you lost yet, Lion? Are you beginning to choke on your fear?"

Sanchia's throat tightened in response to the taunt. *She* was the one choking with fear. She cast a frantic glance over her shoulder at Lion and Marco. She was too far away to determine how near they were to penetrating the hedge.

"We're almost through," Lion called softly as if in answer to her unspoken question. "Damari?"

She realized he hadn't heard Damari's voice over the sound of the chopping. "He's drawing near."

Lion muttered a curse and assaulted the hedge with even more force.

"Your precious Wind Dancer must be a burden to you as you run from me," Damari called mockingly. "Soon you'll be glad to abandon it just to gain a little more strength for the chase."

He couldn't be more than one hedge away, Sancha decided. She would have to warn Lion and Marco.

But they were almost through the hedge and, if they abandoned the attempt, who was to say Damari would not discover the mutilated border and realize they would now be trying the same ploy on the opposite side of the maze. There had to be some other way.

If she could draw Damari and his men away through the maze and then double back . . . She closed her eyes and tried to visualize the passages leading away from the western border. Two right turns would put her on the same path they had traveled previously to reach the storehouse. Then she could circle the small building and come straight down the western border passage and rejoin Lion and Marco. She could give Damari only a glimpse of her skirt going around the corner, or a gleam of the lantern disappearing down the passage and he would think all three of them were still together.

She could hear the clank of armor in the passage diagonally across from the one in which she was standing. If she was going to do it, it must be done now. Her grasp tightened on the handle of the lantern and she drew a shaky breath. An instant later she was flying across the path intersecting the passage Damari's men were traveling.

She heard a shout as one of the guards caught sight of her and then Damari's low, pleased laugh.

The jagged opening in the hedge was scarcely three feet long and two feet wide, but it would have to suffice.

Lion sheathed his sword, picked up the chest containing the Wind Dancer and pushed it through the opening before calling softly over his shoulder, "Sanchia!" He started to crawl through the hedge as he said to Marco, "Watch over Sanchia. I'll go through first and make sure the way is clear and get rid of any guards at the gate." He was already halfway through as he added, "be quick!"

He heard Marco's assent as he wriggled the last two feet, sharp broken twigs and thorny leaves tearing at his jerkin and flesh like daggers. Then he was through the hedge and on his feet. He paused, swiftly looking over the area. They were in luck. As he had hoped, Damari had concentrated his forces at the two entrances and, though he could hear the sound of voices issuing from the far side of the maze, this side of the labyrinth was deserted. He picked up the Wind Dancer's box and moved quickly into the cover of the bushes bordering the fence, then ran at full speed toward the gate. He slowed as he neared the end of the shrubbery, moving cautiously forward. If the gate had been refortified, then there should be signs of the guards soon.

"Do remind me to teach you the rudiments of stalking through a grove without sounding like a pregnant ass." Lorenzo emerged from the bushes beside Lion.

"The guards?" Lion whispered.

"Dead. Behind me in the bushes. I thought there might be something amiss when three of Damari's men appeared and started to search the woods. After I got rid of them I decided to come and see if I could be of assistance. Where are the others?"

"Following. I think I hear them now." Lion looked over his shoulder.

Lorenzo grimaced. "How could you not? They're making even more noise than you did. Still, I think we'll make sure it's not one of Damari's guards." He receded into the bushes.

Seconds later Marco pushed back the screen of branches and bolted into sight. He pulled up at the sight of Lion. "*Dio*, Lion, she wasn't there." He panted. "She was gone. I tried to—"

"What do you mean? Sanchia was only a few yards away from us." His hand closed on Marco's arm with bone crushing force. "What the hell do you mean?"

"They've got her."

"You don't know that." Lion whirled and started back toward the maze. "You *left* her, God damn you."

Lorenzo stepped in front of Lion. "Listen to him, Lion."

"He left her in that maze alone." Lion's voice was trembling with rage. "You whoreson coward, why didn't you look for her?"

"She screamed," Marco said simply. "I was going to try to search for her when I heard her scream. Damari has her, Lion. Should I have stayed and let Damari capture me too? It would have been of no help to her to have me in the same cage."

"And you won't help Sanchia if you let Damari get his hands on you, Lion," Lorenzo said. "You can't do anything at this moment to free her."

Lion glared at him, his eyes wild in his white face. "I promised nothing would happen to her. You're telling me to abandon her?"

"I'm telling you that you'll have to wait until later to help her," Lorenzo said. "Think, Lion. You're not reasoning clearly."

He wasn't reasoning at all, he was only feeling. *She screamed.* "I promised her."

"Then keep your promise," Lorenzo said. "But you won't keep it by letting Damari toss you into his dungeon."

Lion knew he was right. He couldn't help Sanchia, and he was endangering Marco and Lorenzo by lingering. But, Jesus, she needed him and he couldn't help her. The guilt was his, not Marco's.

"Damari won't kill her at once. We both know that's not his way," Lorenzo said. "We have time. You can ride to Mandara and get more men."

No, Lion thought in rage, Damari wouldn't deprive himself by killing her immediately. He would want to go slowly with her, very slowly, and wrench every vile pleasure for himself that he could from Sanchia's torture. Frustration—acid hot, bile bitter—tore through Lion. He whirled and strode toward the gates. "Mandara's too far away. We'll ride for Pisa. Let's go."

Sanchia screamed.

Damari's hand cracked against Sanchia's cheek with such force that she fell to the ground.

"You mustn't scream again. Were you trying to warn your master?" Damari smiled down at her in the moonlight. "But that's not how the game is played. Now, tell me where he is."

"I don't know." Sanchia struggled to raise her head. "We became separated."

"I don't think so," Damari said slowly. "Now that I think back on it, you were a little too slow in getting away from us. We caught far too many glimpses of you before I managed to intercept you. You were leading us away from him, weren't you?" His pitted cheeks creased as his smile widened. "Such inspiring loyalty. Did he tell you to distract us? How unkind of him when he must have known we'd catch you eventually."

Sanchia shook her head, trying to clear it of fear as well as the ringing pain of Damari's blow. "No, we were separated," she repeated hoarsely.

He bent down and effortlessly lifted her to her feet. "You mustn't lie to me." His voice was seductively gentle. "I'll find them anyway, you know. It's amazing that I haven't located them already. It's never taken me this long before." His smiled faded. "But fortune has always been on the side of that bastard. Tell me where you left him."

"I don't know. We were separated and I became lost—"

Agony rocked her when Damari struck her other cheek.

"Tell me." His voice was even more gentle, almost tender. "Was he going toward the north entrance?"

The maze was whirling, blurring around Sanchia. "I don't know."

He struck her again.

She swayed. "We became separated and I lost my way. I don't know where—"

Pain exploded again and she hurtled down into a welcome darkness.

"Come now, wake up. I'm becoming very impatient. You've been unconscious the better part of the night."

Sanchia slowly opened her eyes to see Damari gazing down at her.

"Very good. I was afraid I had done you some grievous physical damage." He waved a hand. "No matter. I had to send for Fra Luis anyway and would not have been able to start."

"Start?" Sanchia whispered. She tried to sit up before realizing with a surge of panic that she couldn't move. She was no longer in the maze but strapped at knees, waist, and shoulders to a hard surface. She glanced wildly around her but could see only the wooden table to which she was bound. The aureole of light cast by a torch in Damari's outstretched hand barely illuminated his face. "Where—"

"In the dungeon." Damari strolled a few yards from the table and thrust the torch into an iron bracket on the wall. "As is proper for a thief."

She became chillingly aware of the darkness surrounding her, the odor of the damp earth, the smell of pitch and decay.

"I'm very angry with you, you know." Damari returned to stand beside her. "I lost not only Andreas but the Wind Dancer. I sent my men riding after him in all directions but he appears to have vanished. All I have is a slave who will be of absolutely no use in getting either back. Lion obviously cares nothing about whether you live or die or he wouldn't have sent you to divert me from his escape." He frowned. "And my lovely hedge is quite ruined. It will take years to replace it with new growth."

He seemed more upset by the damage to his shrubbery than by the escape of Lion and Marco, she thought dazedly. "You lie. They wouldn't have left me."

"Still loyal? They most certainly did leave you. But what did you expect? You're property—far less valuable property than the Wind Dancer. You notice he didn't leave the statue behind. Surely you don't think he'll return for you?"

Lion had promised nothing would happen to her. He had vowed she wouldn't be hurt. She had to believe he'd come back for her or she would be overwhelmed by the terror and despair closing in all around her.

Damari carefully smoothed the hair at her temple. "Poor little slave girl. You're frightened, aren't you?"

He wanted her fear; she could see it in his expression. She didn't answer.

"And you should be." His fingertips drifted lightly over her cheek, leaving pain in their wake. Her bruised flesh was exquisitely sensitive. "I'll get the Wind Dancer back and I'll punish Andreas. It's only a question of time." His fingers had reached her hairline and he reversed the direction, retracing the painful caress. "But I must have some satisfaction to keep me patient."

Her gaze was fixed in helpless terror on his face. Lion had promised her she wouldn't be hurt. Lion had promised her. . . .

"I've always believed punishment should fit the crime. I kept one of Giulia Marzo's whores here at the palazzo for a number of months. She quite enjoyed the pain at first, but alas, it didn't last. She was a pretty little strumpet, though incapable of tolerating more than minor pricks of chastisement. You can understand how this annoyed me when I had paid such a handsome sum for her." His index finger followed the outline of her lower lip. "So I decided I had a right to compensation. Do you know what I did?"

Sanchia couldn't speak, her throat was locked with terror as she gazed up into his pale eyes.

"I stripped her naked and sent her into the maze. Then I sent twelve of my men in to find her. Naturally, they expected reward when they ran her down. A whore's reward." He shrugged. "She died."

He was a monster. Sanchia could imagine the horror of that poor, frightened woman running frantically while she was chased by a pack of taunting, savage animals seeking only to rape.

"A fitting death for a whore, don't you think? But you're not a whore, you're a thief." He lifted her left hand, playing with her fingers. "Tell me, what is the punishment for thieving, Sanchia?"

"*Santa Maria* . . ." She didn't realize she had spoken until she saw him smile again.

"We cut off their hands, don't we?" he asked softly. "I think we'll start with your fingers. One by one." He dropped her hand. "And I have a very skilled companion who will know just how to do it. I met Fra Luis when I was campaigning in Spain and persuaded him to come back to Italy with me. He was much favored by Queen Isabella as a torturer, but he realized there would be more opportunity for advancement in my employ."

Her hands gone. Her worst nightmare— No! This was real. Horribly, hideously real.

She heard the creak of a door beyond her line of vision, and Damari's gaze lifted. "Oh, there you are, Fra Luis, she's awake. We can begin."

Sanchia instinctively began to struggle against the bonds holding her to the table as Fra Luis came to stand beside Damari. He was dressed in a mud-colored monk's robe that only enhanced the unhealthy sallowness of his complexion. His face was full, his lips pouty, and his green eyes coolly objective.

"Greetings, my child." Fra Luis's deep voice resonated hollowly in the chamber. "My Lord Damari tells me you have sinned and must be chastised."

Sanchia shuddered and closed her eyes.

It was going to happen. She was alone and helpless to stop them from torturing her . . . and cutting off her hands.

Lion had abandoned her.

Nine

Her left hand throbbed, waking her. Was it bleeding again? She supposed she should do something to stop it. She rolled over, then slowly, sluggishly, inched herself until she was in an upright position.

Panting, she collapsed back against the damp, slimy wall of the cell. What did it matter? They would be coming for her again soon and then it would start again. What did anything matter?

But it did matter.

It wasn't fair that she should be made to suffer like this. Fury burned away the despair numbing her emotions. What had she done? She had obeyed, as a slave must obey. She had been used, as a slave would be used.

She had been used.

A cockroach scampered over her throat and into her hair. She listlessly shook her head to rid herself of it.

Filth and pain and vermin . . . and betrayal.

Promises to slaves need not be kept. They were nothing, less than nothing.

She tensed, every muscle becoming rigid. She could hear the slap of Fra Luis's sandals on the flagstones of the corridor. He would take her to that room and strap her down on the table, place her hand on the block. He would look down at her with those cool, unfeeling eyes and the agony would begin again.

And Damari would stand there drinking in her pain watching her face, stroking her hair and whispering of pain to come. There was no justice in any of it, she thought fiercely. She did not deserve to be tortured. It was not right that she should submit herself to the will of others when it brought this agony.

The door swung open and Fra Luis's fleshy silhouette was outlined against the flickering amber glow of the torch lighting the corridor.

Sanchia braced herself for the command to rise and follow him. She should be frightened, but the fear had been seared out of her by the anger now possessing every portion of her heart and mind.

"Are you ready, child?"

She rose clumsily to her feet, using only her right hand to push herself from the wall, wanting to hurl herself at him and pound his white, pasty face with her fist. She had done that last night when they had come for her and they had made sure she had paid for it.

But someday she would find a way to escape them. Someday she would escape all the people who had brought her to this.

Until then she could only endure.

Fra Luis held out his hand. "Come, Lord Damari is waiting. He suggests we do the thumb this morning."

"My God!"

It was Lion's voice and yet not Lion's—hoarse, oddly broken . . .

But how could it be his voice when Lion had gone away and left her to Damari? Sanchia tried to fight her way out of the darkness she had purposely drawn about her to shut both madmen away, but the barrier was too solid, too strong. She mustn't lift her lids or move her body or the pain would start again. Pain was hiding everywhere, living in the darkness with the cockroaches and the rats. But she didn't have to open her eyes; she was only dreaming.

"*Jesú*," Lorenzo said. "Don't just kneel there staring at her. *Move*, Lion. We've got to get her out of here before Damari comes back with reinforcements."

"Look at her," Lion whispered.

"She's not dead, and you've seen worse," Lorenzo said impatiently. "Let's get her away from this hellish filth and we'll see what they've done to her."

Terrible things, she wanted to tell them. Cruel and senseless things that had somehow burned away what she had been and left someone else in her place. But it was no use talking to a dream. . . .

She was being gently lifted. Strange. None of her other dreams had seemed so real. Scent too. Leather and soap and that distinctive male fragrance she remembered as belonging to Lion. Perhaps it wasn't a dream after all.

She stirred and tried to lift her head.

"Don't move. You're safe now." Lion's voice was thick, his words muffled. "We're taking you away from here."

She would will the darkness away and see if it was really Lion. Lately she had discovered that her will could triumph when her body failed. She had only to concentrate all her energy and channel it into effort. Slowly her lids lifted and her eyes focused on the face above her.

Dark eyes glittering with a moist brilliance gazed down at her. Lion's eyes. "You . . . you broke your promise."

A muscle jerked in his jaw. "I know." Lion's arm tightened around her. "But I'm here now and I'll take care of you, Sanchia. I'll always take care of you."

She shook her head. "It's too late."

She heard him draw a harsh, strangled breath before her lids fluttered closed again.

The cell was moving, shuddering, falling.

Another nightmare. Sanchia moaned softly, and tried to crowd closer to the wall to keep from falling with the crazily shifting cell.

"Don't be afraid," Lorenzo said. "It's only a small squall, nothing to fear."

A squall was a storm, wasn't it? How could there be a storm in a cell?

Sanchia opened her eyes to see Lorenzo lounging in a chair across the room, one leg thrown over the arm, his booted foot swinging.

"Oh, you're awake. Excellent. I have a craving for conversation. You've been very dull of late, but Lion was most insistent I stay with you until you regained your senses. How do you feel?"

It wasn't a cell, and it wasn't a dream either. The room *was* dipping crazily! She tried to sit up. "What's happ—"

"Lie still." Lorenzo's tone was testy. "I have no desire to have to jump up and run over there to keep you from falling out of bed. When the sea is rough I make a practice of staying in one spot and not moving even if I grow barnacles. It saves a measureless amount of indignity and humiliation."

"Sea?" Sanchia's eyes widened.

"We're on Lion's ship *Dancer* enroute to Genoa."

"Genoa," she echoed. Perhaps she had been wrong about this being a dream. "But how—" She dazedly shook her head. She was immediately sorry as the room swung in sickening circles and she collapsed back against the pillows. "I was in the dungeon."

Lorenzo nodded. "For three days." He grimaced. "All of which time Lion was roaring like his namesake."

She had to have been in that dungeon for more than three days. Cockroaches, slime, the block . . . "No, it was longer than that."

"Stop shaking." Lorenzo frowned. "It's over. Lion managed to get you away from Damari."

It wasn't over. It could never be over now. "How?" she whispered.

"He rode to Pisa and hired a troop of men from Count Brelono and then rode back and attacked the palazzo. Damari realized he was outnumbered and fled with Fra Luis." He sighed. "Which was a pity. When Lion saw what he had done to you I'm sure he would have insisted on a spectacular death worthy of Damari's villainy, if the bastard had remained at hand. I was quite looking forward to it."

Sanchia closed her eyes, trying to understand what he was telling her through the throbbing ache at her temples. "You must have taken him by surprise. He didn't expect you to come back for me. He told me I'd be in the dungeon forever and I was helpless to do anything about it."

"What a sweet-natured bastard he is. Did you tell him he was a liar?"

"No." She opened her eyes. "Because he told the truth. I was there forever."

Lorenzo was silent, studying her face. "It must have seemed so, but truly it was only three days."

She lowered her gaze to the blanket. "Why are we on this ship?"

"Damari's condotti were quartered only twenty miles from the palazzo and Lion reasoned he would ride directly there and return with a sizeable force, far larger than the one we were able to hire so quickly from Brelono. Consequently, we couldn't linger at Solinari but rode to Pisa to get you to a physician. The physician said you were too frail to travel by land so Lion sent Marco home with the Wind Dancer to guard Mandara on the chance that Damari decided to march against it. Then we set sail for Genoa. He intends to settle you comfortably there, safely out of Damari's reach before returning to Mandara."

"Does he think Mandara is in danger?"

Lorenzo shrugged. "Not really. Damari is too crafty to attack a city as strong as Mandara with the condotti he commands. He would need reinforcements from Borgia, and Borgia has too many irons in the fire to release any men right now. Damari will probably wait until he has a good chance of victory before he attacks Mandara."

Condotti, attacks, Borgia. She was too hurt and weary to think about all this strife. She needed to go back to sleep and withdraw until she was healed and could contend with that world. She closed her eyes again.

"Aren't you going to ask how Lion is?"

"No."

"Or about your hand?"

Her eyes opened and she gazed at her bandaged left hand. During those last hours of torture she had tried to pretend it didn't belong to her, that both the pain and the hand itself were not her own. She found that a certain sense of being remote still lingered. "It doesn't hurt any longer."

"It will hurt if you try to move it. The physician splinted the fingers that were broken and snapped the others back into the sockets." He paused. "Would you like to tell me what Damari did to you?"

"You saw what he did to me."

"The thumb and three of the fingers will heal. The little finger was shattered in three pieces, the bones piercing the flesh, and the physician said it was doubtful you'd ever be able to bend or use it."

"The hammer," she said dully. "It bled . . ." She firmly closed her eyes. "I'm going to sleep now."

"Then I'd better try to make my way to the bridge and tell Lion you've awakened to a bright, new world. After your nap I'll help you bathe and dress. Lion purchased a few gowns and shawls from the wife of his shipwright at the yard before we left Pisa, but they're not as elegant as the ones Giulia supplied."

She heard the scrape of his chair as he rose to his feet and then his footsteps as he lurched with evident difficulty toward the door. "It *is* a bright, new world, you know," he said quietly. "Remember that, and be grateful, Sanchia."

She didn't answer and a moment later she heard the door close behind him.

"She's awake."

Lion turned quickly to see Lorenzo clinging desperately to the rail as he struggled toward the forecastle over the rain-slick deck.

"And I hope you appreciate the extreme discomfort I'm suffering to inform you of the fact."

Lion's hands tightened on the tiller. "She is . . . well?"

"If you mean, did Damari succeed in driving her mad while he tortured her, he did not." Lorenzo drew his short cape about him to protect his nape from the cold, driving rain. "I didn't think he'd be able to break her."

Lion's face was a savage mask. "*Cristo*, he tried hard enough. Did she talk about it?"

"No." Then, as Lion continued to look at him, he shrugged. "She said something about a hammer."

Lion felt as though he had been struck in the stomach with the same mallet. "Take the tiller," he said to the seaman standing behind him. He moved to the rail beside Lorenzo, gazing blindly out at the tempest swept sea. "I should have gotten there sooner."

"Three days to ride to Pisa, persuade Brelono to release his troop, and launch an attack on the palazzo smacks of miracles."

Lion reached out to grip the rail with white-knuckled force. "I shouldn't have waited. I should have thought of another way."

"You're becoming boringly repetitive. There was no other way."

Lion hadn't thought so at the time, but that didn't help him to forget the moment when he had found Sanchia curled up unconscious on the floor of the cell. She had looked . . . broken.

And then he had seen her hand.

"I'm going to kill Damari."

"I presumed as much. I suppose you wouldn't let me do it for you?"

"No." Lion released his grip on the rail and turned. "I'm going to the cabin to see Sanchia."

"She's probably asleep again."

"Then I'll wait until she wakes up." He had a hunger to see her, to know she was no longer the pale, shattered child he had carried aboard the *Dancer* two days before.

"Lion."

He glanced over his shoulder.

"She's not mad." Lorenzo hesitated before finally finishing, "But she's different."

"In what way?"

"I'm not certain."

"By all the saints, what do you mean?"

"I think she's . . ." Lorenzo paused again, thinking about it. "I think she's more than she was. There's a strength . . ." He shrugged. "I could be wrong. Judge for yourself."

"You leave me with no other choice." Lion strode down the steps of the bridge and across the deck toward the cabin.

A moment later he stood beside the bed looking down at Sanchia's pale, drawn face. Strength? It must be Lorenzo who had gone mad. Sanchia looked as delicate as the most fragile of blossoms. Rage seared through him as his gaze fell on her bandaged hand. Damari. Dear God, he wanted that son of a bitch.

Sanchia's lids twitched as if she had become aware that someone was watching her. She opened her eyes abruptly. Her gaze was totally alert and without fear.

Lion's muscles locked with tension as her compelling gaze fastened on his face. She stared at him without speaking and Lion suddenly found himself uneasy. He reached out awkwardly and touched her cheek. "Lorenzo tells me you're feeling better."

"Yes."

"Soon you'll be well."

She did not answer.

His hand dropped away from her face. "Is there anything I can get you? Are you thirsty?"

"No." Her gaze moved over him indifferently. "You're very wet."

"It's raining."

"Then you're foolish to be out in it."

"It was necessary. It's not a bad storm but there's always danger. It took me two years to build this ship, and I dislike the idea of its sinking to the bottom of the sea because I am not at the helm."

"I understand." She was silent a moment. "Why are you here?"

The bluntness of the question startled him as much as that first piercing glance had done. "Because I wanted to see for myself that you were on the mend."

"I don't want you here. Will you leave?"

Surprise held him wordless for a moment and then he smiled. "And what will you do if I won't?"

She failed to return his smile. "Nothing." She closed her eyes. "I'm too weak to fight you . . . now."

The last word held an odd quality of threat, Lion realized. Threats from Sanchia who had always been so frightened? So eager to please? "And later?"

"Later I will deal with you." Her eyes remained closed. "Lion."

She had not addressed him as my lord, as was her custom, but Lion. It was the address he had requested from her, but now his name came with no hesitation or prompting. She could not have shown more confidence and authority if she had been raised to be the lady of a great house.

He deliberately turned and sat down in the chair against the wall. "I will stay. You may need me."

"I don't need you. I'll never need you." She deliberately turned on her side. "But stay if you like. Your presence or absence mean nothing to me."

She had closed him out. She had stepped away from him to a place he couldn't follow, Lion realized with a queer twisting sensation in his belly. Nothing could be more clear from the crystalline coldness of her manner toward him. Why should he be surprised that she blamed him for all that happened to her? He knew the fault rested squarely on his shoulders and she was right in her anger. She had suffered and she deserved his patience. "It means something to me," he said gently. "I'll stay by your side, Sanchia."

She didn't answer, and he realized she had stepped even farther away from him into the realm of sleep.

"I brought Sanchia up on deck to get some air. Really, Lion, I'm not the woman's nursemaid." Lorenzo added plaintively, "Though anyone would draw that conclusion from the way I've bathed, dressed, and tended her these last days. If you wanted her cosseted and cared for, you should have brought a servant on board before we left Pisa." He paused. "Or done it yourself. You haven't set foot in her cabin since the first day she woke."

"You know I had no time to find a maid for her with Damari on our heels."

"I notice you don't address my second suggestion."

"She had no desire for my presence." Lion's grip tightened on the tiller. "She made that clear."

"So you meekly run and hide away from her lest your offensive self distress her."

"She's ill, damn you."

"Not any longer." Lorenzo's gaze went to Sanchia, who stood at the rail several yards away. The strong afternoon sunlight stroked her auburn hair with flame as gusts tossed it about. Her face was raised as if she were drinking in both the warmth of the sun and the vigor of the wind. "She has her strength back and she's come alive. Damari did no real damage, except to her hand, and it's healing nicely. She's in a far from delicate state." He nodded toward Sanchia. "Go see for yourself."

Lion looked quickly at her, then away. "For God's sake, quit prodding me. Do you want her in my bed so badly you'd yank her into it when she's still not well?"

"Did I mention bedding?" Lorenzo asked innocently. "Could it be your thoughts aren't as pure as you'd have me believe? She's changed, you know. We both noticed it. Tell me, Lion, has it not occurred to you that it would be like bedding someone else entirely now? The same sweet body but there would be certain differences. You've always had such a curious mind. Would you not like to explore those differences?"

Lion averted his face. "No, it hasn't occurred to me."

"Lies." Lorenzo chuckled. "You'll have to go to confession when you get back to Mandara and be absolved of that sin. Do you think Sanchia will like Mandara?"

"She won't get the opportunity to like or dislike it. She's staying in Genoa, as you well know."

"And we arrive in Genoa the day after tomorrow?"

Lion's lips twisted. "Not enough time for you, Lorenzo?"

"I would prefer more, but it should prove sufficient. However, since you're displaying an unusual amount of resistance, I shall stop being subtle."

"Subtle?"

Lorenzo ignored the sarcasm in Lion's tone. "I will have nothing more to do with Sanchia while we're on board the ship. She's your property and you must care for her as you see fit." He frowned thoughtfully. "Except to change her bandage. I'm having enough trouble contending with these idiotic feelings of responsibility you're experiencing without having you go squeamish. I might never get you to see sense." He turned away. "You notice the wind has come up and Sanchia does not have her shawl. She could take a chill."

"But she's not at all delicate," Lion ironically repeated Lorenzo's words.

Lorenzo shrugged as he walked over to the rail and leaned his elbows on it. "Perhaps she's more fragile than I thought. Who am I to say? I'm no physician."

And he proceeded to gaze placidly out to sea, ignoring both Lion on the forecastle and Sanchia on the deck.

Lion stayed on the forecastle for another fifteen minutes before he said sharply to the seaman behind him, "Take the tiller." He strode past a grinning Lorenzo, down the steps, then across the deck to where Sanchia stood at the rail.

"The wind is sharpening. Go back to your cabin," he said tersely.

"Soon." She didn't look at him. "I like it here. I feel as if I can see forever. What's beyond the horizon?"

His gaze followed hers to the point where the sea met the sky. "It depends on how far you travel. Until recently most men believed that there were only dragons waiting to devour you as you fell off the edge of the earth."

"Tales to frighten children," she said impatiently. "I've heard stories of great explorers who have sailed vast distances and discovered wondrous treasures."

"Lands overflowing with gold and silver, boundless forests, fierce savages." He paused. "And dragons."

"Christopher Columbus found no dragons." She glanced up at him with a frown. "You surely don't believe in such monsters?"

"I believe there are dangers for the unwary whenever you travel the unknown and that you must be prepared for them." He smiled faintly. "And that there are many kinds of dragons."

"But the possibility of dragons wouldn't stop you from seeing what is beyond that horizon?"

"No."

"It wouldn't stop me either. There is so much out there. . . ." The passionate intensity vibrating in Sanchia's voice was reflected in her luminous expression and eyes glowing with eagerness. Bemused, Lion gazed at her. She had come alive, as Lorenzo had said. It was as if she had been asleep before and now had come fully awake.

"Don't you see? There is so much promise in that horizon."

A pang of tenderness stirred within him. He had felt that same sense of revelation on a day over two years ago when he had stood on the dock in Venice and realized a lifetime of dissatisfaction had led him there. "Yes, I do see. Endless promise."

"I want to see all the lands that Columbus saw and more."

He smiled indulgently. "Perhaps someday I'll take

you on a voyage of discovery and we'll find—" He stopped as he watched her expression become shuttered. A poignant sense of loss that withdrawal brought kindled him to sudden anger. "What am I thinking? Voyages of discovery are not for women." He paused before adding with deliberate provocation, "but, if you're very good and obedient, I may bring you back a gift to solace you for what you've missed."

She didn't answer. Her gaze remained fixed on the horizon.

"Why do you not speak?" His tone was taunting. "You know I'm right. Women have no place on great journeys. They must stay at home and weave tapestries and—"

"And where do they have a place?" Sanchia whirled to face him. "In a man's bed, waiting to take his seed? In a dungeon, waiting to take his punishment?"

He felt as if she had struck him and his anger abruptly dissipated. "Sanchia, I would not have left the maze had I known you were in danger. I had no idea Damari was so close."

"Because I chose not to let you know. Because I was foolish enough to try to lead them away to give us all a chance."

Lion gazed at her incredulously. "You led him—" He reached out and grasped her shoulders. "Were you mad? Why didn't you let me know? I could have—"

"You could have done nothing." Sanchia broke free of him and stepped back. "And I knew there was nothing you could do so I led Damari away. I was going to double back and join you, but Damari caught me." She stared into his eyes. "And you left me."

"Sanchia . . ." Lion didn't know what to reply. What could he say to defend himself when the charge was true? "At the time I could see no other way. If they had caught the rest of us, we all could have gone to our deaths."

"Do you think I'm a fool who cannot reason? For a while I was stupid enough to hold on to the blind belief that you'd be coming for me any moment, simply because you had promised me." She drew a deep breath and made an impatient gesture with her bandaged left hand. "But then I forced myself to weigh what was true and what was not true. I had to do so or I would have been destroyed by anger. At times I thought I'd choke and be consumed by rage."

Lion felt a wrenching pity as he looked down at her bandaged hand. "I would have felt the same."

"Yes, you would have known anger, but you have no true idea how I felt in that dungeon." She turned away and gazed out to sea, the line of her spine straight and unyielding. "Because you were never as helpless as I was in that cell, as helpless as I've been all my life. You abandoned me, but I knew it was my fault in part for choosing to lead Damari away without telling you. You're not a man to give a promise lightly, and you probably would have tried to keep it." Her smile was bittersweet. "Even though your promise was given to a slave."

"I had every intention of keeping it."

"So, in a way, it was my choice. It wasn't the broken promise that made me so angry."

His gaze was intent on her face. "Then what?"

"That I was in the maze with you at all."

He stiffened. "You chose to go. I didn't force you."

"Do you know the reason I went?" She laughed incredulously. "It was because you smiled at me. Because I was so grateful you were treating me with kindness and a sort of camaraderie that I would have gone anywhere, done anything to have you continue to treat me so." Her gaze shifted to his face. "And I think you knew that if you were kind to me, I would go with you and you need not feel accountable."

His lips tightened. "You believe me to be so ruthless?"

"Yes." She held his gaze steadily. "I think you would have done anything to get the Wind Dancer back from Damari. In comparison, I had no real value to you. I was only your slave to be used." She shrugged. "Perhaps you didn't even know you were doing it."

Could she be right? He had wanted the Wind Dancer desperately and he had needed her help to retrieve it. Had he tried to woo her with kindness when his promise had kept him from commanding her to come with him? If that were true, then his guilt was even greater than he had thought. "You do have value for me."

"Do I? Now that you have the Wind Dancer back you have no need for a thief. Do you intend to use my body and make me into a whore for your pleasure?"

Her words stung him. "A whore is paid and I have no intention of paying for your services. Both you and Giovanni have already received quite enough from me." He smiled caustically. "And why should I not use you? You didn't seem averse once I showed you the way of it. I found you extremely eager to please. My pleasure was also your pleasure."

The color rose to her cheeks. "You did give me pleasure but . . ." She stopped, searching for words. "It was a false pleasure, a forced pleasure, because I did not choose it. You took my body because you thought you owned it." Her eyes suddenly glittered with cold rage. "You do *not* own it. You do not own me."

Shock ran through him, whatever he had expected it wasn't this complete rejection. "I have a bill of sale that states otherwise."

"I don't care what your bill of sale says. It's wrong for a person to be able to own another person. It should not happen. All my life I accepted being a slave because my mother said I must. She told me I would always be a slave. She said Giovanni had a right to do anything he wanted with us because he had bought us. Well, she was wrong, Giovanni was wrong, and you're wrong. When I was in Damari's filthy dungeon I realized no one has a right to make me do what I don't want to do because of a piece of paper." She drew a deep breath and went on with a rush, "I'm no longer your slave and I won't obey you."

He went still. "The hell you won't," Lion said softly. "You may think of me as the devil himself, but you belong to this particular devil and I'll tolerate no defiance."

"I have to defy you."

"Your memory is short. You gave me your promise of loyalty."

"Not because you bought me but because you helped Elizabet and the others. I paid that debt in Damari's dungeon." She held up her bandaged hand. "You took your Wind Dancer but I was the one who paid its ransom. We're even now, Lion."

He glanced away from her hand and out to sea. "Perhaps in your eyes but not the eyes of the law."

"And in your eyes too," she said fiercely. "You know my debt is paid to you. Why do you not admit it?"

"I do admit it. Your debt is paid," he said quietly. "But the bill of sale remains."

"Then tear it up. Free me."

He shook his head. "Why should I free you?"

"Because it's just," she said. "Dear God, there has to be some justice in the world or nothing makes sense."

"You believe you want to be free now. But think about it. As my slave you're under my protection. Life isn't easy for a woman alone."

"I know. I used to believe a slave was sometimes luckier than a free woman. But I was wrong." She took a step closer. "A free woman has choices. I had none. What I suffered in Damari's dungeon was only because I was your slave—doing what you willed. If I ever have to suffer like that again, it will be because I believe what I'm suffering for is worth the price of my pain." She shook her head. "You would give me no choices. I don't want to be under your protection."

"How very unfortunate, since you most certainly are under my protection and will remain with me."

"You will not free me, even though you know it's right to do so?"

He smiled at her mockingly. "How do I know what is right? What is wrong? Is it right to deprive myself of my own property? Would it not be wrong to take away my protection when Damari would like nothing better than to lay hands on you again?" His mockery faded to be replaced by grimness. "Don't seek to tutor me on what is right, Sanchia. Rightness lies with the holder of power."

"Then I must find a way to obtain power, for I will not let you own me." She gazed at him unflinchingly. "And I will not permit you to use either my body or my mind again. You might as well release me, for I will give you neither pleasure nor service."

"You do not have to give. As your master I'm entitled to take." He paused. "If I so desire. However, there is no hurry. I'll give you opportunity to grow accustomed to me again before I summon you to my bed."

She stared at him in disbelief. "Did you not hear me? I will no longer serve you."

"I heard you." He turned away and strode toward the bridge. "But I've decided not to let you anger me. You've suffered much for my sake and are entitled to a few harsh words."

"I'm entitled to my freedom."

"Then you will be disappointed, for you will not receive it. Go to your cabin. I won't have you catching a chill and falling ill."

"You won't have—"

"No, I won't have it," he repeated deliberately over his shoulder as he started up the steps of the forecastle. "Though you choose to think me as much a monster as Damari, I suffered because Damari captured and hurt you. And you do have value for me."

"As property?" she asked scornfully.

"As . . . Sanchia."

Her eyes widened. She was startled by his revelation. As he motioned the seaman away and took his place at the tiller, she quickly turned her back and gazed out to sea.

"She doesn't appear to be pleased with you," Lorenzo observed as he leaned on the rail to look at Lion. "What did you say to her?"

"She wants her freedom. She says she's no longer a slave and wants me to tear up her paper."

"Hmm, I'm not surprised." Lorenzo frowned. "Though I must admit I'm disappointed she decided to strike her blow for freedom at this particular time. It would have suited me better if she had continued to prove herself willing to render whatever you demanded of her. I take it you didn't give her what she asked?"

Lion's grip tightened on the tiller. "No, I did not."

"Ah, there's hope for you yet. You're not totally lost to the dark joys of corruption."

"She's mine," Lion said harshly. "She has no right to leave me. She—" Sanchia's words came back to him. She had said he had no right to hold her, but she was wrong. Even if the papers didn't exist, a man had the right to win whatever prizes were within his power and then hold on to them. So it had always been and so it would continue forever. Besides, she'd be better off with him than without him. Too many hazards threatened a woman alone in a world populated by men like Caprino, Damari, and Borgia.

And Lionello Andreas.

No, he was no threat to Sanchia. He quickly rejected the ridiculous thought. He would care for her. He would give her gifts of great beauty and fill her life with pleasure.

And fill her body with himself, sate himself in that tight silken sheath until he was rid of the obsession for only Sanchia.

And what was wrong with that? She had been learning all the ways of pleasure and he could not mistake the response she had given him.

False pleasure she had called it.

"Then do you bed her tonight?" Lorenzo asked. "She's well enough. Look at her, there's a bloom about her."

He didn't have to look at Sanchia to remember her clear, glowing beauty as defiance reddened her cheeks. His loins ached as he recalled the sight of her standing naked in the barn gazing up at him with frightened, wondering eyes. He could see her that way again, enter her again, hear her cry out . . .

But she would fight him this time. She would not be too frightened or hesitant to strike out at him, if he tried to force her. No matter what it cost, she would not give him what he wanted from her.

And if he compelled her, he might hurt her.

"Well, she did give you pleasure, didn't she? You were wild enough for her before this experience with Damari."

He was still wild for her. He should be feeling remorse and pity, not lust. Somewhere within him he did feel both those emotions, but the lust was greater. He could not let her go, so he had to find a way to convince her that remaining his slave was best for her. "Yes, she gave me pleasure."

Forced pleasure.

The memory of Sanchia's words knifed through him.

Force meant pain and he could not inflict more pain when she had already suffered so much for his sake.

"I'll not bed her tonight. Though I know it will disappoint you, it will do no harm to show a little patience."

Lorenzo started to say something, but thought better of it, and merely commented, "You're right, of course. It will do no harm and it might do a great deal of good. By all means, take as long as you like. I'm sure the practice of self-restraint will be wonderfully beneficial to the development of your character—and we both know how abstinence affects you, don't we, Lion?"

He didn't wait for an answer but strolled down the steps of the forecastle, a smile of satisfaction returning to his lips.

Ten

The dream came again that night.

Sanchia lay in the darkness, willing her heart to steady its wild cadence. It was only a dream, she told herself over and over. She wasn't in the dungeon, she was on Lion's ship, hundreds of miles away from Solinari. It was only a dream.

It did no good. The walls of the cabin were too close and seemed to be drawing closer with each breath she drew. She had to get *out*.

She got up and began to dress with frantic speed. She would go out on deck and look at the sea and breathe the sharp, clean air and think about what lay beyond the horizon. Freedom and adventure . . .

And perhaps the blessed absence of dreams.

A few minutes later she was standing at the rail looking out at the moonlight-dappled sea. Yes, this was what she had needed. She could feel the peace flow into her, banishing the tumult, blurring the memories she could not forget.

"What are you doing out here? Do you realize it's the middle of the night? You persist in trying to make yourself ill."

Her feelings of serenity were splintered as she recognized Lion's voice. *Dio*, she didn't want him here. Tonight she desired peace and he brought only turbulence. "I'm wearing my shawl." She drew the wrap closer about her. "I'll go in shortly."

He moved to stand beside her at the rail. "Now."

"No!" Then she tried to temper the sharpness of her voice. There must be no conflict now. Peace. Serenity. "I cannot sleep. Leave me and I promise to go in within the next hour."

"Bargains?" A note of surprise colored his tone. "You must already be ill. You were considerably more defiant this afternoon." He suddenly frowned. "Why can't you sleep? Does your hand hurt? Lorenzo said it was healing well."

"My hand doesn't hurt. It grows better every day. I'm just restless."

She could feel his gaze on her face. "Dreams?"

"What difference does it make? Go away. You disturb me."

"You disturb me too." His tone was abstracted. "The same dream? About the thief thrown out of the Stinche?"

"Not the same dream."

"Then what do—"

"Why do you not leave me alone?" She whirled to face him. "I dream of Damari's dungeon, not the Stinche. I dream that the hammer is a sword and Fra Luis is cutting off my fingers one by one. That's what he was going to do, you know. But first they wanted to let me think about it, so they played with me. They brought out the wooden block and put my hand on it and—"

"Hush." She was suddenly in Lion's arms, her cheek pressed against the leather of his jerkin, his fierce voice vibrating low beneath her ear. "Don't talk about it. Don't think about it."

"And after they had finished with me for the time they would take me back to the cell for a few hours so that I could recover and think of the next time they would—"

"I said no!" Lion's palm was suddenly covering her lips. "I don't want to hear any more. I want you to forget it."

She shook her head to rid herself of his hand. "I can't forget. I don't have that capability. I remember everything and, when I refuse to think of it during the day, I dream of it at night." She smiled bitterly. "But I will cease talking about it, if it troubles you."

"It does trouble me. I . . . feel it." Lion gazed down at her, his dark eyes glittering in the moonlight. "Tell me," he demanded suddenly. "Everything. From the first moment you were captured until I came for you. Everything they did to you. Everything you felt."

"Why? You said you didn't want to hear it."

"*Gran Dio*, I don't, but I have to share it. It was my responsibility you were there and I'll not leave you alone with it."

"It will do no good to—"

"Tell me."

And she told him, haltingly at first and then with a feverish rush, releasing all the memories, giving them to him.

And he listened, his expression impassive, his gaze locked to hers. Accepting.

Her words finally dwindled, slowed and then ceased altogether.

"Is it over?" His voice was harsh, strained.

She nodded jerkily. "That's all." She turned her face away from him. She felt lighter, she realized in surprise. As if in some mysterious fashion Lion had managed actually to lift a portion of those hideous memories from her own mind and into his.

"Thank God!" He jerked her back into his arms and held her crushed against him, his fingers buried in her hair. His chest was moving in and out as if he were running, but there was no passion in his embrace. "I did *not* like this. It hurt me."

She found herself laughing shakily. "It hurt me, too." The laughter brought its own easing and diminished Damari's importance in her memory as nothing else would have done.

"I know," he said thickly, then he was pushing her away, his gaze on her face. "Can't you see that it must not happen again? You belong to me and I must protect—"

"I don't belong to you." Yet even as she spoke she realized she felt more bound to him in this moment than when she had held him within her body. She took a panicky step backward. "I belong to no one but myself. I will—"

His hand quickly covered her mouth. "We will not talk about it now. Can you not be still?"

She took another step back and turned her face to elude his hand. "I have no choice, if you persist in covering my mouth with that huge paw," she said tartly. "If you do not wish to hear me speak, then leave me."

He stood looking at her with a scowl. "I don't want to leave you."

Sanchia felt an irrational rush of relief. She found she no longer wanted to be alone and Lion's presence was bringing its own rough comfort. "Then you must let me speak when I wish to speak."

Humor banished the frown from Lion's face. "I've done little else but listen since the moment I came on deck." He took her elbow and propelled her across the deck. "Come."

She tried to pull away from him. "Where are you taking me?"

"Here." He had stopped at the steps leading to the forecastle and now pushed her down on the second step. "Sit." His smile held a hint of little boy mischief. "Did you think I was dragging you to my bed? I'm trying to prove what a patient man I can be. You're safe from me for now." He jerked his head toward the seaman at the tiller a few yards away. "And, since I have no intention of sharing you, it would be cruel to him to take you here in front of him."

She glanced at him curiously. "Have you ever shared a woman with other men?"

He shrugged. "Many times. There are never quite enough camp followers to go around."

He saw the distaste on her face and his own expression hardened as he dropped down on the step beside her. "Yes, I've whored, and killed, and even taken women against their will." He saw her go rigid and continued, "What did you expect? I'm no gentle courtier like Marco. I'm only a rough soldier. When a town is taken, the women are part of the prize."

"It still doesn't make it right," she said clearly. "How did you feel when you were doing it?"

"You get used to it." He paused. "Most of it." He was silent for a moment, remembering, before admitting, "Though only once did I take a woman when she wasn't willing. I was fourteen and drunk with power and victory and hurting for a woman. She was a merchant's wife I found hiding in a shop. I thought, why not? No one else hesitated to take what was theirs by right. I had even seen my father ease himself with comely women, apparently uncaring whether they were willing or unwilling." He hesitated for an instant and then burst out, "But I had no liking for it. Her eyes were empty and she wept. . . . I could not please her. I kept her with me until the condotti left the city and gave her money when we parted. I let no one else touch her but—" He broke off and said again, "I had no liking for it."

Sanchia said nothing.

He turned on her as fiercely as if she had attacked him. "I make no excuses. I am what I am and I do what I have to do. I have little gentleness but I'm honest and return what I'm given, be it good or evil. You must accept me as I am."

She was startled by his sudden intensity. "Why are you telling me this?"

Conflicting emotions darkened his face. "I don't know." He smiled crookedly. "You have a strange effect on me. Lorenzo says I have a great need to go to confession. Perhaps I want you to absolve what cannot be absolved."

Her gaze dropped from his face and silence fell between them again.

"You didn't like being a soldier?" she asked finally.

He shrugged. "I knew nothing else from the time I was a boy. I did it well. My father was pleased with me."

"But you didn't like it?" she insisted. "Is that why you gave up your condotti and began to build ships?"

"The sea has always been in our blood. It was not until my family came from Persia to Italy over a hundred years ago that we moved inland away from the coast." He made a face. "We are not farmers by nature and did not prosper. So my great-grandfather took up the sword. War suited us much better than tilling the land, and we grew rich on it."

"But you gave it up."

"We were rich enough, and I was tired of noblemen who paid me to do battle for them one day and then hired someone to steal my fee the next." He leaned back against the step, his gaze on the sails billowing in the wind. "Then one day I was on the docks in Venice watching a ship from Madagascar sail into port. I had spent the morning squeezing the last half of my fee from the signory coffers and I was sickened to death of the *Serenissima*." He smiled reminiscently. "The wind was lifting the sails, and I could smell the scent of the sea and the cargo of cinnamon being unloaded and suddenly I knew—" He broke off and turned to face her. "Do you think you can sleep now?"

"It's unlikely." She paused, her eyes never leaving his. "Knew what?"

He stood up and reached down to pull her to her feet. "I knew it was time that we returned to the sea where we belonged."

"But why shipbuilding? Why not exploring or trading?"

He shook his head. "We've talked enough. Go to bed."

Sanchia felt a sharp thrust of disappointment. For the first time since she had met him, Lion was becoming more human and less the powerful enigma to her. She was reluctant to let that fleeting glimpse of him out of her sight for fear it would fade away. "I'm not sleepy."

"Neither am I." He added bluntly, "But my body is readying and if you don't want to take me, then leave me now." He smiled faintly as he saw her eyes widen. "Did you think I no longer lusted for you? It's always with me when you are near. You must accept that too."

"I must accept only what I wish to accept."

"What you choose to accept," he amended with soft emphasis. "I can make you 'wish' to accept me."

She gazed up at him, feeling a familiar stirring between her thighs. No, she would not feel like this. She was no longer his leman and must not yield him any response or he would seize on it. "Then I choose not to accept you. I don't want—" She broke off as she met his knowing gaze. "Release me, Lion."

"Come to my bed, Sanchia."

"I cannot."

"And I will not."

She felt a surge of desperation as she looked at him. His expression was without mercy, completely implacable. She wished she had gone to her cabin as he had bade her when he had first come on deck. Before he had shown her comfort, before he had let her glimpse the raw brutality of the life that had carved those jagged edges and helped to make him what he was. Now, though she could not condone, she could understand and, through that understanding, she was drawn to him. "I won't stay in Genoa, you know. I'll run away from you."

He stiffened. "Don't be foolish. You'll be safe in Genoa. Damari won't trouble himself to go so far to seek you out, and I'll make sure you're settled in comfortable lodgings before I leave."

"And when you return?" Sanchia shook her head. "If you want a strumpet, go back to Giulia Marzo and free me."

"I won't free you."

"Then you'll have to send someone to hunt me down. I won't be here when you return." She gazed at him beseechingly. "Why will you not free me? You said you wouldn't be able to bear slavery yourself, that you would run away."

He stiffened. "You know the punishment I could mete out for such a crime?"

"You think I'm afraid of punishment?" She smiled bitterly. "I've learned to deal with pain; Damari was an excellent tutor." She shook her head. "And you would not hurt me."

"You're very sure."

"Yes, so do not threaten what you won't execute, Lion. I do not fear you any longer."

Lion's expression reflected both anger and frustration. "Perhaps I'll have to change my ways. I've obviously become too predictable." He turned on his heel and strode across the deck. "You're a very troublesome woman." He yelled to the seaman at the tiller, "Turn the ship around, dammit. We're returning to Pisa."

"Pisa." Sanchia gazed at him with the same astonishment shown by the sailor at the helm, who was hurrying to do Lion's bidding. "We're only a day away from Genoa."

"And you've just told me you'll run away from Genoa as soon as I sail out of the harbor." His lips tightened. "So I'm keeping you with me."

"In Pisa?"

"I'm going to Pisa only to dock. I can't stay there. I have to make sure Damari hasn't launched an attack on Mandara."

"But Lorenzo said that was extremely unlikely."

"Mandara belongs to me. I have to be sure."

"Then you're taking me to Mandara?"

"You've given me no choice."

The moonlight was strong and full on his face, and Sanchia had never seen a more grim expression on it.

"Yes," he said, "I'm taking you to Mandara."

"There's Mandara, Sanchia." Lorenzo reined in his horse and leaned forward in the saddle, his gaze intent on the walled city in the distance. An odd eagerness warmed the usual remoteness of his features. "It's not as far as it looks. We should be there within thirty minutes."

Lion cast him a less than pleased glance over his shoulder. "Which should make you exceedingly happy."

"Yes, as a matter of fact, it does bring me a good deal of satisfaction." For once there was no mockery in Lorenzo's voice. "Though I'm not at all sure there is any such emotion as happiness." He shrugged. "But there are many words that have no meaning for me."

"It's beautiful." From this slight rise in the foothills Sanchia could see both the walled city of Mandara and, to the north, a large vineyard in the valley. Her gaze shifted to the castle that dominated the city. Her grip unconsciously tightened on the reins and the mare tossed her head in protest. Sanchia deliberately forced herself to relax. She should not be intimidated at the thought of meeting Lion's mother. The woman posed no threat to her. Lion had told Sanchia that she was not even to go to the castle but to occupy a small house in the town itself. It would be obvious to the Lady Caterina that Sanchia's place in Lion's life was too minuscule to be of any importance to her, and she would doubtless ignore her.

She would find a way to leave Mandara. A surge of dismay accompanied the thought as she looked at the high stone walls of the city. Escaping from Lion had proved impossible since they had landed in Pisa and might prove equally difficult now that she was to enter his own domain.

"Give it up, Sanchia."

She turned to see Lion's gazed fixed on her face. "You'll not leave Mandara."

"You're wrong. I'll find a way." Sanchia's gaze shifted back to the castle. "You forget that I'm a very good thief. You'll have difficulty keeping me locked up."

"I don't have to keep you locked up. No keys are needed here. You'll notice the moat and drawbridge and the city gates are guarded by my own men." He smiled pleasantly. "And I'll be careful to tell those guards that I'll be forced to emasculate them if they allow you to step outside the gates of Mandara."

"I think that should prove more than persuasive," Lorenzo said mildly. "Lion's right. Give it up, Sanchia."

She didn't answer as she spurred her horse down the incline toward the distant city.

The gates of Mandara were flung open when they were still some distance away, and two riders rode out of the city. One rider on a huge gray horse immediately spurred ahead of the other and approached them at a hard gallop.

"It seems we're to be honored by a personal escort," Lorenzo murmured. "The Lady Caterina."

Sanchia tensed, her gaze on the rider galloping toward them. She could not distinguish the woman's features from this distance, but there was no doubt this was an *illustrissima*, a great lady. She rode with her spine straight, her carriage indomitable and with the same driving force and skill as her son, Lion. Since the lady was on horseback it was difficult to determine her size, but she appeared tall and slim, her shoulders broad beneath a crimson velvet cloak.

"Courage, Sanchia." Lorenzo's gaze never left the approaching rider. "At least, she's left her mace at home."

"Sanchia won't need courage," Lion said as he urged Tabron forward a few paces. "My mother will do her no harm."

Lorenzo snorted derisively but said no more.

Caterina Andreas reined in her gray stallion a few yards from where Lion sat waiting and Sanchia unconsciously braced herself. Lion's mother needed no weapons to impress and intimidate.

The lady Caterina's features were too strong to be considered beautiful, her jaw too long, her chin too firm, her brows a feminine version of Lion's black slashing ones. She had the bold, authoritative manner of a man, yet there was nothing masculine about the sculptured beauty of her high cheekbones nor the dauntless spirit in her fine dark eyes. Her glossy black hair was threaded with silver but her face was firm and virtually unlined.

Her keen gaze raked Lion's face. "You are well?"

Lion nodded. "Damari?"

"He did not march on Mandara." She shrugged. "The cur would not dare. He prefers to bribe others to do his villainy. Marco sent inquiries to Pisa and we received word that after Damari learned you had set sail for Genoa he left to seek out Borgia." A sudden glint of humor appeared in her eyes. "No doubt to make excuses as to why he cannot produce what he promised. I'd like to have been there when he attempted to explain to his lord how he could not hold on to the Wind Dancer against only three men."

"And one woman," Lorenzo added softly.

Caterina's gaze moved to Lorenzo's face and she nodded formally. "Lorenzo."

He inclined his head in a mocking bow. "My lady."

Then Caterina turned to Sanchia. "You are the slave Sanchia?"

Sanchia drew herself up. "I am Sanchia. I am no longer a slave."

Caterina glanced at Lion. "You freed her? Marco said you had no intention of freeing her."

"I didn't free her." Lion added dryly, "She appears to think saying the words makes it true."

"The debt is paid," Sanchia said. "I am free."

"What does she do here?" Caterina asked Lion. "You were to leave her in Genoa. Marco said—"

"She's here and that's the end of it," Lion cut in harshly. "It will make no difference."

Caterina's gaze narrowed on his face. "You do not bring her to the castle?"

Lion shook his head. "She stays in the town."

"Unless you want to honor her with an invitation as your guest," Lorenzo said. "I'm sure Lion would give in to your urging. He's such a dutiful son."

"No!" Lion said. "Stay out of this, Lorenzo. This isn't your concern."

"Our Messer Vasaro seldom lets that consideration stop him." Caterina asked with dangerous softness, "Is this your doing, Lorenzo?"

Lorenzo merely smiled at her.

"Why?" Caterina turned back to Lion. "If you're

grateful to her for her service to you, then free her, give her money, and let her be on her way. She has no place in Mandara."

"She has a place wherever I choose to give it to her," Lion said. "Let be, Mother."

"I shall not—" She broke off as she heard the clatter of approaching hooves. "I will deal with this later. It is not ended."

"We didn't think it would be," Lorenzo said.

Caterina shot him a lethal glance before wheeling her horse to greet the woman riding toward them. "You were slow, Bianca. You must show more eagerness or Lion will think you're not happy to see him."

"I'm always happy to see Lion, as he very well knows," the woman addressed as Bianca answered serenely. "Do you forget I am not so good a horsewoman that I would dare to ride at breakneck speed as you do?" She smiled warmly at Lion, her deep blue eyes glowing with affection. "Welcome back to Mandara, my lord. We have missed you."

She was possibly the most beautiful woman Sanchia had ever seen. Sunlight shone on the streaks of blond weaving through the ash brown braids wrapped around her small head and revealed the perfection of features that might have graced a statue of Aphrodite. No, not Aphrodite, Sanchia amended her thought with sudden certainty. This woman's face was too innocent to be likened to the worldly goddess of love. She glowed with a childlike purity that was more reminiscent of Psyche.

"I missed you as well, Bianca." Lion smiled gently. "You appear to be flourishing. You have more color than the last time I saw you."

"Oh yes, I'm very well. Marco makes me spend hours in the garden posing for his paintings. I was quite reddened from the last week."

"Marco should take better care of you."

"But she won't have to worry about Marco taking care of her now that you're home, Lion," Caterina said briskly. "You can—"

"Aren't you going to introduce Sanchia to Bianca, Lion?" Lorenzo interrupted. "Where is your courtesy?"

"This is Sanchia?" An eager smile lit Bianca's face. "Marco told me how brave you were in helping to get the Wind Dancer back. How proud I am to meet you. I know we're going to become fast friends."

Sanchia was warmed by Bianca's sincerity; her smile held the same gentle, loving quality Sanchia was accustomed to seeing on Elizabet's face. "I'm most pleased to meet you, my lady."

"But you haven't been introduced," Lorenzo said. "I suppose I must be the one to perform the happy duty. Sanchia, may I present the Lady Bianca?" He paused. "Lion's wife."

Why did she feel so stunned? Sanchia wondered wildly. Just because no one had mentioned that Lion was wed did not mean a marriage did not exist. She quickly forced a smile to hide the shock she knew must be revealed on her face and nodded her head. "My lady."

"Bianca." Lion's wife urged with another smile. "You must call me Bianca."

"Bianca . . ." Sanchia repeated numbly. She would not look at Lion. She would not let him see the pain twisting through her now that the first shock had passed. She felt betrayed . . . more so than she had in the dungeon when she had believed Lion had abandoned her. How stupid and unreasonable she was to feel this way. She should not mind that he had a wife.

"And I will call you Sanchia." Bianca turned to Caterina. "Could we put her in the chamber close to mine? I would dearly like to—"

"She's a slave, Bianca," Caterina cut in harshly.

"Still?" A frown marred the smooth perfection of Bianca's brow. "But I'm certain Lion has only overlooked the formality of freeing her. He has no liking for slavery." She turned to Lion. "Is that not so?"

Lion's face was expressionless. "As you say, there are formalities. But the question of her status is irrelevant at the moment. Sanchia will not stay at the castle."

As Bianca started to protest Lion raised a hand to silence her. "Perhaps later. Sanchia has suffered greatly and needs solitude. I've made arrangements for her to occupy a house off the piazza where she can rest and recover her strength."

Bianca's frown vanished as her gaze went to Sanchia's bandaged hand. "I can understand," she said softly. "You are right, my lord. She must have solitude so that she may commune with God and pray that he return her to full health." She nodded. "I will pray too, Sanchia, and we'll soon have you at the castle."

"Thank you," Sanchia said faintly.

"And I will bring cushions and coverlets from the castle," Bianca went on. "Perhaps a servant. What think you, Lion?"

"I'll arrange for the servant," Lion said. "And you must not trouble yourself, Bianca. Sanchia is my responsibility and I will see to her comfort."

"But I'm sure Bianca doesn't consider it a hardship," Lorenzo said. "Charity is God's will, isn't it, Bianca?"

"Lion is quite right, Bianca," Caterina said with an annoyed look at Lorenzo. "It's not your place to defy him in this."

"Defy him?" Bianca's eyes widened in distress. "I would never defy him. You understand, do you not, my lord? I only thought to—"

"I know, I know," Lion said with sudden impatience. "My mother's words were too harsh. Just accept my will in this."

"Certainly, my lord. Whatever you wish," Bianca said, relieved. "May I send her strengthening food from the kitchens?"

"Send what you like," Lion said between his teeth as he urged Tabron into a trot. "And now, may we end this chatter and continue to the city? I need to question Marco about Damari and speak to the guards at the gate."

The whitewashed house to which Lion led them was small but charming, with window boxes overflowing with coral-red geraniums on the balcony overlooking the piazza.

"I know this house," Caterina said slowly, her gaze

lifting to the curtained doors leading to the balcony. She turned to Lion.

Lion met her gaze and his face softened. "I had no time to find another place. It's this house or the castle."

"I'm not quarreling with your choice. I find it very fitting."

"Mother, it's not my choice. I would—"

"I have no time to linger here. I presume you have the key?"

"Since the house has been empty the key has been held by the shopkeeper next door."

"Then you will have no trouble. Come, Bianca, we must hurry and make sure there is sufficient for supper." Caterina wheeled her stallion and trotted away with Bianca following close behind her.

Lion cursed softly beneath his breath before turning to Lorenzo. "Will you get the key and settle Sanchia before you come to the castle? I must talk to my mother."

Lorenzo nodded, his gaze on Caterina, her back rigidly straight. "I gather the house belonged to your father and was used for the usual purpose?"

Lion nodded. "*Cristo*, why did she have to come to meet me? She wouldn't have had to know Sanchia was occupying the house."

"You thought to hide me?" Sanchia asked clearly. "If I'm proving inconvenient, you have the solution."

Lion gave her a fierce glance. "Don't anger me, Sanchia. I'm having trouble enough without you pricking at me."

Lorenzo's gaze was still on Caterina. "Yes, go after her and give her kind words. I think she has need of them." He turned to smile at Sanchia. "We will deal very well together without you."

"Very well," Sanchia repeated emphatically.

Lion cast her a black look, wheeled his horse, and set out after Lady Caterina and Bianca.

Lorenzo dismounted and came around to lift Sanchia from her mare and tie the horses to the gate post of the iron fence that surrounded the house. "Wait here and I'll get the key."

He was back in a few minutes, not only with the key but with a plump, homely young woman whose sunny smile was only slightly quenched by Lorenzo's chilling presence. "This is Rosa Lanzio. She's the youngest daughter of the owner of the silk shop next door. She will serve you."

Rosa murmured something inaudible and gave Sanchia a quick curtsy.

Sanchia gazed at her, stunned. It was incomprehensible to her that she, who had been a slave for her entire life, was now offered someone to serve her. "I need no servant."

"Lion evidently thinks differently." Lorenzo unlocked the door and wrinkled his nose distastefully as he swung it open. "Come along, Rosa, the entire place needs airing out and a thorough cleaning."

Rosa gave him a frightened glance and then fled wordlessly into the house.

"At least she doesn't chatter," Lorenzo said blandly. "I detest a jabbering woman." He glanced at Sanchia. "Though I should have no complaints about you. You've scarcely uttered a word since I introduced you to Bianca."

"I was . . . surprised."

"I gathered that." Lorenzo smiled. "A lovely child, Bianca, and as good as she is lovely."

"Yes."

"You notice how kind and patient Lion is toward her?"

Sanchia felt a queer jolt of pain. "It's not out of the ordinary for a man to be kind to his wife. He must love her very much."

"Oh yes, everyone loves Bianca."

Sanchia turned to face him. "You didn't want me to know about her until I arrived here."

"I certainly thought it better that you remain in ignorance as long as possible."

"Better for whom?"

"All concerned. You'll understand once you're acquainted with the situation." He looked intently at her.

"But I think you've had quite enough to absorb for the time being."

"I won't be here to come to understand very much about Lord Andreas and his family."

"Oh, I believe you will. Lion will take all the necessary precautions to assure your stay. He's not gone through all this turmoil to see you flit away from him now." He smiled. "So why not enjoy yourself? A pretty house, someone to wait on you, nothing to do but rest. Tomorrow we will look at fabric, and I'll order you gowns so exquisite that Giulia Marzo would gnash her teeth with envy. Are you not tempted?"

"No."

Lorenzo frowned, then his face brightened. "I forgot for a moment you weren't brought up to appreciate the usual female pleasures. Books. I'll bring you several books from the castle to amuse you until I can order your own. There's a skilled young scribe here in Mandara who does both swift and beautiful work and you may choose whatever works please you for him to execute."

"Books?" Sanchia could not keep the eagerness from her tone. A book of her very own! What a delight it would be to possess the magic of words, not only in her mind but on fine parchment, to touch lovingly and keep forever.

"Bound in fine crimson leather," he said persuasively. "With gilt edges."

Sanchia suddenly smiled. "You're surely an emissary from Satan, Lorenzo."

He nodded. "That's what I continually tell Lion, but he prefers not to believe it. So you will take the books and—"

"If I accept the books, it will not keep me from trying to run away," she said quickly. "I must be honest with you."

"Then I am fair warned." Lorenzo shrugged. "Now come with me to the *trattoria* across the piazza and we will have wine and cheese while we wait for Rosa to clean your house. I cannot abide this smell."

"It's not my house," Sanchia said as she fell into step with him.

"It could be, if you'd stop worrying about being free and start worrying about how to please Lion."

Sanchia's lips tightened. "He has a wife to please him."

"True. Sweet, gentle Bianca."

Sanchia walked in silence for a moment before asking abruptly, "Have they been wed long?"

Lorenzo nodded. "Since before I met Lion. I believe he was sixteen and Bianca fourteen. She was Bianca Garlondo, a connection of the Baglioni, and the merging of the families was considered very beneficial to Mandara. The marriage was arranged by Lion's father and, as is the custom, they never saw each other before the contract was signed."

"Are there children?"

"No." Lorenzo smiled. "What a pity. No heir for Mandara. But then Bianca appears almost too beautiful to be subjected to the desecration of childbirth, doesn't she?" His gaze suddenly narrowed on Sanchia's face. "Tell me, what was your first impression when you saw her?"

"Psyche," she answered without thinking.

He looked at her blankly and then chuckled. "You never cease to amaze me. What an interesting comparison."

They had reached the *trattoria*, and he pulled out a chair for her to sit and snapped his fingers for service. "The *vino* is excellent here, much better than in Florence. Mandara is growing famous for its vineyard." He dropped into the chair opposite her. "Now let us speak on a subject that brings us mutual delight. Which books do you most wish to acquire?"

Eleven

The flames of the smoking torches affixed to the stone walls on either side of the tall front doors of Mandara cast an eerie orange-red light on Lion's dark hair. He strode out of the pools of light, hurrying across the courtyard to Lorenzo.

"*Cristo*, you took long enough." Lion motioned for the lackey to take the reins of Lorenzo's horse as he dismounted. "She's settled?"

"As much as she'll let herself be settled. Did you talk to Marco?"

"Yes, Damari is definitely with Borgia. He rode for Cesena directly from Pisa."

"Which means you can't touch him yet without pulling Cesare down on Mandara. You'll have to be patient."

"I don't feel like being patient. I may not be able to touch Damari, but I can drag down

Caprino. I leave for Florence tomorrow at dawn."

"Then do you go to Sanchia tonight?"

"No." Lion turned abruptly and started up the stone steps. "Not tonight."

"Ah, I understand. You wish to spend the evening in the arms of your sweet wife."

"Lorenzo, someday I'll—" Lion stopped. "You have what you wanted, but I'll not give you total victory."

Lorenzo followed him into the great hall. "But the victory will be yours. That will be the beauty of it." He started up the wide oak stairs. "But I admit I'm weary of all this destiny shaping. Even God rested on the seventh day. Do what you wish tonight. I intend to spend the hours before sleep wandering with Dante in his inferno. He doesn't truly understand the nature of hell, but it comforts me to know that someone believes there's a Hades other than the one we make for ourselves. It strikes a certain balance in the universe."

"Sleep well, Lorenzo."

Lorenzo looked down at him from the landing and a rare smile lit his face. "Thank you, my friend, and may your own sleep bring you counsel. It's all so simple, if you would but see it." He continued up the stairs to the chamber he had made his own for the thirteen years he had been with Lion.

It was more than two hours later when the door of Lorenzo's bed chamber was thrown open and Caterina Andreas marched into the room. She wore a splendid midnight blue velvet gown with a low round neckline bordered in sapphires set in filigree silver. Combs ornamented with sapphires held her dark hair smoothly in its bun on her nape and she looked very much the grand lady of the castle. Which had probably been her intention, Lorenzo thought in amusement as he closed his book and leaned back in his chair.

"It was your doing, wasn't it?" She slammed the door behind her. "Lion has never brought a woman to Mandara before. I won't have it. Do you hear me? I won't have it, Lorenzo."

"Good evening, my lady. I trust you had a pleasant evening? I was sorry to miss the joyous homecoming repast." Lorenzo pushed his chair away from the desk. "Sanchia and I had to make do with bread and cheese at the *trattoria*. Sanchia was content, but then she's not accustomed to anything else." He gazed at her in reproach. "Do you not feel guilty in depriving the poor child of a better life here at the castle?"

"I do not. Let her make a better life away from Mandara. Lion spends little enough time here as it is. I won't have him distracted from his duty."

"Duty? Ah, the impregnation of the lovely Bianca. You'd think, considering Lion's appetite for that sport, he would have a dozen offspring by now, wouldn't you?"

"Stop playing, Lorenzo. I *will* have a grandson and Mandara will have an heir. This foolishness has gone on too long."

"My exact words to Lion. It's gone on far too long." He shook his head. "And you know he won't touch Bianca. He regards her as a little sister now."

"That could change." Caterina drew two steps closer, glaring at him. "She's very beautiful."

"She's dull."

"She's gentle and obedient."

"She's a child."

"She's almost as old as Lion, far older than that redhaired urchin you persuaded Lion to bring here."

"In years, perhaps, but Sanchia's upbringing has given her a maturity Bianca will never have. You know that as well as I do." He met her gaze. "And I did not persuade Lion to bring Sanchia here. You should know your son well enough to realize words would not sway him. Circumstances conspired to bring Sanchia here."

"With your help?"

"I certainly offered every encouragement. Sanchia may be the answer to Lion's quandary. She has courage and intelligence and I think they suit very—"

"Sweet Mary, you're surely not telling me he could love her?" Caterina gazed at him in astonishment. "Good God, have you lost your senses? Passion, perhaps, but he's no fool to mistake lust for those mawkish emotions mouthed by troubadours."

"No, he's no fool." Lorenzo smiled. "And we both

know love is a word for fools and children. Still, it could do no harm for him to have a woman who could offer him a mind as well as a body to enjoy."

"Let him have her then," Caterina said. "But not here. I must have an heir for Mandara."

"You could marry again. You're young enough to bear another child."

She suddenly averted her face. "I like my life well enough as it is without bringing in a man to call lord, and perhaps, covet what is Lion's."

"Lion does not want Mandara. He guards it because duty is his nature, but he cares only for that precious shipyard of his in Pisa."

"That's only a whim. He'll tire of it and return to Mandara."

"No, you're wrong. He's found something there he was lacking and from now on he'll return to Mandara only when he must. Mandara is what you want, not what Lion wants. He has no wish to continue your dynasty."

"I desire no dynasty. I want only to keep what I've built here." Her dark eyes blazed at him. "Who do you think protected and nurtured Mandara while my husband and Lion were away fighting their battles? Carlo took Lion from me when he was little more than a baby, and Marco was always absorbed in his painting and music. I have no—" She broke off and then continued with steely determination, "Mandara is my child. It must go on."

"Then you must look elsewhere for the means."

"You will not help me?"

"Are you asking me for help?"

She lifted her chin proudly. "No."

"That is good. I'd hate to refuse such a grand and noble lady. By the way, that gown is truly superb. Was it meant to overwhelm me with your consequence?"

"Yes."

"You've succeeded. I stand abased and chastened."

"You lie." She gazed at him silently for a minute. "Well, aren't you going to ask me to take it off and come to bed?"

"No."

"Do you want me in your bed?"

"Oh, yes." A brilliant smile warmed the coldness of his face as his gaze moved over her caressingly. "Yes, my dear Caterina, it's my most earnest desire."

"Why do you never come to me?" Caterina rubbed her cheek against Lorenzo's naked shoulder with catlike contentment. "Why must I always come to your chamber and ask to be taken to your bed?"

Lorenzo gently stroked her silky hair. "You're a great lady. I would not have your name bandied about by your servants." His index finger moved to lazily trace the straight line of her brow. "And then, too, my self-love is very fragile. What if I should ask and you refuse? I should be devastated."

"I should have known I'd get no satisfaction from that twisted tongue of yours." She raised herself to gaze down at him with a smile. "It's just as well you give me such satisfaction with another part of your anatomy or I would not bother sinking my pride to come to you."

"Such bawdiness." He lifted his head and kissed her lips. "Should the lady of the castle conduct herself so?"

She stiffened and then rolled away from him. "I'm not a bawd. Just because I come to you like this does not mean that I fornicate with all who ask me."

"I did not say it did," Lorenzo murmured. "I jest. You are overly sensitive tonight."

"Yes." She was silent a moment, gazing into the darkness. "It was the house."

"I thought it might be."

"It was the house Carlo kept for his mistresses. I wasn't supposed to know about it." Her voice harshened. "How could I help but know about it? There were always those ready to taunt me with the knowledge of Carlo's latest woman." She paused before continuing fiercely, "There was never affection between us, but I was his wife and he should have spared my pride."

And she had such great pride, Lorenzo thought, as great as the splendid spirit that matched her equally splendid body. "You had no affection for him?"

She shook her head. "There was lust at first. But after the children were born and he had his heirs, he no longer came to my bed. He easily grew tired of a woman and wanted variety."

"A most foolish man."

"I didn't care. I was never so stupid as to think he would be faithful to me. Men are not constant by nature."

"How wise of you to realize and accept our faults." He could feel the rigidity of her muscles against him and sensed the painful tumult the memories had resurrected within her. "Would you turn over? There's a lovely hollow between your shoulder blades that intrigues me."

She turned over on her side with a chuckle. "My shoulder blades?"

"You have magnificent shoulders." He pressed his lips to her right shoulder. "And I could write an ode to your shoulder blades." He brushed his lips against her left shoulder. "And a sonnet to this cunning hollow between them." His lips nuzzled the hollow affection-ately. He could feel the tautness ebbing from her stiff muscles and deliberately kept his tone careless. "Go on, you were telling me of this idiot, Carlo. Though why we're bothering to discuss the boring fellow I don't know. I'm almost sorry I helped Lion dispose of his murderers. He obviously deserved that knife between his ribs." His lips moved down the hollow of her spine. "I suppose you were equally foolish and remained faithful to him?"

She frowned. "Why do you say that? Why should I have remained faithful to him when he was not so to me?"

"You shouldn't, but you probably were. You're the rare creature who finds it impossible to break a vow."

She was silent a moment and then said truculently, "I would have taken a lover, if it had pleased me. I just happened to find no one who roused my lust."

"Until after your husband died and there was no vow to break?"

She suddenly began to laugh helplessly and turned to face him again. "Yes, you villain, but don't gammon yourself that you're the only man who has come to my bed since Carlo died."

His expression was suddenly grave. "You were only generous enough to take me to your bed three years ago and your husband has been dead for many years. I'm glad if you had lovers who could please you in the time before. I hope they brought you joy." His long fingers gently caressed the line of her jaw. "You deserve joy, Caterina."

She went still, gazing at him uncertainly. "Lorenzo?"

For an instant the gravity remained on his face and then he smiled. "And so do I." His hand moved from her face to her throat, his fingertips teasing skillfully. "And I've just thought of yet another way we can both enjoy what we deserve."

She shivered in anticipation. "Indeed?"

His caressing fingers trailed down her shoulders. "I was just pondering your charge that my twisted tongue gave you no satisfaction." His fingertips grazed the very tips of her breast. "I think we must definitely remedy that, Caterina."

"It's time for you to go," Lorenzo said softly. "It's almost morning and the servants will soon be stirring."

"What of it?" Caterina gazed sleepily up at him. "I don't care what people say about me."

"I do. Go now."

She made a face as she slowly sat up, got out of bed and began to dress. "You know I'm still angered by your interference?"

"I know."

"And that I will have my way in this?"

"I know you will try."

Caterina quickly pushed her hair back and fastened it with the sapphire combs. "Why can you not admit that I'm right? Bianca and Lion will deal very well together. They'll have mutual interests, children, and companionship. Nothing else is important in a marriage. It's far more than most marriages offer." She smoothed the velvet skirt of her gown. "We both know you're being stubborn only to annoy me."

"Am I?"

Caterina moved across the room and opened the door. "Do not cross me, Lorenzo." She glanced back over her shoulder. "Why are you smiling?"

"Because it gives me pleasure to look at such a beautiful lady. Are you going to visit me again tomorrow night?"

Her gaze narrowed on his face. "Do you ask me to come?"

"No."

"Then I will not come." She glared at him belligerently. "Well?"

He was silent.

"I *may* come," she said. "If I decide it suits me."

She slammed the door behind her.

Lorenzo immediately closed his eyes tightly, striving to retain that last vision of her. Strong, fiery Caterina. Less fierce and more vulnerable than she would ever admit.

But he must not think of Caterina.

He was always careful not to think of Caterina when she was not with him, for then the loneliness always within him became unbearably intense. He opened his eyes and gazed thoughtfully at the flame of the candle in the copper stand on the table. He could not sleep now, but he had no desire to immerse himself in Dante's journey into the inferno either.

He abruptly sat up, threw back the coverlet and got out of bed. He would dress and go for a walk on the battlements and look out over Caterina's kingdom of Mandara. He would walk until he grew tired enough to return to his chamber and sleep.

But he would not think of Caterina.

"Sanchia."

Sanchia jerked upright in bed with a low cry, her gaze wildly searching the chamber.

"*Dio*, it's only me. I didn't mean to frighten you."

Lion's voice. Lion's big frame silhouetted against the pearl-gray light streaming through the door leading to the balcony. Her relief was suddenly followed by tension. "What do you do here?"

"I'm going to Florence. I just wanted to make sure you were well." His hesitancy in speaking, his awkwardness of movement puzzled her. "I'll return within the week. Lorenzo will care for you while I'm gone and see to your needs."

"I need no one to care for me and you may be sure I'll make every attempt not to be here when you return." She clutched the coverlet to her chin, her tone hostile. "Why shouldn't I be well? You've put me in this fine house, filled with fine tapestries and silver ornaments. You've given me a servant to see to my needs. In payment all I have to do is kneel on the floor and let you thrust into me as Giovanni did my mother. How truly fortunate I am."

"At the moment the thought of you on your knees brings me a good deal of pleasure," Lion said harshly.

"I will not kneel to you. Go home to that poor woman you call wife. She seems eager to do your bidding."

He stiffened. "Bianca has nothing to do with what is between us. It's foolish even to speak of her."

Sanchia felt a sharp pang knife through her. "Why not? She seems a sweet, kind lady. Do you not feel shame at bringing me here to hold her up to humiliation?"

"I had no choice."

"You had a choice. You have it now." The words tumbled from her lips in a wild, fierce stream. "Let me go. Do you think I don't know what the men of your family use this house for? I'm not an ignorant child like your Bianca. I understood what Lorenzo meant. Your father used this place to house his whores and now you use it to house yours. Well, I'm not a whore and I won't be—"

"Hush." He was suddenly kneeling beside the bed. "Cease, I tell you." His hands gripped her bare shoulders and the sudden hard warmth of his palms sent a shiver through her. "You are not my whore." His voice was hoarse, tormented, "You are my . . ." He stopped.

"What? Your slave?"

"*Cristo*, I don't know," he whispered. "I don't know anymore. But I must have you near. I don't think I would have left you in Genoa even if you hadn't threatened to run away." His hands kneaded her bare shoulders yearningly. "Let me look at you. God, it seems a long time since I looked at you."

She caught her breath as a wave of heat tingled through her. "No."

"Yes." One hand left her shoulders to jerk the coverlet down and away from her body and then returned to her shoulders to hold her immobile while his gaze ran lingeringly over her. "Do you remember in the barn when I came into you and—"

"I'll fight you." She could feel her breasts swelling beneath his gaze, ripening, the nipples hardening. No, she must not feel this. In that direction lay a captivity more certain than the bill of sale he held in his possession. "Loose me, Lion."

"In a minute." His head bent slowly to her breasts. "Look how hard and sweet these buds are now. They want attention." His lips enveloped her left breast and he drew on it gently and then more strongly. She gave a low cry, swayed, held upright only by the hands on her shoulders. His lips moved to the right breast and he gave it the same attention. His head lifted, his lips releasing her. "Mine."

"No."

He rubbed his broad cheek back and forth across her breasts with a yearning movement. "Yes." His left hand moved down her body to cup between her thighs as he had in the barn at the farm. "Always."

She closed her eyes as the warmth exuding from his callused hand caused the muscles of her stomach to clench and spasm. He began to rub slowly, teasingly. "Do not do this. It is not my will." She added haltingly, "You . . . shame me."

His hand stilled. She heard the harsh sound of his breathing in the silence of the room. Then his hand was no longer between her thighs and he was releasing her.

Her eyes opened to see him rise to his feet, a massive shadow in the predawn gloom. He moved swiftly across the room to the door and tossed harshly over his shoulder, "Cover yourself."

She drew the coverlet over her, her gaze fixed in bewilderment on his broad back. He had wanted her. She had been sure he would ignore her words and take her. Why had he not done it?

"My mother may come here and try to drive you away." He opened the door. "She does not want you here for reasons of her own. You must not let her words hurt you. I will deal with her when I return."

"It's natural that she wishes to protect Bianca."

His lips twisted cynically. "It's Mandara she wishes to protect." He turned at the door. "I cannot blame her for fighting for what she wants. Life has not been easy for her. We all must . . ." He trailed off, looking at her. "Will you wish me a good journey?"

"You don't need my good wishes."

He flinched, and then shrugged. "You're right. I have done very well without them until now." He started to turn. "Goodbye, Sanchia."

A thread of pain ran beneath the carelessness of his words, waking a strange echoing ache within Sanchia. Her hands gripped the coverlet hard to keep back the words he'd asked of her. They came anyway. "Good journey, Lion."

He stopped and stayed framed in the doorway for an instant. Then he quickly shut the door behind him.

Sanchia sank back against the pillows and turned on her side, gazing at the door leading to the balcony. Her breasts were swollen, the aureoles of her nipples still distended and aching. Santa Maria, she didn't want to feel lust burning through her. It was as unwelcome as the tenderness she felt for him. As unwelcome as the impulse she'd had to call him back.

Sweet Jesus, how she had wanted to call him back.

The winds of dawn blew crisp and cold on Lion's face as he rode out of the gates of the city.

He needed that cold, Lion thought grimly, as he put Tabron to a gallop. He gazed blindly at the sky now turning from pearl to palest pink. Why had he stopped? Unwilling or not, her response had been as strong as his own and he would soon have been able to quench her resistance.

Why had he not done it?

This inner conflict had to end. The emotions Sanchia aroused in him were like nothing he had ever felt before, alternating between lust and a strange, wistful tenderness. It was all madness.

He must think. He must find a way to resolve his dilemma and put an end to this lunacy with Sanchia.

"You no longer have the Wind Dancer?" Borgia asked softly. "I believe I cautioned you about offering it to anyone else, Damari. My father has written expressing interest in it . . . such interest he informs me of his plan to travel to Cesena to inspect it. I don't intend to disappoint him."

"You will not disappoint him, Your Magnificence," Damari said quickly. "If you'll but write him to delay his trip for a few short weeks, I'm sure we will be able to retrieve the Wind Dancer."

"We?" Borgia smiled. "You expect my help? If my help is given, then no further payment is required. Is that what you wish?"

Damari felt the frustration and rage rising in him and sought desperately to control his temper. "Andreas managed to get the statue back through no fault of my own. My information is that it has been returned to Mandara. My condotti is small and the city well guarded. If you could just let me have the service of the forces you've quartered in Cesena, I could—"

"My God, are you mad? I'm surrounded by rebellion and discord here in the Romagna. You wish me to lend you an army when it might mean putting down an insurrection here when you deign to return it?" Borgia shook his head. "You offered me a bargain and I hold you to the terms of it. You supply the Wind Dancer and my father supplies a dukedom."

Damari's eyes widened in excitement. "The holy father agreed to my terms?"

"I told you he had expressed interest." Borgia smiled. "But if you cannot furnish me with the Wind Dancer, perhaps I'll go after it myself. After the Romagna is completely secure, I could launch an attack on Mandara."

"No!" Damari said sharply. "The statue is mine."

"Then bring it to me."

"I must have time to make plans."

"I'll write my father that there's been a slight delay," Borgia told him. "Only a *slight* delay. In five weeks' time I go to Rome with either the Wind Dancer in my hands or you by my side to explain to him why I don't have it in my possession. Tell me, Damari, have you ever been to Rome?"

Damari shook his head. "I have not had that pleasure."

"A magnificent city with a lovely river winding through it. Perhaps you've heard that my own dear brother was found floating in the river Tiber with many knife wounds in his body. No one has ever determined who tossed him into the water since little attention is paid to such an act. So common an occurrence in Rome." He paused. "Do I make myself clear?"

"You always make yourself clear, my lord."

Borgia turned away contemptuously. "Then you may go, Damari."

He was being dismissed like the lowliest lackey. Damari smothered the venom rising within him and forced himself to bow courteously. "Be assured I'll find a way of obtaining the Wind Dancer with no trouble or expense to you. My apologies for suggesting you aid me, my lord duke. I was only concerned for the disappointment of His Holiness."

"You'll gain my forgiveness when I have the Wind Dancer. I expect you here in five weeks' time."

"I'll be here." Damari, bowing obsequiously, backed from the room.

He abruptly straightened after he had closed the door, standing quite still while he fought the bitterness boiling through him. Only a short time ago it had been he who had controlled both Borgia and the pope. Now he was no longer the duke's equal but subservient once more.

And he had come so close!

No matter. He would regain his power and status as soon as he reclaimed the Wind Dancer. There would be no more bowing and scraping once he had what Borgia wanted.

But how to get it?

Bribery had succeeded once, but it was doubtful that Andreas would allow even the most trusted servant close enough to steal the statue again. Damari would be foolish to launch his small condotti against Mandara in the vain hope that luck would carry the day. Andreas was too able a commander and Mandara too strong a fortress to fall without overwhelming numbers launched against it in the field.

Not bribery. Not force. The elimination of both weapons meant he would have to wait and study the situation to find a way to overcome the disadvantages he was facing. In the meantime, a spy could be insinuated into the town, if not into the castle itself, and surely he would be able to think of something before the five weeks Borgia had given him expired. He had not raised himself to his present status by lacking in imagination.

Damari descended the stone steps to the courtyard where a lackey was holding the reins of his horse. Swinging up into the saddle he noted the sky was leaden, clouds roiling, scudding with the wind preceding a storm. He was going to get a wetting before he reached shelter but he refused to go back to Borgia and beg to stay.

He lifted his head and smiled as a gust of moist wind touched his cheeks. Besides, he would not mind riding through the rain. The fact that the storm was heading north was a good portent. Mandara lay due north, safe and snug and arrogant in its small world.

And a storm was coming to Mandara also, as soon as

he thought of a way to send it thundering over Lion Andreas and his bitch of a mother.

And the little slave, Sanchia.

He'd been startled when Andreas had launched an attack on Solinari to get her back. Clearly she was important to his foe.

Yes, he'd have to be sure his plans for the future held a prominent place for the slave girl.

Twelve

I do not wish to look at one more piece of goods," Sanchia said firmly as she turned away from the shop of a leather craftsman.

Lorenzo halted as he saw the determination on Sanchia's face. "Oh, very well. We've bought many lengths of fine fabric, the dressmaker has your measurements now, and she can work 'round the clock without you. Still, I do not understand you in this. You are not behaving with the enthusiasm I thought you'd show, considering your former deprivation."

"I must be careful not to take too much," she said soberly. "It would be foolish to become accustomed to riches that can never be mine."

"How depressingly sensible. They could be yours if you'd be amenable."

She shook her head, beginning to walk

across the square toward her house. "I won't stay here longer than I have to do so."

"Why not? Mandara is a very pleasant place to live. Ask anyone. Lion has built many things of beauty, while he levies few taxes, and his laws are strict but fair. Lady Caterina makes sure the poor are fed and the sick are cared for." He smiled. "Why should you want to go back to Florence when Mandara can give you so much?"

"I may not go back to Florence. I don't know where I'll go, but I won't stay here." She met his gaze. "And you know why, Lorenzo."

"None of us is really free, Sanchia."

"I'd like to see if I could prove you wrong. I don't know anything but servitude and I'll have to learn the way of freedom. When I first awoke on the ship I thought everything was so clear and that I was strong enough to shift the world." She shook her head ruefully. "But now I realize it's as if I have just been born and have to learn everything from the beginning."

"I would wait until Lion freed me before venturing into these realms of knowledge."

"You know he won't do so. I must free myself . . . when the opportunity arises." She paused. "Why did Lion go to Florence?"

"Can't you guess?"

"Caprino?"

Lorenzo nodded. "He can't get his hands on Damari at present, so he's settling for Caprino."

She shivered. "Caprino is a dangerous man."

"But so is Lion," Lorenzo said calmly. "And Caprino will pose no problem for him. Don't worry; if I'd thought otherwise I would have gone with him."

Sanchia quickly averted her eyes. "Why should I worry?"

"You might ask yourself that question. The answer could—" He stopped and then smiled. "I believe you have visitors, Sanchia."

Sanchia's gaze followed Lorenzo's to the two horses tied at the iron garden gate. "Lady Caterina?"

"I'm sure you can expect a call from her shortly, but

that's not her horse. If I'm not mistaken, your visitors are Marco and Bianca."

Sanchia winced. Sweet Mary, she didn't want to see Lion's wife again. The very thought of Bianca brought a surge of unreasoning guilt mixed with an emotion even more incomprehensible and infinitely more base in nature. "What is she doing here?"

"Her charitable duty, no doubt." Lorenzo took Sanchia's elbow and propelled her forward through the shallow garden. "But I'm glad they decided to come. I believe you'll find their visit very illuminating."

"Illuminating?" Sanchia asked, puzzled.

Lorenzo opened the front door and stepped aside for her to precede him. "You have keen eyes, use them."

"Sanchia!" Bianca rushed forward, a smile lighting her face. "I hope you don't mind our visiting so soon. I wanted to go to the cathedral this morning and took the opportunity to bring you a strengthening herbal remedy."

"No, of course I don't mind." Sanchia smiled tentatively. "But it really wasn't necessary. I'm quite well now except for my hand."

"Don't tell her that, Sanchia." Marco strolled into the hall from the direction of the salon. "She delights in concocting foul-tasting remedies for all who will condescend to swallow them."

"It's not foul-tasting," Bianca protested. "I added honey to sweeten it. You aren't kind, Marco."

Marco smiled at her. "You're kind enough for both of us." He turned to Sanchia. "You look well, Sanchia. I think you'll soon have no need for remedies."

Marco's beauty struck her anew as he came forward and bowed. Dressed in a bright blue velvet jerkin and blue-and-white partihose he lit up the small hall with elegance and grace. "Undoubtedly you don't remember our last meeting in that cell at Solinari," he said soberly. "However, it's one I'll never forget. You were very brave, Sanchia. I regret you were forced to suffer for our sake."

She shook her head. "I wasn't brave. It's not brave to endure what must be endured." She smiled with an effort. "But I don't like to think of that time. Did Rosa give you wine? I know nothing about fine wines, but Lorenzo brought a jug last evening and he says it is full of the very best."

Marco shook his head. "We just arrived and cannot stay. Bianca spent hours at the cathedral in the confessional." He shot Bianca a mischievous glance. "She was weighed down by her mountain of sins and required much absolution."

Bianca made a face at him. "You would do well to go to confession yourself. You are puffed up with the sin of pride. Wasn't it only yesterday you were boasting about the beauty of the painting you're working on?"

"It wasn't pride in my skill but in my subject," he said softly. "Bianca, the beautiful."

Bianca smiled radiantly at him. "You tease me. It is the painting that's beautiful." She tore her gaze away from him and turned to Sanchia. "You must see Marco's work. He's a splendid artist."

"I look forward to it," Sanchia said absently, as she looked from Bianca to Marco. They were like two radiant children, filled with the joy of life and with each other. "Are you sure you won't stay and have a goblet of wine?"

Bianca shook her head. "I must return to the castle. It's our day for visiting the sick." She smiled gently. "Good day, Sanchia. Drink my remedy and you'll soon be able to come to the castle and see Marco's beautiful painting."

Marco hesitated. "Will you assist Bianca onto her mount, Lorenzo? I'd like a word with Sanchia."

"It would be my pleasure." Lorenzo opened the door and bowed to Bianca. "If I give her service, perhaps she'll be grateful enough to pray for the forgiveness of my sins."

"God forgives all," Bianca said. "Go to the priest and have him intercede for you."

"I think God would listen more readily to the prayers of the beautiful Bianca. He is, after all, the originator of good taste." Lorenzo's fingers closed on Bianca's elbow and urged her forward. "I'll return shortly, Sanchia."

Marco turned to Sanchia as soon as the door closed behind them. "You're not planning on staying at Mandara?"

"No, I'll leave as soon as possible."

Marco nodded, relieved. "That would be best. If I can help in any way, please call on me."

"I may ask for your help if it becomes necessary."

"You understand I wouldn't want to deprive you of safety or contentment, but Bianca is very innocent."

"I understand." She smiled warmly at him. "And I wouldn't want to hurt her in any way. Believe me, Marco."

"I do believe you." He bowed and crossed the few feet to the door. "Thank you, Sanchia."

A few minutes later Lorenzo entered the hall, closed the door and leaned back against it. "He asked you to go?"

"No, only if I planned to do so." She met his gaze. "He wants to protect her from hurt or shame." She paused. "He loves her?"

"Yes."

"They're quite beautiful together."

"As exquisite as two dancing sunbeams." He smiled. "And with a relationship just as substantial."

Sanchia glanced away. "Does she love him, too?"

"Oh, yes, as much as she can love any man. She won't admit it to herself, of course, for that would be a sin. She's loved Marco since she was brought here to Mandara to marry Lion. They were drawn to each other at once and thrown together constantly as Lion was always away with his father fighting with their condotti."

"Lion knows?"

"Since the first time he came home from battle and saw them together. They were then as they are now."

"Was he very angry?"

"No. Saddened. He loves Marco."

She had seen the affection between the two brothers, but she couldn't believe Lion would react without anger toward anyone who encroached on his property. "But Bianca is his wife. He would not—"

"Psyche," Lorenzo interrupted. "You saw it that first

moment. Pure, childlike. How do you think Psyche would respond to Lion? Bianca is as unsuited to Lion as a woman can be unsuited to a man. If she hadn't been the daughter of a great house she would have gone into a convent. Marco's adoration suits her very well; he is her Cupid for his love is divine, pure."

"I don't want to hear any more." She moistened her lips with her tongue. "This isn't my concern."

"You will hear more because Lion is not one of Bianca's saints; he's my friend and I've grown tired of seeing him give all and get nothing in return." He went on bluntly, "Bianca is not only a Psyche; she's a child who will never grow up. There's something wrong . . . She was only fourteen when she was wed and at first Lion thought her childishness natural, but she's never changed. She's a child in a dream world playing at being a grown woman. He gave Marco endless opportunities to cuckold him during those first years and would have happily accepted Marco's child as his heir." He paused. "But then he realized that Bianca would never accept Marco as her lover. She doesn't understand passion any more than a small child would, and Marco is so filled with tales of courtly love that he'd never try to teach her." He shook his head. "Incredible. So Lion stays away at Pisa and permits them to play like children here at Mandara."

"Perhaps they're all happy with the arrangement as it stands."

"I'm not happy with it, but I would have left it alone if Lady Caterina had not decided to alter the balance. She makes excuses to call Lion back to Mandara at every opportunity. She wants an heir for Mandara and she's clever enough to know Marco will never cuckold Lion to provide her with one nor will the besotted idiot marry anyone else. Which leaves only Lion to be lured back to Bianca's bed and his duty to Mandara." He straightened away from the door. "I agree with Lady Caterina that it's time the situation is resolved, but not in the fashion she's chosen. Lion deserves to be free of this yoke."

"Then in what fashion?"

"You," he said. "A permanent liaison that will discourage Lady Caterina's hopes and free Lion from the responsibility of Mandara. That's why you had to come here, Sanchia. Lion has been very careful not to bring any women to Mandara for fear it would shame Bianca. Lady Caterina must come to recognize that your presence here indicates a shifting in the balance of the situation."

"It means nothing." Sanchia gazed at him, stunned. "You're using me as a pawn."

"Yes," he said calmly. "But you'll be a beautifully cared for pawn and, if you give Lion a child, you'll never again want for anything."

"A child?"

"Had you not thought of that? There's a possibility you might be with child."

"No, I couldn't—" She had not yet had her flux but surely it was not yet her time. So much had happened it was difficult to remember.

"If you're not with child, I'm sure that happy circumstance will occur shortly." Lorenzo added, "And the child would belong to Lion just as you do, Sanchia."

"No! The child of a slave is free."

"Perhaps in Florence, but in almost every other city-state the child would also belong to the mother's master." He paused. "Unless you could convince him to free the child. I don't think you could bear to leave your babe and run away to this dream of freedom you're nurturing. Judging by the way you acquired your band of little friends in Florence, I believe you to have an extremely affectionate and maternal nature."

No, she'd never be able to leave her child, and how could she care for an infant by herself as a runaway slave? What if she became hurt or ill? She had seen the fate of children abandoned to the streets. She could feel the panic rising within her. "There is no child. There will never be a child." She blinked away the tears stinging behind her eyes. "I'm going away and—"

"I'd wait to determine that. It might be too late even now."

"You're very cruel," she whispered.

"No." For an instant his eyes held a distant sympathy. "We can't all have what we want. We have to choose. I choose Lion."

She drew a deep breath. "Well, I do not."

He smiled. "We shall see." He turned to go. "I'll leave you now. I'm sure you'll need time to get over the resentment you're feeling toward me and think about what I've said. I'll return tomorrow to make sure all is well with you." He opened the door. "Good day, Sanchia."

Sanchia gazed blankly at the door that had just shut and then turned and moved slowly, heavily toward the salon. A child? Why had she never considered a child? If she carried his child, Lion would never give up searching for her to claim it. Surely God wouldn't be so cruel as to give her a child. She had only to be patient and Lorenzo's words would prove false.

She had only to wait and be patient.

As Lorenzo had predicted, Lady Caterina called on Sanchia late that afternoon and was ushered into the salon by an excited and awed Rosa.

Sanchia stood up, bracing herself as she closed the book Lorenzo had given her. She smiled determinedly. "You honor me, my lady."

"Yes, I do." Caterina Andreas gazed critically around the room, evaluating the tapestry-cushioned bench and matching hassock, the deeply recessed leaded-glass windows, the polished oak cabinet. Her gaze lingered longest on the huge amethyst on the lid of the silver pitcher on the richly carved Venetian table. "This is furnished quite pleasantly. You must be very content here." She turned back to Sanchia. "Nevertheless, you must leave. I won't have you at Mandara."

Sanchia had been prepared for a dismissal but still found herself startled at the bluntness of the statement. "I have no intention of remaining here," she replied with equal candor. "As soon as I'm permitted to leave, I will do so. You've forgotten I'm not free to make that choice."

Caterina's gaze narrowed on her face. "Yet you said

you considered yourself free even though my son does not."

"I do." She swallowed to ease the sudden tightness of her throat. "But there are certain considerations that may interfere with my attempting to leave at once."

"What considerations?" Caterina asked fiercely. "You like living in this fine house and having Lion pamper you with gowns and jewels? Well, it won't do. I won't permit—"

"No," Sanchia cut through the tirade. "I want nothing." She drew a deep breath. "That's not true. I'd be foolish not to want all of those things. Of course I want them. But not enough to—" She broke off and then said, "You don't have to worry about my staying here, Lady Caterina. Give me a little time and I promise you I'll leave Mandara."

"And what if I don't give you time?"

"Then I'll take it anyway."

A look of surprise crossed Lion's mother's face followed by grudging respect. "You're very bold for a slave."

"I'm not bold at all, but I am determined." Sanchia smiled sadly. "A slave isn't permitted the former and would not survive without the latter."

"Indeed." Caterina studied Sanchia. "The same could be said of a wife."

"I have no experience with which to judge the truth of what you say."

"I have." Caterina whirled toward the door in a flurry of violet silk skirts. "I'm not satisfied, but I'll obviously win no further agreement from you, and I'm not fool enough to waste my breath. I'll hold my peace for a time while you ponder your 'considerations.'" She shot a level look at Sanchia over her shoulder. "But if you're not gone by the end of the fortnight, you may expect me to take action. Be warned."

She didn't wait for a reply or issue a farewell but swept majestically from the room.

Sanchia sighed in relief. She felt as if she had been pummeled. It hadn't been easy to face Lion's noble mother as an equal when she was accustomed to behaving with a show of servility even to shopkeepers. This new life into which she had been tossed had a bewildering number of threats and challenges with which she had to learn to contend, and today she had been confronted with too many of them.

She didn't want to be thrust into the tortured relations of the Andreas family. She didn't want to have to face intimidating women like Caterina while she was still so unsure of herself. She didn't want to be Lorenzo's pawn or Lady Caterina's nemesis.

And dear lord, most of all, she didn't want to be held captive to Lion Andreas by a child within her womb.

"I like her." Caterina wrapped the quilt around her nakedness and slipped out of bed. She padded barefoot over to the table and poured wine into a goblet with one hand while she clutched the quilt to her breasts with the other. "She's no fool."

"She has strength." Lorenzo sat up and leaned back against the carved mahogany headboard. "I thought you'd appreciate Sanchia."

"It means nothing, of course. She still leaves Mandara." Caterina lifted the goblet to her lips and smiled at him over the rim. "She told me she would leave as soon as possible."

"Then I'm sure she'll make the attempt. I've always found Sanchia to be truthful."

Caterina's smile faded. "She also said there were considerations to ponder. Which smacks of your interference."

"Does it?"

She took another sip of wine and strolled back to him. "You're a rogue, Lorenzo." She handed him the goblet and sat down on the side of the bed. "If I were wise, I'd put hemlock in this cup instead of good Mandara wine."

"You are wise." Lorenzo sipped the wine. "Though hemlock is far too obvious a poison for me not to recognize. If you wish to murder me, you must be more subtle, Caterina. I am, after all, a master of the art."

Caterina tried to hide her start of surprise. In all the years she had known him, Lorenzo had never once mentioned his former profession to her. She took the goblet from him, drank a little and returned it to him. "Poison?"

He shrugged. "At times. It's cleaner than most methods and relatively safe. However, there are so many ignorant and bungling practitioners in Italy today that it's no wonder most noblemen and men of means have tasters."

"But you're no bungler."

He met her gaze with eyes as clear and cold as polished stone. "I'm the angel of death himself, my dear Caterina. I am superb."

She drew the blanket more closely around her to shut out the sudden chill. "You're no longer an assassin. You haven't been one for a long time."

"You're wrong. We always remain what we are no matter how our circumstances change. If you lost everything, you would still be a great lady. If I became the pope, I'd still be an assassin."

"Nonsense."

His long slender fingers caressed the raised design on the silver goblet. "Truth. Why are you so belligerent? Does it bother you that you've taken a murderer to your bed? A reformed assassin is acceptable, but a—"

"Why are we talking about this?" she interrupted abruptly. "What you were before you came to Mandara makes no difference to me. It's what you do in this bed that's important."

"What I am makes a difference to many women. It fills some with horror." He smiled. "And it fills others with lust. It's not every woman who's permitted to fornicate with the angel of death and live to boast of it. When you first came to my bed, I thought perhaps you might be one of those women. I admit I was disappointed, for I had great admiration for your strength and courage."

"Then why did you accept me?"

"I'm only a man and you are very beautiful."

"I'm not beautiful. My face is as long as a horse's and I'm as tall as a man."

"If strength and courage have beauty then there's no one more beautiful on this earth than you, Caterina."

She felt uncomfortable with his sudden gravity. "And I was not driven to you by some vile fascination. I came to you because you're clever and amuse me, and I lusted after you. No other reasons."

"One other reason."

She frowned in puzzlement. "What is that?"

"I offered no threat to you or to Mandara either through marriage or a wagging tongue. You were and are safe with me."

"Yes." She bent suddenly and put her lips to his forehead. "I do feel safe with you, Lorenzo. Safer than I have ever felt with any man. I wonder why?"

"No more than I wonder. The knowledge that you trust me fills me with incredulity. No one has felt safe with me since I was a young boy."

"Move over. I'm cold." She took the goblet from him and set it on the floor. "I'm coming back to bed."

She curled up spoon fashion with her back to him, her gaze on the embers glowing in the fireplace across the room. "How young a boy?"

"When I became the angel of death? Eleven. Though I didn't really reach that exalted status without years of practice in my trade. I was quite clumsy at first."

"I don't want to know about your rise in your 'profession,'" she said impatiently. "I want to know why."

"Greed."

"I don't believe that."

"It's the truth. Oh, perhaps not the first one."

"Who was the the first one?"

"Vito Martinado. But don't ask me the name of the last man I killed. I don't remember."

"Who was this Vito Martinado?"

"He was the captain of a merchant ship, a very unpleasant man. He had a fondness for young boys and he picked me up on the dock and took me to his room at the inn and used me for a week or so."

"Used you?"

"It wasn't the first time I had been so used. When you're alone on the streets of Naples, you expect to become prey. If you're lucky they feed and clothe you for a while before they find a new child with which to toy."

The matter-of-factness of his tone touched Caterina far more than any outburst of emotion would have. She felt a painful tightness in her throat.

"But the good captain had the same tastes as Damari. He liked to hurt me."

"Couldn't you run away?"

"He kept me locked in the room when he wasn't at the inn. He must have realized what a unique treasure I was." His hand moved to her throat and began to stroke gently. "You have a magnificent throat. Long and graceful—"

"And you had to kill him to get away?"

"He was hired to captain a galleon going to Bombay and decided to take me with him on the voyage, a decision with which I wasn't in agreement for obvious reasons. I objected. We struggled. I grabbed his knife and stabbed him in the heart." He kissed her behind the ear. "Your hair smells of flowers."

"I washed it today. You weren't punished for it?"

"In Naples? Murder is more common than not on the streets of that illustrious city." He sniffed again. "Lavender?"

"Yes." She swallowed hard. "What did you do then?"

"I had a most unfortunate aversion to being touched with intimacy for quite some time after that, and I had to eat. I decided since I'd committed a mortal sin and was damned to hell anyway I might as well reap the benefits of the trade. Murder was as profitable as it was common and I had great confidence in myself even then. I knew when I'd mastered my trade, no one would practice it with equal intelligence and ingenuity." His fingers moved up the long line of her jaw. "Lavender is delightful, but I think one of the scents from Arabia would suit you even better. They have something of the exotic about them, a maturity that—" He broke off and was silent a moment. "Tears?"

"The chimney must not be drawing well. The smoke . . ."

His fingertips brushed her cheek with a motion that was almost but not quite a caress. "Yes, that must be it. Smoke. For you're far too sensible to weep for a rogue like me."

"Far too sensible."

"And you're far too hardened to feel sympathy for the boy who died in that inn over thirty years ago."

"Far too hardened." She was silent a moment. "Did he die, Lorenzo?"

"Yes, there are some experiences that destroy what we are. Ask Sanchia. She went through that fire at Solinari, but she was born again. I was not. I was too earthbound to rise like the phoenix from the flames. The fire raged through and devoured me and left me empty. And each year that passed I grew more and more hollow until now I sometimes wonder why anyone who looks at me can't see through me as if I were clear water."

Two fingers gently touched her damp lash. "And you've suffered too much not to realize that though we must take what pleasure we can to alleviate the emptiness, we can never really fill it."

Was it a warning or a plea for understanding? She doubted if he would admit to either, and she didn't know if she would dare to answer if he did. "Yes, of course, I know that." Another tear brimmed and then slowly rolled down her cheek. "As I said, it's only the smoke . . ."

Thirteen

Lion returned to Mandara seven days later.

Sanchia was sitting on the balcony enjoying the afternoon sun when she saw Tabron picking his way down the twisting street toward her house. Her gaze rose from horse to master, and she felt a surge of emotion so strong she was dizzy with it. It couldn't be joy. Please God, it mustn't be joy. It had to be relief that Lion had suffered no harm from Caprino.

Lion raised his head and saw her. He reined in Tabron, his expression unreadable as he gazed at her for a long moment. "I've brought you a present." He jerked his head at someone riding behind him. "Though God knows why you would want him. He has the obstinacy of the mule he rides. He would scarcely let me stop to eat or rest in his eagerness to get to you."

Her gaze flew to the small figure

mounted on the mule Lion was leading. "Piero?" she whispered in disbelief. "Piero!" She jumped to her feet and ran toward the doors of the balcony, down the steps and out the front door. By the time she reached the gate Piero was squirming on the small mule's back, obviously trying to figure out how to dismount.

"Hold," Lion said as he slid to the ground. "I didn't bring you all this way to have you crack your stubborn head open on the flagstones." He reached up, plucked Piero from the saddle and set him down. "What good is a present if it's broken?"

Piero hurled himself into Sanchia's arms and held on with all his might. "Sanchia, I want to stay." He added with the fierce tenaciousness she knew so well, "I'm going to stay."

"I told you he was stubborn. He'll probably cling to you like a barnacle." Lion smiled faintly as he stood gazing at the two of them. "Just as he clung to that mule all the way from Florence."

"Piero . . ." Tears were running down Sanchia's cheeks as her palm caressed the little boy's fair hair. She hugged Piero's small, sturdy body closer as she looked over his head at Lion. "Why?"

"You care for him. Is that not reason enough?"

She started to speak, but he went on quickly. "Elizabet is now wed and seems content. Your Bartolomeo is fired with the desire to become the best printer in all of Florence and the *signor* appears well pleased with him."

"You went to see them?" she asked, surprise coloring her voice.

He scowled. "I knew you would want word of them. And after I finished my business I had time to spare to inquire."

"Caprino?"

"Lorenzo told you?" Lion shrugged. "He will no longer trouble you. As I said, the business is finished."

He meant that Caprino was dead. After years of fear Caprino's threat to her was now ended. Strangely, the knowledge brought no feeling of relief only an enormous weariness.

"He betrayed us." Lion's gaze was on her face. "He deserved to die. He was as guilty as Damari."

"What happened at Solinari is over. At first I was so angry I thought I wanted revenge, but now I wish only to forget about it."

"I'm not so gentle-natured. I told you I returned good for good and evil for evil. Solinari will be over when all who are responsible for what happened to you are punished." He swung onto Tabron's back. "I'll visit you this evening. There are things I wish to discuss." He glanced over his shoulder as he turned his horse and tightened his grip on the mule's lead rope. "You'd better feed the boy. He's eaten scarcely a morsel since we set out."

"I will." Her voice was still muffled with tears. "Lion?"

He reined in and looked back at her.

"Why?"

His gaze met hers, his expression impassive. "Solinari."

He turned and rode down the street in the direction of the castle.

"Sanchia." Piero was stepping back, wriggling out of her arms. "I'm staying, Sanchia. He said I could stay, but even if he hadn't, I'd stay anyway. I'm not going back to Elizabet."

"Shh, it's all right." Her palm cupped his cheek. She had forgotten how soft and warm a child's cheek could be. "You don't have to go back. But weren't you happy there? You look well." She grinned. "I can tell you've been living with a baker. You've grown plump as a pigeon since last I saw you."

He shrugged, his gaze fixed on her face. "I didn't belong there. I belong with you. I told him so when he asked me."

"Lion?"

"Lord Andreas asked if I'd be willing to come to you. He said that you'd been hurt and were lonely for me. Have you been lonely, Sanchia?"

"Yes." She hadn't realized how lonely until she had

seen Piero on that mule coming toward her. "I've missed you, too."

"It's because you belong to me and we should be together. That's what I told Lord Andreas," he said solemnly.

"And what did he say?" She lovingly smoothed Piero's hair back from his face.

"He said he understood and that I was going with him to Mandara."

Yes, Lion would understand about belonging and possessing, she thought without bitterness. As she gazed down at Piero, she was too filled with passionate gratitude to have any room for resentment. If Lion had taken much from her, he had also given back. "And you did come to Mandara." She hugged him quickly. "And didn't let Lord Andreas stop or rest until you got here. You're lucky he didn't smack that mule and send it running back to Florence."

Piero's jaw was set with determination. "I wanted to see you."

"And I'm glad you hurried." She rose from her knees and took his hand. "Now, come inside and I'll get you something to eat and a bath to cleanse you of the dust of the road."

He hung back, looking after Lion, who was disappearing into the distance.

"Piero."

"He understood, Sanchia. I didn't think he would, but he did."

She nodded, her gaze following Piero's with joy, bewilderment, and trepidation. She had been trying to develop more resistance to Lion since the day he had left Mandara but now found herself once more disarmed and uncertain. "I know, Piero." Then she turned and pulled him gently toward the door. "I think you'll like living here. It's even prettier than the baker's house."

"My Lord Andreas," Rosa announced and then scurried from the salon.

Lion frowned as he gazed after her. "What's the

matter with the wench? She looked at me as if I sported horns."

"She's only timid." Sanchia rose to her feet. "You should see the way she stares at Lorenzo."

"No doubt that's why he hired her for your service. It amuses him to prey upon the fear in which he's held."

"The fear is well deserved," Sanchia said, remembering how skillfully Lorenzo had kept her from attempting to leave Mandara with a few words a little over a week before. "He's a formidable man."

Lion studied her intently. "Did I detect a note of bitterness? What's Lorenzo been doing to you while I've been gone?"

"Nothing. He's been very kind to me for the most part. He calls on me every day to bring me a book from your library, and teaches me things he thinks I need to know."

"What things?"

"Oh, table manners and how to dance the pavane and the *moresca* and the difference between bad wine and good." She made a face. "Giovanni would have been delighted with that lesson." She met his gaze with bold directness. "He teaches me anything that he believes would prepare me to live in your house as your mistress."

"And you accepted the lessons?"

"Knowledge is never wasted." She paused. "Even though it may never be used in the way intended."

His lips tightened but he failed to rise to the challenge. "My mother tells me she called on you."

"Yes, to tell me she didn't want me here." She smiled. "And I told her I didn't want to be here either. Consequently, we agreed that I would leave as soon as possible."

"You think to annoy me with your defiance? I don't want you here either. We'll return to Pisa next week." He paused. "If you agree to my terms."

She stiffened. "Terms?"

"I've been thinking this last week and . . . I feel something for you that is out of the ordinary for me. There is not only lust, there is . . ." He paused again, searching for words. "Feeling. I don't believe I could be content now with just . . ." He halted again and then burst out with sudden fierceness, "Listen to me. I sound like a stupid, bumbling oaf." He took two steps closer. "Enough of this. I want you to live in my home and sleep in my bed, not only now but for the foreseeable future. I wish you to bear my children. In return I will give you your freedom, honor, and respect. What do you say to that?"

She stared at him, stunned. "I don't know what to say."

He suddenly smiled. "Then say yes. It's a good bargain; you'll never find a better. I have wealth enough to give you whatever you desire, and I won't ask you for more than I told you."

"What of Bianca?" she asked slowly.

His face became shuttered. "There's no need to hurt Bianca. She's content here at Mandara and we'll be equally content in Pisa."

"And will your mother also be content? Lorenzo said she is determined—"

"She will surrender her ambitions in time."

"Or perhaps you will surrender to her ambitions . . . in time."

"Sweet Mary, I have no desire to force Bianca back to my bed." He smiled cynically. "I was even relieved when I discovered Marco was besotted with her. It gave me an excuse to let her go her way and I to go mine."

"Unless you change your mind and decide your mother is right."

"I won't change my mind."

"How do you know? Everything changes. A month ago I was a slave in Giovanni's shop. Today I live in a fine house and Lord Andreas wishes to make me his mistress." Her voice was shaking. "Next month or next year you may decide you want a legitimate heir for Mandara and return to beget it. Then where would I be? Or you might grow bored with me and this 'feeling' would disappear. Would you take my children from me and let me go to another man?" She shivered. "I don't think I would like the life of your mistress any more than I did the life of a slave."

"I would not grow tired of you."

"How can you be certain? You have no knowledge of my mind, only my body, and you're still a stranger to me. I don't really know any more about you than I did when you first came to Giovanni's shop."

He stiffened. "Are you telling me you're refusing me? Perhaps you think to marry some other man who will give you the respectability you seem to crave."

"I have no thought of marriage. Who would marry me? I'm no longer a virgin and there are many women more comely." She moistened her lips. "But there's too much risk in what you offer me. I am to give everything and you may leave me tomorrow. I've been at risk all my life, but this would be different. This would put my children at risk also." She averted her gaze. "And I like Bianca. I would not want to hurt her."

"*Cristo*, not you, too? Everyone is trying to protect Bianca—Marco, my mother, you."

"And you. Why else would you want me to leave Mandara?"

He lifted his shoulders in a weary shrug. "Very well, I don't want to hurt her. God knows I've been careful these past thirteen years to bring no woman here to cause her shame. I saw my mother suffer enough over my father's adulteries." His voice suddenly vibrated with anger and exasperation as he continued, "But, by God, I want you and I *will* have you, Sanchia."

She dumbly shook her head.

Lion's eyes glittered with anger. "I will. You say you have no knowledge of me. Let me tell you of myself. I am not inconstant. I do not tire of things or people I value. But you don't believe me, and it seems I must demonstrate my ardor and steadfastness. How fortunate I have you here in my own house with time to persuade you to my way of thinking."

"Persuade?"

"Is that not how free women are tempted to couple with men?" He took a step closer. "You did not find me displeasing before. I believe we can assume that in future you will again find me pleasing." His hand reached out and gently cupped her breast.

She inhaled sharply and felt the color rush to her cheeks.

He smiled. "I'll tell Lorenzo to stay at the castle tomorrow and come to you myself. I also have lessons I'd like you to learn."

"You cannot change my mind." She tried to ignore Lion's hand fondling her through the fabric of her gown and hoped desperately he couldn't feel the response that caress was kindling. "I was going to take Piero for a walk around the city."

"In the morning. In the afternoon I'll send a groom to take him riding. We have a small pony in the stables that might do better for him than the mule." His gaze narrowed on her face. "Send Rosa away also. I want no one in the house when I come."

"No, I don't—"

"If she's still here, I'll send her away myself." He held her gaze with compelling force. "Don't argue with me, Sanchia. It's not easy for me to leave you tonight. I'll have no interference tomorrow. Not from Rosa." His clasp on her breast compressed gently and then released. "Not from Piero." His hand dropped slowly away from her body and he stepped back. "No one."

He turned and strode toward the door. Before reaching it he stopped abruptly and turned to face her, his gaze searching her face. "You said you wouldn't be here when I got back, but I questioned the captain of the guard, who tells me you made no attempt to leave. Why?"

"Perhaps I was waiting for an opportunity," she said evasively.

He shook his head. "Too tame. You may not think I know you well, but I realize you're not a person who waits for opportunities. You make them."

"I was waiting to find—" she stopped. "What difference does it make? I haven't changed my mind. I still intend to leave Mandara."

"Waiting for what?"

"Lorenzo suggested I might be with child. I was waiting to see if he was right."

His expression became arrested. "A child . . ." His gaze on her abdomen was a lingering caress. "And are you with child, Sanchia?"

"I still don't know."

"That would change things, would it not?" he asked thoughtfully. "A woman burdened with a child would have no easy time of it alone in the world." He suddenly smiled. "Lorenzo did well."

"I don't believe I'm with child." She added defiantly, "And even if I am, it would only mean I'll have to plan my departure carefully for the babe's sake."

He shook his head. "You're wrong, Sanchia. It would mean more than that if you carried my child." His smile widened. "A great deal more than that." He turned back to the door. "Until tomorrow."

When Sanchia opened the door the next afternoon it was to see Lion garbed in the same wine-colored velvet jerkin he had worn the first time she'd seen him in the piazza in Florence. She was immediately deluged with memories of that day: Lion's power and dominance, her own servitude and fear. She wondered resentfully if he had intended to remind her by wearing the garment today.

"Have you sent your servant away?" he asked briskly as he strode past her into the salon.

"Yes, but only because I knew you would—what do you have there?" She noticed for the first time that he was carrying two rolled-up parchment scrolls of about two feet in length under his arm.

He tossed one of the scrolls on the table and began to unroll the second scroll. "Sit down on the floor."

"What?"

"Sit down on the floor." He dropped down on the rug and smoothed out the parchment with careful hands. "How can I teach you, if you can't see what I'm talking about?"

She drew closer and looked warily down at the parchment.

Lion reached out, grasped her wrist and drew her down to her knees beside him. "This is the second Dancer. I call her *Caterina's Dancer*. You sailed to Genoa on the first Dancer I had built. This one will be much larger when it's finished."

She gazed in bewilderment at the sweeping lines and minute mathematical equations inscribed on the parchment. "This is a ship?"

"A design for a ship. The ship itself is only in the first stages at the yard in Pisa. Now." He pointed to one of the many slots in the side of the ship. "This is where the oars will be placed. You notice this is a trireme, which means that each bench on the galley is manned by three rowers, rowing with three separate oars."

"There weren't any oars on the ship that I was on."

"That's because it was a round ship with fully rigged sails, not a galley. I prefer the round ship, but many merchants will ship their goods only by galley because it's safer on the longer trips. The galley depends on the wind to carry it from one port to another, leaving the oars idle most of the time. But the moments when the oars are used are vital. Galleys don't have to sit off a dangerous shore and perhaps be blown onto the rocks or out to sea again. They can maneuver to land at many ports not possible for a round ship and—" He stopped as he glanced up and saw her expression. "What's wrong? Don't you understand?"

"I understand what you're saying, but I don't understand why you're telling me all this."

"You said you didn't know me." He met her gaze. "This is my life now. I thought it best to let you learn this part of me before any other. You must stop me if I go too fast. I fear I'll make an impatient tutor."

"Lessons. I thought you meant—"

"Oh, I did." Rueful humor twisted his lips. "But I decided this would be a better way to proceed. Not the most enjoyable but the least threatening to you. I hope you rid yourself of doubts soon as I don't promise how long my patience will last." He glanced down at the parchment. "There are three kinds of wood used in the building of every ship. Oak for the hull, ribs, stem, stemposts, beams, and planking; larch beams for the wide clamps and interior bracing; and fir for the masts and spars. I try to get my oak from Trevisana, but those forests are running low and I'll soon have to look farther afield. Perhaps the Po valley will yield—"

"I don't need a lesson in shipbuilding in order to learn your way of thinking," she interrupted. "My mind is awhirl with spars, masts, and triremes."

He looked up. "Then what do you need to know? Tell me, and I'll try to give you what you want."

For the first time he was completely open to her, and she suddenly found the temptation to explore his ideas and feelings irresistible. "Why shipbuilding? Why did you not go journeying like Messer Columbus?"

"Someone must build the ships for such enterprises. Safe ships, strong ships, ships that will last a journey around the world and back again." He added simply, "I wanted it to be me." He began to roll up the parchment. "I like the feeling of building something. From the time I was a small boy I knew only destruction. Perhaps I wanted to . . . I like the feel of it."

It was more than liking, Sanchia realized. There was an intensity, an excitement in his expression she had never seen there before. "But you talk of merchants and cargoes, not explorations."

"Commerce feeds discovery. Would Queen Isabella have given Columbus his ships if she hadn't believed there would be riches for her at the end of his journey? The clink of coins is a siren call and I'm not such a fool that I want to go begging myself. A balance can be struck that will give me both." He grinned. "As you can see, I'm an exceptionally greedy man."

He reached up and took the second scroll from the table and spread it out on the floor. "This is the plan for the round ship I'm building at the yard in Marseilles."

She vaguely remembered he had said he was away in France when the Wind Dancer was stolen. "Why did you purchase a shipyard so far away?"

"There's little interference from the local magistrates such as we suffer here, and the guilds are more concerned with the excellence of their members' workmanship and less with their contributions to charity. I've hired a fine shipwright there who will oversee the building of the ships. I expect better production there within the year than in the yard at Pisa."

She hid a smile as he went on in depth with the problems of dealing with the guilds and sailmakers and caulkers. He was so absorbed in describing his ships and the procedures for their construction that he seemed to overlook completely the fact she couldn't possibly comprehend half of what he was explaining to her.

"Then you have to consider the problem of battle engagements. The galley is better built to withstand attack, but the round ship is better in the attack itself. You must weigh the two and decide which is best for you."

"I shall do so," she said solemnly. "As soon as I have the ducats to commission the building of either."

He glanced up with a sheepish smile. "I think you're laughing at me. I'm accustomed to it. Lorenzo finds my enthusiasm very amusing."

It was not enthusiasm, it was a passion, and she was suddenly no longer amused but touched that he would share it with her. "I find it interesting but naturally a little confusing. You're trying to teach me in one afternoon everything you've learned in two years."

He nodded. "I told you I wasn't a patient man."

"I've noticed that lack in you."

He frowned and then suddenly smiled. "You're laughing at me again. I haven't seen you amused since before Solinari."

He was right, she realized with a start of surprise.

"You told me once that you wouldn't let the threat of Caprino rob you of joy," Lion said softly. "Don't let what Damari did to you rob you either, Sanchia. You don't want to give him such a victory."

She gazed at him for a moment and then smiled brilliantly. "No, I don't. I won't let that whoreson take one more thing from me than he already has." She looked down at the plan for the round ship. "Now tell me why this is shaped so differently from the galley."

Lion's gaze rested on her face for a thoughtful moment and then he too glanced down at the scroll and he began to answer her question.

Lion stayed for the rest of the afternoon, but not once did he touch her or betray any hint of intimacy in his speech or manner. When Piero returned to the house he conversed for a few minutes with the boy and then rose to leave.

"Your designs," Sanchia reminded him as she scrambled to her feet and reached for the scrolls.

"Put them in that cabinet." Lion nodded to the polished oak cabinet across the room. "I'll return tomorrow."

She smiled. "You wish to tutor me again in the craft of shipbuilding?"

"No, tomorrow I'll bring something else to show you."

She was lost in bemusement after he left. What an extraordinary afternoon it had been, and what revelations of himself Lion had permitted her. She felt more at ease with him than she ever had before and had been oddly reluctant to see him go.

"Shall I put them away for you, Sanchia?" Piero asked, his gaze on the scrolls in her hands.

"What?" She roused herself and smiled down at him. "No, I'll do it." She crossed the room, opened the cabinet, and placed the scrolls very carefully on the shelf inside. The scrolls were constructed not only of parchment and ink, but of Lion's dreams. Dreams should be well taken care of in a world where so few were realized. She closed the cabinet and, smiling, turned back to Piero. "Did you enjoy your ride? Where did you go?"

At first glance she recognized the mahogany chest Lion carried. How could she possibly forget it?

"The Wind Dancer?" she whispered.

He nodded as he kicked the door shut behind him and carried the chest into the salon. He set the chest on the table and opened the lid. "You suffered much for it. I thought you'd like to see it." He lifted the golden statue out of the box and carefully set it on the table. "The Wind Dancer."

She could see why Marco had thought the statue was alive when he had first seen it as a child. The muscles of the winged horse seemed to flex and flow with life beneath the burnished smoothness of the gold. It issued an irresistible invitation to be touched. Marco had forgotten to tell her the emerald eyes were faceted in such a way that they shimmered as if with an ever-changing expression.

She gazed at the Wind Dancer in silent absorption for several moments before moving slowly across the room to stand before it. She touched the base of the statue with a tentative finger. "It's . . . beautiful. What are these carvings?"

He shrugged. "Some sort of ancient script. It's said there was once a clay tablet that accompanied the Wind Dancer and that one of my ancestors carved the message from the tablet onto the base of the statue after the tablet was broken."

"What does the writing mean?"

"No one knows. Perhaps we'll never know." Lion affectionately touched one filigreed wing. "Perhaps he doesn't want us to know."

Lion was again speaking of the statue as if it were a living being and his touch had been a caress. She gazed with helpless fascination at the breathtakingly beautiful object on the table, and the emerald eyes of the Wind Dancer seemed to be gazing directly back at her.

Lion's gaze shifted to her face. "What's wrong?"

"I suppose it reminds me of Solinari. For some reason, I feel frightened when I look at it." She shrugged uneasily. "Will you put it back in the chest?"

Lion nodded slowly. "Certainly." He started to pick up the statue. "I never meant to—"

"What is that?" Piero stood in the doorway, his gaze fixed curiously on the Wind Dancer. "May I see it?"

Lion nodded and set the statue back on the table. "It's a statue of a horse called the Wind Dancer."

"Why is he called that?"

"Because he's a magical horse who dances on the wind and the clouds. Sanchia thinks he's a little more intimidating than your pony."

"Does that mean frightening?" Piero crossed the room and gazed gravely at the statue. The Wind Dancer and the small boy were almost on eye level, giving Sanchia the uncanny impression they were measuring each other. "He doesn't frighten me. Look, he's smiling."

Sanchia had thought the teeth of the Pegasus were bared, but now she could see how that parting of the lips might be interpreted as a smile. "Aren't you going for your ride this afternoon?"

Piero nodded, his gaze still on the statue. "I came to tell you good-bye. Donato is waiting outside." His index finger poked playfully at the Wind Dancer's muzzle. "I like him. Are we going to keep him?"

"No," she said quickly. "He belongs to Lord Andreas."

Piero looked at her in wonder. "He *does* frighten you. But why? He's beautiful, Sanchia, and he smiles . . ."

Sanchia nodded. "Yes, he's quite beautiful. Now why don't you hurry along? You're keeping Donato waiting, and it's very warm outside today."

Piero moved reluctantly toward the door. "We're going to ride out to the vineyard this afternoon. Good-bye, Lord Andreas." He paused as he opened the door for one last look at the Wind Dancer and then turned and was gone.

"Children always love the Wind Dancer. I did myself." Lion picked up the statue and carefully placed it back in its velvet lined container. "Time will dim the memory of Solinari, Sanchia."

She tried to smile as she avoided looking at the box on the table. "It's already dimming." She turned away. "Would you like a cup of malmsey? Rosa left a pitcher on—" She broke off as she felt his big hands fall on her shoulders.

"I want no malmsey." His voice was rough. "And I'm sorry I brought the Wind Dancer if it frightens you. It's always been a part of my life, and I thought it only fair I share it with you." He paused. "As I want you to share my life." One hand shifted the weight of her hair to one side, his lips lowered to touch the sensitive flesh at her nape with his tongue. "Your skin reminds me of the Wind Dancer. Golden, smooth, infinitely precious. The first time I saw you naked at Guilia's I thought of the Wind Dancer."

"Let's not speak of that time." She quickly stepped forward and away from his grasp. "I put away your designs as you bade me. Would you like me to get them?"

"No. Why are you running away from me?"

"I'm not running away. I only wondered—" A shudder ran through her as she felt his hands on her shoulders again. "Please, don't touch me."

"Why not? I like the feel . . ."

Her laugh held a hint of desperation. "You said that about building your ships."

"It's not the same." His hands moved up to her throat and his thumbs rubbed slowly, sensually, at her nape. "Turn around, Sanchia. I want to see your face so I can fathom your thoughts."

"I'm thinking that this is a mistake." Her voice was shaking. "I told you that you couldn't change my mind. I cannot come to Pisa—" She broke off as she felt his lips on the cord at the side of her neck. The caress felt far more arousing than it should have. The long, hard muscles of his body were pressed against her back and the heat of him enveloped her. She swayed back against him. "It's a mistake."

"No." He turned her around, his gaze on her flushed cheeks and trembling lips. "I'm closer than you believe to persuading you to my way of thinking." He reluctantly released her and stepped back. "And I will most certainly continue. Do you play chess?"

She didn't answer at once, surprised by his change of subject. "No, you forget I had no opportunity to learn such games."

He made a face. "Nor did I, until Lorenzo came into my life. He delights in chastising me regularly at the board. I think it only fair that I pass the punishment on to you. Tomorrow I'll teach you the rudiments of chess." He turned away and picked up the Wind Dancer. "Chess has very interesting tactics both of attack and defense. I believe you'll find it rewarding."

"Attack."

Lion's voice was soft as he moved his ebony knight forward, his gaze lifting to meet Sanchia's across the board.

She braced herself, staring blindly down at the chess board. "I don't believe I like this game. I seem to be always on the defensive."

"That's because you lack concentration." Lion sat back in his chair and smiled. "Why is that, I wonder?"

The smirking devil knew very well why she couldn't concentrate, she thought crossly. Lion worked very hard at making sure her thinking was blurred by her responses to him. Each time he had visited her in the last week it had been the same. He scarcely touched her, but the atmosphere between them was so charged with emotion and memories of what had gone before she had grown increasingly more tense with each passing day. Now, as she looked up and saw him watching her knowingly, she realized she must either surrender or put an end to it.

"Then I obviously should not play." She pushed back her chair and stood up. "And I will not play. You must go back to Lorenzo if you want another game."

He pulled a face. "But Lorenzo trounces me soundly. I'm the one who is on the defensive there." He smiled beguilingly. "Do you not feel pity for me? A man should triumph in at least one arena of endeavor."

She felt a melting within her and quickly averted her eyes from the roughhewn fascination of his face. When had she stopped thinking Lion's face hard and impassive? Of late she had found it was a game to try to catch the sparks of humor, the sudden alertness when something aroused his interest or curiosity, the intensity of his narrowed eyes when he was deep in thought. It was another dangerous sign of the growing disturbance he was capable of arousing in her. A sign she should have heeded long before.

"Not this arena." She turned and moved a few paces away from him, putting distance between them. He hadn't moved from his chair and yet she felt he was in relentless pursuit. "I've decided that you should not visit me any longer."

"Have you? I don't agree." He reached out and picked up her jade queen from the chessboard, his blunt, powerful fingers closing gently about it. "Why do you never wear green? I believe it would become you." His thumb rubbed slowly back and forth, exploring the intricately carved hollows, the smooth texture of the chess piece. "A gown the color of jade."

She gazed in helpless absorption at his fingers caressing the piece. His touch on the queen was light, skilled, infinitely sensual. She found to her surprised dismay that her breasts were suddenly swelling, the nipples peaking, pushing against the material of her undershift. She quickly looked away and crossed her arms over her chest. "Lorenzo chose a length of green velvet and ordered a gown made up of it, but it's far too fine to wear every day. I told him I'd have no use for such a gown, but he wouldn't listen to me."

"It's a fault of Lorenzo's." Lion looked down at the chess piece. "Do you know that some noblemen play chess with human pieces? They lay out their gardens as giant chessboards and choose the most attractive of their servants or loved ones to play the different pieces."

"I've heard tales of such a thing."

"You would make an exquisite queen."

Her gaze was drawn once more to the piece in his hand and her cheeks grew warm. "You're wrong. I'm not at all queenly. The lady Caterina should play that role."

His index finger rimmed the crown on the chess queen's head. "It's true the artist who sculpted these pieces used my mother as a model, but there's more than one kind of majesty." He set the jade queen down on the board.

Sanchia's breath of relief escaped in an audible rush and she immediately felt foolish.

"The idea of such a life-size game appeals to me." Lion smiled at her across the room. "I think we'll play it some day soon."

"I'll not be here to indulge in your fancies."

"No?"

"I told you I wouldn't stay. I told you I was only waiting until I was sure there was no child."

He went still. "And you're certain now?"

"Yes, my flux started three days ago."

"I must admit to disappointment. I was hoping for a child." He gazed at her thoughtfully. "Why did you not tell me before?"

"I did not wish . . . what difference does it make?"

"Could it be that you were enjoying our time together and didn't wish to mar it?"

"No." She ran her fingers nervously through her hair. "I mean, yes. It hasn't been unpleasant but—"

"And you have discovered you have a liking for me?"

She watched him without speaking as he stood up and circled the table to come toward her.

"We've shared laughter and thoughts these past days." Lion stopped before her, studying her expression. "I had hoped you would find something in me to like as well as fear."

"I do not fear you."

"Then why are you standing there barricading yourself against me?" He gently unclasped her arms that were still folded across her breasts and placed them at her sides. "I've never cared before whether any woman had a fondness for me, but I find it necessary that you do." He paused. "At least, you do not dislike me any longer?"

"We have had many pleasant hours together. I found you very . . . amiable."

His hands moved up to cup her shoulders. "Sanchia, tell me truly."

She felt helpless. If she told him the truth, he would be able to wound her and yet he had left himself open to hurt. Abruptly she knew she couldn't inflict pain on him. "I have found many qualities in you to like."

She was rewarded by a brilliant smile. He leaned forward and gave her a quick, hard, honey sweet kiss. Then his hands were gone from her shoulders and he stepped back.

"No more. You see how tame you have me? Soon I'll be caviling at your every frown and composing sonnets to your enchanting eyebrows like a true courtier."

Tame? She almost laughed aloud when she recalled how blatant had been his sensuality as he had toyed with the chess piece. He was tough, amorous, and lusty—and would always be so, no matter how hard he tried to cloak it.

"I haven't noticed you caviling of late."

"Oh, but that's because you haven't been frowning at me. Can't you see how delightfully we deal together? We would enjoy our hours out of bed as much as those in it." His eyes were suddenly twinkling. "Well, a slight exaggeration. Perhaps not *quite* as much."

She shook her head.

"*Dio*, what a stubborn wench you are. I should never have brought Piero here. He's obviously teaching you to be as obstinate as he is."

The words were spoken lightly but their very carelessness aroused her wariness. "You wouldn't take him away?"

He shook his head, his smile fading. "You do not know me as well as I hoped. I don't demand gifts back because none are given in return."

She had hurt him. She had an impulse to reach out in comfort, but she had already yielded too much. "I love him."

"Lucky boy. I have to plead for your admission of your liking for me and he's freely given your love." He shrugged. "Oh, well, I did not ask for love, did I? I suppose I should be grateful that you're teaching me the gentle art of patience." He turned and strode toward the door. "I'll leave you now. I can tell you're becoming nervous of me." He held up his hand as she started to protest. "Why else would you be talking about running away again? It appears I must return to my strategy of attack."

"Attack?"

"Attack and defense. The oldest game on earth. The game we've been playing all this week." He looked intently at her. "But the game is almost over, Sanchia. Why not give up now and save us both time and effort? If you don't do it today, you will tomorrow, or next week or next month." His voice lowered to compelling persuasiveness. "You like me. You lust after me. Why not live with me? There would be no shame in it. I would kill any man who offered you insult. You're a loving woman and, if you cannot love me, would you not like your own child to love?" His gaze swept down her body to her abdomen. "My mother says I'm unnatural not to want an heir of my own, but I have cared nothing for a child before this time." He paused. "Now I believe I'd like to have a child by you."

She swallowed to ease the tautness of her throat. "No."

"Yes," he said softly. "I can give you a babe to love and cherish. You want a child, Sanchia. Let me give you what you need."

His words were weaving velvet ribbons of emotion, binding her, luring her. She shook her head desperately. "There is too much risk to my feelings."

"But the risk seems less now, doesn't it? And, as time passes, coming to me will seem less and less fraught with danger. I have no intention of giving up when I'm so close." He smiled. "One night you'll let me come to your bed, and after that I'll never leave it." He bowed. "*Buona sera, cara.*"

Cara. That sweet, loving endearment he had used only once before to lure her helplessly into a storm of danger.

Now he was drawing her into danger again and she might be incapable of stopping him. Because that danger was gradually being transformed by Lion into a semblance of a welcoming beacon to guide her from the storm itself.

And she suddenly knew Lion was right: some night

soon she would be swept away by his determination and her own tumultuous feelings into welcoming him into her bed.

She turned abruptly from the door and gazed down at the chessboard, her heart pounding hard. She would be caught, held as closely as the jade queen in Lion's grasp.

It mustn't happen. But how to prevent it? She was his property, a captive in his house. He had only to reach out and she was there for the taking, and as long as that opportunity existed so did her danger of yielding.

Yielding. The thought brought a surge of disgust with herself in its wake. She was not a weak ninny who would submit either to her own temptation or to Lion's will. She took a step closer to the table and picked up the knight with which Lion had launched his game. It was time she stopped playing a defensive game and considered what she could do to save herself.

She set the knight back on the board, her brow wrinkling.

Attack?

Fourteen

Why have you come to see me?" Caterina Andreas leaned back in her thronelike chair before the fire. "You know you have no place at the castle. I don't want you here."

"Nor do I want to be here. We've discussed this all before." Sanchia gazed coolly at Lion's mother. "But I found it necessary to seek you out tonight for a reason I'm sure you'll approve. I want to leave Mandara at once. Will you help me?"

Caterina gazed at her silently for a moment. "Why do you need my help?"

Sanchia laughed. "Why would you think? I'm your son's slave and he will not permit me to leave him. Don't you think I could use help?"

Caterina's lips twisted. "Could you not whisper a plea for your freedom when he lies with you? I've heard a man is weak and pliable in his mistress's hands in that moment."

"I do not lie with him." Sanchia added, "Yet."

A flicker of interest crossed Caterina's features. "He goes there every afternoon and does not come home until after nightfall and you claim he does not lie with you?"

"Yet," Sanchia repeated. She moistened her lower lip. "But he . . . stirs me, and I won't deceive you. If I don't leave now, I do not know if I will be able to leave later."

"I see." Caterina studied Sanchia's face. "Then we must be certain Lion doesn't have the opportunity to 'stir' you again."

"You'll help me?"

Caterina nodded slowly. "I want you gone from here."

"Lion has given orders to all the guards not to permit me to leave through any gate. Can you countermand his orders?"

"He's gone that far?" Caterina looked surprised. "Indeed, you *must* be determined."

"Can you do it?"

"No," Caterina said. "Lion is lord of Mandara. If he were not in the city, I might be listened to by the captain of the guard, but not while he's in residence."

"Then can you find a way of helping me slip out of the city unbeknownst to him?"

"That's a possibility." Caterina frowned. "But it will take time to form a plan and make arrangements. A few days at least. Perhaps as long as a week."

"It has to be now. No later than tomorrow."

"I said it couldn't be done. You must be—" Caterina broke off as she noticed the desperation in Sanchia's expression. "Ah, he does stir you. Can you not withstand him for a few more days?"

"I don't know," Sanchia whispered.

"Let me think." Caterina rested her head against the high back of the chair. "Sit down. Together we should be able to find an answer to this problem."

Sanchia sat down on the stool Lion's mother had indicated and folded her hands in her lap. Her position was one of subservience and yet, curiously, she didn't feel at all servile at this moment. The silence between them was companionable and she felt a strong sense of kinship toward Caterina Andreas.

"Ah, I've thought of it." Caterina leaned forward, her dark eyes gleaming in the firelight. "A solution that will suit us both very well and turn the good Messer Vasaro's words back against himself."

Sanchia frowned in puzzlement at the reference to Lorenzo, but leaned forward to listen eagerly as Caterina started to speak.

"Lion!"

About to go out the door, Lion turned at the sound of his mother's voice. She was rushing down the stairs toward him.

"You mustn't leave now. I'll require your presence at supper tonight." Caterina had reached the last step and paused with her beringed fingers resting lightly on the bannister. "We have guests and it would be rude to ignore them."

"Guests?"

"Only a dozen or so. Messer Guido Ralzo and Fra di Bresgano, Lucretia Montagno and her daughter, Mona. Messer Della Rosa and his son who recently has returned from the university at Ferrara."

Lion's eyes narrowed suspiciously. "What are you at, mother? You take little pleasure in entertainments of this kind. I can't remember the last occasion when you invited anyone to sup with us."

"Then it's time I did, isn't it?" Caterina asked with a bland smile. "It's my duty to the citizens of Mandara. And your duty, too, Lion."

"I must go."

"Yes, I know. We've seen little of you since you've come home." Her tone sharpened. "Would it do you harm to sit at the table for one meal with your mother?"

Lion hesitated. "If you had let me know you had invited half the city of Mandara, I would have—"

"A dozen guests is not half the city." She smiled

faintly. "Though I'm planning a more festive entertainment in a week's time to which we'll invite five times the number. Naturally, since I've given you warning, you'll be happy to attend."

"We shall see."

"Yes, we shall see." Caterina moved forward and placed an affectionate hand on her son's arm. "But I think you'll be persuaded to play the host. I don't ask a great deal of you, Lion."

His expression softened as he looked down at her. "No, you ask very little. You rule Mandara much better than I."

"Nonsense. I merely devote time and effort where it's due. If you'd give up this playing at the building of boats and return where you belong, there is no telling what we could do with Mandara."

"But why would you wish to improve on perfection?" Lorenzo asked as he descended the steps. "Besides, what could you have here that you don't have now? If Mandara were larger and more powerful, you'd also have more poverty and corruption." He smiled as he stopped before Caterina and Lion. "No, Lion is right, Lady Caterina. Mandara is truly blossoming under your benevolent rule."

"There are times when I don't feel at all benevolent," she said turning to face Lorenzo. "And this is one of them, Messer Vasaro."

"But I'm sure you'll soon recover to become your usual gracious self." Lorenzo bowed mockingly. "Run along, Lion. With a hostess so exquisite at the table, your presence would be superfluous."

"No," Caterina said through gritted teeth. "At least stay for supper, Lion. I will make no argument if you wish to leave afterward."

Lorenzo looked at her with surprise. "Compromise? Now I wonder why you're willing—"

"I'll stay," Lion interrupted impatiently. "But I'll leave immediately after supper."

"If you like." Caterina's hand squeezed Lion's arm. "It will be delightful to have you with us for even a short time. Thank you, Lion."

"As Lorenzo said, no one will notice I'm at the table but if it pleases you I'll—"

Bianca's excited laughter trilled from the landing. Lion's gaze lifted to see Bianca rounding the curve of the stairwell. "Oh, Lion, is it not wonderful?" She called over her shoulder, "We're having such a superb time, aren't we?"

"A splendid time."

Lion froze as his gaze traveled past Bianca to the woman now coming around the curve of the stairwell.

Sanchia paused for a moment on the stairs to look down and meet Lion's stunned gaze. "My lord." She nodded and then turned to Bianca, who was now affectionately linking her arm with Sanchia's.

Lorenzo murmured an imprecation beneath his breath and then began to laugh softly.

"Is it not a lovely surprise, Lion?" Bianca pulled Sanchia swiftly down the stairs. "Your mother put Sanchia in my dressing room so that I can watch over her until she's completely healed and that sweet little Piero is in the chamber next to mine. Sanchia and I have been chattering and making plans all afternoon."

"Lovely." He stared intently at Sanchia's face. "And yes, a complete surprise."

Sanchia steadily returned his stare. "How could I refuse your mother's kind invitation?"

"Yes, how could you?" Lorenzo asked. "We've just been discussing how charming Lady Caterina can be."

"It's time for Sanchia to be among people who can care for her properly." Caterina stepped forward and gently took Sanchia's hurt hand in her own. "Solitude is all very well, but she'll be much better off here at the castle. Since, unfortunately, Sanchia appears to have no last name, I've chosen to give her one. I've informed my guests I have a young kinswoman here by the name of Sanchia Salmona. Do remember that, won't you, Lion? Now, come along, my dear, and I'll introduce you to our guests. I sent them to wander in my garden while it's still light enough to see how beautiful it is. I'm very proud of my rose garden."

"I'll escort Sanchia, mother." Lion's face was impassive as he stepped forward. "Like the dutiful host you propose to make me."

"I'll come too." Bianca smiled eagerly. "I'll show you the arbor where Marco painted my portrait, Sanchia."

"Yes, of course," Caterina said, "you must show Sanchia everything, Bianca. We want to make certain she knows how welcome she is here."

Lion darted his mother a cold glance. "Come along then, Bianca," he said.

A smile lingered on Caterina's face as she watched the three of them walk away from her.

"A bold move."

Her gaze shifted to Lorenzo. "It was your suggestion that I invite her to the castle, remember?"

"Because I thought it would annoy you." He grimaced. "And because I hadn't thought out the full ramifications."

"Neither had I until she came to see me."

"Sanchia came to you? Interesting. Am I to assume this is a concerted foray?"

"Yes."

"You know, of course, that this move has an element of risk? You're placing Sanchia constantly within Lion's reach."

"Extremely well chaperoned by Bianca, Marco, myself, and some dozen house guests."

"Ah, you didn't mention your guests would be staying at the castle."

"Perhaps I forgot." She looked innocently at him. "Why should I not rejoice in Lion's homecoming by celebrating with a few friends?"

"No reason whatever."

She made a face as she started to follow the others to the garden. "At least you could have the sensibility to behave as though you are properly dismayed and annoyed with me."

"I'm not annoyed. I revel in your cleverness and ingenuity." He fell into step with her. "I was wondering when you were going to make a move to correct the situation to your own satisfaction. You've been entirely too meek and retiring of late."

"You find me retiring? We must discuss that at a more convenient time."

"I'm always willing to be proved wrong by someone of your stature, Lady Caterina."

She paused as she reached the door leading to the garden and glanced at him with a frown. "Are you truly not angry with me?"

He smiled. "I detest disappointing you, but I couldn't be more pleased. This delay will make no difference in the long run, you know."

"It most certainly will."

He shook his head. "They want each other and lust overcomes all obstacles. You've merely made the consummation of that lust more difficult and therefore a thousand times more appealing. One of the foibles of human nature."

"I've made it impossible."

He chuckled. "At any rate, a magnificent challenge I look forward to meeting. Though I'm sure Lion will not be as pleased at your interference."

"Sanchia is pleased."

"She only thinks so, perhaps. Part of her may conspire to aid Lion in achieving his intentions. It's the nature of woman to want to propagate the species."

"You know nothing of a woman's nature. We do have needs besides that of birthing babies and providing a receptacle for a man's—"

"My dear lady, please spare me your lecture. I was speaking of the feminine gender as a whole, not of yourself. We all know how extraordinary a woman you are." He bowed politely. "And now I must mingle with your guests and leave you to play the grand lady. I've been by your side too long."

Without giving her a chance to reply he bowed again and strolled toward a group of ladies and gentlemen standing by the marble fountain in the center of the garden.

Caterina gazed after him a moment, feeling oddly flat. The garden seemed suddenly drained of the vibrancy of its glorious color. She also felt drained of color. When she was with Lorenzo she always felt clever and witty and wonderfully desirable. Perhaps because that was the way she saw herself mirrored in his eyes.

But this was foolishness. She *was* witty and clever and desirable. She certainly needed no man to mirror her qualities in order to pamper her feelings of her own consequences. She needed no man at all.

She deliberately looked away from Lorenzo and strolled down the path toward the arbor where Lion and Sanchia stood watching Marco push Bianca in the flower-garlanded swing hanging from the oak tree several yards away.

"What do you think you're doing here?" Lion asked in a fierce undertone, his stare fixed unseeingly on Marco and Bianca.

"Enjoying the sunshine," Sanchia answered, not looking at him.

"Enjoy it on the balcony of your house on the piazza."

"It has different hues here."

"Sanchia, I'm not—" He drew a deep breath, trying to control his temper. "I don't want you here."

"But I want to be here, your mother wants me here. Even Bianca wants me here."

He was silent a moment. When he spoke again, his voice was cold. "You think to avoid me?"

"It seems for the best. I told you—"

"I weary of what you tell me," he interrupted. "You had no need to run from me. I was giving you time." He turned to look at her. "But I'll give you no more. You've chosen your way. So be it." He turned on his heel and strode up the path, meeting his mother on her way to the arbor. He nodded tersely and would have marched past her had she not stopped him with a hand on his arm.

"It's for the best, Lion," she said quietly.

"Sanchia used those same words." Lion moved to the side so that her hand dropped from his sleeve. "Between the two of you I'm beginning to be convinced you must be correct. You chose for her to come here. Who am I to argue?"

"Lion, you don't want—"

"You don't know what I want. Your ambitions blind you. Yes, *blind* is an excellent word, for you will not see what you've done here today!" He paused. "I've tried for thirteen years to avoid hurting you and Bianca, but I'm done with it. I will not be coerced by you and Sanchia, Mother."

She glanced quickly at a couple who had stopped to admire the roses a few yards away. "Hush, someone will hear."

"Then let them hear. I no longer care."

"Bianca."

"You brought the threat to Bianca here when you took Sanchia from the house on the piazza and settled her so cozily next to my lovely wife. *You* try to keep the threat at bay now." He took a deep breath. "But, by God, you'll not succeed."

"Bianca is very happy you're here."

Sanchia turned from watching Lion stride away to see Marco walking toward her. Bianca was still sitting in the swing, looking dreamily at the boughs of the tree above her. Marco glanced over his shoulder and smiled. He turned to Sanchia. "It would be a kindness if you would not disappoint her."

"I wished to speak to you, Marco. I know I promised I would leave Mandara and that's still my intention. Let me explain why—"

"No explanation is necessary. The situation is more than clear. You came here to escape Lion, not to pursue him." He made a face. "Though my mother and Lion consider me a dreamer, I'm not a fool. As far as I'm concerned you're welcome here as long as you do nothing to hurt Bianca."

"I do not think you a fool." Her gaze went involuntarily to Bianca.

He shook his head. "No, there's nothing of the fool in the way I feel about Bianca." He smiled gently as he, too, looked at the child-woman on the swing. "She's the best part of what I am. She looks at me and sees me as I want to be. I'm not really a wonderful artist, you know. Compared even to the apprentices of Da Vinci and Botticelli I have no talent at all. But I work hard and I do grow better and perhaps someday . . ." He shrugged. "But, if I never develop more skill, if I never receive great inspiration, I'll be enough for Bianca. Just as she'll always be enough for me."

When Sanchia didn't speak, he glanced at her and then nodded slowly. "You find that a surprise? Yes, I know that she'll never be more than a child—though I didn't at first." He paused, searching for words. "When she first came to Mandara I thought she was the most loving, the sweetest maid in all of Italy. She touched my heart and made me feel as if it were always springtime when she was near."

"She is so very lovely."

"Yes." His gaze returned to Bianca. "When I realized she would never change, never become a woman who could be my—" He sighed. "You understand that I would never do anything to hurt my brother, but still there was the smallest hope. And then, suddenly, there was no hope. It wasn't an easy time for me."

Sanchia was unbearably moved. "You don't have to tell me this, Marco."

"Yes, I do. I like and admire you and want you to understand why I seem to be callous to your own needs." Marco shrugged. "We will say no more about it." He started to turn away. "She's becoming restless. I must return to her."

"Marco." Sanchia hesitated. "You said it wasn't easy for you. Why did you decide to stay here with her?"

"But you don't understand. It was too late for me." His smile held sadness as well as sweetness. "And though I know summer will never come, it's not every man who's privileged to live in eternal springtime."

Sanchia watched him walk away from her and heard Bianca's laughing greeting as he came near. A slanting beam of sunlight struck through the leafy branches of the oak tree and surrounded them in a pool of radiance as Marco pulled back the rose garlanded swing. Then, gently but strongly, he pushed Bianca forward so that she left the earth and soared toward the heavens.

"A message?" Borgia asked as he turned away from the window to look at Damari. "Why is it necessary for me to write to my father?"

"A mere precaution." Damari smiled ingratiatingly. "I believe I've found a way to obtain the Wind Dancer with absolutely no expense to you or His Holiness. But there's a certain risk that all of us might be less than adored by the populace should the method become known. Of course soldiers such as ourselves can dispense with the love of the masses, but a pope must be more careful."

"I'm sure your consideration for my father's position will be much appreciated." Borgia dropped onto a chair and looked up sardonically at Damari. "However, he can be persuaded to take a few chances if the rewards are great. What is to be the point of this message of mine?"

"Word has come to me that there are certain conditions prevailing in the small village of Fontana that would aid us in our purpose." Damari began to speak quickly and persuasively, outlining his plan with clear, stark phrases. It took only a few minutes and then he fell silent, waiting for Borgia's response.

Borgia was also silent, thinking. Finally, he nodded slowly. "It could accomplish our purpose. Though it offers a certain danger to you."

"I'm willing to take the chance. As I told you, my lord, I believe in my own destiny."

"You would have to believe very strongly to joust with fate in this fashion. However, as I said, it might possibly work."

"There's no question about it." Damari tried to keep the eagerness from his voice. "Naturally, if you consider the means too dangerous for you or His Holiness, I'll yield to your judgment. But I *can* do this, my lord."

"The sheer boldness of the plan endears it to me."
Borgia nodded. "I'll write to my father and put the
scheme before him."

"Immediately? Time is of the essence, as you can
see."

"At once." Borgia stood up and moved to the
bellrope across the room. "I'll send a messenger with
instructions to wait for an immediate reply. You'll stay
here at Cesena until word comes with my father's
approval."

"Do you think he'll give his approval?"

Borgia smiled. "I can be very persuasive, too, when
I wish."

Damari was reassured. Borgia wanted the statue
enough to take the risk, and everyone knew his influence over his father was growing stronger with every
passing day.

"Perhaps you could emphasize the legendary powers of the Wind Dancer?"

"No need to prod him. He's already mad to have it.
In his last communication to me he was babbling about
some equestrian statue at the Ponte Vecchio in Florence
where Buondelmonti was slain and supposedly started
the feud between Guelph and Ghibelline. He's sure our
fate rests with the Wind Dancer." Borgia sat down at the
desk and drew out a piece of fine parchment from
the middle drawer. "No, he's eager enough to possess
the statue, but he's an old man and grows cautious with
his years. I must stress that your plan can be accomplished without any real danger of discovery of his part
in it." He glanced over his shoulder. "And your plan is
not quite complete, Damari. I can add a few embellish-
ments that will better please my father and myself." He
picked up his quill pen and dipped it in the onyx
inkwell. "You're right. Were my father's part in the
scheme to overcome those at Mandara become known,
he could be forced from the Vatican." He began to write.
"Therefore there must be no knowledge of it."

A lackey came into the room in answer to Borgia's
summons and he said without glancing up, "I want a
messenger at once to take this to His Holiness."

Damari leaned back against the wall and crossed his arms over his chest, a smile of satisfaction on his face. It was truly a brilliant plan and one that would bring him immense enjoyment. What a pity he must wait for word back from that doddering old villain in Rome. He had been tempted to proceed with the venture without informing Borgia but had thought better of it. Both Borgias must be fully involved, fully committed.

"You're very pleased with yourself." Borgia had looked up and was gazing at him with a faint smile. "And well you should be. I could not have thought of a more effective stratagem myself."

"High praise, *Magnifico*."

"Truth." Borgia began writing again. "I had a young Florentine as my guest here this winter who would appreciate your ingenuity as much as I. Unfortunately, he's been recalled by the Signory. At the earliest opportunity, I must remember to introduce you to Messer Machiavelli."

Lion was watching her again.

After that first quick glance at him Sanchia averted her eyes and turned to smile at the younger Della Rosa. "I've never seen such a magnificent scene." She waved a sweeping hand around the great hall, indicating the chandeliers blazing with hundreds of candles, the richly garbed guests, the liveried lackeys rushing back and forth filling silver goblets. "So much color. And the music . . ."

"You speak as if you've never attended a festivity of this nature before," Bernardo Della Rosa said. "It's true that Lady Caterina presides splendidly over the table, but I've seen much more lavish food in Ferrara, and this music is merely tolerable."

"It seems wonderful to me." Sanchia added simply, "And it's true that I've never attended such a gathering before. This whole past week has been like a marvelous dream." She threw back her head and laughed joyously as she put her goblet to her lips and drank deeply. "And I think you lie when you say the music is not excellent.

Surely no musicians this side of heaven could make sweeter sounds, Bernardo."

He gazed in bemusement at her luminous face before admitting, "Perhaps I was overcritical. In Ferrara the musicans are—"

"I don't want to hear about Ferrara. I want to think only about Mandara and the music and—" She hurriedly set her empty goblet on the tray of a passing servant. "The pavane. Escort me to the floor, Bernardo. I should like to dance."

"You always want to dance." Nevertheless he set his own goblet down on the table next to him and took her hand. "I suppose you're going to tell me that you also never danced before you came to Mandara? You must have led a very sheltered life in Florence. Were you brought up in a convent?"

"Not exactly." She wondered what he would say if she told him the truth. She could imagine the distaste on his face and his instant withdrawal. Sanchia Salmano of good family, daughter of a kinswoman of the illustrious Lady Caterina's, was acceptable for flirtation and light-hearted dalliance but the slave-thief, Sanchia, would be instantly ostracized. Still, she refused to dwell on such thoughts now. After she left Mandara, she knew, there would be no more days of richness and splendor, so she must enjoy every moment.

They joined the ladies and gentlemen on the floor and began to tour the hall in the stately steps of the pavane. It was not Sanchia's favorite dance, but the music was lilting, the movements rhythmic, and Bernardo Della Rosa was staring at her as if he thought her beautiful.

Lorenzo was suddenly before her in the set. "You look enchanting tonight. A veritable Circe. You should always wear green."

"I've never seen you dance in public, Lorenzo." She glanced down at her jade green velvet gown with its cream satin undershift embroidered in shimmering gold thread. "And you should recognize this gown. You gave the seamstress every detail you wished to see in the execution of it. Do you not remember those first days at Mandara?"

"But the conception palls before the realization. You glow like a torch." He paused. "But I'd hood my flame when I smiled at young Della Rosa if I were you. I don't like the look on Lion's face."

"I like Bernardo. He makes me feel young. I've never had a chance to dance or play games before." She made a face. "Don't harp, Lorenzo. I'm happy tonight."

"I don't know why I'm bothering to try to save you. It would suit me very well to have Lion lose his patience with the game the two of you have been playing all week." He pointed his toe and led her forward with faultless grace. "But I find I'm reluctant to expose you to needless violence. Is that not peculiar?"

"Very peculiar." She cast a swift glance to the corner where Lion stood. Someone had approached him and he was no longer looking at her. Relief streamed through her, and she was immediately angry at herself. Lion could not hurt her by watching her, which was all he had done since that first evening in the garden. Caterina had kept her surrounded and occupied every waking moment of the last week and made sure she was escorted to Bianca's chamber each night. "But you need not be concerned. Lion has not—" She inhaled sharply as Lion glanced up and met her gaze across the room.

The color flamed in her cheeks and she looked away.

"You see?" Lorenzo asked softly. "Do not anger him more or he will snap, Sanchia." He smiled. "But perhaps that's your aim in dallying with Della Rosa. Perhaps you're weary of being without the sport Lion introduced to you."

"No!" She smiled determinedly. "I do not miss him. I do not want . . . Oh, go away, Lorenzo. Tonight I will be happy and pretend I have no more worries than those pretty girls sitting together near the hearth and giggling at everything one of them says."

"As you command." He shrugged. "But you're not like them. In a fortnight you'll be bored with this masquerade. You've dealt too long with reality to be tolerant of make-believe." The next moment the music signaled a change of set and Lorenzo was gone. Bernardo once more took her hand.

She would not think of Lorenzo's words. He was wrong. She had no wish for Lion to approach her and it certainly was not lust she was feeling toward him. She carefully squelched every thought that came to mind of their time together, and every day she was drawing farther and farther away from him. Soon she would not even notice whether he was staring at her or not.

The music stopped with a little flourish and she turned to Bernardo with a smile. "That was splendid. Now will you go ask them to play the *moresca*? That's so much more lively."

Bernardo nodded and started to move across the hall to where the musicians sat in the gallery.

"Hold." Lion was beside them. "You can dance later. It's time to sit down to supper." He smiled mockingly. "We mustn't spoil my mother's arrangements. I'm sure she's planned something spectacular."

Bernardo frowned. "But there's been no announcement."

"There will be." Lion signaled across the room to a servant and a gong was immediately struck. He turned to Sanchia. "Permit me to take you to your chair."

"She's promised me that honor, my lord," Bernardo said quickly.

Lion ignored him as he took Sanchia's hand and led her toward the table.

"But Lord Andreas, I was given—" Bernardo broke off as Lion turned and fixed him with a cold stare and then continued lamely, "I only thought not to deprive your lovely wife of your escort."

"My wife has an escort and, as you see, Madonna Sanchia has an injured hand." He turned and looked down at Sanchia before adding silkily, "As her host, I feel it my duty to share my trencher with the poor lady and help her in any way I can."

"I need no help." Sanchia moistened her lips as she tried to withdraw her hand. "I've learned to make allowances for my clumsiness."

"See how she protests?" Lion shrugged. "What a truly noble lady she is to struggle in silence with her infirmity. But I really can't allow her to sacrifice herself."

He seated Sanchia in a chair at the long table on the dais and then sat down beside her before motioning Bernardo away with a wave of his hand. "Enjoy your meal, Della Rosa."

Bernardo hesitated and then turned and stalked down to a chair at the far end of the table.

"You go too far," Sanchia said between her teeth. "Do you want to cause a scandal? What will everyone think?"

"Why, that I'm a gracious host aiding my guest. What else should they think? Bianca is clearly not missing my attentions."

Sanchia cast a glance down the table where Bianca and Marco were in animated conversation.

"And your mother?"

Lion glanced down the table at Caterina and met her glare with a bland smile.

"She will ignore us politely once she becomes accustomed to the idea, and her guests will follow her example. She has, after all, been expecting it for more than a week." He turned and dipped his hands in the basin of rosewater offered by a lackey and then dried them on the white linen towel offered by a second servant. "As you have, Sanchia."

"I haven't expect—" she trailed off as she met his gaze. She wouldn't lie. She had expected him to approach her at any time and, when he had not done so, the tension and anticipation had grown to an unbearable magnitude. "I had little time to think about you."

"Because you were playing with that fool Della Rosa." His lids veiled his eyes as the lackey set a silver server of soup before him and then moved to serve Sanchia. "Do you think him comely?"

"He's handsome enough." Sanchia added defiantly, "And he has a lovely voice. He's going to favor us with a song later."

"Intelligence, beauty, and talent." He picked up his

spoon. "And he seems to be enchanted by you. Tell me, do you seek a husband, Sanchia?"

"You know that he would never marry me."

"I'm not so sure. My mother would like to marry you off, and I'm sure she'd managed to scavenge a decent dowry for you even if it meant selling her jewels."

Sanchia laughed uncertainly. "You're jesting."

"No, but I'm glad the idea amuses you." He smiled as he lifted the spoon to his lips. "Because I doubt if your bridegroom would live to make it to the chapel."

She stiffened, her hand clenching the handle of the spoon.

"And if he did, he'd be a cuckold before nightfall. So I'd really not entertain the thought of marriage, if I were you." He paused. "You're not eating. At least try the soup. It's truly delicious."

She automatically lifted her spoon to her lips. She tasted nothing.

"You're not speaking. Why is that? You chattered unceasingly with that prancing coxcomb."

"Why are you doing this?" she whispered. "Why are you trying to hurt me?"

"Did it not occur to you that I, too, could be hurt?" His tone was low but savage. "You said you had a liking for me. I thought you might even—" He was silent for a moment. "Don't talk to me about hurt."

"You forced me to come to your mother."

"I used no force." His left hand had been resting on the table. Now it clenched into a fist. "It was no easy thing for me to show restraint and gentleness with you. All my life I've known only force and the prizes force brings. I wanted something different with you. I wanted your trust."

She didn't know what to say. Sympathy, guilt, fear, assaulted her in an overwhelming tide, deluging her thoughts, drowning her voice. She could only say, "It's dangerous to trust those who have power over you."

"It's more perilous to flaunt those who hold that power." His fist slowly relaxed and he glanced down at Sanchia's hand resting on her lap. "What a prettily decorated splint. That looks like Bianca's touch."

"It is. She used the ivory ribs of an old fan and sent Marco to the seamstress to get strips of the velvet with which my gown is made. Then Bianca fashioned these pretty little bows from those strips. It was very kind of them."

"Oh, yes, they're both exceptionally kind. Finish your soup. The second course is about to be brought in."

"I have finished." She watched numbly as the lackeys collected the soup tureens and with equal disinterest as a parade of lackeys entered the hall with a variety of meat dishes dressed to perfection. Under any other circumstances she would have been as enthralled as the other guests at the sight of roast boar garnished with apples and roses, mouth-watering peacock and, finally, a towering pastry likeness of the castle of Mandara itself, complete with battlements and a miniature garden. The display was met with exclamations and applause as the lackeys proudly toured the hall before repairing to the long carving table on the far side of the room to strip the dishes of their culinary magnificence and carve them to be served. Meanwhile other lackeys were bustling around the table with fresh basins of rosewater and pouring more wine until the trenchers of carved meat and gravy were brought to the dais.

As was the custom, there was one trencher for every two people, and Sanchia found herself staring down at the trencher placed between Lion and herself with dismay. In spite of her claim, it was going to be very difficult to manage knife, spoon, and bread with any measure of dexterity. She started to reach for her knife but Lion stopped her.

"It will be quicker if I feed you," Lion said as he held up the small piece of bread. "Open your mouth."

She found herself opening her lips and taking the bread and then a bit of meat and then bread again. His feeding her was excruciatingly intimate. She wished desperately to have the meal over and done with.

"Again."

His thumb caressed her lower lip as he placed a morsel of meat on her tongue. Her lip began to throb and she instinctively jerked her head away from his hand. "Enough. I want no more."

"I think you do." He smiled at her. "And I certainly want more." He reached for a cluster of grapes, took one, and pressed it to her lips. "Something sweet and full." His gaze moved over the low-cut bodice of her gown. "And firm."

She took the grape, and tart sweetness flooded her tongue. She should look away. The heat tingling between them was thickening in intensity. She realized with desperation that the soft linen of her undershift was abrasive against the sudden sensitivity of her nipples.

She looked down at the table. That was a mistake, too. His big hand still held the cluster of grapes, and memories suddenly assaulted her of those broad, powerful fingers toying with the jade queen, outstretched before the fire encased in heavy leather gauntlets, jerking the neckline of her gown with frantic haste to bare her breasts. . . .

"Your cheeks are flushed," Lion said softly. "Are you warm, *cara*?"

Not warm. Hot, melting. She felt as if the blood was running molten just beneath the surface of her flesh. She quickly picked up her goblet and drank deeply.

"It's a warm evening and will grow warmer. Another grape?"

"No. Nothing." She sat her goblet down and it was immediately refilled by the lackey. "Is it not time for the dancing to start again? It seems we've been at the table a long time."

"It seems a long time to me, too." His hand released the cluster of grapes and dropped casually to his knee. "If we don't leave the table soon I'll have to find something to amuse me. Do you know what I have in mind, Sanchia?" His hand disappeared beneath the heavy damask cloth covering the table and pressed against her upper thigh.

She went rigid, her gaze flying to his face. He was looking straight ahead, his expression bland, only the leaping pulse in his temple betraying his arousal.

The warmth of his palm burned through the layers of velvet and satin, and her limbs began to tremble. Her hand was also trembling as she hurriedly reached for the wine goblet again. "Take . . . your hand off my skirt," she hissed.

"Why? It gives you pleasure. You're quivering like a little bird. Shall I push the skirt of your gown up and touch your flesh, rub those soft, tight curls? No one could see. The table and the linen hides my hand. I could fondle you and bring you even more pleasure." His palm was rubbing slowly back and forth. "Would you like that?"

"No." She could barely force the word past the tightness of her throat.

"I think you would. Of course, you'd have to be careful not to cry out when your pleasure peaked." His nostrils flared and a flush mantled his cheeks. "Why don't we see if you enjoy it? Part your thighs, *cara*, and I'll—"

"The *moresca*!" Lady Caterina was on her feet, motioning to the musicians and guests. "Let us see if we can still manage to move after we've eaten and drunk so heartily."

The announcement was met with laughter and groans by the guests and the wild, spirited strains of the *moresca* from the musicians in the gallery.

Bernardo was suddenly by Sanchia's side. "May I escort you to the floor, Madonna Sanchia?"

Lion's hand on her thigh suddenly tightened. Warmth, strength, demand.

A demand she must not answer. "Yes." Her hand was still trembling as she set her goblet down on the table. Would Lion move his hand and release her? "I love the *moresca*. Did I not tell you?"

Lion's hand dropped from her thigh and he leaned back in his chair.

Sanchia rose hastily to her feet and fled down the long table and the three steps leading from the dais to the floor. She had escaped. Or had she been permitted to escape? A hasty glance over her shoulder revealed Lion still lolling at the table, looking dark, sensual, and slightly sinister in his black velvet slashed jerkin. His expression was lazy, arrogant, as if about to command a performance expressly for his pleasure.

Bernardo snatched four bracelets of bells from the overflowing tray the lackey was extending toward them and slipped one over each of her wrists and then his own. The hall resounded, shimmered, with the merry sound of bells and tambourines, music, and laughter.

Bernardo ran to the other side of the room to join the men, and Sanchia took her place with the women. Bianca was laughing excitedly and even Caterina's dark eyes were glowing with exhilaration as she slipped the bracelets over her wrists, straightened her scarlet velvet skirts and signaled the musicians to start again.

Sanchia lifted her arms over her head, the bells on her wrists jingling. She found herself laughing aloud with the same excitement as Bianca. No, it was not the same. Her excitement was not only with the dance but with the way Lion was looking at her, the way the blood was pounding in her veins, the feel of fabric touching her flesh as she twisted and turned and stamped and whirled. The torches on the walls blurred into blue-orange flame before her eyes, and the bells and the tambourines rang and echoed not only in her ears but in her heart and her body.

The excitement was growing as they all joined hands and circled faster and faster and then broke and whirled by themselves again. The laughter bubbled up in her throat, and she felt almost too breathless to release it. The men and women in the hall were only streaks of violet, crimson, blue, and gold.

A hand grabbed her wrist, pulling her out of the whirling throng and behind a stone pillar.

"What. . . ." She gazed up dizzily to see Lion's face above her. "No, I want—"

His lips were on hers, parting them with his tongue, plunging deep inside with a low groan. His powerful body pressed her back against the pillar and she could feel the tension of his muscles, his arousal rampant. He lifted his head. "This is what you want." He rubbed yearningly against her. "Isn't it, Sanchia?"

She clutched desperately at his shoulders as a wave of heat surged through her. She couldn't think. The bells, the tambourines, the music, the blood singing through her veins were all too loud. "No, someone will see . . ."

"They're all dancing." His lips pressed quick, hard kisses on her temples and cheeks. "No one can see us here. Open your mouth." She didn't realize she had obeyed him until his tongue filled her mouth, toying wildly with her tongue. "I wanted to do this at the table," he muttered. "*This* is how I wanted to feed you."

She tried to stifle the moan trembling in her throat but he heard and lifted his head. "Come with me. You need me. I'll give you what we need." He was already pulling her toward the door.

She shouldn't go. But she found herself stumbling after him and could think of only one protest. "They'll miss us."

"The *moresca* goes on forever, you know that." They were out in the corridor and he was urging her up the stairs. "And what if they do miss us? They've suspected Marco of being Bianca's lover for years. They'll think it only natural that I take my pleasure." He lifted her in his arms as he started up the steps. "It *is* natural, Sanchia. Natural and beautiful and right. Don't you know that?"

She didn't know anything anymore. Her mind was whirling as if she were still dancing, and her heart was slamming against her ribs until she thought it would burst. She should resist Lion and this lust cascading through her. It was madness to lie pliant and helpless in his arms.

But she wasn't helpless. She could fight him if she chose.

Yet she knew with a sudden despair that she wouldn't fight him. Not tonight.

She murmured his name and closed her eyes as she buried her face against the black velvet of his jerkin.

Fifteen

You appear to be looking for someone, my lady. May I be of some small service?"

Caterina whirled to face Lorenzo. "You know very well who I'm looking for, you demon from hell. Where are they?"

"Lion and Sanchia? I have no idea. How many hundreds of chambers does this huge castle contain? However, wherever they are I'm sure they're in no danger of being disturbed. Lion is your son and would have provided against that possibility."

Caterina's hands clenched into fists at her sides. "You saw them leave the hall?"

Lorenzo nodded. "I spared a glance or two for them when I wasn't looking at you. By the way, you do dance the *moresca* splendidly. Your vigor gave the steps a certain glorious—"

"I should not have danced at all. I should have been more watchful. I saw what was going on between them earlier this evening."

"Do you really think you could have stopped Lion? You were fortunate he didn't act sooner. We both know it was only a question of time until he broke free of the chains you wound around him." He smiled faintly. "No, you should have done exactly what you did do tonight: smiled and danced and made us all happy to see your joy."

She gazed at him, startled. "Happy?"

He looked surprised himself. "Did I say that? How very common of me." He thought about it. "But perhaps it comes closest to what I was feeling as I watched you."

She frowned suspiciously. "Do you seek to distract me?"

"Have I ever lied to you?"

"No," she said slowly. "Never."

"Nor shall I ever." He turned. "And now I'm going for a walk in your lovely garden. Would you like to follow me or do you intend to tear through the castle, searching chamber to chamber for your missing offspring? It would do no good and make you look exceedingly undignified."

She hesitated, glancing around the crowded room.

"They will not miss you as long as the wine is flowing and the musicians play." He added softly, "And I will miss you if you don't join me, Caterina."

He turned, walked away from her and was soon lost to view in the throng.

Caterina stood very still. The hall was suddenly too hot, the music too loud, the company far too boring to tolerate.

He would miss her if she did not come to him. Lorenzo had never before indicated her company was important enough to him to miss.

She started slowly across the hall, nodding and smiling as she skirted the dancers on her way to the garden where Lorenzo waited.

Lion set Sanchia down before turning and slamming the chamber door. He was breathing heavily, his chest rising and falling as he leaned back against the door. "*Dio*, I think my heart may burst. You're heavier than you look."

She gazed at him in astonishment and then burst into laughter. Those blunt, unvarnished words were so typical of Lion. "You didn't have to carry me up those thousands of stairs. We must be at the very top of the castle."

"We are." He turned and shot the bolt. "This is the tower where we keep the Wind Dancer." He turned to face her. "And I was afraid if I made you walk up all those stairs you might change your mind." He crossed to the stone fireplace and knelt to light the logs laid in readiness. "You're already having second thoughts, aren't you?"

The wood caught, flared, revealing the broad, strong planes of his cheekbones, the glittering darkness of his eyes as he turned to look at her. She drew a deep breath. "I don't think I had a first thought. I wasn't thinking at all."

"That was my intention." He stood up and came toward her. "And I shall endeavor to make sure you remain in that state."

She took a hurried step back. "Lion, this is not—"

"It is." His hands cupped her cheeks and he tilted her face up to look into her eyes. "Trust me, *cara*."

She could see in his eyes twin flames reflected from the fire. She felt helpless in her fascination.

"Is it so difficult to trust me?"

"Yes. I . . . I think I've had too much wine."

"You're not drunk." His lips feathered her temple. "*In vino veritas.*"

But was that the truth? There was only chaos in what she was feeling. She was hot, tingling, as dizzy as when she was dancing the *moresca*.

"I like your gown. I knew you'd look wonderful in that color." He pushed her away from him and took a step back. "Jade queen, shall we start our play?"

"But you always win."

"Not this time." He took off his black velvet jerkin and threw it aside. "This time we both win. Do you remember when I had you undress for me in the barn?"

She felt a tightening in her chest. "Yes."

"You were frightened." He took off his fine white linen shirt and dropped it on top of the jerkin. He stood before her in only steel gray hose and calf-length black boots whose soft leather molded his legs with the same delineation as the hose. "I wanted you to be frightened. I wanted you to be so afraid that you'd never forget you belonged to me."

The dark hair thatching his chest looked soft and springy and she felt a tingling in her hands. She wanted to touch him, run her fingers through that curly mat, explore the powerful muscles cording his chest and shoulders.

He took off his boots and began to untie the points of his hose. "You don't look frightened now."

But she was frightened. More frightened than she had been in the barn when she had acted on his command. Because she suddenly knew he wouldn't command her now. What she did would be by her own will.

The steel gray hose were gone now and he was naked. "Come to me, *cara.*"

She couldn't move. Her gaze traveled down his chest to the tightness of his muscular belly. Then down . . .

"You can't be shy." Lion stood with his legs apart, blatantly aroused, the essence of bold masculinity. "Attack, Sanchia, I stand defenseless."

"But not weaponless," she murmured, her gaze fixed on him in total absorption.

"Then let me sheath my weapon." His eyes were suddenly glinting with humor. "You have the means. Do I have to come to you?" He held out his hand. "*Cara?*"

She took one step forward, then another, and suddenly she was directly in front of him.

He took her right hand and raised it slowly to his lips. He kissed her palm lingeringly, his gaze never leaving hers. "Square one, jade queen. Not so hard, was it?" He moved her hand to his chest and she felt the pounding of his heart beneath her palm.

"I belong to you." He said softly. "Say it."

Her eyes widened. "What?"

"It's true, you know. I belong to you, just as you belong to me. Say it."

"You . . . belong to me."

"Forever."

Stunned, she gazed speechlessly at him.

He pressed her palm harder against his chest. The beating of his heart seemed in some mysterious fashion to beat within her. "Forever, Sanchia."

"It cannot be."

"We will talk of it later." He slid her hand slowly down his body to clasp it around his manhood. He held it there as a shudder racked through him. "Dear God, I can't wait any longer. Will you take me into you?"

His face was drawn as if in pain, and she felt a sudden surge of tenderness that swept away her last reservations. Why was she hesitating when she had known when she left the hall she would not be able to stop herself from yielding? "I think I . . . must."

"Thank the saints." He took her hand from him and stepped forward, his hands on her gown. He stopped. "Remove it quickly or I swear I'll have to push up your skirts and take you as I did on that pile of hay in the barn. *Cristo*, what I'd give for a bed at this moment."

There was no furniture at all in the chamber, she realized as she glanced around dazedly, only a rug thrown down before the hearth.

"Hurry, I cannot wait long and my hands are shaking so that I can do nothing but fumble."

Her hands were trembling, too, but she managed to strip off the gown and undershift. She was reaching down to take off her slippers when she felt his hands on her waist lifting her. "Clasp me," he muttered. "Your legs . . ."

Her limbs encircled his hips and he was pressing against her, into her, with frantic urgency. He sank home.

Her neck arched back as she gave a low cry. Ridged fullness. Deep. So deep.

His palms cupped her buttocks and held her to him,

forcing her to take all of him. She heard him mutter something beneath his breath. A curse, a prayer . . . She could not tell which it was.

"Hold on." His palms kneaded the rounded flesh of her buttocks as he stood still, his eyes shut, his nostrils flaring with each breath. "Tighter."

"I cannot . . ." Still, she tried, and heard him groan deep in his throat as if he were in agony.

Then he was sinking to his knees on the floor, lowering her so that her naked back rested on the rug as he plunged in and out of her body in a rhythm both primitive and forceful.

Completion. Joining. Sanchia bit her lower lip to keep from screaming as jolt after jolt of sensation rocked through her. His hands were petting her, his fingers pressing, rotating. "Sanchia, it must . . ." His hips moved back and forth in a flurry of short, hard thrusts. "May I give to you? Please let . . ."

He was entreating her. The knowledge filled her with wonder. He moved with raw, blind sensuality, taking, giving and yet he was pleading with her for acceptance.

"Give . . . to me." Her words were little more than a whisper as her limbs tightened strongly around his hips. "Give!" She arched up helplessly as the pleasure burst through her, spasming, exploding.

He pulled her upright on him again, crushing her close as his own pleasure peaked and then soared.

He rocked her back and forth, breathing low, whispering love words into her ear. His lips moved yearningly across her cheek to the corner of her lips. "Sanchia, did I not tell you? We must have this. How can we live without it?"

At the moment she didn't think she could live without it. She was part of him. He was part of her. Pleasure . . . possession . . . passion . . . Nothing had ever seemed more natural than having Lion within her, having his hands caressing her naked back, having his lips on her lips.

He raised his head. "Thank you, *cara*." His voice was grave.

She buried her cheek on the soft wiry mat on his chest and his fingers reached up to tangle in her hair. "Why do you not speak?"

"I don't know what to say. I'm too full—" She broke off as she felt the reverberation of his laughter beneath her ear and she realized her unintentional play on words. "Well, that too."

He flexed lazily within her. "If you think I'm going to leave you yet, you are very much mistaken. I've waited too long to reach this haven to withdraw until I've sated both of us." He pushed her away from him to smile down at her with surprising sweetness. "I think you'll like this game far better than chess. Shall we move to another square? There are many strategies left to test."

"Not yet. I'm not sure how I even came to this point."

"I am sure." His hands cupped her breasts. "And it was not the *vino*. I seduced you. I think I did it very well considering I've never attempted to lure a woman to my bed before. My nature is usually too rough and blunt for seduction. I would never have succeeded if you hadn't already wanted me as much as I wanted you." His hand moved down and began to stroke her belly. "Do you believe it possible I've given you a child?" He laughed softly. "Do you feel me stir? I grow ready just thinking about my child moving in you and—" He broke off as he felt her stiffening against him. "Sanchia?"

"I didn't consider a child. I didn't . . ." Panic was rising within her. "How could I be so stupid?" She began to struggle but he held her immovable against him. "Let me go, Lion."

"No." His voice was fierce. "You want to be here." His hand lay heavy on her belly and he began to rub slowly back and forth. "And you want my child in your womb. I used no force. You took my seed willingly."

"The child would be a bastard and I a whore. I've lived only a shadow life since the moment I was born, and now you want me to live in those shadows for the rest of my life." Her hands pushed at his shoulders. "I should not have done this. I should not have let you—"

"Do you think I would not give you marriage if I

could?" His hands grasped her shoulders with bruising force. "Do you want me to murder Bianca so that I can take you as my wife?"

Her eyes widened in horror. "No, I didn't mean—"

"I cannot undo my marriage. As God is my witness, I wish I could." His eyes were fierce in his set face. "I cannot make you my wife. I can only make you my love."

"Love?" she whispered.

"It must be love. I told you I had feeling for you. What else could it be?"

"You did not say you loved me."

"The word is hard for me." His hands opened and closed on her shoulders. "I've never said it before." He burst out, "I've never felt it before. I can't say I like it. It twists my gut and makes me want to smash something."

"It doesn't sound like love."

The fierceness faded from his expression as he looked down at her. "It also makes me wish to . . . treasure you. To care for your needs and protect and defend you." He slowly lifted her off him. "And to have you feel something besides lust for me. I know I can rouse you to want to lie with me but—Why do you sit there and say nothing?"

"I'm confused. I never expected you to say these words."

"And I never expected to say them." He gazed at her directly. "You have no love for me?"

"I don't know." She shivered. "*Dio*, I hope not."

A flicker of pain crossed his face. "You are honest, at least." He shrugged. "So I must depend on lust to draw you to me. It was no more than I anticipated. Lust and perhaps my child in your body." He turned toward the fire.

She began dressing quickly, in a fever to be gone.

He glanced over his shoulder. "You're in a great hurry. Do you think I mean to keep you locked here in my tower room to use for my pleasure?"

"Of course not." Her trembling fingers made a futile attempt to tidy her hair. "I've already been in one prison for your sake. You would not cast me into another." She moved toward the door.

"Unless I cast myself into it with you."

She undid the bolt and threw open the door. "And you would not do such a foolish thing. You love your freedom too much."

"Sanchia."

She stopped, not looking at him.

"Do you believe me when I say I love you?"

"I don't know." She turned to face him. "I have a question for you. Was it your intention to lure me here only to get me with child?"

"What do you think?"

"I think you capable of it."

"You're quite right." His smile was bittersweet. "I'm capable of most acts of ruthlessness, but I thought you knew I had no liking for deception."

She was again aware of pain beneath the toughness he wore like armor, and that perception awoke an answering hurt within herself so sharp she instinctively took a half step toward him. "I do know you're an honest man. I did not mean . . ." She shook her head wearily. "I spoke without thinking. I didn't believe I would be so weak as to let you couple with me again. It frightens me to realize I'm not as strong as I thought I was." She straightened and gazed intently at him. "But it will not happen again. I am on guard now."

"It will happen again," he said quietly. "And again and again. I'll waylay you in the garden, I'll pull you into any vacant chamber that has a bed, a quilt, or a cushion on the floor. It will keep on happening until you admit you want what we're doing more than food or drink or sleep. Until you let me take you away from here to live with me."

He meant it. Once again Sanchia felt panic rising within her. She muttered an exclamation that was half despair, half protest, turned and fled from the chamber and down the spiral steps.

She stopped at the bottom of the first flight of stairs and leaned her cheek against the cold stone of the wall. She could not go back to the hall and face Caterina and Bianca. She had betrayed both of them. She had betrayed herself. She could feel the tears sting her eyes as she ran down two more flights of stairs and along the corridor toward Bianca's chamber. She would go to bed. She would go to sleep and not think of Lion or the way his face had looked when he had said he loved her or her own agonizing response to his words. It couldn't be love between them. Wouldn't love bring joy? Marco and Bianca loved each other and the joy shone from their faces. Surely if she loved Lion, it would be the same?

The tears were running down Sanchia's cheeks as she paused outside Bianca's chamber. She had forgotten Bianca's maid, Anna, would be waiting up for her mistress. Sanchia could not arouse Anna's curiosity with these stupid tears or she would doubtless mention it to Bianca.

She turned and ran down the hall to the chamber which Piero occupied next door, quietly opened the door, and slipped into the room. The fire in the fireplace had burned low and only the orange-red embers sparked up the chimney. The faint glow revealed Piero's fair hair gleaming on the pillow on the big bed across the room, and Sanchia immediately felt as if a cool, soothing hand had been laid upon her heart. Here was a love with no pain, a love that would leave her with honor *and* independence. Whole. She moved closer to the bed and looked down at Piero. His long lashes curved on his round cheek, and he appeared even younger than his six years now that she could no longer see the wariness in those bright blue eyes.

Even as the thought occurred to her, his eyes opened to gaze up at her. He was instantly awake. "Sanchia."

"Shh, all is well. I wanted to make sure you were sleeping." She tucked the coverlet more closely around him. "It was a fine, splendid party. I'll tell you all about it in the morning."

He raised himself on one elbow. "Why are you crying?"

She wiped her eyes swiftly with the back of her hand. "No reason. I'm merely tired."

"You don't cry when you're tired. Is your hand hurting?"

"No, next week I'll take off the splints and it will be

quite well." She reached out and smoothed his hair. "Go back to sleep. I'll sit here awhile."

His gaze searched her face and then he shook his head. "Lie down. I want you to hold me until I go to sleep. Will you do that, Sanchia?"

She hesitated and then lay down on the bed beside him. "Why do you want me to hold you? Are you afraid of the dark?"

"Of course not. I'm not afraid of anything." The denial came fiercely. "I just thought it would be . . . nice." His arms came around her and he held her tightly. "Good night, Sanchia."

"Good night, Piero," she whispered. Her throat was so tight she could scarcely speak. She was obviously not lying here to comfort, but to be comforted. Piero, with that instinctive wisdom he had learned so young, had comprehended her pain and bewilderment and was trying to soothe it in the only way he knew how. Her heart swelled with poignant tenderness as she nestled closer to the warmth of Piero's small body.

Yes, this was the only love she wanted in her life. This was the best kind of love.

"You've made this garden into an Elysian field." Lorenzo's gaze ran admiringly over the rows and rows of brilliant blooms as they walked slowly toward the arbor. "I've always liked to stroll among your roses."

"You've phrased it well. For over thirty years I've wrested peace and forgetfulness from this earth." Caterina's proud gaze followed Lorenzo's. "The castle grounds were overgrown, a tangle of thorn bushes when I came here as a bride." She paused to touch the petals of one full-blown damask rose before strolling on. "And the castle was in little better condition than the grounds. Carlo's father had been without a wife for over ten years and the servants had grown lazy without a mistress. It was foul as a pigsty. But I set to work and soon had it in order."

"I'm sure you did." Lorenzo smiled at her. "I can see

you tearing through the castle with a broom in one hand and a whip in the other."

She shook her head. "I was not then as I am now. I had just reached my thirteenth year when I was given to Carlo in marriage and my home was very different from Mandara."

"How different?"

"Serene, well ordered. My mother would never have permitted conditions such as I found at Mandara, and she would have swooned if she had seen the kitchen."

Lorenzo chuckled. "Do you think to make me pity that thirteen-year-old bride? You are not your mother. If you had not had a challenge to overcome, you would have ridden out and found one."

"What a hardhearted rogue you are." She suddenly laughed. "But you're right. In those early days I would have gone mad if I hadn't had a great deal to do. I can remember kneeling in the dirt and digging and stabbing my spade into the earth. I spilled out all my rage and sorrow and loneliness to feed and water this garden. It's a wonder anything at all grew."

"But you brought forth beauty."

"Yes, it's strange how indifferent nature is to why we nurture it. It simply keeps on blossoming and giving as if we had lavished it with love instead of hate or despair." She was thoughtful for a moment. "And then one day we look around and see all this beauty we've helped to create and suddenly the love is there. Is that not queer, Lorenzo?"

"It's the way nature tricks us into slaving to do her bidding. Children are the same. Nature makes infants winsome and amusing so that they won't be strangled when they bring so much trouble to their unfortunate parents."

"Lion was a terrible baby, but Marco was as even-tempered as an angel."

"But you preferred Lion."

"I did not say that," she said quickly. They walked in silence for a moment. "Lion was so like me. Impatient, wild, curious. It was natural I should feel close to him."

"Very natural. You're still very much alike."

She shook her head. "But we grew away from each other when Carlo spirited him off." She dropped down on the marble bench beneath the arch of the arbor. "Lion was only seven when Carlo insisted on taking him on his first campaign. Scarcely more than a baby. He said Lion must learn the ways of war early as Carlo had done from his father. I screamed and ranted but it did no good."

"And what did you do?"

"I cleared another tract of land for an increase of my garden." She indicated a place to the left of the arbor in which roses of a deep red flourished. "And I dug in the earth from dawn until sunset every day for two months and every time I tore into the earth I pretended it was Carlo's heart. When he came back in the spring he told me how glad he was I had found such a gentle, womanly occupation to keep me from meddling in men's affairs."

Lorenzo laughed and sat down on the bench beside her. "*Cristo*, what a dullard the man must have been."

She pointed to the graceful marble fountain in the center of the garden. "Marco designed that fountain when he was only fifteen. He was . . ." She stopped and her hand dropped to her lap. "Why am I out here chatting about flowers and fountains? I should be doing something. Lion is somewhere inside—"

"My dear Caterina, as inflamed as Lion was when he dragged Sanchia away, you can be sure the act has already been done. He's every bit as passionate as his mother. What is that pleasant little jingle I've been hearing?"

Her gaze lowered to her left wrist. "I've forgotten to take off one of my bell bracelets." As she slipped the slender circlet from her wrist it gave off a silvery tinkle. She held the circlet between her slim, nervous fingers and turned it around and around, gazing down at it unseeingly. "Did I give up too easily?"

"You've not given up at all. Tomorrow you'll be planning and plotting how to separate them again."

"Yes, but perhaps I should have done something

before this. I don't know why I was so lacking in determination. Am I getting old, Lorenzo?"

"No, Caterina, no one is younger than you."

"I have gray in my hair."

"You have steel in your soul."

"I think I saw a line beside my mouth this morning when I looked in the mirror."

"Impossible. It was a crack in the mirror."

She was silent a moment, and then burst out laughing. "What sweet lies you tell me, and you say you always speak the truth."

"I am telling the truth. Is your garden any less beautiful now than in its first flowering thirty years ago?" He shook his head. "It has only changed, grown, matured. It's been disciplined by harsh winters and your own hand, but each spring it renews itself. You're like your garden, Caterina." He looked out over the acres of flowers. "Perhaps you *are* this garden."

She glanced at him in surprise before her gaze shifted back to the bells in her hands. "Trust you to be extravagant. You compare me not to a single rose but to an entire garden."

"And the rich earth that nourishes it and the sharp thorns that protect it."

"Lorenzo, I . . ." She stopped and shook her head. "I value our friendship."

"Friendship is a fine thing."

"It is so pleasant sitting here in my garden with you."

"You don't have to make polite conversation with me. I am only Lorenzo. Sit and be at peace."

She nodded and tilted her head to look up at the night sky. So many stars, remote and uncaring, as they shone down on a turbulent world. But no turbulence existed tonight in this garden. There was only Lorenzo, moonlight, the scent of roses, and the silvery music of the bracelet of bells she turned slowly in her fingers.

"You must send me away," Sanchia said as soon as she entered Caterina's chamber the next morning. "Now. Today."

Caterina looked coolly at her as she put her quill pen back onto the ivory inkstand. "I wasn't sure you hadn't changed your mind. You didn't appear overeager to leave Lion last night."

A flush stained Sanchia's cheeks. "I made a mistake. I told you he makes me . . . That's why I must leave now before it happens again. You said you could find a way to smuggle me out of the city. It's been over a week since I came to the castle. Surely you've discovered some way for me and Piero to leave."

Caterina nodded slowly. "The day after tomorrow, Messer Kalando's merchant caravan goes to Venice to sell wine from our vineyard. I'll send for the man and see if I can slip you out of the city with his train. However, they'll be moving too slowly for Lion not to overtake them, so you and Piero must branch off and hide until Lion has stopped searching the immediate area. Then you can rejoin the caravan before it reaches Venice." She paused. "You're welcome to leave Piero here. I've grown very fond of him in the last week."

"He wouldn't stay. He says we belong together," Sanchia said. "But, if I find I cannot give him a good life, I'll send him back to you in spite of his protests. It's kind of you to offer him shelter."

"I am not kind." Caterina rose to her feet and closed the account book. "Piero is welcome here because I like and admire the child." She met Sanchia's gaze. "As you would have been welcome under other circumstances."

Sanchia's eyes widened in surprise, but she was given no chance to reply. Caterina was reaching into a drawer and taking out a soft leather pouch. "There are a hundred ducats here together with a ruby pendant worth ten times that amount. It should keep you very well until you find gainful employment." She held out the pouch. "Well, take it. Did you think I meant to send you out in the world to beg or steal?"

Sanchia reached out mechanically to take the purse. "Thank you. I'll return the money as soon as I—"

"It's a gift, not a loan." Caterina frowned. "Have the courtesy to accept it as such and say no more about it."

She came around the desk and strode toward the door. "Now set to packing. I'll try to send your baggage to Messer Kalando this evening." She opened the door and stood waiting for Sanchia to depart. "This is the wisest thing for you to do, Sanchia."

"I know it is." Sanchia crossed the room and would have left the chamber if Caterina hadn't stopped her by placing a hand on her arm.

"If you have need of anything, you must send word to me. I will know no guilt over sending you away."

Sanchia smiled with genuine warmth. "It's my choice. There is no guilt, Lady Caterina."

Caterina gazed at her with a fierceness that suddenly reminded Sanchia of Piero's challenging glare. Was Lion's mother's ferocity used as the same armor? "I thank you for your help and I'm sorry if I brought you worry and pain. Good-bye, Lady Caterina."

"It's not good-bye yet. You cannot leave until tomorrow night." Caterina hesitated. "I visit the sick today. Perhaps you'd like to delay your packing and accompany me." She added quickly, "It would keep you out of Lion's way."

"I think I'd like to go with you." Sanchia was again conscious of that sense of companionship that was close to kinship blossoming between them. "If I'd be no trouble."

"If I thought you'd be trouble, I would not have suggested you come," Caterina said gruffly. "I'll meet you in the courtyard when the chapel bell tolls the half hour." She released Sanchia's arm and almost pushed her from the room. "See that you don't keep me waiting."

The door slammed in her face, and Sanchia turned and moved quickly down the hall. She understood Lion's mother even less than she understood Lion himself, but both of them fascinated her. It would do no harm to try to get to know Caterina a little better on this last day before she left Mandara. After tomorrow, it was unlikely that she would see either of them ever again.

Not see Lion again? She was wrenched with agony

and drew a deep breath to try to stifle her betraying response. Lion would never give up, and she would not have the strength to withstand him if she stayed here at Mandara.

Yes, she and Piero must leave the city—and Lion as soon as possible.

Sixteen

In the afternoon Piero disappeared.

Sanchia, Caterina, and Bianca did not return to the castle until almost dusk, and Rosa was waiting when they rode into the courtyard.

"It wasn't my fault," Rosa said as soon as she saw Sanchia. "It was that stupid groom's duty to watch over the boy. I couldn't be expected to trot after him into the town, could I?"

Sanchia felt her heart leap and then begin to pound wildly. "Piero?" She got down from the mare and ran over to where Rosa stood on the steps. "What are you talking about? What's happened to Piero?"

"It wasn't my fault. I always watch him like a hawk. You know that, Madonna Sanchia." Tears were streaming down Rosa's cheeks. "It was that stupid Donato who—"

Sanchia grabbed Rosa's shoulders and

shook her. "Stop babbling and tell me what's happened to Piero."

"I don't know." Rosa gulped and her face twisted in an ugly grimace as she tried to suppress her sobbing. "He was out riding with Donato and the oaf lost him. He should have kept better watch over the boy. If I had been there, I would have—"

"How could he lose him?" Sanchia shook her again. "Piero's not foolish. He wouldn't just wander away. How long has he been gone?"

"All afternoon," Rosa said. "Donato told me they were in the *mercato* and he turned his back for an instant and Piero was gone."

"All afternoon? Why did no one send for me?"

"A good question," Caterina said grimly. "And has anyone told Lord Andreas the boy's disappeared?"

Rosa shook her head miserably. "Donato rode into the courtyard only five minutes before you came. He's been scouring the city for the child. He thought to find him before dark and had to return without him. I sent him to find Lord Andreas and confess he had lost Piero."

"Surely nothing could have happened to Piero," Bianca said comfortingly. "After all, he's only a child. Perhaps he wandered away. I've often become intrigued watching all the tradesmen working at their crafts in their windows and found myself going farther than I intended."

"Piero wouldn't have done that." Sanchia's hands dropped from Rosa's shoulders. "He would never—"

"We'll find him, Sanchia." Lion was coming down the steps, pulling on his leather gauntlets. He gave a crisp order over his shoulder and Donato started on the double across the courtyard. Lion turned to Bianca. "Find Marco and have him meet me at the stable. I last saw him painting in the garden."

Bianca nodded and ran to the castle.

"Piero is a sensible child," Caterina said sharply. "Sanchia is right. Why couldn't that dimwitted groom find him?"

"We'll soon know," Lorenzo said as he joined Lion.

"The people in the city know Piero is under the protection of this family, so no harm should come to him."

"How do you know? So many things can happen to a child alone in the streets," Sanchia said fiercely. "You know that, Lorenzo."

"Yes," Lorenzo said gently. "Evil things can happen anywhere, but Mandara is safer than the streets of Naples or Florence, Sanchia. Trust me. It is true."

Sanchia turned to Lion. "I'm going back with you. Perhaps something frightened Piero and he's afraid to answer when called. He'll know my voice and come to me."

Lion nodded. "Come then." He came a step closer, lifted her onto her horse and handed her the reins. He gazed steadily at her. "We'll find him, Sanchia. I promise you. We'll search until we do."

"He's so little." Sanchia blinked back the tears. "We've got to find him, Lion. I love him so."

"I know you do." For the briefest instant Lion's hand covered Sanchia's and then he was gone, striding across the courtyard in the direction of the stable.

They found no sign of Piero that evening, though Lion ordered the search to go on far into the night. The next morning they returned to the city and searched the houses and shops from cellars to roofs.

Piero was not found.

In the late afternoon Lion rode at the head of a troop of men out the city gates to look for him in the countryside surrounding Mandara. It was to no avail.

Piero was not found.

Four more days passed while Lion searched neighboring villages and then in desperation traveled to a Franciscan monastery some eight hours distant.

"You must get some sleep," Caterina said briskly as she strode out on the battlement toward Sanchia. "You've scarcely rested since the boy disappeared. Getting ill won't bring Piero back."

Sanchia's gaze remained fixed on the vineyards to

the north of the city. She lifted her hand to rub her temple. "I can't remember if they tried the winery."

"The second day." Caterina paused. "Even the vats."

Sanchia shuddered. "He's dead, isn't he? He must be dead or we would have found him."

"Nonsense. We should have found him even if he was dead. So not finding him proves nothing."

Caterina's abrasiveness was oddly comforting. "That's right. They would have found his bo—" She couldn't say the word. Her hands clenched on the stone ledge, trying to fight down the sickness the thought brought. "Bianca told me she's praying for him. I tried to pray, but I'm not sure God listens to me anymore. I've broken so many of his laws. I've stolen and lied." Her voice lowered to a whisper, "I've committed adultery."

"I've never been sure God hears me either. I have an idea He leaves alone the people capable of solving their own problems and concentrates on those who can't. It may not seem just to us, but we should not argue with Him." Caterina drew her crimson cloak more closely about her. "It's growing cooler now that the sun has gone down. Come in and sup with me. You can do no good out here. Lion will return when he returns and not before."

"I'll join you shortly." Sanchia turned and once more gazed out over the countryside. She suddenly stiffened. "Is that someone coming?"

Caterina squinted at the puff of dust barely discernible as horses and riders at a distance. "Possibly. Yes, I think those are horsemen."

"Lion!" Sanchia turned and ran toward the door leading to the stairs.

"He's still far away," Caterina called after her. "Be careful. You'll hear nothing if you fall down those stairs and crack your head."

"I'll be careful but I must . . ." Sanchia's words trailed behind her as she left the battlements and started down the first curving flight of stairs.

It was almost an hour later when Lion rode into the courtyard. Sanchia ran forward, her gaze searching Lion's face. "Piero?"

Lion smiled. "We found him. He's well, Sanchia."

Sanchia swayed and reached out to clutch at Tabron's saddle. "Where?"

"He'll be here soon. I rode on ahead to tell you." Lion swung down from the saddle and put his arm around Sanchia's waist to steady her. "Marco's bringing him. Piero wouldn't ride any longer in the wagon in which we found him, so Marco took him up behind him."

"You found him at the monastery?"

Lion shook his head. "Not three miles from here. We were returning from the monastery when we saw a wagon pulled over on the shoulder of the road. Piero was in the bed of the wagon lying on a pile of blankets. He was bound hand and foot and blindfolded."

"Bound." She was stunned. "But why would anyone do that to Piero?"

Lion shook his head. "God knows." His lips tightened. "But I intend to find out."

For the first time Sanchia noticed the deep lines of exhaustion graven on either side of Lion's mouth and the dark circles beneath his eyes. Lion had been searching unceasingly for five days with even less sleep than she had gotten. She took a step nearer and laid a hesitant hand on his cheek. "You must rest. You look so weary."

"Now I can rest. The boy—"

"Sanchia!"

Sanchia's gaze flew to the mounted men who had just galloped into the courtyard. Lorenzo and Marco, and behind Marco clutching at his waist a small, beloved figure.

"Piero!" She dashed across the courtyard.

Piero released his grip on Marco and swiftly slid off the horse into Sanchia arms. "I'm back." His arms were so tight around her she could scarcely breathe. "They took me away but I'm back, Sanchia."

"Where have you been?" Her hands moved over him anxiously. "Are you all right?" She wrinkled her nose, half laughing, half crying. "You smell *terrible*, and where did you get those horrible rags?"

"I don't know." Piero's hands were moving over her hair caressingly. "I don't know anything. I was walking in the market . . . and then my head hurt—" He took a step back and looked at her gravely. "I couldn't see anything when I woke up. I thought I was blind. Then I heard them talking about the blindfold and then I knew—"

"*Gran Dio*, the boy is filthy." Caterina came down the steps to the courtyard. "Ask him questions after he's had a bath and a meal."

"A good idea." Marco said, making a face. "And a bath for me too. I must smell as bad as Piero after having him cling to me all this way." He looked around the courtyard. "Where's Bianca?"

"In the chapel praying." Sanchia took Piero's hand and gripped it tightly. "Why don't you go tell her Piero's back safely?"

"Well, perhaps I shall just stop by." He dismounted and tossed the reins of his horse to a hovering groom. "She'll want to know her prayers have borne fruit."

Lorenzo sniffed. "Rather overripe fruit. Be sure not to get too close or you'll overpower her."

Marco grinned and started toward the chapel.

A small wagon pulled by a shaggy horse was being driven into the courtyard; it was followed by the eight riders Lion had taken with him that morning. Sanchia looked hard at the wagon as her hand tightened on Piero's. Why had he been tied up and left in the wagon? More, why had he been taken in the first place?

"The bath," Caterina said firmly. She knelt and gave Piero a vigorous hug, then rose and took his other hand. "Rosa will be very glad to see you. She's been weeping and wailing ever since you disappeared, young Messer Piero. Come along now."

Sanchia hesitated as she passed Lion, her gaze on his strained, weary face. "Thank you," she whispered. "I'll always remember—" Her voice broke and she turned and hurried up the steps with Piero and Caterina.

There would be time later to tell Lion how much Piero's return meant.

"I must see you."

Lion stood in the doorway to Piero's chamber. He was fully dressed, even to his cloak and gauntlets and Sanchia hurriedly stood up from her chair beside the child's bed and moved toward him. "What is it?" she whispered.

"I'm leaving for Pisa with a company of men." He drew her from the room and shut the door softly. "A messenger arrived only minutes ago from Basala, my shipwright at the yard."

"What message?"

"Damari has set a torch to all the ships in the yard."

"Oh no!" She grasped his arm, her eyes misting with tears. No wonder Lion's face was set in lines of suffering. Damari might just as well have attacked Lion's family as those ships. "All of them?"

"All four," he said hoarsely.

"Is Basala sure that Damari is responsible for the fire?"

"Damari made certain Basala *knew* who was responsible. He boasted he was going to come back and burn the yard itself." He grimaced. "He may have done it by now."

"And if he has?"

"I'll follow him and set a torch to the bastard." He paused. "Will you be here when I return?"

Sanchia hesitated, realizing he wasn't asking for an answer to a question, but a promise. Her heart went out to him. He had spent five days in exhaustive search for Piero and now must leave to face still another catastrophe. At this moment she would promise him anything. "I'll be here."

"Good." He started to turn away, but stopped abruptly and asked, "How is the boy?"

"He is very tired. However, children have great recuperative powers and I'm sure he'll be better after a night's rest." She frowned. "I don't understand any of this, Lion. Who took Piero? None of it makes sense."

"What did he tell you?"

"Only that he was blindfolded the entire time he was gone. He heard nothing to indicate where he was or who did this to him. He was evidently kept in a room by himself most of the time and only taken out among people once or twice."

"That's all he knows?"

"He said he heard heavy breathing, moans . . ." She sighed in disappointment. "Maybe he'll remember more in the morning."

"Perhaps. Go to bed now. You can accomplish nothing by sitting and watching him sleep."

"I don't want to leave him yet. I just got him back and I don't want to let him out of my sight."

"I'm leaving Marco and a full company of men here in Mandara with orders to watch over all of you. They won't let anything happen to him." His hand touched her cheek gently. "I should be back within a fortnight even if I have to chase Damari back to Solinari."

"First the Wind Dancer and now the shipyard. Why does Damari hate you so much?"

His lips twisted. "Because of who I am—my father's son and therefore the master of Mandara. And because of who he is. His mother once lived in the pretty house you occupy on the piazza."

Her eyes widened in astonishment. "He's your brother?"

"*Dio*, no! His mother was the widow of a shopkeeper and he was two years old when she became my father's mistress. She was a coarse, earthy woman but she held my father longer than most." His expression darkened. "She flaunted the association and those years were very difficult for my mother. Damari was seven when my father finally gave in to my mother's pleas and sent him and his mother away from Mandara, but he came back when he was twelve years old and asked to be taken into my father's service."

"And he wants whatever is yours."

"But he'll not get it." Lion turned away. "Good-bye, Sanchia."

"Lion." She didn't want him to leave. She had a

sudden vision of Damari's face as he stood over her in the dungeon. Malevolence. Evil. Death.

He looked at her inquiringly. No matter what she said, he would still go after Damari, she realized. "Go with God," she whispered.

A brilliant smile lit his face, then he was striding away from her down the corridor.

"How is Piero?" Caterina asked as Sanchia entered the hall the next morning.

"Still sleeping. I thought I'd pamper him and bring breakfast to him in his chamber."

"A little pampering can do no harm." Caterina paused. "You know that Lion left for Pisa last night?"

Sanchia nodded. "Damari."

"I would not have had this happen." Caterina frowned. "The shipyard was troublesome to me, but I would not have had Lion lose it at the hand of that bastard."

"I know you would not," Sanchia answered. "And Lion knows it as well. He's too much your son not to realize your thinking on the matter."

Caterina's brow cleared. "You're right, Lion is not fool enough to think I mean him harm." She took an apple from the bowl and put it on the trencher with a piece of melon. "Go feed the boy. I'll be along soon to see how he does and put a few questions to him. We have to get to the end of this coil."

True to her word Caterina arrived in Piero's chamber only a quarter of an hour later.

"Still in bed?" She swept into the room with a smile and strode toward the bed.

"No!" Sanchia said sharply. "Don't come any closer." Her gaze never left Piero's face.

Caterina stopped short. "What's wrong?" Her gaze raked Piero's flushed face and glittering eyes. "The boy is sick."

Sanchia nodded jerkily. "The blankets in the wagon where Lion found him. What did you do with them?"

Caterina frowned. "Why, I sent a lackey last evening

to distribute them among the poor. They were well-woven wool and—Why do you ask?"

"Piero said his left arm is sore." Sanchia's voice was low, the words barely audible. She took the child's arm and raised it carefully over his head.

"Mother of God!"

A red and pus-filled boil as large as a hen's egg lay in the curve of Piero's armpit.

"Thirsty." Piero jerked his arm away and turned on his side. "Drink, Sanchia."

"Right away, *carino*." Sanchia moved toward the door. "I'll be back in a moment."

Caterina followed her out into the hall and closed the door.

Sanchia whirled to face her. "Is it what I think?"

"I'm not sure," Caterina said slowly. "I've never seen anyone who actually had it. I was only a child when it came to Florence in 1470 and it never spread to Mandara, thank God."

"But I've heard stories." Sanchia pressed her palms back against the panels of the door. "That's how it starts."

"Sometimes. Sometimes there are no boils at all." Caterina turned away, her movement sluggish for someone who was usually so brisk and forceful. "I have to . . . to do something."

"What?" asked Sanchia. "What can you do?"

"I'll send someone to collect those blankets. No, I'll do it myself. Perhaps it's not too late."

"I've heard anything spreads it. The wind . . . the touch of befouled clothing . . ." Sanchia's eyes widened in horror. "The rags we took off Piero. I sent Rosa to burn them. She'll be in danger too."

"Rosa, Marco, Bianca, and you and me," Caterina enumerated. "We all touched Piero. Perhaps even Lion . . . Who knows who's safe from it?"

Sanchia closed her eyes and sank back against the door. "Pray God we're wrong."

"Well, we'll soon know. The plague isn't shy about making its presence felt."

Rosa fell ill that night and died at dawn the next day. No one else in the castle appeared to be ill, nor was there any sign of illness in the city.

Caterina came into Piero's chamber to give Sanchia the news that no one besides Rosa was ill. She lingered to stand looking down at Piero. "How does he?"

"I don't know." Sanchia shook her head wearily. "He's in great pain. He wakes and sleeps and wakes again."

"He's fighting hard. It is said the plague has two heads and the one that produces the boils is not so deadly as the other."

Two heads. It brought to mind a picture of a monster Medusa lying in wait to pounce on the unwary.

"I'll prepare another poultice for the boils." Caterina turned away. "And then return to sit with him while you rest."

"No." Sanchia sat down in the chair by the bed. "He knows when I'm not here and grows more restless."

"You should—" Caterina shrugged. "Send word to me, if you change your mind."

As she left the room, Sanchia leaned her head against the high back of the chair. Who would she send? Sanchia wondered dully. No servants would come near this chamber.

"Sanchia."

Her gaze flew to Piero's face. His lids had opened and he was looking at her with those brightly burning blue eyes.

"More water, love?"

He shook his head. "I'm sick, aren't I?" he asked hoarsely. "Very sick."

She nodded.

His jaw set stubbornly. "I won't die. You'll see, I won't die."

"Of course you won't." She smiled shakily. "You're much too willful to allow any sickness to best you."

"But it would help if you'd lie down and hold me. Would you do that?"

"Of course, *carino*." She got up from the chair and lay down beside him on the bed. Her throat ached as she felt his arms go around her with the same loving protection he had shown the night before he had been taken away from her.

"I won't leave you," he muttered as his eyes closed. "I know you need me."

"Yes, stay, love." Her voice broke. "I do need you so much."

"I won't die . . ."

Piero died six hours later, after experiencing so much pain Sanchia was almost glad to let him go.

Caterina was there at the end, and it was she who closed the fierce blue eyes for the last time and led a numbed Sanchia from the room. "Can you weep? Sometimes it's better if you can."

Sanchia shook her head.

"Then keep busy. Wash him and prepare him and take him to the chapel. I've had several men building coffins for the last few hours. I thought we might have need of them." She paused. "After you've finished come to Marco's chamber. That's what I came to tell you."

"Marco," Sanchia repeated numbly.

Caterina nodded. "Marco has fallen ill. He needs you. He needs us both."

"Plague?"

"Yes. We aren't as fortunate as I had hoped. There doesn't seem to be any pattern about the length of time it takes to strike someone down." She turned and her voice was slightly uneven. "I must go to my son. Come when you can. You're needed there now and will probably be needed even more later."

Bianca was in Marco's chamber when Sanchia returned from taking Piero's body to the chapel. In her yellow silk gown she looked as incongruously lovely as a buttercup. She insisted on staying in the chair beside Marco's bed in spite of their protests.

At one point Marco begged Caterina to send Bianca away. "She won't understand," he whispered. "She's not meant to. . . ." Once more he lapsed into unconsciousness.

"Bianca, do go sit in the garden," Caterina suggested gently. "Sanchia and I will tend to Marco's needs."

Bianca shook her head, her hand tightening around Marco's.

"We'll take wonderful care of him." Sanchia's hand clasped Bianca's shoulder. "I promise you, *cara*."

"But why should I go to the garden?" Bianca glanced up at Sanchia in wonder. "Marco won't be there. I can't go there without Marco."

Sanchia had a sudden poignant memory of Bianca and Marco laughing and playing on the flower-garlanded swing.

"Marco is sick," Bianca said with dignity. "I'll stay with him until he's better."

"But he may not—" Sanchia's eyes widened. Bianca *knew*. The knowledge that Marco might not live was there in the serenity of Bianca's face. Marco had been wrong about how much of the true world Bianca could understand. She not only had understood but had accepted.

Marco opened his eyes at that moment and Bianca turned swiftly back to him. "They wanted me to go to the garden. Isn't that silly?" She smiled down at him. "We can always go to the garden another time when you're well enough to paint me. You said you wanted to paint me in the swing, remember?"

"Yes." His gaze caressed her face. "Beautiful. So beautiful . . ."

"But right now we can sit here and think about all the flowers and your lovely fountain, can't we?" Her palm caressed his feverish forehead. "It's so hot today. Why don't you try to think of the water flowing and the smell of the roses?"

"I will."

"And we'll be sitting there on the bench together beside the fountain and you'll be teasing me."

"Together . . ."

"Oh, yes, we'll always be together. God is good. He'd never make us part."

His eyes closed. "Together."

They were together four hours later when Marco died.

Caterina stepped forward and gently unclasped Marco's hand from Bianca's. "Take her to her chamber, Sanchia." She closed her eyes tightly for an instant before opening them to say huskily, "I must stay here and prepare my son."

Bianca nodded obediently. "Yes, I'll go now." She stood up and looked down at Marco's face. "*Arrivederci*, Marco."

Not good-bye. Just till we meet again. Sanchia was barely able to suppress her tears as she gently took Bianca's arm and propelled her toward the door. Bianca's step was unsteady and Sanchia glanced up, expecting to see her face contorted with sorrow. Bianca's expression was serene. "Sanchia, I'd like to see the priest."

"We sent to the cathedral for him several hours ago, but he didn't come." Sanchia added gently, "Marco was a good man, Bianca. God will accept him without the last rites."

"God has already accepted him," Bianca said. "The priest is for me. I'd like to take confession before I die."

Sanchia gazed at her in shock. "Bianca, what—"

"I do not feel well. I told Marco the truth: God *is* good." She smiled radiantly at Sanchia. "Together."

Sanchia's hand tightened on Bianca's arm. "As soon as I put you to bed I myself will get the priest."

Bianca collapsed on reaching her chamber and lingered for another two days before she was devoured by the monster ravaging Mandara.

It was proving to be a virulent, insatiable, indiscriminate monster, bringing down servants, soldiers, women, children. Fully half of those in the castle had been struck down by the third day and Caterina told Sanchia the townfolk had been as tragically affected. Sanchia was left with the nursing of Bianca while Caterina tried to ease the suffering of her people beyond the walls of the castle.

Sanchia was forced to send for Caterina at the hour of Bianca's death.

"Dear God," Caterina said softly as she opened the door and the foul stench assaulted her. "Dear God in heaven."

"I need more water. The servants were bringing me a pitcher of water every few hours and setting it outside the door, but they haven't come back since last night." Sanchia was dabbing futilely with a towel at the black suppurations on Bianca's body. "I've got to make her beautiful again. How can I make her beautiful, if I have no water to wash her?"

"Her boils burst." Caterina swallowed hard and then came forward to stand beside Sanchia. "Most of them die before that happens."

"I need water."

"There is no water. The well in the city is fouled. I am permitting everyone to come to the castle and use the cistern in the courtyard for their needs. The cistern is dry now, too." Caterina gently closed Bianca's lips which were stretched wide in a silent scream. "We'll have to take a wagon to the vineyard and bring back water from the well there."

"I must get her clean. She was so beautiful . . ."

"Shh, I'll help you." Caterina took the towel away from Sanchia. "But this little cloth won't do. I'll try to find a sheet and perhaps some water in a ewer in one of the bedchambers." She turned and left Bianca's chamber to return in only minutes.

"She kept asking for the priest," Sanchia said numbly as they washed Bianca's pitifully boil-covered body. "I couldn't tell her the priest was either gone or hiding, so I lied to her. When she was in such pain that she couldn't tell the difference, I pretended the priest was here and took her confession myself. Was I wrong, Lady Caterina?"

"Caterina." Lion's mother shook her head. "I would have done the same. God is too busy striking us down to bother with confessions at the moment." She turned to Sanchia. "You'll have to help me build a coffin for her. The men who were building them in the courtyard appear to have run away, and there's no one to do my bidding. Do you know anything of carpentry, Sanchia?"

Sanchia shook her head.

"Neither do I, but it can't be so difficult if those cowardly louts were able to do it." Caterina shrugged. "There must be some dignity in death. We're not savages to pile our dead on the door stoops or leave them in the gutters as those beleaguered souls in the city are doing."

"Is that what's happening?"

Caterina nodded. "There is no sanity. There's weeping and wailing from some and drunkenness and rape from others." She straightened. "I'll get my needle and thread and we'll sew a shroud from this sheet. Then we'll try our hands at fashioning a coffin. Where's Anna? She can help us with the sewing."

Sanchia tried to focus her mind on something besides the last harrowing hours with Bianca. She hadn't seen Bianca's maid, Anna, since a short while after Bianca collapsed. "I think she may have run away too. She was frightened."

"We're all frightened." Caterina went to the door. "We'll probably have to carry Bianca down to the chapel ourselves. Perhaps we'd better build the coffin in the chapel." She opened the door and left the chamber.

Sanchia sat in the chair beside the bed and closed her eyes. *Please, God, you've taken the innocent, the shining, the beautiful. Please, no more.*

"Are you ill?" It was Caterina's sharp voice behind her.

"No." Sanchia opened her eyes to see Caterina in the doorway carrying her sewing basket. She straightened in the chair. "I was only resting a moment."

"There will be time for rest later." Caterina strode forward and set the basket on the bed. "Help me wrap the sheet around her."

It was well after dark when Bianca lay secure in her clumsily crafted coffin in the chapel.

"Come, do not linger here. They're no longer with us. Do you not feel it?" Caterina pulled Sanchia from the chapel and down the steps to the courtyard.

No torches lit the darkness.

No footsteps of grooms or guards sounded on the cobblestones.

Sanchia ran her hand wearily through her hair. "Perhaps I'm too tired to feel anything."

Caterina nodded. "We must rest." Her hand dropped from Sanchia's arm. "But first come with me."

Sanchia followed Caterina into the castle and up the stairs, but instead of going toward the bedchambers Caterina went to the door at the end of the hall leading to the tower.

"Caterina?"

"Come."

Sanchia followed her up the steps, past the chamber where Lion had carried her the evening that seemed so long ago. They stopped at a door at the very top of the tower.

Caterina opened it and preceded Sanchia into the room.

It was the chamber of the Wind Dancer.

The statue was not in its chest but sitting atop a pedestal. Across the moonlit chamber the eyes of the Pegasus appeared to shimmer with life as it stared blindly at them.

Sanchia took an instinctive step back. "I don't want to stay here."

"Please, if you would be so kind. I need someone here with me. I'll try not to be long." Caterina's voice was unsteady. "I have to say good-bye to my son. There's been no time before this. Marco liked this room."

Sanchia felt a rush of sympathy. Both she and Caterina had been forced to submerge their grief for the dead to help the living. She, too, had need to say good-bye. "Of course." She shut the door. "We'll stay as long as you like."

"Sit down and rest." Caterina indicated a chair across the room. She dropped down on the rug and leaned her head back against the stone wall. "And I'll sit here. Have you ever noticed children will never sit on chairs when they can sit on the floor? I used to bring Marco here when he was a small child to see the Wind

Dancer and we would sit here on the floor together for hours and talk and play games."

Sanchia sat down beside Caterina. "I know. Piero used to sit on the floor beside my chair at the scribe table when I was copying and I would reach down and stroke his hair." She had to stop for a moment to steady her voice. "His hair was as soft as spring air beneath my fingers."

"Marco's skin felt like rose petals to the touch."

"Piero's voice was hoarse as a frog's when he first got up in the morning."

"Marco's fingers were always stained with paint when he came to meals."

"Piero was so terribly stubborn."

"Marco was so very gentle."

There was a long silence in the room.

Caterina said, "I can remember how Marco used to stare at the statue and make me tell him all the stories about the Wind Dancer that Carlo's father had told me. There were so many stories. . . . I was afraid I'd forget them, so I had a scribe set them down on parchment and had them bound in a book."

"And you gave it to Marco?"

Caterina shook her head. "Lion has them somewhere among his papers at the shipyard. By that time, Marco was no longer coming here. He had begun to paint and the Wind Dancer no longer gave him pleasure, only pain."

"Why?"

"I asked him that question once. He said he knew he'd never be able to fashion anything one tenth as beautiful and the knowledge of his own inadequacy filled him with sadness." Caterina paused, gazing at the statue. "It filled me with sadness too. For I knew I'd lost those hours with him and he'd grow away from me just as Lion was doing. Marco was never again as much mine as he was during those hours in this room."

Sanchia's gaze shifted from the Wind Dancer to see Caterina's eyes glistening in the dimness of the chamber. She did not know what to say. "Marco loved you. He seemed to love everyone."

"Yes, but Bianca most of all. I should not have tried to take Bianca from him. I thought it was for the best." Caterina's eyes closed. "Now I don't know what is for the best. Nothing is clear."

"No, nothing is clear." Sanchia reached out tentatively and covered Caterina's hand with her own.

Caterina stiffened and for a moment Sanchia thought she'd pull away. Then Caterina sank back against the stone wall, her fingers clinging to Sanchia's. "Is it selfish of me to want to mourn my son when so many others are dying? Surely a son's death deserves a private grief." She paused and when she spoke again her voice vibrated with pain. "*Marco!*"

Sanchia could feel the tears running down her cheeks as the grief of her own loss welled up within her in an overwhelming tide. Her shoulders began to shake as great sobs racked her body and she wept for all of them. Piero and Bianca and Marco . . . and all those whose names she did not even know.

And the emerald eyes of the Wind Dancer gazed serenely at Caterina and Sanchia as they huddled together, silently sharing their grief, until neither had more tears to shed.

The next morning after waking from an exhausted sleep Caterina and Sanchia left the tower room and the Wind Dancer and went out again to face the Medusa.

The first order of the day was the fetching of the water from the well in the vineyards. They hitched a horse to a wagon and Caterina drove into the city.

Mandara was silent, the hooves of the horse clattering noisily on the cobblestones as the wagon wound through the twisting streets leading to the outer gates.

Rats and birds swarmed in the streets. Occasionally Sanchia would see a corpse left lying in the gutter or on a stoep as Caterina had described. She hastily looked away, especially when she caught sight of scurrying motion near the bodies.

The city gates were unguarded, thrown wide. They passed through, immediately bearing north to traverse the few miles to the vineyard at as fast a clip as the lone horse could manage.

"It appears deserted," Sanchia said as they approached the large fieldstone winery. "How many men work in the vineyard?"

"Only one or two at this time of year. Of course, at picking time there are many more." Caterina reined in the horse and wagon before the well. She raised her voice and called loudly, "Ho! Is anyone here? Leonardo!"

No answer.

Caterina shrugged. "It seems we'll have no help." She leapt down from the wagon. "I had hoped for better luck. We'll be able to manage only the small casks by ourselves." She strode toward the winery. "Start drawing water from the well. I'll roll the casks out and you fill them."

The task of drawing buckets of water from the well and pouring them into the casks was not so difficult after Sanchia developed a rhythm for the work. However, it was when the casks were sealed that the real labor began. Even the small casks weighed well over a hundred pounds when filled. Lifting the casks onto the bed of the wagon was an unbearable strain on Sanchia's and Caterina's muscles. The sweat was running down their faces and soaking through their gowns in dark patches when the last cask was stowed.

Caterina leaned against the wagon, her breath coming in gasps. "*Cristo*, I'm glad that's over. I never realized water could be so—What's wrong with your hand? It's bleeding."

Sanchia glanced down. A small cut bled freely on her right palm. "I don't know. I must have cut it on one of the casks. Perhaps it's a splinter. It's not important."

Caterina frowned. "What do you mean it's not important? It could fester." She lifted her skirt and began tearing at her undershift. "I've seen splinters that have laid low strong men. Do you want to go to your deathbed, you foolish—" She gazed at Sanchia in bafflement.

Sanchia laughed. She laughed so hard she was

forced to cling to the side of the wagon to keep from falling to the ground. "Caterina, you can't . . ." Laughter continued to overwhelm her.

"I see nothing the least bit amusing."

"Caterina, *madre di Dio,* if I go to my deathbed in Mandara it won't be due to a splinter. There's *plague.*"

Caterina's eyes widened and then she began to chuckle. "I believe I've heard rumors to that effect." In another moment she too was laughing helplessly, tears running down her cheeks. "I didn't think." She shook her head. "A splinter. Sweet Mary, a tiny splinter . . ."

"We shouldn't be laughing," Sanchia gasped. "There's nothing at all funny." She started to laugh again. "Why can't I stop?"

"Lorenzo once said something about how nature protects." Caterina wiped her cheeks with the back of her hand. "Perhaps laughter is the way nature keeps us sane when there's too much sorrow to be borne." She shook her head. "Anyway, I feel the better for it. Now give me your hand and let me bind it. If the plague doesn't kill you, I won't have this idiotic splinter doing so."

Sanchia offered her hand and stood patiently while Caterina cleaned and bandaged the tiny cut.

"You could stay here, you know," Caterina said in a low voice as she tied the knot in the makeshift bandage. "You might be safe here away from the city."

"And I might not."

"It's not your home. No duty holds you at Mandara."

"You need me."

"Yes, I need you," Caterina said wearily. "And God knows I don't want you to leave. You . . . comfort me."

Sanchia nodded, feeling great affection for Caterina as she looked at her. The woman before her was no longer the elegant, queenly lady of Mandara. Caterina's amber silk gown was stained and her face carved with deep lines of weariness and suffering. Yet Caterina had never looked more the *illustrissima* than she did at this moment. "And you comfort me. Therefore it only makes sense that we stay together." She gently took

Caterina's arm. "We'd better go. They need the water in the city. Where shall we unload it?"

"On the steps of the cathedral. We'll keep two of the casks for the castle and leave the others."

"Should it not be rationed?"

"Who is to ration it? The priest is gone and we'll be too busy nursing the sick." Caterina turned and strode to the wagon. "We'll make a trip every day and draw fresh water." She climbed into the driver's seat. "Unless this well also runs dry or becomes polluted. It wouldn't surprise me. Good fortune seems to have forgotten Mandara."

Sanchia found her life in the days to follow a despairing round of fetching water, nursing the sick, preparing the dead, and building their coffins. Only one young scullery maid recovered from the disease, and Sanchia had no faith her cure was permanent. Death was everywhere. Why should anyone be spared? She knew it was only a matter of time until the Medusa touched her as well. When children as innocent as Piero and Bianca were taken there was no doubt a sinner such as she would be taken, too.

And poor, shining Marco . . .

"I went to the piazza to fetch the physician for young Donato. To no avail, I see," Caterina said as she knelt beside Sanchia on the cobblestones of the court-yard. "Here let me help you with that." She began to bathe the body of the groom, who had died only minutes ago. "It's strange how we no longer notice the stench," she said absently. She looked up. "The physician has fled the city."

"He could not help anyway." Sanchia shrugged. "But fleeing will do him no good." She looked up at Caterina. "We're all going to die, aren't we?"

"Probably. But I resent the whoreson giving up the battle before it's lost. I didn't. You didn't." She tossed the cleaning cloth back into the water in the basin. "The city is almost deserted. Those who aren't dying or cowering in their houses have fled like the physician."

Sanchia spread a clean linen sheet over the body of Donato. She supposed she should say a prayer over him, but she couldn't seem to think of any words.

"Some of the sick have crawled to the steps of the cathedral and lie there begging God and the saints for aid. I doubt if God will answer. Perhaps you'd better go and see if you can substitute."

"Me? Alone?"

Caterina nodded. "I'll soon be of no help to you."

Sanchia stiffened, her gaze flying to Caterina's face. She had thought she had become numb to all sorrow but she found she was wrong. "When?"

"When did I notice this pesky boil beneath my armpit? Last night."

But Caterina had kept on working unceasingly, probably on strength of will alone. Sanchia studied Caterina's face and for the first time noticed the flush mantling her cheeks and the lines of pain drawn around her lips. "I won't leave you."

"I didn't think you would." Caterina's smile lit her strained face with sudden brilliance. "I suppose I should try to persuade you to do so and go to those who have more need, but I think I'll indulge myself by dying with a friend nearby. I have no desire to die alone and smothered by four walls." Her smile faded and she held out her hand to Sanchia. "Will you come with me to my garden . . . friend?"

Sanchia slowly stood up and took Caterina's hand. She held it very tightly as they walked to where the Medusa waited in the sunlight, among the roses for Caterina.

"Why didn't he come back?" Lion murmured, his gaze on the charred skeleton of the *Dancer* at the dock. "He said he was returning to burn the shipyard. Why didn't he do it?"

Lorenzo shrugged. "Perhaps Borgia snapped his fingers and he had to come running. Damari is clever enough to put aside his own personal vengeance where his ambitions are concerned."

"Or perhaps he wanted to draw me to Solinari where he had set his trap."

"Basala said he had only a small troop of men when he raided the shipyard. Do you think he had a larger force at—"

"I don't like it," Lion cut in with sudden violence. "Any of it. It doesn't feel right."

Lorenzo's gaze went back to the wreckage of the ship and then to the other blackened hulls sitting in the shipyard. "This has hurt you. Consider that you may not be thinking clearly."

Lion's hand tightened on the reins. "Damari meant to hurt me," he said hoarsely. "And he's depending on me to rush wildly to Solinari after him. Why?"

Lorenzo merely gazed at him.

"And why didn't he burn the ships and shipyard when he came here and discovered we'd taken the *Dancer* and sailed for Genoa? It would have been a better opportunity. Why did he hold his hand then and strike now?"

"He could have wanted to destroy the *Dancer* as well."

Lion shook his head. "I don't think so."

"Then do we go to Solinari and reconnoiter?"

Lion was silent, his gaze on the *Dancer*. "What if Damari meant to draw us not to Solinari but away from Mandara?"

Lorenzo stiffened, his gaze whipping to Lion's face. "You think he might have persuaded Borgia to give him reinforcements to attack the city?"

"I don't know what he's done, but all this has an odd feel to me." Lion suddenly called over his shoulder at the men milling around the shipyard, "Mount up! We're going back to Mandara."

Seventeen

Sanchia was sitting on the steps of the chapel, her head resting back against the stone wall, when Damari rode into the courtyard.

The setting sun was behind him, and at first he appeared only as a squat, dark figure against the blood-red orb. Then, as he drew closer, she recognized him, but oddly felt not the least surprised. It seemed fitting that he should be here in this place of death and sorrow.

"Ah, Sanchia, how pleasant it is to see you." Damari swung down from his horse. "You'll forgive me if I don't come any closer. It's only wise to take certain precautions. Tell me, do you have the disease as yet?"

"Probably." Sanchia shook her head wearily. "I don't know."

"And the Lady Caterina?"

"Dead. Yesterday." She paused. "I think

it was yesterday. They're all dead. Marco, Bianca . . . Piero."

He nodded. "Excellent. I was hoping the lady had been taken. Now, if you'll excuse me, I have business inside the castle, I'll rejoin you shortly."

He crossed the courtyard and went briskly up the stone steps and into the castle.

Sanchia leaned her head back against the wall and closed her eyes. She should probably go back down to the piazza and see if any more victims had been brought to the cathedral. She would go soon, but it was comforting to sit there next to the chapel. She didn't feel so alone when she was this close to Caterina and Piero.

"Wake up and bid me good-bye, Sanchia."

She opened her eyes to see Damari tying a familiar mahogany chest on the hindquarters of his stallion. The Wind Dancer.

"You see I have it again. I told you I'd get it back."

He seemed absurdly pleased, she thought with vague surprise. Did he think the loss of the statue mattered now?

"You didn't believe me, did you?" He glanced up as he tightened the rope. "I'm truly glad you're here to see my triumph. I was afraid there would be no one left alive to appreciate my cleverness."

"No one is alive."

"Well, you're half alive. That will do." He smiled. "Tell me, did the boy die at once? I thought he was ill when my men put him in the wagon."

Piero. He was talking about Piero. "Not right away." She managed to focus on what he was saying. "It was you who took Piero?"

"One of my men, actually. It was truly a brilliant plan. It had come to my ears that the plague had attacked a tiny coastal village not far from Solinari and it was only necessary that we spread the disease here. Now who would make a better carrier than the child you had taken to your bosom? My informant had already told me that both you and the child were here at the castle. We had only to steal the child, smuggle him out of the city, and transport him to Fontana. We kept him in the charnel house there for two days, making sure he was properly exposed to the disease."

It was Damari who was the monster of death. The horror of his words pierced her apathy and exhaustion. She gasped. "How could anyone do such an evil thing?"

"Of course, it was necessary to conduct the plan with the most exquisite precision and timing," Damari went on calmly. "I returned to Pisa to raid Andreas's shipyard and draw him and a goodly portion of his men from Mandara. Then I sent two of my men with the wagon and orders to abandon it a few miles from the city gates. After the raid I had to bring my men back here to stop those who were fleeing the city."

"Fleeing . . ."

"But of course. The disease couldn't be allowed to spread. Borgia and His Holiness were afraid there would be an outcry if the disease were carried into another city." He smiled. "I assured them that wouldn't happen, so I waited in the hills and when the scared rabbits came streaming out of the city we eliminated them with a barrage of arrows. I had to be careful to keep my men at a distance. Those who I find it necessary to bring close to the plague will also have to be eliminated."

"But you're here now."

"Ah, but I'm not afraid of the disease." He rubbed his pitted cheek. "If I was meant to die of any disease, the pox would have gotten me when I was a child and that Lady bitch persuaded her husband to send my mother and me away from Mandara to a pox-ridden village. No, I was spared to do great things, to lead armies, to create kingdoms."

Sanchia shook her head. "You'll die here, like all the rest. Everyone dies here."

For a moment an expression of uneasiness crossed Damari's face because of the certainty in her tone. "Not me. I have another fate awaiting me." He gave a final tug to the rope and swung onto the saddle. "Do you smell the smoke yet?"

"No."

"I do." He lifted his head and sniffed. "I set fire to

the castle and to the gardens. My men are torching the city now. Another precaution His Holiness insisted on my taking. Naturally, we torched the village of Fontana after we took the boy from the charnel house."

"Lion . . ."

"You're wondering why I let Andreas leave when he too might have become infected?" He shrugged. "I had to accept the risk. I had to draw his forces away so I could be sure of walking into the castle unopposed. If he does carry the plague elsewhere, we'll merely put out a story that he fled in terror from the disease and it was his fault the sickness was brought to more innocents." He smiled. "I will, of course, now proceed back to Solinari and dispose of him at my leisure."

As he gazed down at her a flicker of regret passed over his face. "I'd really like to take you with me. I quite enjoyed our time together in the dungeon. It's not often that one runs across a woman with the courage and endurance you possess. I had promised myself another such experience after Andreas took you from me." He shook his head. "Too bad. But Borgia would be most irate if he learned I'd let anyone live who knew of his and his father's involvement."

"You're going to kill me?"

"I've already killed you," Damari said. "I was merely considering resurrecting you for a few day's amusement. Good-bye, Sanchia. If you're fortunate, the fire may end your life before the plague does. I hear the plague gives a very painful death."

"Yes." She closed her eyes again, trying not to see the pictures his words brought to mind. "Yes, it's very painful."

She heard the clatter of Damari's horse's hooves on the flagstones as he left the courtyard. A moment later the first acrid wisp of smoke drifted to her nostrils.

They came upon the first dead seven miles from Mandara.

Lion looked down at the body of a child of perhaps eight years crumpled in the road beside a wagon. An arrow had pierced her narrow chest, pinning her to the wood of the wagon wheel.

Lorenzo reined in beside him. "A man, a woman, and two more children are lying farther down the road."

"Arrows?"

Lorenzo nodded. "The wagon is piled high with furniture and household goods. It looks as though everything was tossed into the wagon with great speed. They obviously left the city in a hurry with no intention of returning."

"And were waylaid and murdered." Lion looked away from the child lying against the wagon wheel. "Women and children too. Nothing appears to have been stolen. Why would they have been murdered?"

"Shall I order them buried?"

"No." Lion turned his horse. "Later. We have to find out why they were running from Mandara. Hurry."

They came upon two more bodies a mile down the road and then an entire family butchered a quarter of a mile farther. After that, Lion stopped counting the dead that littered the road and gullies and spurred on toward Mandara.

They first saw the glow lighting the night sky as they left the foothills.

Lion heard Lorenzo's harsh imprecation but couldn't tear his gaze from the macabre, obscene beauty of the sight before him.

"Mandara." Lorenzo gazed stonily at the burning city in the distance.

Lion heard the shocked murmur of the men riding behind him. They had wives, friends, families in that inferno just as he did, he thought dully. Sanchia, his mother, Marco, Bianca . . .

"Caterina," Lorenzo said hoarsely. "There have to be prisoners."

Lion felt a spring of hope. Lorenzo was right. None of them had to be in the burning city. He spurred forward and put Tabron into a dead run.

"Lion," Lorenzo shouted above the thunder of the horse's hooves. "If it was Damari, where's the condotti?"

The same thing was bothering Lion. On this level

plain the torches and movement of an attacking army should clearly be visible. There was nothing. No army. No horses. No catapults or other war machines. Nothing.

Nothing but Mandara being devoured by flames.

Lion saw Sanchia when they were within three miles of the city.

She was plodding slowly, blindly down the road and, if the illumination from the burning Mandara had not lit the countryside with unusual clarity, the troop would have ridden her into the ground.

"Sanchia!" Lion held up his hand to halt the troop and reined in Tabron. "*Dio*, what's happened here?"

She didn't seem to hear him. She kept walking, her gaze fixed on something he couldn't see. Her brown velvet gown was torn, filthy, her hair a wild tangle of grease and soot.

"Sanchia." Lion dismounted and strode toward her. "Are you hurt?"

She kept plodding forward.

Lion stopped before her and grasped her shoulders. "*Santa Maria*, answer me. Are you hurt?"

Her blank gaze finally focused on his face. "Lion?" she whispered. "I thought you were dead. I thought everyone was dead but Damari. It's not right that he should live, you know. He shouldn't be allowed to live when everyone else in the world is dead."

"Everyone isn't dead, Sanchia. You're alive."

She looked at him in wonder. "No, I'm not. Damari killed me just as he did everyone else. Caterina, Marco, Piero, Bianca."

Agony tore through him as his gaze went over her head to Mandara. "All dead?"

"Of course," she said, surprised that he should ask. "Everyone is dead."

He felt the tears sting his eyes even as he shook her. "You're *not* dead, Sanchia. We're both alive."

"That's right, you're alive. You told me." She suddenly stiffened, her eyes going wide with horror. "No!"

She tore out of his grasp and backed away. "Don't touch me. Are you mad? The plague . . ."

Lion went icy cold. "Plague? You said Damari, Sanchia."

But she had turned and was running wildly back toward Mandara, the skirts of her tattered gown flying behind her.

Lion pounded after her. "*Cristo*, Sanchia. Stop. No one is going to hurt you." He drew even with her and grabbed her in his arms. "Sanchia *cara*—"

"You don't understand." She was struggling desperately to free herself. "I'll kill you. I don't want to kill you. Only Damari. Let me go!"

The tears were now running unashamedly down Lion's cheeks. "*Cara*, no . . ." He drew her closer, his hands feverishly stroking her sooty hair. "Shh . . ."

She abruptly gave up, slumping against him. "It's too late anyway. You've touched me. Even Damari was afraid to touch me. Medusa . . ."

He caught her as she swayed, collapsing into unconsciousness.

The bitter odor of smoke was gone. Now the air was pervaded with the odor of wood and something fruity, yet musty.

Sanchia opened her eyes to see Lion bending over her, bathing her forehead. Dusk enveloped them. The only light piercing the dimness was the sunlight pouring through two small windows high above her. Dust motes danced in the dual brilliant streams of sunlight and she gazed at them in dreamy fascination.

Two dancing sunbeams . . .

Lorenzo had said that about Bianca and Marco, hadn't he? But those sunbeams were no longer dancing; they lay still and quiet in the chapel.

But was there a chapel? Would the stone have withstood the heat of the flames that engulfed Mandara?

"Fire . . ." Her throat was raw, and it hurt to speak. Had she been screaming? She had felt the screams welling up inside her, but she believed she had kept them from coming out.

"No more fire, Sanchia," Lion said gently. "You're not in Mandara any longer."

"Where?"

"The winery." He smoothed the damp cloth on her temples. "You remember the winery?"

"Yes." She looked around and could discern the shadowy outline of a huge wooden vat and oak casks in the dimness.

"Keep covered. It's cool here." He pulled the blanket over her and she suddenly became aware she was nude beneath it.

Lion was without clothes, too, she realized in bewilderment. Strange.

"Do you know who I am?" Lion asked.

"Lion."

Relief lightened his expression. "And what happened at Mandara?"

How could she forget? How could anyone forget. "Plague." She was suddenly jarred into full wakefulness. "Get away from me!" She sat upright and tried to slide farther from him. "Plague!"

"Be easy. I've been with you here for over a week." Lion said gently. "If I'm fated to fall to the disease then I'm already infected."

She looked at him, stricken. "A week?" She closed her eyes. "Dear God, why?"

"Why did you stay in Mandara to care for those I loved?"

"I was there."

"And I am here. Open your eyes and look at me, Sanchia. Do I appear ill or racked with the disease?"

She opened her eyes. He looked strong and vigorous in spite of the lines of weariness and sorrow she saw in his face. "Sometimes it doesn't happen right away."

"And sometimes it doesn't happen at all. Was everyone stricken in Mandara?"

"It seemed as if they were." She shook her head in confusion. "There were a few that were not ill but, as I said, sometimes it takes more time for one or the other. I don't know if any lived or not."

"I think it likely some survived, if the fire didn't kill them."

The fire. "Damari and his men set the fire. I watched him do it but I couldn't seem to move. Then it came to me that if Damari lived, he could do this again. I couldn't let him repeat such a monstrous act. So many died . . . Did I tell you about Piero?"

"Yes, you told me everything." Lion's eyes glittered brightly in the dimness of the room. "You raved and ranted until I thought I could not bear to hear any more. I believed you would very likely go mad."

"Perhaps I did. I keep seeing—"

"No," he said fiercely. "You will heal in mind and you will heal in body. I will not lose you, too. Do you hear me? You will heal!"

The passionate force of his voice almost convinced her he could hold both death and madness at bay. Poor Lion. He had lost so much. His family. His ships. His home.

She had thought she was incapable of feeling ever again, but to her surprise she felt a faint stirring within her. She looked away from him. "Why do we have no clothing?"

"I burned the clothes you were wearing and the ones I had on when I found you."

When she looked at him inquiringly, he shrugged. "It seemed a good idea at the time. I know nothing about plague." He paused. "I bathed us both in hot water every day and clothing would have just gotten in the way. It seemed a sensible precaution to take. When you swooned I told Lorenzo and the men not to come near us and brought you here to the winery. They're encamped beyond the vineyard. Lorenzo comes every day with fresh food and water and sets it outside the door." He nodded at a pile of blankets against the wall. "I've boiled those blankets and dried them in the sun. If you like, I suppose I could fashion you something to wear from one of them."

"Soon." She felt no discomfort in either Lion's nudity or her own. More than her clothing had been stripped from her in the past weeks. "How long are we to remain here?"

"Another week. Then, if neither of us falls ill, it will be reasonable to assume you did not carry the plague."

"Reasonable." She looked at him and found herself suddenly shaking. "There's no reason or justice connected with that monster. It strikes the good, the innocent, the strong. Caterina—" She choked back a sob. "Forgive me. I know it must hurt to have me speak of her. She was your mother, and she—"

"Hush." He was suddenly holding her in his arms, his fingers tangled in her hair as he rocked her back and forth in an agony of sympathy. "I know she was not kind to you. She meant well—".

"No, you don't understand," Sanchia whispered. "I loved her, too. We became so close those last days that when she died it was almost like losing Piero again. I loved her."

"I wish I had said good-bye to them," Lion said hoarsely. "I should have taken the time to say good-bye. If I had known—"

Sanchia felt something warm and wet on her temple. *If.* The eternal word of regret. Sanchia's arms slowly went around his shoulders to comfort as well as take comfort. Caterina had said something about regrets that she must think about and then share with Lion and Lorenzo. But not now. The pain was too fresh and new. Later there would be time enough.

Why, she was thinking about the future, she realized with astonishment. Perhaps she was beginning to believe that Lion could in some magical way keep the Medusa from taking them both.

But she must not let her hopes rise, for that was another way the Medusa tricked and deceived, giving a little only to take away all. Sanchia would not allow herself to hope until she was sure the monster had passed them by and would not look over its shoulder to smite them down.

Later that night, they sat before the small fire Lion had lit in the center of the winery. Lion had draped her in one of the blankets to protect her from the cold, and his arm around her formed another comforting barrier.

She did not look away from the fire as she said haltingly, "I do love you, you know."

He stiffened and then his arm tightened around her. "No, I didn't know."

"I knew I loved you in that first moment when I thought you might also get the plague. I believe I didn't realize it before because love was different from what I had thought it would be." She gazed pensively into the flames. "It's not sweet and gentle like the emotion Dante felt for his Beatrice, is it?"

"No."

"It twists and turns and makes you ache with lust and then with tenderness, but still the love remains. Somehow I thought there would be . . ." She stopped, thinking about it. "A splendor."

"Perhaps there is splendor for people who have an easier path to tread than we."

"Perhaps."

They were silent.

"I thought it important that you know I love you before we die," she said. "I think we should—"

"We aren't going to die."

"Oh. Well, if we do." She leaned her head back against his chest and closed her eyes. "No, it's not at all like Dante said. I didn't even think of you very often once Caterina and I set to nurse the dying in Mandara. Only now and then when there was time." She paused. "But when I did think of you, it was with love. I want you to know."

"I do know." Lion's voice was thick as his arms clasped her closer still. "I know, Sanchia."

"Good." She opened her eyes to gaze wistfully once again into the heart of the fire. "Still, it would have been quite wonderful if there had been splendor . . ."

A week later Sanchia and Lion walked out of the half dusk of the winery into the full sunlight.

Lorenzo was waiting with the reins of two horses in one hand, a pile of clothing for Lion in the other, and a smile on his lips for Sanchia. "Ah, how . . . interesting you look." His gaze flicked to Sanchia's hair before shifting to the coarse gray blanket Lion had slit in the middle and then slipped over her head to form a loose robe. "That garment has a kind of barbaric charm when combined with her wild red hair, don't you think, Lion? Yes, she'd definitely be a fit mate for Attila the Hun."

She gazed at Lorenzo in wonder. He was behaving exactly as he had before. Everything in the world had changed since that time . . . except Lorenzo.

"Why are you looking at me like that?" he asked mockingly. "Are your wits so dazed you cannot give me my proper set-down? I suppose I must make allowances for your recent ordeal. However, I hope you will not be long about it, or I'll be forced to deprive you of my company. You know how I detest being bored."

He turned to Lion, who had discarded his blanket and was quickly dressing in the clothes he'd brought. "I've taken the liberty of sending the troop to Pisa with instructions for your steward to give them each a small sum to start a new life somewhere else." His gaze went to the blackened stone of the walls of Mandara. "They obviously have no future here, and you have no immediate use for them."

Lion nodded. "You did well." He pulled on boots. "Have you found other survivors of the fire?"

"Only a handful. We quartered them in a field a few miles from here and as yet there's been no sign of the plague among them." He grimaced. "And we spent most of the week burying the bodies in the foothills we chanced upon when coming here. There were eighty-seven of them."

"The population of Mandara numbered well over a thousand," Lion said. "Damari has claimed a high toll."

"What do we do now?" Lorenzo asked. "I admit I'm abysmally weary of sitting around and waiting for you two to rise like Lazarus from the tomb. Damari?"

"Not yet. We go to Pisa. But first, I have to visit the survivors and see how all goes with them." Lion swung onto Tabron's back.

Lion's sense of responsibility again, Sanchia thought.

There was no longer a Mandara, but as long as his people needed him he was ready to give. "Should I go with you?"

Lion shook his head. "Sit in the sun and rest. Lorenzo and I will be back shortly."

"I've done little but rest for the past two weeks."

"Tarry here. It will do you no harm and will save me worry. Lorenzo said these people 'appeared' to be free of the plague. I'll not go close, but I don't want you within miles of them."

Sanchia nodded in acceptance. Lion would go no matter what she said or did, and she had no desire to see the refugees from Mandara. The sight would stir too many memories of those last days. "I'll stay here."

"*Santa Maria*, such meekness." Lorenzo mounted his horse. "Where is your spirit, your tartness? What a disappointment you're proving, Sanchia. And you, too, Lion. You have the settled air of a couple married a decade or so."

Sanchia's gaze met Lion's and the faintest smile touched her lips. In a strange way she felt Lorenzo was right. During their week of isolation together they had known only sorrow and fear and the need to comfort each other. The bond between them had toughened and yet become more supple, like fine leather after years of use.

As if he had read her mind, Lion nodded imperceptively. "We'll return soon," he said as he and Lorenzo set off.

Sanchia sat down on the bench beside the door of the winery and closed her eyes as she lifted her face to let the rays of the sun bathe her cheeks. The air was clean and sweet, and a feeling of peace gradually settled over her. With it came the strange certainty that the plague was gone.

The Medusa had moved on.

Lion returned alone two hours later. When she inquired into Lorenzo's whereabouts, Lion shrugged as he reined up before her. "He's gone to Mandara. God knows why. There's nothing there but ashes and ruins. He said he had a whim to see it one more time before we left."

"A whim." Sanchia turned to look thoughtfully at
Mandara. She could not imagine anyone wanting to go
back to that charred wasteland. Then, suddenly, she
knew why Lorenzo had returned. "I have to go back too.
Will you take me?"

"No!" Lion turned to look at her in amazement.
"Why, by all the saints, would you be mad enough to do
that?"

"Not madness. And not a whim," she said soberly.
"But I have to go back. There's no danger there now.
Not even the plague could have lived through the
inferno."

"You can't be certain."

"No, but I feel it so strongly." She smiled. "It has
passed us by, Lion."

"If you have to go, then I'll go with you."

"No." She held up her arms and he muttered a
curse as he swung her up before him on the saddle. "You
can take me to where the city gates once were." She
settled herself back against him. "And wait for me there,
as I waited for you here."

Lorenzo was sitting on his horse looking at the
blackened ruins of the rose garden when Sanchia
guided Tabron through the rubble to draw even with
him.

She flinched as she looked around the garden. The
devastation of the town had moved her terribly when
she was riding through it, but this ruin had much more
emotional meaning for her. Where there had been
flowering beauty there was now only charred bushes,
blackened fountains, cracked benches. The wooden
arch over the arbor had crashed down to bury the
marble bench beneath, and there was no sign of the
pretty garlanded swing where she had watched Bianca
and Marco at play that first afternoon.

Lorenzo didn't look at her. "I don't want you here."

"She did," Sanchia said quietly. "She called me
friend and held out her hand to me and said, 'Come
with me to my garden, for I don't want to die alone.'

And I took her hand and we stayed here together and talked of many things until she could no longer speak sensibly. But even then she held my hand tightly and would not let it go until she was taken. I wrapped her in a sheet and dragged her to the chapel to lie with the others. I had to make her coffin with my own hands. She—"

"Be quiet. I don't want to hear this," Lorenzo said hoarsely. "Leave me."

"I cannot leave you. What she said in this garden has worth and meaning for all of us. She said she had no regrets about anything she had done. She only wished that she had taken more time to nurture and appreciate the people around her as she had this garden."

"Is that all she said?"

"No, but it was all much the same. Live in the rose gardens of life, live fully and well, and do not fear the thorns." She paused. "She did say one more thing. But that was much later, when the pain had nearly crazed her and she no longer knew of what she spoke. She said, 'I love you, Lorenzo.'"

He stiffened as if she had struck him. "She was . . . an extraordinary woman and my very good friend." His voice was uneven. "Naturally, you will not repeat her words, as they could be misunderstood."

"You don't have to protect her any longer, Lorenzo," Sanchia said softly. "And certainly not from me. I would not even tell Lion this, but you have the right to know. Because I think you are one of the gardens Caterina didn't get a chance to nurture and bring into full bloom."

He was silent, gazing out over the charred garden. "It was not an easy death?"

"No, none of them died easily."

Lorenzo's hands suddenly clenched on the reins. "She was—" When he spoke again his voice was so low she had to strain to hear. "I thought I was . . . empty inside, but she was there all the time."

"She'll still be there as long as we remember her."

"Yes." Lorenzo turned his horse and Sanchia felt a thrill of pity as she saw the stark desolation in his usually expressionless face. "But she's not here in this garden any more. I thought perhaps she might be."

Sanchia turned Tabron to follow him, but he suddenly reined in and glanced sharply over his shoulder at the blackened wreckage of the marble bench in the arbor. He tilted his head to one side as if he were listening.

"What is it?" Sanchia asked, puzzled.

"Nothing." His gaze was still on the arbor. "I thought I heard something."

"What?"

"Bells." He turned and rode slowly out of the garden. "It must have been the wind rustling through those burned bushes, though I could have sworn I heard the jingle of bells. . . ."

Eighteen

I'm sorry, Lion," Sanchia said softly as her gaze first wandered over the blackened remains of the *Dancer* at the dock and then to the wreckage of the three ships in the yard. Seeing this senseless devastation filled her with the same sadness she had felt when riding through the streets of Mandara. "Is there nothing you can salvage?"

"As you can see, the shipyard is still intact. But what is a shipyard with no ships? It takes a good two years to build just one and nothing to show for it until it's sold. I'd have to start over." He got off Tabron and lifted Sanchia down. "And I'm not sure I have the heart for it."

"You have the heart for it," Lorenzo said as he dismounted. "Wounds may leave scars, but they don't change what we are." He grimaced. "And what I am now is stiff, odorous, bad-tempered and likely to become more so if my needs are not met quickly. Where is your shipwright? No wonder Damari wreaked such havoc when we're able to ride into the yard in bright daylight unchallenged."

"I hired Basala because he was an excellent shipwright, not a soldier, Lorenzo. It's just a little past dawn, and he's probably still asleep." Lion nodded toward the small brick house a short distance away. "Why don't you go see if you can rouse him?"

"I shall." Lorenzo strode toward the house. "Which service will certainly entitle me to the first bath."

Lion turned to look back at the *Dancer* and said haltingly, "I cannot offer you a great deal now. Everything I owned at Mandara was destroyed. My only wealth lies in the shipyard in Marseilles, and it may bear no fruit for many years. I can give you no more than a plain roof over your head and plain food on the table."

Sanchia gazed at him in disbelief. "*Dio*, Lion, I have never had anything of my own. A roof over my head is all I'd ever ask. I knew the life I tasted in Mandara could never be mine."

"It *will* be yours," Lion said as he whirled and faced her. "Someday I'll build you a castle more beautiful than Mandara and you'll reign there like a queen."

"Like Caterina?" Sanchia shook her head. "It's not the life I want and it wasn't the life she wanted either. Not at the end."

A spasm of pain crossed Lion's face at the thought of his mother's death. "What do you want then?"

"Work. Peace. Children." Sanchia found the tears stinging her eyes. "Yes, children. I think I should like a son like Piero."

Lion touched her cheek with gentle fingers. "Lorenzo is right. Wounds heal, *cara*."

"I'm already healing." Her lips trembled as she tried to smile. "It will take time and there will be scars, but I will heal. Thank you for being so very kind to me."

"Kind?" He frowned. "Did you think I'd use you ill after all you've been through?"

"No, I only wanted to—"

He cut through her words. "You'll have work

aplenty during our first years and, if God is willing, you'll have your children, but I can't promise you peace. I'm not a peaceable man." He put his fingers on her lips as she started to speak. "And there's no reason you shouldn't have the castle, too. If you have no inclination to rule it yourself, then raise one of our children to watch over it."

She studied his face. He was healing also, but it was perhaps even more difficult for him than for her. He had suffered not only the loss of his loved ones but all that he had built these last years. She remembered the expression on his face when he told her of the joy he took in building after a life filled with destruction. Now in order for his wounds to heal he must build again and with a lavish hand. "That seems a sensible plan. I will take your castle." She pretended to think. "And a stable full of fine horses, and a palazzo in the country and—"

"Stop." He was smiling faintly. "You'll have to give me many sons to work in my shipyard to make it flourish enough to provide you with all those riches."

She smiled back at him. "That was my intention. One to be master of the castle, one to send exploring to distant lands, one to help you in the family business. I think we should have at least five children if that would be of no bother to you. Shall we—"

"Lord Andreas, you honor me with your presence." Basala was hurrying toward them, a warm smile on his thin, intelligent face as he struggled into his leather jerkin. "May I express my regret at your loss? God has not been kind to you of late. When your man arrived here with the news of the burning of Mandara"—he shook his head—"what a blow to you, my lord."

Lion nodded. "You issued them the sum Lorenzo requested?"

Basala nodded. "But there is not much left in the coffers." He hesitated. "Have you decided what you'll do here? I do not wish to hurry you, but the guilds have been most insistent I either release their members or put them to work again."

"We will talk of that later." Lion gestured to Sanchia. "You remember Madonna Sanchia. As you can see, she's once more in dire need of clothing. Can your good wife find something for her to wear?"

"If she has nothing herself, I'm sure she can persuade the master carpenter's wife to accommodate the madonna."

"That would be most generous of her," Sanchia said. "I understand your wife furnished me with two gowns when we left for Genoa. I'm sorry I was too ill to thank her at that time."

"She was glad to be of help and my lord was most generous. He gave her thrice their value." Basala studied Sanchia. "May I say you look considerably more robust than you did then? You were so pale and wan I thought you'd surely die before you reached Genoa. Is your hand healed?"

"Entirely, except for a slight stiffness in one of the fingers."

"But it must have been a long and terrible illness to turn that pretty hair white. The same thing happened to my second cousin who underwent—"

"White?"

"Madonna Sanchia needs to bathe and rest, then break her fast," Lion said quickly as his hand grasped Sanchia's arm and urged her forward. "If you please, Messer Basala."

"Of course, of course. This way. I believe my wife is already heating water for a bath for Messer Vasaro." The shipwright hurriedly led them toward the house.

"White?" Sanchia asked in bewilderment. "What did he mean?"

"It doesn't matter, *cara*. It only makes you more beautiful."

Then they were in the house and Sanchia was meeting the shipwright's cheerful, vigorous wife, Lisa. It was not until Lisa Basala led Sanchia to a small antechamber for her bath and left to go to the kitchen to heat more water that Sanchia's question was fully answered.

She stood before a highly polished oval of brass and gazed at her reflection with wondering eyes. The face in the mirror was the same face she had always known, smooth, unlined, the face of a woman still in her sixteenth year. It was the hair framing her face that was changed. A single lock of startling white shone against the dark auburn of the hair brushed back from her left temple.

So the Medusa had not left her untouched after all.

"I told you it only made you more beautiful." Lion stood in the doorway behind her.

"Why didn't you tell me?"

"Women are sometimes strange about such things. I didn't want to disturb you. It wasn't important."

She reached up to touch the shining white streak. "Another scar."

"No." He moved behind her and pressed his lips to her left temple with the same infinite gentleness he had displayed toward her since she had awakened in the winery. "A medallion of courage." Then he was gone, leaving her to gaze at the familiar stranger.

Lion and Lorenzo were deep in conversation when she entered the salon two hours later but broke off immediately when they saw her.

"That shade of blue is entrancing on you, but I admit I do miss your barbaric blanket," Lorenzo said as he rose to his feet. "Gowns are rather ordinary, are they not?"

"Basala and his wife will return shortly and we will have dinner," Lion said. "I sent him to make a few arrangements, and his wife went to the *mercato* to see about having shoes made for you."

Sanchia came forward and stood before them. "Those 'arrangements' wouldn't be concerned with purchasing passage for me on the first ship to Marseilles?"

Lion stiffened. "And if they are?"

"I would not go." She held up her hand to stop his protests. "Do you think me so simple I wouldn't guess your plan? You intend to whisk me off to a place where you think I'll be safe while you both go after Damari. I would have had to be blind and deaf not to notice the two of you whispering and plotting on the way here from Mandara."

"We didn't want to disturb you," Lion said. "You said yourself you wanted peace."

"But not until I've earned it."

"*Santa Maria*, who could have earned it more than you? What you went through at Mandara should have earned you a lifetime of peace."

"Not while Damari's alive."

"Lorenzo and I will attend to—"

"No." Sanchia met his gaze. "After Solinari I just wanted to forget what Damari had done to me, but for what happened at Mandara there can be neither forgiveness nor forgetfulness."

"*Cristo*, Sanchia. I will not involve you again with that bastard."

"Then I'll involve myself," she said fiercely. "You forget I was *there*. I have memories that will be with me all my life and there must be justice. I will not be able to bear to remember what he did unless I can remember he was justly punished and I had a part in seeing to his punishment. Do you realize what he did to Piero? He was only six years old and—"

"Shh, we know, *cara*. We know."

"And Caterina. She didn't deserve to die. None of them deserved to die."

"She's right," Lorenzo said abruptly. "She's entitled to her part in this, Lion."

"And is she entitled to the danger? You saw what happened to her at Solinari and then we had ducats aplenty to pave our way. Now we only have our wits against Damari and his condotti."

"Then they'd better be exceedingly sharp wits." Lorenzo moved over to the window to stand looking out at the ruined hulls in the shipyard. "And we obviously need all the help we can muster. If you won't take her, then I will."

Lion made a violent motion with his hand. "Damn you, Lorenzo, what if I—" He broke off as if afraid to speak the thought gripping his mind.

"What if you lose her, too? Don't worry. You're so

besotted with Sanchia that you'd probably die gloriously defending her and therefore have no time for foolish regrets."

Sanchia gazed at Lorenzo blankly and then began to laugh. The laughter was tentative, rusty, but still it was laughter and she felt the knot of anger and sorrow within her miraculously loosen. "That has all the macabre logic I would expect of you, Lorenzo."

"I am always logical."

"I don't like it." Lion shook his head wearily. "But I obviously can't move either of you."

"It's very wise of you to surrender, for you may well need Sanchia." Lorenzo turned away from the window. "Because I won't be able to help you with Damari."

Lion's gaze narrowed on his face. "That is your choice, of course."

"You think I back away from the task?" Lorenzo shook his head. "But you speak only of Damari. You've forgotten that he wouldn't have been able to do what he did if he hadn't had the approval and support of Borgia and the pope. Damari was the sword, but the Borgias were the ones who wielded it. In my eyes it's Cesare and Alexander who bear the brunt of the blame."

"Certainly a good portion of the blame."

"And consider this, throughout his entire career Cesare Borgia has adopted whatever methods he found at hand to conquer the cities in his path. The ploy Damari used to defeat Mandara had the advantages of economy and complete devastation. Who is to say Borgia will not choose to use the plague again if the need arises?"

"Dear God," Sanchia whispered.

"Exactly. If justice is to be done, it must be done to all three." Lorenzo smiled. "And, as I'm the most qualified for the task, I'll volunteer to be the dispenser of justice to the noble house of Borgia."

Sanchia and Lion gazed at him in astonishment.

"You would kill the pope?" Sanchia whispered.

"Do you not believe he deserves it? He's totally corrupt, a man who has lusted for power his whole life long. Did he not buy the papacy with blood and ducats?

Does he not have the blood of any number of people on his hands?"

"No one is saying the world would not be better off without him." Lion hesitated. "But, *Dio*, it would be hazardous, if not impossible. Both Borgias are surrounded by guards at all times. How would you manage it?"

"I have no idea. Something will come to me. I'm most ingenious when offered a challenge of this magnitude." Lorenzo paused. "But you may be sure their deaths will not be easy."

He had asked if Caterina's death had been easy, Sanchia remembered, and she had told him that none of the deaths at Mandara had been easy.

"So Damari is mine," Lion said.

"And Sanchia's. Don't be selfish, Lion." Lorenzo turned toward the door. "I'm going to Cesena to make a few inquiries regarding the whereabouts of Duke Valentino. I should be back in a few days. Will you still be here?"

Lion nodded. "I've decided to sell the shipyard to Basala and keep only the one in Marseilles. It will take that long to complete the transaction."

Sanchia looked at him in surprise. "You're leaving Italy?"

"*We're* leaving Italy. There's nothing here for us now. I told you once that Mandara was my country." He shrugged. "And now there is no more Mandara."

Lorenzo nodded. "It's best to put Mandara behind you." He opened the door. "We'll talk more when I return."

Lorenzo returned on the evening of the third day as he had promised.

"Borgia has left for Rome," he announced. "He departed almost immediately after he was paid a visit by Damari. The good duke was said to be in excellent spirits, so it's safe to assume that he journeyed to his father with the Wind Dancer."

"And Damari?" Lion asked.

"He was planning on returning to Solinari 'to dispose of Andreas at leisure,'" Sanchia quoted bitterly.

"But he won't stay there long. It will worry him that I haven't launched an attack on Solinari, and he'll need to know if I've spread the disease so he can take steps to protect the Borgias. He'll probably come here to Pisa first." Lion frowned. "And bring enough men to make sure we have no chance to resist him."

"Then I believe it's time to complete our plans," Lorenzo said with a faint smile.

Lion nodded. "And to put them into motion."

The next morning Lorenzo left Pisa for Rome.

The following day Lion and Sanchia departed for Florence.

It felt very strange to Sanchia to be riding through the same Porto San Friano from which she had departed those many months ago. Yet it had not actually been so long, she realized with a slight sense of shock. They had left Florence through this gate in early March and it was now only late July. It seemed a lifetime since Lion had come to Giovanni's shop for that frightened, nervous child.

She was thinking of that other Sanchia as if she were some other person entirely, she thought sadly. Well, and so she was.

"You're very quiet." Lion asked, "Are you weary?"

Anxiety threaded his voice and Sanchia tried to smother the impatience it aroused in her. His cosseting at first had brought her a sense of security and comfort she had badly needed, but now that she was stronger it was unbearable. "I was thinking about how many things have happened since I left Florence. I'm no longer the same person."

He flinched. "Who would not change after the punishment I've dealt you?"

"You meant me no harm."

"That didn't stop harm from coming to you. I am to blame."

Sanchia sucked in her breath. Lion's pampering,

the way he avoided touching her as if she were one of the holy saints instead of a woman he wanted, all stemmed from his sense of blame. "Who knows what would have happened to me if I had stayed here?" she asked softly. "It could have been as bad. No place is entirely safe."

"If I hadn't taken you away, you would never have known Damari."

"But there was already a Caprino in my life."

"It's not the same."

Dio, the man was stubborn. It would obviously take more than words to change his mind. "Do you think Giulia will help us?"

"We'll find out shortly. Her *casa* is—" He broke off with the sharp intake of breath of a man struck an unexpected blow.

Sanchia looked at him in alarm. "What is it?"

"Nothing. I just forgot about the doors." Lion reined in and sat looking at the magnificent bronze doors of the baptistery of the cathedral of Florence, his eyes glittering with sudden moisture. "Ghiberti's Gates of Paradise. When Marco and I were boys my father brought us to Florence whenever he visited Lorenzo de' Medici. My father insisted I go with him to the palace to learn the ways of dealing with princes, but he permitted Marco to run free. Marco was giddy with joy. He was drunk with the art of Michelozzi and the ideas of Alberti, the beautiful statues and the paintings." He stopped, unable to go on for a moment. "And most of all he loved those bronze doors. He'd get up before daybreak so he could see the first light of dawn strike them, he'd go four streets out of his way to catch a glimpse of them. Once he said to me, 'Lion, if I could sculpt something as beautiful as those doors I'd never ask for heaven. I'd stand outside all day long and ask everyone who passed, Did you see them? Did you really look at them?'"

Sanchia swallowed to ease the sudden tightness of her throat. "I grew so accustomed to walking by the cathedral that I scarcely noticed the doors."

"Not Marco. Beautiful things were always new to

him." He shook his head. "But most of us do forget to take notice of what is familiar to us. It's only when they're lost that we realize how we valued them."

"That's true." Sanchia wanted desperately to comfort but knew there was nothing she could say to ease the depth of suffering she sensed in him at this moment. "But perhaps if we remember that, we can learn to—"

"It's not *enough*. It's too late." His hand tightened with sudden violence on the reins. "I want him back! I want all of them back, Sanchia."

She was silent, gazing at him in an agony of tenderness.

Then he straightened his shoulders and deliberately loosened his grip on the reins. "I'm behaving foolishly," he said gruffly. "I'm not a boy to cry for what's beyond my reach." His gaze shifted to her face. "I've distressed you."

"Distressed *me*?" She was exasperated. She could feel the tension and sorrow coiled within him, but he allowed her only an occasional fleeting glimpse before he walled it up inside himself again. "It's you who are in distress."

"Nonsense. All goes well with me." He nudged Tabron forward. "Come along. Giulia's *casa* is on the next street."

Giulia Marzo looked up warily from her account book as the maid showed Lion and Sanchia into her chamber. "What a surprise to see you, Lion. I believe you stated the intention of never visiting me again." She looked from Sanchia to Lion. "I see you still have your little slave. Has she brought you pleasure?"

"More than I've brought her." He gently pushed Sanchia down on a chair by the door. "Sit down, *cara*. Since Giulia is failing in courtesy, we must take our comfort where we may."

"When did you do otherwise?" Giulia asked dryly. "As I remember, you always did exactly as you pleased." She paused. "As it pleased you to kill Caprino."

"Did his death disturb you?"

She shook her head. "In truth, you did me a favor. I moved quickly and took over a number of Caprino's enterprises. Being a woman, I was not able to assume fully Caprino's place, but let us say I now possess considerably more power than when last you saw me."

"I rejoice in both your success and my small part in it." Lion's tone was mocking. "Though I must confess I was tempted to slice your pretty throat as I did Caprino's."

She stiffened, and her gaze darted to the bellrope across the room. She forced a smile. "Why would you want to do that?"

"Caprino had only one way of learning that our destination was Solinari. Naturally, I put a few questions to him about the name of his informant." Lion smiled. "The only reason I didn't come after you, Giulia, was that I blamed myself for mentioning it within your hearing, and Caprino said he suspected you withheld the information until you thought it would do him no good. His venom was so great that I was forced to believe him."

Giulia let her breath out in a rush of relief. "I meant no harm. It was only business."

"And you're an excellent businesswoman, are you not?" Lion took a step closer. "That's why I'm here. I have a proposition to make."

Giulia's eyes glinted with sudden interest as she leaned back in her chair. "I'm always ready to listen to a proposition as long as there's profit in it."

"There's profit. I wish you to draw Damari to Florence. Sanchia said you had dealings with the man at one time."

"Once." Giulia made a face. "However, I acted through Caprino."

"But he knows your name?"

"Of course, everyone knows of my casa. He asked Caprino specifically for one of my women."

"Do you know what he did to her?" Sanchia asked fiercely.

"It was not my concern," Giulia said quickly. "The girl made no objection to going. In truth, she was filled with happy anticipation."

"She could not have known—" Sanchia shook her head. "He is a monster."

"It was not my concern," Giulia repeated, adding in a lower tone, "he was not supposed to kill her. He cheated me."

Sanchia gazed at her in disbelief and opened her mouth to speak, but Lion cut in quickly, "We wish you to send a message to Damari telling him you have Lionello Andreas and his slave, Sanchia, under your roof. Say we fled to Florence and begged you to take us in, and that you hear he will pay dearly to get both into his hands."

"Why would you come to me instead of Mandara?"

"There is no longer a Mandara."

"Indeed?" Giulia was clearly astonished. "It seems you have more reason to want vengeance against Damari than I believed. What is your purpose in drawing him here?"

"What do you suppose?"

Giulia nodded. "And he wants you enough to come here to capture you?"

"More than enough."

"And how much are you willing to pay for my help?"

"Five hundred ducats."

"It's not enough. There is risk aplenty."

"It will have to do. I have no more to give you."

"I will think on it." Giulia stood up. "Come back tomorrow."

"I want your answer now," Lion said bluntly. "And I'll have it now."

Giulia smiled faintly. "You were not always so impatient." She hesitated, a frown furrowing her wide brow. "Very well, the bargain is struck."

"Good. We'll speak more on this later." Lion helped Sanchia to her feet. "We have no place to stay until Damari arrives. Will you give us two chambers?"

"Two?" Giulia's smile became malicious. "If you require two chambers, she must not be giving you as much pleasure as you claim. I warned you it would be ）."

"Sanchia has been ill." Lion turned to the door.

"And she is not well yet. Will you give us accommodation or not?"

"Certainly. It will be my pleasure." Giulia moved gracefully to the door. "Perhaps it's best that I have you under my eye. I don't think it would be safe to tease Damari with a prize he wants and then not be able to produce it."

"You have only to offer, not produce." A sudden sharpness had edged Lion's tone.

Giulia smiled sweetly over her shoulder. "A mere slip of the tongue, *caro*. Come this way. You'll naturally occupy the chamber that pleased you in the past, and we'll find something suitable for the girl."

"I am *not* ill," Sanchia hissed at Lion as they followed Giulia down the hall. "I'm quite well now. Why did you tell her—"

Giulia had stopped before a door and abruptly turned to face them. "This will do for you, Sanchia." She opened the door. "I'll send up a tub and hot water for a bath." She sniffed delicately. "That horse odor is quite reminiscent of the way you smelled when first you came here. I do hope you've gotten over your aversion to soap and water."

Sanchia bit her lip to keep back the stinging reply that trembled on her tongue. She must not let the woman anger her. Lion had said they needed Giulia. "Thank you, I would like a bath."

"Will you need me?" Lion asked, the familiar frown of concern on his face.

"No, I will *not* need you. I'm perfectly well." Sanchia entered the room and slammed the door behind her, immediately resenting the sound of Giulia's low laugh.

Why was she so angry? She should have ignored Giulia, not let the woman's manners prick her. Yet there was no doubt Giulia's spite had disturbed her composure. It was stupid to let Giulia trouble her when she had not done so in the past.

But then she had not known she loved Lion.

And she had not known how it felt to have him inside her body, the hot, dizzy pleasure as he plunged and lifted her to his every stroke.

Santa Maria, her body was coming alive, stirring with lust and anticipation at the thought of the next time Lion would come into her.

Not only her body, but her emotions were being reborn. She was experiencing lust, anger, jealousy. Yes, jealousy of the hours Lion had spent in Giulia's bed. Jealousy of her beauty and her knowledge of how to please him. It was clear the woman wanted him still; she had made no overtures, but the invitation had definitely been implied. Would that invitation be accepted?

Lion had possessed no woman since he had taken Sanchia that night in the tower room, and no one knew better than Sanchia that he was a man of strong desires. Sorrow had emptied them both of everything but tenderness and the desire to comfort and receive comfort, but, if she was coming alive, who was to say that Lion's desires were not also awakening?

Cristo, and what a damnably inconvenient time for that to happen with Giulia Marzo at hand not only to stoke but to appease his lust.

Sanchia took herself to task—she had been through so much she had thought she was done with petty emotions.

She knew suddenly she wanted desperately to live fully . . . to feel, to nurture her rose gardens as Caterina had told her to do. She wanted to bear children and know love as it was meant to be.

The Medusa had left her alive and by all that was holy she would *live* that life.

Nineteen

"Forgive me, Messer, but I understand you have a room to let."

"Then your understanding is at fault." Luigi Sarponi had a deeply creased, heavily jowled face, and the scowl now twisting it was obviously meant to discourage and intimidate. "I have no room to let and, if I did, it would not please you. My house is not for such as you. Find somewhere else to stay. There are plenty of lodgings going begging since summer is here. Rome in summer isn't a healthy place to be."

"Are you not Luigi Sarponi?"

"I am."

"And did you not work in the kitchens of His Holiness until the month of April three years ago?"

Luigi nodded warily. "I did."

"Then you're exactly the man to whom I wish to speak. Allow me to present myself. I am Lorenzo Vasaro." Lorenzo took a step forward and, as the light from the candle on the table fell fully on Lorenzo's face, Luigi instinctively took a step back.

"We have many matters to discuss." Lorenzo smiled. "And I think after we have had that discussion you will find you do have a room to let."

"You speak in riddles." Luigi Sarponi poured wine in Lorenzo's wooden goblet and then his own before sitting down at the scarred table across from him. "What do you want of me?"

"Only what you want for yourself." Lorenzo leaned forward across the table. The light from the tallow candle cast shadows beneath his high cheekbones and lit the crystal coldness of his eyes. "What you've wanted for over three years."

"And what is that?"

"The death of the Borgias."

Sarponi went rigid. His gaze searched Lorenzo's impassive face. "You are misinformed."

"Because you've not shouted your hatred of them to the four winds? If you had done so, I would have no use for you." Lorenzo smiled. "But if I should be wrong and you have no interest in the subject, I've no wish to bore you. Should I leave your house?"

Sarponi lowered his gaze to his goblet. "Why did you come to me?"

"I've been asking questions, very discreet questions, but I find my inquiries are usually answered."

"I can see how they would be," Sarponi said sourly. "And after you leave, they cross themselves and pray to the saints you'll never come back."

"Exactly." Lorenzo chuckled. "But you do not fear me, do you, Luigi? I did not think you would. I've heard you're a surly, bad-tempered rascal who fears neither God nor the devil."

Sarponi lifted his goblet to his lips. "Neither God nor the devil can do any more to me than they've done already."

"Which of them took your son, Luigi?" Lorenzo asked softly.

Sarponi paused for an instant and then drank deeply and set his empty goblet down on the table. "The devil." He looked up to meet Lorenzo's eyes. "What do you know of my Mario?"

"I know he was murdered one night by a masked band roving the streets of Rome. They killed and mutilated for the pleasure of it, and I know that shortly after his death you resigned your position as second cook in the kitchens of His Holiness to take a far less lucrative position in the kitchens of Messer Obano. You gave no reason for leaving the Vatican, and it was assumed Messer Obano paid you a fat bonus to come to him."

"But you do not believe it?"

Lorenzo shook his head. "Rumor has it that Cesare Borgia led the band that murdered your son. Indeed, there are stories he and his bodyguards still find it amusing to indulge their tastes in that fashion, but now they tend to go abroad to do so."

"They are not stories," Sarponi said hoarsely. "It is the truth. What is the blinding of an artist or the murder of a boy to the great Il Valentino? The duke and his father are in league. Alexander sits on the papal throne and we kiss his feet and he lets his beloved son indulge in any act of cruelty and—" He halted the rush of words and drew a deep breath. "Mario was not like me. He possessed a sweet nature and always had a smile for everyone. He was apprenticed to become a cobbler. I told him he should become a cook like me, but he said as long as people had to walk he would not go hungry."

"You're sure it was Borgia who killed him?"

"He was attacked only a short distance from here and was not dead when he was brought home to me. He had eight sword thrusts through his body but he was not dead." Luigi gazed blindly at the flickering flame of the candle. "They toyed with him. They felt safe because of their masks, you see."

"But he still recognized Borgia?"

"No, it was the medal. Borgia's cloak fell open and

Mario saw the order of St. Michael that the French king had given the duke. Il Valentino takes great pride in the gift and wears it always."

"But you said nothing to anyone?"

Luigi's lips twisted. "Who would I tell? His Holiness? Or perhaps Michelotto Corella, the duke's favorite assassin? No, I would only have ended up in the Tiber. But I will no longer serve either that serpent in the Vatican or his vile offspring." His gaze shifted from the candle to Lorenzo. "Are you going to kill me now?"

"Why should I do that?"

Luigi shrugged. "It occurred to me you might be one of Borgia's assassins tying up loose ends."

"But still you spoke to me."

"I have no great fondness for life anymore. I have no wife and my son is dead." He rubbed his neck. "I work, I come home, I sleep. There's little reason to fight to hold on to such a life."

"I have no intention of killing you."

A spark of interest flickered in Luigi's dark eyes at Lorenzo's slight emphasis on the last word. "Borgia? Truly?"

"Both Borgias." Lorenzo smiled. "With your help. Do you not think this project could stir a bit of interest in you?"

"Possibly," Luigi said cautiously. "But how can they be murdered? Both go about with guards."

"I wasn't thinking about a knife between the ribs."

"Poison? There's no taster at the Vatican, but that's because none is needed. One of the guards is in the kitchen the entire time the meal is prepared and accompanies the servants to the dining hall."

"Hmm, I didn't know that. It's a circumstance that may present difficulties."

"Difficulties?" Luigi laughed shortly. "The guard never takes his eyes off us. It will be impossible."

"The Borgias will be dead within a month's time."

Luigi started to argue, then stopped and studied Lorenzo's face. "I . . . I believe you."

"But will you help me?"

Luigi hesitated. "You want me to go back to work at the kitchen of His Holiness?"

Lorenzo nodded. "And help me to get work as a cook's helper there also. I understand the duke has been dining with his Holiness at almost every meal since his return from the Romagna."

"They say his pox has flared up again and he won't be seen abroad." Luigi shook his head. "You don't look the part of a kitchen lackey."

"Then you must help me to change my appearance so that I do."

Luigi regarded him critically. "Perhaps if you don't gaze at anyone directly. Your eyes—"

"I'll be as shifty-eyed as you could want me to be."

"And you're too clean. You must have clean hands, but a bit of grease and dirt on your face and hair would help." He smiled maliciously. "And no more baths for you. You smell too sweet."

Lorenzo flinched as he glanced at Luigi's unkempt gray hair. "I'm sure no one is a greater authority on the subject of dirt. I place myself entirely at your disposal." Lorenzo paused. "Agreed?"

Luigi nodded slowly. "Agreed."

"*Bellissima*," Lion said as Sanchia opened the door at his knock.

Sanchia made a face. "At least I no longer smell of horse."

"I thought you would like to visit Elizabet and Bartolomeo this evening. Then we could sup at the tavern on the piazza. It will be more pleasant than eating here."

Sanchia brightened. "Could we? I was going to visit them tomorrow, but I would like to see them right away."

"And they will want to see you."

Her smile faded. "I'll have to tell them about Piero."

"I've already paid them a short visit to advise them you were coming. I informed them of Piero's death."

Sanchia felt a surge of warmth at his thoughtfulness. Then Lion gently took her arm in a protective clasp and escorted her down the hall. "You've suffered enough. Now it's time to lean on me and let me take the burdens."

He was doing it again, she thought worriedly, treating her as if she were the helpless child Bianca had been. She must do something to put a stop to it.

Yet after they had paid their visit to Elizabet and Bartolomeo she was passionately grateful to have his strength to lean on again.

"What's wrong?" Lion's gaze was fixed anxiously on her face as he led her toward the piazza. "You seemed happy enough when you were with the newlyweds, but now you look . . ." He seemed to search for a word. "Melancholy."

"It's nothing." She felt the foolish tears brimming and determinedly blinked them back. "It's stupid of me, but I suddenly feel . . . alone. Elizabet and Bartolomeo are so happy and busy with their own lives. They don't need me anymore, do they?"

"Didn't you want it so?"

"Oh, yes. I told you I was being foolish." She walked faster, not looking at him. "I suppose it's because I feel they're now as lost to me as Piero."

"Sanchia." Lion's hand grasped her arm. "You're not alone while you have me."

She swallowed. He was showing her that exquisite gentleness and sweetness again, as if she were a frail invalid who needed great care or she would slip away from him. Perhaps that was the way he did view her, she thought with sudden panic. What if he felt no passion for her, only guilt and responsibility?

Suddenly, she saw where she must lead them.

"You're right. I'm not alone. I have you and Lorenzo." She walked faster. "No, I don't really have Lorenzo. No one has Lorenzo now. Except perhaps you. Do you think he does well in Rome? I did not like—"

"It's not only Elizabet and Bartolomeo, you've been acting strangely since we arrived at Giulia's *casa*. If you wish to withdraw from the plan, only tell me and I will go another way."

"I don't wish to withdraw. Why do you persist in thinking I'm afraid? I'm not afraid of Damari."

"Then what do you fear?"

"Nothing." She broke away from him and hurried on ahead. "And I'm not hungry. I think I'll go back to the *casa* and go to bed. You go to the tavern without me."

"You should eat. You've had nothing since—"

"I'm not hungry." She was running, dodging through the crowds of people as she had when she was a thief in these very same streets.

"Sanchia!"

She ignored Lion's shout and kept on running. She heard his steps pounding behind her on the flagstones but he did not overtake her until she was running up the stairs to the second floor of Giulia's *casa*.

His hand was rough on her shoulder as he spun her around. "What in God's name is wrong with you? Are you ill?"

"No, I'm not ill." She pulled away from him and finished climbing the stairs. "I'm not weak or afraid." She hurried down the corridor toward her chamber. "And I'm not going to shatter if you say a harsh word to me."

He had caught up with her again and his hand on her arm brought her to a halt. "That's fortunate, for I'm about to say a number of harsh words." His eyes were glittering with anger as he dragged her down the hall, threw open the door to his own chamber, and pulled her inside. "I do not deserve this, Sanchia." He slammed the door. "I know your state is delicate but—"

"My state is not delicate," she said through her teeth. "How many times must I tell you? But perhaps you wish to think me delicate so you have the excuse not to touch me. Then you will feel free to summon Giulia Marzo here and—"

"I don't want Giulia in my bed," he shouted.

"Why not? You told me once that you would not touch me if she was near."

"I lied. I was angry that you stirred me so."

"But now I do not stir you with anything but pity. So why should you not take Giulia to your bed?"

His hands hovered around her throat as if he'd like to strangle her. "*Cristo*, is this my reward for patience? You do not stir me? *Madre di Dio*, I even wanted to take you in the winery when you were helpless and grieving and balanced on the edge of madness. I, too, was grieving but my body did not recognize or respect that grief." He dragged her into his arms, and her hands slid to his tight, muscular buttocks. "I'm so angry with you I want to beat you, but still I want you." He pulled her into the hollow of his hips and she felt the hardness of his arousal against her. "Tell me, am I stirred, Sanchia?" He did not wait for her answer but lifted her in his arms and carried her to the bed. "I do not want Giulia. I want you!"

He tossed her on the bed and flipped up the skirt of her gown and undershift. He untied his points and his manhood sprang boldly free. He moved quickly between her thighs. "Does this feel as if I'm stirred, Sanchia?"

He plunged deep, wildly grinding his hips to reach the quick of her.

She cried out, her hands reaching out blindly to clutch at his shoulders.

He froze. "Did I hurt you?" His fingers moved between them, petting her, arousing her. "It's your own fault. Did I hurt you, dammit?"

"No," she whispered. "It's only—"

"Then *take* me."

The rhythm was wild, hard, almost brutal in its hunger and passion. Her head thrashed back and forth on the pillow as she attempted to keep from screaming with the intensity of the lust shuddering through every muscle and nerve in her body. She tried to help him but she was shaking too badly to do anything but hold him. He was trembling, too, she realized dimly, his breathing harsh, his chest moving in and out as if he were running.

He cried out and threw his head back, his strong

neck arching, his body going rigid as if he had been struck by an arrow. "Sanchia, I can't hold—"

"Don't!" Her own pleasure exploded in a fiery release that left her stunned and weak.

Minutes later she felt him leave her and carefully pull down her skirts but she was still too dazed to open her eyes. Something cold and metallic pressed against her lips. "Drink this; it will restore you."

She opened her eyes to see his set face above her. He was still angry with her, she realized dazedly. She raised herself on one elbow and took the silver goblet. "I have need of restoration."

He flinched. "You made me angry."

"I believe it. You weren't gentle."

"It was your own fault," he said fiercely. "What manner of man do you think I am? You could expect nothing else."

She took another sip of wine. "I remember you told me I must take you into me whenever you had need. At least, you didn't push me up against a tree this time."

He scowled. "I suppose you're going to try to leave me again. Well, I won't permit it. If you want me to tear up your bondage papers, you must wed me." He glanced away from her. "It will not be a bad life. If you do not anger me, I'll try to be gentle with you."

"Wed you?"

"Why are you surprised? I told you I would give you marriage if I could. *Dio*, we even spoke of children."

She shook her head. "I never thought of marriage for me. It seems strange . . ."

"Then think on it now. For I will not let you go."

She nodded solemnly, her lashes lowering to veil her eyes. "I shall think of it."

He frowned. "You've thought long enough. What say you? I'm no longer as wealthy as—"

"Yes."

"You agree?" He gazed at her uncertainly. "You're not angry with me?"

She tried to smother a smile. "What would be the use? You would not change." She paused. "Thank the saints."

His gaze narrowed on her face. "You do not mind my roughness?"

She shook her head. "It is a part of you. I cannot separate the roughness from the gentleness. I cannot say 'Yes, I will love this side of Lion Andreas, but no, I will not love the other side.' I love the entire man."

A slow smile lit his face. "Truly?"

"Truly," she said softly. "I love the lust and the gentleness and the stubbornness and the—What are you doing?"

"Undressing you." His laughter was joyous. "I wish to give you more lust to love. We will deal with the rest later." He met her gaze and said softly, "But this time we will take our time and I will also show you gentleness." He grimaced. "If I can."

And Sanchia's laughter joined Lion's as she fell back on the bed and welcomed him once more into her arms and into her body.

"Why did you do it?" Lion's fingers were gently stroking the shining white lock at her temple. "I'm not a fool. I know you deliberately forced me to anger when I only wanted to show you I could give you honor and sweet words."

"I wanted to bring you back to me and it was the only way I could think to do it. I realized I was coming back to life and I wished you to travel the same road with me." She paused. "And perhaps I was a little afraid. You were so different . . ."

"Most women would have applauded the difference. Why would you be fearful of it?"

She laughed shakily, and brushed her lips against his bare shoulder. "I am a slave. Slaves are not treated with gentleness and sweet words. It made me uneasy." She paused. "For a while I even wondered if perhaps you felt it your duty to care for me because of the service I did at Mandara."

"Not duty—love. I honor you for what you did at Mandara, but I loved you long before." He was silent a moment. "Will you wed me?"

She raised her head to look at him in surprise. "Of course. I told you I—"

"Now. We have time before Damari comes. We will go to the priest tomorrow and make the arrangements."

She gazed searchingly at him. His expression was taut, strained. "Why do you feel the need for such haste?"

"I want you to be mine. Is that not reason enough?"

And he wanted her to be protected by his name if by chance they were not successful in killing Damari, she realized, chilled. He wanted her safe, if death took him from her. Her cheek lowered to nestle in the hollow of his shoulder. "It is reason enough. I would like to feel you are mine also," she whispered. "Yes, let us go to see the priest tomorrow."

"What do we do here?" Luigi asked testily. "The sun is too hot for strolling in the woods. I have no liking for all this greenery and fresh air."

"You have no liking for anything that you cannot brew in a pot or cauldron." Lorenzo's reply was absent as his gaze searched the trees and shrubbery on either side of the path. "I wonder how you ever came to beget a son. You like neither man, woman, nor beast."

"I concocted a fine mulled cider one night and imbibed so much the scullery maid appeared as appetizing to me as a glazed piglet with an apple in its mouth. She birthed Mario nine months later and left him in a basket in the kitchen when she ran away with a sailor. A father at my age!" Luigi mournfully shook his head. "I was so angry when I saw the babe that I burned the goose I was roasting."

"What a charming love story. It arouses not only pathos but also the palate. I'm sure you were a splendid father."

"I got used to it," Luigi said in a growl. "After a time I even . . . liked it."

Lorenzo darted him a glance. "How old was the boy when he was killed?"

"Seventeen." Luigi walked in silence for awhile. "I talked to Simonedo about you yesterday."

"Ah, the illustrious master of the kitchen. What does he think of my work?"

"He thinks your wits are addled. He says you sidle around the kitchen like a scared snake and never say a word."

"Well, you told me not to look at anyone. I thought it best not to speak either."

Luigi grunted.

"You do not agree?"

"Maybe. It's true your tongue has the sting of a scorpion. Simonedo says you work hard enough, and he thanked me for my recommendation. What think you of the guard who watches the food preparation?"

"An extremely sharp-eyed individual."

Luigi nodded. "Laraba has the eyes of a falcon. The Borgias have used poison often enough themselves not to be careful in choosing a good man, and with Laraba, we'll have to be magicians in order to slip poison into the food."

"I agree." Lorenzo had stopped, his gaze on a tall shrub abounding with clusters of delicate pale rose blossoms. "Is that not a pretty sight, Luigi? I wasn't sure I could find this beauty here on the outskirts of Rome. In my own birthplace of Naples you see these bushes frequently, indeed they grew in my garden. Ah, how lovely it was to see the first flowering in spring. Hand me the hatchet."

Luigi scowled as he handed the hatchet to Lorenzo. "I don't know why I had to carry the hatchet anyway."

"It was only sensible. You're built like a bull and have a comparable strength. Why should I be the beast of burden when you're far more suited to it?"

"And now you're taking the cuttings of silly bushes? I warn you, I'll not let you plant them in my little patch of a garden. That's only for my herbs."

"Luigi, I'm truly hurt you won't share your plot of earth with me." Lorenzo was quickly chopping several large branches from the bush. "Now what is better? A spot of blossoming beauty for the eyes or herbs and vegetables for the stomach?"

"The stomach. You'll not plant your stupid flowers in my garden."

Lorenzo sighed as he handed Luigi back the hatchet. "Oh, very well." He gathered the branches up in his arms. "I guess I'll have to find something else to do with them."

"I've sent the message to Damari," Giulia said as soon as Lion opened the door in answer to her knock. "Santini is to deliver my letter. Caprino used him once before, so Damari will recognize him and perhaps feel safer." She smiled. "Santini is one of the assets I acquired from Caprino's demise. He's a reliable man and trustworthy as long as an opponent's bribe is not too great."

"We cannot ask more than that, can we?" Lion asked. "A bribe or a threat can be equally effective to control a wavering loyalty."

Giulia's smile faded. "What is your meaning? Do you think to threaten me?"

"Only if it's needed."

Giulia's gaze went past his shoulder to Sanchia, who still occupied the big bed across the chamber. Her lips tightened. "I see you will no longer have need of the other chamber."

"No." Lion paused. "We go to the priest today. We plan to wed before the week ends."

"Wed?" Her eyes widened. "You'll wed her? But why should you—" She quickly schooled her angry expression. "I suppose you must do as you think best." She turned away. "I will tell you when I receive word from Damari."

"You're getting twigs and branches all over my floor," Luigi complained. "I won't pick them up, you know."

"My dear Luigi, I'm well aware you keep nothing clean in this hovel but your pots and trenchers." Lorenzo chopped another outcrop of lance-shaped leaves from the branch between his knees. "And I'm sure you'll suffer no profound distress from the mess I'm adding to this disaster of a room."

"I didn't ask you to move in here." Luigi added, "Mario kept the house clean. I tried to tell him it was unhealthy but he would laugh and say, 'Papa, your fine food will have a foul taste if seasoned with dust. Come, we will spend the evening sweeping and polishing.'"

"And you've obviously done neither since he died." Lorenzo tore off a delicate pink blossom from the branch and tossed it at Luigi, striking him on his cheek. "Admit that you like having me here. I give you someone on whom to vent your bilious spleen."

"I do not like you here. Why should I?" Luigi picked up the blossom and sniffed at it. "You're not good company as was my Mario. You only waste my hard-earned money by burning my candles to read your fine books and speak only to make mock of me."

"But I also eat your delicious cooking with an appreciation you don't encounter every day."

"That is true," Luigi said grudgingly. "You're no fool when it comes to the important things of life. Perhaps that's why I tolerate you."

"Perhaps." Lorenzo put the now denuded branch aside. "Hand me that other branch, will you?"

Luigi pushed the branch toward him across the table. "But I will go for no more walks with you in the woods. I could have spent the morning in far more important occupations."

"I realize it was a great sacrifice for you."

"And for what?" Luigi stood up and began to gather the discarded twigs and branches from the floor. "To give you something to whittle." He carried the bundle of branches to the hearth and dumped them on the stones.

"What are you doing?" Lorenzo asked mildly.

"I'm certainly not tidying up after you," Luigi said quickly. "You can clean up your own mess. I only thought to save myself from carrying in fresh wood for the evening fire."

"A very practical thought." Lorenzo lowered his

gaze to the branch between his knees as he sliced off another twig. "But I really wouldn't do that if I were you."

"Why not?"

"Because, if you strike flint to those branches," Lorenzo cut off another blossoming twig, "within a very short time we will both be conspicuously dead."

"You're trembling." Lion's hand tightened on Sanchia's as they walked up the steps to the cathedral. "There's no reason to be frightened." He smiled. "After you've braved the plague, marriage to me cannot be so bad."

"It's not fear." Sanchia moistened her lips with her tongue. "I don't know why I feel so uneasy."

"Are you not content with this marriage?"

She nodded. "More. I am happy with this marriage. I love you. I will always love you, *caro*."

He leaned forward and brushed his lips to her temple. "As I will always love you." He stopped as they entered the dimness of the cathedral. "Wait here. I will talk to the priest." He genuflected and moved swiftly down the aisle.

She watched him walk down the marble aisle toward the priest, who had turned away from the altar and was gazing curiously at them. Lion was all that was strong, forceful, and beloved. She had never dreamed she would possess a love so powerful and passionate as this. Why then was she feeling this sudden anxiety at the thought of linking her life to Lion's?

Perhaps it was because she had read too many stories of noble courtly love and her own love was so very much of the earth and the living.

A ray of sunlight struck the stained-glass windows, and as it passed through, it turned into a rainbow, effulgently bathing Lion and the robed priest. The scent of flowers, incense, and candles drifted to Sanchia, enfolding her in their heady fragrance.

Lion turned away from the priest and held out his hand to her.

She genuflected and started down the aisle, her gaze fixed on Lion's face.

Then he smiled at her and she was suddenly filled with a sense of wonder and a joy as radiant as the light streaming through the windows. The radiance swept through her, lifting her up, until she felt as if she was sparkling with the same jewellike brilliance as the light surrounding Lion and the priest.

Dear God, it was so simple. Why hadn't she understood before what was so clear now?

Love, like life, was composed of plateaus and valleys, of serene silences as well as the clarion peal of trumpets. Pain and turmoil were necessary. . . . How else would they learn to appreciate moments such as this?

Splendor.

Twenty

"Why have you chosen to meet me here?" Damari gazed at Giulia with suspicion. "Why not at your own *casa*?"

"This is a pleasant enough inn, a safe distance from Florence." Giulia turned away from the window overlooking the stable yard. "I see you've brought a sizeable detachment of your men. I assumed it would be so."

"I will not lose Andreas or the woman again."

"But you cannot lose what you do not have." Giulia paused. "Yet."

"I *will* have them."

"If the price is high enough." She motioned to the men in the courtyard. "And you'll not take them away from me with those numbers. I have the money to muster thrice this force to guard what is mine."

"You? A whore?"

"Did you not recognize Santini? He's only

a sample of what I've taken from Caprino. I shall soon be the most powerful woman in Florence. Caprino was a clever man and I learned much from observing him over the years."

"I do not deal with women."

"I know. You prefer to abuse them." She shrugged. "I've not forgiven you for Laurette. It will drive my price higher."

Damari hesitated. "You have them? Truly?"

"In the palm of my hand. They came to me to ask me to help them lure you into their net. They offered me five hundred ducats. I warned them it was not enough to satisfy me, but Lion was foolish enough to believe me when I finally agreed."

"And how much would satisfy you?"

"Fifteen hundred ducats."

"Ridiculous. You'll take far less."

She shook her head. "If you want Andreas and his whore, you will pay my price."

Damari seethed with fury. The greedy slut meant what she said. "Where are they?"

"Safe from you." She smiled. "But not from me."

Damari's hands closed into fists at his sides. "I will pay a thousand ducats, you filthy strumpet."

"I don't like being insulted. The price will now be sixteen hundred ducats."

"You daughter of filth, you cannot—" Damari, seeing her expression, tried to smother his rage. "I will pay your price."

"Excellent."

"But I do not have that large an amount with me. You'll have to wait for payment. When I return to Solinari I'll send you the fee."

She laughed in genuine amusement. "I am to trust you?" She shook her head. "By all means go back to Solinari, but without what you came for."

"I tell you, I do not have the ducats here."

"Then we will have to think of something else." She was silent a moment. "I will bring them to you at Solinari. We will exchange the merchandise for the ducats on the spot."

"How will you get them there? Andreas is no fool."

"But he trusts me." She added, "With reservations. It's difficult for a man to believe a woman who has given him pleasure would betray him."

"I want his woman too. For such a price I'll not be cheated of her."

"The woman also," Giulia agreed. "God knows I have no fondness for her."

"How will you do it?"

"As you so delicately pointed out, I am a whore and therefore familiar with many powders and potions to make the women in my house more compliant. A little bigger dosage and Lion and his little slave will sleep all the way to Solinari." She lifted a brow. "Unless you want me to kill them? It's all the same to me."

"No," Damari said. "I want them alive."

"I thought that would be your wish. Well, you'll soon have them both at Solinari to do with as you please."

Damari felt a sweet surge of pleasure that almost submerged his anger and frustration at the arrogance of the bitch. Well, perhaps the whore would have a surprise waiting for her when she rode through the gates of Solinari. She had a streak of iron within her that might be very exciting to break. "When?"

"Give me a day or two to ease their suspicions and then I'll slip the powders in their wine." She moved toward the door. "It can be no longer, as they're expecting me to receive a message from you any day."

"Then in a week's time?"

She nodded as she opened the door. "If all goes well, you can expect them to be delivered to you one day next week."

"Why not slip the branches into the pile meant for the fires in their bedchambers?" Luigi asked. "You said the smoke would kill."

"It's not a certain enough method," Lorenzo said. "It is August and a fire is not needed often. We might wait weeks for a fire to be lit and even then, if the chimney is clean and draws well or if they do not come too close, the fumes might only make them ill. No, it's best to use the branch as a spit to roast the meat for the table. The wood of the branch will poison the food as it cooks."

Luigi stooped and picked up one of the long branches, gazing at it in fascination. "What bush is it that bears death as well as pretty flowers?"

"The oleander." Lorenzo smiled at him. "A very useful plant. There's not one part of it that's not deadly. One leaf will kill a man. Even the nectar of those 'pretty' flowers will send a man to his grave."

"You're sure they'll get enough poison in the meat to do the task?"

"No, but it's our best chance." Lorenzo lifted his goblet to his lips and gazed at Luigi over the rim. "Now you remember what you're to do?"

"I'm not stupid. You've told me enough times," Luigi said sourly. "I slip the branches into the kitchen woodpile tomorrow morning."

"But today you make sure the chimney in the kitchen is drawing strongly." Lorenzo added grimly, "Even if you have to sweep it yourself. If you don't, I may find myself as dead as His Holiness since I'll be tending the spit."

"You know the scullery maid usually tends the spit."

"Tomorrow I will tend the spit. Create a new sauce with which to baste the meat and insist to Simonedo that you cannot trust the maid with the task. That will give you a reason to keep others away from the hearth. We don't want anyone breathing the smoke and becoming ill before the meat is done. Immediately after the meat goes on the spit you claim illness and leave the kitchen. I'll slip away as soon as the meat leaves the kitchen and join you here. Be ready to depart Rome at once."

"A new sauce is not created overnight," Luigi said, outraged and ignoring all the details except the one most important to him. "It takes time and many efforts before the right mixture is blended in the right proportions. Anyone who knows anything about fine cooking knows you cannot create a sauce—"

"Perhaps for common, ordinary cooks, but you tell me you're extraordinary."

"You know I'm extraordinary."

"Then prove it. A new sauce by tomorrow morning."

Luigi scowled. "You believe you are very clever. Well, I refuse to commit the sin of desecrating one of my dishes. We will murder the Borgias next week."

Lorenzo shook his head. "Everyone knows Cesare is importuning his father for fresh funds for a new campaign. He may not be in Rome next week."

"But I cannot concoct . . ." Luigi frowned fiercely. "Honey. Perhaps I can use honey with just a sprinkle of cinnamon . . ."

Lorenzo smiled with satisfaction as he leaned lazily back in his chair and stretched his legs out before him.

"Why is Giulia being so kind to me?" Sanchia asked as she turned in a circle before Lion. "Look at this gown. It must be one of the finest in her wardrobe, yet she not only gifted me with it but also sent a servant to alter it. Do you not think that's strange?"

"It's a very pretty gown. I like those blue ribbons on the bodice. Perhaps white does not become her as it does you."

"She looks beautiful in anything." Sanchia made a face. "And don't tell me you haven't noticed."

"I notice only the beauty of my own wife, as is proper in a virtuous married man." A glint of mischief appeared in his dark eyes. "Though I admit I prefer you without the gown. It could be that Giulia is not being kind to you, but cruel to me." He tilted his head and looked at her critically. "Yes, you're entirely too fully clothed. Send the gown back to her and we'll—"

A knock interrupted and they both turned as the door opened to Giulia's touch. She carried a silver tray which held three silver goblets and smiled as she moved gracefully toward them. "That gown looks enchanting on you, Sanchia. It never suited me." She set the tray on the polished table and picked up two of the goblets, handing one to Sanchia and one to Lion. "I found this Mandara wine you brought the last time you came to see me, Lion. You always liked it better than any wine Florence could boast." She picked up her own goblet. "Drink," she said softly, her smile lighting the luminous beauty of her face. "And then I'll tell you of the good news that's come to my ears regarding our friend Damari."

The whoreson chimney was not drawing well!

Dio, only minutes ago the flames had been drawing perfectly, and now it was casting thin billows of smoke into the kitchen!

Lorenzo turned his face away from the spit on which the honey-basted lamb was roasting and took a deep breath. Then, holding that breath, he turned back and leaned closer to the flames to peer up the chimney and try to see where the blockage occurred.

"How goes the lamb?"

Lorenzo turned to see the head cook, Simonedo, frowning impatiently at him.

Lorenzo hurriedly averted his gaze and muttered, "It's almost done, only a few more minutes, but the chimney . . ."

"What? Speak up, dolt."

"The chimney does not draw well."

"It's probably only another pigeon." Simonedo turned away. "There's a crook in the chimney and every now and then a pigeon flies down and becomes caught. We'll send a sweep up tomorrow to remove it. Douse the fire after the lamb is done."

A pigeon. Mother of God, a pigeon!

Lorenzo smiled grimly as he settled before the fire, carefully blocking the fumes from the rest of the kitchen with his body and trying to avert his face and take shallow breaths.

Cristo, if this smoke continued to billow, it was not only the lamb that would be done this night.

The pounding on the door was oddly erratic.

When Luigi threw open the door he saw Lorenzo on his doorstep.

"*Santa Maria,* why are you knocking? You've never showed me such courtesy since that first night you barged into my life. Where have you been? You should have been here hours ago. Did all go well?" Luigi grinned. "My sauce was superb. It's too bad the duke and His Holiness won't appreciate it. I was tempted to stay and hear the outcry." He paused. "Why are you just standing there? Come in and I'll give you a glass of spiced wine and you can tell me how Cesare choked on his own bile. You told me not to stay, but you couldn't resist lingering yourself, could you? It's just like you to deny me the pleasure but take it yourself."

"I did not stay."

"Then where have you been?"

"I became . . . lost."

"Lost? How could you become—" Luigi broke off and suddenly reached out a hand and pulled Lorenzo into the room and into the circle of light from the candle. He inhaled sharply. Greasy sweat coated Lorenzo's face and blank, dilated pupils dominated the gray of his eyes. "What happened?"

"A pigeon. Is that not amusing? A pigeon . . . in the chimney. I thought of everything but—"

"Why did you not leave or make some excuse to douse the fire?"

"We were too close."

"*Stupido. Idiotto.*" Luigi's dark eyes glittered in the candlelight. "You tell me to stop and get out if anything goes wrong and then you do this. You have the brains of an ox and no more sense than a beheaded chicken."

"I truly wish you would stop . . . calling me vile names." Lorenzo swayed, his eyes glazing. "I'm sure it's not proper behavior"—his knees buckled—"toward . . . a dying man."

"Madonna Giulia Marzo is at the gates with a wagon, my lord."

Damari felt a rush of excitement. "I've been expecting her." He stood up and motioned for the lackey to leave. "Let her in."

"She has a company of men with her."

"What!"

"She says she will not enter your gates without protection."

"How many men?"

"Fifteen."

The bitch was craftier than he had thought. Fifteen men were no threat to the palazzo, but there was a possibility he would have to let her return safely to her *casa* in Florence.

Damari cursed steadily beneath his breath as he strode out of the palazzo and across the grounds, his gaze fixed on the multitude of torches held by the soldiers beyond the gates.

He stood just inside the gates and shouted. "You have brought me what you promised?"

Giulia Marzo rode her horse forward from her position beside the wagon and smiled at him in the torchlight. "In the bed of the wagon. See for yourself."

"I will. Draw your soldiers away from the wagon." He turned to the guard. "Open the gate. Four of you come out and surround me while I'm beyond the gates."

A moment later he was kneeling on the hay in the wagon and peering down at Lionello Andreas and Sanchia. They appeared to be in a deep sleep, but he had to make quite sure.

He raised his hand and then brought it cracking down with vicious force onto Sanchia's left cheek.

She did not stir.

"Satisfied?" Giulia edged her horse closer. "My powders do not fail me. Now, my money."

"Come in and get it." He smiled. "But naturally I can't permit your hired soldiers to accompany you."

"Then I cannot permit you to take my merchandise." Her lips tightened. "I've gone to much trouble to bring them here, and you're beginning to make me angry. Perhaps I should forget our bargain and return them to Florence. I'm sure Lion is desperate enough to take your life to reinstate his offer of five hundred ducats."

"No!" He jumped down from the wagon. "Open the

gates," he called out as he strode through the soldiers toward the gate. "Someday, Madonna Giulia, I'll take great pleasure in introducing you to my friend, Fra Luis. As a matter of fact, he's at the palazzo now awaiting the arrival of Andreas and Sanchia. A pity you cannot stay and join us."

He stood aside and watched as the wagon and the riders rode through the gates.

He took a step nearer to the wagon, his gaze searching Andreas's face. "They're lying very still. You haven't killed them, have you? I want them ali—"

A sword was pointed only inches from his throat!

Lion's dark eyes glared fiercely at him as his blade jabbed at Damari's throat. How had that whoreson Andreas snatched a sword from beneath the hay and moved so swiftly? Damari's hand dropped instinctively to the hilt of his own sword.

"Do not draw it," Andreas said coldly. "I'd like nothing better than to slit your gullet."

"To me!" Damari screamed. "You fools! To me!"

"They're occupied at the moment," Lion said as he again pricked Damari's throat with the sword. "That was my first instruction to Giulia's men. As soon as we were through the gates, a sword point at the back of every guard."

Andreas's words were confirmed by the glance Damari darted them out of the corner of his eye. "You fool, there are more guards in the palazzo. You cannot fight all of them. We outnumber you."

"You won't for long." Andreas motioned to one of the soldiers, who immediately rode to the open gates and waved a torch in a wide arc three times. "There are some seventy-seven men waiting in the woods who will be here shortly. That should be a sufficient number since your men are hired men just as are these soldiers of Giulia's. They owe no loyalty to you, and I imagine the first thing they'll do once you're dead is strike a bargain so they can have their share of the sacking of the palazzo. They certainly won't waste time trying to vanquish a dead man's foes."

Sanchia was wriggling out of the wagon to stand

beside Lion. A livid bruise marked her left cheek, but her expression was as cold as Andreas's. "*Buona sera,* Damari. You said you wanted to spend more time with me, and I could think of no better place than Solinari."

"You seem very pleased with yourself," Damari snarled. "I must commend you on your endurance. You didn't flutter an eyelash when I struck you."

"I was expecting it." Sanchia gazed at him steadily. "And I should thank you. It was you who taught me endurance, Damari."

"And will teach you more. Fra Luis waits for you in the dungeon. You remember Fra Luis?"

"I remember." Sanchia shook her head in wonder. "Do you not realize that it's over? You're going to die, Damari."

He shook his head. "It's not my fate to die by the hand of such as you. I have a great destiny. I'll follow the Borgias to power no one could dream exists. My men will soon rush out of the palazzo and rescue me."

"They don't seem in any great hurry."

"Let's get it over." Giulia rode forward and reined in beside them. "I have no liking for violence."

"You betrayed me, you whore." Damari's face twisted with anger as he looked at her. "We had a bargain and you betrayed me."

"As you would have betrayed me," Giulia said. "In truth, I was close to aligning myself with you, but suddenly I asked myself why I should receive only sixteen hundred ducats when your palazzo must have so much more?" She motioned and a half dozen of the soldiers dismounted. "The maze. Beware, it's guarded."

She watched as the men drew their swords and started at a trot toward the south entrance of the labyrinth. "Sanchia obligingly drew a map for them to follow and Lion still had the key to the storehouse. We even have a wagon to carry away your treasures. The only question was whether I could obtain the services of this company of soldiers in time for our departure. Fortunately, that was resolved four days ago when they were unexpectedly released from the service of Lord

Gondolfo." She smiled mockingly. "Destiny, my lord Damari."

"You should have taken my ducats. This way you'll get nothing but a short sojourn in my dungeon."

"I'll get half of the treasure." Giulia paused. "But even if the reward were not great, I still might have sided with them against you."

"Then you're a fool as well as a whore."

She shook her head. "Laurette. Caprino told me once it was bad business to let any defeat go unpunished." She lifted her head and smiled again as she saw the rest of the company of soldiers thundering down the road toward the open gates. "You cheated me, but no one will ever try to cheat me again after they learn what happens here."

"Enough of this chatter," Lion said impatiently. He called to the captain at the head of the column, "Bind those guards and secure the palazzo." He turned to Damari. "And you will accompany us to the maze to wait for the treasure to be brought out of the storehouse."

An hour later the palazzo had been secured and the wagon loaded with paintings, large coffers of ducats, jewels, and golden plates.

Damari watched, agape, as treasure after treasure was carried past him. "It will do you no good. I'll get it all back. Just as I got the Wind Dancer back." He smiled maliciously. "Your Wind Dancer is gone forever, Andreas. It rests in the pope's private treasury and will stay there."

"I wouldn't be too certain. Forever is a long time, and it's said the Wind Dancer always returns to my family . . . eventually."

"Bah! It's gone forever. You will see."

"Perhaps, but you will not," Sanchia said. "Take off your clothes."

Damari whirled on her. "What?"

She motioned with the torch in her hand. "Your clothing. Take it off. Everything."

"I will not!"

She took a step closer. "Then let us see if your

destiny will guard your skin from a scorching." She shoved the flaming torch perilously close to his face.

He took a hurried step back and felt the point of Andreas's sword in his back.

"Bitch." Andreas's sword bit through Damari's jerkin and shirt and pain lanced through him. He began to undress, tearing off his clothing piece by piece in rhythm with his muttered curses. Finally he stood naked between the two of them.

"Light the north entrance of the maze," Lion called over his shoulder.

Damari watched as one of the soldiers loading the wagon seized a torch from a companion and ran toward the corner of the labyrinth.

"Now," Lion said softly. "Into the maze, Damari. You shouldn't object to dying there. As I remember, it's a place for which you have a great fondness."

"You're going to chase me through the maze?"

"Oh, no." Lion shook his head. "We're going to let the flames chase you. There's been little rain this last month. The hedges should take the flames easily . . . and spread rapidly, Damari. The north entrance will be blocked by flames in a few minutes." He nodded toward the opening in front of them. "We'll fire this entrance as soon as you pass through."

"If I pass through."

"Your choice. The sword or the maze. Does that not sound familiar? I admit I would prefer you to choose the maze. There's a certain justice in it." Lion's expression hardened. "I'll enjoy seeing you burn as Mandara burned."

"Perhaps the flames will spare you for your great destiny," Sanchia said softly. "As you spared the people of Mandara, as you spared that poor Laurette."

"They *will* spare me. You think you've bested me?" Damari shook his head as he turned and strode toward the entrance. "I'll live to see you all dead."

He smelled the smoke, heard the crackle of flames in the shrubbery behind him as soon as he entered the maze. The bitch and Andreas were wasting no time.

He could see a flare lighting the night sky ahead of

him. The north entrance was burning. He instinctively started to run, thorns tearing at his naked flesh as he brushed against the hedges. He would escape. He had to escape. His destiny must be fulfilled.

Those fools had forgotten there was a way out other than the entrances they had set afire. The west hedge through which Andreas and his brother had escaped had not been replanted. He could wriggle through the hedge and then hide in the shrubbery until they were gone.

His breathing grew painful as he ran. The damned smoke was growing thicker, causing his eyes to tear and sting.

Ah, just ahead was the hole in the hedge!

He sprinted forward and started wriggling frantically through the opening. He cried out as the thorns pierced his legs and buttocks and stabbed into his genitals. He would kill them for this outrage! He would kill them all!

"No, Damari."

He looked up and froze, no longer feeling the bite of the thorns and sharp twigs.

Sanchia was standing outside the circular opening in the hedge, a torch in her hand. Her expression was stern as she slowly shook her head. "There has to be justice." She lit the branches at the top of the opening. "Piero." She lit the left side. "Bianca." She touched the torch to the right side. "Marco." Finally she touched the flames to the bottom of the circle. "Caterina."

"No!" Damari heard himself screaming as he backed out of the opening as the flames licked at him.

The bitch stood there beyond the flaming circle looking as delicate and fragile in her white gown as the figure on a cameo.

"One more," she said quietly. She tossed the torch into the center of the opening. "Mandara."

The hedge blazed high, a solid sheet of flame.

He was going to die, Damari thought dazedly. No, it could not be true. He scrambled away from the flaming hedge and onto the path. He began to run down the path, trying to see through the ever-thickening smoke.

There had to be a way out. He was screaming the words, he realized.

The burning hedges were all around him now, the fire coming closer, still closer.

He turned the corner.

Another wall of flame!

No matter how swiftly he ran, he could not get away from it. The flame touched the naked flesh of his back, and in agony he threw back his head and howled. The rest of his flesh was catching fire as easily as had the hedges.

No, it could not be. He had a destiny. . . .

Lorenzo opened his eyes to see Luigi's scowling face above him. He swallowed and moistened his dry lips. "I take it I've yet to depart this earth, as you bear not the slightest resemblance to an angel."

"Why would you think you deserve heaven?"

"For killing two arch demons?"

Luigi shook his head.

Lorenzo made a face. "They didn't die?"

"Well, you didn't totally fail. The pope will probably die at any moment. They say he was administered extreme unction at vespers today." Luigi lifted a goblet of wine to Lorenzo's lips and fed him a sip. "And Cesare may yet succumb. The servants say he didn't eat as much of the lamb as his father, but he lies gravely ill in a sickroom above the Borgia apartments."

"How long has it been?"

"You've been ill for five days."

"And we're still in your house?" Lorenzo's gaze searched Luigi's face. "I told you to leave Rome at once."

"And why should I obey a man who's stupid enough to poison himself?"

"You stayed to care for me?"

"I stayed because I had no need to go. The fools think both His Holiness and his son fell victim to the same bad-air illness that's struck down nearly everyone in Rome." He grinned. "I told you that Rome in summer wasn't a healthy place to be."

Lorenzo began to laugh weakly. "No one is thinking it peculiar that they both fell ill on the same day?"

Luigi shrugged. "There are those few who murmur of poison, but they speak of the banquet that Alexander and the duke enjoyed at the vineyards of Cardinal Adriano Corneto on August fifth. They say the Borgias wished to poison Corneto but the goblets became switched. Corneto also—conveniently—has fallen ill."

"*Jesú*, that thought is as foolish as the other. Even I couldn't brew a poison that would delay the effect for almost two weeks." Lorenzo hesitated, considering the advantages of such a potion. "Though it would be a challenge to develop one. Since Cesare is still alive, perhaps I should think about it."

"Think about going back to sleep and getting well."

"Ah, you worry about me."

"I care nothing if you live or die." Luigi gave him another sip of wine and then gently wiped Lorenzo's lips with a surprisingly clean cloth. "Why should I? I just grow tired of cleaning up your vomit and hearing you moan. Who is Caterina?"

Lorenzo was silent.

"Don't answer me then. It's not really as if I want to know anything about you." Luigi set down the goblet on the floor and stood up. "Go back to sleep, and if you vomit again you can wipe it up yourself."

"Luigi."

Luigi turned to face him.

"I . . . thank you."

Luigi looked quickly away. "It will be much easier to get rid of you when you're on your feet than to drag your stinking carcass out the door."

"Have I ever mentioned the sweet eloquence of your discourse?" Lorenzo closed his eyes and rolled over on his side. "I'll sleep for a while, but awaken me in a few hours. There's something I must do."

"You can do nothing. You're as weak as a starving kitten mewling for its mother's teat."

"What a truly denigrating comparison." Lorenzo didn't open his eyes. "If I cannot do the task myself, then you must help me. Wake me . . ."

"Hold the lantern higher. It's black as a chimney in this alley. Do you want me to stumble into the Tiber and drown?" Luigi tightened his grip around Lorenzo's slender form. "I know you have no fear for yourself. You'd probably float. They say the devil guards his own."

"My dear Luigi, it's humiliating enough having to submit to being carried like an infant without being insulted as well. Are we nearing the Vatican?"

"Just ahead," Luigi panted. "And you're heavier than an infant. About the weight of a boar dressed for serving or a side of beef before it's spitted and—"

"Stop." Lorenzo's tone was pained. "I realize you're enjoying my plight, but please refrain from comparing me to one of your dishes." He peered into the darkness ahead but could see nothing beyond the circle of the lantern light except the warm mist rising from the river. "If you continue in this vein, I'll be forced to walk and deprive you of this purely temporary feeling of superiority."

Luigi grunted. "And fall into a heap on the floor as you did when you tried to get out of bed?"

"I can walk—" He halted as Luigi snorted and then conceded, "A little. I just have to become accustomed to the idea that my limbs have only the consistency of pasta dough. I'm sure you appreciate that comparis—Ah, there it is."

Luigi stopped short. "This is stupidity. We have no business here at this time of the evening, and those Swiss guards will cleave our heads like melons with their halberds. Let me take you back to the house."

"After I've patiently suffered all the insults and vilification you've heaped upon my hapless head? We will definitely go on." Lorenzo paused. "Or I'll go on. I don't think the situation will be as perilous as you believe, but, if you prefer, you can put me down and I'll go on alone."

Luigi muttered curses as he started toward the gates. "You have the brains of a peahen. The pope may lie dying but he's still the pope. The Vatican is guarded more closely than any palace in all of Italy, and Cesare's guards have formed a cordon around him while he lies helpless. There's no way you can kill him now."

"I know I cannot kill him. I must wait for another opportunity. That's not why we came."

"Then, by all the saints, what are we doing here?"

"The pope has something I want, and this is the best time to pluck it from his treasury."

"And now you think of robbing the papal treasury?" Luigi shook his head. "*Cristo,* do you know how difficult that will be?"

"Not difficult at all, if our timing is correct." Lorenzo's gaze searched the darkness of the courtyard. "And I believe it very well may be. Where are the Swiss guards, Luigi? Where are the mighty forces that guard His Holiness?"

Luigi frowned as his gaze wandered over the empty courtyard. "Why, I don't know . . ."

"It's as I thought: Confusion, turmoil, and disorder. When a great house falls it leaves terror and chaos behind. Take me to the Torre Borgia."

"The private apartments?"

"We must determine whether the pope is dead. Cesare wouldn't act while there was even a chance his father would live."

"Cesare is ill in his bed and almost as weak as you."

"But I'm here. Do you think Cesare is less determined than I? If he isn't there himself, his lieutenants will be hovering around the pope's chamber like vultures."

Luigi continued to mutter obscenities while he made for the Torre Borgia.

A loud crashing and excited laughter could be heard as soon as they entered the apartments.

"Judging by all this merriment, it's safe to assume Alexander is dead," Lorenzo said. "Put me down in that chair and go to the bedchamber and see what information you can gather from those poor souls attending His Holiness. No doubt they've become crazed with grief or they'd never see mirth in this sad occasion."

Luigi set him in the highback cushioned chair Lorenzo had indicated. "You will be all right?"

"Certainly. I shall sit here and enjoy studying Pinturicchio's magnificent murals. I'd heard they're truly the best things he's ever done."

"Murals! You study pretty pictures when the Swiss guards could rush in at any minute and cut off our heads?"

"Well, what else is there to do?" Lorenzo leaned back in the chair. "And I imagine you might find a Swiss guard or two in the bed chamber of the pope, but I seriously doubt if they'll be guarding him." He set the lantern on the table beside him and tilted his head to look critically at the mural. "I hear Alexander posed for that figure in the *Resurrection*. Do you think Pinturicchio caught his likeness?"

Lorenzo smiled as Luigi threw up his arms, turned and strode from the room.

Luigi returned only five minutes later. "The pope is dead and his valets are sacking his chambers. Burchard, the master of ceremony, is the only official on hand and he cannot stop it. He says the entire Vatican has gone mad. They're all trying to salvage what wealth they can before Alexander's death becomes widely known." He paused. "Michelotto Corella demanded the key to the papal treasury on behalf of Cesare not thirty minutes ago."

"Ah, then we're in time." Lorenzo straightened in the chair. "By all means let's proceed to the treasury."

"I was afraid you were going to say that. You're insane, you know. Corella is Borgia's assassin, his bravo, and obeys Cesare's orders without question. Rumor has it he even garrotted Madonna Lucretia's second husband when the man lay helpless in his bed."

"I've never admired stranglers. They lack subtlety and imagination and rely only on physical strength. I'm sure we can overcome such a dullard." Lorenzo struggled to his feet and stood, swaying. "Shall we go?"

"You expect to overcome Corella when you stand there weaving as drunkenly as a thieving butler of the wines?" Luigi sighed and picked Lorenzo up again in his arms. "Madness."

The doors of the treasury were thrown wide, and a stream of men wearing the scarlet-and-yellow colors of the house of Borgia were hurrying from the chamber carrying plates of silver and gold and large coffers.

"I told you this was madness," Luigi whispered as he set Lorenzo down in the shadows beyond a turn in the long hall. "There are too many of them."

"I only need one," Lorenzo said absently as he gazed surreptitiously around the corner. "That guard appears to be of my height and weight and there's no one coming down the hall behind him." He nodded at the man striding toward them down the hall before leaning down and reaching into his boot. "Be prepared to grab the coffer he's carrying. It's probably filled with ducats and we don't want them spilling out and scattering all over the floor."

"Why should he—"

The soldier came even with them and Lorenzo stepped swiftly forward, encircling the guard's neck from behind and jerking him the two paces around the turn of the hall. His poniard moved with lethal accuracy and his victim made no sound other than a soft expulsion of breath as the dagger entered his heart.

Luigi caught the coffer as it fell from the dead guard's hands. "*Maraviglioso*. What an artist you are. What a splendid butcher you would have made!"

"Drag him into that chamber and strip him." Lorenzo leaned weakly back against the wall. "Quickly."

Ten minutes later, with Luigi's help, Lorenzo had struggled into the guard's uniform and Luigi had hidden the naked corpse in a window embrasure.

"Now what?" Luigi whispered.

"Now I go to the treasury and get the prize for which I came." Lorenzo smiled. "And you stay here, my friend."

"You cannot even walk without staggering."

"Corella was obviously in a hurry and did not bother

lighting many torches. The hall is so dimly lit no one will notice whether I stagger or not."

"When you enter that chamber Corella will see you're not one of his men and throttle you."

"Then you'll not have to worry about carrying me back." Lorenzo started down the hall. "Stay here. If I don't return in ten minutes, leave the Vatican without me."

"I'll do it," Luigi vowed. "Why should I endanger my life for a madman? The minute you go into the treasury, I'll be gone."

The treasury seemed as far distant as hell from heaven to Lorenzo. Another Borgia guard strode out of the treasury staggering under the weight of the enormous pile of gold plates he was bearing. Lorenzo hastily averted his face but the soldier hurried by him without giving him so much as a glance.

Dio, the floor was quaking beneath his boots. Each step drained a little more of Lorenzo's strength, and by the time he reached the treasury door his limbs were shaking uncontrollably.

"It has to be here somewhere. His Grace said we were to be sure to bring it to him." A powerfully built man across the huge room was pushing aside heavy trunks filled with jewels and plates. "Search harder. It's a plain mahogany chest."

Corella, Lorenzo thought, as he stared at the bravo's grim expression. Relief flooded him as he realized he could not make out the features of either Corella or the other two soldiers in the chamber. There were only a few candles scattered about the enormous room and, if Lorenzo couldn't see Corella and his men clearly, then he must be equally cloaked by the gloom.

He stepped deeper into the shadow to the left of the door and bent over as if searching among the trunks and coffers as the other two guards were doing. His head started to swim and he clutched desperately at a large trunk until his vision cleared.

"There it is!" Corella pointed to the mahogany chest half hidden behind a five-foot golden vase on which a depiction of the Last Supper had been sculpted. "Take it."

As Lorenzo straightened and moved quickly forward, a short, stocky soldier also headed for the chest from the opposite corner of the room.

Mother of God, Lorenzo thought. He could scarcely walk and now he was being forced to run races!

Lorenzo reached the chest first, snatched it up, whirled, and started toward the door.

"Wait!"

Lorenzo froze, keeping his back toward Corella.

"Perhaps we can pour some of these ducats into the chest. We must make every trip count. Open it and see if there's room."

Lorenzo set the chest on the floor, unfastened the latch, and opened the lid. The emerald eyes of the Wind Dancer twinkled up at him as if in amusement at his predicament.

"No room," he said hoarsely. He slammed the lid shut, his fingers fumbling as he fastened it.

He picked up the chest and staggered toward the door.

"Is it so heavy? If you drop it, I'll lop off your *coglios, stupido*."

"Heavy," Lorenzo muttered as he weaved out of the room. Perspiration beaded his forehead and he could feel the bile rising in his throat. The few steps remaining to the turn in the hall might just as well have been a mile.

He wasn't going to make it.

He couldn't make it.

He made it!

He felt himself jerked around the turn in the corridor and the chest plucked from his hands.

"*Santa Maria*, you're stubborn." Luigi tucked the chest beneath his right arm as his left arm encircled Lorenzo's waist. "Why couldn't you give up?" He walked Lorenzo down the hall. "Is it because you wish to make my life even more miserable than it is already?"

"You said you were going to leave."

"I decided I was in no hurry. I needed to rest after hauling your scrawny carcass across Rome."

"I see." Lorenzo smiled. "How fortunate for me. Could you loose your grip around my middle? You're cracking my ribs. I haven't been held so tightly by a man since my childhood in Naples. Are you sure you have no romantic inclinations toward the male sex?"

"For that insult I should loose you and let you sprawl at my feet." Luigi added quickly, "And I'd do it, but then I'd have to go to the bother of picking you up again. If I left you here, someone would remember that I recommended you for the pope's kitchen and I'd end up in the dungeons of Sant' Angelo too. It's certainly not that I care what happens to you."

"Certainly not." The moist night air felt good on Lorenzo's face, and he breathed deeply as they left the confines of the palace behind them. "I'd never make that mistake in judgment."

"That is good." Luigi's powerful arm tightened around Lorenzo's waist to support more of his weight. "A man would have to be a dunce to care what happens to a madman who'd risk having his neck twisted off by Corella just to steal from the papal treasury. What's in this chest to make you take such a chance?"

Lorenzo saw the dull, gleaming waters of the Tiber directly ahead and exultation surged through him as he realized there was no sound of pursuit behind.

Per Dio, they had done it!

"There's a gift in the chest. A special gift for a very good friend."

Twenty-One

Do you think he will come?" Sanchia leaned over the rail, her gaze anxiously searching the crowd milling on the dock below. "I don't see him and it's almost time to sail."

Lion gently pulled the hood of the laurel green cloak over Sanchia's shining auburn tresses. "Lorenzo always keeps his promises. He'll be here."

"But what if—there he is!" She pointed to the familiar elegant figure moving lithely through the crowd. "He looks well. I was afraid the illness might have lingered."

"You worry about everything these days," Lion said indulgently. "He wrote months ago that he had recovered his health."

"Then why did he stay in Rome? Alexander was dead and he could not touch Borgia after the duke doubled his guards. I thought he might be ill and not wishing to worry—he's carrying something." Sanchia's eyes widened as she recognized the familiar mahogany chest. "Dear lord, it's—"

"The Wind Dancer." Lion's expression lit with excitement. "*Santa Maria*, he has the Wind Dancer!"

Pain knifed through Sanchia as memories swelled. The dungeon at Solinari, Piero's solemn, wondering eyes as he had gazed at the statue in the salon, the Pegasus staring sightlessly at Caterina and herself as they wept for their dead, Damari tying the Wind Dancer on his saddle as he unfolded horror after horror to Sanchia. Her hands clutched at the wooden rail with white-knuckled force.

"How in Hades did he manage this?" Lion turned and saw her face. "What's wrong? Are you ill again?"

"No." She tried to smile. "It brings back so many memories. Mandara . . ."

Lion's hand covered her own on the rail. "Mandara's gone. We're starting a new life, *cara*. The memories will fade."

"*Dio*, married over four months and still holding hands and cooing like turtledoves."

They turned to see Lorenzo striding up the gangplank. "It's enough to make me shudder." He came toward them, a smile on his face. "Or, as my friend Luigi would say more crudely, vomit."

"You are well?" Sanchia asked.

Lorenzo put the chest containing the Wind Dancer down on the deck. "Very well." His gaze searched her face. "And you, my dear Sanchia, are blooming."

"I'm with child," she said simply.

"Ah, that is good. Renewal." He turned to Lion. "I've brought you a present."

"I see you have." Lion clapped him on the shoulder. "*Madre di Dio*, how on earth did you get it?"

"On the night Alexander died I went back to the Vatican." Lorenzo grimaced. "Or rather Luigi carried me to the palace, for I was not yet myself. Michelotto Corella demanded the keys to the pope's private treasury the moment Alexander breathed his last and made off with a hundred thousand ducats, together with a fortune in plates and gems, and took them to his master, who was too ill to accompany him. I managed to appropriate the Wind Dancer while Corella was stealing whatever else his men could carry." A pleased smile touched Lorenzo's lips. "I understand Borgia was most irate with Corella for failing to bring him the statue with the other treasures."

"I imagine he *was* a trifle upset," Lion said dryly. "Borgia needs every asset he has since the papal monies have been cut off. I've heard he scrambled desperately to save his power even to striking a bargain with the new Pope Julius."

Lorenzo nodded. "I've been watching with great interest as he starts his slide to hell. You know that Julius has now imprisoned Borgia until he agrees to give the passwords that will cause his commanders to yield Borgia's strongholds in the Romagna?"

"You think he will do it?"

"Eventually. But that doesn't mean Borgia will be defeated. He's a brilliant man with a will of iron. It takes a great deal to rend iron, but I now have the time to make his destruction complete." He paused. "I've come to say farewell."

Lion stiffened. "It was planned that you come with us. You've changed your mind?"

"Borgia still lives."

"But you said yourself he's losing power."

"His destruction is not certain. I must make sure." Lorenzo met Lion's gaze. "Damari's death was too easy."

"I assure you he didn't find it so."

"He didn't have time to see everything he had built falling away from him. I'll make sure Borgia will be aware of every step of his downfall."

"Where do you go? Rome?"

"Perhaps." Lorenzo gazed down at the crowds on the dock. "Though I've been thinking about returning to Mandara."

"Mandara!" Sanchia gazed at him in bewilderment. "But there's nothing there."

"The vineyard is still there, and the winery. I could build a small cottage."

Lion shook his head. "You? In the country?"

"There's an order and symmetry to the growing of the grapes that has a certain appeal for me. The process is much like the bringing to harvest of any bold endeavor." Lorenzo started to turn away. "The vineyard's as good a place as any to watch and wait for opportunity to ripen."

"Wait." Lion gestured to the chest on the deck. "Take this with you."

Shock jarred Sanchia. "Lion . . ."

Lorenzo swung back to face him. "You don't want it?"

"Of course he wants it." Sanchia tried to steady her voice. "He loves the Wind Dancer."

"But I also love my wife."

"It's part of your family," Sanchia said. "You told me—" She drew a deep breath. "I would not deprive you of it."

A tender smile lit his face. "It's my choice, Sanchia. It would please me if you could feel toward the Wind Dancer as I do, but you cannot." He paused. "And I will not have it always near to remind you of what you suffered. You told me once that what I felt for you didn't compare with what I felt for the Wind Dancer. Perhaps you might have been right then, but you'd be wrong in saying it now."

"No, it will be fine. I can—"

"Hush, *cara mia*." His left hand reached up to gently smooth the silver lock at her temple. "It's settled. There's a legend that says the Wind Dancer always returns to my family. Its return now won't be by my will." He turned back to Lorenzo. "The Wind Dancer is yours, if you will accept it."

"I will accept it."

"I wasn't sure you'd want it." Lion smiled crookedly. "I seem to remember your saying you believed it was a siren luring men to destruction. After Mandara, I thought your belief would be doubly reinforced."

"I've changed my mind." Lorenzo gazed thoughtfully down at the chest. "It wasn't really the Wind Dancer that caused the destruction of Mandara. It was the ambition and greed of men. Damari and Cesare's ambition and Alexander's greed. Together the three of them might have conquered all of Europe. But in a convoluted fashion, it was the Wind Dancer that put a halt to all their plans." He stooped and picked up the chest. "I promise I'll find a good use for it."

"Lorenzo." Lion took an impulsive step forward. "Come with us."

Lorenzo shook his head. "You don't need me. Perhaps I'll come to visit you someday so that I may learn how fortunate I am to be free of the chains of domestic bliss."

"You will be welcome." Lion's voice was husky. "Always."

"Lion, you grow maudlin," Lorenzo said mockingly. "I must leave before you burst into tears and—"

"I would do so, if it would make you come with us," Lion said simply.

The smile faded from Lorenzo's face. "That was a foul blow. You . . . unman me."

"I love you well."

"Another blow." A sudden warm smile lit Lorenzo's face. "Farewell, my friend." He turned and strode away from them.

"Stop him." Sanchia clutched at Lion's arm. "Don't let him leave like this."

"I cannot stop him." Lion's eyes glittered moistly as he watched Lorenzo stride down the deck. "He's made his choice."

"And you're too honorable to try to make him waver in it." Sanchia's tone was exasperated. "You love him. He belongs to you. Have you not lost enough people who belong to you?"

"This is different. It's his right to decide."

"It's different only because you have the chance to claim him again." She saw the stubbornness in his expression and grew impatient. "If you'll not do it, then I will. I will not lose him too." She took a step forward. "Lorenzo!"

He looked over his shoulder.

"If you will not come now, promise you'll come when you finish what you have to do."

"Perhaps." He turned away again.

"Not perhaps. We *do* have need of you. Lion has a fancy to build me a fine castle. You know I have no training to run such an establishment. You must teach me."

"You will learn by yourself." He continued to walk away from them.

"It's going to have the finest rose garden in all of France. I'll need your help in planting it."

His stride faltered for an instant and then he continued walking.

"If our child is a boy, we'll call him Lorenzo."

"God help him."

"No, *you* must help him."

Lorenzo started down the gangplank.

"And if the child is a girl, we'll call her Caterina."

He stopped on the gangplank, the line of his spine suddenly rigid. It was a moment before he turned to face them. "Ah, Sanchia, I always did say you were a clever urchin."

His gaze was a warm caress, embracing them both Then he turned and strode down the gangplank to be lost from sight a moment later in the crowd on the dock.

"Oh, Lion," Sanchia whispered. "Will we ever see him again?"

Lion's arms went around her from behind and drew her back against him. "I don't know." His lips gently brushed her temple. "You did your best."

"Because I love him, too."

They stood watching, still hoping he would return or that they might have a last glimpse of him. They watched even after the gangplank had been raised . . . even as the ship put out to sea.

"The breeze is cold," Lion said. "You should go to the cabin."

It was cold, she thought. The sky was as leaden gray as the sea, and the wind had a sharp bite to it. Not a promising day to start a journey.

"Soon. I want to stand here until I can no longer see the land. It seems strange to realize I may never return."

"Does that thought make you sad?"

"No." She hesitated. "Yes. I don't know." She nestled back against him. "My feelings change from moment to moment. Only one thing is certain. I want to be with you. All the rest will fall into place."

The coastline was barely visible now and she had to strain her eyes to see it. Soon it would be gone and they would sail into the unknown.

Dragons waited in the unknown, Lion had said on that night they had sailed toward Genoa.

Well, she and Lion were strong enough to defeat any dragon who dared hurl his flames at them. There might be struggles ahead in that unknown, but there would also be great rewards.

"You're very quiet," Lion said. "What are you thinking, *cara*?"

"Of dragons." She straightened and squared her shoulders as she turned to smile into his eyes. "And of splendor."

Epilogue

THE BUDDING

On April 12, 1504, the major strongholds of Borgia's forces in the Romagna were yielded to Pope Julius, and Borgia was released from his imprisonment. People expected Duke Valentino to flee immediately to his old friend and comrade in arms, King Louis XII of France, but for some mysterious reason, instead he sailed south to Naples, then in the hands of Spain.

On May 26, 1504, the Spanish forces in Naples arrested Borgia. They sent him by galley to be imprisoned at the Castle of Seville and later at the fortress of Medina del Campo.

October 23, 1504
The Vineyard, Mandara

"There's a messenger waiting for you in the stable yard," Luigi said sourly. "I suppose this means you'll let my dinner get cold."

"Not necessarily." Lorenzo pushed his chair back from the desk and strode across the room.

"I'll not keep it hot for you," Luigi called after him. "I'll throw it to the pigs."

"We have no pigs," Lorenzo shouted back at him.

"And whose fault is that? I've told you that we should have pigs. If you will buy no pigs, how can I make pork dishes? Thanks to your miserliness I'll soon forget all my skills."

Lorenzo stepped onto the stoop of the cottage and accepted a folded and sealed piece of parchment from a freckle-faced messenger who was little more than a boy.

"Dismount and come inside and refresh yourself."

The young man quickly shook his head. "I have orders to wait for an immediate reply, Messer."

Lorenzo broke the seal and opened out the fine leaf. Unsigned, the message consisted of only one line of script.

Is it enough?

"I'll return in a moment." Lorenzo wheeled and went inside the house to his desk. On the bottom of the letter he scrawled in bold, decisive script.

It is not enough.

He returned to hand the parchment to the messenger.

He did not bother to watch the young man's departure as he closed the door of the cottage.

THE FLOWERING

After Queen Isabella's death, King Ferdinand of Spain decided it would be a brilliant move to release Borgia and take advantage of his military acumen to make him his generalissimo in Italy. However, fate once again intervened to strike down Borgia's ambitions. The Castle Medina del Campo in which he was imprisoned was in Castile, and under the control of Ferdinand's daughter, Juana. There appeared to be no reason for her to turn on Borgia with such venom, but she did. On the day Ferdinand asked for the prisoner to be released, she had Cesare indicted on charges that he had conspired in the deaths of his brother, The Duke of Gandia, and Alfonso of Bisceglie, his brother-in-law. On September 4, 1506, Ferdinand finally abandoned his efforts to obtain Cesare's freedom and set sail for Naples without him.

October 15, 1506
The Vineyard, Mandara

The messenger from whom Lorenzo took the letter this time was not a boy, but a man in his prime who accepted a cup of mulled wine from a grudging Luigi while Lorenzo broke the seal and scanned the contents of the dispatch.

"Wait here." Lorenzo went into the cottage and straight to his desk. The terse message he had received was exactly what he had expected.

Enough?

The answer Lorenzo scrawled on the bottom of the letter was almost as brief.

Not enough.

He strode back out into the stable yard, gave the letter to the liveried messenger, and sent him on his way.

THE VINTAGE

Six weeks after Ferdinand sailed for Naples, Cesare Borgia escaped from the Medina del Campo and fled to Pampeluna, the capital city of his wife's brother Jean D'Albret, the king of Navarre. His brother-in-law welcomed him with wild enthusiasm, seeing the chance of using Borgia's military genius to further his own ambitions. The king spoke of supplying Borgia with new armies to start him once more on the road to conquest. However, Navarre was very poor, and in desperation Borgia sent an envoy to his sister Lucretia in Italy asking her to speed to him enough of the family art treasures to yield three hundred thousand ducats from their sale. The messenger was arrested on Pope Julius's orders.

Borgia also sent a message to King Louis of France begging him to pay the one hundred thousand ducats owed him as part of his bride Charlotte's dowry and also the sizeable revenues of his dukedom of Valentinois so that he might regain his former power and affluence. King Louis not only refused to pay either sum, he revoked Borgia's title, taking away his dukedom of Valentinois and stripping him of royal arms.

By March 1507 Cesare Borgia at the age of thirty-one was ravaged by the swiftly progressing and debilitating French pox and was without power, money, or land. Shortly after he received word from his steward, Don Jaime de Requesnez, of his loss of Valentinois, Borgia was ordered by the king of Navarre to subdue the rebel lord, Don Juan, count of Beaumont at Viana. Borgia was heading a garrison at Viana when an alarm was sounded that the garrison was being attacked. He jumped out of bed, dressed, and giving no orders to his men, flung himself on a horse and rode alone through the city gates. It was said later that Borgia was screaming and cursing and appeared completely mad. He rode alone into the enemy camp in a ravine nearby and attacked them, still shouting wildly and uttering oaths.

At dawn Borgia's soldiers rode out of the city and soon found Cesare Borgia's naked corpse hacked and pierced with twenty-three bloody, hideous wounds.

April 7, 1507
The Vineyard, Mandara

I grow impatient. What more could you desire? Enough?

Lorenzo's gaze lifted from the letter to the window across from his desk through which the scarred and blackened city walls of Mandara could be seen.

Then, with a faint smile on his lips, he picked up his

pen and scrawled a single word at the bottom of the parchment.

Enough.

Lorenzo strolled down the long, gleaming corridor, his gaze lingering in admiration on the splendid paintings on the wall of the gallery.

The liveried page stopped and looked reproachfully back at him over his shoulder. "Please, Monsieur Vasaro, His Majesty is most anxious."

Lorenzo nodded, but his pace failed to quicken. "His Majesty has many fine paintings. Is that a da Vinci?"

The page nodded. "His Majesty admires Monsieur da Vinci very much indeed. However, there are many more beautiful objects in His Majesty's private apartments."

The page threw open the tall, beautifully paneled doors at the end of the corridor. "Monsieur Vasaro, Your Majesty."

King Louis hurried forward. "*Mon Dieu*, Vasaro, you took your time about it." He stared eagerly at the chest Lorenzo carried. "Is that it?"

Lorenzo nodded as he crossed to a Carrara marble table and set the chest on it. "Yes." He unfastened the chest and opened the lid. "As I promised."

He started to lift the Wind Dancer out, but Louis forestalled him. "No, let me." With reverent care Louis took the Wind Dancer from its velvet nest. "Ah, it's as exquisite as I remembered. I thought perhaps anticipation might be playing tricks with my memory." He cast Lorenzo a resentful glance. "Your obstinacy in this matter did not please me. Three years is a long time to wait."

"For me, also, Your Majesty." Lorenzo smiled. "But a bargain is a bargain."

"You could have relented. You didn't have to have everything to your exact specifications," Louis said peevishly. "I did what you asked. I told Borgia he would not be welcome here and forced him into Spanish hands. That should have been enough for you."

Lorenzo was silent.

"And do you know how difficult it was for my envoy in Juana's court to manipulate her into turning against Borgia? The woman is now tottering on the verge of madness."

"But he managed the task."

"Because I told him I would have his head if he didn't." Louis carried the Wind Dancer across the room and set it on a black marble pedestal. He took a step back, looking at the statue appraisingly. "I had this pedestal carved two years ago for the Wind Dancer. How do you think it looks?"

"Superb. You have exquisite taste, Your Majesty."

Louis was silent for a long time, staring at the statue. "Do you know that the soldiers at Viana who saw Borgia ride out that night think he meant to end his own life?"

"Then he's effectively barred his way to heaven, if he had not done so before."

"You would condemn his soul to hell as you did his body to the grave?"

Lorenzo did not answer.

"When he first came to my court I thought him the most charming, the most brilliant man I had ever met." Louis's gaze remained on the Wind Dancer. "He would have been destroyed even if I hadn't aided you, wouldn't he?"

"Perhaps, but it's not likely."

"You're a hard man." Louis grimaced. "And as sharp and cutting as a Toledo blade. I have use for you in my retinue. What say you to a post at my court?"

Lorenzo shook his head. "I have a fancy to go to Marseilles to visit friends who have recently been blessed with a child."

"A boy?"

Lorenzo shook his head. "A girl. They've named

her Caterina after the child's grandmother and say she resembles her in many ways."

"A pity it was not a boy. They must be disappointed."

Lorenzo smiled. "They don't appear to be."

"You are tired of your vineyard?"

"Let us say, it's time I nurtured something other than grapes. Perhaps I will plant a rose garden."

"You'll be disappointed. There is little profit in flowers."

"We shall see."

Louis took a few more paces back, frowning with dissatisfaction at the statue. "It does not look as well on the pedestal as I thought it would. The pedestal is not worthy of it. The Wind Dancer overshadows everything around it."

"So it does."

Louis fell silent again before bursting out with sudden defensiveness, "I did only what was for the best in destroying Borgia. It's only right and proper the Wind Dancer should be here at the royal court of France. All of the Italian city-states are fading in power, but France is beginning to shine like the sun. The Wind Dancer should belong to such a nation. Do you not agree, Vasaro?"

Lorenzo gazed at the statue and a curious smile touched his lips. "Yes, Your Majesty, I believe that France is now exactly the right place for the Wind Dancer."

An errant beam of sunlight streaming through the long windows surrounded the Wind Dancer in an aura of radiance, kindling the emerald eyes to brilliant life and striking the parted lips of the Pegasus at an angle.

And, for the briefest instant, the Wind Dancer seemed to smile.

AN AFTERWORD
FROM THE AUTHOR

I have interwoven fiction and fact so closely in *The Wind Dancer* that I believe clarification may be in order.

The historical customs, costumes, and political events of the day are as accurate as my research could make them.

Actually the black death devastated Europe's population during the fourteenth century, but there were still isolated outbreaks of plague during the fifteenth and sixteenth centuries.

As for the Borgias, the brilliance, greed, brutality, and ruthlessness of Pope Alexander and his son, Cesare, are well documented. Although there is no record of their sanctioning such an atrocity as occurred at Mandara, it's certainly not beyond the realm of possibility they would have done so. Both father and son did fall ill on that fateful day in August, and it was indeed assumed they had been poisoned. Many historians still cling stubbornly to the theory of attempted assassination, while others believe the Borgias succumbed to malaria after being bitten by mosquitoes while dining al fresco with Cardinal Adriano Corneto at his vineyards. Medical knowledge and records were so scanty at the time that neither claim can be substantiated.

Cesare Borgia's bravo, Michelotto Corella, did raid the treasury on the night of the pope's death. Alexander's apartments in the Torre Borgia were ransacked by his valets, and his body lay unattended all through the night. It's entirely possible that someone could have infiltrated the Vatican during that chaotic period.

The oleander is as deadly as I've indicated, and it did grow in Italy during the period of the Renaissance. Though, as Lorenzo says, the poisoners of the day were principally bunglers and lacking in skill, a master assassin such as Lorenzo Vasaro might well have discovered and used the plant to his advantage.

So much for fact.

Could the fictional portions of *The Wind Dancer* really have happened?

The Renaissance was an age of velvet and armor, of abject poverty and untold wealth, of plague and assassination, of saints and sinners, of Michelangelo and Machiavelli. It was a time when the world was being reborn and boldly shaped to fit the needs of the men and women strong enough to conquer and hold it.

Of course this story could have happened.

Storm Winds

ONE

The emerald eyes of the golden horse looked down at her, as if he knew her every hope, her every sorrow, Juliette thought. Lips parted in a smile of fierce joy, filigree wings folded back against his body, the Pegasus stood on a tall marble pedestal in the gallery, deserted now. Juliette could hear the tinkling music of a clavichord and women singing, but she paid no attention to anything except the beautiful golden horse.

She had caught glimpses of herself in the seventeen mirrors gracing the long gallery as she'd dashed moments ago to the sheltering presence of the Pegasus. How helpless and stupid she looked with tears running down her face, she thought.

She hated to cry as much as she hated to feel helpless. Marguerite, her nurse, liked to see her cry, Juliette had realized recently. When the old woman goaded and tormented until she succeeded in making her break down and weep, she seemed to Juliette to puff up with satisfaction as if those childish tears somehow watered and nourished her. Someday, Juliette vowed, when she was a woman grown like her mother and Marguerite, she would never let anyone see her this helpless or frightened.

She ducked behind the tall pedestal, gathering her nightgown close to her shivering body and crouched on the floor, trying to hide in the shadows. Her breath coming in harsh sobs, she cradled a precious brown clay pot against her chest. She prayed Marguerite wouldn't find her and soon would stop searching. Then she would run into the garden and find a safe hiding place for the pot in the vast beds of flowers.

She could see only a narrow slice of the long hall glittering with mirrors, the candles shimmering starlike in crystal chandeliers. Juliette had eluded Marguerite in the corridors below, but an army of footmen and at least three Swiss guards would be able to set her nurse on the right path if she stopped to inquire. She peeped cautiously around the pedestal and sighed with relief.

No Marguerite.

"I tell you I *did* see something, Axel." A woman's light voice, very close, faintly impatient. "I looked up from the clavichord and I saw . . . I don't know . . . something."

Juliette tensed, pressing back against the wall and holding her breath.

"I would not think of arguing with you." A man's amused voice. "I'm sure those blue eyes are as keen as they are beautiful. Perhaps it was a servant."

"No, it was much closer to the floor."

"A pup? God knows your court seems to abound with them and none of them worth a franc in the hunting field."

A pair of white satin shoes, diamond buckles gleaming in the candlelight, appeared in Juliette's line of vision. Her gaze traveled from the gleaming buckles to the hem of enormously wide azure satin skirts decorated with square-cut sapphires set in circlets of violets.

"It was just a glimpse, but I know— Well, what have we here?"

Sparkling blue eyes peered down into the shadows at her. The lady knelt in a flurry of satin skirts. "Here's your puppy, Axel. It's a child."

Wild despair tore through Juliette. It was clear she had been found by a lady of the court. The rich gown and stylish white wig were so like her mother's. This woman would be bound to find her mother, Juliette thought desperately. She braced herself, the muscles of her calves tensing to spring, her hands clutching the clay pot so tightly her knuckles turned white.

"A very small child." The lady reached forward and gently touched Juliette's wet cheek. "What are you doing here, *ma petite*? It's almost midnight and little girls should be in bed."

Juliette drew back, huddling against the wall.

"Don't be frightened." The lady drew closer. "I have a little girl too. My Marie Thérèse is only a year old, but later perhaps you and she could play together when . . ." The words trailed off as the lady looked down at her damp fingertips that had caressed Juliette's cheek. "Mother of God, there's blood on my fingers, Axel. The child's hurt. Give me your handkerchief."

"Bring her out and let's have a look at her." The man came into view, tall, handsomely dressed in a brilliant emerald-green coat. He handed the lady a spotless lace-trimmed handkerchief and knelt beside her.

"Come out, *ma petite*." The lady held out her arms to Juliette. "No one is going to hurt you."

Hurt? Juliette didn't care about the pain. She was used to pain and it was nothing compared to the disaster facing her now.

"What's your name?" The lady's hand gently pushed back the riotous dark curls from Juliette's forehead. The touch was so tender Juliette wanted to lean into it.

"Juliette," she whispered.

"A pretty name for a pretty little girl."

"I'm not pretty."

"No?"

"My nose turns up and my mouth is too big."

"Well, I think you're pretty. You have exquisite skin and lovely brown eyes. You are such a big girl, Juliette."

"Almost seven."

"A great age." The lady dabbed at Juliette's lip with the handkerchief. "Your lip is bleeding. Did someone hurt you?"

Juliette looked away. "No, I fell against the door."

"What door?"

"I . . . don't remember." Juliette had learned a long time before that all bruises and cuts must be explained away in this fashion. Why was the lady so interested in her? In Juliette's experience, adults accepted any untruth that made them most comfortable.

"Never mind." The lady held out her arms again. "Won't you come out from behind the Wind Dancer and let me hold you? I like children. Nothing will happen to you, I promise."

The lady's arms were as white and plump and well-formed as those on the statues of the goddesses in the garden, although they were not as beautiful as the golden wings of the Pegasus, Juliette thought. Suddenly, though, she was drawn to those open arms as she had been drawn to the statue the lady had called the Wind Dancer.

She inched out of the shadows.

"That's right." The lady drew Juliette into her embrace. The scent of violets, roses, and perfumed powder surrounded Juliette. Her mother sometimes smelled of violets, Juliette thought wistfully. If she closed her eyes, perhaps she could pretend this lady holding her with such tenderness was her mother. She would run away soon but it would do no harm to stay for just another moment.

"What a sweet, shy child you are."

Juliette knew she was not a sweet child. Marguerite always called her an obstinate spawn of the devil. The lady would find out her mistake soon enough and push Juliette away. If her own mother considered her too wicked to be pleasing, she would not be able to deceive a stranger for any length of time.

A mirrored door next to the statue was thrown open, and a burst of laughter and music entered the gallery along with a woman.

"Your Majesty, we miss your lovely voice in our harmonies."

Her mother!

Juliette stiffened and burrowed her head in the lady's powdered shoulder.

"In a moment, Celeste. We have a small problem here."

"May I help? What pro—Juliette!"

"You know this child?" The lady stood up, still holding Juliette by the hand. "It seems she's in great distress."

"Juliette is my daughter." Celeste de Clement came forward, her exquisitely shaped mouth tight with displeasure. "Forgive her, Your Majesty, she's not usually so naughty and uncontrolled. I'll send for her nurse who must be searching the palace for her."

"I'll go, Your Majesty." The handsome man rose to his feet, smiled, bowed. "It's my pleasure to serve you." He paused. "Always."

"Thank you, Count Fersen." A faint smile on her lips, the lady's gaze followed him as he turned and strode down the hall. When he vanished from sight she looked again at Juliette. "I think we must find out why she's so unhappy, Celeste. Why were you hiding, child?"

Your Majesty. This lady was the *queen?* Juliette swallowed. "Marguerite said she was going to take away my paints."

Marie Antoinette looked down at her. "Paints?"

Juliette held out her clay pot. "I have to have my paints. She cannot take them away." Tears of helplessness and anger began to well in her eyes again. "I won't let her do it. I'll run away and hide them where she'll never find them."

"Hush." Her mother's voice was harsh. "Have you not shamed me enough with your behavior?" She turned to the queen. "My father gave her an artist's brush and that pot of red paint when we visited him in Andorra and the child does nothing but cover every scrap of parchment in our apartments with her daubs. I told Marguerite to take them away from her so she wouldn't disfigure your beautiful walls."

"I'd never do that." Juliette looked pleadingly at Marie Antoinette. "I want to paint splendid pictures. I wouldn't waste my paint on your walls."

Marie Antoinette burst into laughter. "That relieves me exceedingly."

"She's done nothing but wander about the palace, gazing at the paintings and sculptures, since we arrived here at Versailles a fortnight ago." A veil of tears turned Celeste's blue-violet eyes moistly brilliant. "I know she's unruly, but since my dear Henri was taken from me I fear I've neglected her supervision. It's not easy being a woman alone in the world."

The queen's expression softened as she looked at Celeste. "I, too, am a woman who knows the trials of being a mother." She reached out and took Celeste's hand in both her own and raised it to her cheek. "We'll have to endeavor to make things easier for you, my dear Celeste."

"Your Majesty is too kind." Celeste smiled sweetly through her tears. "Indeed, it's enough reward to be allowed to be close to you. After all, I'm not even of French birth. I'd heard Spaniards were not popular at Versailles, and I never imagined when I came to court that the honor of being near you would be accorded me."

How did her mother manage to keep the tears misting her eyes? Why did they not spill over and run down her cheeks? Juliette had noticed this many times before and it baffled her.

"I was a foreigner also when I came here as a bride from Austria. Both you and I became French when we married." Marie Antoinette pressed an affectionate kiss on Celeste's palm. "It is but one more bond between us. Our court is infinitely richer for your enchanting presence, Celeste. We would have been devastated if you'd chosen to stay in that horrid château in Normandy."

The two women exchanged a glance of intimate

understanding before the queen reluctantly released Celeste's hand.

"And now I think we must do something to dry your daughter's tears." She dropped to her knees again, grasped Juliette's shoulders, staring at her with mock sternness. "I do think such a passionate love for beauty should be rewarded, but your mother is right. A paintbrush should be allowed in the hands of a child only under a careful eye. I shall have my friend, Elizabeth Vigée Le Brun, give you lessons. She's a splendid artist and very kind as well."

Juliette gazed at the queen in disbelief. "I may keep my paint?"

"Well, you could hardly create pictures without it. I'll send you more paints and canvases and I'm sure someday you shall paint many splendid treasures for me." The queen ruffled Juliette's curls. "But you must meet one condition."

Disappointment made Juliette almost ill. It wasn't going to happen. She should have known the queen was toying with her. Grown-ups seldom told the truth to children. Why should this lady be any different?

"Don't look so tragic." Marie Antoinette chuckled. "I ask only that you promise to be my friend."

Juliette went still. "Your . . . friend?"

"Is that so impossible a task?"

"No!" Her heart was pounding so hard she could scarcely breathe. Paints, canvas, a friend. It was too much. For a brief moment she felt as if she were soaring up to the high-arched ceiling. Quickly she hurtled back to earth. "You probably won't want to be my friend for long."

"Why not?"

"I say things people don't like."

"Why do you say things people don't like when you know they'll be upset with you?"

"Because it's stupid to tell lies." Juliette met the queen's gaze, and her voice held desperation as she continued. "But I'll try to be whatever you want me to be. I'll be so good, I promise."

"Shh, I have no desire for anything but your

honesty." The queen's voice was suddenly weary. "There's little enough of that commodity in Versailles."

"Ah, here's Marguerite." Celeste's voice sounded relieved. But Juliette winced at the sight of the tall, black-gowned figure of Marguerite Duclos, escorted by the handsome man the queen had called Axel.

Celeste took Juliette's hand. "My dear child must be put to bed. I'm sure your kindness has excited her until it will be impossible for her to sleep. I shall return as quickly as possible, Your Majesty."

"Do hurry." Marie Antoinette patted Juliette's cheek but her gaze was already fixed dreamily on Axel. "I think we shall play a game of backgammon before we retire."

"An excellent idea." Celeste pulled Juliette the few paces to where Marguerite waited at a respectful distance from the queen.

Her mother was still angry, Juliette realized. Yet she was so full of joy, she could not worry. Paints, canvas, and a friend!

"You incompetent fool," Celeste whispered to Marguerite as she released Juliette into the nurse's custody. "If you cannot raise my daughter to display some semblance of meekness and decorum, I shall send you back to Andorra and find someone who can do so."

Marguerite's thin, sallow face flushed in distress. "I do my best. She's not the sweet girl you were as a child," she mumbled. "It was those paints. She was like a wild thing when I tried to take them away from her."

"Well, now you must let her keep them until the queen loses interest in her. If you'd done your duty well, I would not have been put to this embarrassment."

"The queen didn't appear angry. I could not—"

"I want no excuses. Punish the child," Celeste ordered as she whirled on her heel in a fury of violet brocade. "And keep her away from the queen. It's fortunate Count Fersen was here tonight to put Her Majesty in a felicitous mood. I'll not have Juliette with her bold ways spoil my chances of becoming the queen's favorite. I have enough to contend with. That mewling Princess de Lambelle preys on the queen's sympathy at every turn." She paused, glaring at Juliette. "You're staring at me again. Why do you always stare at me?"

Juliette averted her gaze. She had displeased her mother again. Usually that knowledge brought an aching sense of loss, but tonight the hurt was less. The queen had not found Juliette either ugly or displeasing.

A brilliant smile lit Celeste's exquisite face as she swept back down the hall toward the queen. "All is well, Your Majesty. How can I thank you for making my little girl so happy?"

Marguerite propelled Juliette forward, her clasp cruelly tight. "Are you satisfied now, you imp from hell? Making your sweet mother unhappy and disturbing the queen of France."

"I didn't disturb her. She liked me. She's my friend."

"She's not your friend. She's the queen."

Juliette was silent, still in a warm, cozy haze of delight. No matter what Marguerite said, the queen *was* her friend. Hadn't she held Juliette in her arms and dried her tears? Hadn't she said she was pretty and sweet? Wasn't she going to have her taught to paint beautiful pictures?

"And do you think your mother will really let you have those nasty paints after you've been so naughty?" Marguerite's lips tightened until they formed a thin line. "You don't deserve gifts."

"She'll let me have the paints whether I deserve them or not. She won't want to displease the queen." Juliette gave a hop and skip to keep up with Marguerite's long stride as they moved quickly down the Hall of Mirrors. Juliette's fascinated gaze clung to their images moving from one of the seventeen mirrors to the next as they walked along the gleaming hall. It surprised her to see how small and unimportant she looked. She certainly did not feel small inside now. She felt every bit as big and important as her mother and Marguerite. How unfair that the mirror did not reflect the change. Marguerite looked much more interesting, Juliette decided. Her black-gowned body was lean and angled like one of the stone gargoyles Juliette had seen on a column of the grand cathedral of Notre Dame. How fortunate she had felt when her mother had instructed the coachman to detour to the cathedral on his way through Paris to Versailles. Perhaps, she could persuade Madame Vigée Le Brun to show her how to paint Marguerite as a gargoyle.

"Your arms are going to be black and blue for a fortnight," Marguerite muttered with satisfaction. "I'll show you that you can't shame me in front of your mother."

Juliette looked down at the long, strong fingers of Marguerite's hand holding her own and felt an instant of fear. She drew a deep breath and quickly suppressed the terror before it overcame her. The pain of the pinching would be over quickly, and all the time she was undergoing it she would be thinking of her paints and canvas and the lessons to come.

But in her very first painting she would most definitely paint Marguerite as a gargoyle.

Ile du Lion, France
June 10, 1787

Jean Marc Andreas strode around the pedestal, studying the statue from every angle. The jewel-encrusted Pegasus was superb.

From its flying mane to the exquisite detail of the gold filigree clouds on which the horse danced, it was a masterful piece of work.

"You've done well, Desedero," Andreas said. "It's perfect."

The sculptor whom some called a mere goldsmith shook his head. "You're wrong, Monsieur. I've failed."

"Nonsense. This copy is identical to the Wind Dancer, is it not?"

"It is as close a copy as could be made, even to the peculiar cut of the facets of the jewels," Desedero said. "I had to journey to India to locate emeralds large and perfect enough to use as the eyes of the Wind Dancer and spent over a year crafting the body of the statue."

"And the inscription engraved on the base?"

Desedero shrugged. "I reproduced the markings with great precision, but since the script is indecipherable that is a minor point, I believe."

"Nothing is minor. My father knows the Wind Dancer in its every detail," Andreas said dryly. "I paid you four million livres to duplicate the Wind Dancer—and I always get my money's worth."

Desedero knew those words to be true. Jean Marc Andreas was a young man, no more than twenty and five, but he had established himself as a formidable force in the world of finance since taking over the reins of the Andreas shipping and banking empire three years before from his ailing father. He was reputed to be both brilliant and ruthless. Desedero had found him exceptionally demanding, yet he did not resent Andreas. Perhaps it was because the young man's commission challenged the artist in him. Certainly Andreas's desperation to please his father was touching. Desedero had loved his own father very much and understood such deep and profound affection. He was much impressed by Jean Marc Andreas's wholehearted zeal for replicating the Wind Dancer to please his ill and aging father.

"I regret to say I do not believe you have gotten your money's worth this time, Monsieur Andreas."

"Don't say such a thing, sir." A muscle jerked in Andreas's jaw. "You have succeeded. *We've* succeeded. My father will never know the difference between this Wind Dancer and the one at Versailles."

Desedero shook his head. "Tell me, have you ever seen the real Wind Dancer?"

"No, I've never visited Versailles."

Desedero's gaze returned to the statue on the pedestal. "I remember vividly the first time I saw it some forty-two years ago. I was only a lad of ten and my father took me to Versailles to see the treasures that were dazzling the world. I saw the Hall of Mirrors." He paused. "And I saw the Wind Dancer. What an experience. When you walked into my studio some year and a half ago with your offer of a commission to create a copy of the Wind Dancer, I could not pass it by. To replicate the Wind Dancer would have been sublime."

"And you've done it."

"You don't understand. Had you ever seen the original, you would know the difference instantly. The Wind Dancer has . . ." He searched for a word. "Presence. One cannot look away from it. It captures, it holds"—he smiled crookedly—"as it's held me for these forty-two years."

"And my father," Andreas whispered. "He saw it once as a young man and has wanted it ever since." He turned away. "And by God, he'll have it. She took everything from him—but he *shall* have the Wind Dancer."

Desedero discreetly ignored the last remark, though he was well aware of the lady to whom Andreas referred. Charlotte, Denis Andreas's wife, Jean Marc's stepmother, had been dead over five years. Still the stories of her greed and treachery were much passed about.

Sighing, Desedero shook his head. "You have only a *copy* of the Wind Dancer to give to your father."

"There's no difference." A hint of desperation colored Andreas's voice. "My father will never see the two statues side by side. He'll think he has the Wind Dancer until the day he—" He broke off, his lips suddenly pinched.

"Your father is worse?" Desedero asked gently.

"Yes, the physicians think he has no more than six months to live. He's begun to cough blood." He tried to smile. "So it's fortunate you have finished the statue and could bring it now to the Ile du Lion. Yes?"

Desedero had an impulse to reach out and touch him in comfort, but he knew Andreas was not a man who could accept such a gesture, so he merely said, "Very fortunate."

"Sit down." Andreas picked up the statue and started toward the door of the salon. "I'll take this to my father in his study. That's where he keeps all the things he treasures most. Then I'll return and tell you how wrong you were about your work."

"I hope I'm wrong," Desedero said with a shrug. "Perhaps only the eye of an artist can perceive the difference." He sat down in the straight chair his patron had indicated and stretched out his short legs. "Don't hurry, Monsieur. You have many beautiful objects here for me to study. Is that a Botticelli on the far wall?"

"Yes. My father purchased it several years ago. He much admires the Italian masters." Andreas moved toward the door, carefully cradling the statue in his arms. "I'll send a servant with wine, Signor Desedero."

The door closed behind him and Desedero leaned back in his chair, gazing blindly at the Botticelli. Perhaps the old man was too ill to detect the fraud being thrust upon him. Whole and well, he would have seen it instantly, Desedero realized, because everything in this house revealed Denis Andreas's exquisite sensitivity and love of beauty. Such a man would have been as helplessly entranced with the Wind Dancer as Desedero always had been. Sometimes his own memories of his first visit to Versailles were bathed in mist from which only the Wind Dancer emerged clearly.

He hoped for Jean Marc Andreas's sake that his father's memories had dimmed along with his sight.

Jean Marc opened the door of the library, and beauty and serenity flowed over him. This room was both haven and treasure house for his father. A fine Savonnerie carpet in delicate shades of rose, ivory, and beige stretched across the highly polished parquet floor, and a Gobelin tapestry depicting the four seasons covered one wall. Splendid furniture crafted by Jacobs and Boulard was placed for beauty—and comfort—in the room. A fragile crystal swan rested on a cupboard of rosewood and Chinese lacquer marquetry. The desk, wrought in mahogany, ebony, and gilded bronze with mother-of-pearl inserts, might have been the focal point of the room if it had not been for the portrait of Charlotte Andreas. It was dramatically framed and placed over a fireplace whose mantel of Pyrenees marble drew the eye.

Denis Andreas always complained of the cold these days and, although it was the end of June, a fire burned in the hearth. He sat in a huge crimson brocade-cushioned armchair, reading before the fire, his slippered feet resting on a matching footstool.

Jean Marc braced himself, then stepped into the room and closed the door. "I've brought you a gift."

His father looked up with a smile that froze on his lips as he looked at the statue in Jean Marc's arms. "I see you have."

Jean Marc strode over to the table beside his father's chair and set the statue carefully on the malachite surface. He could feel tension coiling painfully in his every muscle as his father gazed at the Pegasus. He forced a smile. "Well, do say something, sir. Aren't you pleased with me? It was far from easy to persuade King Louis to part with the statue. Bardot has virtually lived at court this past year waiting for the opportunity to pounce."

"You must have paid a good deal for it." Denis Andreas reached out and touched a filigree wing with a gentle finger.

His father's hands had always been delicate-looking, the hands of an artist, Jean Marc thought. But now they were nearly transparent, the protruding veins poignantly emphasizing their frailty. He quickly looked from those scrawny hands to his father's face. His face was also thin, the cheeks hollowed, but his eyes still held the gentleness and wonder they always had.

"I paid no more than we could afford." Jean Marc sat down on the chair across from his father. "And Louis needed the livres to pay the American war debt." At least, that was true enough. Louis's aid to the American revolutionaries along with his other extravagant expenditures had set France tottering on the edge of bankruptcy. "Where should we put it? I thought a white Carrara marble pedestal by the window. The sunlight shining on the gold and emeralds would make it come alive."

"The Wind Dancer *is* alive," his father said gently. "All beauty lives, Jean Marc."

"By the window then?"

"No."

"Where?"

His father's gaze shifted to Jean Marc's face. "You didn't have to do this." He smiled. "But it fills me with joy that you did."

"What's a few million livres?" Jean Marc asked lightly. "You wanted it."

"No, I have it." Denis Andreas tapped the center of his forehead with his index finger. "Here. I didn't need this splendid imitation, my son."

Jean Marc went still. "Imitation?"

His father looked again at the statue. "A glorious imitation. Who did it? Balzar?"

Jean Marc was silent a moment before he said hoarsely, "Desedero."

"Ah, a magnificent sculptor when working in gold. I'm surprised he accepted the commission."

Frustration and despair rose in Jean Marc until he could scarcely bear it. "He was afraid you would recognize the difference but I felt I had no choice. I offered the king enough to buy a thousand statues, but Bardot reported that Louis wouldn't consider selling the Wind Dancer at any price. According to His Majesty, the queen has a particular fondness for it." His hands closed tightly on the arms of the chair. "But, dammit, it's the *same*."

Denis Andreas shook his head. "It's a very good copy. But, my son, the Wind Dancer is . . ." He shrugged. "I think it has a soul."

"Mother of God, it's only a statue!"

"I can't explain. The Wind Dancer has seen so many centuries pass, seen so many members of our family born into the world, live out their lives . . . and die. Perhaps it has come to be much more than an object, Jean Marc. Perhaps it has become . . . a dream."

"I failed you."

"No." His father shook his head. "It was a splendid gesture, a loving gesture."

"I failed you. It hurt me to know you couldn't have

the one thing you so wished—" Jean Marc broke off and attempted to steady his voice. "I wanted to give something to you, something that you'd always wanted."

"You *have* given me something. Don't you see?"

"I've given you disappointment and chicanery and God knows you've had enough of both in your life." Denis flinched and Jean Marc's lips twisted. "You see, even I hurt you."

"You've always demanded too much of yourself. You've been a good and loyal son." He looked Jean Marc in the eye. "And I've had a good life. I've been fortunate enough to have the means to surround myself with treasures, and I have a son who loves me enough to try to deceive me ever so sweetly." He nodded at the statue. "And now why don't you take that lovely thing out to the salon and find a place to show it to advantage?"

"You don't want it in here?"

Denis slowly shook his head. "Looking at it would disturb the fine and fragile fabric of the dream." His gaze drifted to the portrait of Charlotte Andreas over the fireplace. "You never understood why I did it, did you? You never understood about dreams."

Looking intently at his father, Jean Marc felt pain and sorrow roll over him in a relentless tide. "No, I suppose I didn't."

"That hurt you. It shouldn't." He once again opened the leather-bound volume he had closed when Jean Marc came into the study. "There must always be a balance between the dreamers and the realists. In this world strength may serve a man far better than dreams."

Jean Marc stood up and moved toward the table on which he had set the statue. "I'll just get this out of your way. It's almost time for your medicine. You'll be sure to remember to take it?"

Denis nodded, his gaze on the page of his book. "You must do something about Catherine, Jean Marc."

"Catherine?"

"She's been a joy to me but she's only a child of three and ten. She shouldn't be here when it happens."

Jean Marc opened his mouth to speak, then closed

it abruptly. It was the first time his father had indicated he knew the end was near.

"Please do something about our Catherine, Jean Marc."

"I will. I promise you," Jean Marc said thickly.

"Good." Denis looked up. "I'm reading Sanchia's journal, about old Lorenzo Vasaro and his Caterina."

"Again?" Jean Marc picked up the statue and carried it toward the door. "You must have read those old family journals a hundred times."

"More. I never tire of them." His father paused and smiled. "Ah, our ancestor believed in dreams, my son."

With effort Jean Marc smiled. "Like you." He opened the door. "I don't have to return to Marseilles until evening. Would you like to have dinner on the terrace? The fresh air and sunshine will be good for you."

But Denis was once more deeply absorbed in the journal and didn't answer.

Jean Marc closed the door and stood a moment, fighting the agony he felt. His father's last remarks shouldn't have hurt him, for they were true. He was no dreamer; he was a man of action.

His hand clenched on the base of the statue. Then he squared his shoulders. The pain was fading. Just as he had known it would. Just as it had so many times before. He strode across the wide foyer and threw open the door to the salon.

Desedero's gaze was searching. "He knew?"

"Yes." Jean Marc set the statue back on the pedestal. "I'll have my agent in Marseilles give you a letter of credit to our bank in Venice for the remainder of the money I owe you."

"I don't wish any more money," Desedero said. "I cheated you."

"Nonsense. You did what you were paid to do." Jean Marc's smile was filled with irony. "You were given my livres to create a statue, not a dream."

"Ah, yes." Desedero nodded in understanding. "The dream . . ."

"Well, I'm only a man of business who doesn't

understand these idealistic vagaries. It appears a duplicate won't do, so I will have to get the Wind Dancer for
him."

"What will you do?"

"What I should have done in the beginning. Go to
Versailles myself and find a way to persuade the queen
to sell the Wind Dancer. I didn't want to leave my father
when—" He broke off, his hands again slowly clenching.
"I knew he didn't have much time left."

"But how can you expect to succeed when she's
clearly so determined to keep it?" Desedero asked
gently.

"Information." Jean Marc's lips twisted in a cynical
smile. "I'll find out what she most desires and give it to
her in exchange for the statue. I'll take lodgings in an
inn near the palace and before two weeks are gone I'll
know more about the court and Her Majesty than King
Louis does himself, even if I have to bribe every groom
and maid in the palace."

Desedero gestured to the statue on the pedestal.
"And this?"

Jean Marc avoided looking at the Pegasus as he
strode to the door. "I never want to see it again. You
may sell off the jewels and melt it down." He jerked
open the door. "God knows, I may need the additional
gold to tempt Louis into selling the Wind Dancer."

The door slammed behind him.

TWO

"You're spoiling the lad." Marguerite's thin lips pursed as she gazed at Louis Charles's fair head nestled against Juliette's breast. "His nurse won't thank you for this coddling when we get him back to Versailles."

"He's been ill." Juliette's arms tightened protectively around the baby's warm, firm body. Not really a baby any longer, she thought wistfully. The queen's second son was over two, but he still felt endearingly small and silken in her arms. "He deserves a little extra attention. The motion of the coach upsets his stomach."

"Nonsense. The doctor at Fontainebleau pronounced the prince fit for travel."

"That doesn't mean he's completely well again." Juliette glared at Marguerite on the seat across from her. "Only two weeks ago he was running a fever high enough for the queen to fear for his life."

"Measles don't always kill. You had them twice and survived."

Louis Charles stirred and murmured something into Juliette's shoulder.

Juliette looked down, a smile illuminating her face. "Shh, *bébé*, we'll soon have you back with your *maman*. All is well."

"Yes, now that we're returning to Versailles," Marguerite agreed sourly. "So contrary of you to offer to stay with the child at Fontainebleau when the court returned to Versailles. You knew I'd have to stay with you no matter how much your mother needed my services."

Juliette rocked the little boy back and forth, her fingers tangled in his downy, soft curls. It would do no good to argue with Marguerite, she thought wearily. The woman cared for naught but her mother's comfort and welfare and was never happy except in her presence. It didn't matter to her that the queen had been worried to distraction when Louis Charles had fallen ill. Marie Antoinette's baby daughter, Sophie, had died only four months before and Louis Joseph, dauphin and heir to the throne, whose health had always been fragile, was failing rapidly. When Her Majesty's ever-robust youngest son had succumbed to the measles, she had been in despair.

"Put him down on the seat," Marguerite ordered.

Juliette's lips set stubbornly. "He's still not well. Her Majesty said I was to use my own judgment as to his care."

"A flighty chit of fourteen has no business caring for a prince."

"I'm not putting him down." Juliette's lips firmed as she avoided Marguerite's stare and looked out the window of the carriage. She knew silence would serve her better than quarreling, but meekness was never easy for her. Thank the saints they were close to the town of Versailles now and the palace was just a short distance beyond. She would try to ignore Marguerite and think only of the painting in her trunk on the roof of the carriage. Much of the detail on the trees in the work was still to be finished; she could paint sunlight filtering through the top leaves of the trees revealing the naked skeletal spines. It would be an interesting effect, suggesting the lack of truth in the characters of the figures she had painted lolling below the boughs of the trees.

"You always think you know best," Marguerite grumbled. "Ever since you were a child scarcely older than the prince. Do you believe the queen would have trusted you to stay with Louis Charles if the child's nurse had not come down with the sickness? Her Majesty will find you out someday. You may amuse her right now with your drawings and bold tongue, but she's easily bored and will— You're not listening to me."

Juliette shifted her gaze to the thick green shrubbery bordering the bluff on the far side of the road. "No." She wished Marguerite would cease her acid discourse and let her enjoy these moments of holding the little boy in her arms. She had never had anyone of her own to care for, and during the past few weeks she had actually felt as if Louis Charles belonged to her. But his time of recuperation was over now, she thought wistfully, and in only a few hours she would have to return Louis Charles to his mother and the attention of the royal court.

Marguerite's palm cracked against Juliette's cheek.

Juliette's head snapped back, her arms involuntarily loosening about the baby.

"You're not too old to be punished for your insolence." Marguerite smiled with satisfaction at Juliette's stunned expression. "Your mother trusts me to know how to school you in spite of the spoiling Her Majesty gives you."

Juliette's arms quickly tightened again around Louis Charles. She had not expected the slap. She had clearly misjudged the degree of anger and frustration building in Marguerite since she had been commanded to stay with Juliette at Fontainebleau. "Don't ever strike me again while I'm holding the boy." She tried to keep her voice from shaking with anger. "I could have hurt him badly if you'd caused me to drop him."

"You're giving me orders?"

"I think the queen would be interested to know the reason if Louis Charles suffered any harm, don't you?"

Marguerite's baleful gaze sidled away from Juliette's stare. "You'll soon not be able to hide behind the prince. You never would have gotten so out of hand if your mother hadn't required my services."

"I'm not hiding from—"

A horse neighed in agony.

The coach lurched and shuddered to a halt, throwing Juliette to her knees on the floor.

Louis Charles awoke and began to whimper. "Jul . . ."

"What is it?" Marguerite thrust her head out the window of the carriage. "You fool of a coachman, what—"

The blade of a scythe pierced the wood beside her head, burying its curving length through the side of the coach.

Marguerite shrieked and jerked back from the window.

"What's happening?" Crouched on the floor of the coach still, Juliette gazed at the blade. She could hear shouts, metal clashing against metal, the screams of the horses.

A bullet suddenly splintered the wooden frame of the door.

"Farmers. Peasants. Hundreds of them. They're attacking the carriage." Marguerite's voice rose in terror. "They're going to kill me, and it's all your fault. If you hadn't insisted on staying with that brat, I'd be safe at Versailles with your mother."

"Hush." Juliette had to stem the panic rising in her. She had to think. Stories abounded of carriages and châteaus being attacked by the famine-stricken peasants but never a royal carriage accompanied by the Swiss guard. "We'll be safe. They can't overcome the soldiers that—"

"You fool. There are *hundreds* of them."

Juliette crept closer to the window and looked for herself. Not hundreds but certainly too many to assess at one glance. The scene was total confusion. Coarsely dressed men and women on foot battled the mounted uniformed Swiss guard with scythes and pitchforks. Men on horseback garbed in mesh armor were plunging through the melee, striking with swords at the peasants on either side of them. Two of the four horses pulling the coach were lying dead and bloody on the ground.

Black Velvet.

Her gaze was caught and held by the only still, inviolate figure in this scene of blood and death. A tall, lean man wearing a sable velvet cape and polished black knee-boots sat on his horse at the edge of the crowd. The man's dark eyes gazed without expression at the battle.

Another bullet exploded in the wood just above the seat where Juliette had been sitting. She ducked lower, her body covering the sobbing child. If they stayed in the carriage, how long before one of those bullets hit Louis Charles, she wondered desperately. She couldn't stay and wait for it to happen. She had to do something. All the fighting was taking place to the right of the carriage, so the Swiss guard must have kept the mob from surrounding it. The thicket bordering the bluff . . .

Juliette crawled toward the door, clutching Louis Charles tightly.

"Where are you going?" Marguerite asked.

"I'm trying to escape into the woods bordering the bluff." Juliette ripped off the linen kerchief from her gown and tied it around the boy's mouth, muffling his wails. "It's not safe here for Louis Charles."

"Are you mad?"

Juliette opened the door a crack and peered out cautiously. The shrubbery started only a few feet away, and there seemed to be no one in sight.

"Don't go."

"Be silent or come with us. One or the other." Juliette clasped Louis Charles's small body tighter and opened the door wider. She drew a deep breath, leapt from the carriage, and darted across the dusty road and into the shrubbery. Branches lashed her face and clawed at her arms as she pushed through the bushes.

"Come back to the carriage at once! You can't leave me."

Juliette muttered an oath as she bolted through the shrubbery. Even in the cacophony of shouts and clatter of sabers Marguerite's shrill voice carried clearly. If Juliette could hear it, she would be foolish to believe none of the attackers would.

Louis Charles whimpered beneath the gag, and she automatically pressed him closer. Poor baby, he didn't understand any of this madness. Well, she didn't either, but she wouldn't let those murderers harm either the child or herself.

"Stop!"

A sudden chill gripped her and she glanced over her shoulder.

Black Velvet.

The man who had sat watching the battle was now crashing through the underbrush behind her, his cloak flying behind him like the wings of a great bird of prey.

Juliette ran faster, trying desperately to outdistance the man in black.

Tears were running down Louis Charles's cheeks.

She jumped over a hollow log, staggered, and almost fell as she landed in an unseen hollow behind it. She regained her balance and ran on. Pain stitched through her side.

"*Merde,* stop. I mean you no—" The man broke off, cursing.

A glance over her shoulder revealed he had fallen to his knees in the hollow that had almost been her own undoing.

She felt a surge of primitive satisfaction. She hoped the villain had broken his leg. It would serve him well if—

A bullet whistled by her ear, striking the tree next to her.

"The boy. Give me the boy."

The guttural voice came not from behind but ahead of her!

A huge, burly man dressed in ragged trousers and a coarse white tunic stood only a yard in front of her, holding a smoking pistol in his hand. He threw the empty pistol aside and drew a dagger from his belt.

Juliette froze, her gaze on the gleaming blade of the knife.

She couldn't go back toward the man in black. She desperately sought some way to escape.

The branch lying on the path a few feet away!

"Don't hurt me, Monsieur. See, I'm putting the child down." She set Louis Charles on the ground at her feet.

The huge man grunted with satisfaction and took a step forward.

Juliette snatched up the branch and brought it up between the man's legs with all her might.

He screamed, clutching his groin and dropping the knife.

Juliette picked up Louis Charles again and darted past her victim.

Only seconds later she heard the man cursing as he pounded after her. How had the lout recovered so quickly? She knew how disabling a blow to that part of a man's anatomy could be. Only a few months earlier the Duc de Gramont . . . A stream to jump. Her skirts trailed behind her in the water.

Within seconds she heard the splashing of heavy boots in the water.

He was closer!

A meaty hand grasped her shoulder, jerking her to a halt.

"Bitch! Whore!"

She caught the gleam of metal from the corner of her eye as he raised his dagger to plunge it into her back.

Sweet Mary, she was going to die!

The dagger never fell.

She was jerked and whirled away from the peasant's blade with such force she fell to her knees on the ground.

Black Velvet.

She gazed in stunned amazement at the bloody stain spreading on the shoulder of the black velvet cloak worn by the man who had thrust her aside to take the peasant's blade himself.

Pain wrenched the tall, lean man's features into a grimace even as his own dagger plunged into the other man's broad chest.

The burly peasant groaned, then slumped to the ground.

The man in black velvet stood there, swaying, before staggering to lean against a pine tree a few feet away. One hand clutched at his left shoulder from which the dagger still protruded. His olive skin had faded to a sickeningly sallow shade, his lips drawn thin. "My dear Mademoiselle de Clement. May . . . I say." His voice faded. "That . . . you . . . make it damnably hard for a man to . . . rescue you?"

Her eyes widened. "Rescue?"

"I brought reinforcements to help the guard when I learned of the plan to attack the carriage. If you'd stayed in the coach—" His palm clutched blindly at the bark of the tree as his face convulsed with pain. "The battle should be . . . over by now."

"I didn't know what was going on," Juliette whispered. "Whom to trust. Who are you? Where did you come from?"

"Jean Marc . . . Andreas. An inn nearby . . . Inn of the Blind Owl . . ." His gaze shifted to the peasant lying on the ground a few feet away. "Not clever. Boots . . ."

His eyes closed and he slid slowly down the tree trunk in a dead faint.

"Don't argue with me. You must send for the physician in the village and I'll need hot water and clean linen."

Jean Marc opened his eyes to see Juliette de Clement belligerently confronting a large, stout man. Jean Marc dimly recognized him as Monsieur Guilleme, the proprietor of the inn where he had been residing for the last few weeks.

The innkeeper shook his head. "I've no wish to

offend His Majesty by sending for the physician in the village if Monsieur Andreas truly saved the life of the prince. We must wait for the court physician to arrive."

"The palace is too far. Do you wish to be responsible if he dies?"

Why, she was scarcely more than a child, Jean Marc realized hazily. When he had first caught sight of the girl running through the forest his only impression had been of a thin, graceful form, a storm of shining dark brown curls and wide, frightened eyes. Now, although she stood with spine straight, shoulders squared as if to compensate for the fact that the top of her head barely came to the third button on the innkeeper's shirt, it was clear her slim body bespoke only the faintest hint of the maturity to come.

"Can't you see the man's lifeblood is pouring onto your floor?"

Jean Marc shifted and became aware he was being held upright by two soldiers dressed in the uniform of the Swiss guard, both of whom were grinning as they watched the confrontation. "What a truly depressing . . . picture," he whispered. "I devoutly hope . . . you're not referring to myself, Mademoiselle."

Juliette whirled to face Jean Marc, and an expression of profound relief lightened the tension in her face. "You're awake. I was afraid . . ." She turned back to Monsieur Guilleme. "Why do you just stand there? He must have the dagger removed from his shoulder immediately."

Monsieur Guilleme spoke soothingly. "Believe me, sending for the court physician is best. You're too young to realize—"

"I'm not too young to realize you're more afraid for your own skin than for his," Juliette interrupted fiercely. "And I'll not have him bleeding to death while you stand there dithering."

Jean Marc grimaced. "I do wish you'd stop talking about my pending demise. It's not . . . at all comforting."

"Be silent." Juliette glanced back at him, her brown

eyes blazing. "I'm sure speaking is not good for you. You're behaving as foolishly as this innkeeper."

Jean Marc's eyes widened in surprise.

"That's better." She nodded to the two soldiers supporting Jean Marc. "Take him to his chamber. I'll follow as soon as I deal with the innkeeper. And be gentle with him or, by the saints, you'll answer to me."

The soldiers' grins faded and they began to bristle with annoyance as the girl's fierceness turned on them. Christ, in another minute the chit would have the men dropping him in a heap on the floor. He flinched at the thought and asked hastily, "The prince?"

"I told you not to—" She met Jean Marc's gaze and nodded curtly. "He's safe. I sent him on to the palace with my nurse and the captain of the guard. I thought it safer for him."

"Good." Jean Marc's knees sagged and his eyes closed wearily. He let the soldiers bear the brunt of his weight as they half dragged, half carried him toward the stairs.

The next ten minutes proved to be an agony unsurpassed in Jean Marc's experience, and when he was finally lying naked beneath the covers on the wide bed in his chamber he was barely on the edge of awareness.

"You won't die."

He opened his eyes to see Juliette de Clement frowning down at him with a determination that was strangely more comforting than tenderness would have been. "I hope you're right. I have no—"

"No." Her fingers quickly covered his lips and he found the touch infinitely gentle in spite of its firmness. "I told the innkeeper you were bleeding to death only to make him move with some haste. He wouldn't listen to me. He thought me only a stupid child."

"A grave error in judgment."

"You're joking." She gazed curiously at him. "I think you must be a very odd man to joke with a dagger sticking in your shoulder."

Her image wavered before him like the horizon on a hot day. "Only because I find myself in an odd predicament. I'm not at all a heroic man, and yet I'm thrown into a position where I must"—he stopped as the room tilted and then began to darken—"act the hero."

"You do not consider yourself heroic?" Juliette's tone was thoughtful. "I see."

"I wish I could. It's growing fiendishly dark. I believe I'm going to—"

"Go to sleep." Her hand swiftly moved to cover his eyes. "I'll stay and make sure no harm comes to you. You can trust me."

She lied. He could trust no woman, he thought hazily.

But Juliette was not yet a woman, she was still a child. A strong, brave child whose hands were as gentle as her tone was sharp.

Yes, for the moment he could trust Juliette de Clement.

He let go and sank into the waiting darkness.

When he next opened his eyes Juliette was kneeling by the bed. "I was hoping you wouldn't wake up yet," she whispered. "The village physician's here."

"So you . . . won."

"Of course. The man appears even more foppish than the court physician, but I hope he's not a fool." She hesitated. "He's going to pull out the dagger now."

Jean Marc stiffened, his gaze flying across the room. A small, rotund man dressed in a violet brocade coat and wearing an elaborately curled white wig stood by the hearth warming his bejeweled hands before the blaze. "I've no doubt I, too, will be wishing I hadn't regained my senses in a few minutes. I have no fondness for pain."

"Of course not. You'd be a twisted soul if you did." Still kneeling, she frowned thoughtfully. "Listen to me. It will hurt, but there are ways of making the pain less. You must try to think of something else, something beautiful."

The physician straightened his cravat and turned away from the fire. Jean Marc braced himself.

"No, you mustn't tense, that will only make it hurt more." Juliette reached out and took both Jean Marc's hands in her own. "Think of something beautiful. Think of— No, I can't tell you what to think. It has to be your own beautiful picture."

Jean Marc watched the physician stroll toward the bed.

"I'm afraid I can't oblige you," Jean Marc said dryly. "Would you settle for panic? Beauty evades me at the moment."

"It shouldn't. There are a great many beautiful things in the world." Her hands tightened on his. "I always think of how I feel when I'm painting or when I look at the Wind Dancer."

"The Wind Dancer?" Jean Marc's muscles contracted, his gaze shifting from the approaching physician to Juliette's face.

"You're heard of it?" Eagerness illuminated her face. "It's the most beautiful statue in the world. Sometimes I look at it and wonder—" She broke off and fell silent.

"Wonder what?"

"Nothing."

"No, tell me."

"It's just that I don't see how any man or woman could create such beauty," she said simply. "It's more than beauty, it's—"

"Don't tell me." Jean Marc's lips twisted. "The dream."

She nodded. "You *have* seen it. Then perhaps you could think of the Wind Dancer."

He shook his head. "I regret I've never seen your Wind Dancer."

Her face clouded with disappointment.

"Well, Monsieur, I see you're awake." The physician stood beside the bed, smiling cheerfully. "I'm Gaston St. Leure and I'll soon have that dagger out of your shoulder." He stepped closer. "Now, brace yourself while I—"

"No, don't listen to him," Juliette said fiercely. "Look at me."

Jean Marc's gaze was drawn by the sheer intensity of her manner. Her brown eyes were brilliant, sparkling with vitality in her thin face. The high color in her cheeks glowed rose against cream skin, and he could see the tracery of blue veins at her temple pounding with agitation.

"Something beautiful," she said urgently. "What's the most beautiful thing you've ever seen?"

"The sea."

"Then think of the sea." She shifted her grasp so that his hands encircled her wrists. "Hold on to me and tell me about the sea. Tell me how you remember it."

"Storm . . . power . . . The waves dashing against the ship. Gray-blue water shimmering in th—"

Searing, white-hot pain!

"The sea," Juliette whispered, her gaze holding his own. "Remember the sea."

"One more pull," the physician said cheerfully as his grasp tightened on the hilt of the dagger.

"Hush." Juliette's gaze never left Jean Marc's. "Tell me more about the sea."

"In the sunlight on a calm day it's . . . as if we were floating on a giant sapphire."

Sparkling brown eyes holding the pain at bay.

He moistened his dry lips with his tongue. "And when the ship draws near the shore . . ."

Her skin, a rose resting in a bowl of cream, glowing like candlelight.

"The water turns to . . . emerald. You're never certain—"

Pain!

Jean Marc's back arched off the bed as the dagger came free of his flesh.

"That does it." The physician turned away from the bed, the bloody dagger in his hand. "Now I'll get rid of this thing and clean and bandage you."

Jean Marc lay panting, the room whirling about him. He could feel the blood well from the wound and run down his shoulder.

"You'll have to let me go," Juliette said.

Jean Marc stared at her uncomprehendingly.

She tugged, wriggling her wrists to escape his grasp. "I can't help the physician if you don't release me."

He hadn't realized he was still holding her arms. He slowly opened his hands and let her go.

She sat back on her heels. Sighing with relief, she briskly massaged her left wrist. "That's better. The worst is over now."

"Is it?" He felt terribly alone without the girl's touch and wanted to take her hands again and hold on to her. Strange. He couldn't remember when he had ever accepted solace from a woman. "That's comforting to know. I should certainly hate to think the worst was yet to come. I told you I wasn't fashioned of the stuff of heroes."

"Not many men would have borne such pain without crying out."

A faint smile touched his lips as his eyes closed. "Why should I bellow? I was thinking of . . . something beautiful."

Juliette straightened in the chair, arching her spine to rid it of stiffness. The movement did little to ease her discomfort after the hours of sitting immobile. She really should get up and walk about the chamber, but to do so might wake the man lying on the bed. Andreas's sleep had been restless and fitful since the physician had left some hours before. Her glance wandered about the large chamber, seeking something to distract her. The furnishings of the room were quite luxurious for a country inn, and the chamber probably the best Monsieur Guilleme had to offer, but it held little of interest to her.

Her gaze drifted back to Andreas's face, studying it with the same fascination that had caught and held her even in that first moment of panic and danger in the carriage. *Mon Dieu,* how she would love to paint him.

Excitement banished her weariness as she studied his face. How she wished she had a sketching pad. She had given up painting recognizable likenesses of people because she almost always offended her subjects. So she had decided it was not worth the bother to paint faces from life. Yet she knew that here was a man who would not care how cruelly she portrayed him, how brutally honest her brush strokes. He had no need for flattery because he knew exactly what and who he was and cared not a whit what others thought of him.

His bronze face was too long, his cheekbones too high, his lips too well defined, his dark eyes too sharp and determined beneath straight black brows and heavy lids. His features, taken individually, were all wrong, but fit together in perfect harmony to form a whole far more compelling than one that was merely beauty.

What a challenge he would be to paint, to peel off the cynical armor and see what lay beneath, to solve the mysteries beyond those black eyes. He wouldn't readily reveal those secrets, yet, given a little time, she was sure she'd be able to paint the man, not the mask.

But what if she were not given the time? Any deep wound was a hazard, and he might well be taken from her before—

His lids flicked open to reveal those black eyes, totally alert and wide awake. "What are you thinking?"

She was startled and blurted out, "I was hoping you wouldn't die before I could paint you."

"What a truly touching sentiment. Go to bed."

She stiffened and then forced herself to relax. "Don't be foolish. The physician said you might run a fever. Do you think I'd go to such great trouble to save you and then let you die for lack of care?"

He smiled weakly. "My apologies. I'll try to refrain from departing this temporal plane and causing you to waste your time."

"I didn't mean—" She bit her lower lip. "I don't always put things in the correct way. Marguerite says I have the tongue of an asp."

"Who's Marguerite?"

"Marguerite Duclos, my nurse. Well, not really my nurse any longer. She serves my mother more than me."

"And this Marguerite disapproves of your bluntness?"

"Yes." She frowned. "You should go back to sleep and cease this chatter."

"I don't feel like sleeping." His gaze searched her face. "Why don't you amuse me?"

She looked at him in astonishment. "Amuse?"

He started to chuckle and then flinched with pain. "Perhaps you'd better not amuse me. Humor appears exceptionally painful at the moment."

"Since you refuse to sleep, you might as well answer my questions. You said before you fainted that you had learned of the attack. Who told you?"

Jean Marc shifted in the bed to ease his shoulder. "A servant in the palace at Versailles."

"How could a servant in the palace know there would be a peasant attack so far from Versailles?"

"An interesting question. One might also ask how some of the lads in the mob came to have pistols rather than their pitchforks." His lips twisted. "And why the poor starving peasant who slipped a dagger into my shoulder appeared exceedingly well fed and wore boots made of finer leather than my own."

So that had been the reason for those last cryptic words he had uttered before he had collapsed, Juliette thought. "Or why the servant came to you instead of His Majesty with the information."

"That's no mystery. Money." Jean Marc smiled mockingly. "King Louis gives medals and expressions of eternal gratitude for such loyalty. I let it be known I'd give fat bribes for any information of interest regarding the royal family. Money buys comfort and a fast horse to take the informant far away from the swords of the people he's betrayed."

"And this servant didn't tell you who was responsible for the attack?"

"A man in high place. He would say nothing other than that the carriage bearing the prince and Mademoiselle de Clement would be set upon enroute to Versailles. I gathered a company of hirelings and set out like a *grand chevalier* to the rescue."

She studied his face. "Are you never serious? You saved the life of the prince." She paused. "And my life also."

"Not because of my nobility of soul." He gazed at her calmly. "I'm a man of business who never takes action without the promise of return. I'll even admit I was most annoyed with you when you made my task so difficult."

"And what return do you expect to receive from rescuing the prince?"

"Her Majesty's profound gratitude and good will. I have a favor to ask of her."

She gazed at him without speaking for a moment. "I think you're not so hard as you'd like me to believe. You were truly concerned about Louis Charles though you were nigh out of your head with pain."

"I have no liking for child killers."

"And you took the knife thrust meant for me. Is that the behavior of a man who never takes action without the promise of return?"

He grimaced. "No, that's the behavior of a man who acted on impulse and was soundly punished for it." He shook his head. "Don't make the mistake of thinking me something I'm not. I'm neither a warrior nor a hero."

"I'll think what I please." She frowned uncertainly as she studied his face. "But I can't read you. I don't know what you're thinking."

"And that disturbs you?"

She nodded. "I usually have no problem. Most people are easy to read. It's important that I be able to see beneath the surface."

"Why?"

"Because I'm going to be a great artist," she said simply.

He started to laugh, then stopped as he met her clear, steady gaze. "I recall you said something about painting me when I first awoke. You wish to be an artist?"

"I am an artist. I am *going* to be a great artist. I

intend to study and work until I'm as great as Da Vinci or Del Sarto."

"I admire your confidence."

A sudden smile lit her face. "You mean you think I have no modesty. Artists can't have modesty or their talent withers. Men persist in believing women can paint only shallow daubs. I do not— Why are you looking at me in such a peculiar way?"

"I was wondering how old you are."

She frowned. "Four and ten. What does that matter?"

"It may matter a great deal." He closed his eyes.

"What do you mean?"

"I think I can sleep now. Run along to your own chamber."

She did not move.

He opened his eyes again. "I said for you to go. I think it will be for the best if you leave for the palace tomorrow morning."

She felt an odd pang. "You want me to go?"

"Yes." His voice was rough. "I have no need of you here."

Her jaw set stubbornly. "You *do* need me. Look at you, weak as a babe and still mouthing nonsense. I won't leave you. Do you think I want to remember I owed you my life and let you die before I could repay you? I'm not my mother. I take nothing without giving something in return."

His gaze narrowed on her face. "Your mother?"

She shook her head impatiently. "I did not mean to mention her. My mother has nothing to do with this." She raised her chin. "You did me a service. Therefore, I must do one for you in return. I've already sent word to the queen that I'll stay here until you're well enough to go to Versailles and receive her thanks."

"You'll soon regret staying. I'm not a good patient. I detest being ill."

"And I detest bad-tempered patients. I shall be as foul-natured as you, and you'll get well quickly so that you can rid yourself of my services."

A reluctant smile touched his lips. "There's something in what you say." He suddenly gave in. "Stay if you like. Who am I to refuse the gentle ministrations of a damsel for whom I've given my life's blood?"

"I have little gentleness, but on no account will I allow you to die." She straightened briskly in the chair. "Naturally, I can't have my painting interrupted while I care for you. I think I shall set up my easel in that corner by the window. The light should be very good there." She smiled. "I'm sure we'll deal very well together, and I'm glad you've come to your senses."

"As I told you, I'm a man who seldom denies himself for chivalry's sake." He settled more comfortably, wearily closing his eyes. "Someday I may remind you that I tried to send you away."

"Someday?" She shook her head. "You'll be well and hearty in a fortnight or so and we shall part. There will be no someday."

"That's right. I must not be thinking clearly. Perhaps I do have a fever."

"Truly?" An anxious frown wrinkled Juliette's brow as she reached out to touch him. She sighed with relief. "Not yet."

"No?" His eyes remained closed, but he smiled, curiously, Juliette thought.

"Not yet," he murmured. "Someday . . ."

Jean Marc's temperature began to rise in the late evening.

Juliette bathed him with cool water and tried desperately to keep him from tossing and spilling out of the bed onto the floor.

During the middle of the night the fever receded and severe chills took its place. The chills racked him, and his great convulsive shudders worried Juliette more than the fever had.

"I—have—no liking—for this." Jean Marc's teeth were clenched to keep them from chattering. "It should teach me well the foolishness of—" He broke off as another shudder ran through him. "Give—me another blanket."

"You have three already." Juliette abruptly made a decision. She stood up. "Move over."

"What?" He gazed at her blankly.

She drew back the covers, lay down beside Jean Marc, and drew him into her arms. "Be at ease," she said impatiently as she felt him stiffen against her. "I'm not going to hurt you. I only seek to warm you. I often held Louis Charles like this when he had the night chills."

"I'm not a child of two."

"You're as weak as a puling infant. What difference does it make?"

"I believe a great many people would be happy to enumerate the—differences."

"Then we shall not tell them. Are you not warmer with me here?"

"Yes, much warmer."

"Good." His shivering had almost stopped, she noticed with relief. "I'll hold you until you go to sleep." She reached up and gently stroked his hair as she did Louis Charles's. A few minutes later she said impatiently, "You're not at ease. I can feel you hard as a stone against me."

"How extraordinary. Perhaps I'm not accustomed to females slipping into my bed only in order to 'ease' me."

"As you say, the situation is extraordinary." Juliette levered herself up on one elbow and gazed sternly down at him. "You must not think of me as a female. It's not good for you."

His lips twitched. "I'll endeavor to dismiss your gender from my mind. I'll think of you as a thick woolen blanket or a hot, warming brick."

She nodded and again lay down beside him. "That's right."

"Or a smelly sheepskin rug."

"I do not think I smell." She frowned. "Do I?"

"Or a horse lathered from a long run."

"Do you have the fever again?"

"No, I was merely carrying the image to greater lengths. I feel much more comfortable with you now."

"You laugh at the most peculiar things."

"You're a most peculiar fem—sheepskin rug."

"You *are* feverish."

"Perhaps."

But his brow felt only slightly warm to the touch, and the shaking of his body had stopped almost entirely.

"Go to sleep," she whispered. "I'm here. All is well."

A few moments later she felt him relax, his breathing deepen.

At last he had fallen into a deep slumber.

THREE

You've painted long enough. Come here and play a hand of faro with me."

Juliette didn't look at Jean Marc as she added more yellow to the green of the trees in the painting on the easel before her. "What?"

"Play cards with me."

She cast a glance over her shoulder at Jean Marc lying on the bed across the room. "I'm busy."

"You've been busy for four hours," Jean Marc said dryly. "And will probably be at that easel for another four if I don't assert my rights."

"What rights?"

"The rights of a bored, irritable patient who is being neglected in favor of your precious paints and canvas."

"In a moment."

She was aware of his gaze on the middle of her back as she resumed painting.

"Tell me what it's like," he said suddenly.

"What?"

"Painting. I watched your face as you worked. Your expression was extraordinary."

Juliette was jarred out of her absorption into uneasiness. He had been lying in that bed watching her for hours every day and never before made comment. Her art was a private, intensely personal passion, and realizing he had been studying her emotions as she worked made her feel oddly naked. "Painting is . . . pleasant."

He laughed softly. "I hardly think that's the correct term. You looked as exultant as a saint ascending the steps to heaven."

She didn't look at him. "That's blasphemy. I'm sure you know nothing of how a saint would feel."

"But you do?" He coaxed, "Tell me."

She was silent a moment. She had never tried to put her feelings about her work into words, but suddenly she realized she wanted him to know. "It's as if I were swathed in moonlight and sunlight . . . drinking a rainbow and becoming intoxicated on all the hues in the world. Sometimes it goes well and the feeling's so exquisite it hurts." She kept her gaze on the painting so she wouldn't know if he was laughing at her. "And sometimes I can do nothing right and that hurts too."

"It sounds like an exceedingly painful pastime. But it's worth it to you?"

She nodded jerkily. "Oh, yes, it's worth it."

"Something beautiful?" he asked softly.

She finally glanced at him and found no sign of amusement in his intent regard. She nodded again. "A struggle to achieve something beautiful."

A brilliant smile lit his lean, dark face, and she gazed at him in fascination. Jean Marc's thick black hair was rumpled, his white linen shirt open nearly to the waist to reveal the bandage and a glimpse of the triangle of dark hair thatching his chest. Yet, in spite of his disarray, he still managed to exude an air of elegance. Dear heaven, how she wanted to paint the man. She had persistently asked him to permit her to sketch him ever since he had started to mend and he had just as persistently refused her.

"Well, I feel it my duty to rescue you from this painful pleasure," he said. "Come and play faro with me."

"Shortly, I wish to finish this lit—"

"Now."

"You're fortunate that I play with you at all. You've grown very spoiled in recent days. But then, I think you were already spoiled before you became ill."

"Spoiled?" Jean Marc levered himself upright against the headboard. "*I'm* not the queen's favorite. How could a poor bourgeois man of business become spoiled?"

"I'm not the queen's favorite either. She's kind to me but it's my mother who has her affection," Juliette said. "And Monsieur Guilleme says there are few noblemen in France who are as rich as you are."

"You shouldn't listen to gossip."

"Why not? You will tell me nothing of yourself. You're like the glass in the Hall of Mirrors at Versailles. You reflect but reveal nothing of yourself."

"And it's your duty as an artist to uncover my hidden soul?"

"You're laughing at me again." She turned back to the painting. "But it's quite true. I've already learned some things about you."

"Indeed?" His smile faded. "I'd be curious as to the nature of your discoveries."

"You're spoiled."

"I beg to differ."

"You hate anyone to see you weak and helpless."

"Is that extraordinary?"

"No, I feel much the same. And you're not nearly as hard as you appear."

"You said that once before." His lips twisted. "I assure you it's not a safe assumption to make about me."

She shook her head. "You asked Monsieur Guilleme yesterday about the plight of the peasants in the area and gave him a purse of gold to distribute among those in need."

He shrugged. "Some of those poor clods attacking the carriage were walking skeletons. It was little wonder they let themselves be whipped into a frenzy."

She continued to enumerate. "And you bear pain much better than boredom."

"Now, that truth I will own. Come and play cards with me."

His smile was coaxing, banishing all hardness and lighting his face with rare beauty. Juliette dragged her gaze from his face and back to her canvas. "Why should I play with you when I could be painting?"

"Because I wish it, and you're all that's gentle and obliging."

"I'm not oblig—" She stopped as she saw the wicked arch of his black brow. "The physician said you could get up for a little while tomorrow. Soon you'll be able to do without me entirely."

"And you'll go back to Versailles?"

She nodded vigorously. "And I shall be very glad to see the last of you. You laugh at me. You take me away from my work. You make me amuse you as if I were—"

"It was your decision to stay," he reminded her. "I told you I'd be a bad patient."

"And you told God's truth."

"I regret you've suffered so grievously at my hands. I'm sure every minute has been an interminable strain."

The devil knew very well it had been no such thing, Juliette thought with exasperation. It was not fair Jean Marc should be able to understand her with such ease when she was able to see only a little beyond the hard, glittering surface he displayed to the world. He knew she enjoyed both the sharp-edged banter and the comforting silences. Being with him stimulated and excited her in some strange fashion. She never knew how he would treat her. At times he teased her as if she were a small child; at other times he seemed to forget the difference in age between them and talked to her as if she were a woman grown. She looked forward to his company in the same way she looked forward to immersing herself in her painting, knowing she would be swept away but still eager to yield to the force. Now he was treating her with an annoying indulgent amusement, and she had a sudden desire to shock him. "I haven't finished telling all I know of you." She paused and then said in a rush, "I believe you've fornicated with that tavern maid who serves our meals."

His smile vanished. "Germaine?"

"Is that her name? The one with breasts like Juno."

Jean Marc was silent for a moment. "Women of quality don't speak of fornication, Juliette, and certainly not to gentlemen."

"I know." Her hand was shaking slightly as she added white to her brush. "But I do speak of it. Have you?"

"Why do you think I have?"

"She stares at you as if she'd like to eat you."

"Look at me, Juliette."

"I'm too busy."

"Look at me."

Juliette glanced over her shoulder and inhaled sharply as she saw the expression on his face.

"No," he enunciated softly and with great precision. "You don't want to wander down that path. Not unless you wish to learn exactly what I did with Germaine."

Juliette felt a hot flush rush to her cheeks. "I only wondered. I need no description."

"Description? I wasn't speaking of words."

Juliette pulled her gaze away. "You're teasing me again."

"Am I?"

"Yes." She added white to the blue of the sky in the painting, hunting desperately for a change of subject. "If my presence is so boring, perhaps I should let Marguerite tend to your needs."

"You would not be so cruel. How can you stand having that gloomy-faced harridan about? She stalks around the inn like a crow scratching for worms. Does the woman never smile?"

His tone was teasing again and Juliette breathed a sigh of relief. "She smiles at my mother. She was my mother's nurse since the day she was born and loves her very much. Most of the time I see very little of her when we're at the palace." Juliette kept her gaze carefully averted. "Marguerite doesn't like being here, but the queen thought I should have a woman in attendance while I saw to your needs, so she sent Marguerite back to the inn to serve as my chaperone."

"Quite proper. However, totally unnecessary. You're scarce more than a child."

Juliette didn't argue with him though she couldn't remember a time when she had thought of herself as a child—and it was not as a child that he had looked at her a few moments before. "The queen believes in being discreet."

Jean Marc raised his eyebrows.

"She does," Juliette insisted. "You mustn't believe what those horrible pamphleteers write about her. She's kind and a good mother and—"

"Foolishly extravagant and self-indulgent."

"She doesn't understand about money."

"Then she had better learn. The country's on the edge of bankruptcy and she still plays at being a shepherdess in her fairy-tale garden at Versailles."

"She gave to the relief of the hungry from her own allowance." Juliette put her brush down and turned to face him. "You don't know her. She gave me paints and a tutor. She's *kind,* I tell you."

"We'll not argue about it." Jean Marc's gaze narrowed on her flushed face. "I have a feeling if I say anything more about Her Sublime Majesty, you may take a dagger to my other shoulder."

"You'll see for yourself when you go to Versailles," Juliette said earnestly. "She's not what she is portrayed to be."

"Perhaps not to you." Jean Marc raised his hand as she opened her lips to protest. "As you say, I'll judge when I'm admitted to the queen's august presence."

Juliette frowned at him, not satisfied. "She doesn't understand. She's as a butterfly who always has lived in a garden filled with flowers. You wouldn't expect a butterfly to understand why—"

"I wouldn't expect a butterfly to be queen of the greatest country in Europe," Jean Marc said mildly.

"Yet you have no hesitation about asking a boon of that butterfly just as all the rest of the world does. What do you wish from her? A patent of nobility? A great estate?"

"The Wind Dancer."

She gazed at him in astonishment. "She will never give it to you. Not the Wind Dancer."

"We shall see." He changed the subject. "But your threat to inflict your Marguerite on me will not come to pass. I've sent word to Paris for my cousin, Catherine Vasaro, to be brought here tomorrow. Perhaps she'll be more sympathetic to the ennui of a poor wounded man."

Juliette became still. "Your cousin?"

He nodded. "A distant cousin and my father's ward. My nephew, Philippe, escorted her from my home in Marseilles to Paris, and I received word yesterday they had arrived." He smiled teasingly. "Catherine's everything that's gentle and kind. Not at all like you."

Juliette suddenly had a vision of a woman as tall and voluptuous as the tavern maid with a radiant halo suspended above her lovely head. The thought ignited within her the bewildering pain of envy. Why should it matter to her if this Catherine was as virtuous as a saint? She carefully hid any hint of her pain as she raised her chin. "Then I'll leave you to your gentle Catherine and return to Versailles at once."

"I think not. You said you wouldn't desert me until I was ready to leave the inn. Catherine is of such a delicate nature, I doubt she'll prove of much value." He added softly, "Surely, you wouldn't leave me when I still need you?"

He was looking at her with that rare, brilliant smile she had found herself watching and waiting for in the last few days. She felt her resistance melting away and quickly lowered her lashes to veil her eyes. "No, I would not leave you . . . if you truly needed me."

"I do. Now come here and play faro with me."

She hesitated, feeling the same half-sad, half-possessive regret she had known at the thought of giving up Louis Charles after his illness. Jean Marc, too, had belonged to her alone for so many days, and now she must let him go. It wasn't fair that—What was she thinking? She should be glad she wouldn't have to bear the intimacy of his company. She was accustomed to being alone. She could paint uninterrupted.

Still, it would do no harm to indulge Jean Marc with a little extra attention on this last evening, when he would be completely her own . . . responsibility. She moved briskly toward the bed. "I'll play a game or two with you before supper." She sat down on the chair beside his bed and reached for the deck of cards on the table. "You must understand it's not because you ask it, but only because I'm weary of painting and wish to play."

His dark, watchful gaze searched her face before a curiously gentle smile touched his lips. "I do understand, *ma petite*. I assure you that your motives are completely clear to me."

Holy Mother of God, she couldn't breathe!

Catherine Vasaro leaned back on the cushions of the coach and tried to keep from panting. Why had she been so foolish? She should have protested, but she had wanted to appear as womanly and beautiful as the ladies Philippe usually admired. Now she couldn't—

"Why are you looking so troubled, Catherine?" Philippe Andreas asked gently. "Jean Marc's message said he was in no danger and well on the mend."

Oh, dear, how wicked she had been to indulge in vanity when she should have been thinking only of Jean Marc. She tried to smile. "I know he will be fine. Jean Marc is so . . . invulnerable. I cannot imagine him allowing anything to hurt him."

Philippe's eyes twinkled. "Is that why you tiptoe around him with eyes as big as china plates?"

"He does make me feel nervous." She rushed on. "Not that he isn't extremely solicitous of me. No one could be more kind."

"Not even my humble self? You cut me to the quick, Mademoiselle Catherine."

"Oh, no, I didn't mean that you—" She stopped when he threw back his head and laughed. He had been teasing her and she had not had the sense to realize it, she thought in disgust. No wonder he treated her only with indulgent amusement when she behaved like a gaping idiot whenever he appeared in view. But how could she help it when he was as handsome as one of the ancient gods in one of Cousin Denis's books? However, Philippe was no unapproachable deity; his classic features were generally lit with an easy smile and his blue eyes with good humor.

Always fashionably dressed, he looked particularly elegant today, she thought. The sea-blue silk cutaway coat and gold brocade vest he wore flattered his tall, manly figure. The black satin trousers lovingly followed the line of his thighs ending below the knee to display white silk stockings that admirably showed off his muscular calves.

"Shall I get your fan from the valise? You look a trifle pale."

She sat up straighter. "I'm just distracted. I'm concerned about Jean Marc's wound. . . ." God would most certainly punish her for that falsehood, she thought gloomily.

Philippe nodded. "It hasn't been an easy time for you. First the long journey from Marseilles and then to hear of Jean Marc's wound immediately upon your arrival."

"Yes." Catherine was silent for a moment, staring blindly out the window. "And I didn't want to leave Cousin Denis at this time."

"No?"

"He's dying, Philippe. They think I don't know, but

Cousin Denis is dying." She shifted her gaze to meet his. "Isn't he?"

"Nonsense. He has many—" Philippe broke off and nodded. "Yes, Jean Marc says he hasn't long to live."

"Cousin Denis has always been so kind to me," she whispered, her eyes shining with tears. "I wanted to stay with him until the end, but he seemed not to want me there. So I feigned ignorance when he told me I was to go away to school. Sometimes it's difficult to know what's best to do, isn't it, Philippe?"

Philippe reached out and touched her hand. "You're doing very well, *ma chou*. Death's not easy for us to face at any age."

Warmth spread through Catherine. Philippe's comforting clasp gave her feelings of golden serenity.

"We're approaching the inn," Philippe said, leaning back in the seat. "You'll feel better when you see for yourself that Jean Marc's wound isn't serious."

Of course she would feel easier to know Jean Marc was getting better. She was very fond of Jean Marc.

And it was wicked to want the journey to go on and on so that she could remain within the warmth of Philippe's luminous smile.

"They're here." Juliette stood at the window gazing down at the coach that had just stopped before the door of the inn. She frowned as she saw the footman help a fragile-looking, splendidly gowned girl from the coach. "Or perhaps not."

Jean Marc moved haltingly to the window and glanced out to see Philippe take Catherine's arm and escort her. "Yes, that's Catherine." He quickly sat down on the closest chair. "You seem surprised."

"She's not what I expected." No voluptuous angel but a beautiful, frail child no older than herself. Juliette quickly masked the relief surging through her and turned away from the window to look at Jean Marc. When she had gone into his chamber that morning and seen him fully dressed, it had given her a queer shock. Lean, elegant, powerful, the bandage hidden by the fine linen of his white shirt, he had appeared independent and totally in command. However, now she noticed the paleness of his complexion and the weariness of his posture as he slumped in the chair, and these signs of his weakness brought her another freshet of relief. She hadn't lost him yet. He would still belong to her for a while longer. "You've been up long enough. Lie down and rest."

"Presently. Are you not going down to welcome our guests?"

"They're your guests, not mine." She crossed to the easel and picked up her brush. "Monsieur Guilleme will bring them to your chamber."

"Juliette . . ." Jean Marc shook his head with a faint smile. "You can't hide behind your painting and that gruff tongue forever."

"I don't know what you mean. I just don't wish to—"

"Jean Marc, what idiocy have you been about?" Philippe Andreas threw open the door and allowed Catherine to precede him into the chamber. "It's not at all like you to involve yourself in physical combat. You much prefer a battle of wits."

"An error I have no intention of repeating," Jean Marc said dryly. He frowned as he looked at Catherine. "You're well, Catherine? You look a bit pale."

"It's you who are ill, Jean Marc." Catherine's gaze moved from the painting that had immediately captured her attention to her cousin's face. "I do hope you've recovered."

"As well as could be expected, I suppose. I'd like to present Mademoiselle Juliette de Clement, who has been both my salvation and my torm—Catherine! Catch her, Philippe!"

Catherine swayed but remained on her feet, clinging desperately to Philippe's arm. "I'll be fine. Perhaps it's the heat." Her breath was coming in shallow bursts. "If I could sit down . . ."

"Why didn't you say at once that you weren't feeling well?" Jean Marc demanded.

Catherine's eyes widened in distress as her gaze

shifted to Jean Marc. "You're angry. I didn't mean to make you angry. I'm sorry—"

"I'm not angry." Jean Marc was obviously trying to keep the exasperation from his voice. "Is your stomach upset?"

"No. Yes. Perhaps a little." Catherine seemed barely to get the words past her pale lips. "I'm sorry, Jean Marc."

"It's not your fault. I'll send for the physician."

"Oh, no, I'm sure I'll be quite recovered in a few moments." Tears rose to Catherine's eyes. "I should never—" She stopped and swayed again. "Jean Marc, I think . . ."

"It's her corset."

Jean Marc turned at Juliette's clear voice. "I beg your pardon."

She ignored him, scowling at Catherine in disgust. "Why don't you tell him you can't breathe?"

Another blush tinted Catherine's delicate skin. "Please, I can . . ." She trailed off miserably.

"Oh, for the love of God." Juliette turned to Philippe. "Give me your dagger."

"What?"

"Your dagger," she repeated as she stretched out her paint-smeared hand. "There's no time to unlace her. Do you want her flopping like a fish at your feet?"

"The idea certainly doesn't appeal to me," Jean Marc said lightly. "Are you saying her corset's laced too tightly?"

She cast him an impatient glance. "Of course, can't you see she can get little air?"

Philippe began to chuckle and Catherine's blush deepened to bright scarlet.

Jean Marc turned to Catherine. "Is that what—" He stopped as he saw the tears begin to roll down her cheeks. "*Sacre bleu*. Why didn't you tell us?"

Miserable, Catherine gazed up at him. "It would have been indelicate. My governess, Claire, says such subjects are never discussed in polite company. I was afraid you'd think—" She broke off as a sob robbed her of the little breath she still possessed.

"The knife." Juliette's fingers wriggled demandingly, and this time Philippe unsheathed his jeweled dress dagger and placed it in her hand.

Juliette dropped the dagger on the bed and was immediately behind Catherine, unfastening her peach-colored brocade gown. "You know you're very stupid to let them do this to you? Why did you not fight them?"

"It was only for a short time." Catherine gasped. "Claire said every woman should be willing to suffer to look attractive."

"Hush," Juliette said. "Save your breath." She cast a glance over her shoulder at Jean Marc. "Tell your father this Claire is a fool and should be dismissed. It's clear the girl's too gentle to fight for herself."

Catherine's gown was finally unfastened and Juliette started to spread the material to reveal the lacings of the corset.

Catherine suddenly stiffened and whirled to face them. "No."

Juliette scowled. "Stop this foolishness. Do you wish—"

"Philippe must go away. It's not proper he should see me in dishabille."

Juliette gazed at her in astonishment. "Proper? He'll see you gasping like a chicken with its neck wrung if you don't get these lacings undone."

Catherine's jaw set. "It's not proper."

"Go away and come back in fifteen minutes, Philippe," Jean Marc said quickly.

Philippe nodded and gave Catherine an understanding smile before leaving the chamber.

Juliette muttered something beneath her breath that sounded remarkably like an oath as she picked up the dagger from the bed and began to saw through the lacings of the corset. A moment later she had cut through the last lacing and the corset sprang open. "There, that's over."

Catherine drew a deep shuddering breath. *"Merci."*

"Don't thank me. You should never have been bound in the first place. From now on, when someone tries to bind you, cut yourself free. How old are you?"

"Three and ten."

"I'm four and ten and I haven't worn a corset since I was seven. It took six months before Marguerite finally gave up trying to lace me into one, but it's foolish to let them take your breath just because fashion decrees you must." She turned to Jean Marc and demanded, "Well, will you fight for her?"

"As well as I can. I travel a great deal and my father is ill." Jean Marc smiled enigmatically. "Though I see now my cousin definitely needs a champion. Perhaps I can arrange something."

"Truly, Claire is usually very kind," Catherine said, troubled. "I wouldn't want her to suffer because of my foolishness. I should have told her the lacings were too tight."

"She should have seen it." Juliette started to refasten Catherine's gown and then stopped. *Bon Dieu!*"

"What's wrong?" Catherine glanced anxiously over her shoulder.

"The gown won't fasten now," Juliette said in disgust. "I can't even get it closed."

"Claire stitched me into it after the corset was fastened." Catherine sighed resignedly. "Perhaps you'd better try to lace up the corset again."

Juliette shook her head. "Monsieur Guilleme's given you a chamber a few doors from here. We'll go there and you can rest until the servants can bring your trunks from the carriage." She pushed Catherine toward the door and glanced at Jean Marc over her shoulder. "Don't overtire yourself. I have no desire to have two of you gasping for breath."

"As you command," Jean Marc replied sardonically.

Juliette turned back to Catherine, ignoring his tone. "You still look pale, take deep breaths."

In another moment Juliette had whisked Catherine from the chamber.

"How is she?" A frown of genuine concern clouded Philippe's classical features as he came back into Jean Marc's room a few minutes later. "Poor little cabbage.

We should have guessed what was troubling her." His blue eyes were suddenly twinkling. "God knows, we've both undone our share of corsets."

"I'd say you've undone more than your share," Jean Marc said dryly. "You have no discrimination. Any pair of thighs are fine as long as they welcome you."

"Untrue." Philippe's grin widened. "The thighs must be shapely and the lady clean and sweet-smelling. Other than that I have no prejudices." He added simply, "I like them all."

And women liked Philippe, Jean Marc thought. Females young and old seemed to sense Philippe's fascination with their sex and responded generously with both their bodies and their company. "Do you have the legal agreements I asked you to bring from my office in Paris?"

"They're still in my cases in the carriage." Philippe made a face. "Only you would be concerned with business while you lie there with a dagger wound. Are you trying to become the richest man in France?"

"No." Jean Marc smiled. "The richest man in all Europe."

Philippe chuckled. "You'll probably do it. As for myself, I'm content to be the poor connection. It gives me more time to enjoy the pleasures of life." His gaze wandered to the painting on the easel in the corner. "Exceptional, isn't it? Though I can't say I like it. I prefer my art pretty and comfortable. Pictures like that have a tendency to make one think. Very fatiguing."

Jean Marc shot his nephew an amused glance. "Thinking. An occupation much to be avoided."

Philippe nodded placidly. "One must conserve one's energy for the important things in life."

Jean Marc looked at Juliette's painting. No, the painting wasn't at all comfortable to view. The picture portrayed several richly dressed ladies and gentlemen lolling in a forest glade but, other than the pastoral setting, it held none of the lush sentimentality popular with artists favored by the nobility. Strong beams of sunlight poured through the branches of the oak trees. Some leaves were unscathed, others were stark, the illumination revealing skeletal stems beneath the green foliage. When the sunlight reached the painted, powdered faces of the courtiers below the branches, the effect was even harsher. The expressions of those in the shadow were smiling and bland but the faces in the sunlight were stripped of their conventional masks, nakedly revealing pettishness, boredom, even cruelty. Yet, in spite of its brutal revelations, the painting had a certain austere beauty about it. Juliette's brush had made the sunlight into a living entity that shone pure, undefiled as truth itself.

"It's not often you see a woman painting at all, much less doing a painting of this nature," Philippe said. "She's . . . interesting, isn't she?"

"But far too young for you," Jean Marc said quickly, his gaze leaving the painting to return to Philippe's face.

"I'm not so corrupt," Philippe said indignantly. "She has practically no breasts. I, at least, wait until a woman blossoms."

Jean Marc chuckled. "Well, this child will no doubt have some sharp thorns when she blossoms."

"All the more interesting to pluck. But it's you who enjoys difficult women. I would never have attempted to tame that little virago you're keeping in such splendor in Marseilles. Too much effort."

Jean Marc smiled reminiscently. "A challenge is never too much effort. Léonie is exceptional." Jean Marc's smile faded as he recalled that Philippe had a very good idea why he chose the type of women he did to bed.

"So is a beauteous wolf but I wouldn't want to bed her. Don't you ever choose a woman with less—" He stopped. "I'm looking forward to sampling the favors of the ladies of the court at Versailles."

"They have no liking for bourgeoisie like ourselves. You're better off at Vasaro with your Maisonette des Fleurs than you would be in those noblewomen's bedchambers. They'd devour you."

"Would they? What a blissful prospect," Philippe murmured. His smile faded and his big white teeth pressed worriedly into his lower lip. "I didn't know you were aware of my little cottage, Jean Marc. I assure you it's only a small indulgence and it doesn't interfere with my running Vasaro."

"I know it doesn't. You're doing fine work caring for Catherine's inheritance. If you weren't, you would have heard from me before."

"And why am I hearing from you now?"

"I want no outraged fathers applying to me for aid for their ravished daughters."

"Ravished?" Philippe's tone was indignant. "I seduce, not rape. No unwilling woman has ever come to Les Fleurs."

"Make sure the circumstances remain unchanged, and you'll have no argument from me."

"I wouldn't cause you distress, Jean Marc." Philippe gravely met his gaze. "I know how fortunate I am to have this post. I enjoy my life at Vasaro."

"And Vasaro evidently enjoys you." Jean Marc suddenly smiled. "At least the female population of Vasaro does. I simply thought it best we clarify the situation."

Philippe's gaze narrowed on Jean Marc's face. "Is that why you asked me to leave Vasaro and accompany Catherine here?"

"I asked you because I knew you would guard Catherine and I find your company stimulating."

"And because you wished to issue a warning to keep my pleasures separate from my duties." Philippe smiled slowly. "So why not accomplish a threefold purpose, eh?"

"Why not, indeed?"

"Don't you ever tire of these convoluted maneuvers to shape the world to suit yourself?"

"On occasion, but the prize is usually worth the game."

"Not to me." Philippe made a face. "Which is why you're busy gobbling up all the wealth of Europe while I labor humbly at your command."

"At Catherine's command. Vasaro belongs to her, not to the Andreas family."

"Does it? I wasn't sure you knew the difference."

"It's tradition for our family to guard the heiress of Vasaro."

"But you care nothing for tradition," Philippe said softly. "I wonder what you do care about, Jean Marc."

"Shall I tell you?" Jean Marc's tone was mocking. "I care about the French livre, the British pound, and the Italian florin. I'm also rapidly acquiring a passion for the Russian ruble."

"And nothing else?"

Jean Marc was silent a moment, thinking. "The family. I suppose I care for the well-being of the Andreas family more than I care for anything else."

"And your father?"

Jean Marc kept his expression guarded. "He's a member of my family, is he not?" He glanced coolly at Philippe. "Don't expect cloying sentimentality from me, Philippe. I'm not a sentimental man."

"Yet, you're capable of friendship. You call me your friend."

Jean Marc shrugged, then winced. He had forgotten momentarily that his wound would be long in healing.

"But, of course, I'm an exceptionally charming fellow." Philippe continued. "How could you restrain yourself from feeling affection, not to say admiration, respect, amusement, and—"

"Enough." Jean Marc raised his hand to stop the flow of words. "I'll grant you the amusement, at least. Pour all your charm into the task of cajoling Her Majesty and I'll be content."

"I have no intention of exerting myself in such a profitless endeavor. Gentlemen who make cuckolds of royalty often end with their heads on pikes. Tell me, do you think the queen really prefers women to men?"

"Why ask me?"

"Because I know you well. Undoubtedly you've made it your business to discover everything about everyone down to the lowest groom in the stable at that splendid palace. You never go into any venture without a full knowledge of your opponent."

"Opponent?" Jean Marc murmured. "Her Majesty is my sovereign and I her loyal servant."

Philippe snorted.

"You don't believe me? I paid no bribe to learn the secrets of the Queen's bedchamber. It would have reaped me little benefit. However, I did find she's written several extremely passionate letters and given very lavish gifts to the Princess de Lambelle, Yolande Polignac, and Celeste de Clement."

"De Clement?" Philippe's eyes widened as his gaze flew back to the painting. "Then that child is—"

"She's Celeste de Clement's daughter. I understand the marquise was the daughter of a wealthy Spanish merchant who became the second wife of an impoverished nobleman. His son and heir was less than well disposed toward the lovely Celeste and her offspring. When his father died, he gave his stepmother a carriage, a wardrobe of fine gowns, and bid her and her child a final adieu."

"Do you think the little firebrand is being brought up to her mother's persuasion?" Philippe asked idly. "I hear Sappho's daughters delight in—"

"No!" The violence of Jean Marc's rejection surprised him as much as it did Philippe. He felt as if Philippe had besmirched something peculiarly his own. He quickly brought his tone under control. "I didn't say Celeste de Clement has unnatural tastes. She's been the mistress of several wealthy and generous gentlemen of the court since she arrived there several years ago. I'd judge her passion is for acquisition and not the pleasures of the flesh."

"Like Jean Marc Andreas?"

"The Marquise de Clement and I have a similar passion, but I don't prostitute myself to pursue it. I prefer not to manipulate emotions, but circumstances."

"Yet, you manipulate both if it suits you."

"The legal agreements, Philippe."

Philippe made a face and turned toward the door. "I'll go get them. By the way, I caught sight of a deliciously robust servant girl as we came into the inn. I don't suppose you'd object if I invited her to occupy my bed while I'm waiting here for you to recover?"

"Not as long as you use discretion and don't offend Catherine. The woman's name is Germaine."

Philippe opened the door. "Have you tried her?"

"When I first came to the inn. Pleasant, eager, but boringly docile." Jean Marc's lips twisted ruefully. "Needless to say, I've not been tempted to repeat the experience in my present state of health."

"I've no objection to docility." Philippe grinned as he started to close the door. "And I enthusiastically embrace eagerness."

Juliette closed the door of Catherine's chamber and turned to face the upset girl. "Sit down over there." She gestured to the chair across the room. She gazed at Catherine's flushed face. "Your color is better."

Catherine sat down in the chair. "I feel as if my face is on fire. I'm so ashamed."

"Why?" Juliette plumped down on the bed. "Because you were idiot enough to let yourself be too tightly laced into your corset?"

"And because Jean Marc and Philippe must surely think ill of me."

"It's done now." Juliette crossed her legs tailor-fashion and tilted her head critically. "You don't bear any resemblance to either Jean Marc or Philippe Andreas."

"We're only distantly related."

"You're a handsome family. He's quite beautiful. I'd like to paint him."

"Philippe?" Catherine nodded eagerly. "Oh, yes, I've never seen such a handsome man. His hair is as golden as sunlight when it's not powdered. And he's very kind too, he's never impatient and sharp with me as Jean Marc sometimes is. Philippe once brought me a lovely pair of scented gloves from Vasaro when he came to the Ile du Lion."

Juliette shook her head. "Not Philippe. I was speaking of Jean Marc."

"Jean Marc?" Catherine looked at her in disbelief. "But Philippe is much finer-looking. Why would you want to paint Jean Marc?"

Why would she not want to paint him? Jean Marc

was mystery cloaked in his black velvet, cynical wisdom, wicked wit, and, infrequently, a gentleness all the more precious for its rarity. Juliette realized she had scarcely noticed Philippe Andreas while he was in the same room with Jean Marc, and now she had to struggle to recall what he looked like. "Your Philippe is comely enough, I suppose."

"He's much handsomer than Jean Marc."

"Where is this Ile du Lion?" Juliette asked in order to change the subject.

"It's in the Golfe du Lion, off the coast of Marseilles."

"It's your home?"

"No, my home is in Vasaro, near Grasse." A note of pride sounded in Catherine's voice. "Perhaps you've heard of Vasaro? We grow flowers for the making of perfume. Philippe says Vasaro is quite famous for its essences."

"I've never heard of it." Juliette glanced back at Catherine and grimaced. "But that's not unusual. The ladies and gentlemen of the court seldom converse about the outside world. They gossip only about themselves."

"I hear Versailles is the most beautiful place on the earth," Catherine said softly. "How lucky you are to live with such magnificence."

"If your home is in Grasse, why do you live at Ile du Lion?"

"My parents died of smallpox when I was four and Jean Marc's father brought me to live with him and Jean Marc on the Ile du Lion. I'll live there until I'm old enough to manage Vasaro myself. They have a splendid château that's much grander than the manor house at Vasaro." She hurried on as if afraid she had hurt Juliette's feelings. "But, of course, I'm sure your home at Versailles is much nicer than the château or Vasaro."

"Home?" Juliette experienced a sense of loss that startled her. What would it be like to have one settled place in which to live, not to have to travel from Paris to

Versailles to Fontainebleau and all the other royal residences at the whim of Her Majesty? "I have no home
there. We occupy a small apartment in the palace." She
shrugged. "Not that it matters. I have my paints."

"I noticed your painting when I first came into Jean
Marc's chamber. It's quite wonderful. You are very
clever."

"Yes, I am."

Catherine suddenly laughed. "You shouldn't agree
with me. My governess says a young lady should be
modest about her accomplishments."

"But we've already discovered what a fool your
governess is." A twinkle appeared in Juliette's eyes. "You
should have learned your lesson not to pay her any
heed."

Catherine's eyes widened in horror. "You think I
should not obey her?"

"Of course, you should not o—" Juliette stopped as
she met Catherine's gaze. The girl's fragility reminded
her of one of the Chinese vases in the queen's cabinet,
and if Claire was anything like Marguerite . . . Juliette
decided to temper her words. "Perhaps you should fight
her only on important matters." She frowned. "But you
must not let her bind you again."

"I shouldn't have been so vain. I'm sure she didn't
mean to cause me distress."

"No?" Juliette tried to keep the skepticism from her
voice. Perhaps this Claire wasn't a gargoyle like Marguerite but she was obviously not overly intelligent. "Then
you must make sure she knows when you're in distress.
Do you understand?"

"I'm not a fool," Catherine said with dignity. "I
know I should have told Jean Marc the corset was too
tight."

"Then why didn't you?"

Bright scarlet flowed once again under Catherine's
fair skin. "Philippe . . ."

Juliette started to laugh. "You're besotted with that
handsome peacock."

Catherine rounded on her fiercely. "He's not a
peacock. He's kind and manly and—"

Juliette held up her hand to stop the passionate flow. "I meant no disrespect. It's just my way. Tell me, have you lain with him yet?"

Catherine frowned in puzzlement. "I don't know what you mean."

Juliette gestured impatiently. "Has he tried to bed you?"

Catherine stiffened in shock. "Do you mean fornication?"

She was truly horrified, Juliette realized. "He's not attempted you, then?"

"No, of course not. He'd never . . ." She swallowed hard before she could continue. "He's a gentleman, and gentlemen do not do those things. Even if I were a woman grown, he would not—"

"You jest."

Catherine shook her head emphatically and then asked curiously, "Have you ever—" She stopped, obviously shocked at the question she had been about to broach. "Of course, you haven't."

Juliette nodded. "You're right. I've never fornicated with any man. Nor shall I." She smiled fiercely. "The Duc de Gramont slipped beneath the covers of my bed and tried to caress me one night a few months ago, but I kicked him in his private parts and then ran away and hid in the garden."

"Perhaps he was just being affectionate."

Juliette gazed at her incredulously. "All the court knows he's fond of young girls."

"Well, there you are," Catherine said triumphantly. "He was merely being kind."

"You don't understand. He has a taste for . . ." Juliette smiled in genuine amusement even as she felt a surge of pity that the girl was so ignorant.

"If you were frightened, you should have called your nurse and she would have explained there was nothing to fear."

"Marguerite wouldn't have come."

"Why not?"

"Because the duke is one of my mother's protectors and she wouldn't dare offend him."

"Your mother's protector?"

"Her lover," Juliette said in exasperation. "She lets him fornicate with her and then he gives her jewels and money. Don't you know anything?"

Catherine straightened, her chin rising. "I think you must be mistaken. People of honor do not behave in that fashion, and I'm sure noblemen and ladies would not. You're very lucky to have a mother alive and well and you shouldn't malign her."

"Malign her? My mother *sent* His Grace to my bed. He told me so."

"Then I was correct. His Grace was merely being—"

"Kindly?" Juliette finished, gazing dazedly at Catherine's stubbornly set lips and stern frown. Then she began to chuckle. "I like you."

Catherine appeared surprised at the abrupt change of subject. "You do?"

Juliette nodded. "You may be blind, but you're not stupid and you don't back down."

"Thank you," Catherine said doubtfully. "I find you very interesting also."

"But you don't like me." Juliette made a face. "I'm used to that. I know I'm not a likable person." She glanced away. "I suppose you have a great many friends on the Ile du Lion?"

"Claire won't let me consort with the servants' children and there's no one else."

"I have no friends at the palace either. Not that I care. They're all very stupid." Juliette turned to look at Catherine. "Will you be staying at Versailles long?"

Catherine shook her head. "We leave for Jean Marc's house in Paris directly after he has his audience with Her Majesty."

Juliette tried to ignore the sharp thrust of disappointment she felt. She had no need for friends as long as she had her painting, she told herself. And she certainly had no need for a friend who couldn't see the ugly truths behind the veil of feigned honor and pretended virtue. She would no doubt be constantly arguing with the ninny if she stayed around.

"Do you know Her Majesty?" Catherine asked. "Is she as beautiful as everyone says?"

"She's not unattractive and she has a lovely laugh."

"You have affection for her?"

Juliette's expression softened. "Yes, she gave me my paints and had me taught by a fine teacher. She even hung one of my paintings of the lake in the billiard room at Petit Trianon."

Catherine was impressed. "You must be pleased. That's a great honor."

"Not really. It wasn't a particularly good painting. I painted the lake at sundown and it looked . . ." Juliette grimaced as she finished. "Pretty."

Catherine giggled. "You don't like pretty things?"

"Pretty is . . . it has no depth. Beauty has meaning, even ugliness has meaning, but pretty is . . ." She scowled. "Why are you laughing?"

Catherine sobered. "I'm sorry. It's just that I find you a trifle peculiar. You're so serious about everything."

"Aren't you?"

"Not like you. I'm not at all like you. I like pretty things and I hate ugly ones."

"You're wrong. You shouldn't hate ugliness. It can be very interesting if you look at it the right way. For instance, I once painted an old, fat count who had a face as ugly as a frog, but every line told a story of its own. I tried to—" She broke off as she heard the sound of footsteps in the hall. "The servants must be bringing your trunks. I'll see." She frowned as she got off the bed and moved toward the door. "I suppose you'll wish me to leave you to rest?"

Catherine shook her head. "I'm not tired."

Juliette's expression brightened. "Then perhaps you'd like to go for a walk with me before it gets dark and I could show you what I mean. There's a sway-backed horse in the field beyond the inn that's as ugly as sin itself but he's far more interesting than the more handsome ones." She opened the door. "Change your gown and meet me in the common room as soon as you can." She looked back over her shoulder, suddenly uncertain. "If you want to come with me?"

A radiant smile lit Catherine's face as she rose to her feet. "Oh, yes, please. I do want to come with you."

FOUR

"May I speak to you, Jean Marc?" Catherine stood in the doorway, her hand nervously fiddling with the knob. "I know you're working and I promise I'll take only a moment. I have something to ask of you."

Jean Marc carefully smothered his impatience and pushed the papers in front of him aside. "You wish to know when we're going to Versailles? I should be well enough to travel within a few days. Have you been bored here at the inn?"

"No, I've been very happy here." Catherine closed the door and came forward to perch on the edge of the chair beside his bed, clasping her hands together on her lap. "It's . . . different being with Juliette."

Jean Marc chuckled. "I'd say *different* is an apt word to describe Juliette. You've certainly spent enough time with her in the past two days to judge."

"I *like* her, Jean Marc." Catherine's hands twisted together. "She does not deserve—" She broke off. "Have you ever noticed she always wears gowns with sleeves down to her wrists?"

Jean Marc's smile faded. "What are you trying to tell me?"

"Marguerite." Catherine met Jean Marc's gaze. "Why would she want to hurt Juliette? I haven't been punished by Claire since I was a small child." She paused and then said in a rush, "Juliette's arms are covered with bruises."

Jean Marc went still. "You're sure of this?"

"I've seen her arms. They have terrible bruises. I felt ill. . . ." Catherine shook her head. "I asked her what happened and she shrugged and said Marguerite had been bad-tempered since she had been forced to leave the palace and stay at the inn."

The intensity of the anger searing through Jean Marc astonished him. Christ, Juliette had said Marguerite was not pleased to be here, but he had paid no attention. He had joked and dismissed the subject. Why in thunderation hadn't she told him what the black-hearted bitch was doing to her?

"I didn't know what was for the best," Catherine whispered. "She told me I could do nothing and to forget it. But it isn't right. Can you help her, Jean Marc?"

"Yes." What he'd like to do was break that harridan's scrawny neck, he thought grimly, a solution that was clearly impossible under the circumstances. "Don't worry, I'll take care of it."

"Soon?"

"Tonight."

"Thank you, Jean Marc." Catherine stood up and moved hurriedly toward the door. "I'm sorry to have troubled you. I'll leave you to your work now. I only thought . . ."

The door closed behind her.

It had not been easy for Catherine to come to him, Jean Marc thought as he stared absently at the panels of the door. She had always been a shy, gentle child and, for some reason, particularly intimidated by him. Perhaps some of Juliette's boldness had rubbed off on her during their association of the last few days.

Or perhaps she had been so horrified by Juliette's mistreatment she could not bear the thought of not doing something to help her.

Think of something beautiful.

No wonder Juliette knew so well how to combat pain. She had obviously experienced it for the major part of her life.

His grip tightened on the coverlet as he remembered Catherine's words.

"Terrible bruises."

"I felt ill."

"The wound's healing very well." Juliette tied the fresh bandage, helped Jean Marc into his linen shirt, and began to fasten the buttons. "You should be able to travel soon."

"Day after the morrow, I believe," Jean Marc said without expression. "I've arranged for a carriage to send you and Marguerite to Versailles tomorrow morning."

Juliette's fingers froze on the button she was fastening. "Tomorrow?" She shook her head. "Next week, perhaps. You're not well enough to—"

"You leave tomorrow." Jean Marc's lips thinned. "And your kindly Marguerite can toddle happily back to your mother instead of devoting her questionable attentions to you."

Juliette frowned. "Catherine told you? She shouldn't have done that. Bruises are nothing—"

"Not to me." Jean Marc cut fiercely through her words. "I'll not have you suffer for my sake. What do you think—" He broke off. "You leave tomorrow."

Juliette's fingers fell away from his shirt as she gazed in wonder at him. "Why are you so angry? There's nothing to be upset about."

Jean Marc was silent for a moment, his expression shuttered. "Good night, Juliette. I'll not say good-bye because I trust we'll see each other at Versailles."

"Yes," Juliette said dully. It was over. The days of

companionship with Catherine, the hours of exhilarating conversation with Jean Marc. She tried to smile. "I cannot persuade you how foolish it is to rush your recovery in this fashion?"

"No."

"Then I'll not waste my time." She started to turn away.

He caught her hand. "Not yet." His usually mocking expression was surprisingly grave. "Not before I express my appreciation."

She determinedly blinked her eyes. "That's unnecessary. I didn't do it for you. I owed you a debt and I paid it. Why should I—" She broke off as he pushed up the loose sleeve of her gown. He stared at the deep purple-yellow marks marring her smooth flesh. "Only bruises. I've had much worse. I bruise very easily." She pointed to a faint yellow mark on her wrist. "You see? You did that yourself when you held on to me when the physician was removing the dagger."

He looked sick. "*I* did that?"

"You didn't mean to do it. I told you, one has only to touch me to leave a bruise." She tried to keep the desperation from her voice. "So there's no reason for you to press on to Versailles until you're entirely well."

"No reason at all," he said thickly, his gaze never leaving her arm. "Except that I've always thought you had the most exquisite skin I have ever seen. Roses on cream . . . glowing with life. I find I can't bear this atrocity. I can't stand seeing . . ." He trailed off as he turned her arm over and stared at the marks on the more delicate flesh of her inner arm. Then, slowly, he lifted her arm and pressed his lips onto one of the most livid bruises.

She stiffened in shock, staring down at the dark hair of his head bent over her arm. She was suddenly acutely aware of the scent of tallow of the candles on the table by the bed, the play of light and shadow on the planes of his cheekbones, the sound of her own breathing in the silence of the room. His lips felt warm, firm, gentle on her flesh, and yet they caused an odd tingling to spread up her arm and through her body.

He looked up and smiled crookedly as he saw her expression. "You see? Who knows? If you stay, there may come a time when I'd be more dangerous to you than your dragon, Marguerite." He released her arm and leaned back against the headboard. *"Bonne nuit, ma petite."*

She didn't want to leave him. She wanted him to touch her again with those strong, graceful hands. She wanted to tell him . . .

Merde, she did not know what she wanted to tell him. It was clear he wished to be rid of her and she would not beg him to let her remain.

She turned on her heel, the skirts of her black gown flying. "I didn't really want to stay. You've been nothing but trouble to me and Catherine is only a stupid girl who knows nothing. Nothing!" She grabbed her painting from the easel and strode toward the door. "Marguerite said the queen is at Le Hameau now. She can be at ease there with few of the strictures of the main palace and will probably receive you at the queen's cottage." She opened the door and glanced at him over her shoulder. Her eyes were shining with unshed tears. "But it will do you little good to see her. She will never give you the Wind Dancer."

Juliette stood with spine straight and head high, waiting on the wooden bridge leading to the queen's cottage as Jean Marc, Catherine, and Philippe strolled into view.

Jean Marc experienced a mixture of sharp pleasure and deep regret as he saw her. He had carefully avoided thinking of the girl since the evening three nights past when he had told her she must leave the inn. Now the sight of her was like a sudden blow.

"Juliette!" Catherine rushed toward her. "I was so afraid I wouldn't see you again. Why did you leave the inn without a word of farewell?"

"I knew I'd see you here." Juliette smiled at her. "I couldn't allow you to see the queen without me being present." She gazed challengingly at Jean Marc over

Catherine's head. "Jean Marc would probably have managed to get all of you put into chains."

Philippe chuckled. "You clearly have little respect for his tact. I assure you Jean Marc can be very diplomatic when it serves him."

"But he likes his own way and so does the queen. I'm not about to let him throw away his life after I've worked so hard to save it. Come along. She's on the terrace." Juliette turned and walked quickly across the quaint bridge arching over the mirrorlike lake. She led them over carefully tended lawns toward the queen's cottage.

The cottage actually consisted of two buildings linked by a gallery that could be reached by an external spiral staircase, Jean Marc noticed. He had heard much of this village the queen had built at such extravagant expense a short distance from the small palace of the Petit Trianon. Le Hameau was everything he expected— charming, bucolic, a fairy-tale peasant village where the animals smelled sweet and the containers used to milk the cows were of fine Sèvres china.

A fleecy snow-white lamb wearing a pink bow lay at Marie Antoinette's slippered feet, and a brown and white milk cow grazed a few yards away from the terrace. Yellow silk cushions occupied the space directly in front of the queen, and sprawled on the cushions was Louis Charles sound asleep.

Jean Marc stopped in surprise, then recovered and moved forward. Le Hameau may have been predictable, but Marie Antoinette definitely wasn't what he expected. The woman sitting beside the rosewood table appeared almost matronly in her simple white muslin gown with its white silk sash. The only note of fashionable extravagance about her attire was her huge straw hat with its curving white plumes. The queen's ash-brown hair was unpowdered, but pulled back in the currently fashionable style.

She looked up with a teasing smile when Juliette approached and curtsied. "So you have seen fit to escort your brave rescuer into my presence, Juliette."

"This is Monsieur Jean Marc Andreas, Your Majesty." Juliette sank to the terrace beside the heap of pillows, her expression reflecting her disappointment as she looked down at the sleeping child. "Oh, he's taking his nap. I wanted to play with him."

The queen shook her head in amusement. "Why are you so fond of babies when you have no use at all for older children?"

"Babies don't know how to be cruel. I guess they have to learn it. I like babies." Juliette gently stroked the little boy's silken hair. "And Louis Charles likes me too."

The queen gazed over Juliette's head at Jean Marc. "*Bonjour*, Monsieur Andreas. You're most welcome at Versailles. Such a brave man always is. And we are greatly in your debt."

Jean Marc bowed low. "Your Majesty is very gracious to receive me. I was happy to be of service."

"But not so happy you do not wish a reward. Juliette tells me you have a boon to ask of me." Marie Antoinette reached down and patted the head of the pink-ribboned lamb at her feet. "What can I grant you that my husband cannot?"

Jean Marc hesitated and then said in a rush, "The Wind Dancer. I wish to purchase it."

The queen's eyes widened. "Surely you jest. The Wind Dancer has belonged to the court of France for almost three hundred years."

"And it belonged to the Andreas family much longer than that."

"You're challenging our right to the statue?"

Jean Marc shook his head "It was given to Louis XII by Lorenzo Vasaro in 1507, who had been given the statue in turn by Lionello Andreas. However, we do wish the statue returned to our family. My father has a passion for antiquities, and it's always been his fondest wish to find a way to repurchase the Wind Dancer. He offered to buy the statue from His Majesty's father but he was refused. And I've made two offers myself." He paused. "I judged this an excellent opportunity to repeat the offer."

The queen's lips tightened. "You have no need for another treasure. The Andreas family is rich as Croesus with all their shipyards and vineyards, and you yourself have tripled the family fortunes since you expanded your endeavors into moneylending and banking."

Jean Marc inclined his head. "Your Majesty is well informed."

"I'm no ignorant fool. My husband relies heavily on my judgment and advice." She frowned. "I have no intention of giving you the Wind Dancer. I have a great fondness for it and I believe it brings good fortune to the royal household."

"Indeed?"

Marie Antoinette nodded emphatically. "My husband's father gave the statue into the custody of Madame Du Barry a short time before his death. Do you not think that is significant?"

"Men do die. Even kings are not immortal."

"He should never have given it to that woman." She scowled. "On his death I took it from her and banished her to a convent."

"So I heard."

"It's not a matter for your amusement."

"Forgive me, Your Majesty. I admit the thought of Jeanne Du Barry in a convent strikes me as a trifle humorous. You, too, must have come to believe the convent a highly inappropriate abode for her as you released her after only a short time in which she could consider her wicked past."

"I am not unkindly."

"I'm sure you're the soul of mercy and nobility."

"Well, I was very happy myself at the time," she said, mollified. "I knew the statue would bring good fortune back to the royal household, and I was correct. Only a few years after I retrieved the Wind Dancer I discovered I was with child."

Jean Marc quickly suppressed a start of surprise. It was common knowledge Louis had not been able to consummate his marriage until he had undergone a surgical procedure, yet the queen sounded as if she truly believed she owed both the consummation and her beloved children to the Wind Dancer.

"May I suggest it could have been due to circumstances other than the recovery of the Wind Dancer that—"

"No, you may not," Marie Antoinette interrupted sharply. "And I will not relinquish my statue." She smiled with an effort. "However, I cannot turn you away with nothing after your service. Suppose we give you a patent of nobility? As a nobleman you will no longer have to pay taxes, and you cannot deny it is a great boon I grant. I understand you bourgeoisie are always clamoring to avoid paying your rightful share of the tariff."

"Your Majesty is too kind."

"Well, then you will take the patent," the queen said with satisfaction. "It's settled."

He shook his head regretfully. "I'm a simple man and would feel uncomfortable in such august company."

Marie Antoinette's gaze narrowed on his face. "Are you mocking the honor I give you?"

"Never. However, I do prefer to be what I am."

"What you are is an arrogant upstart of a—"

Juliette made a sudden motion with her hand, and Louis Charles stirred and murmured on his bed of pillows.

The queen's expression immediately softened as she leaned over to look at him. "Shh, Louis Charles. What happened, Juliette?"

"I believe your tone of voice awakened him." Juliette kept her gaze lowered as she tucked the lacy quilt about the little boy.

"Doucement, bébé." Marie Antoinette's expression glowed with affection as she gazed at her son. "Nothing is wrong." The boy drifted back to sleep and the queen looked up at Jean Marc. "You will not accept the patent?"

"May I counter with another suggestion?" Jean Marc carefully hid the tension gripping him. "The court is desperately in need of funds to pay the war debts and seeking a sizable loan. Suppose I give His Majesty the money he requested as a loan and add another million livres to sweeten the bargain." His voice became low. "I beg Your Majesty to reconsider."

"Beg? I'd wager pleading doesn't come easily to you. You must want the Wind Dancer very much."

"My father is very ill."

"A magnificent offer." She gazed at him thoughtfully before shaking her head. "I won't give it up."

"Two million."

She frowned. "Be done with it. I'm no haggling shopkeeper."

Jean Marc's disappointment was so intense he couldn't speak for a moment. He had known he was going too far, but desperation had driven him. "As you will, Your Majesty. My father will be very disappointed." He paused. "If you still wish to reward me, I have another boon to ask." He motioned for Catherine to come forward. "This is my kinswoman, Catherine Vasaro."

Marie Antoinette's expression softened as Catherine moved forward and curtsied deeply. When she rose, the queen stared into Catherine's widely set blue eyes, then she looked at the girl's light brown hair braided and pinned into a coronet about her head. "She's truly a lovely child. You wish a place for her at Versailles?"

Jean Marc shook his head. "It's come to my attention that you've taken an interest in a certain convent, the Abbaye de la Reine just outside Paris, where young ladies of noble blood are given an education far above the ordinary for a female. I thought I might persuade you to use your influence to get the Reverend Mother to accept my cousin Catherine at the convent."

"But you've just taken pains to point out that you're not of noble birth. I assume the same applies to this child?"

Jean Marc nodded. "But she'll become the head of the House of Vasaro and must be prepared to take her place. It's difficult enough for a woman to rule without burdening her with ignorance."

"She will be the head of her house?" The queen was intrigued. "How is that?"

"The same Lorenzo Vasaro who gifted the court of France with the Wind Dancer settled in Grasse and began to raise flowers for the perfume trade. He prospered but never married, and when he died he left Vasaro to Caterina Andreas, the child of his friend, Lionello Andreas. He stipulated one condition: The property had to be passed down from the oldest daughter to the oldest daughter. The only requirement was that the female child retain the surname of Vasaro even after marriage and be named Caterina or some variation of the name."

"How extraordinary!" Marie Antoinette's blue eyes misted with tears of sentiment. "The poor man must have been deeply in love with this Andreas child."

Jean Marc shrugged. "Perhaps. The fact remains that a woman who rules is threatened from all sides and needs the protection of knowledge as well as wisdom."

"Yes, she does. I was very poorly educated when I came to France and I suffered greatly for it. That's why I gave the abbey my favor." A frown creased her forehead. "But I meant it only for the nobility."

Jean Marc took a quick step forward, drawing a small golden casque from beneath his coat. "I understand Your Majesty is fond of the scent of violets. I took the liberty of having the master perfumer at Vasaro prepare a scent that may please you." He handed her the golden casque and stepped back. "A humble gift of allegiance."

She gazed at his bland face suspiciously before opening the casque. "Humble?" An amused smile lit her face as she looked at an exquisite crystal vial stoppered by an enormous ruby cut in the shape of a teardrop. "I'm enchanted with your gift of perfume, Monsieur."

"Catherine's gift," Jean Marc corrected. "The container was provided by me but the scent is from Vasaro."

"Catherine . . ." The queen's gaze shifted to Catherine. "Do you wish to go to the convent, *ma petite?*"

"Yes, Your Majesty." Catherine hesitated. "Of course, I'm frightened of going away from the Ile du Lion, but Jean Marc says there are things I must learn."

"Hmmm, I see." Marie Antoinette lifted the ruby stopper and bent down to dab a bit of scent behind the ear of the white lamb at her feet. "And what your kinsman says is always the truth?"

"Jean Marc knows what is best for me."

A dry smile appeared on the queen's face. "I'm inclined to agree that this child is direly in need of educating. I'll advise the Reverend Mother your cousin is to be admitted to the abbey."

"Your Majesty is too kind." Jean Marc bowed low. "You have my eternal gratitude."

"Yes, yes, I know. You may go." She held up the ruby stopper and watched admiringly as its glittering facets caught fire in the sunlight. "Is it not pretty, Juliette?"

"Splendid," Juliette murmured.

Jean Marc bowed low and backed across the terrace. He had failed, he thought dully.

Merde, but he could *not* fail.

He was several yards away when Philippe and Catherine fell in step with him.

"I'm sorry, Jean Marc," Philippe said soberly. "I know how disappointed you are."

Jean Marc forced a smile. "My father said he didn't really need the Wind Dancer. I suppose he'll have to be satisfied with his dream."

"Dream?"

"Never mind."

"That jewel you gave her was worth fully half the amount Louis needs to pay his war debt. Will she give it to him?"

"I doubt if it will occur to her. She sees it only as an amusement." Jean Marc smiled crookedly. "Like her lamb and her cow."

"You could suggest it to her."

"If I chose to interfere. I do not. The Andreas family has always taken care of its own, let the Bourbons do likewise."

"Is that not a trifle ruthless?"

"To choose survival? Why do you think our house has existed through centuries of war and political strife when others have been destroyed? Because we've never aligned ourselves with either warring faction and devoted ourselves to preserving what we had built. It's not the kings who rule the world but the bankers."

"So you became a banker."

"Exactly. I can't escape the taxes, but I can offset them by charging the nobles and clergy fat interest rates. I thought it only fair. Don't you sympathize with—"

"Wait!"

Juliette de Clement was running toward them, her mop of dark brown curls flopping about her flushed face. She stopped as she came up to them and looked squarely at Jean Marc. "You shouldn't make Catherine go to the abbey. They won't be kind to her there."

"The good sisters?"

"No, the other students." Juliette made an impatient motion with her hand. "She's bourgeoisie. Do you think the other pupils will like having her there as their equal? They'll treat her as they do the lackeys and pages here at Versailles. They'll treat her as they do me in a cruel fashion and—" She caught her breath and continued urgently. "Can't you see? She won't know how to fight them. She can't even tell a servant to loosen her corset, for heaven's sake."

Catherine flushed. "I'm sure they won't be unkind. Why should they?"

"I told you. Because you're not one of them. That's reason enough."

"You're of the nobility and you've treated me kindly."

"But I'm not one of them either. My mother is a Spaniard and the queen loves her. Everyone is jealous of the queen's affection for my mother and contemptuous of me. They do try to hurt me but I won't let them." She turned fiercely to Jean Marc. "Tell her. She doesn't *know*."

"However you know, do you not?" Jean Marc's gaze narrowed on Juliette's intense face. "By the way, did you pinch that poor child when Her Majesty was lowering the royal wrath on my head?"

"I wouldn't pinch Louis Charles. I like him. I merely nudged him." Juliette frowned. "You were behaving very foolishly, Jean Marc. In another moment she would have sent you away and told the king to punish you. He's very good-natured but he usually does what she tells him to do." She returned to the main issue. "Catherine will be unhappy at the convent. Don't send her there."

"I'll consider your objection. I admit it has a certain merit. Catherine has obviously never learned to do battle."

Catherine smiled gently at Juliette. "Thank you for your concern."

"De rien." Juliette lingered a moment, gazing at Catherine. "Listen to me. If you go, you mustn't believe the best of them. Strike first and they may leave you alone."

Catherine frowned and shook her head.

"You see?" Juliette rounded on Jean Marc. *"C'est impossible!"* She turned and strode away from them.

"Juliette!"

She glanced back over her shoulder at Jean Marc.

"Are you not going to bid us *adieu?"* he asked softly.

"I have no liking for farewells." Juliette's eyes were suspiciously bright. "I've said what I wished to say."

The next moment she was running back toward the queen's cottage.

Jean Marc watched her until she was out of sight, then turned and began walking again.

"She's unhappy here," Catherine said.

He stopped and looked at Catherine. "Did she tell you that?"

"No." Catherine hesitated. "But she has many strange ideas about her mother and the people here. It must be very bewildering to live at this great place." A frown marred her wide forehead. "And that horrid Marguerite isn't kind to her."

Jean Marc's expression hardened. "No, she's not. You have a fondness for the girl?"

Catherine blinked to rid her eyes of tears. "Oh, yes. I've never met anyone like Juliette. I wish I could see her again. She wouldn't admit it, but I think she must be very lonely here. Is there no way you can help her, Jean Marc?"

"Perhaps." He smiled recklessly as he came to a

decision. God knows, he had done his best to put the girl beyond his reach. "Who am I to battle destiny when it knocks so persistently?" They walked in silence for a few minutes before Jean Marc asked suddenly, "Tell me, Philippe, did you bring more than one vial of perfume from Vasaro?"

Three days later Jean Marc Andreas sent a message to the queen and begged another audience for that same afternoon. When he departed Her Majesty's presence, it was noted that another silver flask of superb beauty rested on the table beside Marie Antoinette's chair. It was agreed by all who saw it that the magnificent sapphire serving as the bottle's stopper admirably matched Her Majesty's sparkling blue eyes.

The next day Juliette de Clement was informed by the queen she was being sent to the Abbaye de la Reine to receive the education befitting the daughter of a noblewoman serving the queen of France.

Eight months after Juliette de Clement arrived at the Abbaye de la Reine, a clumsily wrapped package was delivered by a street urchin to Jean Marc at his residence at the Place Royale in Paris. The gift was not accompanied by a message of any sort, but when he unwrapped the object a smile of amusement lit his face.

It was a painting of the Wind Dancer.

Abbaye de la Reine
January 7, 1789

Catherine!
It had to be Catherine.
The coach rumbled up the hill toward the north gate of the abbey at a fast clip, the muscles of the two black horses straining with effort, their nostrils quivering, their breath curling and pluming as it joined the snowflakes filling the air. Lanterns on the coach were

already lit, two pinpoints of fire illuminating the pristine snow-filled twilight.

Juliette drew her gray cloak closer about her as she straightened away from the pillar and moved restlessly within the overhanging arcade. She staggered, her feet refusing to obey her. Her limbs were as cold and numb as the rest of her body, but the long watch was over now and soon she and Catherine would be inside and out of this bone-chilling wind. She moved onto the courtyard and was immediately engulfed, absorbed into the thick, swirling fall of snow, the plump wet flakes splattering on her cheeks and catching in her dark curls.

The coach rumbled through the open gateway, the horses' hooves thudding softly on the snow-covered cobblestones.

It *was* Catherine!

Juliette recognized the muffled and cloaked footman and coachman as the same who had come to fetch Catherine three weeks before to take her to Jean Marc's residence in Paris for Christmas festivities.

She hurried forward, slipping and sliding on the icy stones. Reaching the door of the carriage before the footman could get down from his perch, she threw it open. "You're late. You said you'd be here at noon. Have the sisters not taught you to—" She broke off in surprise as she saw a second passenger

Jean Marc Andreas sat opposite Catherine. Juliette had not seen him since that day at Versailles two years ago. He appeared not to have changed an iota. His mocking black eyes glittered like the blade of a jewel-encrusted Toledo dagger.

"Good afternoon, Juliette." Jean Marc smiled and nodded his head. "How delightful of you to come and greet us." He threw aside the tawny fur lap rug covering him and leaned forward to extricate Catherine from the furs enveloping her. "Or should I be more formal and address you as Mademoiselle de Clement now that you've become such a young lady?"

"Don't be foolish. I'm no different than I was two years ago." She dragged her gaze from him to look at

Catherine. "You're late. You told me you'd start from Paris this morning."

"Jean Marc had business to conduct this morning and, as he wanted to speak to the Reverend Mother, we didn't—"

"Why does he want to see the Reverend Mother?" Juliette felt a ripple of panic as her gaze flew back to Jean Marc. "You're not taking Catherine away?"

Jean Marc turned to study her. "Would it matter so much to you if I did?"

Juliette's lashes quickly lowered to veil her eyes. "The nuns say Catherine is their best pupil. It would be a pity if she couldn't stay and learn all she could from them."

"And what of you? Aren't you also a fine pupil?"

"Not like Catherine."

"Because you don't apply yourself." Catherine made a face. "If you'd listen to the sisters instead of studying them to see how you'd like to paint them, you'd be much better off."

"I listen." Juliette grinned. "Sometimes." Her smile faded as she stepped back to permit Jean Marc to get out of the carriage. "You're taking her back to the Ile du Lion?"

"The château on the Ile du Lion is closed. When my father died I found it inconvenient to keep it open." Jean Marc helped Catherine from the carriage. "I spend most of my time in Marseilles and Paris now."

"Then where will Catherine—"

"He's only teasing you," Catherine said quickly. "Jean Marc says I'm to stay here at the abbey until I reach my eighteenth year. . . ."

Relief surged through Juliette. "That's good." She caught Jean Marc's gaze narrowed on her face and continued quickly. "For Catherine, of course."

"Of course," Jean Marc echoed softly.

"Your hair's becoming damp." Juliette stepped nearer and gently pulled up the hood of Catherine's cloak to cover her hair. "Have you supped? They're all in the hall eating now. You could still join them."

"We had an enormous dinner before we left Paris."

Catherine smiled. "Why are you out here in the courtyard instead of at supper? I suppose you were painting
and forgot to eat again?"

Juliette nodded. "I wasn't hungry."

"If you were so absorbed in your artistic endeavors,
how is it you were in the courtyard when we arrived?"
Jean Marc asked with a quizzical smile. "You wouldn't,
by any chance, have been waiting for Catherine?"

"No, of course not." Juliette lifted her chin and
gazed at him defiantly. "I wouldn't be so foolish as to
linger in this cold. I was merely passing by when I saw
the coach approaching."

"How fortunate for us." Jean Marc motioned to the
footman. "Get the basket of fruit from the carriage.
Even though the mademoiselle has no hunger, perhaps
she'll be able to force down an apple or pear later."

"Perhaps." Juliette turned to Catherine. "Say good-
bye and come along. It's too cold out here for you."

Catherine nodded and tentatively addressed Jean
Marc. "It was very kind of you to have me for Christmas,
Jean Marc. I enjoyed myself tremendously."

"You're easily pleased. I thought it time I paid some
attention to you. I've not been an overly attentive
guardian these last years."

"Oh, no, you're always so kind to me. I knew you
were busy." Catherine's gentle smile was radiant. "And
I've been very happy here at the abbey."

"I doubt if you'd tell me even if you weren't." Jean
Marc took the large covered straw basket from the
footman. "But I'm sure the Reverend Mother will be less
concerned for my feelings. She'll scold me for lack of
attention but will give me honesty regarding your contentment here."

"Catherine's not dishonest," Juliette said fiercely.
"She would say nothing at all rather than lie to you."

"I'm not maligning her." A curious expression on
his face, Jean Marc gazed into Juliette's blazing eyes.
"And if she's happy here, I imagine her contentment
has much to do with you." He handed the basket to
Catherine. "If I'm still in Paris, I'll send for you again at

Easter. Now, run along. Juliette's right. There is bitter cold in this wind."

"*Au revoir*, Jean Marc." Catherine whirled and hurried across the courtyard toward the shelter of the arcade, calling over her shoulder, "Hurry, Juliette, I have so much to tell you. Jean Marc let me act as hostess at supper one evening and bought me a wonderful blue satin gown."

"I'm coming." Juliette started after her.

"Wait."

Juliette stiffened when Jean Marc touched her arm. "Catherine is waiting for me."

"I'll keep you only a moment." The snow fell heavily, cocooning and veiling them from Catherine's view. Star-shaped flakes caught in Jean Marc's thick dark hair and shimmered on his black cloak. He gazed intently at Juliette. "As usual, you've piqued my curiosity. You see, I don't believe in this particular coincidence."

She moistened her lips with her tongue. "No?"

"I think you've been standing here for most of the afternoon waiting for Catherine to come." His hands slipped down her arms and he took her slim hands in his. His lips tightened. "Your hands are like blocks of ice. Where are your gloves? Have you no sense?"

His warm, hard grasp spread a disquieting heat through her wrists and forearms. Heat should have brought only comfort, but this sensation was somehow . . . different. She tried to pull her hands away. "I'm not cold. I . . . like the snow. I'm studying it to paint."

"Juliette," Catherine called from beyond the spiraling curtain of snowflakes.

"I have to go now."

"Presently." Jean Marc's hands tightened on hers. "Are you as happy as Catherine here at the abbey?"

"One place is as good as another. I think that—" She met his compelling gaze and nodded jerkily. "Yes."

"Was that so difficult to confess?" Jean Marc's sudden smile flashed in his dark face. "I think it must have been. Happiness doesn't necessarily go away if you admit to possessing it."

"Doesn't it?" She smiled with an effort. "Of course it doesn't. I know that."

"Catherine tells me you've not heard from the queen since you came here."

"I didn't think I'd hear from her," she said quickly. "She's always too busy to—"

"And a butterfly has a very short memory." He smiled faintly.

"It doesn't matter if she's forgotten me. I expected nothing else." She tugged again and this time he let her go. She backed away from him. "I have been happy at the abbey and I thank you for persuading her to send me here."

He lifted a black brow. "I see you don't make the mistake of lauding my kindness as Catherine did."

"No, I know you wanted me here to protect Catherine."

"Indeed?"

She nodded gravely. "I've not failed you. I've done what you wished."

"Then Catherine and I are both fortunate. Did it never occur to you that I might have another reason?"

She glanced away. "No."

"Aren't you going to ask me if I did?"

"I must go." Yet she suddenly realized she did not want to go. She wanted to stand there and look at him, try to glimpse and interpret the expressions flickering across his magnificent face. His dark features were still, intent; his tall, lean body absolutely motionless. His immobility should have given the impression of forbidding coldness, but instead she had a sense of smoldering intensity. She half expected the drifting snowflakes to melt as they touched him.

"Shall I tell you?" He drew even closer. "A man of business must sometimes wait for his investment to mature so he may reap a profit."

"But I told you I was protecting Catherine. You are reaping the profit."

He lifted the hood of Juliette's cloak to cover her hair with the same gentleness with which Juliette had covered Catherine's a short time before. "Am I?" He gazed into her eyes. "How old are you, Juliette?"

She felt suddenly breathless and swallowed to ease the tightness of her throat. "I'll have my sixteenth natal day soon."

He gazed at her for a long moment before abruptly turning away. "Go and get out of this cold. I must seek out the Reverend Mother and pay my respects as a dutiful guardian." His voice roughened. "And, Mother of God, eat some of Catherine's fruit. I won't have you starving as well as freezing for her sake."

"I told you I didn't stand here all—" She broke off as he glanced over his shoulder and then said simply, "She's my friend. I missed her."

"Ah, the truth at last." Jean Marc's lips twisted. "Excellent. I thought you'd never stop hiding beyond those prickly barriers. Perhaps I won't have to be as patient as I thought."

Juliette looked at him in bewilderment, but in another moment Jean Marc had disappeared into the swirling snow. She could hear the crunch of his boots on the ice-encrusted cobblestones as he moved quickly across the courtyard. She felt suddenly hollow, as if he had taken some part of her with him.

What an idiotic thought, she told herself impatiently. Nothing had been taken from her. Jean Marc Andreas was a man whose powerful personality colored everything around him, and it was natural she should feel a little drained and flat at his departure.

"Juliette, you'll freeze in that wind," Catherine called in exasperated concern.

Juliette was abruptly jarred from her bemusement and turned to hurry to Catherine's side. She ducked beneath the arcade and shook her head, deliberately letting the hood of the cape Jean Marc had drawn over her head fall once again to her shoulders. She and Catherine moved down the walkway toward the ancient stone building housing the students' cells. "Now tell me all about your supper party. Who were the guests at the table the night you were Jean Marc's hostess?"

Jean Marc gazed out the window of the coach, noticing ruefully that the snow was no longer a gentle fall but near blizzard. He knew very well he should have given in to the Reverend Mother's urgings and sheltered at the abbey instead of attempting to return to Paris.

But he had found the thought of a hard pallet in an austere cell intolerable this night. Instead, he would go straight to the house on the Place Royale occupied by his current mistress, Jeanne Louise. She would greet him with the usual challenge which would melt into surrender and desire before the night waned. The challenge was always as important to him as the surrender, and tonight he needed a sensual struggle with an intensity that startled him.

He gazed blindly out at the falling snow, seeing not the lush beauty of Jeanne Louise he would enjoy in a few hours but the innocent appeal of Juliette de Clement. He had been expecting to see the girl when he had accompanied Catherine back to the abbey, but the actual encounter had still come as a shock. Her slim body, even cloaked in that hideous gray garment, betrayed womanhood on the brink.

He felt a stir of arousal at the memory of Juliette standing in the courtyard facing him, bold, defiant, yet touchingly vulnerable, her cheeks flushed plum bright with cold and her eyes blazing with a will that could be yielded but never subdued. He had avoided examining his complex emotions and actions involving the girl in the past and he found himself doing the same thing now. He did not want to know why she stirred him and touched him at the same time.

But, at least, he had not committed the ultimate folly. For a moment, as she had looked up at him, he had the insane impulse to take her back with him to Paris.

Why not? Perhaps it was not so insane a thought after all. She had no money and he could provide handsomely for her. According to Catherine, both Juliette's mother and the queen evidently had forgotten her existence since she had left Versailles. She was more vulnerable to him than she dreamed and could be made to realize the seductive nature of the bond forged between them those two years earlier. He knew the skills to make a woman want him, and she would be a superb mistress and a challenge *extraordinaire*. He had seen a foreshadowing of the woman Juliette would become, but now that flowering had almost come to pass.

Almost.

Merde, and he was not such a libertine that he seduced an innocent from her nunnery, he thought with self-disgust. Whatever lay ahead for the two of them must wait until she was an adversary worthy of his steel. Until that time he would be content with the challenges offered by the Jeanne Louises of the world.

Yet, for the first time, he had the odd feeling the victory he would wrest from Jeanne Louise would provide neither contentment nor satisfaction.

FIVE

I'll not ask where Juliette can be found, Catherine." Sister Mary Magdalene deliberately avoided Catherine's pleading gaze as she turned back toward the chapel. "But I wish to see her in the scullery before the midday bell tolls or her punishment will be doubled. Do you understand?"

"I'm sure she never meant to miss morning prayers," Catherine said anxiously. "When she's painting she loses all track of time."

"Then she must be taught to remember. God has given her a great gift, but appreciation for His gifts must be shown in worship and humility."

Humility. Juliette? If Catherine hadn't been so exasperated with her friend she would have laughed aloud. "Juliette strives always to improve her gift. Isn't that a form of worship, too, Reverend Mother?"

Sister Mary Magdalene's lined face softened as she glanced over her shoulder. "Your loyalty does you credit, Catherine." For an instant a twinkle appeared in her fine gray eyes. "Consider it fortunate I don't test your loyalty by asking where Juliette is hiding this time or you might find yourself on your knees scrubbing the stones of the scullery with your friend." She shrugged. "Not that I believe the punishment will serve to teach her any great lesson. With scrub brush in hand she must have prayed her way over every inch of the abbey these last five years."

"But Juliette never complains," Catherine reminded her. "She serves the Lord joyfully. Surely that must—"

"I agree she suffers her punishment cheerfully enough." The Reverend Mother was amused. "But have you noticed how true to life the stone walls and floors in her paintings have become? I believe she uses the time on her knees to study their composition and texture instead of praying."

Catherine had noticed, but she had hoped no one else had. She smiled weakly. "You said the acquisition of knowledge is a blessing."

"Don't throw my words back at me. We both know Juliette has been most wicked. When the bell tolls!" She turned and vanished into the chapel.

Catherine ran to the south courtyard, then through the gates, all the while muttering imprecations beneath her breath. When she had seen Juliette creeping out of the abbey before dawn that morning, she'd sternly reminded her to be back in time for prayers. But would her headstrong friend listen? No, she must get them both in trouble with the Reverend Mother.

The dew-wet grass dampened Catherine's slippers and darkened the hem of her gray uniform as she ran through the vegetable garden, then up the hill toward the stone wall bordering the abbey's cemetery.

Straggly weeds caught on her long skirts as she streaked toward the column of ancient crypts at the rear of the cemetery. When she had first come to the abbey five years before, there had been no weeds, the cemetery had been well tended and money had been plentiful for the nuns to hire workers to keep the abbey in good repair. All that had changed when the Bastille was attacked. With the queen a virtual prisoner in the Palace of the Tuileries in Paris, her charities had ceased and the nuns were forced to rely on contributions from the parents of their students to keep food on the table and the abbey in minimal repair.

As Catherine approached the crypts she felt a familiar clenching of the muscles of her stomach. She would tell Juliette it was time to learn restraint and discipline. No one could go on forever doing exactly as they wished, and the Reverend Mother's tolerance had been stretched to the limit.

The white marble crypt at the far end of the row had been weathered by time and the elements to a dirty gray; the winged statue of the angel Gabriel hovering over the door gazed menacingly down with blind, pupilless eyes, Catherine thought. She paused to get her breath before the rusty iron door, steeling herself to go into the vault. She *hated* coming here. Blast Juliette! The bolt had been drawn and the door was open a crack, but it was terribly heavy and took Catherine a moment to widen it enough to slip into the crypt.

"You can close the door." Juliette didn't look up from the painting on the easel before her. "I'm doing shadows and don't need the light for this bit. The candle will do very well."

"I'm *not* closing the door." Catherine shivered as she stepped gingerly around the marble sarcophagus with its upraised likeness of Sister Bernadette in serene state. Sweet heaven, the candle Juliette had mentioned had actually been placed between the folded hands of the effigy, casting a soft glow over the stern chiseled features. "How can you stay here for hours?"

"I like it here."

"But it's a tomb."

"What difference does that make?" Juliette added a bit more yellow to the brown on her brush. "It's quiet and it's the one place I don't have to worry about the sisters coming to find me."

"Sister Mary Magdalene would call it sacrilege. The dead should be left in peace."

"How do you know?" Juliette grinned at Catherine over her shoulder. "Peace is dreadfully dull." She patted the smooth marble cheek of the nun. "Sister Bernadette and I understand each other. I think she's glad I come to visit her after lying here alone for over a hundred years. Did you know she died when she was only eight and ten?"

"No." Catherine was immediately distracted as she looked at the figure on the sarcophagus. She had been concerned only with the forbidding atmosphere in the crypt and never thought about the life of the woman whose remains it contained. What a tragedy to be forced to leave this earth for heaven when one had scarcely started to live. "How sad. So young."

Juliette made a face. "I shouldn't have told you. Now when you come here you'll be all misty-eyed and doleful instead of scared. It's far more amusing to see you big-eyed and trembling."

"I'm not frightened," Catherine said indignantly, the tears vanishing. "And even if I were, it's unkind of you to be so scornful. I don't know why I took the time to come after you. I should have told Reverend Mother where you were so that you couldn't hide and—"

Juliette's gaze returned to the canvas. "She noticed I wasn't at morning prayers?"

"Of course she noticed," Catherine said crossly. "It was different when there were more students at the abbey. Since our number has dwindled to thirty-six, it's obvious when one is missing matins or vespers or meals. Sister Mathilde always makes sure Reverend Mother knows when you're not where you're supposed to be."

"She doesn't like me." Juliette paused, looking unseeingly at the painting of the abbey. "Thirty-six. There were forty-two last week. Soon everyone will be gone."

Catherine nodded. "Cecile de Montard's father came for her just after matins. Even now they are packing her bandboxes and loading her other things into the huge berlin drawn by four horses her father arrived in. Her family is leaving for Paris. She said they would go to Switzerland."

Juliette didn't look at her as she said in a low voice, "I'm surprised Jean Marc hasn't sent someone for you. He must have received the Reverend Mother's message telling him the National Assembly has closed the convents. Perhaps he has already sent for you. Marseilles is a great distance. Someone may come for you at any moment."

Catherine frowned. Juliette was speaking very strangely. "Nonsense. Jean Marc probably intends for me to stay at the abbey for another year."

"Things have changed. Everything has changed." Juliette's tone became suddenly fierce as she said, "I thought I'd taught you to rid yourself of that blind stupidity."

"And I thought I'd taught you not to be rude to me." Catherine held up her hand as Juliette started to protest. "And don't tell me truthfulness isn't rudeness. I've already heard it a score of times and I believe it no more now than I ever did."

A reluctant smile touched Juliette's lips. "Well, it *is* stupid of you not to realize we can't go on forever here at the abbey."

"Not forever. But I don't see why we can't stay another year. The nuns can no longer give us lessons, but I'm sure they'd let us remain here anyway. After all, I'm not of the nobility and there's certainly no reason for me to flee the country." Catherine glanced away from Juliette as she continued. "And you said your mother now has the protection of that wealthy merchant who can guarantee her safety in Paris. So she'll surely not take you away either."

"Undoubtedly, my mother has forgotten she has a daughter."

"Oh, no." Catherine's eyes widened in distress. "I know she never sends for you, but perhaps it's because she feels it wouldn't be proper . . . under the circumstances."

Juliette shook her head. "Stop looking as if you're

about to weep. I don't care. I'm glad she never makes me leave the abbey. I like it here." She blew out the candle. "Let's get out of here. How do you expect me to work when your knees knock so loudly the sound disturbs my concentration?"

"I am not afraid." Catherine moved quickly toward the door, sighing with relief as she crossed the threshold into the sunlight. "But we'd better get back to the abbey. The Reverend Mother said she'd double your punishment if you failed to report by the time the midday bell tolls."

"Not yet." Juliette followed her from the crypt, closed the heavy door, and shot the bolt. She sat on the ground and leaned comfortably against the wall of the crypt. "Stay with me for a while." She tilted her head back, closing her eyes and letting the sunlight bathe her face. "I need to garner my strength. Heaven knows how many miles of stones I'll be set to scrub this time."

"Perhaps Reverend Mother will let me help you."

"Why should you want to help me?" Juliette's eyes remained closed but she smiled. "I'm rude and sacrilegious and cause you no end of trouble."

Juliette was obviously not going to be hurried, Catherine realized resignedly. She dropped down opposite her. "Perhaps you've not rid me of my stupidity after all."

Juliette's smile faded. "Why?"

"When I had that terrible cough last winter, why did you stay up night after night and nurse me?"

"That's different. *You're* different. Everybody wants to help you."

"It's not different. Why do you pretend to be so uncaring? When that poor peasant woman ran away from her husband and gave birth at the abbey you refused to leave her and cared for the babe yourself until she was well enough to leave the abbey."

"I like babies."

"And the mother? You spent almost a year teaching her to read so that she could find employment in Paris at a decent wage."

"Well, I couldn't let Yolande go back to her lazy lout of a husband. He would have beaten her to death within days and the baby would have starved. Then I quite probably would have stuck a pitchfork in her pig husband and the Reverend Mother would have been forced to send me away from the abbey." Her eyes sparked with sudden mischief. "So you see I was just being selfish. Give it up, Catherine. I'll never be the saint you are."

Catherine felt her cheeks heat. She gazed at Juliette in bewilderment, unable to remember her ever being in such a mood as this. "I try to do what's right. I'm not such a saint as you make me out to be."

"Close enough." Juliette wrinkled her nose. "But I forgive you, for you're not at all boring." She glanced away, her gaze fastening on the abbey looming in the distance. "I shall miss you."

"I told you I was—"

"You always think everything is going to be fine. We've been lucky we've had these years. At least, I've been lucky. I've liked being here at the abbey." Juliette looked down at the paint-smeared hands folded on her lap. "When I first arrived I thought I'd hate it. All the rules and the kneeling and the scraping."

Catherine chuckled. "You break nearly every rule, and most of your kneeling and scraping is done only when you're caught."

Juliette wasn't listening. "And then I tried to find the ugliness in the sisters, but I found there wasn't any. They're . . . good. Even Sister Mathilde doesn't realize she dislikes me. She thinks she's punishing me only for the good of my immortal soul."

"Perhaps she does like you. She's often cross with me too."

Juliette shook her head. "She's younger and more clever than the other nuns. She can see how selfish I am."

Catherine felt helpless. Juliette, who never needed anything, needed something from her now, but she didn't have the least notion what it might be.

Juliette chuckled. "I see you give me no argument."

"You can be wondrously kind when it pleases you. But at times you are so involved with your painting that you forget the needs of others."

"And you think too much of the needs of others. It's a dangerous practice. It's much safer to close everyone out and live only for yourself."

"You don't close me out."

"I probably would if I could. You won't let me." The fingers threaded together on Juliette's lap suddenly contracted. "I closed *her* out."

"Her?"

"The queen," Juliette whispered. "I closed her out and refused to think about her. I was never happy anywhere before I came to the abbey. Don't I have the right to be happy? I want to stay here with the sisters and paint wonderful pictures and tease you when you become too odiously prim and proper. I don't want to have to leave here and go to help her."

"The Reverend Mother said the National Assembly put the queen and the rest of the royal family in the Temple for their protection."

"That's what they said when they forced them to leave Versailles for the Tuileries. But that was to go to another palace, not to a prison. The tower of the Temple is so gloomy, so grim."

"You couldn't do anything to help her, even if you did leave the abbey." Catherine added, "And they may not be quite as comfortable in the tower, but I'm certain they're in no danger."

"I may be selfish, but I'll not lie to myself."

"But the Reverend Mother said no one would hurt—"

"I don't want to talk about it. I've already decided I won't leave here until Jean Marc takes you away." Her gaze returned to the rose-pink stone walls of the abbey and some of the tension left her face. "There are silences here. Beautiful silences. I didn't know anyone could paint a silence until I came here."

Catherine understood. Some of Juliette's recent

paintings possessed a tranquility as hushed as the stillness of the chapel at dawn.

"I have a present for you."

"A present?"

Juliette fumbled in the pocket of her gray gown and handed her a paint-stained, knotted linen handkerchief. "I'll remember you, but I thought you'd probably need something to remind you of me. You'll marry your handsome Philippe and have ten children and—"

"You're speaking foolishly. I haven't seen Philippe more than three times since I came to the abbey. He thinks of me as a child."

"You're an heiress. He'll change his mind." Juliette bit her lower lip. "I didn't mean to say that. You know my unruly tongue. Perhaps your Philippe is as honorable as he is comely. How do I know?"

"You'll marry too. Most women marry except the nuns."

"I shall probably never marry. Who would marry me? I'm not at all pretty and I have no dowry." Juliette lifted her chin defiantly. "Besides, I see no advantage in being a man's chattel. It seems to me Madame de Pompadour and Madame Du Barry lived much more interesting lives than mere wives would." She suddenly grinned. "I'll be no man's slave. Instead, I shall become a famous painter like Madame Vigée Le Brun. No, much more famous."

Catherine finally got the knot in the handkerchief undone. "You mean only a quarter of what you say." She began unfolding the handkerchief. "And you delight in making me—" She broke off as she looked down at the circle of gold on which a single spray of lilac was exquisitely carved. She recognized the necklace immediately. Juliette had only one piece of jewelry, and Catherine had seen it on rare occasions through the years. "I can't take it. You told me Her Majesty gave this to you for your eighth natal day."

Juliette's expression became shuttered. "I'm not sentimental. The queen has forgotten me. It was always my mother she loved and she never gave me a thought unless I was underfoot." She shrugged dismissively, her gaze fixed eagerly on Catherine's face. "Open it."

"It's a locket? I thought it only a necklace. The opening is almost seamless. . . ." Catherine stopped as the locket sprang open between her fingers. She stared down in disbelief at the painted miniature in the locket. She whispered, "It is I. It is . . . beautiful."

"It's executed well enough, I suppose. I've never worked on a miniature before. It was quite interest—" Juliette stared at Catherine in disgust. "Holy Mother, you're not going to cry?"

"Yes." Catherine looked up, the tears running down her face. "I'll weep if I wish to weep."

"I did it only because I wanted to learn how to paint a miniature and I wouldn't have given it to you if I'd known you were going to blubber like this."

"Well, I won't give it back." Catherine slipped the long, delicate chain over her head and settled the locket on her breast. "Not ever. And when I'm a very old lady I'll show it to my grandchildren and tell them it was painted by my dearest friend." She wiped her cheeks with the rumpled linen handkerchief. "And, when they ask me why she painted me as so much more beautiful than I could ever hope to be"—Catherine paused and met Juliette's gaze—"I shall tell them that my friend was a little peculiar and could find no other way to tell me she loved me as much as I loved her."

Juliette stared at her in astonishment for a minute before she shifted her gaze to the locket. "It's nothing. I'm . . . glad you're pleased with it." She jumped to her feet. "I'd better get back to the abbey. Sister Mary Magdalene will be . . ." She trailed off as she plunged into the long grass and straggly weeds. Jumping over low tombstones, she hurried toward the gate in the stone wall enclosing the cemetery.

Juliette was running away. Catherine rose slowly to her feet, her palm closing caressingly around the smooth warmth of the golden locket at her breast. The locket's warmth came from being in Juliette's pocket, close to her friend's body. How long had Juliette been

carrying that paint-smudged, clumsily knotted handkerchief around with her? How like Juliette to do something thoughtful and kind, then claim it as selfishness.
Juliette was so much braver than she when confronted
with life and death but scurried away like a frightened
squirrel at the slightest hint of sentiment. Affection
swelled through Catherine, tightening her throat and
bringing the tears Juliette so despised to her eyes again.
She cupped her mouth with her hand and called to
Juliette, who had now reached the gate. "Remember to
wash the paint off your hands before you go see the
Reverend Mother."

Juliette turned and waved in acknowledgment, the
sunlight glinting on her wild mop of dark curls. Then
she was running across the vegetable garden toward the
abbey, her skirts flying.

Catherine started after her, picking her way carefully among the crosses. As she reached the gate of the
cemetery, the Comte de Montard's large berlin, now
burdened with his daughter's bags, was lumbering out
the south courtyard gates. The coachman snapped his
whip, urging the horses to a faster clip. Cecile de
Montard was on her way to Switzerland via Paris.

Change. Catherine suddenly felt a chill similar to
the one she had experienced when she opened the
door to the crypt. She didn't understand anything
about this tempest threatening to disrupt their lives.
Great and terrible changes had swept through France
since the fall of the Bastille that signaled the beginning
of the revolution. Riots and hunger, peasant uprisings,
massacres, religious orders suppressed, the shifting of
power from the king and nobles to the Legislative
Assembly, the declaration of war against Austria and
Prussia.

The nuns had taught them the revolution was
caused by a combination of many things but most of
them seemed to concern hunger. The terrible hunger
for bread by the starving peasants, the bourgeoisie's
hunger for equal power with the nobles, the hunger of
the nobles for additional power from the king, the

hunger of the idealists for rights such as the ones won in America's war for independence.

Catherine wished them all well with their aims, particularly those poor peasants, but none of it really touched her here at the abbey. She just wished all this turmoil would disperse, leaving tranquility in its wake.

She began to run toward the high, secure walls surrounding the abbey, feeling the blood tingling in her veins as the cool morning wind tore at her hair and stung her cheeks. There was really nothing to worry about. The sun was shining, she and Juliette were both young and strong, and they would be friends forever and ever and ever.

The bells were ringing!

Juliette opened her eyes to the pitch darkness of her cell. The darkness was not unusual. They always rose before dawn for matins.

It was the screams that were unusual.

Raw screams of terror shredded the silence. Was the abbey on fire?

Juliette shook her head to clear it of the last vestiges of sleep and scrambled off her pallet. Fire was always a danger. An ember left smoldering in the huge fireplace in the scullery, a lighted candle forgotten in the chapel.

She lit the candle in the copper holder on the rough cedar table before pulling on her gown, her fingers fumbling frantically with the fastenings.

"Juliette!" Catherine was at the door of her cell, her long pale brown hair tumbling about her shoulders, her eyes wide with fright. "The bells . . . the screaming. What's happening?"

"How do I know?" Juliette jammed her feet into her slippers and grabbed the candle. "Come quickly. I have no desire to be roasted alive if the abbey's on fire."

"Do you think—"

"I'll think later." Juliette grabbed Catherine's hand and pulled her into the corridor. A crush of frightened girls in various states of undress clogged the narrow passage.

"We'll never get through to the courtyard. Come." Juliette turned and began shoving her way in the opposite direction toward a small arched oak door. "The chamber of learning. There's a window."

Catherine followed her down the hall and into the deserted room. They dodged long writing tables as they raced to the deeply recessed window. Juliette slid back the bolt and threw open the wooden shutters. "It *is* a fire. Look at the—"

Torches. Men with torches. Men with swords. Men dressed in rough striped trousers and flowing linen shirts, some with strange red woolen caps. It seemed there were hundreds of men. Shouts. Laughter. Curses.

And screams.

"Dear God," Juliette whispered. "Sister Mathilde . . ."

The nun was lying on the cobblestones, her habit in rags, her legs obscenely parted and held by two laughing men as a third man wearing a red woolen cap brutally plunged his member into her body.

"We've got to help her." Catherine started to clamber onto the recessed windowsill. "We can't stay here. We've got to help all of them."

The same horror was happening all over the courtyard. The nuns were being dragged from their cells, stripped, pulled to the cobblestones.

"We can't help them." Juliette jerked Catherine back into the room away from the window. "Can't you see there are too many of them to fight? But we can try to stop those silly sheep in the hall from joining them." She turned back toward the hallway.

Catherine grabbed her arm. "Wait," she whispered. "It's too late."

The young girls had already reached the courtyard. They stopped in bewildered horror at the sight that met their eyes.

A laughing shout from one of the men. "Fresh meat. Leave the old crows."

"Here's pretty young pullets for the plucking."

And new screams shrilled through the courtyard.

"Why?" Catherine asked. "Why are they doing this? They're *hurting* them."

"Because they're beasts who want only to rut," Juliette muttered, trying desperately to think what to do. "We can't go through the north courtyard and we can't hide here. They may come searching."

"Henriette Balvour." Catherine couldn't take her gaze from the horror outside in the courtyard. "Look what those two men are doing to her. She's only ten years old."

"I'm not going to look. And neither will you." Juliette pulled Catherine farther away from the window and slammed the shutter. She blew out the candle and set it on the windowsill. "We can't help them, but we may be able to help ourselves."

"She's only ten years old," Catherine repeated dully.

Juliette took her by the shoulders and shook her. "If we go out there and try to help, the same thing's going to happen to us. Do you want that to happen?"

"No, but we—"

"Then no arguments. I *won't* let them do that to you." Juliette tried to ignore the sounds filtering through the wooden shutters. The screams were awful but the whimpering was worse. Someone was sobbing for her mother. Little Henriette? "We have to find a place to hide."

"Where? There's no place . . ."

Juliette seized Catherine's hand and led her down the corridor toward the north courtyard.

Catherine tried to pull away. "We can't go there. You just said—"

"We're not going into the courtyard. We're going to run down the arcade to the bell tower. It's only a few yards away and there's a back entrance that leads from the tower to the south courtyard."

"What if . . . this is happening in the south courtyard too?"

"We'll worry about that then. We can't be any worse off than we are now."

The door leading to the north courtyard had been left open, and as they reached it, Juliette pulled Catherine to one side, pressing against the wall and into the shadows.

Catherine shivered. "What if they see us? I'm so frightened, Juliette."

"So am I." Juliette cautiously peered out into the courtyard. No one was under the arcade. All the women had been pulled into the courtyard where the rapine was going on. "Run as fast as you can for the bell tower and dart between the stone columns. I'll be right behind you. If they catch me, don't stop. You won't be able to help, and there's no need for both of us to . . ." Catherine was frantically shaking her head and Juliette glared at her. "Do what I tell you. Promise me."

"I couldn't let them hurt you." Catherine was trembling uncontrollably but her voice was firm. "I'd have to try to stop it."

"Oh, God in heaven," Juliette said in exasperation. "If those pigs catch you, do you want me to fling myself in their arms to rescue you?"

"No, but I can't—"

"Then it's agreed. If we become separated, we try to save ourselves."

Catherine was silent.

"You know I'd never let those *canailles* defeat me," Juliette said. "I'd find a way to get free. Now, we don't have time to argue. Yes?"

Catherine hesitated and then reluctantly nodded.

"Good." Juliette's hand compressed bracingly around Catherine's. "When you get through the south courtyard, run for the cemetery."

"The cemetery?"

Juliette nodded. "We'll let Sister Bernadette hide us until this is over and they've gone away."

"They may not go away." Catherine shuddered as she lifted her hands to her ears to shut out the screams. "It seems as if it's already been going on forever."

"They'll go away. Men tire of fornicating. My mother once said—" Juliette broke off. This wasn't the same as the rutting that had taken place in the bedchambers at Versailles. In those scented, silk-hung rooms the men and women had at least made a pretense of tenderness. Here there was only a fever of violence and brutality. "Leave the door of the bell tower open and be sure and look outside before you go into the south courtyard. Remember to wait for me at the tomb. Are you ready?"

Catherine nodded.

"Go!"

Catherine streaked out the door, keeping close to the wall.

Juliette waited tensely for a shout to go up or one of the men to detach himself from the orgy and run after her.

Catherine reached the door of the bell tower, threw it open, and disappeared inside.

Juliette's fear lessened a fraction, but she waited to be sure no notice had been taken and no tardy pursuit was to follow. Then she bolted across the few yards separating the students' cells from the bell tower, ran up the three stone steps, crossed the threshold, and slammed the door behind her. Darkness.

Her heart pounded painfully as she leaned back against the brass-studded oak door in an agony of relief. Gradually her eyes became accustomed to the gloom and she could discern the long flight of spiraling open wooden stairs a few yards away leading to the belfry. Beyond the staircase moonlight streamed through an open doorway. Catherine must have found the south courtyard deserted and taken the second step to freedom. Juliette straightened and started eagerly for the open doorway.

"You weren't thinking of leaving, Citizeness?"

Juliette froze.

A small, slender shadow detached itself from the darkness beneath the spiraling stairs. It held a sword in one hand and a coil of rope in the other. "Not after I've gone to so much trouble and been waiting so patiently," the voice continued. Juliette now watched as the figure waved the sword toward the open doorway. "Your little friend was in such a hurry, I wasn't able to get down the steps from the belfry in time to detain her. However, I'm sure someone else will intercept the little flower before she gets too far. From the glimpse I caught before she ran out the door I'd say she was quite pretty. I was about to go after her myself when you ran into the bell tower."

Juliette took a step back, her gaze fixed on the sword. She had been so close to freedom. Mother of God, she didn't want to die.

"Ah, well, you're a little thin but not unattractive yourself. Permit me to introduce myself. I'm Raoul Dupree. And what's your name, little one?" The man stepped forward, peering at her face.

Juliette didn't answer.

"Tell me, do you wish me to throw you to that mob in the courtyard?"

"Don't be absurd. Of course I don't."

"Very wise. I'm afraid the good sisters and your fellow schoolmates are having a dreadful time of it. It's regrettable, but the only way I could get my patriots to travel from Paris to do their duty was to offer them the opportunity to quench their lusts on these fine aristos."

"They're raping the nuns too."

"Well, the Marseilles are none too fond of the church." Dupree shook his head. "I must admit the sight of so much carnal revelry has aroused me, but I have a distaste for seconds. That's why I rang the bell." He chuckled. "I thought I'd catch a sweet little virgin for my very own. Unfortunately, your friends were seen almost as soon as they poured out the door and I feared I was going to be deprived of my pleasure." He pressed the tip of his sword to Juliette's throat. "Are you afraid? You're not speaking."

Juliette swallowed. "Of course I'm afraid. I'd be stupid not to be frightened."

"And you're not stupid or you'd have run bleating into the arms of those louts like all the others. I think I shall enjoy you, little aristo."

"You'll get no pleasure from me."

"You're wrong." He held out the coil of rope to

her. "However, I have no time now. I must see to organizing the trials. Form a loop in the rope and slip it around your wrists."

Juliette didn't move.

"Shall I tell you what will happen to you if you don't do as I command? One of two things. I'll either plunge this sword into your throat or I'll march you out to the courtyard and toss you to the Marseilles. I really don't want to make that choice. What I'd like to do is tie you up and leave you here. Then, when I have time to indulge myself, I'll return to your eager arms. Now, which shall it be?"

Juliette quickly considered her situation. Dupree intended to save her for himself. While he was gone she might be able to escape the ropes. He might even forget she was there once he joined the frenzy outside. In any event, she had little choice. She took the rope, formed a noose, and slipped it over her wrists.

"Very sensible." Dupree tightened the noose about her wrists and then wound the rope around her torso. "But if you weren't sensible, you'd be out in the courtyard with the rest, wouldn't you? Come over here beneath the steps." He sheathed the sword and jerked her into the dark recess beneath the staircase. He passed the rope three times around the fifth step before knotting it. "That should be adequate. Now, all you have to do is stand here and wait for me." He leaned forward and patted her cheek and then stopped to stroke it. "What soft skin. Don't scream or you'll attract some of those crude fellows in the courtyard. We wouldn't want that, would we?"

She didn't answer, surreptitiously testing the thick ropes binding her wrists.

"No, we wouldn't want that." Dupree moved toward the door to the north courtyard, his steps precise, mincing. He opened the door and the light from the torches in the courtyard allowed her to get her first clear look at him. He reminded her of a cat with his thin, triangular face and slightly slanted hazel eyes. Even his body was catlike, small, wiry almost to the point of scrawniness. Instead of the rough loose trousers and coarse shirts of the men in the courtyard, he was dressed in an elegant light blue coat trimmed in gold brocade and dark blue knee breeches. "*Au revoir,* Citizeness. I'll return as soon as I can lure these good men from their pleasure to their duty in starting the trials."

He shut the door firmly behind him.

Trial. It was the second time Dupree had mentioned a trial. Juliette dismissed the thought as she concentrated on her own predicament. The ropes were too strong to break and the knots dismayingly secure.

She bent her head forward and began to gnaw with her teeth at the loop of the rope wound around the step.

There were men in the south courtyard too!

Catherine skidded to a stop halfway across the courtyard and shrank into the shadow of the tall cistern. She'd thought the courtyard was deserted but there was no mistaking the sound of a woman sobbing and masculine laughter coming from the direction of the passage linking the north and south courtyards.

The gate seemed a hundred miles away as she glanced longingly at it. The atrocity going on seemed to be limited to four or five men gathered around the supine body of a nude woman, but she couldn't risk one of them glancing toward the gate.

She could tell by the pleas, sobs, and prayers tumbling in an indiscriminate stream from the woman's lips that she was one of the nuns but she didn't know which one. Sister Thérèse? Sister Hélène? It would be a sin not to help that poor woman.

Catherine took an impulsive step forward and then stopped in an agony of indecision. She had the right to risk herself but not Juliette. If Juliette saw Catherine in trouble, she knew she would forget every practical argument and rush to save her. Juliette had great confidence in her own abilities and was more gallant than she knew herself to be. A choice. She and Juliette or that poor woman being assaulted by those beasts?

She fell to her knees by the cistern, trying to close out both the sobs of the woman and the coarse remarks of the men. She would wait and hope they would leave the courtyard quickly after they were done with the nun.

She closed her eyes, her lips forming the silent words of prayer. Sweet Jesus, deliver us from evil . . .

Where was Juliette? Had she seen the men and remained in the bell tower, waiting for them to begone?

Go to Sister Bernadette, Juliette had said. Yes, she'd be safe in the tomb. Why had she ever been afraid of the dead when life was so much more savage? She wrapped her arms around herself, trying to stop the shudders racking her body.

Please come, Juliette. I'm so alone.

Mary, Mother of God, let them not find me.

Let Juliette be safe.

Let all those poor women stop suffering.

"Well, what do we have here?"

The sudden shout caused Catherine's heart to lurch sickeningly.

"How very naughty. You shouldn't have dragged her out of the courtyard around here. You know the agreement. We're all to share and share alike."

There was a burst of laughter from one of the men. "There's not much to share. She's only a stringy old crow of a woman."

"Still, she belongs with the rest of the spoils."

Catherine leaned forward to venture a swift glance around the curve of the cistern. She could make out two silhouettes moving toward the men. Whoever the new arrivals were, they seemed to be in positions of authority.

"Now, stop ramming her and bring her back to the courtyard."

There was a grumbling among the men, but they began to stir from the spread-eagled body of the nun. "Get up, whore."

"She won't move." A coarse chuckle. "You see? She doesn't want to go back to the rest. She likes us."

"Then carry her."

More grumbling, then the naked woman was lifted by one of the brawnier men and carried toward the two men waiting in the shadows. "What difference does it make? There are plenty of women to go around."

"Rules are rules."

Catherine tensed, her gaze fixed eagerly on the departing figures. They entered the shadows. Soon their footsteps faded. She jumped to her feet and streaked toward the open gate.

A shout!

Dear Mary, someone had seen her!

Footsteps on the cobblestones.

Please God, don't let them catch me.

She tore through the vegetable garden.

She couldn't hear them behind her any longer. Was it because they were running on the soft earth instead of on the cobblestones or was she not their prey?

Her heart pounded so hard she was sure it would burst.

The blood drummed in her temples.

She was running among the graves. Why had she never noticed the moss growing on the crosses looked like rivulets of blood?

Sister Bernadette. She must reach Sister Bernadette.

She heard something behind her. A laugh? She was afraid to glance over her shoulder to see.

It could have been the wind.

Oh, let it be the wind.

Gabriel's marble wings shining in the moonlight. Sister Bernadette's tomb. She frantically shoved the bolt aside, dashed into the crypt, and slammed the door behind her.

No bolt on the inside.

Of course not. The dead needed no locks.

She backed away from the door.

Her hip collided with the marble sarcophagus.

She scarcely felt the pain as she sank to her knees beside Juliette's easel. The darkness pressed in on her, taking her breath.

She leaned her hot cheek against the cold marble of the sarcophagus, her gaze straining toward the door.

Protect me, Sister Bernadette. You were only ten

and eight when you died. You must have wanted to live too.

Protect me. Don't let them find me.

Dear God, *why* had she come here? This tomb wasn't a sanctuary.

It was a trap.

The door of the crypt swung open.

SIX

"*Sacre bleu*, you've almost got the rope gnawed through. What an industrious vixen you are." Raoul Dupree held the lantern in his hand closer to the ropes and smiled at Juliette as he cut the bonds with his sword. "If I'd been gone only a few minutes more, you might have freed yourself. But life is filled with might-have-beens, isn't it?"

Juliette hastened to mask her disappointment. She refused to give the *canaille* the satisfaction. "You might as well have stayed away. I'll give you no pleasure."

"Oh, but you will." Dupree stripped her of the ropes and pulled her toward the door. "However, not the immediate carnal pleasure I'd anticipated. Unfortunately, I indulged my appetites while I was going about my duties. I'll have to have time to regain my virility before I'm ready to enjoy you, Citizeness . . . ?" Dupree lifted a questioning brow. "What did you say your name was?"

"I didn't say."

"No matter. We'll give you another name. You shall be Citizeness Justice." His pouty lips tilted up in a feline smile. "Every court needs a symbol, and you shall be ours. I think it very fitting under the circumstances. Sweet, pure Citizeness Justice."

"Court?"

"Let me explain. We're going to have a trial. It's come to the ears of the Paris commune that the nuns of the abbey, in order to help their former patroness, the queen, have turned this establishment into a bordello. They've offered their own bodies and that of their students to sway young, gullible patriots from fighting for the revolutionary cause and deserting to the Austrians."

Juliette gazed at him incredulously. "That's ridiculous. No one will believe you."

He chuckled. "Why not? Every man here can testify there are no virgins at the Abbaye de la Reine."

She spat in his face.

He went rigid. "I did not like that." He reached in his pocket, drew out a lace-trimmed handkerchief, and wiped the spittle from his left cheek. "You must behave with better decorum if you're going to survive a few hours longer." He jerked her forward. "Every insolence will be met with punishment. Every obedience a reward. You understand?"

"No."

"You will, Citizeness. You will."

The golden chalice of the holy sacrament was filled to the brim with dark red liquid.

"Drink it," Dupree said softly. "And perhaps we'll spare the next one."

She couldn't drink it. They were probably lying to her anyway. These monsters would spare none of them.

She shook her head.

Dupree nodded to the man wearing a red patriot's

bonnet bearing a tricolored revolutionary cockade. The man immediately started toward the Reverend Mother kneeling naked before the tribunal table.

"Wait!" Juliette took the cup and brought it quickly to her lips.

A cheer went up from the men in the courtyard.

The liquid smelled sickeningly of copper. Dear God, she couldn't . . .

She closed her eyes and drained every drop.

"Very good," Dupree murmured.

Juliette's stomach rebelled. She turned quickly aside from the tribunal table and violently vomited up the contents of her stomach onto the stones of the courtyard.

"I'm afraid that won't do," Dupree said regretfully. "You cheated, Citizeness Justice. You'll have to try again."

He motioned to the man wearing the red bonnet.

The man grinned, flexed the brawny muscles of his arms, and took two steps forward toward the Reverend Mother.

Juliette screamed.

The travesty of justice was over, disintegrating into a brutal slaughter with clubs and swords. Juliette gazed at the sea of faces of the men in the courtyard as they went about their carnage. She had once told Catherine she possessed the vision to comprehend and appreciate the subtle nuances of ugliness. Now she knew that until this night she had been ignorant about true ugliness.

"Come along, my sweet." Dupree took her elbow and propelled her toward the bell tower. "I have an impulse to enjoy you before Citizeness Justice goes beneath the sword."

She walked beside him without speaking.

"You're suddenly quite meek. I do hope you're going to show a little spirit when I'm between your thighs."

Dupree closed the door of the bell tower and placed his sword on one of the spiral steps. "Lie down."

She stretched out on the cold flagstones and closed her eyes.

Blood.

She felt the heat of Dupree's body as he lay down and took her in his arms.

Screams from the children. Screams from the nuns. Blood.

Dupree's hand closed on her breast. "Open your eyes. I want to see you looking at me, Citizeness."

She obediently opened her eyes. He was bending over her, his cat face only inches from hers. He was smiling.

"Your eyes are glittering. Are you weeping, little Citi—"

She sank her teeth into his throat. The coppery taste was in her mouth again, but now she welcomed it.

He shrieked. He tried to shake her off his neck, but she followed him, her teeth biting deeper.

"Bitch." He began cursing. "Animal." He tried to lift her off but her arms closed fiercely around him in a mockery of an embrace.

The blood was pouring onto his shoulder. She shook her head savagely to tear his flesh. Then, as he gasped with pain, she pushed him aside, leapt to her feet, and grabbed the sword from the step. Dupree opened his lips to scream, but the flat of the sword came down on his temple before he could utter a sound. He slumped to the side and lay still.

Pity. She had meant to strike him with the edge of the blade.

She turned and fled out the door leading to the south courtyard which was deserted. She ran across the cobblestones to the gates, through the vegetable garden and up the hill to the cemetery.

Catherine had to be in the crypt, she thought desperately. She must have reached safety or she would have been brought to trial with the others at that mockery of a tribunal.

The door of the crypt was open.

Profound relief made Juliette's pace falter momentarily. Catherine was always so afraid of the dark, but she should have closed it, Juliette thought impatiently. Didn't she realize the open door would be noticed?

"Bitch, don't just lie there." The sound of flesh striking flesh. "Move."

Juliette froze. She could barely discern the heavy form of a man humping over the figure of a woman, moving rhythmically between her pale thighs.

Catherine. The woman had to be Catherine.

"No!"

Juliette didn't realize she had screamed out the word until the stout man looked over his shoulder in startled dismay. "What! Who are—"

Juliette didn't make the same mistake this time. The sword came down on his neck blade first. He slumped over, covering Catherine's slender body like an obscene blanket.

Juliette ran forward, pushing his heavy carcass off Catherine. "Filth! *Canaille!*" She knelt, cradling Catherine's still body, rocking her back and forth in an agony of sympathy. "Sweet Jesus, they're all filth. Are you hurt?"

Catherine shuddered and didn't answer.

"A stupid question. Of course you're hurt." Juliette smoothed Catherine's hair back from her face. "But you're safe now. I'm here."

"Filth," Catherine whispered. "You're right. Dirty. I'm so dirty."

"No, not you. Them," Juliette said fiercely. She pulled Catherine's gown down about her thighs and sat her up. "Listen, we have no time. They'll be looking for us soon. We must get away from here."

"It's too late."

Juliette shook her. "It's not too late. We're not going to let them best us. I'm not going to let them kill you."

"Filth. I won't ever be clean again, will I?"

"Shh." Juliette gave Catherine a quick hug, picked up the sword again, and rose. "Can you stand up?"

Catherine looked at her dumbly.

Juliette took her wrist and yanked her to her feet. "Do you want them to catch me? Do you want them to do the same thing to me they did to you?"

Catherine slowly shook her head.

"Then come with me and do as I say." Juliette didn't wait for an answer but pulled Catherine stumbling from the tomb. "We have to hurry or they'll—" She stopped, her gaze fixed on the abbey. "*Bon Dieu,* they've set fire to it."

The abbey wasn't fully ablaze yet. Only intermittent flames showed in the windows of the chapel. Well, what had she expected? This final desecration was no less terrible than what had gone before. It might even be for the best. Perhaps Dupree would think she had been butchered like the rest or burned up in the fire and wouldn't search the surrounding countryside. She turned away, pulling Catherine through the gates of the cemetery. "We'll skirt the road and try to make our way to the forest. Then after they've left we'll walk toward Paris."

"They're singing."

"It's easier to hide in the city than it is in the open countryside, and it will—" Juliette broke off. Dear God, they *were* singing. The stirring strains of the song lent a macabre beauty to the destruction below. She knew if she lived to be an old woman she would never forget standing on this hillside and listening to those murderers singing their song of liberty and revolution.

"Filth," Catherine murmured, rubbing frantically at the front of her gown.

"Shh. We're too close." Juliette pulled her forward through the vegetable garden, angling past the abbey wall south toward the forest. "Just be quiet a little longer and we'll—"

"Wait. You're going the wrong way."

At the deep masculine voice Juliette whirled to face a man standing in the shadows of the convent wall. Only one man, she realized with relief. Juliette's grasp tightened on Catherine's wrist as she lifted the sword. "Take a step toward us and I'll slice your heart out."

"I have no intention of attacking you." He paused. "You're the Citizeness Justice that Dupree had sitting at the tribunal. You carry Dupree's sword?"

"Yes."

"Did you kill him?"

"No. You're not going to stop us. I won't let—"

"I'm not trying to stop you." His voice was heavy with weariness. "I'm only trying to tell you that you're going the wrong way. Dupree's set a watch. They will capture you if you are within a stone's throw of this road."

She gazed at him suspiciously. "I don't believe you. Why should you tell me the truth if you were in the courtyard with those . . ." She searched for a word, but there was none vile enough. "Why are you here? Did you grow bored with slaughtering innocent women?"

"I didn't kill anyone. I don't—" He stopped. "I came into the courtyard just before Dupree took you from the tribunal. I was sent here to witness—I didn't know it was going to be like this."

Juliette stared at him in disbelief.

"I tell you I didn't know," he said fiercely. "I have no love for either you aristos or the church, but I don't murder the helpless."

"Murder." Catherine's words came haltingly. "They . . . killed them?"

"Yes." Juliette shot her a worried glance, but the news seemed to have little impact on Catherine's shocked state.

"All of them?"

"I think so." Juliette's gaze shifted to the man in the shadows. "He should know better than I."

"I didn't stay to count the dead."

"You didn't stay to help the living either."

"I couldn't help them. Could you have helped them?"

"You're one of them. They might have listened to you. Why should—" A sudden shout caused Juliette to stiffen with fear.

"Hurry. Come with me." The stranger stepped from the shadows and Juliette registered a swift impression of a man above medium height with a square, hard jaw. His eyes were arresting. They were fierce, light-colored, the eyes of an old man in a young man's face. "They'll probably come streaming out of the gate any moment. I have a carriage waiting around the turn of the road about a quarter of a mile from here."

He wore a dark brown cutaway coat, well-fitting trousers, knee-high boots, a fine white linen shirt. He didn't look like those *canailles* in the courtyard, but Dupree had also been dressed in the guise of a gentleman and he was even more monstrous than the others. "I don't trust you."

"Then die here," he said harshly. "What are two more aristos to me? Why should I care if you're bludgeoned like cows in the marketplace? I don't know what impulse made me offer my aid in the first place." He turned on his heel and strode away in the direction he had indicated the carriage waited.

Juliette hesitated. It could be that he was like Dupree and merely wanted the exclusive use of their bodies before he dispatched them.

Another shout. This one sounded dangerously close.

"Wait." She hurried after him, dragging Catherine along with her, her other hand clutching the handle of the sword. As long as she had a weapon, the danger of trusting him was not so great. She could always split the bastard as she had the man in the tomb. "We're going with you."

He didn't look at her. "Then be quick. I have no desire to be found with you and have my own throat cut."

"We are hurrying." She turned to Catherine. "It's going to be all right, Catherine. We'll be safe soon."

Catherine looked at her blankly.

"What's wrong with her?" The young man's gaze was fixed on Catherine's face.

"What do you think is wrong?" Juliette stared at him scornfully. "She's been treated as gently as those other women have been treated. She'll be fortunate if she keeps her senses."

His gaze slid away from Catherine. "I've always found women have a greater strength than we men think they have. She'll survive to get her own back."

"She wouldn't know how. I'd have to teach her."

Juliette smiled grimly. "I may do it. Oh, yes, I'd delight in sending you all to perdition after this night."

"I can understand how you'd feel that." The heaviness of his voice startled her. They reached the curve of the road and he stopped abruptly. "Stay here. I have to get rid of Laurent."

"Who is Laurent?"

"The coachman. I don't want word of my helping you getting back to Paris. I'll send him to the abbey on some pretext or other."

"A massacre is permitted, but a rescue is forbidden?"

"Stay hidden in the shrubbery until I return." Without another glance he disappeared beyond the turn of the road.

Juliette pulled Catherine behind the screen of holly bushes at the side of the road. They were still too close to the abbey. She could hear the sound of shouts and the dull roar as the flames engulfed the buildings of the convent.

"Dirty," Catherine whispered.

"It's not true." Juliette gently pushed a strand of light brown hair back from Catherine's face. "You're clean, Catherine."

Catherine shook her head.

Juliette opened her lips to argue but closed them again without speaking. She wasn't sure there were words to pierce the stupor enveloping Catherine. She would have to worry about Catherine's sanity later. Now she had to keep them both alive.

She stiffened as she saw a figure hurrying around the bend of the road. The man was tall, lanky. The coachman Laurent? Whoever he was, he hurried past them down the road in the direction of the abbey.

Three minutes later two men followed him around the turn. One man was powerfully built, deep-chested, a veritable giant with a huge leonine head. The other she recognized as the young man who had led them from the abbey. He now carried a coach lantern, and the flickering flame lit the square planes of his cheekbones and deepened the green of his eyes.

Juliette stepped out of the shrubbery to confront them. "Can we go now?"

The larger man stopped in surprise. "*Bon Dieu.* What have we here?"

Juliette gave him an impatient glance. He was probably the ugliest man she had ever seen. A scar twisted his upper lip into a permanent sneer, his nose was smashed into his face. Smallpox scars added to the ruin of his visage. "We have no time to chatter. We're still too close to the abbey."

"I see. My young friend didn't explain the exact nature of the situation."

"There wasn't time, Georges Jacques."

"I think we must take time." The older man glanced at the sword Juliette still clutched. "Introduce me to the ladies, François."

"I don't know their names. We should be on our way while the confusion—"

"Stop hurrying me, François." Steel layered the softness of the ugly man's voice. "We have a situation here that may be very dangerous for me and I think you know it." His gaze switched to Juliette. "Let us introduce ourselves, shall we? I'm Georges Jacques Danton and this fierce young man is François Etchelet."

"Juliette de Clement. Catherine Vasaro." Juliette's gaze narrowed on Danton's face. "I don't care how dangerous it is for you. I'm not going to let you take us back there."

"No? I didn't say I would turn you over to the tender hands of the Marseilles. Though the possibility does exist."

"No, Georges Jacques." François Etchelet shook his head. "It does not exist. We're taking them back to Paris."

Danton glanced at him in surprise. "Indeed?"

François looked at Juliette. "The carriage is down the road. Wait for us there."

Juliette gazed at him suspiciously. Then she turned away and led Catherine in the direction he'd indicated.

François waited until they had vanished from view before he whirled back to face Danton. "You didn't tell me it would be a slaughter."

Danton went still. "Was it? I had hoped Dupree would be content with rapine here."

"He was not. The debauchery and slaughter sickened my very soul."

"How extraordinary when you're quite accustomed to violence."

Etchelet's eyes were suddenly blazing. "Not like this. I want no part of it."

"You're already a part of it. You were eager enough to go to the abbey when I sent you." Danton smiled grimly. "You were like a hound scenting a stag in the forest."

"I didn't realize they would . . ." Etchelet gestured impatiently with his free hand. "What does it matter? We must get these young women away before Dupree discovers they've escaped."

"You're upset." Danton shrugged. "Truly, I did not imagine it would be so bad when I sent you to represent me. Actually, knowing how hot-blooded you are, I hoped to give you enough of a taste of the savagery of these affairs to make you shy away from Marat's other parties."

"Parties? There are going to be more?"

Danton nodded. "One at the Abbaye Saint Germain-des-Prés this afternoon and another at the convent of Carmel earlier this evening. There will be others."

François felt the nausea rise in his throat as he remembered the horrors he had just witnessed. "In the name of God, why?"

"Who knows? Marat claims the aristos and clergy within France are plotting to overthrow the government and hand the country over to the Austrian armies. He calls it a necessary elimination of the royalist scum in the prisons."

"And that was why thousands of aristos and priests were rounded up last week and thrown into prisons?"

"But if my memory serves me, you made no objection to the arrests, François. Are you becoming softhearted by any chance?"

"No!" François made no attempt to hide the violence in his tone. He drew a deep breath. "A convent is not a prison. Nuns are not aristos."

"It was Marat's choice which places would be attacked." Danton glanced away. "We made a bargain. I would not interfere if he kept his hands off the Girondins in the assembly. You know without the Girondins the assembly would be dangerously unbalanced."

"I cannot understand you. Why would you sanction this atrocity? I thought—"

"You thought Madame Revolution was all shining virtue?" Danton shook his massive head. "Only her soul is pure. Her body is that of the lowliest whore, passed from man to man and gowned in the tawdriest compromises."

"I have no use for this particular compromise."

"Nor do I." Danton's gaze went to the turn of the road where the two women had disappeared. "And so I'm willing to give you a sop to your conscience as long as it can be done safely. What excuse is Dupree giving for the massacre of the women of the abbey?"

"Prostitution and treason."

"Flimsy. However, the war hysteria is high enough in Paris for them to accept anything Marat tells them— which means your ladies in distress will likely be condemned as enemies of the revolution." He shrugged. "I'll drive to make sure you get through Dupree's sentries. My ugly face is known well enough so they probably won't stop the coach. If they do, I'll let you deal with them."

"It will be my pleasure."

"I'm sure it will." Danton smiled sardonically. "I can see your temper is not of the best." He started walking to the bend in the road. "I think you'd better ride in the coach with your highborn waifs, my young firebrand. I want no more deaths unless I deem them necessary."

"They're not 'my waifs.' After we get them to Paris, they can take their own risks. I'm done with them."

"We shall see." Danton shot François a speculative glance as he climbed up onto the driver's seat. "Before

now I would never have believed you'd have turned
knight for any aristo. It's clearly an evening for sur-
prises."

François had scarcely seated himself opposite Juliette and Catherine when the coach started with an
abruptness that sent him lurching back against the
cushions.

Juliette waited for him to speak.

He said nothing.

Juliette gazed at him in exasperation. The hard,
stormy intensity François Etchelet radiated would ordi-
narily have intrigued her artist's eye, but at the moment
it served only to annoy her. "Well?"

He gave her a glance. "Georges Jacques will get us
through the sentries." He did not elaborate.

"How can you be sure?"

"He is Danton."

Juliette tried to restrain her irritation. "And what
does that mean?"

"He's the hero of the revolution."

She gazed at him scornfully. "Heroes don't partici-
pate in massacres."

"He's the Minister of Justice, the head of the
Executive Council, and a very great man. Today he
spoke before the entire assembly and saved the revolution. The representatives were like frightened sheep
because the Prussians had taken Verdun and might
march on Paris. They would have disbanded the assembly and surrendered. He wouldn't let them."

"I don't care about your revolution." Her arm
tightened around Catherine's shoulders. "I care only
about her . . . and about myself and the Reverend
Mother and all those—"

"You don't understand."

"Do you?"

"Most of the time I do." He shook his head wearily.
"Not tonight. Why were you even at the abbey? You
should have taken warning when they forbade the nuns

to teach you. To be an aristocrat in France today is to be in peril. You should not—"

"Catherine is no aristocrat." Juliette cut through his words. "Her family is in the perfume trade in Grasse, but your fine patriots didn't question her heritage before they raped her."

François's gaze shifted to Catherine. "She's not of the nobility?"

Juliette shook her head. "It scarcely matters now."

"No, it doesn't matter." He looked at Catherine with a curious intentness that bewildered Juliette. Catherine *was* a sight to stir sympathy in the hardest breast—sitting so still, pale as the moonlight streaming through the windows of the coach. She reminded Juliette of Sister Bernadette's effigy.

However, Juliette somehow doubted if François Etchelet could be easily moved by any woman. Still, she sensed he was no immediate threat to Catherine. Lethargy was attacking Juliette's body and she forced herself to sit up straighter in the seat. She mustn't give in to it. There were still threats to be faced and decisions to be made.

And this François Etchelet could very well be one of the greatest dangers of all. Whatever had motivated him to save them, it certainly wasn't gallantry, and it was clear he resented being thrown into the role of rescuer. "Where are you taking us?"

Etchelet's gaze was still on Catherine's face as he answered Juliette's question with one of his own. "Do you have a family in Paris?"

"Only my mother. The Marquise Celeste de Clement."

"A marquise? Well, she should be able to find a safe place for you to hide. We'll take you both to her."

"It will do no good. She won't want me."

"Your arrival may prove inconvenient, but I don't doubt she'll take you in."

"You're wrong. She doesn't—" She stopped as she saw his closed expression. He wouldn't listen. He was eager to be rid of them. She leaned back and wearily closed her eyes. "You'll see."

"Where does she live?"

"Fourteen rue de Richelieu."

"One of the finest addresses in Paris. I should expect nothing less of a marquise." François leaned forward and drew the heavy velvet curtains over the windows. "However, there's no longer a rue de Richelieu. The government's changed the name to the rue de la Loi. There are many such changes in Paris."

Juliette was too weary to give the scathing comment that occurred to her regarding those changes. She would save her strength for what awaited her arrival at her mother's house.

The coach was challenged only once as they passed Dupree's sentries. Danton met the challenge with boisterous good humor and a ribald remark about his distaste for the carnal talents of the nuns and his eagerness to get back to his wife in Paris. They were allowed to pass.

It was only a few hours before dawn when they arrived at 14 rue de la Loi. The elegant three-story town house sat imposingly among other equally impressive houses on the tree-lined street. However, the other houses were dark, as befitted the lateness of the hour, while Number 14 was ablaze with light.

"Trouble?" Danton smiled mockingly down at François as he lifted Juliette from the coach.

"We've had nothing else. Why should this be different? Are you coming?"

Danton shook his head. "I'll stay here. I have no desire to be connected by anyone with this endeavor. Besides, we may have need of a hurried departure."

Without question and despite his words Danton was enjoying the situation, François thought. He did not wait for Juliette but strode up the six stone steps and knocked on the elaborately carved door.

There was no answer.

He knocked again. Louder.

No answer.

The thunder of the third knock could be heard halfway down the street.

The door was thrown open by a tall, lean woman in a black gown. "Stop," she hissed. "Do you want to wake the neighborhood. Go away."

"I must see the Marquise de Clement."

"In the middle of the night?" The woman was outraged. "This is no time for calls."

"Let us see my mother, Marguerite." Juliette pushed in front of him into the light. "Where is she?"

"In her bedchamber, but you can't—"

Juliette brushed her aside and entered the elegant, venetian-tiled foyer. "Upstairs?"

"Yes, but you're not to disturb her. The poor lamb has enough to worry about without you coming to torment her." Marguerite's disdainful gaze traveled over the torn, bloodstained ruin of Juliette's gray gown. "I see those nuns haven't been able to make a gentle-woman out of you in all these years. What trouble are you in now?"

"This is Marguerite, my mother's servant," Juliette said to François as she moved toward the stairs. "Come along, you won't be satisfied until you see for yourself."

She quickly climbed the stairs, her back very straight.

"She has no time for you," Marguerite called from the bottom of the stairs. "She's sent a footman to hire a carriage to take her away from this horrible city and it will be here any moment."

A door at the head of the stairs flew open. "Marguerite, what is that—" Celeste de Clement stopped in mid-sentence as she caught sight of Juliette. "Good God, what are you doing here?"

Juliette had not seen her mother since she had entered the abbey but there appeared to be little change in her. She might be even more beautiful. Celeste's sea-green velvet gown flattered her tiny waist and a cream-colored lace fichu framed the smooth olive skin of her shoulders. Her shining dark hair was unpow-dered and fell in fashionable ringlets about her heart-shaped face. "I've come to throw myself on your loving protection." Juliette's tone was threaded with irony. "The Abbaye de la Reine was attacked by a mob tonight, and my friend, Catherine, and I need a place to hide."

"They're killing everyone in the prisons." Celeste shuddered. "I didn't know they'd attacked the abbey too. No one told me."

"I believe it's considered customary to express curiosity about one's daughter's welfare in these circumstances. If someone had told you, would you have come running to my aid?"

Her mother bit her lower lip. "Why are you here? You know I can't help you. I can barely help myself. Do you realize that *canaille* Berthold has told me to leave his house? He says the times are growing too dangerous for him to risk harboring a marquise." Her violet eyes glittered with anger. "After I lowered myself to welcome that bourgeois pig to my bed, he abandons me when I most need him. Now I must return to Spain to that boring house in Andorra until I can think what next to do."

She stiffened as her gaze fell on François standing on the steps behind Juliette. "Who is this man?"

"François Etchelet. He brought me here from the abbey."

"Then let him help you." Her mother whirled in a flurry of sea-green velvet, marched back into her chamber, and slammed the door.

"Are you satisfied?" Juliette asked François without expression.

"No." Frustration and exasperation sharpened François's voice. "You're her responsibility and she has to care for you." He climbed the staircase two steps at a time and yanked open the door to the bedchamber.

Celeste de Clement looked up with wide, startled eyes from the portmanteau she was packing.

"How dare you? I told you—"

"She needs your help," François said curtly. "She'll probably be arrested if she's found in Paris in the next few days."

"What about me?" Celeste asked shrilly. "Do you know how dangerous it is for me to be here without protection? Do you realize how many members of the nobility have been arrested in the past week? And now those horrid beasts are murdering and killing and—"

"Raping," Juliette finished from the doorway.

"Well, I'm sure you weren't troubled, *ma fille.*" Her mother tossed a yellow taffeta petticoat into the bag. "After all, you're not at all pretty."

Pretty? What did appearances have to do with that horror at the abbey? Juliette gazed at her in disbelief as she remembered the child Henriette and the Reverend Mother. She turned to François. "May we go now?"

François stubbornly shook his head, his gaze on her mother. "She's your daughter. Take her with you."

"Impossible. No aristocrats are being given passes to leave the city. I had to make a bargain with that beast Marat to get one for myself. It's not at all fair. That pig thinks I'll send it, but he'll find I'm not so easily cowed—" She broke off and turned back to her packing. "Juliette will have to shift for herself."

When had she ever done anything else? Juliette walked out of the room and down the stairs.

François was behind her by the time she reached the bottom of the staircase. "She has no right to refuse you. The two of you are no longer my responsibility," he said fiercely.

"Then leave us in the street and go about your business." Juliette's tone was equally fierce. Strange how raw she felt after seeing her mother. The interview had gone just as she expected, and she should really be numb to pain after the events of this night.

Marguerite smiled smugly as she held open the door for them. "I told you it would do you no good to see her. You were stupid to think—"

Etchelet's breath exploded in a harsh rush. Juliette saw only a blur of movement. Yet Marguerite was suddenly jammed up against the wall with a dagger pressed to her long neck. "You said? I don't believe I could have heard you correctly."

Marguerite squealed, her eyes bulging as she gazed down at the knife.

Etchelet pressed the knife until a drop of blood ran down Marguerite's neck. "You said, Citizeness?"

"Nothing," she squeaked. "I said nothing."

Juliette watched the wildness flicker in Etchelet's taut face. For an instant she thought he would push the blade home, but he slowly lowered it and stepped back. A moment later he slammed the door behind them.

François sheathed his knife in his boot. "I lost my temper. I've been trying to keep from striking out since I arrived at that abbey and of a sudden I snapped. But I shouldn't have frightened the servant when it was the mistress I wanted to skewer."

"You didn't like my mother?" Juliette asked. "How extraordinary. Most gentlemen do."

"Do you have any friends or other relations in Paris?"

Juliette shook her head.

"There must be someone. What of Citizeness Vasaro?"

"Catherine's guardian is Jean Marc Andreas. He has a house on the Place Royale but he's not in residence at present."

"Not the Place Royale." François's brow was creased in thought as he told her absently, "It's the Place de l'Indivisibilité now."

"Mother of God, not again? How does anyone find his way around the city? Such stupidity." Juliette enunciated precisely. "Number Eighteen Place Royale."

"Are there servants?"

Juliette shrugged. "I don't know and I can't ask Catherine."

"No, you can't ask her." François's gaze went to the carriage and Juliette again noticed that curiously intent expression on his face. "She's not . . . well."

Danton gazed quizzically down at them as they approached. "The marquise was not obliging?"

François shook his head. "The marquise is a bitch."

"What a pity. I suppose you'll just have to take these forlorn women to your bosom and care for them yourself."

"The devil I will." François opened the door of the

carriage and half lifted, half pushed Juliette onto the seat next to Catherine. For the briefest instant his gaze rested on Catherine's delicate features before he continued. "I detest spoiling your amusement, Georges Jacques, but when you feel you can bestir yourself, take us to the Place Royale."

Danton's lips twitched. "Place Royale? I do believe you're being corrupted by these aristos."

"I mean the Place de l'Indivisibilité." François slammed the door of the carriage shut.

SEVEN

Thirty-six houses surrounded the elegant square. All were similar in architecture with their steeply slanted slate roofs and dormer windows but each possessed unique trimmings . . . and secrets. Beyond the brick and stone façades lay delightful courtyards and enchanting gardens where graceful fountains sprayed sparkling water and one could sit on marble benches and breathe in the intoxicating fragrance of roses and violets.

How did she know about those gardens? Catherine wondered numbly. Then she realized it was because Jean Marc lived in one of these houses. They were standing before the door of Jean Marc's house on the Place Royale and someone was pounding on the front door. She hadn't gone there since Jean Marc had invited her for Christmas three years before. He had surprised her with a splendid blue gown made from measurements the seamstress had received from the Mother Superior. She had been so disappointed Philippe had not been there to see her in it. Philippe had once told her he liked her in blue and she had—

Philippe.

Pain spiraled through her and she quickly drew the mist of numbness about her again.

François was forced to knock repeatedly before the door was opened a narrow crack to reveal the frightened face of a man in his twilight years. Wrinkles seamed his thin face and sparse white hair clung in tufts to his shiny pink scalp. As soon as he caught sight of François through the crack, he started to swing the door shut.

François pushed the door open and stepped into the marble foyer. "Make up two bedchambers." He pulled Juliette and Catherine into the hall. "These ladies will be staying here for the next few days. However, as far as anyone else is concerned, the house is still unoccupied. Do you understand?"

"See here, you can't walk in here and . . ." He met François's gaze and his words trailed off as his glance slid away toward Juliette and Catherine. He stiffened and raised the candelabrum in his hand higher. "Mademoiselle Catherine?"

Juliette stepped forward. "She's been injured and needs to be nursed. What's your name?"

"Robert Dameraux. I'm head gardener for Monsieur Andreas and I care for the house when he's in Marseilles." His gaze was still fixed on Catherine. "*Pauvre petite.* So pale . . ."

"Robert." Catherine's vague gaze focused on his deeply lined face. "Violets. You gave me white violets."

The old man nodded. "When you were a child you loved my flowers."

"They looked so . . . clean. Like nothing had touched them since the beginning of time. I thought—" She swayed and would have fallen if the young man had not caught and steadied her. She couldn't remember who he was. François, yes, that was his name. He and Juliette had been arguing in the coach. . . .

"A bedchamber," he repeated curtly as he lifted Catherine in his arms.

Robert nodded and scurried ahead of them across the foyer and up the staircase.

François tightened his grip around Catherine's body and started across the foyer. Catherine saw their reflections in the gilt-framed mirror affixed to the far wall. She could hardly recognize her own tattered, dirty image while he looked solid, dark, and formidably male. Catherine stiffened as panic soared through her. She mustn't let him touch her. She mustn't let any man touch her. Pain. Filth. She'd never be clean again.

"Stop trembling. I won't hurt you." His low voice was rough, but there was such raw force in his words, Catherine found herself relaxing. Juliette was right behind them on the stairs and was not objecting. If the man was a threat, Juliette would not have let him carry her. She could trust Juliette, if not the man who held her.

He was very strong, she thought remotely, stronger than he looked, the sinewy muscles hard and inflexible beneath the wool of his coat. His throat was only a few inches away, and she could see the throb of his heart in the hollow. She found herself staring at that rhythmic pulse in fascination. Life. She had never seen anyone so robustly alive. His face was hard, shuttered, and yet those glittering green eyes betrayed a restless male energy beneath the expressionless features.

Male. She shuddered and suddenly those fierce eyes were fastened on her face. He stared at her intently for a moment before shifting his gaze to Robert, who had reached the landing at the top of the stairs.

A moment later Robert opened the third door on the left and preceded them into a chamber. "You remember this room, Mademoiselle? You always liked a room overlooking my garden."

Yes. She dimly recalled the wall hangings and bed-covers of blue watered silk with lilac and silver borders, the Sèvres plaque on the wall. She had sat for hours on that window seat, watching Robert work in the garden.

"*Dieu,* it smells musty in here." Juliette crossed the room and threw open the casement window.

"The house has been closed for over a year," Robert said defensively. "You gave us no warning. You can't expect it to—"

"I'll need warm water and clean linen, something for us both to sleep in and wear tomorrow. Anything will do," Juliette interrupted. "Are there any other servants in the house?"

"My wife, Marie. She's still in bed and—"

"I can't do everything myself for Mademoiselle Catherine." Juliette strode toward the door. "Come, we'll roust your wife from her bed."

Juliette was ordering everyone about again, Catherine realized dimly. Poor Robert, she should really say something to Juliette.

"Why are you just standing there holding her?" Juliette tossed over her shoulder at François. "Put her down on the bed." She didn't wait for an answer as she marched from the chamber.

François muttered something under his breath as he strode toward the bed.

"Don't be angry with her. It's her way," Catherine whispered as he laid her on the silken coverlet.

"A virago's way."

"No, she means well." Why was she defending Juliette? What did it matter what this stranger thought? She closed her eyes and tried to go back into the comforting, mindless haze she had managed to gather about her in the coach.

She thought the young man had gone away, until he suddenly broke the silence. "You look like a corpse."

She opened her eyes to see him gazing down at her. "*Pardon?*"

"You lay there like a dead woman. The pain will go away. Woman is made to take a man into her body. You will heal."

Catherine shook her head. She would heal but she'd never be as she was. She would always carry this sickening stain. "You're wrong."

"No, I'm right. Don't be foolish. The fault was not

yours and you have no reason to feel shame. Inside you're the same. What you are has nothing to do with your body."

She gazed at him in bewilderment. His words carried the same soft vehemence that had swayed her downstairs.

"Do you hear me? You're just the same. Nothing has been taken from you that's of any importance."

"Why are you shouting at her?" Juliette came back into the room carrying a basin of water and clean cloths. "Have you no sense? She's had enough to endure without you bothering her."

"I wasn't shouting."

Juliette sat down on the bed beside Catherine. "Go away. I have to wash her and get her to bed. Wait for me downstairs."

François gave her a level glance before he turned and left the room.

She shouldn't be lying here letting Juliette take care of her, Catherine thought. Dark circles ringed Juliette's eyes and her hands were shaking as she dropped a cloth into the basin of water. Juliette was clearly exhausted and the horror of this night had taken its toll on her strength. Catherine reached for the cloth. "I can do it."

Juliette slapped her hand aside. "Lie still." She closed her lids tightly for an instant and then opened them to reveal tear-bright eyes. "Mother of God, I'm sorry."

"No, I'm the one who should be sorry," Catherine whispered. "I'm being such a bother to you. I'll try to help—"

"Hush." Juliette smiled shakily. "You can help me by not fighting over the little I can do for you. I don't seem to have much strength to argue."

A phantom of a smile touched Catherine's lips. "How unusual. I never thought I'd hear you say that."

"See, you're laughing at me. Things can't be so terrible if you can still laugh. Just lie still and let me help you."

Catherine closed her eyes and let the mists close about her and Juliette have her way.

"Well, what are you going to do?" Juliette strode into the salon close to an hour later and halted directly before François. "You can't leave her here alone and unprotected."

"She has you," François said. "I'm surprised you think anyone else is necessary."

"I'm not stupid enough to believe I can get us out of Paris to safety." She met his gaze. "And we won't be safe here, will we? You say Danton is one of the heroes of the revolution. If men that powerful are involved in what happened tonight . . ." She stopped, pushed back the memories flooding back to her and drew a deep breath. "Then the whole world has gone mad." He didn't answer and she braced herself to attack again. "I have to know what I'm fighting. Who were those men who attacked the abbey? Dupree called them Marseilles."

"They're hirelings from Marseilles and Genoa. Most of them are the spawn of the prisons. The Girondins hired them to come to Paris and protect them against the Paris Commune's National Guard. Unfortunately, as soon as they arrived in Paris, Marat upped the Girondins' offer and they now belong to him."

"Girondins?"

"Even in the convent you must have heard of the Girondins."

"Why should I have been interested in your idiotic politics? Tell me."

"The National Assembly is run by members who belong to several different political clubs. There are actually three principal parties in the assembly. The Girondins, who want to walk a middle road and keep both the constitution and the monarchy. The Jacobins, who are radicals and want to dispose of the monarchy."

"And this Paris Commune?"

"Most of them are Cordeliers. They control the National Guard and therefore Paris." He smiled crookedly. "The threat of the sword can be more persuasive than the most eloquent oratory."

"Dupree is a Cordelier?"

François nodded. "Jean Paul Marat controls the Paris Commune and Dupree is his agent."

"And to what party does your great Danton belong?"

"He's the leader of the Cordeliers and belongs to the Paris Commune." He rushed on. "But he's not a radical. He believes only in doing what's best for the revolution."

"And butchering women is best for the revolution." She waved his protest aside. "Can I appeal to these Girondins for protection?"

"Not against the Commune. They talk a lot but do little."

"So I obviously cannot count on sanity from anyone in the government. Catherine and I must protect ourselves." A frown wrinkled her brow. "You must make sure no one knows we're here and then find us a way to leave Paris at the earliest opportunity."

"Indeed, and why must I do all this? You're fortunate that I saw fit to intervene tonight."

"I don't consider myself fortunate." Her hands clenched into fists at her sides. "I'm angry and someone must pay. *You* must pay."

"Why?"

"Because you were there. If you didn't expect to pay for that atrocity, you should never have gone to the abbey tonight." She smiled grimly. "And if you wish another reason why you should help us, perhaps I should tell you that I killed the man who raped Catherine tonight. Do you think your Commune would take kindly to your aiding the murderess of one of its number?"

He turned on his heel and strode toward the door.

Juliette called to him. "One more thing. Before you leave, talk to that old man, Robert. It would do no harm to be a little threatening."

"I'm not accustomed to frightening old men."

"Yes, you are. I think you're accustomed to frightening anyone who stands in your way."

François paused at the door of the salon. "The old

man presents no danger. He appears fond of your friend."

"Fear will make him more cautious with his tongue than will affection."

"What a gentle nature you have, Citizeness."

"Catherine is gentle. Did it save her?" Her fingers rose to rub her temples wearily. "I can't really trust anyone. Everything is different now, isn't it?"

François gazed at her for a moment. "Yes." He turned. "I'll have a word with Robert."

As he left the room Juliette could feel the tension flow from her muscles, and a wave of exhaustion caused her to sway. She reached out blindly to clutch at the table next to her. She mustn't give in to weakness. Catherine needed her, and the saints knew there was no one else she could count on. François Etchelet's aid had been grudging at best, and he might balk at any moment. Danton obviously would help only to the extent Etchelet could persuade him, and Jean Marc Andreas was somewhere flitting around the countryside when Catherine needed him. Those strangers had no connection with Catherine, but Jean Marc had a responsibility toward her. Why hadn't he come to the abbey for her before this monstrous thing could happen?

The surge of anger against Jean Marc momentarily banished her exhaustion and she welcomed it. She could deal with anger as she could not with fear and frustration. She needed to hold on for just a little longer and then she could rest. She would talk to Marie and Robert and then go find a bedchamber for herself. She would wash and then sleep and gain strength for the morrow.

She had picked up the candelabrum from the table and started for the door when a glimmer of color in the corner of the room caught her eye. She stopped abruptly, her gaze on the wall to the left of the doorway. Holding the candelabrum higher, she moved slowly forward until she stood before the small painting on the wall.

The Wind Dancer.

She could execute it much better now, but it was

not such a bad effort. Still, it was not as superior as the Bouchers, Doyens, Fragonards, and other artists whose works graced the walls. She frowned in puzzlement as she glanced around the room. The salon was decorated with restrained good taste, its white-paneled walls covered with exquisite gold arabesques, the furniture carefully fashioned of finest woods. Everything in the room whispered of excellence. So why had Jean Marc Andreas hung her painting here? She moved her shoulders uneasily. For that matter, why had she painted it for him? It was the real Wind Dancer he had wanted, not its likeness. She had told herself it was gratitude for arranging for her to be sent to the abbey, but was it something else? The memory of those days and nights at the inn had never entirely left her. Had she wanted him to remember her as she had remembered him over the years?

Nonsense. It was fascination with his face that held her enthralled. Nothing else. She had paid her debt and they were quits. She walked quickly from the room, returning the painting of the Wind Dancer to darkness.

"Your wounded lambs are settled?" Danton asked as François reached the carriage.

François nodded curtly.

"You don't appear to be pleased to be rid of them."

"I'm not rid of them. Juliette de Clement just told me she killed a man before she left the abbey."

Danton gave a low whistle. "Which means we've not only aided an enemy of the state but a murderess of a hero of the revolution." He chuckled. "I admit to respect for our little aristo. She has claws and is willing to use them."

"On us."

"Dupree's been known to bargain. You could turn them over to him in return for forgetting our part in their escape."

François had a sudden memory of Catherine Vasaro's strained, bewildered expression in that last moment before Juliette had come back into the room. He knew well how she would fare in Dupree's hands.

"Well?"

François climbed onto the driver's seat beside Danton. "It would give Dupree a weapon to hold over our heads later. The more reasonable course would be to get the women safely out of Paris."

Danton gave him a shrewd glance. "And we're both reasonable men, are we not?" His lips twisted in an ironic smile. "Why else would we be here amid these 'reasonable' men who guard our nation?" He snapped the whip and the horses lurched forward. "Do what you will. But if you involve me in your downfall, I'll deny you."

"As Peter did Jesus?"

"Exactly."

François slowly shook his head. "No, you wouldn't deny me."

"You think not?"

"You might curse me, you might even lay open my head with a bludgeon, but you wouldn't deny me." He shot Danton a sidewise glance and smiled faintly. "Why do you think I chose to come to you when I arrived in Paris two years ago? Everyone knows of your loyalty, Georges Jacques."

Danton grimaced. "Life is not always so simple. Loyalty can waver in trying times."

François didn't reply.

"You stubborn idiot, listen to me. I'm like any other man. I became frightened and weary and greedy. And who should know better than you how corrupt I can be? Don't trust me. Don't trust anyone."

François only smiled.

Danton sighed. "Very well. How do you intend we should get them out of Paris?"

François shrugged. "Something will occur to me."

"Well, don't wait to construct your usual convoluted plan. Whoever said Basques were simple folk? You never take the straight path if you find one that's twisted."

"The twisted path is far less boring and safer in the long run."

Danton shook his head and snapped the whip to urge on the horses.

"We've found no trace of Citizeness Justice," Pirard said to Dupree. "I've sent men to scour the outlying villages. But do not worry, we'll find her."

"I'm not worried. The bitch can't have gone far on foot." The fine chain of the golden necklace in Pirard's hands was broken and flecked with blood. Dupree took the necklace and balanced the circlet hanging from the chain in his palm. "You found this in the tomb with Malpan?"

The Marseilles nodded. "Beneath his body."

"Anything else?"

"A painting of the abbey," Pirard chuckled. "Crazy thing to be in a nun's tomb. But then, a woman has to be a little crazy in the head to become a nun, isn't that true, Citizen?"

"Yes." Dupree's tone was absent as he held up the necklace to catch the first tentative light of dawn. It was an exquisitely delicate piece of jewelry, fit for the throat of a princess, he thought. In fact, the woman who had worn it, if not a princess, had probably been the daughter of a count or marquis or perhaps even a duke.

"Shall I throw the painting in the wagon with the rest of the loot for the Commune?"

"What? Oh, yes, go ahead."

"And the necklace?"

Dupree's hand closed possessively on the fine golden chain. This necklace had probably belonged to a child of glory, a child of nobility, a child accustomed to the company of kings and queens. If he gave it up, it would only be melted down or stolen to grace the fat neck of some shopkeeper's wife. Such a necklace deserved a better fate. "Forget you found the necklace. I'll dispose of it."

Pirard grinned slyly. "And we'll see it hanging on the bosom of that little actress you find so accommodating?"

Dupree shot Pirard a contemptuous glance. Didn't

he realize a prize like this must be given to someone worthy of its glory? Camille Cadeaux occupied a necessary place in his life but that place was dark and secret and had nothing to do with glory. Pirard was not only a fool but was becoming insultingly intimate since he'd been chosen as Dupree's lieutenant. He would have to do something about the man.

"No, I have no intention of giving it to Camille." He would have the chain repaired and cleaned, then have the gold polished until it was as bright and shining as when it might have been worn at Versailles. "I shall give it to the only woman in France who is blameless enough to wear it with honor."

"And who is that?"

Dupree took his lace-trimmed handkerchief from his pocket and carefully began to rub at a dried spot of blood on the spray of lilac engraved on the gold surface. "My mother."

Catherine was screaming.

Juliette was out of her bed and halfway across her chamber before she was fully awake. What could it be now? Catherine had been sleeping soundly when she had peeked in on her before going to her own chamber.

Robert Damereaux stood outside Catherine's door that Juliette had left ajar. He wrung his hands. "Mademoiselle Catherine, she's not—"

"She has the fever," Juliette said as she brushed past him. "I'll take care of her. Go back to bed."

"Bed?" he asked in a high, surprised tone. "I was not in bed. My Marie and I were sitting down to our supper when we heard Mademoiselle Catherine screaming."

Supper? Then the half darkness mantling the hall was not dawn but twilight. They had slept the entire day through.

Catherine screamed again.

"I don't need you." Juliette threw open the door. "Bring soup and wine for Mademoiselle Catherine after you finish your meal." She slammed the door behind her, then flinched as the sound bludgeoned her throbbing temples. Her tongue felt coated and sour. *Dieu,* she didn't want to face this right now.

Catherine moaned, turned restlessly on her side but did not wake.

Juliette straightened and moved across the room toward the bed. "The windows are open. Do you want the entire neighborhood to know we're here? Wake up." She reached down, grasped Catherine's shoulders, and shook her. Catherine's lids flicked open to reveal wild, glittering eyes and Juliette's irritation melted away as if it had never been. "You're safe now. Well, as safe as we can be in this city of madmen."

"Juliette?" Catherine whispered. "I dreamed . . ." She shuddered. "But it was real, wasn't it?"

Juliette sat down on the bed beside her. "It was real."

"They hurt me." Catherine's tone was wondering, childlike. "Like they hurt Henriette and Sister Mathilde."

Juliette's hand closed on Catherine's. "Yes."

"They tore my clothes and then they tore . . . me."

"Yes." Juliette's grip tightened. "But you're alive and I killed the *canaille* who did it."

"Murder." Catherine's eyes glistened with tears. "It's a mortal sin. I made you commit a mortal sin."

"You made me do nothing. It was my choice."

"No, I was to blame. You would have never—"

"I wanted to do it," Juliette interrupted. "I enjoyed doing it. I wish I could have killed all of them."

"You don't mean that."

"I do," Juliette said fiercely. "I want them all dead. I want them all burning in hell. Do you think I should forgive them? Are you going to forgive that loathsome slug who raped you?"

"I . . . don't want to think about him." Catherine turned her gaze toward the window. "I don't want to think of either of them."

Juliette stiffened. Them. She had been so weary she hadn't realized Catherine had been speaking in the plural. "Catherine, how many men . . . hurt you?"

Catherine's voice was barely audible. "Two."

Fury surged through Juliette, taking her breath, sending the blood pounding in her temples. "There was only one man in the tomb."

"There was another before him. He left after . . ." Catherine's voice broke. "But the other one stayed. He did it over and over until I—"

"Shh. Go to sleep." Juliette enfolded her in a close embrace. "He can't hurt you now."

"Yes, he can. I dreamed about him. He was there above me. Hurting me. Looking down at me with no face." Catherine was trembling uncontrollably. "No face. He had no face."

"He had a face. It was just too dark to see in the tomb."

"They were shadows. They didn't have faces. I thought if I could see their expressions I'd know why they were doing this to me. I thought I'd be able to make some sense out of it, but they had no faces." She was panting as if she were running. "And then I realized I had no face either. I was nothing. I was something to use and throw away. It didn't matter what they did to me because I was already so soiled that I couldn't get dirtier, more fouled, or—"

"It's not true," Juliette said. "None of that is true. It wasn't your fault."

"What difference does that make? You know it's a woman's duty to keep herself pure for her husband. Do you think any man would take a woman to wife who had been so used?"

Juliette hesitated. She could not lie to Catherine and tell her it would make no difference. The world was neither fair nor gentle to women in most instances, and men were particularly unfair in matters of chastity. "No one need know. At Versailles there were tricks the women used to fool a bridegroom into believing he was getting a virgin. We could—"

"I couldn't lie. I'm already stained enough without adding falsehoods to my sins. Besides, I could never marry." Catherine's eyes twitched beneath their lids like an animal in mortal terror. "He would hurt me. I couldn't let him do that. I don't want anyone to touch me ever again."

Juliette swallowed to ease the tightness of her throat. "No one's going to hurt you. Rest now and try to sleep. Robert is going to bring soup and wine."

"I'm not hungry. You won't leave me?" Catherine whispered, her eyes closing. "I'm afraid I'll dream . . ."

She was already half asleep, Juliette noticed. She supposed it was natural after Catherine's hideous experience for her to wish to hide away, but she was embracing sleep with an eagerness that made Juliette uneasy.

Catherine opened suddenly anxious eyes. "Juliette, they didn't hurt you? You got away without them—"

Blood.

The Reverend Mother kneeling before the tribunal.

The golden chalice of the holy sacrament.

Dupree's delicate hand motioning to the man with the red bonnet.

Juliette firmly banished the memory and smiled down at Catherine. "Of course they didn't hurt me. Do you think I'd be so easy to catch?"

Catherine relaxed. "No, I didn't think so. You wouldn't let anyone hurt you. You're too strong."

Blood.

Juliette's hand tightened around Catherine's. "You're strong too, Catherine. You'll get over this."

"That's what he said." Catherine's words were nearly inaudible.

"Who?"

"That man. François."

Juliette hid a start of surprise. Etchelet had not impressed her as a man who would pass words of comfort. He would expect everyone to respond to adversity with the same toughness that seemed inherent in his own character. "Then he has more sense than I thought."

"He was angry. I don't know why . . ."

"Don't worry about it." Juliette released Catherine's hand and stood up. "Don't worry about anything. I'll sit in the chair across the room and—"

"It's gone." Catherine's hand was fumbling at the high neck of her nightgown. "My locket. It's gone!"

Juliette stiffened in sudden fear. Why hadn't she noticed the previous night that the locket was no longer around Catherine's neck? If Dupree found the locket next to the corpse in the tomb, he would have Catherine's likeness in the palm of his hand! She mustn't panic. The locket could have been lost anywhere and, even if found, the miniature might never be discovered. The catch of the locket was hard to find and the opening almost seamless.

"I love my locket. I wanted to wear it forever and now it's gone."

Catherine had obviously not made the dangerous connection of the loss and the body in the tomb and Juliette was certainly not going to bring it to her attention. "I'll paint you another miniature."

"It won't be the same." Catherine closed her eyes and turned her face away. "Nothing will ever be the same."

Juliette sat down in the chair and leaned her head wearily against the high back. Catherine's words were almost identical to the ones Juliette had uttered in the salon the previous night. She wished she could argue with her, but how, when Catherine only spoke the truth.

The flame of the candle burned above her bed, hanging like a shimmering topaz teardrop on the velvet of the darkness. She should really concentrate on learning to paint fire, Juliette thought drowsily. She had tried once or twice but the elements were terribly difficult to master. Fire kept changing from gold to emerald, to amber to ruby red. People were much easier once you got beyond their surface and . . .

"Are you well?"

A deep masculine voice, taut with tension, issued from somewhere beyond the flame.

Juliette's gaze jerked from the flame to the face behind the candle. High intriguing planes, bold black eyes, and that beautifully cynical mouth.

Jean Marc!

He was here. Wild joy—as instinctive as it was bewildering—soared through her. After all the years of waiting, he was here.

"Answer me!"

She sat bolt upright in bed, jarred wide awake and into anger by the sharpness of his tone. "Why did you not come for her? She's your responsibility and it wasn't right of you to—"

"Hush." Jean Marc's fingers were shaking as they pressed her lips. "For God's sake, don't rail at me. I've just come from the abbey and I thought you both dead. I rushed here and—Philippe came in time then?"

"Philippe?"

"I sent Philippe to—" He broke off as he saw her bewildered expression. "My God, he *didn't* come for you."

"I told you, no one came for Catherine." She gazed at him fiercely. "You let those *canailles* rape her. And if they had killed her too, it would have been your fault. For weeks the carriages came and took the students away, but none came for Catherine."

Jean Marc was rigid with shock. "Raped?" His rich olive complexion looked suddenly muddy in the candlelight. "My God, that . . . child."

"They raped old women and children."

"What about you? Are you well?"

"How could I be well after seeing—"

"*Merde!* Juliette, did they hurt you?"

"Catherine was raped by two men and she's—"

"You told me about Catherine. I asked about you." He grabbed her shoulders and made her look into his eyes. "*Tell me,* were you raped?"

"No."

His breath escaped in an explosive rush and his grip on her shoulders loosened. "One blessing. I have enough guilt to bear without adding your assault to it."

"More than enough guilt. Why didn't you come?"

"I had urgent business in Toulon. When the Reverend Mother's message reached me, I stopped at Vasaro and sent Philippe to fetch you and Catherine from the abbey. He should have been here days ago."

"Perhaps he had 'business' too and didn't think Catherine's welfare important enough to waste his time."

"I don't know why he isn't here." Jean Marc's lips tightened grimly. "But I intend to find out."

"It's too late. Two days too late." Juliette could feel her eyes filling with tears and determinedly blinked them back. "They *hurt* her, Jean Marc."

"I know they did." Jean Marc looked intently at her. "There's no use saying I'll regret what's happened for the rest of my life. All I can do is try to heal the harm that's been done. You're sure nothing happened to you?"

"Nothing important." She frowned. "Oh, I forgot. I had to kill a man."

The faintest smile broke the somberness of Jean Marc's expression. "You don't consider killing a man of importance?"

"He was a *canaille*. He was raping Catherine."

Jean Marc's smile vanished. "A *canaille*, indeed. I regret you deprived me of the pleasure."

"There was another man. If you can find out who he is, you can kill him."

He bowed. "Such generosity, Juliette. Now, tell me how you escaped being butchered at the abbey."

She briefly related the events and roles of François Etchelet and Danton in their flight.

"François Etchelet," he murmured thoughtfully. "I owe him a debt."

"I assure you his rescue was most reluctant."

"Reluctant or not, he saved you."

"True." She threw back the covers and jumped out of bed. "We must talk. Come down to the scullery and I'll find you something to eat."

"I'm going to be allowed to break my fast? I thought my laggardliness had put me beyond redemption in your eyes."

Profound weariness and sadness lay beneath the mockery in Jean Marc's voice and, for the first time, Juliette noticed the deep shadows beneath his eyes, the layer of dust mantling his elegant dark blue cloak. She suddenly felt a rush of protectiveness that banished both anger and resentment. "You care for Catherine. I know you would not hurt her deliberately. You were merely stupid, I suppose."

A faint smile indented his lips. "I'd forgotten that sharp tongue of yours. I remembered only . . ." He fell silent for a moment, looking at her. "How kind of you to acquit me of malice, if not witlessness."

"You *should* have come for her. What business could be so important that you—"

"The assembly's confiscated eight of my ships for their navy in the past year," Jean Marc interrupted. "I was hoping to salvage some of my cargoes stored in the warehouses at Toulon before those greedy bastards managed to steal those too." He shook his head wearily. "It seemed very important at the time."

"*Eight* ships? That's a great many."

"They would have taken the lot if I hadn't seen this coming and sent most of the Andreas fleet to Charleston harbor two years ago."

"You knew they would steal your ships?"

He nodded grimly. "Oh, yes, at the first opportunity or excuse. The majority of the illustrious members of the assembly are as corrupt as the nobles of the court they supplanted. The only way to deal with them is by bribery and evasion."

She shivered. "The world seems filled with thieves and murderers. François tried to tell me why the abbey had been attacked but I couldn't understand it. I'll never understand it."

"It was madness. How can anyone understand madness?" His gaze met her own. "As God is my witness, I never suspected the abbey would be attacked, Juliette. I sent Philippe to fetch you both to Vasaro merely as a precaution because of the unrest in Paris. If I'd thought there was any real danger, I would have come myself." His lips twisted. "You're right, I was stupid."

The pain and the bitter denunciation in his tone hurt her in some odd way, and she said quickly, "Maybe you weren't completely at fault."

"Are you softening?" He shook his head. "The blame was mine and you had the right to condemn me." He reached out and wound his forefinger in one of the tight curls at her left temple. "You have much too tender a heart beneath all those thorns, you know."

The tip of his finger was resting lightly against her cheekbone while he lazily tested the silky texture of the curl between his thumb and forefinger. The action was almost unbearably intimate. She swallowed. "Nonsense."

"But you must never show that softness. Not to me." His gaze was mesmerizingly intent as it held hers. "It's dangerous for you. Never let me see a weakness, Juliette."

"I don't . . . understand what you're saying."

"I know you don't." He smiled cynically. He released the curl and it instantly sprang back into its former tight ringlet. "And only God knows why I'm saying it. It must be a combination of guilt and shock that has me behaving with such uncharacteristic gallantry. I guarantee after I've slept a while I'll be fully myself again and you'll find me a fit antagonist."

"Antagonist?" Juliette frowned at him. "I don't wish to fight you."

"Yes, you do," he said softly. "You've fought me from the beginning. It's all part of the game."

"Game?"

He turned away and moved toward the door. "Not now."

He had said those words before, she remembered vaguely. Not now. Someday. "I don't understand a tenth of what you're saying. You're being most exasperating." She took a hasty step forward as she saw him open the door. "And you can't leave now. I'll find you something to eat and then we must speak of Catherine."

"I have no intention of discussing Catherine or anything else at the moment. I'm too weary either too eat or think right now," Jean Marc said firmly as he moved toward the door. "Since I left Toulon I've been riding day and night and I'm sure half the dirt of the road is still clinging to my person. I intend to wash and then sleep for the next dozen hours."

"*A dozen hours?* You can't! We need to discuss what's to be done about Catherine."

"My dear Juliette." His caressing tone failed to hide its steely determination. "It's just as well you learn immediately that I do exactly as I wish and I abhor the word *can't.*"

She could understand that, Juliette thought grudgingly. She had a dislike for the word herself. "As I do, but if you'd—"

"Tomorrow. *Bonne nuit,* Juliette." The door closed softly behind him.

Juliette gazed at the door in astonishment, tempted to go after him and make him listen to her. Then she slowly turned, got into bed, and pulled the covers back over her. She had forgotten how obstinate the man could be. She knew Jean Marc could not be forced to do anything and quite possibly would do the exact opposite if she pushed him too far.

She turned on her side, a tiny pinwheel of excitement spiraling through her. He was here! Beautiful, glittering, and as darkly enigmatic as she remembered him. Even as she had been railing at him she had been drinking in the unusual molding of his cheekbones, trying to probe the secrets behind his glittering black eyes. She had wanted to reach out and touch the hard plane of his cheek, the corded muscles of his thighs.

Touch? She quickly rejected the thought and then brought it back to examine it more closely. Perhaps she had wanted to explore his body, but surely it had been only an artist's curiosity regarding physique.

She closed her eyes and willed herself to sleep. Yes, it wasn't excitement she was feeling at all, merely the curiosity of the artist who had rediscovered a fascinating challenge and relief for the help Jean Marc's arrival could offer Catherine.

Jean Marc's hands slowly clenched into fists as he stood looking down at Catherine. Why was he here? He should have gone straight to bed as he had told Juliette he would. He certainly didn't intend to wake Catherine and face her silent accusations.

No, Catherine would never rail, accusing him of negligence. She was gentle, as his father had been gentle. Like him, she would suffer and be destroyed before uttering a word of blame.

Yet the blame had been Jean Marc's and he did know why he was here. He had wanted reassurance that Catherine had not been destroyed by his carelessness and he was not receiving that reassurance. Catherine was enveloped in a pale fragility in cruel contrast to Juliette's vibrant vitality.

Juliette.

Strange, how after all these years fate had driven her once more into his circle of power and protection as it had at the inn so many years earlier. Strange and damnably frustrating; her vulnerability shielded her from him now even as her youth had in the past. It almost made one believe in a guardian angel for the innocents of the world.

Almost. Catherine was also an innocent and the angels hadn't protected her.

He reached out and gently stroked Catherine's fair hair flowing over the pillow. He hadn't been the guardian his father would have wanted him to be. He had always been too busy, too impatient, moving from place to place. Even when Catherine had come home for visits from the abbey he'd given her cursory attention, never stopping to see if she needed a word of kindness or understanding.

He swallowed to ease the aching tightness in his throat and turned away. Self-recrimination could not help now. At least, Catherine and Juliette were alive.

They must accept what had happened and find a way to go on.

EIGHT

Philippe Andreas arrived early the next morning, white-faced, sober, and infinitely relieved when Jean Marc told him Catherine and Juliette had escaped the massacre at the abbey.

"You're right to be angry, Jean Marc," Philippe said miserably. "When I heard of the massacre as I entered the city I felt—you can't blame me any more than I blame myself."

"You're damned right I can. Mother of God, what the hell delayed you?"

Philippe flushed as his teeth sank into his lower lip.

Jean Marc gazed at him in astonishment. "A woman?"

"One of the pickers. She was . . . I didn't think it would matter. It was only two nights . . ."

Jean Marc laughed mirthlessly. "Christ, I hope you found your dalliance with a flower picker worth what happened to Catherine." Jean Marc's lips tightened. "You can't simply say you're sorry and walk away from this, Philippe. My God, why the *hell* didn't you do what I told you to do?"

"I didn't believe this could happen," Philippe said simply. "You know how it is at Vasaro. The war and revolution seem not to exist there."

"*Damn* you, I told you to leave at once and—" Jean Marc broke off as he saw Philippe's forlorn expression. Why was he shouting at Philippe? Jean Marc was the one who should have gone directly to the abbey. Philippe was so far removed from the turmoil of the revolution in his Garden of Eden that undoubtedly he had been blind to the harm his delay could do. Jean Marc had no such excuse. He'd had experience with the fanatics and the money grubbers of the assembly, and the mobs of starving rabble roaming city streets and country roads.

He straightened and relaxed his clenched fists. "All right, it's done. Now let's try to repair the damage. Juliette told me they were helped by a man named François Etchelet who is in league with Georges Jacques Danton. I want to see him. Go find him and bring him here."

"Do you think that's wise? Danton has publicly stated he approves of the massacres."

"We need help and Etchelet has a reason for giving it."

Philippe turned to go and then hesitated. "May I go up and see Catherine first? I want to tell her how much I regret—"

"I don't think she'll want to see you." Juliette stood in the doorway, gazing accusingly at him. "I remember you. You're Philippe. I'm Juliette de Clement."

Philippe nodded and bowed. "I recall you as well, Mademoiselle. I can't tell—"

"Why, by all the saints, didn't you come for her?"

He flushed. "I was . . . delayed."

"And Catherine was raped."

"Jean Marc told me. I can't tell you how sorry—"

"Go, Philippe," Jean Marc said. "I want Etchelet here before dinner."

Philippe bowed again to Juliette and quickly escaped from the room.

Juliette turned to Jean Marc. "You sent for Etchelet? Good. Why didn't you— What are you looking at?"

"You."

"Do I have a smudge on my face?" She lifted a hand to her cheek. "I was scrubbing the floor of the foyer this morning and—"

"Scrubbing?"

"Why not? Robert and Marie are no longer in their first youth, and we must not bring any other servants into the house. I'm very good at scrubbing floors. I did it all the time at the abbey." Her hand fell away from her cheek. "I can wash it off later. One smudge doesn't matter."

"No, it doesn't matter." Jean Marc doubted he would have noticed if she was as painted as the savages brought back from the wilds of America. He had always loved her skin, roses and cream with a texture glowing as if burnished by a loving hand. The night before in the candlelight she had been all tumbled shining curls and curious brown eyes, brave and impatient in her white, high-necked, long-sleeved gown. This morning the strong sunlight streaming through the windows revealed a Juliette of enticing beauty. The shabby brown wool gown she wore hugged her small waist and fitted snugly over the slight swell of her breasts. She was of medium height but appeared taller, for she carried herself boldly, proudly, and with a grace at once impetuous and defiant.

Christ, he could feel himself harden just looking at her. So much for her shield of innocence and dependence.

Her gaze as she lifted her head to face him was as defiant as her bearing. "You should have listened to me last night, you know."

"I make it a practice never to give attention when it's demanded of me. I react much more kindly to requests." He smiled faintly. "You should have said, 'Jean Marc, *s'il vous plaît*,' or 'Jean Marc, would you be so kind?' Then I'm sure I'd never have been able to resist hearing what you had to say."

To his amazement, her cheeks turned scarlet. "Don't be ridiculous. Perhaps your mistresses speak to you with *s'il vous plaîts*, but you'll never hear from me."

"No?" He lifted his brow. "How unfortunate. Then I fear you'll get far less than you would like from me."

"I don't want anything from—" She stopped and drew a deep breath. "I know you're mocking me. You like to play with words, to thrust and then step back and watch, don't you?"

"Do I?" At the moment the only thrusting he was interested in had nothing to do with words. He wished she looked less challenging and more vulnerable. He found it difficult to remember her recent suffering when he was experiencing his own immediate painful physical response.

"I think so." Her hands clenched into tight fists at her sides. "I can't *read* you. I'm not sure what you're thinking. It's even worse than when we were at the inn."

"A mirror. I think that's what you once called me." He tilted his head. "No, I believe it was an entire gallery of mirrors. I suppose I should be grateful you granted me a multiplicity of images."

"You're laughing at me." She lifted her chin. "You see, I'm learning. I'll find a way to know you."

"I could suggest a number of fascinating ways to accomplish that goal, but until such a felicitous time I suggest you try '*s'il vous plaît*, Jean Marc.'"

She looked hurriedly away. "No, I couldn't—" She broke off as she looked back at him and found him still watching her intently. She drew a deep breath and then slowly let it out. "What are you going to do about Catherine?"

He was suddenly filled with self-disgust. What was wrong with him? Danger existed all around them and he could think only of his pleasure in rutting with her. His mocking smile vanished. "I'll get Catherine out of Paris as soon as possible. She'll be safe at Vasaro."

He had spoken only of Catherine, he realized at once. *Merde*, he couldn't actually be thinking of keeping

Juliette in Paris, where she would be in constant danger, just because he lusted after her.

"I'm not sure she'll ever be safe." Juliette shivered. "You don't know Dupree."

"No, I've seen him a time or two at the Hôtel de Ville with Marat, but we've never been introduced." Jean Marc's gaze narrowed on her face. "But you clearly know him very well indeed. What happened at the Abbaye de la Reine, Juliette?"

"You know. I told you about Catherine."

"But not about Juliette."

Her glance slid away. "There's nothing to tell."

"I believe there may be a great deal to tell."

"Why are you asking me these questions? It's Catherine who's important."

"So I've been told." Jean Marc paused. "All right, let's talk about Catherine. You're worried that Dupree might pursue her to Vasaro?"

"If he finds out she's one of the students from the abbey. He wants no witnesses to refute the charges against the nuns."

"Then we'll have to make sure he doesn't find out. As soon as it's safe, she'll go to Vasaro."

"I want her to leave right away. She needs to get away from everything that could remind her of the abbey. You don't understand." Juliette's teeth pressed hard into her lower lip. "I'm afraid for her here. For the last two days she's been like a spirit, walking around in a dream. She shuts me out. She shuts everyone out."

"She'll recover in time. I have no intention of sending her through the barriers until it's safe."

"And what will make it safe?"

Jean Marc grimaced and shook his head. "I have no idea. I'll have to explore the situation and then think about it."

"Think? *Do* something."

"I've already done something. I've sent for Etchelet."

She hesitated and then gave up the battle. "Call me when he arrives. I have to go to Catherine. She didn't touch her breakfast again this morning, and I must coax her to eat something." She turned away and then abruptly whirled again to face him. "Why did you keep it?"

"I beg your pardon?"

"My painting of the Wind Dancer." She gestured to the corner of the salon, where the painting hung. "Oh, not that it isn't excellent, but it lacks the mastery of the other paintings in this room."

His gaze went to the painting across the room. "I like it. It pleases me to see it here whenever I come to Paris."

"Because it's a painting of the Wind Dancer?"

"Perhaps." He smiled faintly. "Maybe beneath my 'mirror' I'm as sentimental as my father regarding the family treasures."

She looked at him skeptically.

"You don't believe I have a sentimental soul?"

She ignored the question and moved across the salon to stand before the painting. "Where is it now?"

"The statue? No one knows. It disappeared mysteriously the day the royal family was forced by the mob to quit Versailles for Paris. Rumor has it the queen hid it somewhere in the palace or on the grounds rather than have it fall into the hands of the revolutionaries."

"Well, why shouldn't she?" Juliette demanded. "It belonged to the queen. They took everything else from her. Why shouldn't she be allowed to keep the Wind Dancer?"

"Let's say, it didn't improve her position in the eyes of the assembly. I understand some of those good gentlemen wished to use the Wind Dancer as a symbol of the revolution."

"They have enough symbols. She has nothing now."

"Still loyal to the monarchy?" His smile faded. "That, too, is a dangerous position today. I'd reconsider if I were you."

"I care nothing for either the monarchy or the republic. I care nothing for politics. I would have been quite happy to have been left alone at the abbey if those murdering *canailles* hadn't seen fit to descend upon us."

"I can't envision you donning a wimple and scapular."

"I didn't say I wished to be a nun. I wanted only to be left in peace without— Oh, you're laughing at me again." She turned away from the painting. "You don't appear to be upset that the statue has disappeared. Don't you want it any longer?"

"I want it. I promised my father before he died that I'd see to its return to the family." He paused. "But I've learned if I'm patient, I usually get what I want."

"I'm not patient. I hate to wait for things to happen."

He smiled. "Ah, and so do I, *ma petite*. But one must weigh the value of what one desires against the irritation of waiting for it."

She felt suddenly breathless as she realized he was no longer speaking of the Wind Dancer. She desperately veered back to the primary subject. "It's foolish not to realize that Catherine needs something done now."

"You never give up, do you? In spite of what you deem my 'foolishness,' I'll continue on the course I've set." Jean Marc smiled ironically. "I regret I can't take your excellent advice. How delightful it must be to know you're always right."

"I'm not always right." She turned and walked across the salon toward the door. "*Almost* always, however."

"What is this?" Juliette gazed in bewilderment at the pile of packages Robert carried into Catherine's chamber three hours later.

"Clothing. Monsieur Philippe has returned and is in the gold salon with Monsieur Etchelet."

"Philippe!" Catherine's gaze flew to Juliette. "You didn't tell me Philippe was here."

"I was going to tell you later."

"Monsieur Philippe said he took the liberty of purchasing a few items of apparel for you and Mademoiselle Catherine." Robert smiled at Catherine as he set the packages on the padded bench by the window. "Evidently he didn't approve of my Marie's gown."

"But where did he get them? He's been gone only a few hours." Juliette opened a package to reveal a silk gown in a vibrant shade of cinnamon. Intricate gold embroidery bordered a low neck and delicate lace frothed at the hems of three-quarter-length sleeves. The gown was as fine as any she had seen at Versailles, and she knew very well how many hours of work had gone into the embroidery. Rose Bertin, the queen's favorite dressmaker, would have demanded many fortnights to produce such a gown. "This must have been meant for another client. I'd like to know how he managed to find a dressmaker obliging enough to offend another customer to sell him such a gown."

"Oh, the ladies have always been most obliging for Monsieur Philippe. Shall I tell the gentlemen you'll join them as soon as you've changed?"

"No." Juliette turned and moved toward the door. "I'm decently covered. Your wife's gown will do very well for me."

Robert nodded. "I thought as much. I informed Monsieur Andreas you'd be down immediately."

Juliette stopped and looked suspiciously at him over her shoulder. It could be dangerous to have a servant so perceptive. "How clever of you."

Robert smiled gently. "You don't have to be afraid of me, Mademoiselle Juliette. I would never tell anyone you were from the abbey."

Juliette's gaze narrowed on his face. "And what do you know of what happened at the abbey?"

"Only what I hear in the market."

"And what is that?"

"I think you know. All of Paris is talking of the massacres. Don't worry, I would never say anything to hurt Mademoiselle Catherine. Nor would I believe such slander against her or the nuns. I have no liking for these pompous men of the assembly who command me to say *tu* instead of *vous* and call myself Citizen when I've always found Monsieur good enough in my sixty years."

Juliette felt a surge of warmth. "Thank you, Robert.

It's not easy to trust anyone." She hesitated and then turned to Catherine. "Philippe wishes to see you."

"No!" Catherine sat bolt upright on the bed, her cheeks flaming, her eyes brimming with tears. "Send him away."

"Catherine, I admit he's been—"

"I *won't* see him. I don't ever want to see him again. Don't bring Philippe here, Juliette. Don't make me—"

"I'm not going to make you do anything you don't wish to do." Juliette cast her an anxious glance as she started for the door. "I'll be back soon."

"Don't bring him back with you. Don't let him see me. He'll—" Catherine broke off, the tears running down her cheeks. "Sweet heaven, I'm sorry. I know you hate for me to blubber like a baby, but I can't seem to stop. Forgive me for being such a burden to you."

"You're not a burden and, if you feel like blubbering, do it. You have reason."

Catherine's eyes sparkled like sapphires in the rain as she whispered, "Please, don't make me face him, Juliette."

"I won't bring him here." Juliette swallowed to ease the tightness in her throat before turning to Robert. "Fetch your wife to stay with Mademoiselle Catherine in my stead."

He nodded. "My Marie was always fond of Mademoiselle Catherine. She'll take good care of *la petite.*"

"Good." Juliette was already halfway down the corridor. "I want her fed, bathed, and calmed by the time I return."

"We'll endeavor to accomplish at least the first two tasks, Mademoiselle." The faintest shade of dry humor colored Robert's tone.

No fear, no scurrying to obey. The old man might have more courage than had first been evident, Juliette thought with respect. Courage could be a problem if not accompanied by loyalty, but still she liked dealing with it more than cowardice. She grinned at Robert over her shoulder. "And I'll take care of all else."

She straightened her shoulders as she marched down the stairs to face the three men in the salon.

But only François Etchelet and Philippe Andreas were in the Gold Salon, standing in uneasy silence, looking as alien to each other as panther and peacock.

The image intrigued Juliette, and she found herself pausing in the arched doorway before making her presence known. Philippe, radiantly golden and brilliant as a sunset in his crimson silk coat, pearl-gray trousers, and polished black boots. Etchelet dressed in black, anonymous serge, wearing his fierceness like the sleek coat of a great cat so that his clothing appeared totally unimportant. Interesting.

She must have made some sound, for François suddenly whirled. "I should inform you, Mademoiselle, I dislike being sent for as if I were a stable boy bound to do your bidding." His eyes glittered in the candlelight as he took a step forward. Panther's eyes, Juliette thought, all black iris and shimmering menace. "*If* I decide to help you, it won't be because you demand it."

"We needed to speak to you," Juliette said. "And it wasn't I who sent Philippe after you. It was Jean Ma—"

"Ah, Monsieur Etchelet." Jean Marc suddenly materialized beside Juliette and strolled leisurely toward François. "How kind of you to come. I'm Jean Marc Andreas and I wished to give you my heartfelt thanks for your services to my cousin and Mademoiselle de Clement."

"Monsieur Andreas." Etchelet bowed, his gaze wary. "The circumstances were such that I could do nothing else."

"And I am sure he would have made every effort to avoid his involvement," Juliette said sweetly, "I suppose we should be grateful he saw fit not to send us back to his friend, the butcher."

"I'm sure Mademoiselle de Clement means no offense." Philippe stepped forward protectively. "She's overcome by the horrors she's undergone."

Juliette bristled. "Overcome? I'm not overcome. I'm tired and angry, but I'm not about to swoon because this man scowls at me."

François suddenly smiled. "No, I think it would take considerably more to make you swoon."

"So do I," Jean Marc said dryly. "Don't you think it's time to put differences aside and concentrate on the task at hand? Your words do not help Catherine, Juliette."

François turned abruptly away, walked over to the window, and stood looking out into the street.

"Philippe says it's very difficult getting through the checkpoints without proper papers," Jean Marc said to François's back. "Can you get them for us?"

"No."

"Can Danton get them for us?"

"Probably. But he won't risk it. Not now."

"Why not?" Juliette asked.

"It's too dangerous. In addition to the regular guard, Dupree has at least one man of his own at every gate and there's no telling when or where he will appear to make checks personally. Georges Jacques mustn't be connected with you or he'll lose what he's gained."

"And what is that?" Jean Marc asked.

"The Girondins. If the assembly loses the Girondins, the extremist radicals like Marat and Robespierre will gain power."

"I don't care about these Girondins," Juliette said. "I want Catherine out of Paris. What do we do?"

"Wait."

It was easy for him to say, Juliette thought in frustration. "I don't want to wait."

François whirled to face her. "Then you shouldn't have killed one of the Marseilles."

She stiffened. "They found him?"

"Oh, yes, they found him. They've been searching the countryside for his murderess. Georges Jacques says Dupree was highly displeased. He likes everything neat and tidy."

"I doubt if those words would apply to a massacre." Juliette nibbled at her lower lip. "Does he know who killed the pig?"

"He doesn't know your true identity, but he does suspect 'Citizeness Justice.'"

"No one else?"

François shook his head.

Then Dupree must not have found the locket, she thought with relief. "The sword. Dupree knows I took his sword." A frown knitted her brow. "But he can't be sure Catherine was at the tomb. He saw her for only an instant in the bell tower—unless he remembers she wasn't in the courtyard at the tribunal."

"Dupree has an excellent memory for detail. He posted a reward for both of you this morning with full descriptions."

"Citizeness Justice?" Jean Marc asked.

"Mademoiselle de Clement," François said. "It's the only name by which Dupree knows her."

Jean Marc's gaze shifted with sudden intentness to Juliette. "Why Citizeness Justice?"

"It's only a name Dupree found it amusing to call me. But that's not important." Juliette frowned. "Then Dupree can't know we're in Paris."

François nodded. "Which is why it's safe to wait."

"Wait for what?"

"Georges Jacques is going to arrange to intercede with Marat to have Dupree sent out of the city as soon as possible. He's the only man who can recognize you."

"There's a courtyard of men who can recognize me. *You* recognized me."

"The Marseilles were busier at that moment than I."

Juliette's stomach clenched as she remembered the tasks that had occupied those men in the courtyard. "Yes, very busy."

"They're still busy." François's lips set grimly. "I'm sure in a few days the events at the abbey will blur into one red haze."

Juliette's gaze flew to his face. "Dear God, more?"

François nodded. "After they left the abbey that morning they marched on *La Force*. They killed the Princess de Lambelle, stuck her head on a pike, and carried it to the Temple to show it to Marie Antoinette."

Juliette swallowed bile. Her mother had always hated the gentle princess who had given the queen her love and loyalty since girlhood. Juliette had not understood the woman's high-strung delicacy but never questioned the princess's genuine affection for Her Majesty.

"You should not have told her," Philippe said. "Can't you see how it's upset her?"

"The queen?" Juliette asked. "Did they kill the queen?"

"No, the Temple is well guarded. None of the royal family was hurt."

Relief rushed through Juliette. The queen and Louis Charles were still alive. "How disappointed those butchers must have been."

François avoided her glance. "Marat won't permit Dupree to be sent away until he's satisfied that his job is done. You must not step foot out of the house until there isn't the least possibility you could encounter him."

"Is bribery feasible?" Jean Marc asked.

"Not now. Perhaps later."

"So we're to stay here until Dupree is sent out of Paris?" Juliette tried to gather her thoughts into some kind of order. "I don't like it. There are too many residences around the square and we can't stay here very long in secret. No matter how careful we are, people are bound to realize we're in the house."

Jean Marc thought for a moment and then said, "I can tell Robert to put it about that Philippe came from Vasaro to be of assistance to his two sisters who were forced to flee from their homes in the north after the Prussians took Verdun."

"It's possible," François said. "Providing no official inquiry is undertaken regarding them." He turned to Philippe. "You'll stay here to lend the story credence?"

Philippe nodded. "Of course. I'll stay as long as I'm needed."

"Catherine won't want you here," Juliette said. "She does not wish to see you."

"I'll stay out of her way." Philippe's tone was firm. "But my place is here helping Jean Marc and Catherine to—"

"The story will have to do for the time being," Jean

Marc said. "You'll let me know if there's any danger, Etchelet?"

"I assure you neither Georges Jacques nor I wish to have the women apprehended. It would be a distinct embarrassment." François turned toward the door. "I'll inform you when Dupree has left Paris."

"Wait." Juliette took a step forward. "That's not enough. Philippe is a stranger in Paris and it may be known that Jean Marc's ward was at the abbey. It's you who must lend our presence here credence. You must be well known if you work for Danton. Call on us at least every other day."

"I have no time for—"

"Call on us as frequently as possible and stay but briefly." She smiled mockingly. "Do wear one of your tricolored cockades so that everyone can see how loyal to the government the members of this household must be. A fine revolutionary gentleman like yourself should be displaying one anyway."

He met her gaze. "I don't have to wear my convictions on my hat."

"It won't hurt you to do so for the next few weeks. Don't worry, we don't want to see you any more than you do us. Have Marie show you to the garden and spend the time in contemplation." Her smile faded. "Yes, contemplate why you were at the Abbaye de la Reine."

He gazed at her silently for a moment. "I may drop in occasionally if I'm in the neighborhood."

He turned and left the salon.

"Wait." Juliette suddenly remembered something and followed him into the foyer. To her surprise, she found him standing at the foot of the curving staircase, looking up.

"How is she?" he asked in a low tone.

"Not good. How do you expect her to be? She dreams and wakes up screaming. She won't eat or—" Juliette drew a deep breath and tried to regain her control. "This man I killed, who was he?"

"A Marseilles. His name was Etienne Malpan."

"Do you know what he looked like?"

"Yes."

"Describe him."

"Dead."

"Very amusing."

"I find death lends a certain anonymity of appearance to everyone. Why are you suddenly so curious about his looks?"

"It was dark in the tomb and Catherine couldn't see who attacked her. She said they had no faces and for some reason it bothers her."

"So you're trying to put faces to them for her?" He was silent a moment. "Etienne Malpan was fair, about forty, a big, beefy man."

"I remember he was large. What color were his eyes?"

"I don't remember."

"Find out."

"I'm to go to the graveyard and, providing they haven't buried him yet, have them pry open his lids?"

"She needs a face, a complete face. You don't impress me as being overly squeamish."

François shook his head. "Do you never give up?"

"She needs a face."

François opened the door.

"Will you do it?"

"Stop *badgering* me."

The slam of the door echoed in the high-ceilinged hall.

"You should be more cautious. He's a dangerous man."

Juliette turned to see a frowning Philippe behind her in the foyer.

"I asked a few questions about Etchelet when I was trying to locate his lodgings. He's well known among the representatives of the assembly."

"Well known in what way?"

"He's nominally Danton's agent and clerk, but that's not his primary duty."

"I'm not surprised. He didn't impress me as a clerk."

"He gathers information for Danton."

"A spy?"

"He also intimidates. He's fought five duels in the past two years, all with men Danton found convenient to have out of the way. Needless to say, he was not content merely to inflict token wounds to have honor satisfied."

That information didn't surprise her either. "He'll not challenge me to a duel. Nor do I have any important information he can steal."

"Two of those duels concerned women. Etchelet presumably seduced the women in order to prod his prey into challenging him so that he would have the choice of weapons." Philippe shook his head. "None of it was honorably done."

"That he used the women to get what he wanted?" Juliette could not see Etchelet in the role of seducer. In spite of his physical attractiveness, he radiated a blunt honesty that seemed at odds with the deceit needed for such schemes. "But did you not do the same? How else did you get those gowns Robert brought to my chamber."

"That was different," Philippe protested. "I merely explained my need to the ladies in the shop."

He believed what he was saying, Juliette realized with amazement. Philippe had merely charmed and cajoled and smiled sweetly and the deed was done. "At which shop did you purchase them?"

"Julie Lamartine's. I remembered Jean Marc uses her to clothe his—" Philippe stopped and then continued lamely. "She'll begin fitting you both with a complete wardrobe as soon as I provide her with your present measurements."

He had gone to the shop where Jean Marc sent his mistresses. Juliette felt a sudden jab of pain. No, it couldn't have been pain. She was tired and confused. All rich men had mistresses, and most courtesans had better taste in fashion than wives. The dressmaker would do very well to outfit Catherine before she left Paris. "I'll have Catherine's measurements for you tomorrow."

Philippe nodded. "And yours."

"I can make do with one of Marie's gowns."

"My sisters would not be ill dressed."

Juliette's gaze traveled over his impeccable attire, and she was forced to smile, albeit faintly. "I can see how you would be filled with shame at such ignominy." She started up the stairs. "Very well, you'll have my measurements too."

She had almost reached the landing when she heard Jean Marc's voice behind her. "Juliette."

She glanced down to see Jean Marc standing in the doorway of the salon and unconsciously tensed. "Yes?"

His dark eyes narrowed on her face. "Why Citizeness Justice?" he asked softly.

Juliette quickly glanced away. "I told you it wasn't important."

"No? I'm beginning to wonder just what you do consider important."

"My painting. Catherine."

"And nothing else?"

"Nothing else."

Jean Marc's lips were lifted in a faint smile, and there was something in his expression that was both intimate and challenging. She became suddenly aware of the physical presence he exuded, the wideness of his shoulders beneath the smooth fit of his gray coat, the sinewy muscles of his thighs outlined by the clinging doeskin of his trousers, the flatness of his belly. She found herself gazing at him in helpless fascination unable to look away.

His intent gaze held hers for another moment. "How interesting. And challenging. We really must attempt to widen your horizons." He turned and strode back into the salon.

Her breath expelled in a little rush as if his departure had forced its release.

"Did you ask if she'd see me?"

To her amazement, she had forgotten Philippe was there the moment Jean Marc had appeared in the foyer. The knowledge sent a tingle of uneasiness through her. Jean Marc had been there only one day and he was already overshadowing everyone and everything around her.

Philippe took a step forward. "I'd still like to express my shame for my—"

"Shame? Let me tell you about shame." Juliette's hand tightened on the oak banister as she looked down at him. "Catherine is so full of shame she can't look you in the face. I can't make her understand the shame belongs to the guilty, not to the victim. For some reason she thinks you're a gentleman of such nicety of character you'll find her abhorrent."

"Then let me tell her differently." Philippe took another step forward. "Let me tell her I'm the one to blame."

"She wouldn't believe you. Do you know her so little? She would see your shame and think it a reflection of her own."

"Tell her— Never mind. There's nothing I can say, is there?"

"No." Juliette hesitated. To her surprise the desolation in his expression moved her. Everyone mentioned that Philippe had a way with women, but she had not thought herself vulnerable to his charm. "Perhaps you may try in a few days."

His expression brightened. "And you'll tell me if there's anything I can do for either of you? It would be my great pleasure to serve you in any way."

"If there is, I shall tell you." As Juliette climbed the stairs she could feel his wistful gaze on her back.

Peacock and panther, she mused. And dominating both of them was the darkly glittering, enigmatic mirror who was Jean Marc Andreas.

She abruptly stopped and looked down as she reached the head of the stairs. "Paints and canvas."

Philippe was startled. "What?"

"If I'm to be imprisoned here in this house for any time, I must have paints and canvas. Will you see to it?"

She didn't wait for an answer but turned on her heel and moved down the hall toward Catherine's chamber.

"Monsieur Jean Marc is not at home. Will you wait in the salon while I tell Mademoiselle Juliette you've arrived?" Robert asked as he took François's hat and gloves and laid them on the table in the center of the foyer. "I believe she's upstairs in the—"

"No." François certainly didn't need Juliette de Clement lashing out at him today. He had come directly from the assembly and was already raw enough with the talk of Dupree's latest massacre. He didn't know why he called now. He'd had no intention of obeying Juliette's command to appear at frequent intervals at the Place Royale, and it had been only two days since he had slammed this very door and stalked out of the house. Still, now that he was there, he might just as well stay for a brief time. "Show me to the garden."

Robert blinked and then nodded. "Oh, you wish to see Mademoiselle Catherine? Certainly, Monsieur. This way."

François hesitated as Robert started across the foyer. He had no desire to see Catherine Vasaro either. He had thought he was too hardened for either pity or regret to touch him, but looking at Catherine filled him with a strange poignant desire to soothe and protect.

Robert was looking at him inquiringly over his shoulder.

François slowly followed him across the foyer toward the glass-paned double doors leading to the garden.

Catherine Vasaro sat on a marble bench by the fountain in the center of the garden, her hands folded on her lap. He was vaguely aware she was dressed in something blue and soft and that the sunlight threaded glints of gold through her light brown hair.

"It's Monsieur Etchelet," Robert said gently as he paused before Catherine. "He's come to see you, Mademoiselle Catherine."

"Has he?" Catherine lifted her gaze from her folded hands to look beyond Robert's shoulder at Etchelet. Her brow furrowed in puzzlement. "François. Your name is François, isn't it?"

"Yes." He stood looking at her as Robert turned and walked back toward the house. She appeared even more fragile than when he had last seen her. Dark shadows underscored her eyes, and she appeared thinner, the bones of her wrists breakable. "You've not been eating."

"I've been eating a little. I don't seem to be very hungry." She looked down at her hands again. "I remember now. You were angry with me. Why were you angry?"

"I wasn't angry." He dropped down on the marble bench across the path from her. "Well, perhaps a little."

"Why?"

"You gave up. You can't ever give up. No matter how much it hurts, you have to endure. That's the only way to survive to avenge yourself."

She looked up at him. "But I don't want revenge."

"Of course you do," he said harshly. "It's only human to want it. Anyone would—" He stopped as he realized she was staring at him as if he were speaking in a language foreign to her. The comparison was apt, for she looked like some serene, gentle being from a land alien to any he knew. A land where there were no Duprees, no compromises, no jostling for power, no bloody massacres.

He glanced away from her, filled with the sense of sick premonition that she would be destroyed. This world had no tolerance for gentleness. Forgiveness was a weakness. And he was helpless to change any of it.

"I'm . . . sorry." Her voice was hesitant. "I've made you angry again, haven't I?"

"Why should you care if I'm angry? For the love of God, worry about yourself."

Her hands were opening and closing nervously on her lap. "It's more than anger. You have . . . pain."

"Nonsense."

She didn't seem to hear him. "This garden helps. For the past few days I've come here to sit for hours. The feel of the sunlight on my face and the sound of the birds in the trees . . . Sometimes you can wrap the silence around you and close the pain out." A gentle smile turned her face luminous. "Perhaps the garden will help you too."

Dieu, she was going through an inward agony and yet she was still trying to help him banish the unrest she sensed in him. François suddenly realized Catherine was like the garden she had just described—beautiful, serene, lit by sun and yet vulnerable to every cruel wind. He could feel her serenity flow over him, soothing the rawness he had brought with him.

He sat silently, gazing at her with the same expression of bewilderment and wonder with which she'd looked at him. He suddenly knew he *wanted* to stay there. He wanted to sit in that garden and look at Catherine Vasaro and let peace and silence replace the turbulence of the outside world. Yet how could he do so when he had chosen his battleground?

He stood up abruptly. "No, *merci*. I won't stay in your garden. You can sit here and close yourself away from the world, but I have things to do with my life."

Some untranslatable emotion flickered across her face before she once more lowered her gaze to the hands folded on her lap.

He stared at her for a moment, an inexplicable frustration aching in him. He left her then without a word.

It didn't improve his temper to encounter Juliette de Clement in the foyer.

"I was wondering when you would see fit to visit us," Juliette said. "We could have been—"

"Blue."

Juliette blinked. "What?"

François picked up his hat and gloves from the table and turned toward the front door. "Etienne Malpan's eyes were blue."

"Oh, you did go to the graveyard." Juliette paused on the bottom step, her gaze narrowed on his face. "What about the other man? Can you find out who he was?"

"Are you never satisfied? There were over two hundred men at the massacre at the abbey."

"Catherine has nightmares every single night. She's obsessed that those two men have no faces for her." Her lips tightened. "Besides, *I* want to know."

"I've given you one face. You'll have to be content with Malpan." François opened the door. "I've better things to do with my time than conduct an inquiry that not only could take months but also arouse suspicion among Dupree's men."

The door was swinging shut as she called, "François."

"I told you I won't—"

"Thank you."

He looked at her warily but could detect no mockery in her expression.

"I know you didn't have to do that for Catherine," she said simply. "I suppose I can wait to find out about the other man."

"I'm glad I did something to please you."

"Oh, you did." Her eyes were suddenly twinkling with mischief. "But you didn't do everything I asked. Your hat has no cockade and—"

The slam of the door cut off Juliette's final words.

NINE

"I have to talk to you, Jean Marc."

Jean Marc looked up from the document he was studying to see Juliette standing in the doorway of the study. The emerald green of her gown contrasted magnificently with her skin and unruly dark curls which seemed to shimmer while her eyes sparkled. He had been deliberately avoiding Juliette for the whole month past; now her sheer vitality sent a sensual shock through him. He felt every muscle tense as he fought the response she always provoked in him. "Can't it wait? I'm busy."

"Don't tell me you're busy." Juliette moved across the study toward the desk. "You're always busy. You work in here day and night and I never get a chance to talk to you. Not once in the past month have you even had supper with Philippe and me."

Jean Marc leaned back in his chair. "My

dear Juliette, those damned Jacobins have taken over the government and I'm trying to keep them from stealing everything I own." He smiled. "However, I didn't realize I'd been missed. Perhaps if you'd said *s'il vous plaît*, Jean Marc, I would have—"

"I believe Catherine's with child."

Jean Marc went still. "No."

"I am afraid it is so. She's not had her flux due a fortnight ago. At first I couldn't believe it." Juliette smiled bitterly. "You'd think God had given her enough to bear and would spare her this. What are you going to do?"

"I must think about it."

"Think? *Do* something. Catherine is so filled with shame, she's drowning in it. She wakes screaming every night."

"I said that I must think."

Juliette took a step closer. "And while you're thinking, what if it occurs to her that she's with child and she kills herself? Do you wish such a thing to happen?"

Anger surged through Jean Marc. "And what should I do? Find a dirty old woman in one of the back streets to kill the child in her womb? Did it ever occur to you to kill the child might also kill Catherine?"

"Don't be foolish—or misunderstand me in this. Catherine would never accept the murder of her babe, but she can't be made to suffer even greater shame. I've been thinking about it." Juliette paused. "You must find her a husband."

"Indeed? Who?"

"How do I know? It's your responsibility. You're the one who was too busy to come when she needed you. Now you should be the one to help her."

He lifted a brow. "Are you suggesting I offer myself on the marital altar?"

"*Bon Dieu,* no! She already quakes when you frown at her. She'd snap like the ribs of a fan before you'd been wed a month."

"I'm not an ogre and I don't appreciate you—" Jean Marc stopped, his gaze narrowing thoughtfully. "But if not me, perhaps she could—"

"No!" Juliette immediately realized where his logic was leading. "You're thinking of Philippe. She wouldn't marry him."

"Why not? She's always been fond of him."

"Fond? She *adores* him. She's besotted with him. She blushes at the mere mention of his name."

"Good. Then it's settled. It's time Philippe married and it will be an advantageous match for them both. He always has loved Vasaro and will continue to be an excellent manager."

"Settled? You haven't even discussed it with him."

"I'll speak to him immediately. I'm sure there will be no problem. Philippe likes Catherine and he appears genuinely remorseful for—"

Juliette adamantly shook her head. "Anyone else. Not Philippe."

"You make no sense whatsoever." Jean Marc frowned. "Philippe will treat her with the greatest tenderness."

"Haven't you been listening to me? She loves that beautiful peacock. Do you think she'd force herself on him in marriage when she won't even allow herself to be in the same room with him?"

"I'll talk to her." He started for the door. "It's an excellent solution and it's unreasonable of her to—"

"Dear heaven, she's in *pain*. How do you expect her to be reasonable?" She rushed after him. "You must not tell her she's with child."

He stopped with his hand on the knob of the door. "You're sure she doesn't know?"

Juliette shook her head. "She's like a child herself now. You shouldn't tell her. She'll accept that she has to wed to hide her shame. She mustn't know there's anything else to hide."

"It's not something you can hide indefinitely."

"Perhaps she'll be better soon," Juliette said desperately, her eyes glittering with unshed tears. "She has to get better, doesn't she?"

Jean Marc was strangely moved. Juliette, too, was like a child frantically seeking reassurance. Mother of God, he wanted to think only of her strengths, not her weaknesses. Yet he found he couldn't deny her comfort. "We will find a way to make sure she gets better."

Juliette's gaze clung to Jean Marc's. Abruptly, then, she glanced away and stepped back. She moistened her lips. "You won't speak to her about Philippe? It will only make her weep."

"I'll wait until after I speak to Philippe at least."

"I don't know why you even bother getting his approval on the disposition of his life." Her tone was especially tart. "Doesn't everyone do as you wish them to do?"

He smothered a smile. "For the most part, but one must display a certain courtesy. I shall speak to Philippe and then talk to Catherine."

She sighed and shook her head. "You're making a mistake."

Jean Marc frowned as he came down the steps toward Juliette and Philippe, waiting for him in the foyer.

"I told you it would do no good," Juliette said, reading his expression. "You should have listened to me."

"I'm getting exceptionally tired of listening to you," Jean Marc said in a clipped tone. "I wonder the nuns were able to tolerate you for more than a fortnight."

"They considered me a scourge, good for their souls."

An unexpected smile banished the look of annoyance from Jean Marc's face. "As do I."

Juliette's own exasperation melted away as she looked at him. It was difficult to be angry at a man who could smile after being proved wrong. "I suppose you made her cry."

Jean Marc grimaced. "I never imagined she would become so upset. Perhaps you'd better go to her. She seems distraught."

Philippe took a step forward. "Perhaps I should go up and explain that this marriage is entirely by my will.

I can't understand why she has so suddenly taken this dislike to me. I only want to help *la pauvre petite*."

"And have her see you pitying her?" Juliette started up the stairs. "Even Jean Marc would be a better husband to her than you."

"You've reconsidered my eligibility, then?" Jean Marc asked.

"You needn't be sarcastic just because you were wrong and I was right. You'd do much better to channel your thoughts to finding a solution to Catherine's predicament. I don't see that a husband should be a problem. François says you're very good at bribery. Buy her one."

"Oh, now I should buy her one. At a slave market on the vast Arabian desert? Where am I to find this convenient husband?"

"That's your affair. I've told you what's needed. It's your place to supply it."

The door to Catherine's chamber closed behind Juliette and she stood there silently cursing Jean Marc and mankind in general. Catherine was lying on the bed sobbing in an attitude of complete desolation, her slight body shuddering with sobs.

"Stop it." Juliette strode forward. "There's no reason to weep. All the stupidity is over."

Catherine quickly rolled over and sat up. "I can't do it, Juliette. Jean Marc is angry with me, but I can't do it."

"I know you can't." Juliette picked up a linen handkerchief from the table beside the bed and gently wiped Catherine's cheeks. "No one is going to make you marry Philippe if you don't wish to."

"How could Jean Marc ask him to do such a thing?" Catherine asked wonderingly. "He loves Philippe. Philippe deserves a wife who can come to him clean and free from the taint—"

"Philippe would be fortunate beyond belief to wed you."

"No, I'm not fit—"

"Stop spouting this nonsense." Juliette tried to temper her impatience. "I won't try to persuade you to marry Philippe, but you do realize it's necessary for you to marry someone?"

Catherine shook her head. "I shall never marry."

"You *must* marry."

"That's what Jean Marc said. Is it because of what they did to me? Because I'm disgraced?"

"Yes, it's because of what they did to you."

"It doesn't seem . . . fair."

"No."

"I don't wish to marry."

"I know, Catherine." Juliette sat down on the bed beside her and took both Catherine's hands in her own. "But you realize I'd never ask you to do anything that wasn't for the best?"

Catherine nodded listlessly.

"Then you'll do as I ask?"

"Not Philippe."

"No, not Philippe." Juliette's hands tightened around Catherine's. "Someone else."

Catherine tensed. "He won't hurt me?"

Juliette's rush of fury was followed immediately by passionate tenderness. "I promise you won't be hurt."

Catherine relaxed. "I couldn't bear to be touched like that again."

"It won't happen. Trust me."

"I do trust you. I'll do whatever you wish." Catherine withdrew her hands from Juliette's clasp and Juliette realized she was already drifting away again. "I think I'd like to go sit in the garden now."

"Be sure to take your shawl." Juliette rose to her feet. "Will you join us for supper?"

"What? Oh, no, thank you. I shall go to sleep early, I think."

She was asleep now, Juliette thought in despair. When would she wake? "Would you like me to come and brush your hair after supper? It sometimes helps you to sleep peacefully."

"No, thank you. I'd rather be alone." Catherine's gaze slid away from Juliette's. "Unless you think it necessary."

This from Catherine, who so hated to be alone she

had sometimes sought out Juliette's company in Sister Bernadette's tomb. "No, it's not necessary. I simply thought you might like it." Juliette moved toward the door. "I'll tell Marie you'll have supper in your room."

She was halfway down the stairs when the idea occurred to her.

It was too absurd.

But was it?

She continued down the stairs, a thoughtful frown on her brow.

"You can't work through this meal, Jean Marc," Juliette said as she opened the door of the study the next evening. "You must have supper with us tonight."

"Must?" Jean Marc repeated silkily.

Juliette nodded. "We have a guest."

"What guest?" Jean Marc's chair screeched as he pushed it away from the desk. "Dammit, you know we can't have guests with you and Catherine in the house."

"Join us in the Gold Salon in a few minutes." Juliette left the study.

François Etchelet looked surprisingly elegant when he was shown in. His dark brown hair was drawn back from his face and fastened with a black tie, and his dark blue coat fitted his shoulders as impeccably as did Jean Marc's or Philippe's. The gracefulness of his bow betrayed an easy worldliness, and Juliette had a sudden memory of Philippe's words regarding François's reputed seductions. Evidently the panther did indeed have hidden facets to his character.

"Good evening, Monsieur Andreas," François said to Jean Marc and then continued impatiently. "This travesty of a social supper isn't necessary. Let's get on with it. Why did you send for me?"

"I didn't send for you."

"Then why am I here?"

"I have no idea." Jean Marc turned to Juliette. "Suppose we ask Mademoiselle de Clement?"

"Later," Juliette said, her gaze fixed on François. "Talk. I'm still thinking about it."

"As you command. We wouldn't wish to disturb your concentration." Jean Marc began to pour wine from the silver pitcher into the goblets Marie had set in readiness on the rosewood table. "Dupree is still in Paris, Etchelet?"

"Not much longer perhaps. Georges Jacques is concerned about how the war is going and may leave for the front shortly. He'll ask Marat to delegate Dupree to his entourage."

"Perhaps?" Jean Marc grimaced. "I don't like to depend on uncertainties. Can't we hurry things a bit? How much would it cost to get the guards at the gates to look the other way?"

"It can't be done."

"I could be very generous."

"Impossible."

"There are no incorruptible men."

François inclined his head. "And no one knows that better than you, do they? You frequent the National Convention more than most of the delegates themselves."

Jean Marc stiffened. "You object to me bettering the fortunes of your fellow revolutionaries?" he asked softly.

"Georges Jacques says I think the revolution is all shining virtue." François shook his head. "He's wrong. I know exactly how corrupt some of the men of the convention can be."

"And you have no quarrel with it?"

"I accept it." François paused. "As long as it doesn't strike at the heart of the revolution. Bribe whomever you will to circumvent tax levies and trade embargoes. I do not care. Just stay away from the Rights of Man and the Constitution."

Jean Marc's eyes narrowed on François's face. "And what would you do if I decided I needed to make a few adjustments in those august documents?"

François smiled pleasantly. "Cut your heart out."

Jean Marc braced. Slowly, he relaxed. Finally, he smiled. "I don't believe I need to tamper with your Rights of Man. For the most part, I approve."

"How fortunate for both of us."

Juliette had been following the exchange with keen interest. The two men were completely different in character and philosophy, yet they were smiling at each other with complete understanding. However, she must stop this verbal minuet and bring them back to the principal topic. "Why is it impossible to bribe the soldiers at the gates?"

François turned to her. "Because they're more afraid of Dupree than greedy for Monsieur's francs. Greed is universal but there are certain limits."

"Not extensive ones." Jean Marc held out one of the silver goblets of wine he had poured for Juliette. "Perhaps you can persuade them to— What's wrong?"

"Nothing." Juliette couldn't stop staring at the deep red of the wine in the goblet. Sickness caused her stomach to clench and then churn helplessly. She mustn't be sick.

"You're ill." Jean Marc's gaze was on her face. "You've turned white. Take a sip of the wine."

"No!" She pushed the goblet from her and stepped back. "I'm not ill. I won't be ill."

"Very well. You needn't become violent about it. I only thought a drop of wine would brace you."

"Juliette doesn't like wine," Philippe said. "I've often teased her about it. She always has water with her meals."

"How unusual." Jean Marc studied Juliette's face. "And unhealthy. Water from the abbey must have been a good deal more pure than that of Paris."

Juliette swallowed and looked away from the goblet. "I don't know if it is or not."

"I recall Catherine saying the wine of the abbey was excellent. That the nuns grew their own grapes and that—"

"I'll take it." François stepped forward and took the goblet from Jean Marc. "We poor republicans get little opportunity to sample the wine cellars of merchant princes." He lifted the cup to his lips and sipped the wine. "Excellent."

To Juliette's relief Jean Marc's attention swung

immediately to François. "I'm delighted that a republican can appreciate something besides the Rights of Man."

François smiled. "I'm a Basque. No one can enjoy the pleasures of life more than a Basque."

François had deliberately diverted Jean Marc's attention to himself when he'd realized Juliette was upset, an act that seemed totally out of character. But was it? She stared at the man thoughtfully. "It's time for supper," she said abruptly. "Marie's a fine cook, François. Better than you can find in the kitchen of any eating establishment in Paris."

All three men looked at her in surprise.

"Come along." She turned and led the way through the arched doorway connecting the dining room to the salon. "You can talk to Jean Marc over the meal about ways of getting Catherine out of Paris."

Marie had served the fourth course when Juliette suddenly broke the silence she had maintained throughout the meal. "François."

François glanced at her across the table. "Yes?"

She ignored him as she turned to Jean Marc at the head of the table. "I've decided we'll use François."

"I dislike the word use," François said. "I've agreed to give you my assistance, but it will be in the way I choose. I am not one to be 'used.'"

"Oh, hush, I meant nothing by the word. I'm not always as silver-tongued as I might be."

"Not always?" Jean Marc murmured. "Rarely."

"That doesn't matter now." Juliette leaned forward, her expression suddenly eager. "Are you wed, François?"

He frowned warily. "No."

"Good, that would have ruined everything. Make him an offer, Jean Marc."

Jean Marc leaned back in his chair and studied François calmly. "Of marriage? I think not. He does not appeal to me."

François's lips twitched. "Thank God. I believe I'd

put your tampering with my person on the same level as tampering with the Rights of Man."

"This is no time to be joking." Juliette glanced at Jean Marc impatiently. "Catherine."

Jean Marc's lids lowered to veil his eyes. "An interesting choice."

"No!" Philippe threw his napkin on the table. "It's madness, Juliette. He's a stranger to her. He's a stranger to all of us."

"I can make her accept him," Juliette said.

"She wouldn't accept me," Philippe said.

"That was different."

"How?" Philippe demanded. "She's too ill to—"

"May I inquire as to just what you're discussing?" François demanded.

"I'll have no part of it." Philippe scraped his chair from the table and rose to his feet. "And neither will Catherine."

Juliette watched him stride angrily from the room. "Good. Now we can get on with it." She took a deep breath. "Don't you see, Jean Marc? What could be better? A civil marriage. Robert told me that the new assembly—no, they call it the convention now—that the convention has passed a law that makes it very easy to marry and divorce. One merely has to appear before the civil authorities and sign certain contracts. Is that not true?"

"So I've heard." Jean Marc continued to stare at François.

"And, married to François, Catherine would be under the protection of a member of the revolutionary government. Wouldn't it be reasonable for him to send her away from Paris if her health was not as good as it should be?"

"Wait," François said sharply. "You wish me to wed Mademoiselle Vasaro?"

"Of course! Have you not listened to what I've been saying?" She turned back to Jean Marc. "Catherine probably wouldn't regard the contract as making a marriage since a priest wouldn't preside. It would be only a matter of pretense to her."

François said with measured precision, "Since I seem to be central to your plan, perhaps you should include me in your discussion."

Juliette leaned back in her chair again. "He's right. Make him an offer, Jean Marc."

Jean Marc lifted his goblet to his lips. "I think Juliette may be correct. You may be the answer. How much does Danton pay you, Etchelet?"

"Enough for my needs. What does that—"

"Six hundred thousand livres," Jean Marc said quietly. "A dowry large enough to make you a moderately rich man and the marriage need last only long enough to spread a cloak of safety over Catherine and Vasaro. The marriage contract will read that you're entitled to keep the entire dowry in case of a divorce. It's a very generous offer."

An expression of surprise crossed Etchelet's face before he could school his features. "An amazing offer."

Juliette nodded. "And it will remove Catherine from Paris, where her presence is a threat to both you and Danton. Your wife wouldn't be stopped at the gates and questioned closely, would she? Can't you see it's the perfect solution?"

"It could work if the way were carefully prepared." François's tone was impassive. "And you could accompany her from the city as her maidservant."

"What? Oh, yes, I could." Juliette rushed on, "Then you'll do it?"

"I didn't say that." François looked at Jean Marc. "A rather expensive solution when waiting a short time might accomplish the same goal. Why?"

"It's become necessary."

"Why?" François repeated.

"Catherine . . ." Jean Marc frowned slightly before continuing. "Catherine is very likely with child."

François remained expressionless. "I thought as much. So she must have a husband. Why not your nephew? He seems to be willing. I can't believe you'd choose me over a member of your own family."

"I admit Philippe was my first thought. You heard Juliette. Catherine won't have him."

"Why not?" François asked Juliette.

"Catherine has a *tendre* for him. She wishes to save him from the stigma of wedding a woman of shame. However, you're nothing to her and will do very well." She shrugged. "We'll tell her Jean Marc 'bought' you."

"Like a jeweled fan or a feathered bonnet?" François asked ironically. "I don't believe I'm overfond of your choice of words, Mademoiselle de Clement."

"This is no time for quibbling over words. Jean Marc *is* buying you and the price is generous. Will you do it?"

François was silent.

"Give him more money, Jean Marc."

"You're very eager to spend my livres. I don't believe it's greed that's causing Monsieur Etchelet to hesitate, Juliette." Jean Marc sipped his wine. "Let the man think about it."

"But we *need* him. You know that Catherine needs him."

François glanced down at the wine in his glass. "I haven't seen Mademoiselle Vasaro for some time. Is she no better?"

"No, she grows more withdrawn every day and she . . ." Juliette faltered and then tried to steady her voice. "She doesn't even know she's with child. If she did, I'm not sure . . ." She took a deep breath. "You saw her. She cannot bear any more pain. She must be protected. *You* must protect her." She turned to Jean Marc. "Give him more money."

Jean Marc shrugged. "Eight hundred thousand livres."

François remained silent, his brow furrowed in thought.

"Why are you hesitating?" Juliette asked. "You'll be rich and your Danton will be safe."

François didn't answer for an instant, and Juliette once more opened her lips to speak.

François held up his hand. "Enough."

"You'll wed her?"

François smiled mockingly. "How can I resist? As Monsieur Andreas knows, every man wishes to be rich."

Juliette breathed a sigh of relief. "It's settled, then."

"If you can persuade Mademoiselle Vasaro to accept me," François said gravely.

"Catherine. Her name is Catherine. You're more formal than that pompous Comtesse de Noailles. Everyone at Versailles called her Madame Etiquette."

"I've been taught well to give proper respect to my betters."

"You think you have no betters," Juliette scoffed. She stood up. "I'll go talk to Catherine."

"I wish to see her myself," François said.

"Tomorrow. Call on her tomorrow. Give her time to become accustomed to the idea."

A silence fell after she had left the room. "I don't begrudge Catherine the dowry, Monsieur Etchelet," Jean Marc said softly, "but I'll expect good value for my money. I detest being cheated."

"You think I'll cheat you?"

Jean Marc gazed at him thoughtfully. "I believe you're more than you appear to be."

"Are we not all more than we appear to be . . . Jean Marc."

Jean Marc noted both the familiarity and the mockery of François's tone and nodded slowly. "I think you should be made aware that I am very fond of Catherine. I should be most unhappy if Juliette's solution proved an unhappy one for my cousin."

"You shall get what you paid for." François met his gaze. "But I will be no puppet for you. I go my own path."

"Somehow I didn't think you'd display a predilection for strings."

François rose to his feet and bowed. "Then, since our understanding is complete, I believe it's time I bid you *au revoir* until tomorrow."

Catherine sat as usual on the marble bench in the garden. Her gaze was fixed dreamily on the border of pink rosebushes beyond the fountain when François arrived at the Place Royal. The sight of her brought back a sudden vivid memory of that afternoon when he had sat opposite her in this garden. Her gown today was not blue but a simple white muslin with a sash of sunshine yellow. A matching yellow ribbon held back her hair.

The gaze she turned on him was childlike as he walked toward her down the garden path.

He bowed formally. "Good afternoon, Catherine. Did Mademoiselle de Clem—Juliette—tell you I would call today?"

Catherine nodded, her gaze returning to the roses. "It's a lovely afternoon, isn't it? Robert says soon the frosts will come, but it's difficult to believe on a day such as this."

"Did she inform you of—" He broke off. Catherine appeared to be paying no attention to him, and he felt something twist within him. She had changed. That afternoon in the garden she had been subdued but still alive and caring. Now she appeared polite but as remote as the stars. "Catherine."

She glanced at him, her stare vague. "Philippe told me once there are fields and fields of flowers at Vasaro that are beautiful beyond belief, but I scarcely remember them. Did I mention to you that I left there when I was only four? Here the garden is very nice, but I think I should like to see—"

"Catherine, you're to wed me in two days' time." He paused. "If you wish it."

For a moment the dreaminess vanished from her expression. "I do not wish it, but Juliette and Jean Marc know what's best for me." She straightened her shoulders and turned away to point to a spot beneath the high stone wall. "Robert's going to plant white violets there next spring. He says they generally grow well, but this year the winter was harsh and killed them." She frowned. "Harshness does kill, doesn't it?"

"No!" François found his fists were clenched and forced himself to relax them. "Not if you fight it. Then it only makes you grow stronger."

"The violets died."

"People aren't flowers."

"But weren't we talking about violets?" Catherine asked, puzzled. "Yes, I'm sure we were speaking of violets. I said Robert was planning—"

"I don't wish to talk of flowers," François interrupted. "I want to know if you—" He started again. "Will you trust me to do what's best for you?"

"Juliette trusts you, so I suppose I must."

"No, not Juliette. You." He took her chin in his fingers and turned her face up so that she was forced to look into his eyes. "*You* must trust me." He could sense her withdrawal at his touch like a cold wind blowing through the autumn-shrouded garden.

"I wish you would leave me now. You . . . disturb me."

"But you'll trust me?"

"You and Juliette. Why do you keep pushing at me? Why won't you realize I wish only to be left alone? I don't—" She drew away from his hand. "Oh, very well, I'll trust you. Now will you go away?"

"And you'll do as I say?"

She nodded jerkily, not looking at him.

François drew a deep breath and took a step back. "Then I'll bid you good day, Catherine."

"Good day."

François turned on his heel and strode toward the door leading to the house. Before he reached it, Catherine's gaze was once again fixed dreamily on the last roses of autumn.

Two mornings later at the Hôtel de Ville François Etchelet posted an announcement of his intention to marry Catherine Vasaro late that same afternoon. At shortly after four, as agreed, he and Danton met Jean Marc and Catherine outside the hall.

"It won't take long." François didn't give Catherine more than a passing glance as he took her elbow and threw open the door of the municipal chamber. Shrill laughter, chatter, the scent of perfume, and unwashed humanity assaulted them as they entered the crowded room. "I deliberately chose a time when the officials would be busy. The municipal authorities don't like to waste time, so there will be at least forty marriages conducted at one ceremony this afternoon. The official makes a short speech and then asks us all whether we wish to marry. We answer yes and it's over."

"Interesting. Impersonal but interesting. A veritable Greek chorus of 'yeses' portending marital bliss." Jean Marc's lips twitched as his gaze fell on a grim-faced, rifle-bearing soldier of the National Guard standing beside an ornate statue of Hymen bearing flowers and a torch. "And they seem prepared for any eventuality."

Danton gestured at a long table occupied by several gentlemen busily engaged in perusing and signing documents beneath the upraised pedestal where the municipal official presided. "The contracts, gentlemen. I had them drawn up myself to make sure they'd be in order."

Jean Marc nodded. "And who would dare question the legality of a document drawn up by the Minister of Justice?"

Danton smiled. "I was sure you'd understand. Shall we get the formalities over with so that we can enjoy seeing these two beautiful children united?"

It took longer for Jean Marc to read and sign the contracts than it did for Catherine and François to be joined in marriage.

Jean Marc kept a careful eye on Catherine during the brief ceremony, but she appeared calm and composed and did not look out of place with the other brides in the crowded hall. Juliette had dressed her in a simple dark blue gown, pulled her hair back in a smooth knot and then tucked it beneath a straw bonnet with a wide brim that shadowed her face.

What was she thinking? Jean Marc wondered. She had been silent from the moment Juliette had brought her downstairs and given her into his keeping. It was difficult to know what she was feeling at any time these days. Juliette was right. Catherine would let no one break through that protective shell to the girl they had once known.

The marriage ceremony was ending and Catherine

gave the required assent in a low tone that held no expression.

The hall exploded into immediate confusion as the couples dispersed and new brides and grooms were ushered into the room.

Danton laughed his big, booming laugh, slapped the municipal official on the shoulder, and made a few ribald remarks before whisking their party from the chamber and out onto the street. His demeanor immediately sobered as they reached the Place de la Grève. "It went well, I think."

Jean Marc nodded. "If the authorities remember anyone in that melee, it will be you and not Catherine."

The driver of the carriage Jean Marc had hired hurried to open the door as he saw them approaching.

Jean Marc glanced sardonically at Danton. "I'm surprised you chose to come, Danton. After all, there was a certain risk."

"Everyone knows François is in my employ, and it would have been regarded as unusual for me to ignore the ceremony," Danton said. "If it was to be done, it had to be done right."

Jean Marc took Catherine's elbow to help her into the coach. "I agree. Let's hope Catherine and Juliette's departure from Paris tomorrow goes as well. Have you—" He stopped as François deliberately stepped before him in the street. His gaze narrowed on François's face. "You're blocking our way, Etchelet."

François motioned to the driver of the carriage to mount to the driver's seat. "That was my intention." He took Catherine's hand and pulled her away from Jean Marc. "Catherine won't be returning to your house tonight."

"Indeed? And where will she be spending the night?"

"I'm taking her to an inn next door to the café owned by Georges Jacques's father-in-law."

Jean Marc stiffened. "You made no mention of this before."

François glanced at the driver to make sure he was out of hearing range. "We've made arrangements for

Dupree's men who'll be guarding the barrier tomorrow evening to be brought to the common room of the inn tonight. I want them to see Catherine with me."

"Is that necessary?"

"Everyone must be made to believe the marriage is a real one." François's face was expressionless. "And a bridegroom doesn't spend his wedding night alone."

"You could come to my house."

"No." François turned away and propelled Catherine toward Danton's carriage a few yards behind Jean Marc's. "It will be better my way. I'll return Catherine to you in the morning."

"As long as your way is best for Catherine." Menace layered the softness of Jean Marc's tone.

François glanced back at Jean Marc and smiled mockingly as he lifted Catherine into Danton's carriage. "Doesn't a husband always know what's best for his wife?"

"We shall see." Jean Marc watched him climb into the coach, his brow furrowed in thought. François's move had disconcerted him and he didn't like to be caught off guard. Yet there was logic in Etchelet's plan, and there was no doubt the women's departure from Paris would be made safer if the groundwork was carefully prepared with the guards at the barriers.

Danton paused before joining François and Catherine in the carriage to gaze at Jean Marc in amusement. "You appear disturbed, Citizen. Were you not aware of the character of my friend François? He delights in doing the unexpected. At times it's a great trial to me." He climbed into the carriage and the coachman slammed the door shut.

In another moment Danton's carriage was rumbling over the cobblestones.

Jean Marc stood looking after it, still frowning ruefully. He had an idea this particular action of Etchelet's was going to prove a trial to him as well.

Because it was Jean Marc who was going to have to tell Juliette that Catherine was not to spend her wedding night safely under the Andreas roof.

"Go after her," Juliette ordered, glaring at Jean Marc. "I can't believe you'd be so stupid as to let him—" She stopped and drew a deep breath. "I promised her she'd be safe from harm."

"I believe she is safe from harm."

"If you won't go after her, I'll do it myself."

"I think not," Jean Marc said quietly. "Not unless you want to endanger both Catherine and yourself by your foolishness."

"She'll be frightened. What if he—"

"Demands a bridegroom's rights?" Jean Marc finished. "I don't think he will. It would be the act of a barbarian to enjoy taking a woman who is no more alive than a statue."

"Perhaps he *is* a barbarian. You don't know what he is. He's a stranger to you."

"That sounds familiar. May I remind you that Etchelet was your choice?"

"Because I thought we could control him."

"Etchelet's obviously not a man who can be controlled."

"Then why are you just standing there? Go get Catherine and bring her back."

"They're wed. I have no rights and Etchelet does."

"Rights? What if he rapes her?"

Jean Marc said calmly, "Then I'll kill him. Very slowly."

"What good will that do Catherine? You must—"

"Juliette. Catherine stays with Etchelet tonight because I am sure it's best for both of you. If that wasn't my belief, I wouldn't have let Etchelet take her. The discussion is closed."

"It's not closed." Juliette whirled toward the door. "I'll get Philippe to—"

"No." Jean Marc's hand closed on her arm. "Believe me, this is one of those rare times when you are *not* right. Give it up."

She tried to pull away. "I can't give it up. I made

her a promise. If something happens to her, I will have failed her. She needs me. I can't—"

"Shh, it's all right." To his surprise, he found she was trembling with emotion. He could feel the tension, the flutter of her pulse on the wrist beneath his thumb, the feverish warmth of her skin. "Etchelet is a risk that had to be taken."

"Risk? You don't know what you're talking about. You weren't *there*. You don't know what they . . . " She broke away from him and turned and ran toward the stairway.

"Juliette!"

She glanced back over her shoulder. "If he hurts her, I won't forgive you." Her eyes were blazing in her white face. "I'll never forgive you for making me guilty again. Do you hear me? I'll never forgive you for the rest of my life."

She dashed up the stairs and a moment later he heard the door of her chamber slam.

Jean Marc frowned thoughtfully as he looked up the stairs. Guilty *again*?

TEN

"I didn't like those men," Catherine said suddenly. Those were the first words she had uttered since the maidservant at the inn had brought their supper and left their chamber.

François sipped his wine. "Who?"

"Those men downstairs in the common room. They reminded me of— I didn't like them."

"I didn't expect you to like them." He met her gaze. "Did they frighten you?"

The intonation in the question was merely polite. He didn't care if they had frightened her, she thought with resentment. He had deliberately lingered with those horrible men, encouraging their crude jests about brides in general and Catherine in particular until they had progressed from ribald to obscene. At first she'd only been vaguely aware of them in the same way she'd been aware of the other events of the day. Then, as François had not rushed to protect her from the abuse, she had gradually begun to catch a remark here and there and felt a tiny stirring of indignation and resentment. She repeated, "I didn't like them."

"You won't have to see them again."

"Thank you." She looked at her food.

"You've not eaten more than a few bites. Eat your beef. The sauce is quite good. Georges Jacques arranged to have the meal sent over from the Café Charpentier next door. One of the reasons he began to frequent the café was the food." A sudden smile lit his face. "The other reason was the proprietor's daughter who cooked it. Now he has both."

She didn't pick up her fork. "I don't wish to stay here any longer. May we go now?"

François studied her over the rim of his goblet. "No."

Her long lashes rose. "I'm not comfortable here. I want to see Juliette."

"You'll see her tomorrow." François set his goblet down. "Did you understand what I told Jean Marc?"

She shook her head.

"I didn't think so. You've been walking around in a daze all day." François's hand tightened on the stem of his goblet. "If you didn't understand, then why the hell did you come with me?"

"Jean Marc and Juliette said you wouldn't hurt me."

"And how do Jean Marc and Juliette know what I will or will not do?"

Her eyes widened. "Are you going to hurt me?"

"No." He lifted his goblet to his lips, drained it, and then set it down on the table with a crash. "For God's sake, stop looking at me like that. I mean you no harm."

"Then why do you keep shouting at me?"

"Because you drive me to—" He swallowed, seemed to be searching for words, and then said wearily, "I promise I won't hurt you. You said you'd trust me."

"But I don't *know* you."

"You know the man I am tonight."

"I don't understand."

"You know the angry Basque, the man who hates aristos and spies for Danton. You know that man, Catherine."

"You're confusing me."

"I mean that we're all many people." François gazed at her intently as if willing her to understand. "I can't help you if you won't trust me." François looked down into his empty goblet. "When the servant comes back to clear the dishes, she must see us in that bed together." He heard the soft intake of her breath, but he didn't look up. "She'll giggle and then go back downstairs and tell the others. There will be more jests and winks." He paused. "And tomorrow at the barrier those men you found so offensive will remember François Etchelet's pretty little wife and comment on how weary she looks after her romp between the sheets." He stared into her eyes. She was clearly alarmed. "And then they'll open the barrier and let you go home to your Vasaro. That's what you wish, isn't it?"

"Yes," she whispered.

He pushed back his chair and stood up. "Then let's set about it." He held out his hand. "Come. It won't be so terrible."

She gazed at his hand as if it were a striking serpent and then slowly placed her hand in his grasp.

"You see, it didn't hurt." François pulled her to her feet. "Now, can you undress yourself or must I help?"

"I can do it."

"Good." He gave her a push toward the bed and then sat back down and poured himself more wine. "Call me when you're in bed."

He was speaking to her as if she were a small child. Why was he pretending to be gentle when he was not a gentle man? "I don't believe it's necessary to do this."

"I do. If you won't obey me for your own sake, then do it for your friend Juliette. She'll also be in that coach, and her risk is greater than yours if she's captured." He kept his gaze straight ahead. "Everything."

"What?"

"Take off everything."

"I don't think—"

"Undress!"

The command was so sharp she worked more quickly to unfasten her gown. She could hear the panicky sound of her own breathing in the quiet room. Why was she doing this? She should never have come here. She wanted to run away back to the house on the Place Royale. Juliette would help her. Juliette would never let this rude, violent man order her about.

Juliette. Juliette had killed a man for Catherine's sake and must be kept safe. Was François right that this act would help keep Juliette from being questioned at the barrier? She suddenly realized she was entirely naked and hurried across the room toward the bed, dove beneath the covers, and pulled up the sheet.

François continued to look straight ahead, slowly sipping his wine.

Minutes passed, the silence unbroken.

Catherine was suddenly irritated. "Well, it's done."

He stood up and her annoyance was submerged in panic.

"It's all right, Catherine. I'm not going to hurt you." His tone was no longer sharp but soothing again. "Are you entirely undressed?" He slowly turned to face her.

She sat rigidly upright in bed, holding the sheet to her chin, her gaze fixed suspiciously on him.

He looked at the smooth flesh of her shoulders bared by the sheet. "I see you are."

He walked slowly toward her.

She tensed and backed against the oaken headboard.

He sat down on the bed beside her. "I'm not going to hurry you. We have time."

She looked at him wordlessly.

"Are you cold? Should I build a fire?"

She shook her head.

"Would you like some wine?"

"No."

He had to bend closer to hear her and she froze. *"Sacre bleu!"* The curse exploded from him as he jumped to his feet. "Will you stop shaking? I told you there was nothing to fear. Do you think this is easy for me? Mother of God, I—"

"Stop cursing!" His violence suddenly ignited an answering response. She glared at him. "I won't stand for it. First you let those horrid men say filthy things to me, then you order me about, and now you curse in my presence as no gentleman would."

He was staring at her in astonishment.

She gestured to the bed. "And this may be necessary but it's not at all easy for me either."

"Well, it's certainly not my fault. I've behaved every bit as gently as that fine buck Philippe. I can't remember ever using such soft words to any woman."

"That's quite clear. You do it very badly."

The anger abruptly faded from his expression as his gaze narrowed on her face. "You prefer me to be rude?"

"It seems more natural. You make me uneasy when you pretend to be something you're not."

"Do I?"

"Has no one ever accused you of being rude before? Why are you staring at me like that?"

"I believe I've just made a discovery." He gave her a curious smile. "And yes, it's no secret among my acquaintance that I'm neither sweet-mannered nor a gentleman. Now, since you're no longer quivering and quaking, may I get you a glass of wine?"

"I don't rest well if I drink wine before I go to sleep."

"You don't look as if you rest well anyway." He paused. "Do you still dream?"

"Yes." Her gaze slid away from his and she changed the subject. "That's why Juliette sometimes brushes my hair at night before I go to sleep. It . . . relaxes me."

"Are you suggesting I take over her duty?"

She looked back at him, startled. "No."

"I think you are." His smile widened with amusement. "I think you're angry with me for ordering you about and wish to humble me."

Was he right? Catherine had not thought she was

capable of wishing to see anyone humbled, but there was no doubt François's arrogance had annoyed her exceedingly. "I was merely making a remark."

He bowed mockingly. "Like any patriotic republican I'm not ashamed to discharge lowly tasks." He strolled toward the highboy across the room. "Tonight we'll pretend I'm Juliette." He picked up the horsehair brush on the highboy and turned to face her. "I'll even promise not to tongue-lash you as she might."

She gazed at him uncertainly as she watched him come toward the bed. Her hand tightened on the sheet. "Juliette doesn't tongue-lash me."

"Then she makes you the sole exception." He began to take out the pins binding her hair in its tight bun. "Why are you trembling? I'm only going to brush your hair."

She closed her eyes tightly as the loosened hair tumbled down her back.

"I have no desire to touch you." The brush began to move through her hair in long, deep strokes. For many minutes the only sound in the room was the sibilant whisper of the bristles in the thickness of her hair.

"I like that," she whispered. "Thank you."

"You're very welcome."

"What did you mean when you said we're all many people?"

"What I said." He brushed the hair back from her temple. "Look at yourself. You're Juliette's friend and Jean Marc's meek little cousin. They each see you differently."

"And how do people see you?"

"They see what they want to see." He reached up and shifted the heavy swath of her hair over her right shoulder, his warm fingertips brushing her nape and igniting a faint tingling sensation that made her shiver. Then the light touch was gone and the bristles of the brush were once again moving through her hair.

"How do you see me?" she asked impulsively.

He hesitated in mid-stroke. "I see you in a garden."

"Because you wish to see me there?"

"Perhaps. There haven't been many gardens in my life."

"But you said you wouldn't choose to live in—"

"I'm not always logical."

"Juliette says you're clever and kinder than you pretend."

"And do you always trust Juliette's judgments?"

"I have been lately. It's . . . easier."

"I can see how it would be. If you want to remain a child forever."

"I'm not a child."

"Because you were raped?"

She stiffened. "It's not kind of you to mention—"

"If you find me lacking in kindness, then could it be that Juliette's judgment isn't infallible?"

She frowned as she glanced at him over her shoulder. "Why are you arguing with me?"

"Because evidently no one else does. They just pity the poor, wounded Mademoiselle. Do you wish me to pity you too?"

The corners of her lips suddenly turned up with rueful humor. "No, but if I did, it would do me no good. You obviously will do as you please."

"Ah, now we understand each other. No pity."

Catherine abruptly felt lighter, as if some tremendous burden had been lifted. "No pity."

He put the brush on the nightstand. "There, I've done my penance for offending you. Tell me, for what sin is Juliette paying penance?"

She frowned in bewilderment. "Sin?"

"It doesn't seem unnatural to you that she cossets you as if you were a small child?"

"I don't demand she do anything. She says—"

"It's time." He stripped off his coat. "The servant woman will be back to clear away soon. Lie down and turn your back to me."

She gazed at him in confusion.

He was stripping off his shirt. "Mother of God, can't you see I'm trying to spare your delicacy of feelings? Do you want to see me naked?"

"You're cursing again." She hurriedly scooted down

and turned her back to him. She could hear his movements behind her. He was undressing. Soon he'd slip naked beside her in this bed. She supposed she should be frightened, but she was too bewildered to know what she was feeling.

"Move over." He was standing beside the bed.

She hurriedly rolled to the far side of the bed. A cool draft chilled her as the covers were lifted and he slipped beneath them. She could feel the waves of heat his body emitted though he was not touching her. Sweet heaven, she *was* frightened. She began to tremble again.

"Stop that." His tone was rough, yet, in an odd way, comforting. "It will be over soon."

"Yes."

"I don't want you. It's only pretense. Skinny women don't please me. Men don't want every woman they see, you know."

"The Marseilles at the abbey were—"

"That was different. That was a sickness, a fever."

"Henriette was only ten years old."

"Not all men are the same. Some men are aroused by only one kind of woman. Some men, like Robespierre, are totally abstinent. There are other men who don't like women at all but prefer men."

She was startled. "Really? Do you prefer—"

"No, I'm not a sodomite."

"Oh," she hesitated. "Then you . . ." She stopped, shivering in distaste. "You like to hurt women."

"It doesn't have to hurt. If a woman pleases me, I can make her enjoy what happens between us."

She was silent.

"It's true. I tell you, there's no—" A soft knock halted the soft vehemence of his voice.

"Quick!" He was over her, flesh pressed to flesh before she knew what was happening. "Come in."

The door opened to admit the same stout servant woman who had served their meal. She stopped and murmured something before rapidly clearing the table.

"Hurry." François's voice was thick with impatience.

The servant woman giggled and her motions deliberately slowed.

A wild cascade of sensations and thoughts tumbled through Catherine as the warm, hard musculature of François's chest pressed against her softness.

The tomb! She opened her lips to scream.

His gaze bore down as he whispered, "No!"

Her lips closed as she gazed helplessly up at him. Slowly the terror began to ebb away. It was the same, yet totally different, she realized. This body was warm, sleek, nude, not dressed in rough clothes that scratched her flesh. This body was hard and masculine, yet carefully withheld to save her both unnecessary contact and weight. This was no anonymous stranger above her. This was François, his face square, bold, its fierceness clearly defined in the candlelight. It was odd how that very fierceness offered her the comfort of blessed familiarity.

"Blow out the candles and begone," François ordered over his shoulder.

Another giggle and the room was suddenly plunged into darkness. The door closed.

François settled as far from her as possible on the bed. "There, it's over. I told you it wouldn't be so bad."

He had left her so quickly, it was clear he found the physical intimacy as distasteful as she had, Catherine thought. Her nipples still tingled from the warm texture of his skin against hers, the slight abrasion of the tight curly hair that thatched his chest. Yet she discovered to her surprise that the feeling wasn't totally unpleasant. The entire experience had not been the horror she had thought and, as he said, it was now over. She breathed in a sigh of relief. "Do we go to sleep now?"

"If we can."

She was beginning to think she would have no trouble sleeping that night. The ordeal was over, and every muscle in her body felt heavy, sluggish. "Do you stay here with me?"

"There's only one bed."

She closed her eyes. "Yes, of course."

There was a long silence in the room before she spoke again. "May I ask a question?"'

"Yes."

"Why are you always so angry with me?"

He didn't answer for such a long time she was beginning to think he was ignoring the question.

"Because I bleed inside when I look at you."

"What?"

"Go to sleep."

Another silence fell between them.

"I'm sorry I was so foolish. I didn't understand."

"Understand?"

"That you didn't want to hurt me." She turned on her side to face the wall. "I thought all men desired women only because they were women. I'm glad you explained. I feel more at ease with you now."

"Do you?"

"Yes," she whispered drowsily. "I'm glad I don't please you and you don't want me."

"No, I don't want you."

As she drifted off to sleep she heard him repeat the words. Strange, on his lips they sounded like one of the holy litanies the nuns had taught her.

"You don't please me.

"And I don't want you."

Juliette met them at the door when François and Catherine arrived at the Place Royale the next morning.

"Is all well with you?" Juliette's gaze anxiously searched Catherine's face. She felt a surge of relief. Catherine showed no sign of ill treatment. In truth, her expression was surprisingly alert. "He did you no harm?"

"Other than stinging my ears with his foul language, he did me no harm," Catherine said. "He has a more unruly tongue than even you, Juliette."

"I've had a few more years to practice." François smiled faintly. "And I didn't spend my childhood in a nunnery."

Catherine frowned. "Still, you should not—"

"Well, it's done." Juliette pulled Catherine into the foyer, untied her bonnet, and took it off. "You're home safe and I'll take care of you. Are you tired?"

Catherine looked at her uncertainly. "I don't think so. I slept very well."

"Good. But perhaps you should rest anyway. Jean Marc and Philippe are at Monsieur Bardot's place of business arranging for funds for your stay at Vasaro. When they return we'll have dinner and then be on our way. Run along to your room and I'll be up in a moment."

The vivaciousness faded from Catherine's expression. "If you think it best." She turned obediently toward the stairs.

"Wait. Don't do it," François said softly. "Tell her no, Catherine."

Juliette frowned. "Why should she? You know she's not been well. She should rest before the trip. Look at her, she's fading more by the minute."

"Perhaps I am a little tired." Catherine ignored François's frown as she started heavily up the stairs. "I'd like to go to the garden before we leave for Vasaro. Do I have time, Juliette?"

"After your rest." Juliette turned to François. "I'd like to speak to you."

"I thought you would." His gaze was following Catherine as she slowly climbed the steps. "I believe I'd like to talk to you as well. Come along."

He turned and strode into the salon.

Juliette hesitated in surprise at his assumption of command before hurrying after him. "You shouldn't have taken her away last night. You had no right. You could have frightened her."

"I did frighten her."

Juliette stiffened. "What did you do to her?"

"Oh, I didn't force myself upon her, if that's what you suspect." François met Juliette's gaze. "But I frightened her, and made her angry, and made her face unpleasantness." He paused. "Just as you've been facing it since you left the abbey."

"I'm able to face it. Catherine's not strong enough to deal with it yet."

"She's stronger than you think. Last night she came alive. If she's as fragile as you seem to think, she should have wept or swooned and she did neither. And I think

I discovered why she's been getting worse instead of better." He paused. "It's you."

"Me!"

"You've been smothering her."

Juliette gazed at him incredulously. "That's not true. You know nothing about her. She needs me."

"Does she?" François said softly. "Or do you need her?"

Juliette's hands clenched into fists. "You're wrong. She can't do without my help. She's with child."

"She did without you last night." François studied Juliette with cool objectivity. "I don't doubt you care for her, but no one is worse for her at the moment than you. She needs to stop leaning and stand by herself, and I don't believe you're capable of letting her do that."

"You lie! I'm capable of doing anything that will help her."

He slowly shook his head. "You'll smother her with attention and soon she won't be able to live without it. You're beginning to destroy her. You care too much for her to force her to stand alone."

"And you wouldn't care if she did fall when she found she hadn't the strength to stand alone."

He shrugged, his expression bland. "Why should I care? We both know I married her for the dowry. Once you leave this afternoon, I'll be done with all of you. I offer you the benefit of my experience only as a disinterested observer."

"As a spy." Juliette's voice was shaking. "Philippe said you were Danton's spy."

"True."

"And an assassin."

"I've killed men."

"Yet you presume to tell me I'm—"

"You might ask yourself why you're so upset that you're hurling names at me." François turned toward the door. "If you really care for Catherine's welfare, you'll find a way of leaving her to fend for herself once you've arrived at Vasaro."

He walked out of the salon and a moment later she heard the door close behind him.

It wasn't true. Catherine *did* need her.

Yet Catherine had looked surprisingly well when she arrived that morning. Not withdrawn and without spirit as she had been when she left the house the previous afternoon. It had been only when Juliette had begun to take charge and make suggestions that Catherine's lethargy had returned.

Juliette could feel the tears burn her eyes and she blinked them away angrily. There could be other explanations. François didn't have to be correct. She didn't have to give up Catherine just because what he said had a few grains of truth.

You smother her.

You're beginning to destroy her.

No one is worse for Catherine than you.

Or is it you who need her?

She had thought she was doing what was best for Catherine. Now she wasn't sure of anything. François's words had struck a chord that vibrated with the ring of truth.

She walked slowly from the salon and up the stairs.

Catherine lay on the bed staring at the ceiling, her gaze blank and dreamy. She was in the state Juliette had become accustomed to seeing her in the last few weeks. Now, after glimpsing the vivaciousness of her expression when she'd arrived so few minutes before with François, it came as a fresh shock.

Juliette smiled with an effort and came to sit on the bed beside her. "François said you were frightened last night."

"Yes, there were some men at the inn who reminded me of—" Catherine stopped. "I wanted to run back here, but François wouldn't let me. I knew you wouldn't allow anyone to hurt me."

"And I make you feel safe?"

"Oh, yes, always. I never have to worry about anything when you're with me. You keep everything away from me."

You won't let her stand alone.

Juliette felt her hopes plummet as she reached out

and took Catherine's hand. "Tell me what happened last night."

Catherine didn't look at her. "I'd rather not talk. May I go down to the garden now?"

Catherine would go down to the garden and sit in dreamy silence. She would go to Vasaro and the silence would journey with her. Why? Because Juliette would be there to keep anything that might break the silence away from Catherine.

"Yes, you may go to the garden," Juliette said numbly.

Mother of God, she hadn't wanted Etchelet to be right.

Jean Marc helped Catherine into the carriage and looked beyond her at Philippe on the opposite seat. "Send a messenger as soon as you arrive safely at Vasaro. I wish to know at once."

Philippe nodded. "I'll take care of them, Jean Marc."

"You're damned right you will. Where's Juliette?"

"She went back inside to fetch the shawl Catherine left in the garden."

"Etchelet's meeting you shortly before you reach the barriers to make sure you get through without difficulty. You have the papers?"

"I'm not a fool, Jean Marc."

Jean Marc didn't answer as he turned and started to climb the steps. He met Juliette coming out of the front door as he reached the top step. She wore a dark green traveling gown and matching bonnet, and a blue silk shawl was draped over her left arm. "You have it? Good, get in the carriage."

"Why aren't you going with her, Jean Marc?" Juliette's voice was low, her face shadowed by the brim of her bonnet. "You should be the one to go with her. After all, she's your responsibility."

"I believe you've pointed that out before," Jean Marc said dryly. "I can't leave Paris now. The National Convention's in the middle of a debate about whether to confiscate more ships for the navy. If I'm not here to stop it, they'll strip my shipyards even of the ships under construction."

"Business again?"

"Philippe will send for me if there's a problem. Once you're beyond the barriers, you'll be safe. Vasaro is a world of its own."

"I'm not worried about being safe." She started down the steps, her head bent, her gaze on the carriage. "I just think you should—"

"Look at me." Jean Marc's hand grasped her arm. "I want to see your face. You're being entirely too subdued."

She lifted her head and he saw tears swimming in her eyes. "She needs you, Jean Marc."

He shook his head. "She has you and I'll come to Vasaro in a few months' time. It's best, *ma petite*. I can't go on this way much longer. You're still wounded and I'm not accustomed to walking the virtuous path."

"I don't know what you mean."

He smiled crookedly. "I know you don't. But, if I went with you to Vasaro, you'd find out inside a few days. I might even decide to borrow Philippe's Cottage of Flowers."

She avoided his gaze. "I'm not wounded."

"Is that an invitation?"

The blood scorched her cheeks as she started down the steps again. "All this has nothing to do with Catherine. You speak in riddles."

"But a riddle you could easily decipher if you cared to make the effort. You've known the answer all along, but you chose to ignore it." He followed her and stopped beside her as she reached the carriage. "And I chose to let you ignore it. By permitting you to leave Paris without me, I'm letting you ignore it again." He lifted Juliette into the carriage onto the seat next to Catherine. "I've no doubt you'll manage quite well without me at Vasaro." He smiled faintly. "*Au revoir,* Juliette."

"*Au revoir.*" Juliette's gaze clung to his with desperation. "I didn't mean I couldn't manage without you. I only meant it was your responsibility and not mine to care for Catherine. I think you should—"

"*Au revoir,* Juliette," Jean Marc repeated as he slammed the carriage door and motioned to the driver.

Juliette stuck her head out the window and he was astonished to see the tears that had been brimming were now running down her cheeks. It was completely unlike Juliette to allow herself to display weakness. "You never listen to me. I'm trying to tell you—"

As the carriage lurched, Jean Marc stepped back to avoid its wheels. Juliette sank back in the coach; Jean Marc stood in the street looking after them.

All would be well. Etchelet would send him a message as soon as they had passed the barriers. Nothing should go wrong. Still, he had a nagging sense of anxiety and unease as he remembered Juliette's desperate expression. He suddenly wished he had gone with them.

He was being foolish. His place was not at Vasaro with Juliette, but here in Paris attending to his own business concerns.

Dark was falling when Robert came into the study where Jean Marc was working at his desk and began to light the candles. "A message has just come from Monsieur Etchelet."

Jean Marc stiffened. "Yes?"

"The carriage was permitted through the barrier."

The tension uncoiled within him. "Thank God."

Robert nodded. "Shall I tell Marie you'll have your supper now?"

Jean Marc picked up his pen. "Soon. I have some work to finish. Perhaps in an hour."

Robert stood hesitating as he reached the door. "I wondered what I should do with the painting, Monsieur?"

Jean Marc looked up. "Painting?"

"The painting Mademoiselle Juliette was doing of me. She left it on the easel in the garden. She must have forgotten it."

"Yes." Juliette cared too much about her work to treat it so carelessly—and for her to forget a painting in progress was extraordinary. She must have been even more upset than he'd supposed. "You'd better put it in her chamber."

"Yes, Monsieur." Robert closed the door.

Her chamber? Juliette had been a guest in this house for only a short time, and yet everything she touched seemed stamped with an indelible impression. Stubborn, exasperating, willful, she managed in some way to touch him as no woman ever had. The house seemed oddly silent without her vibrant, demanding presence, and he was experiencing a restlessness out of all proportion. He heard the door open.

"I'm hungry. Will you tell Marie to fix supper?"

Jean Marc froze and slowly his gaze lifted from the document on the desk in front of him.

Juliette stood in the doorway of the study, gazing at him defiantly. She had removed her dark green bonnet and was swinging it by its ribbons. As he watched, she ran nervous fingers through her tousled dark curls. "You needn't glare at me. I told you that you were the one who should go with her but you wouldn't listen to me. Now she has only Philippe and you know how she feels about him, but—"

"What the devil are you doing here?"

"I'm going to stay here."

He felt a leap of emotion he refused to identify. "Not likely."

"Well, where else am I to go?"

"Vasaro."

"I can't go to Vasaro. François said I'm smothering Catherine, and I'm not sure he's right, but I—" She stopped. "No, that's not true. He *is* right."

"Nonsense."

She shook her head, her fingers opening and closing on the ribbons of her bonnet. "I don't know how to let go. I wasn't sure I could let her go even when I knew I should. Do you think it was easy for me to do this? I've never had anyone but Catherine and I didn't want to believe him."

"I can see I'm going to have to have a discussion with Monsieur Etchelet," Jean Marc said grimly as he set his pen back in its holder. "I suppose he brought you back here from the barrier?"

She shook her head. "François doesn't know I didn't go with them. I had the carriage stop on the street before we reached the barrier. I got out and watched until they let Catherine through, then I started back. François was talking to the guards and never looked into the coach."

"And just how did you make your way here?"

"I walked. I believed you would be angry, so I thought it best if the carriage were well on its way before you knew I wasn't on it. You are angry, aren't you?"

"Exceedingly."

"Then I was right to—"

"You were not right," he interrupted icily. "You were thoughtless and stupid and reckless. Why the hell have we been keeping you off the streets of Paris? What if you'd been recognized or—"

"I was careful. I wore my bonnet and kept my head down." She frowned. "And I didn't even ask directions when I became lost."

"*Merde,* it's a wonder you weren't captured and thrown into prison. Do you have any idea how we're going to get you out of Paris now that you've seen fit to destroy our plans?"

"I'm not going to leave Paris. At least, not right away. Do you think I'd upset Catherine and walk halfway across the city to turn around and meekly follow them to Vasaro?"

"And just what is your intention?"

She gazed at him warily. "I think we'd better discuss this after supper."

"Now."

"I'm hungry," she said. "And I'm tired and my feet hurt. I'm going to wash and eat and then we'll talk." She whirled on her heel. "Tell Marie to fix supper."

"Juliette."

She glanced over her shoulder.

His tone was soft but edged with steel. "I'll wait to

talk to you, but this is the last time you'll ever give me orders in this house."

Pink rose to color her cheeks. She started to speak, but thought better of it. Her gaze clung to his and suddenly he was startled to see the bravado fade into desperation. She looked hurriedly away and gave a careless shrug. "I doubt it."

ELEVEN

"May we talk now?" Jean Marc's tone was impeccably polite as he placed his napkin beside his plate and leaned back in his chair.

Juliette reluctantly set down her spoon. "You didn't eat very much. Are you sure you won't have some more of Marie's lemon syllabub? It is—"

"I don't want lemon syllabub. I want to know why you're not on your way to Vasaro. Three days ago you were in a frenzy of worry about Catherine and today you abandon her."

"I didn't abandon her," Juliette said, stung. "I told you why I didn't go with her. She'll be better off without me for a while. In a few months I'll join her at Vasaro and stay with her until the child is born."

"And what if she realizes she's with child before you decide to grace Vasaro with your presence?"

Panic speared through Juliette and she

couldn't speak for a moment. "I could be wrong. She might not be with child. We weren't absolutely sure."

Jean Marc gazed at her in disbelief.

"And if she is, then she'll just have to face it alone. She has Vasaro and Philippe. Philippe said he would send for his mother as soon as they arrived. I couldn't be expected to stay with her. She has to face what happened to her sometime, doesn't she? She's stronger than we think. You should have seen her this morning when François brought her—"

"Juliette." Jean Marc's voice cut through her feverish dialogue.

Jean Marc's face blurred and Juliette fought back the tears stinging her eyes. She whispered, "I'm so frightened, Jean Marc. What if I'm wrong? When I told her I wasn't going with her to Vasaro she looked so bewildered. I tried to explain it to her, but I know she didn't understand."

"I'm having a good deal of trouble understanding myself."

"You see, I thought she needed me."

"She does need you."

"Does she?" Juliette swallowed and shook her head. "She did at the beginning, but now I can't stop sheltering her. I'm too selfish."

"Selfish?"

"I *liked* having her need me. It made me feel so good to be important to her." She drew a deep shaky breath. "I thought about it a long time today and I realized François was probably right about me being bad for her. At first I decided I'd go to Vasaro anyway, but I knew that wouldn't do. I don't give up easily what I want. I had to cut the ties and let her go alone." She tried to smile. "And if I am wrong, Philippe will send you a message and I'll find a way to get to her at once."

"May I point out you'd been a virtual prisoner in this house for almost six weeks before we could arrange to get you safely out of Paris?"

"We wouldn't have to be nearly so careful with me as we were with Catherine."

"No?" For an instant the sarcasm was arrested on

Jean Marc's expression, and he quickly glanced away. "I suppose I'd forgotten that no care need be taken for your welfare."

She nodded briskly. "So you see my being here isn't nearly as foolhardy as you might think. I can stay here for a few months and when Dupree leaves Paris we'll have François get me papers that—"

"No."

"But why? I've explained why it's best for Catherine that I stay here."

"But you haven't explained why it would be best for me. Why should I harbor an enemy of the republic? Every minute you stay in my house, everything I own is in danger." He smiled cynically. "Including my head. Personally, I don't believe the claims the guillotine is the most humane way to die. I think it lacks a certain dignity."

Juliette hadn't considered the possibility that her presence might put Jean Marc in actual physical danger. She found the idea hard to accept. "You have too many friends in the government to be in jeopardy."

"When a house topples, everyone scurries to get out of the way, not prop it up."

"We could find a way to—"

"You've been fortunate not to have been discovered already." Jean Marc's lips tightened. "Particularly when you decide to stroll about the streets of Paris in broad daylight."

"I told you why I took that risk."

"I don't regard your reasoning as either clear or prudent." He shook his head. "Prudent? *Merde*, what am I thinking of? You don't know the meaning of the word."

Juliette frowned. "I suppose I could try to find some other place to live. Perhaps Robert would help—"

"No!" Jean Marc's hand clenched on the stem of his goblet. "You're leaving for Vasaro as soon as possible."

"Maybe you're right. I guess Robert could be connected back to you. Besides, I wouldn't want to endanger him." She met his gaze across the table. "Very well,

I'll admit I could be a danger to you. What would make the danger worth tolerating?"

He looked down at the wine in his glass. "Nothing."

"There must be something you want. You're very greedy."

"Thank you."

"Oh, I approve of greed. All the best artists were greedy. They took whatever they needed from life and from the people around them and put it into their work. It's really quite fair when you consider what they gave back. That's the most sublime form of avarice."

He looked startled. "And is my greed sublime?"

"Well, perhaps not sublime, but I've never heard talk of you cheating anyone, so surely it's a good, honest greed."

He smiled faintly. "Well, since I'm afraid you don't have anything to feed my greed, you'll just have to go—"

"The Wind Dancer!" Juliette's eyes were suddenly alight with excitement as she leaned forward in her chair. "Of course. You want the Wind Dancer!"

A flicker of surprise crossed his face. "And you don't have it."

"But perhaps I could think of a way to get it for you."

His gaze narrowed on her face. "I thought you said Marie Antoinette had the right to keep her treasure?"

"It's not doing her any good in the Temple, is it?" She was thinking quickly. "How much would you be willing to give to get the Wind Dancer back? I can't remember how much you offered the queen."

"Two million livres. Plus the loan I made to the king."

"And you didn't get any of the loan back?"

He shrugged. "I knew it was a risk."

"Two million livres." Juliette gnawed at her lower lip. "It's a great deal of money. Would you pay me two million livres for the Wind Dancer?"

Jean Marc was silent a moment. "Yes."

Her gaze flew to his face. "You *do* want it. It wasn't

only your father who wished it returned to the family.
You want it too."

Jean Marc sipped his wine.

"You must want it very badly." Juliette's gaze was
still fastened on his face. "Why?"

"I don't like being thwarted."

"No, I think it's more than that."

"If it is, then I refuse to let you probe it out of me.
A man must have a few secrets."

Jean Marc had more than his share and Juliette had
never wanted more to uncover them than at that moment. In the candlelight his black eyes shimmered
with cynical amusement and those beautifully shaped
lips smiled mockingly. Yet, beneath it all, she sensed
something . . .

He shifted his shoulders impatiently. "This conversation is useless. You're trying to sell me something you
don't possess."

"I'll want two million livres for it," Juliette said
slowly. "And I want to stay in this house under your
protection for as long as I wish. That's my price for the
Wind Dancer. Would you pay it?"

Jean Marc frowned impatiently. "You're being ridiculous. You don't have any idea who has the statue."

"Would you pay it?"

"The revolutionary government has been searching
for the Wind Dancer ever since it disappeared."

"Would you pay it?"

"Yes," he snapped.

"Then it's a bargain." Juliette smiled with relief.
"Now, all I have to worry about is how I'm going to find
it for you."

Suddenly Jean Marc began to chuckle. "*Merde*, for a
moment I was taking this nonsense seriously."

"I am serious. I see nothing to laugh about."

"It's impossible."

"I don't see why." Juliette frowned. "Though I
admit I'll have to think about it."

"I'm sure you will. And, in the meantime, you won't
mind my making plans for sending you immediately to
Vasaro?"

"But I'll need time to—"

"You have no time." Jean Marc's smile faded. "I'll not risk having you in my house a moment longer than necessary. You'll be on your way to Vasaro before the week is gone."

"Only a week?"

"Surely that's enough time. After all, you said it wasn't an impossible task." He smiled recklessly and suddenly leaned forward and offered her his wine. "Shall we toast your success?"

She jerked back away from the goblet. "I don't like wine."

He was watching her. "Not even to toast such a splendid enterprise? Just a sip?"

"No!" Juliette tried to steady her voice. "You're making mock of me."

"No." He lifted the wine to his own lips. "But I admit to curiosity. I delight in complexity and I find you the most intriguing of puzzles, Juliette."

"I'm not particularly complex. I'm not even clever with books, like Catherine." Juliette pushed back her chair and stood up. "You're the puzzle."

A smile so wickedly sensual it took her breath lit his lean face. "Then perhaps we should attempt to merge our complexities to form a felicitous whole."

She stared at him in fascination, a sudden tightness constricting her chest. She was acutely aware of the lithe power of his physique beneath his air of elegant indolence, the grace of his long, tanned fingers toying with the fragile stem of the crystal goblet. "How?"

"In the usual manner. I'm not one who demands a bizarre repertoire of—" He stopped as he noticed her expression. "What did you expect?" he asked softly. "If you didn't want to solve the puzzle, you should have gone on to Vasaro. You knew what awaited you here with me." He paused. "Didn't you?"

She *had* known, she realized. She had not wanted to acknowledge it, but he was right, she had known. "You want to . . . fornicate with me."

"Blunt, but precise." He leaned back in his chair. "To be even more precise, I wish to fornicate with you for a long, long time and in ways which you may not even be aware exist."

Her heart was pounding so hard she could scarcely breathe. "I doubt it. I'm not like Catherine. At court I heard and saw many . . ." She trailed off and swallowed hard. "Why? I'm not at all pretty."

"You think not? Then why do I find you desirable?" His voice thickened. "Why do I grow hard when I look at you?"

Her eyes widened, instinctively shifting to his lower body hidden by the damask tablecloth. "Do you?"

He smiled and pushed his chair back. "Come and see."

Her gaze quickly fell to the plate in front of her. "I think not. I have no wish to fornicate with any man."

His smile widened as he rose to his feet. "No? Let's see, shall we?" He was beside her chair in three strides, pulling her to her feet. He sat down in the chair from which he had just evicted her and pulled her down onto his lap. "If you won't look at me, *feel* me."

She stiffened with shock. Even through the multitude of layers of clothing separating them she could feel the bold arousal pressing against her womanhood. And where he touched her she tingled, burned, ached. She should be fighting him, she thought hazily. But Jean Marc wasn't the Duc de Gramont; he wouldn't take what she didn't want to give. "This is foolish."

"Infinitely." He unfastened the top of her gown and bared her throat. "And we've only just started. I wonder what you'd say to the other foolish positions I've been imagining you in of late." His head lowered and his tongue licked delicately at the pulse rioting in the hollow of her throat.

She inhaled sharply and he looked up and nodded slowly. "You like that? Let me free your breasts and I'll do other things you'll like."

She could feel the tension of his every muscle, see the pulse that was pounding in his temple as he wrapped his arms around her. "Why are you doing this?"

He looked down at her. "Because you refused to

understand," he said quietly. "This is what we are together. This is what we've been since you cared for me at the inn over five years ago." His hands cupped her hips and he pressed her down on himself. "I warned you. If you let me, I'll take until you have no more to give. It's my way."

He was pulsing, hard, alive against her, and his eyes were glittering wildly in his taut face. Juliette couldn't move, couldn't look away. She was beginning to feel a heavy, hot languor sweeping through her and her breasts were swelling, ripening.

His gaze was suddenly intent on the bodice of the gown. "Let me see your breasts. They want me, don't they? See how they're pushing against—"

"You should not speak in this way."

He chuckled. "Since your own tongue is far from discreet, I can't see how you can reprove me."

"I did not ask to see your—" She broke off, her color rising even higher. "I mean I—"

"I know exactly what you mean." His eyes were twinkling as his teeth closed on her left earlobe. "You do not have to ask. I'm at your disposal at any time."

His teeth were hard as he gnawed gently at the softness of her lobe, and she suddenly felt the warm tip of his tongue in her ear. A hot shiver rippled down her nape and through her body. "Let . . . me go."

He immediately released her and leaned lazily back in the chair. "I have no intention of taking you on this chair in the dining room. Robert and Marie might wander in and be shocked."

She jumped off his lap and whirled to face him. His dark hair was slightly tousled, and his black eyes glittered with recklessness as he stared at her. She could see the hard length of his manhood outlined against the fitted tightness of his silk trousers and had a sudden tingling memory of how he had felt against her only a moment before. He was savage need clothed in silken elegance. She realized at that moment he wouldn't care if the entire city saw him have his way with her. The knowledge brought her a queer, half-terrifying excitement. "You are not— I don't think you'd care!"

"Shall we see if you care?" he challenged softly.

She backed away from him, her gaze fastened on his face. She couldn't seem to look away from him. She had never really seen this Jean Marc before. She had always known he was there waiting for her. He had even allowed her fleeting glimpses she had chosen to ignore.

But she could ignore them no longer. This was the man to whom innumerable mistresses had whispered pleas and entreaties, the Jean Marc capable of any excess of primitive hunger and sensual indulgence. His eyes appeared to be growing darker, more glittering, dominating the room, dominating her. "No, I don't want to—" She broke off and shook her head. "This is not why I stayed in Paris."

"But it's what you'll get if you remain." He looked down at his lower body. "All of it, all the time. Would you like me to tell you all the ways I mean to have you?"

She laughed shakily. "You're just trying to frighten me into going to Vasaro."

"You know better." His gaze rose to her face. "One week. If you're not on your way to Vasaro in one week, you'll become my mistress." He shrugged. "It will happen sometime, it may as well be now. God knows, I feel as if I've waited a century already."

"You're not stupid and will probably come to your senses in time."

"I doubt it. I haven't recovered them in the last five years. You were always there in the back of my mind."

"Well, I wish you'd let me return to the back of your mind. I've no desire to be any man's mistress. I want only to paint and—"

"I will give you one week before I send you to Vasaro." He stood up and took a step toward her. "Naturally, during that time I'll feel free to indulge myself freely with your enchanting person." His fingers reached out and caressed her throat. "I must have some compensation for the danger you place me in and it will prepare you for more extensive intimacies to come."

His stroking was gentle and his touch as light as if he were fondling something precious and loved. She wanted to stay there, letting him caress her, letting him look at her with that expression of intoxicating posses-siveness.

"You look like a child lifting her face up to be kissed," he whispered.

"I'm not a child."

His smile faded. "I know and you never were. That's always been the problem. I could never keep from wanting you even while I tried to perceive you as a child in need. You always managed to tear me in two."

"I was never in need. I could care for myself always." She pulled her gaze away and backed away from him toward the door. "I'm tired and I have to think. I believe I'll go to my chamber and—"

She broke off. He was chuckling softly and she glanced at him with a sudden surge of anger. "Stop laughing at me. I don't like it." She drew a deep, trembling breath. "I think you're capable of being very, very cruel, Jean Marc."

"You may not realize it, but you also have that potential. Which is another reason I want you from under my roof. We could quite possibly rip at each other, and you're not strong enough for the battle yet. Strange, but I find I don't want to hurt you."

Juliette felt as if she had been kicked in the stomach. Her breath vanished and another rush of blood scorched her cheeks. What was wrong with her? It couldn't be Jean Marc who was affecting her in this manner. She would not allow it to be Jean Marc. It must have been the long walk that afternoon that made her knees suddenly weak and trembling.

"This is all nonsense. I have to think," she mut-tered, and turned and fled from the room.

Danton rose to his feet and ruefully shook his head as his wife closed the door of his study behind Juliette. "I admit to being so ungallant as to wish never to see you again, Citizeness de Clement. François made no mention to me that you were still in Paris."

"He doesn't know." Juliette threw back the hood of

her brown cloak. "May I sit down? I walked from the Place Royale and I'm a trifle weary."

"By all means." Danton watched her cross the study and plop down in a cushioned chair. "I assume Andreas doesn't know of your visit here or he would have provided you with a carriage."

"Jean Marc wasn't pleased I decided to stay in Paris. He'd prefer I let him hide me away until he can arrange to send me to Vasaro. I thought it wiser to slip away when I decided to see you." She shrugged. "It wasn't difficult. All day he's either been closeted in his study with huge mountains of documents or speeding off in his carriage to meet someone or other."

"I'm afraid I concur with Andreas. I'd prefer you hide away also." His expression hardened. "And I don't appreciate you coming to my home and risking both your discovery and my own. Raoul Dupree has come to call almost every day of late and I'd not like to give him reason to ask me awkward questions."

"Well, I could hardly go to the assembly, and I had to see you."

He folded his arms across his chest and leaned back against the mantel. "I'd be fascinated to learn why."

"I need your help."

"To leave Paris?"

"No." She gestured impatiently. "You sound like Jean Marc. I'm not ready to leave Paris yet. I have something to do first."

"Indeed?"

"I want to speak to the queen."

He gazed at her incredulously and then chuckled. "So you've come to me? What makes you think I'll help you?"

"I'm going to find a way to speak to her no matter what. I thought you might prefer to arrange a safe way for me to get into the Temple and out again." She smiled sweetly. "You wouldn't want me to be caught. It might be awkward for you."

"A good point. And exactly what subject do you wish to discuss with Her Majesty?"

"That's my concern."

"What if I demand to know as a price for my help?"

"I'll find help at a cheaper price."

Danton laughed. "*Merde*, but you have audacity. It's a quality I admire."

"You'll help me?"

His smile vanished. "Don't rush me. I'm thinking about it. You wish only to speak to the queen? You have no intention of trying to arrange helping her escape?"

Juliette hesitated. "Not at this time." She rushed on. "Though you should not have placed them in that horrible place."

"It's not so terrible. They have many comforts." Juliette de Clement was clearly involved in a plot of some sort and reckless enough to risk all their heads if it suited her. Still, audacity often carried the day, and it had always been his opinion it would be better for France if the royal family did escape before the Jacobins sent Louis to the guillotine. The moment the king was beheaded, Danton hadn't the slightest doubt that both England and Spain would declare war. "Why do you think I'll be able to get you into the Temple?"

"You're a man who wants to know everything that's going on around him. Why else would you hire François Etchelet? The royal family is a danger to your new republic and you make sure you know everything concerning them. Isn't that true?"

Danton nodded. "You're very perceptive. I did have François study their situation at the Temple in some depth when they were transferred there from the Tuileries."

"And you can get me in?"

"We can get almost anyone into the Temple, according to François. Hebert's precautions are laughable. Entry cards are issued to practically anyone who asks." He paused. "But it would be impossible to get any member of the royal family out. They're very closely guarded."

"I don't want to get anyone out except myself."

Danton thought for a moment. "The lamplighter who goes every evening to the Temple often takes members of his family along, and I understand the faces of the members of his family change with his fortunes. A small bribe should suffice."

"I don't have any money and I don't want to ask Jean Marc. He mustn't know about this."

"Why not?"

"If he doesn't want me to go out on the street, do you think he'd want me to go to the Temple?" She frowned. "He's not being at all reasonable regarding this matter."

Danton smothered a smile. "I regret not being able to offer you any funds, but I'm only a poor republican official."

"Let me think." Juliette was silent a moment. "François. Jean Marc gave him a fortune for marrying Catherine. He can pay the bribe."

"Perhaps. If he wishes to become involved."

"He's already involved."

"That doesn't mean he'll help you. François is a brilliant man, but he can be blind to practicalities on occasion. Two years ago he showed up on my doorstep fresh from the Basque country, burning with the fever of the revolution, begging to serve me in any way I asked of him." Danton's lips twisted in a half smile. "Some of the things I asked were not exactly as pure as his ideals, but he never said no to me. He believes the republic will live forever because the Rights of Man are just and good."

"And you don't?"

"I believe the republic will be what we make it whether good or evil." He tilted his head. "And what do you believe in, Citizeness?"

She rose to her feet. "I believe people should be left in peace to do what they wish to do." She drew her hood over her head. "And I believe that people who take away that peace should be punished. Will you speak to François or shall I?"

"I haven't said I'd cooperate with you."

"But you will?"

Danton hesitated and then nodded slowly. "And I'll speak to François. I've noticed you lack a certain diplomacy of expression."

She nodded briskly. "When? It must be soon."

"Today. And if all goes well, you'll go to the Temple tomorrow evening. I'll see that the queen receives a message to the effect that if she goes for a walk in the courtyard when the sun is about to set, she may be pleasantly surprised." He bowed mockingly. "If that will suit your convenience."

She nodded. "I'll be here at—"

"No, I'll tell François to meet you down the street from the Andreas house just before dusk. I have no wish to have you on my doorstep again." His lips twisted. "Your disguise leaves a great deal to be desired."

"I had no time to think about disguises."

"I suggest you take the time if you intend to continue to dash about Paris."

"I will." She started for the door. "I suppose you're right and it would be wise to—"

A soft knock sounded at the door and his wife opened the door. "Georges Jacques, it's Citizen Dupree." Her tone was stilted. "Shall I show him in?"

"In a moment, *chérie*. Don't tell him of our visitor."

"I'll not speak to him at all. It makes me ill to look at him." Gabrielle shut the door.

Nor did she speak often to her own husband anymore, Danton thought with a wrenching pang. She shrank away from him as she did from anyone connected with the massacres.

He turned abruptly away and gestured toward the door on the other side of the study. "That door leads to a small garden with a gate that lets out onto the street. Hurry."

Juliette moved quickly across the room. "Tomorrow."

Danton nodded and then watched dully as the door closed behind her. He was not thinking of his rash young visitor, but of his wife. Gabrielle would forgive him in time. Their love was too deep to be lost because of politics. In a few months she would be fine again.

"Georges Jacques, I dropped by to bring you the latest copy of 'Père Duchesne'." Danton turned to see Dupree standing in the doorway. Dupree moved forward and dropped a copy of Marat's inflammatory pamphlet on the desk. "I was in the neighborhood and thought I'd give you one of the first copies."

"You're too kind, Citizen."

Dupree shrugged. "I believe in serving my friends well." He crossed to the window. "I'll be glad to wait for—" He broke off, stiffening, his gaze on the street.

"What's wrong?" Danton quickly crossed the study to stand beside Dupree. Juliette de Clement was disappearing around the corner, but nothing was visible except the back of her cloak, he noticed with relief. "Is something amiss, Citizen?"

"Perhaps not." Dupree frowned. "That woman looked familiar."

"Which woman?"

"The woman in the brown cloak. She's gone now."

"You know her?"

"There was something in the way she moved."

"You frequent the Comédie Française. Perhaps she's an actress you've had occasion to see there."

"Possibly." Dupree shrugged. "However, if I do know her, I'll eventually remember. I have an excellent memory."

"I'm sure you will." Danton strolled to the desk and picked up the pamphlet. "What's the subject of Marat's ravings today?"

Dupree turned immediately from the window. "You should not speak of him in that way. He's a true friend of the republic."

"But sometimes we must forget loyalties toward one friend when we make another." Danton paused meaningfully. "I have no liking for Marat."

Dupree hesitated and then smiled ingratiatingly. "Naturally, I would not care to display my dislike of being in his service until I had a position I esteemed more."

Mother of God, the man would betray the devil himself if offered a higher place. Danton was careful to mask his disgust. "I can understand your caution."

"But this wouldn't be a suitable time to relinquish my position. I'm leaving tomorrow for Andorra on a very important mission. Perhaps we can talk when I return?"

"Andorra?" Danton frowned. "Spain? What business has Marat with the Spaniards?"

"A concern of great importance to France, and naturally he would trust it to no one but me."

"Naturally." Dupree was evidently not going to confide the nature of that concern, Danton thought with annoyance. What the devil was Marat doing with his filthy fingers in foreign affairs? "You said you'll leave tomorrow?"

Dupree nodded. "Marat's given me permission to stop off and spend a fortnight of rest with my mother, who lives on the outskirts of Paris in the village of Clairemont. It's a difficult trip across the Pyrenees."

Then the "concern" while important was not urgent. "After your efforts of last month I can see how you'd need a rest," Danton said without expression as he picked up his hat and gloves. "Come, it's time we started for the convention."

Marie Antoinette's hair was white.

"Keep your head down," the lamplighter whispered. "I told you not to look up once we were in the courtyard."

Juliette hastily lowered her gaze and reached up to tie the woolen kerchief more securely under her chin. Her hands were trembling and her throat tight with tears. The queen's hair was white. It wasn't perfumed or powdered. She didn't have on a wig as Juliette had seen her wear on so many occasions when she had first come to Versailles. Marie Antoinette was only thirty-six and she looked twice those years.

"Stop gaping at her." The lamplighter lit the lamp to the left of the gate. "Do you want to get thrown into the Tower with her?"

"She looks so different."

"Stand over there in the shadows. I'll send her over to have a word with you. But only five minutes, you understand? When I finish lighting my lamps, we leave."

Juliette obediently moved into the shadows beneath the looming Tower. Dusk had completely claimed the courtyard of the Temple and in her drab brown gown and kerchief she knew she'd be virtually invisible to any but the closest observer.

The queen was not ill dressed. Her black cloak was well made and the muff she carried was of marten fur, but her garments might as well have belonged to a prosperous innkeeper's wife instead of the queen of France. Poor Marie Antoinette had lost everything but her family—and even some of them had been taken from her. The king's brothers, the Comte de Provence and the Comte d'Artois, had escaped to Austria and his spinster sisters to Italy. Marie Antoinette's firstborn son, Louis Joseph, the dauphin, had died tragically in 1789 at the same time the queen's entire world was vanishing around her.

Now Marie Antoinette had only her big, gentle husband, her sister-in-law, Madame Elizabeth, her daughter Marie Thérèse, and little Louis Charles, who was now the dauphin and heir apparent to the throne.

"Juliette?" Marie Antoinette peered into the shadows. "Is it truly you? All that dirt on your face . . ."

Juliette started to curtsy and then caught herself. The daughter of a republican lamplighter would hardly show respect for royalty. "It's I. The lamplighter thought I looked too clean, so he rubbed some soot on my cheeks."

"More than a little. You look like a street urchin." The queen came forward and reached out to gently touch Juliette's left cheek. "But yes, I know those bold eyes. I thought you were dead. They told me of the massacre at the abbey and I thought . . ." She trailed off and shivered. "Did you hear what those brutes did to the Princess de Lambelle?"

"Yes."

"Her head was on a pike and they told me they shot her limbs from a cannon." Tears misted the queen's eyes. "She was safe in England and returned to stay by my side and they killed her for it. They're killing everyone. Soon there will be no one left." She closed her eyes tightly and when she opened them the tears had vanished. "And how is my sweet Celeste? Is your mother well, Juliette?"

"Yes."

"And safe?"

"Yes, she fled France for Spain during the massacres."

"*Bon.* I often think of her and pray for her safety."

"Are you comfortable here?"

"Oh, yes, it is not too bad. They see that we have decent enough food and the guards are not too unpleasant. They even brought me a clavichord from the Louvre." She frowned. "Of course, they stare a great deal. I do not like to be stared at."

She had never liked excessive attention, Juliette remembered. That was why she would run away from the principal palace to the smaller palace of Petit Trianon or the village of Le Hameau to play among her flowers and lavish toys. "Perhaps they've never seen a queen before."

Marie Antoinette raised her head. "Well, they've seen one now. I'll show them how a queen deports herself." Then the momentary regalness vanished and she was once more only a sad-faced woman who was older than her years. "You must go, child. It was kind of you to come and see me, but it's dangerous for you to stay. That grotesque Hebert is in charge of our captivity. He's a true *canaille.* He would like nothing better than to cause me more pain by hurting you."

Juliette drew a deep breath. "I came for a reason," she rushed on. "I want the Wind Dancer."

The queen stiffened. "You always did. Even as a child you loved my statue." Her expression became cold. "The Wind Dancer is mine. I won't give it up."

"Jean Marc Andreas still wishes to own it. You remember Jean Marc?"

"How could I forget him?" Marie Antoinette said dryly. "He's not a man who slips readily from one's memory."

"He's willing to give me two million livres for the statue. Wouldn't that be enough money to buy your way out of prison and help you to escape to Austria?"

The queen went still. "Perhaps. The guards have been willing to accept small bribes to provide us with additional comforts."

"Tell me where the Wind Dancer is and I'll go and get it. I'll sell it to Jean Marc and then give you the money."

"Not to me." The queen frowned in thought. "I could do nothing with it here. However, there's a group loyal to me in the city who would possibly help. Go to the Café du Chat on the Pont Neuf and ask for William Darrell."

The lamplighter had finished his round and was walking slowly toward them across the courtyard.

"There's not much time. Where may I find the Wind Dancer?"

Marie Antoinette's gaze searched Juliette's. "Can I trust you, Juliette? I meant to save the Wind Dancer for my little Louis Charles. He may not ever be the king of France, but the Wind Dancer would provide for him."

"It's better to save yourself and the rest of the royal household than a statue."

"Yes, I suppose . . ."

"He's coming. Be quick."

"It's in the Belvedere. I had Monsieur Minque include a cache beneath the sphinx when he first designed it. I had the Wind Dancer hidden there when they told me that horrible mob was marching on Versailles."

Juliette was thinking frantically, trying to remember. The Belvedere was a pavilion behind the Petit Trianon but there were several sphinxes flanking the steps of the Belvedere. "Which sphinx?"

"The one on the left of the door directly facing the lake."

The queen put her hands in her fur muff. "Do not betray me, Juliette. I have so few people I can trust."

She turned and hurried away, and a moment later she disappeared into the entrance of the large Tower.

Juliette gazed after her, her emotions in tumult. She had not expected to feel such melancholy. Over the years she had tried to vanquish the affection she felt for the queen. She had told herself it was foolish for her to care for someone who had no more fondness for her than she did for the lambs of Le Hameau. She had told herself that only her painting was important and Marie Antoinette didn't matter in her life. Yet today all she could remember was that long-ago night when she had first met Marie Antoinette and the queen had taken her in her arms and cradled her and asked her to be her friend. Poor butterfly. All the brilliant flowers of her garden had withered and now she, too, was fading away.

"Here now. Don't just stand there. Come along," the lamplighter said, low and harsh.

Juliette reluctantly turned away from the doorway through which Marie Antoinette had disappeared. She fell meekly into step behind the lamplighter, following him across the courtyard toward the gate.

François Etchelet was as grimly silent on the drive from the Temple as he had been when he had met Juliette earlier. Clearly, he was not pleased with her. At first his reticence suited Juliette very well. She was finding it difficult to shake off the depression that had settled on her since she had met with the queen. They were near the Place Royale when Juliette finally roused herself to speak. "I don't see why you're angry with me. It was you who told me I shouldn't remain with Catherine."

"I didn't tell you not to go to Vasaro." He looked straight ahead. "And I most certainly didn't tell you to stay in Paris and embroil us all in treasonous activities."

"I'm not embroiling anyone in treason." She tilted her head to gaze shrewdly at him. "And if you objected so heartily to my going to see the queen, why did you arrange the bribe?"

"It was Georges Jacques's decision. He thought it safer to indulge you in this stupidity." He gazed at her face. "And was your conversation with Citizeness Capet worth the risk to all of us?"

"Her Majesty," she corrected him. "And don't tell me that's one of the things your precious republic has changed, for I won't believe it. Being a citizeness wouldn't suit her at all. She doesn't know how to be anything but a queen."

"I'll call her whatever—" He stopped and shrugged. "Perhaps that's her tragedy. Do you know her well?"

"Since I was a small child. She was kind to me."

"You can't help her, you know."

Juliette was silent.

"Guards in the courtyard, commissioners from the Commune, are on duty in their apartments day and night."

"Just like Versailles," Juliette said softly. "She always hated all those people gaping at her when she arose in the morning and went to bed at night. Some of those silly women of the court used to quarrel over who would hand the queen her chemise in the morning."

"I assure you the commissioners aren't acting as maidservants to her." The sarcasm vanished from his tone as he looked at her soberly. "This is the end, Juliette. You'll get no more help from either Georges Jacques or myself. It's too dangerous. Ever since the royal family tried to escape from the Tuileries last year, the Commune has been seeing plots behind every bush."

"Did I ask for help?"

"Not yet. But that doesn't mean you won't. I'll be very glad when Jean Marc sends you on your way to Vasaro. I received a message from him this morning asking me to call on him tomorrow."

"He probably wants you to arrange departure papers for me."

"Now, that's a service I'll be happy to render. Passing the barriers should be safe enough for you now. Dupree left Paris this morning."

"Danton arranged it?"

François shook his head. "Marat sent him on a

mission. Andreas could have saved himself a handsome dowry if he'd waited a few days."

"But we didn't know that." Juliette frowned. "You won't tell Jean Marc about my going to the Temple? It would serve no purpose and only cause problems for me."

"I'll keep silent." He paused. "If you give me your word you won't try to see the queen again before you leave Paris."

She nodded. "You have it. I have no need to go back there." She shivered. "And it made me too sad. She's not the same as she was at Versailles."

His gaze narrowed on her face. "Nothing is the same. No one can bring back the past, and those who try will face the guillotine."

She wrinkled her nose at him. "And you would release the blade."

"If necessary." He added soberly, "But it would not be by my will. In many ways I've come to admire you."

She looked at him in surprise.

"Your courage." He smiled faintly. "Not your good sense."

She burst out laughing. "And I admire your honesty, if not your tact. It greatly relieves me to know that you'd regret parting my head from my shoulders."

His smile faded. "You've been nearer the guillotine than you think. Georges Jacques said Dupree caught a glimpse of you yesterday." He saw her stiffen and shook his head. "He didn't recognize you, but it was very close."

She shrugged. "I can't hide myself away any longer. It's not my way. If I hadn't had Catherine to care for these last weeks, I would have gone mad in that house."

The carriage stopped in front of Jean Marc's house and she gathered her cloak around her. "I should have told him to stop down the street again. Oh, well, perhaps Jean Marc hasn't come back from seeing Monsieur Bardot as yet. *Au revoir,* François."

Laurent opened the door to the carriage and helped her down to the sidewalk.

"Not *au revoir.*" Grimness inflected François's voice

as he watched her hurry up the steps. "I most earnestly hope it's *adieu*, Juliette."

The lanterns affixed on either side of the door on the walls of the alcove revealed both Juliette's deplorably dirty face and the mischievous glance she cast him over her shoulder.

"But how often are our hopes realized in this world, François?"

She entered the house and with utmost care to be silent, closed the front door.

TWELVE

Juliette dashed across the foyer and started to mount the staircase two steps at a time.

"What an intriguing ensemble. Don't tell me that gown came from Julie Lamartine's?"

Juliette stopped on the eighth step. *Merde,* she should have known events were going too well. She sighed and turned to face Jean Marc, who stood leaning against the jamb of the archway of the salon, his arms folded across his chest.

His gaze traveled slowly over her. "If it did come from Julie's establishment, then I've been grossly cheated."

"It's one of Marie's old gowns."

"Rags. Is that the latest fashion? I've always been fascinated by the vagaries of ladies' apparel. Come down and let me get a closer look at you."

Jean Marc's tone was silky but his lips were tight with displeasure. Juliette hesitated and then came slowly down the stairs and across the foyer to stop before him. "Don't be ridiculous. I've been out. This is my disguise."

"Is it?" He reached out, touched her cheek, and then looked at the soot on his fingertips. "Who were you supposed to be? A chimney sweep?"

She merely gazed at him.

He took a linen handkerchief from his pocket and carefully wiped his fingers. "I thought I'd expressed my wishes very clearly regarding your venturing from this house. And just where have you been? Perhaps for a walk on the square?"

She didn't answer.

"Or a ride in a carriage? Please, don't bother to lie. I discovered you were gone more than an hour ago and was watching out the window when the carriage drew up in front of the house." He paused. "Danton's carriage, I believe. I recognized his driver. Was Danton in the coach?"

"No, it was François."

"And where had you been with our friend François?"

There was no avoiding it. Jean Marc was obviously not going to give up. "It was your own fault I had to sneak out of the house. If you'd been reasonable, I could have gone without—"

"Where did you go?"

"To the Temple."

Jean Marc froze. "The Temple?"

"Well, I had to see the queen. How else was I to find out where she'd hidden the Wind Dancer? You told me she was the only one who knew its whereabouts."

"So you went to the Temple to ask her." Jean Marc's words were measured. "It didn't occur to you that if you'd been caught you'd almost certainly been taken before the Commune and recognized by Dupree?"

"Why are you so upset? You were quite safe. If I had been caught, I would never have told them you sheltered me."

"*I* was safe? What about—" He broke off, and when

he spoke again his tone was expressionless. "That relieves my mind completely, of course."

Juliette nodded with satisfaction. "I thought it would." She started to turn away. "Now I'll go bathe and change my gown. Will you tell Marie to hold supper?"

"No, I will not tell Marie anything." Jean Marc's hands closed on Juliette's shoulders and whirled her back to face him. "You persuaded François to help you in this folly?"

"It wasn't folly. It was entirely reasonable." She tried to wriggle away from him. "And actually I went to Danton and he persuaded François into helping. Though I think Danton would have done it anyway. He's a very strange man. I got the impression he wouldn't be averse to—"

"You told him about the Wind Dancer?"

"Of course not. I'm not a fool. You told me the republic wanted the statue for a symbol. Since he's the Minister of Justice, he might have decided he wanted it for himself. I just told him it would be safer for him if I wasn't captured when I went to the Temple, and he agreed with me." She frowned. "But I can't count on either of them for any more help. I'd hoped to find a way to persuade François to take me to Versailles, but he was very adamant—"

"Versailles?"

Juliette nodded. "The queen hid the Wind Dancer at Versailles just as everyone thought."

"And she told you where?" he asked incredulously.

"Of course she did."

"There's no of course about it. She's refused to tell anyone what happened to it for the last two years. Christ, I never thought you'd be able to do it." Jean Marc's gaze narrowed on her face. "Why should she tell you?"

"Because she knows I wouldn't betray her," Juliette said simply.

"You were willing to sell me her statue."

She looked at him in surprise. "But I thought you'd know the money would go to her."

"You didn't mention that aspect of our arrangement."

"I wouldn't *steal* from her."

"My apologies." Jean Marc's grip on her shoulders loosened slightly. "My faith in human nature isn't of the highest, and two million livres is a very tempting sum."

Her gaze searched his face. "You wanted to believe that of me, didn't you?"

"Perhaps I did." He smiled faintly. "I do have occasional stirrings of conscience regarding my intentions toward you. It would have been comforting to find you lacking integrity."

Juliette glanced away from him. "She looked terrible," she whispered. "I wish I hadn't gone. It was much easier remembering her the way she was at Versailles. I can't ignore her any longer."

"And you wish to ignore her?"

"I thought I did. She ignored me all those years I was at the abbey and that . . . hurt me. Perhaps if I give her the money to escape from that horrible place I can forget her." She paused. "I *have* to forget her. She gets in the way of my painting."

"And nothing must get in the way of your painting."

"Would you let anything get in the way of your business concerns?"

"*Touché.*" Jean Marc smiled faintly. "We're much alike, *n'est-ce pas?*"

She nodded and shifted her shoulders uneasily. She wished he'd release her and step away. His grasp was not painful but her flesh was tingling oddly beneath his hands. She took a step back and his hands fell away from her. "Are there soldiers at Versailles?"

"Only a company of National Guard to prevent theft."

"Good. Then perhaps I can manage without help."

"You're going alone to retrieve the Wind Dancer?"

"I told you François wouldn't help me with anything but papers to get beyond the barriers. It should be much safer now. François said Dupree has left Paris on a mission for Marat. Perhaps you could ask François to—"

"If I can get papers to get you beyond the barriers to go to Versailles, you'll continue on to Vasaro."

She should have known Jean Marc would not easily give up his determination to get her away from Paris. "How can I go to Vasaro when I have to bring the Wind Dancer back to Paris to give to you?"

"I'm going with you."

"You'll help me? Ah, that is good." Juliette suddenly frowned. "Why? That wasn't in our agreement."

"I can alter the agreement if I so desire. After all, I'm the one who's paying the ransom for the Wind Dancer."

"But you'll still pay me the two million livres, even if you help me? The agreement will still stand?"

He was silent a moment. "You believe I'd cheat you? I thought you judged my greed to be an honest one."

Did a flicker of hurt cross his face? No. She had to be mistaken, for his tone had reflected only mockery.

"I suppose my faith in human nature isn't of the highest either, and I've never really understood you, have I?"

"All you have to understand is that I want the Wind Dancer," he said. "If you're captured with it in your possession, I'd have a devil of a time getting it back from the National Convention. It's more sensible for me to help you find it and make sure I get it instead."

"That's true." Her brow knitted in thought. "You mustn't tell François we're going to Versailles. When you ask him for papers, tell him to have them made out to us as husband and wife. Let's see . . . we'll be Citizen Henri and Madeleine La Croix and pretend we work at Versailles for one of the nobility. I'll decide which one later. I'll wear my plainest gown and cape and you must wear something much less elegant also. Perhaps you can arrange to bribe one of the guards at the gate at Versailles. You seem to be very good at bribing people." Her eyes began to sparkle. "It's rather like a painting, isn't it? First we do the background and then we sketch in the foreground and add color and texture. It will be very amusing."

"Amusing?"

"Well, interesting anyway."

Jean Marc smiled. "You remind me of a child eager to dress up for a masquerade." His smile faded. "One more thing. Before I give you the money for the Wind Dancer, I want a writ of separation from the royal coffers for the statue signed by Marie Antoinette."

"What good would that do? The republic would confiscate the statue anyway if they knew you possessed it."

"The Wind Dancer has existed thousands of years, republics and monarchies coming and going. Who knows how long this one will exist? I want the document."

"You want me to go back to the Temple?"

"*Merde,* no! It may take time, but I'll find a way to get a message from you into the Temple asking the queen for the bill of sale. Agreed?"

"Agreed."

"We'll have supper soon. Go wash that dirt off your face. It bothers me."

"Do you think it doesn't bother me?" Juliette said indignantly. "I had to pretend to be the lamplighter's daughter. Do you think I'm wearing these smudges as beauty patches? It was part of my disguise."

"You don't need beauty patches." His gaze was suddenly intent. "They would be redundant."

Juliette felt a queer ripple of heat go through her. She knew she was no beauty but he still found her pleasing. How quickly his manner had switched from cool incisiveness to sensuality. "I agree." She quickly turned toward the steps. "I'm aware that no artifice would make me beautiful like Catherine or my mother. Nor would I wish to be. It would only get in my way." She was mounting the steps quickly, not looking back at him. "You're fortunate I'm not a beauty or you'd be without your supper until midnight. Even with the help of three maids my mother took at least four hours each day at her toilette."

"Yes, I'm very fortunate."

The weariness in his tone caused her to look back at him but his face was mirror-smooth.

The emblem of the Sun King on the zenith of the gates shone in golden splendor in the moonlight, and for a moment Juliette was wafted back to those other times she'd stopped at that very spot. The memory was so strong it was a shock to see not the Swiss guard, but a soldier wearing a black cocked hat flourishing a revolutionary cockade and a uniform sporting a tricolored sash.

Juliette tensed as the guard approached with crisp military precision the wagon she and Jean Marc rode. The light cast from the lantern he carried revealed a face weathered by sun and time with a long nose and slablike cheekbones. His eyes narrowed as he examined the papers Jean Marc handed him.

Juliette drew the woolen cloak more closely about her as a chill of apprehension ran through her. The guard was taking a long time with the papers and he didn't seem the sort of man who could be easily bribed. What if it was the wrong guard? The papers he was examining had been hurriedly and clumsily forged, but Jean Marc had assured her it wouldn't matter. The papers were only to give an appearance of authenticity in case there was more than one guard at the gate. There wasn't. If this was the one who had accepted Jean Marc's bribe, there was no need for subterfuge.

"You come very late, Citizen. Eight bells tolled only moments ago." The guard held the papers closer to the lantern.

"We're on our way to Vendée and wished to claim the belongings we left here two years ago, when our master fled the palace."

The guard's gaze was cold as it shifted to Jean Marc's face. "It says here you were employed by the Duc de Gramont as his coachman."

Jean Marc shrugged. "The times were bad, and it was better than starving. Thank God for the revolution. My wife and I have now opened a fine café on the rue de Rivoli, where we grovel to no one."

"Then why do you go to Vendée?"

"It's only for a visit. Vendée was the place of my birth, and we thought to give these belongings to my brother, who has not been as fortunate as we."

It *was* the wrong guard. He was asking too many questions.

The guard lifted his lantern to shine on Juliette's face. "This is your wife? She was also in the service of the Duc de Gramont? In what capacity?"

"Maidservant."

The guard's expression was growing more suspicious by the moment.

"Why lie to him?" Juliette asked suddenly.

Jean Marc stiffened and turned to look at her.

"Everyone knows what a *canaille* the duke was. He kept me at court to use me as his strumpet. I was only eleven years old when he forced his way into my bed." She cuddled lovingly close to Jean Marc on the seat of the wagon. "I know you're trying to hide my shame, but this good man must have heard how the duke used children to soothe his lust."

"It's true. I've heard many such stories about the duke since I was assigned here." The guard smiled wolfishly. "It must have pleased you that the duke was beheaded at La Force last month, Citizeness."

"It wasn't his head I wanted struck from his body."

The guard chuckled and lowered the lantern. "Pass through, Citizen." He handed Jean Marc the papers. "Go to the queen's vestibule. There will be someone there to direct you to the chamber where all the boxes are kept. You know where it is?"

Jean Marc nodded. "Of course."

"If the guard's not on duty, call out for him. He'll probably be in the guardroom playing cards."

"I'll do that." Jean Marc snapped the reins and the wagon rolled slowly through the gates into the Cour Royale.

The wheels creaked as the wagon lumbered over the cobblestones of the vast courtyard.

"It was the wrong guard," Juliette whispered.

"You can't always be sure a bribe will work. Anything can happen. Sometimes they'll become frightened.

Sometimes their duty will be changed." Jean Marc shrugged. "It was fortunate you knew of the Duc de Gramont's lascivious tastes. Your lie disarmed him completely."

"It was no lie." Her gaze was searching the massive bulk of the palace just ahead. Light streamed from a few windows on the lower floors, but the other windows were dark, empty of life. "Pull into the shadows over there by the east wing. We can't chance encountering anyone else on the way to the Belvedere while we're in this wagon. We'll have to walk the rest of the way."

His expression was suddenly harsh. "What do you mean, it was no lie? De Gramont raped you?"

"What? Oh, de Gramont was my mother's lover, you know."

"So that gave him the right to—"

"We have no time to talk of trivialities," Juliette said impatiently as she jumped down from the wagon and started across the courtyard. "If we hurry, we should be able to make it to the Belvedere in forty minutes. Take the lantern but don't light it until we need it."

"Trivialities? I don't regard the rape of a child as a—" He broke off as he noticed she was almost out of earshot. He grabbed the lantern from the wagon and caught up with her by the time she reached the corner of the wing. "We'll discuss this later."

"If you like." For so cynical a man Jean Marc was reacting most peculiarly. The idea of her in the duke's bed clearly bothered him and the knowledge filled her with inexplicable excitement. The Neptune Basin was just ahead and her pace quickened. "Do you think the gates of the smaller palaces will be guarded?"

"Perhaps. I couldn't gather any detailed information without incurring suspicion. If they are, will that be a problem?"

Juliette shook her head. "I know the grounds of the Petit Trianon very well." She grinned. "I hid from Marguerite in every glade, fountain, and building at one time or another."

"Marguerite?" Jean Marc nodded. "Oh, yes, your charming nurse. Whatever happened to her?"

"She fled to Spain with my mother the night of the massacre at the abbey." Juliette turned left at the Basin. "François tried to persuade my mother to take Catherine and me with them, but she wouldn't agree. He became very annoyed with both of them."

"I can understand his feelings."

"I told him it would do no good." She frowned. "We should go faster. Are you able?"

"Able?"

She carefully avoided looking at him. "Well, you must be over thirty and you get no exercise."

"I'm thirty-two, which is no great age." Jean Marc's tone was icy. "And how do you know I get no exercise?"

The excitement was growing within her. "You take carriages everywhere and you work for hours in your study. You cannot be very fit."

"I don't spend all my time with my ledger books. Perhaps I should demonstrate my fitness to you," he said silkily. "I assure you I'm no aging de Gramont."

Jean Marc appeared unable to let the subject of de Gramont alone and was obviously sensitive regarding his own age. Juliette thoroughly enjoyed turning the tables, pricking at his aplomb now when usually she was the one on the defensive. "Oh, I know that. The duke was in his fifties." She pretended to think about it. "But he hunted a great deal and his body was amazingly strong for—"

"Set the pace," Jean Marc grated between his teeth. "I assure you I'll keep up."

She cast a sidewise glance at his grim expression and then thought it best not to answer at all. She increased her speed until she was almost running past the silent fountains and ghostly statues toward the gates of the Petit Trianon.

The Belvedere was an enchanting enclosed pavilion crowning a grassy hillock. The graceful octagonal structure overlooked a small rivulet issuing from a pond behind the Petit Trianon. Four steps surrounded the Belvedere with pairs of sphinxes set at intervals.

"She said it's under one of the sphinxes on the stairs facing the pond," Juliette whispered as she strode down the winding walk bordering the lake. "The one on the left."

"Buried?"

"No, a hidden cache."

They had reached the four steps of the pavilion and Jean Marc halted beside a sphinx. "It appears—"

"Hush! I hear something." Juliette glanced over her shoulder across the rivulet toward the palace of the Petit Trianon. Dots of light punctuated the darkness. "Mother of God! Lanterns! Come with me." She flew up the steps of the pavilion. What if the doors were locked? The knob turned under her hand and she pulled Jean Marc inside and closed the glass-paneled door.

Jean Marc pushed her to the side and peered through the glass. "Soldiers."

Juliette's heart skipped a beat. "Searching for us?"

"Possibly." Jean Marc watched for a moment and then shook his head. "There's no urgency. Probably a patrol making rounds. We were lucky not to have run into them coming from the palace."

Being in the pavilion was no real shelter, she thought desperately. Not only were the four doors glass-paneled, but the long windows were almost floor to ceiling and separated by only narrow strips of wall. It was as if they were captured in a crystal box.

"Are they coming here?"

"I don't kn—yes!" Jean Marc ducked away from the door as a beam of light played on the glass illuminating the interior of the pavilion. He dragged Juliette to the right of the door, pressing her against the wall.

She could hear voices outside, then the crunch of booted feet on the steps. The door beside them was flung open.

Juliette was afraid to breathe. A huge figure appeared in the doorway. Light played on the glittering panes of the door directly across the room. She could see the flame of the lantern reflecting on the glass.

And Jean Marc's and her own reflection barely discernible in the shadows.

Juliette could feel Jean Marc's muscles tense as he readied to spring.

"All secure, Corporal?"

"All secure, sir." The soldier stepped back and shut the door. His boots clattered on the steps as he rejoined the patrol.

Juliette's heart was beating so hard she marveled the men outside didn't hear it.

Jean Marc peered carefully through the glass of the window to their right. "They're going away."

"Toward the palace?"

"No, toward Le Hameau. We'll wait a minute until they move farther away and then we'll have to be quick. We don't want to run into them on our way back to the gates."

"I thought for sure he'd seen us."

"He wasn't looking hard. He saw only what he expected to see."

Juliette sank to the floor and leaned back against the wall, trying to steady her breathing. She was shaking and the icy cold of the mosaic marble floor seemed to pierce through her woolen gown to her bones. She wondered if Jean Marc could see how frightened she was as he stared so intently at her. She moistened her lips. "It's the same."

"What?"

"This pavilion. Versailles. Even the gardens are still well cared for." She gestured to the exquisite arabesques painted on the wall, the clear blue sky drifting with fleeting clouds on the cupola above them. "I expected it to be defaced. Paris has changed so much. The queen used to have wonderful parties in the gardens of the Trianon and she had a concealed trench dug around this pavilion. Faggots were lit so that it looked as if it were floating on a cloud of light." She wished he would stop staring at her. He mustn't see how weak she felt. It was dangerous to show anyone her weaknesses but most of all Jean Marc. "I tried to paint it once, but I'm not good at fire."

"I'd say your incendiary capabilities are extraordinary." To her relief, Jean Marc finally shifted his gaze. "Do I detect a hint of sentiment?"

She shook her head. "It's very beautiful here, but I liked the abbey better." She was silent a moment. "Why did you intercede with the queen to have me sent there?"

"Why do you think?"

"Because of Catherine."

"It was partly Catherine." His voice was suddenly rough as his gaze returned to her face. "Stop chattering. It doesn't matter if you're frightened."

She should have realized she couldn't deceive him. "I'm only a little frightened."

"But you won't give in to it. You won't let anyone see." He knelt beside her and pulled her into his arms, cradling her against his chest. "Christ, stop trying to hide it."

He felt hard and strong and smelled of spice and the night. She buried her face in his shoulder. "You told me not to let you see any weakness."

"Did I?" His hand gently stroked her hair. "Ah, yes, I'd forgotten. I'm not usually so generous as to give warnings. Never mind, this isn't the kind of battleground I was speaking about."

"I'll be all right soon. It was the surprise . . ."

"I was scared out of my wits too."

She looked up at him in surprise. "You were? You didn't show it."

"I've had a few more years of practice hiding my feelings than you have."

She didn't know any other man who would have admitted to fear, but he had never been like other men. He had always been only Jean Marc, and the gift he was giving her tonight was as unique as the man himself. He had saved her pride by his simple admission of fear. "You're a strange man."

"You've said that before."

"Because it's true." She nestled closer into his arms. "I never know what you're going to do next."

"Nothing at the moment. Hush."

She fell silent for a moment, absorbing his comfort

and strength. Warmth flowed through her, not the tingling heat of lust but something deeper, cozier. She suddenly chuckled. "I feel very foolish kneeling here like this. We must look like two porcelain figures in a music box."

"You must be feeling better if you're thinking in pictures." Jean Marc cast a glance out the window and then rose to his feet and opened the door. "I believe it's safe to leave now."

Juliette scrambled to her feet and grabbed the lantern. "Shall I light it?"

Jean Marc was already going down the steps. "Not if we can avoid it. It might be seen." Jean Marc knelt by the sphinx again, examining it closely. "I see no levers." He pushed at the base. "The foundation is solid." He pushed sideways on the body of the sphinx.

It moved!

He pushed again, harder.

The statue swung to the side at a right angle, revealing a deep cavity measuring a good two feet square.

"I can't see. Light the lantern."

Juliette's hands were trembling as she obeyed him. She drew closer to the sphinx, blocking the light with her body as she held the lantern directly over the dark cavity.

She heard Jean Marc mutter a curse but she was too shocked to speak.

The cache was empty.

Jean Marc smiled and waved at the guard at the front gate as the wagon passed under the Sun King's golden emblem.

He snapped the whip and the horses picked up speed. As the wagon began to rumble through the streets of the town Jean Marc's smile vanished. "So where is it?"

"I don't know. She said it was at the Belvedere."

"Then you're evidently mistaken about her trusting you. She sent you on a fool's errand."

"I don't think so."

Jean Marc shot her an impatient glance. "The Wind Dancer wasn't there, Juliette."

"But I'm certain she didn't realize it wasn't still where she put—" Juliette stopped, her eyes widening as she remembered the queen's exact wording. "But she didn't put it in the cache herself."

"No?"

Juliette shook her head. "She said, 'I had it hidden in the Belvedere.' Someone else must have hidden it for her."

"And then taken it out unbeknownst to her. Who?"

"Someone she trusted." Juliette shrugged. "It could have been anyone. The queen's never been overly shrewd and trusted almost everyone at court. Her ladies-in-waiting, a servant, her family. We'll have to ask her."

"And how do you propose to do that?"

"I'll go back to the Temple."

"No." Jean Marc's tone was sharp as a scythe. "You most certainly will not."

"But I'll have to ask—" She stopped. "But François said he wouldn't help me another time. I suppose you're right. I won't be able to visit her again, but there must be another way to find out." She frowned. "William Darrell quite likely has access to Her Majesty."

"Who in perdition is William Darrell?"

"I'm not sure. The name sounds English, doesn't it? The queen told me to give him the money I received from you. If he's trying to help her escape, he must be able to get a message to her."

"Perhaps. Did she tell you where to reach him?"

Juliette nodded. "I'm to ask for him at a café on the Pont Neuf. I'll go there tomorrow."

Jean Marc smiled sardonically. "In your chimney-sweep disguise?"

"Of course not. That wouldn't be at all suitable. I'll have to think of something else."

"I'm the one who'll go."

Juliette shook her head. "I won't tell you where he can be found unless you promise to let me go too."

"This place is no doubt a hotbed of royalist sympathizers with every agent of the Commune sniffing about."

"You exaggerate. So far I've found the Commune to be composed of bumblers and lummoxes. Look how easily I got in to see the queen. And tonight we danced past that guard at the gate—"

"And were almost captured by the patrol," Jean Marc finished. "They're not all bumblers. You forget our friends François and Danton."

"But they're no threat to us. It's worth the risk. You want the Wind Dancer and I want the two million livres."

They reached the outskirts of the town and Jean Marc turned the wagon toward Paris. "I believe I'm going to regret this. I should leave you at an inn here with funds enough to take you to Vasaro on the coach."

"I'd only follow you."

"On foot?"

"Why not? I'm young and strong and—"

"Not a doddering man of thirty—"

"Thirty-two."

"I was going to say that."

"You needn't snap at me."

He glanced sidewise at her. "Why not? You've certainly recovered your equanimity and you're clearly trying to annoy me. I should think it would offer you satisfaction." He smiled crookedly. "Enjoy it, Juliette. When you realize why you are doing this, I think it will bring you little pleasure."

She had already begun to suspect why drawing fire from him had brought her such a feeling of exhilaration. But now she realized since that moment when he had held her in the pavilion the excitement and satisfaction of taunting him had entirely vanished. She looked away from him. "It doesn't matter. I'm going back to Paris with you tonight, and tomorrow night I'm going to the café to see this William Darrell. The discussion is closed."

"Not quite."

Juliette gazed at him warily.

"It's a long trip back to Paris. I wish to be amused.

Tell me a few anecdotes of your interesting past at Versailles."

"It wasn't very interesting. All I did was paint."

"But you had many fascinating acquaintances," Jean Marc said softly. "For instance, I think it's time you told me all about the 'triviality.' Who was the Duc de Gramont?"

THIRTEEN

The hair of the stylishly coiffed wig was so pale a shade of gold, it shimmered silver beneath the candles of the chandelier of the foyer.

"Take it off," Jean Marc said flatly.

"Don't be foolish, it's part of my disguise." Juliette drew the wine-colored velvet cloak more closely about her as she came down the staircase toward him. "I think it looks quite splendid. Marie said Madame Lamartine obtained the hair for the wig from a village in Sweden where all the women have hair of this color."

"Everyone at the café will be staring at you."

As Jean Marc was staring at her now. Juliette's heart began to pound harder, and the excitement she had known the previous night suddenly returned. She could see an emotion other than displeasure in his expression. "Oh, but they'll be staring at Jean Marc Andreas's latest mistress, not at Citizeness Justice."

"My mistress?"

"Danton said I needed a more clever disguise, and you were most insulting about my dirty face." Juliette strolled over to the ornate gilt-framed Venetian mirror on the wall and patted the long curls spiraling in glossy clusters to touch her bare shoulders. "I look completely different. I believe I like this much better than being the lamplight's daughter. Yes, this will be my permanent disguise."

"The one is as bad as the other. I dislike fair hair intensely."

Juliette gazed at Jean Marc's reflection in the mirror. "But why? It's a very fine wig and a very fine disguise. You're a rich man who has had many mistresses. I live in your house. Therefore, isn't it natural I should occupy your bed?"

"Entirely natural." His gaze narrowed on her face. "What are you trying to do, Juliette? I'm not a man you can tease with impunity."

"I'm not teasing you. I wouldn't know how. What's your objection to my pretending to be your mistress?" Juliette suddenly snapped her fingers. "I know, you don't think I'm *ravissante* enough. It's true I'm not pretty, but that needn't make any difference."

"No?"

She shook her head. "There were a few women at Versailles who weren't pretty but still seemed to fascinate gentlemen." She frowned. "I wish I'd paid more attention to how they deported themselves." Her brow cleared. "Oh, well, I'm sure I'll play the role very well. I'm not unintelligent, and if I do something wrong, you can always tell me. You've had more experience dealing with the demimonde than I."

"I'm to be your instructor, then?"

"No, you must only—" She broke off as she met his gaze in the mirror. She realized she had gone too far. What demon prompted her to goad Jean Marc in the direction she had no intention of traveling? He was looking at her as he had that night in the dining room, and she again experienced the strange hot breathlessness. She glanced hurriedly away. "Never mind, I'll probably do very well alone."

His black eyes glittered as he took a step toward her; the movement was stalking, predatory. "But the role you've chosen requires my complete cooperation."

"Not necessarily." She turned quickly and started for the front door. "Only when we're in public must you pretend to find me *très intéressante.* You can do that."

Jean Marc opened the door. "Oh, yes, I can do that."

The Café du Chat was brightly lit, noisy, and the patrons a mixed group of students, workers, and well-dressed merchants who were accompanied by ladies of various stations ranging from poorly dressed stolid peasants to flamboyant birds of paradise who laid no claim to domesticity.

"You see, I'm not at all out of place." Juliette sat down at a small damask-covered table in the corner of the room. "I'm certain that red-haired woman with the short fat gentleman is not his wife." She tilted her head. "Perhaps I should study her."

"Don't bother. I'd never consider her for a mistress." Jean Marc motioned to a burly man wearing a leather waistcoat and white apron who was bearing a tray to another table. "And we're not here to further your knowledge of demimondaines."

"What's wrong with her?" Juliette unfastened her cloak and let it slip from her shoulders to the back of her chair. "Her face is a trifle hard but very pretty and has— Why are you laughing?"

His gaze was on the low square neckline of her wine-colored gown. "Forgive me, but have you not . . . blossomed?"

"You think it's too much? I have a small bosom, so I stuffed six handkerchiefs down my front to push me up and make me appear more womanly. Don't gentlemen prefer ladies with large breasts?"

"I believe you can dispense with the handkerchiefs." His gaze lingered on the bared flesh glowing against the wine-colored velvet. "Large breasts are not required."

"That's a relief." She made a face. "The handkerchiefs are not at all comfortable. The lace borders scratch and make me want to pull them out."

"What an interesting—" He stopped as the burly man he'd summoned appeared at his elbow. "A bottle of wine and fruit juice for the citizeness." He paused and lowered his voice. "And a word with Citizen William Darrell."

The man's chubby, cheerful face didn't change expression. "Will you have some of my fine lamb stew? It's the best in all of Paris."

"I think not."

The man turned and wound his way across the room to the kegs against the wall. He returned and set a bottle of wine and two glasses on the table. "It's too late in the year for fruit juice."

"Water," Juliette said impatiently. "And William Darrell."

"Water?" The waiter shrugged and turned away. "I will see."

"What's wrong with the man? He's not paying any attention to us."

Jean Marc poured wine into one of the glasses. "You should really get over your aversion to wine."

Juliette's gaze was following the waiter. "He's serving someone else. Why doesn't he—"

"A lovely fan for the citizeness?" A tall woman with glossy chestnut hair plopped down onto the chair between Jean Marc and Juliette and placed her straw tray of paper fans on the table. "Every citizeness wants a pretty fan to show where her loyalty lies." She unfurled the fan in her hand. "Here's one of the glorious capture of the Bastille. I painted it myself. See the red glow of the torches and the—"

"The citizeness doesn't want a fan," Jean Marc said.

"Perhaps one of Danton or Robespierre." The woman fumbled through her tray and triumphantly withdrew a fan. "Here's Citizen Danton. Notice the noble brow."

"This is a *terrible* painting." Juliette took the crudely executed fan and shook her head. "And it doesn't even look like Danton. Danton is ugly."

"But such a man has noble thoughts." An engaging grin lit the woman's freckled face. "I paint the ideal, not the man."

"You paint carelessly, and ideals do not excuse such a terrible misuse of color and form. Have you no respect for your craft? How can you offer—"

"If you don't like Danton . . ." The woman fumbled among her merchandise again and extracted another fan and unfurled it with a flourish. "The Temple, where our patriots hold those bloody tyrants."

"These towers are completely out of proportion. You have them almost the same size, and this one is much larger."

"Wait." Jean Marc took the fan and looked at it more closely. "This one has a certain charm. Observe the pigeons, my dear." He lifted his gaze to meet Juliette's. "Four pigeons taking flight from the large tower."

Juliette's gaze flew to the fan vendor's face.

The woman smiled. "You wish to buy this fan?"

"I haven't decided." Juliette studied the woman with more care.

The woman was well worth a second look, Jean Marc thought. She seemed to be a trifle under thirty, certainly not in her first youth, yet her yellow woolen gown flattered both her shining brown hair and full, statuesque figure. Her features were nondescript and her cheeks and snub nose liberally dusted with freckles, but the expression in her hazel eyes was lively and her smile full of humor.

Jean Marc leaned forward in his chair. "Show us something else, Citizeness . . . ?"

"Nana Sarpelier."

"I'm Jean Marc Andreas, and this is Citizeness Juliette de Clement."

The woman unfurled another fan. "This one may please you. It's a ship of our glorious navy. Notice the sails battened by the wind and the figurehead of Virtue Incarnate."

"And the name of the ship on the bow," Jean Marc said softly.

"The *Darrell*." Juliette pounced. "Where is he? We want to see him."

"Who sent you here?" Nana Sarpelier unfurled another fan and batted her long lashes flirtatiously over the rim as she fanned herself.

"The lady in the Tower," Jean Marc said.

The fan seller opened another fan. "That's difficult to believe."

"How else would we know to come here?" Juliette asked. "We need to speak to William Darrell."

"There is no William Darrell. The name's only a password." The fan vendor closed the fan. "However, there are certain people with the same interests in fans as yourselves who might be able to help you. Give me your message."

"I need to ask the queen something and I have no way to get back into the Temple to see her," Juliette said. "But your group must be able to do so."

"We don't risk contact unless it's important."

"Would two million livres pouring into your coffers for our common purpose be considered of importance?"

Nana Sarpelier didn't change expression. "It's certainly a good deal of money. Still, it would have to be discussed."

"When?"

"I'm not sure. What message do you wish us to give to her?"

"A question." Juliette leaned forward. "Tell her Juliette needs to know who placed the object in the cache. The name of the person. The name."

The fan vendor took back from Jean Marc the fan depicting the Temple, gave him the one of Danton, and held out her hand palm up. "Give me a few francs." She put the money Jean Marc gave her on her tray and stood up. "*Merci*, Citizen. The lady will be the envy of all when she displays my fan."

"When?" Juliette persisted.

"*If* we decide to help"—Nana Sarpelier picked up the tray—"I'll let you know when we've accomplished the task. Leave your address with Raymond."

"Raymond?"

"Raymond Jordaneau, the man who served you. He owns the café and is one of us." She picked up the tray and sauntered through the crowded tables, stopping here and there with a smile and a word.

"It's done." Jean Marc sipped his wine. "And now we wait."

Juliette nodded and reached for the paper fan portraying Danton's face. "It's perfectly dreadful. Do you suppose she really sells any of them?"

Jean Marc smothered a smile as he watched Nana Sarpelier move about the room. "She probably does a very good business."

"But the work is shoddy and she . . ." Juliette glanced at Jean Marc's face and then at Nana, who was bending over the obese gentleman escorting the red-haired demimondaine. "He's buying a fan from her."

"Yes." Jean Marc took another sip of wine. "So I noticed."

"Do you suppose he's looking for William Darrell too?"

Jean Marc chuckled. "No, I think he's looking for a pleasant romp in any convenient bed or alcove."

"Oh." Juliette looked at the fan vendor with new interest. "Why with her and not his red-haired lady? His companion is far prettier."

"Because a man can tell when a woman will open her thighs because she enjoys a man and when she does it because she enjoys the clink of coins."

"Does it make such a difference?"

Jean Marc finished the wine in his glass and motioned to the man who had served them. "Yes, Juliette, it makes a great difference."

"How long do you think we'll have to wait to hear?" Juliette turned to face Jean Marc as he closed the front door. "We should have urged her to hurry."

Jean Marc crossed the foyer and dropped his cloak and gloves on the tapestry-cushioned bench beneath the oval mirror. "It would have done no good." He turned and walked toward her.

"But we could have— What are you doing?"

"Unfastening your cloak."

"I can do that." She could feel the heat of his body and catch the scents clinging to him. He smelled different from the men at court. Not overly sweet, just clean and . . . pleasant.

"But you must become accustomed to these small attentions." Jean Marc slowly slipped the cloak from her shoulders, letting her feel the caress of the velvet on her bare shoulders before he tossed it atop his on the bench. "It's only what I would accord any woman who gave me pleasure. It's courtesy to return kindness with kindness, and I consider it my duty to see to your comfort."

He hadn't moved away and she was experiencing a warm languor as she looked up at him. "It was . . . only pretense."

"Was it? I take my role most seriously. For instance, you mentioned experiencing a certain discomfort in the café. I didn't think it fitting to aid you there, but now there's no reason to hesitate."

"What discom—" She inhaled sharply.

He had dipped his thumb and forefinger into the bodice of her gown, grazing her nipple as he searched for and then found one of the handkerchiefs. An instant of warm, hard flesh pressing against the soft underside of her breast, then the tug of material, the delicate abrasion of the lace as it slid slowly over her nipple.

The muscles of her stomach clenched in response which wasn't at all reasonable. He wasn't even touching her stomach. He wasn't really touching her breasts either, yet they were beginning to feel heavy, full, and tingling. He was pulling a second handkerchief from her bodice, and she gazed up at him helplessly while sensation after sensation moved through her.

A faint flush mantled his cheeks, and she could see the rapid throb of a pulse in his temple as he slid the third handkerchief from her bodice. "Almost over. Three more. Six in all, you said?" His voice sounded thick, rough. His fingers searched beneath her other breast, deliberately rubbing the hard ball of his palm against the nipple.

She swayed forward, biting her lower lip to stifle a cry.

His gaze rose to her face as he pulled the handkerchief over her nipple, soothing and inciting at the same time. "As I said, you don't need these. If you wish to appear more womanly in public, there are things I can do to help you accomplish your goal." He pulled another handkerchief from her bodice. "Look at yourself," he whispered.

She looked down at her breasts and found them ripe, engorged.

"Next time we go to the café, I'll close the curtains of the carriage." He was pulling the final handkerchief from her bodice with excruciating slowness. "There are things I can do with my hands." He suddenly whipped the handkerchief past her nipple, leaving a streak of fire in its wake. "And with my mouth. Would you like that?" His nostrils were flaring slightly and his black eyes shimmered in the candlelight. "I think you would. Shall I show you?"

The air around them seemed to be thickening, darkening, vibrating. "You make me feel . . . strange."

"But you like it?"

"Yes. No. I'm not sure."

He pushed her gently down on the third step of the staircase and sat down beside her. "I'm sure. You wish to play the game. I knew you were ready to make the first moves the moment I saw you walk down the stairs tonight." His head lowered slowly until his lips were hovering over the exposed flesh swelling from the bodice. His breath was merely warm; it shouldn't have burned her. Yet it did burn and caused her to shiver as if with a fever. "You're trembling."

His lips touched her flesh.

She made a low sound and involuntarily arched upward. "Jean Marc . . ."

"Shh." His warm, wet tongue moved over her left breast, into the valley between, and then shifted to caress the right breast. "I used to wonder how you'd taste. Warm, sweet . . ." His hands slowly pushed down the bodice of the gown. "I want to *see* you."

Her breasts tumbled from the gown, the nipples pointing up at him, hard, erect. She felt heat sear her cheeks, her throat, her shoulders as she lay on the steps, her breasts lifting and falling with her quickened breathing.

He carefully arranged the velvet gown so that the low neckline was beneath her breasts, framing and lifting them into prominence. "Now, there's a lovely picture." His voice was thick as he looked down at her. "White velvet and exquisite pink flowers. But they don't have to remain pink. Let's see if we can make them the same wine color as your gown, shall we?"

His mouth closed on her right nipple.

Fire, fierce hunger.

She arched helplessly upward as he sucked, bit, tongued. She could hear the low groans he uttered deep in his throat as his hands cupped, squeezed, as his mouth worked its own sensual magic.

He lifted his head to gaze down at her with glazed eyes. "Look at yourself."

Her nipples were deep, deep red, pointed and flaunting. As she watched he slowly took one between his teeth and gently tugged upward.

She gasped as hot pleasure rippled through her.

"I've pleased you." He licked delicately at the engorged tip. "Now it's time to please me."

She looked at him in bewilderment.

"I only want you to ask me to pleasure you," he whispered. "Isn't that fair? I'll give you the words and you only have to say them."

"I don't—" She broke off as she saw his expression

that contained desire, hunger, and something else. Something reckless, bitter, and infinitely darker in nature.

"Why are you doing this? Why do you want to make me feel this way?"

"How do you feel?"

"Weak, trembling, as if I want—" She stopped, stiffening as she saw a flicker of satisfaction on his face. "That's the way you want me to feel."

His beautifully shaped hand, olive dark against her fairness, squeezed and released her breast. "Yes."

Her gaze searched his face. "It's lust but not lust. It's something else too." She pushed him away, sat up, and drew a deep breath. "You want to hurt me. Why?"

"I wouldn't hurt you."

"Why?"

"Why do I want to bed you?" He smiled crookedly. "Because you taunt me and challenge me. Because one moment I think of you as a child I have to protect and the next as a woman I've no intention of protecting." He paused. "And because you're perhaps the strongest woman I've ever encountered."

She pulled her bodice back up over her breasts. "And that's important to you? Do you want to break me just because I have strength?"

"I didn't say I wanted you to break. It's only the game."

"What game?"

He smiled at her. "Why, the one men and women always play with one another. There's always a victor and a loser in that most interesting of battles. I prefer to be the victor." He lowered his lips to brush her shoulder. "No one needs to be broken. I know how to win without crushing my antagonist."

"But you'd hurt me. Not my body, perhaps. You would try to wound me in some other ways. I can feel the anger in you." She moistened her lips. "I don't believe you are able to feel true affection for any woman. You just want to conquer me as my mother used to conquer all those men she brought to her bed. It was a game for her too." She stood up, her hands nervously smoothing the skirts of her gown. "It's a game I don't know how to play."

"You'll learn," he said cynically as he rose to his feet. "Believe me, you have a greater instinct for the game than anyone I've ever known."

She was fumbling for the pins that held her wig in place. "But I don't want to learn. It would get in my way."

His lips curved in a sensual smile. "Yes, it most certainly would."

"You needn't feel so satisfied with yourself. I didn't really feel anything. Oh, perhaps a little, but it was all a part of the pretense." His knowing glance lingered on her breasts, and she wished desperately they'd cease betraying her. "Like the gown and the handkerchiefs." She jerked off the blond wig. "And this thing. None of it is me."

"I believe it's very much—" He stopped as his gaze rose from her breasts to her hair. "My God, what have you done to yourself?"

"I had Marie cut it all off." She ran her hand through the short dark curls that clung to her fingers and formed riotous wisps at her brow and cheekbones. "The wig was hot and since I'm going to be wearing it all the time I shall be much more comfortable without my own hair beneath it."

"You look no more than eight years old."

"I was right to cut it." She glanced in the mirror on the wall across the foyer. She did look surprisingly young. The shortness of her hair made her eyes appear enormous and her retroussé nose and bare throat enhanced the air of youthful vulnerability. "It got in my way."

Jean Marc started to laugh, and she glanced at him warily.

"Don't worry, our passage of arms is over." He shrugged. "You've disarmed me. How can I seduce a child? I'm no Duc de Gramont. I told you that you had an instinct for the game."

She smiled uncertainly. "We'll both be much more content if this evening is forgotten."

"Can you forget it?"

"Of course." Juliette turned and started up the stairs.

"Juliette."

She glanced over her shoulder.

Jean Marc was smiling faintly. "I have no intention of forgetting. You knew very well what you were starting when you came down those stairs this evening. You're not the child you look and, as soon as I can force myself to get beyond that barrier, the game resumes."

She should be angry with him. He clearly had no honor where women were concerned and would think little of taking her virtue.

She wasn't angry. Whatever she was feeling was more complicated than mere anger; elements of fear, anticipation, and finally a heady exhilaration at the prospect of the challenge to come.

She veiled her eyes with her lashes so that he wouldn't see her reaction to the challenge he'd flung down and turned and ran up the steps.

"She's impatient." Nana Sarpelier began to unfasten her woolen gown. "If we don't get her the information she needs, she'll try herself. She's not going to wait long."

"What's her name?" William Darrell's brow knotted in a thoughtful frown as he lazily raised himself on his elbow on the bed to watch her undress. It always excited her to have him look at her as she readied herself for him, and she felt a tiny tingle of heat begin between her thighs.

"Juliette de Clement." She turned around in front of him. "I can't get this last hook. Will you help me, William?"

William's deft fingers accomplished the task quickly and efficiently, and the gown slipped from her shoulders. She looked down at his hand that had fallen to the coverlet. It was square and powerful, the hand of a soldier or a man who worked with the soil. A little shiver of anticipation surged through her at the thought of

what those fingers were going to do to her in a few
minutes. She had never known as skilled a lover as
William, or one who could read a woman's responses
with such accuracy. She had been married to a man
twice her age for five long years and when widowed
swore she would never marry again. Yet sometimes with
William she wondered what she would do if he demanded sole ownership of her body.

Not that he would demand it. William wanted only
what she wanted. To come occasionally to this small,
shabby inn where no one asked questions, to exchange
information, and then take from her body the same
intense pleasure he gave her. If there were times when
they shared an instant of warm companionship or a
fleeting moment of laughter, it was only a bagatelle.
"The man was Jean Marc Andreas. I think she's his
mistress."

William kissed her shoulder blade. "Really?"

She nodded. "There's something between them."
She stepped away from him and took off the gown. "Do
you think the risk is worth the money?"

"Perhaps. She didn't tell you what the object was?"

"No. Should I have pursued it?"

"No, you did well. We can find out anything we need
to know once we have the information to bargain with."

"You're going to send a message to the queen?"

"For two million livres? Of course. We always need
money. Monsieur is not as generous as he should
be—and with so much at stake."

"You could always send a message to London to the
prime minister." Nana's eyes were twinkling as she
glanced over her shoulder at him. She finished undressing. "I should think a fine English gentleman like
yourself would have many avenues to explore."

"If you'll come to bed, I'll show you an avenue or
two we can explore together, minx."

She giggled as she moved naked toward the bed.
"I'm not sure you know the way of it. You know how
fond I am of bedding Frenchmen. Now, *they* know how
to please a woman. You English are too—" She shrieked
with laughter as he pulled her down on the bed, parted

her thighs, and entered her with one bold stroke. No teasing anticipation tonight, just a hard, hot stroking until she was whimpering for release. She hadn't known she had wanted it this way tonight, but William had known. William always knew. She bit her lips to keep from screaming as the rapture climaxed, leaving her weak and mindless with contentment.

It was several minutes before her breathing became steady enough to speak. "A very interesting 'avenue.'" She nestled her cheek in the hollow of his shoulder. "Will you stay with me for a while?"

"Yes." His fingers touched her cheek. "I don't want to be alone tonight."

She lifted her head and looked down into his face. It was a peculiar thing for William to say. Except for carnal pleasures, he had never appeared to need anyone. He did the tasks given him by Monsieur with a keen intelligence that caused all the group to lean upon him for leadership, but she had never seen him show emotion regarding those duties. Now that she thought about it, there had been a restlessness about William ever since the last message had come from Monsieur.

"Why do you . . ." She trailed off as she saw his expression become shuttered. He didn't want either her curiosity or her help. They worked well together and they gave each other pleasure. It was enough. She kissed his shoulder and made her tone deliberately light. "It's just as well you're staying. You can't leave me in this state."

He looked at her in surprise. "You weren't satisfied?"

"Oh, you did very well." She winked at him. "For an Englishman." She rolled over and held out her arms to him. "But come here and let me show you how much better this Parisian can be."

The front door was opening.

Jean Marc frowned as he looked up from his ledger to the clock on the mantel of the study. It was the middle of the night. Who could be about at this hour? The sound had been very faint through the closed door of the study. Perhaps he had been mistaken. He had locked the front door himself after Juliette had run up the stairs and left him in a state of frustration so intense he'd known he'd not sleep.

No, dammit, he wasn't mistaken. It *had* been a door opening.

He pushed the ledger away, rose to his feet, and strode across the study, out the door, and into the dark foyer.

"Robert?"

No answer.

The front door was open wide and a bitterly cold rain was driving into the foyer, forming puddles on the marble floor.

A thief? No, he was sure he had locked that door. He crossed the foyer and stood in the doorway, the wind whipping his shirt against his body, his gaze searching the empty street.

No, it was not quite empty.

A glimmer of white shone in the darkness a few yards away.

Juliette!

Dressed only in a billowing white nightgown, Juliette was trudging determinedly down the street.

"Christ!" He ran down the steps and tore down the street after her. She had reached the corner by the time he caught up with her. He grabbed her shoulder and spun her around to face him. "What idiocy are you committing now? Mother of God, you don't even have shoes on! Where do you think you're going?"

"The abbey."

"What? I can't hear you." His hand slid from her shoulder to her wrist and tightened around it. "Do you wish to become ill? I've never seen such a stupid—"

"The abbey. I have to go to the abbey."

"There is no abbey, dammit." He turned and began pulling her back toward the house.

"No, I have to go. It's not finished . . . I can do better this time."

He dragged her stumbling up the steps and into the foyer.

"Let me go. I have to go to the abbey."

He slammed the door and locked it behind them. "Be quiet. I'm cold and wet and not at all pleased with this ploy, Juliette." He pulled flint from his pocket and sparked it to light the candles in the silver candelabrum on the table beside the door. "You're a woman who behaves impulsively but not irrationally. You meant me to hear you leave and did this for a purpose. Now, where were you—" He broke off as he saw her face for the first time.

Juliette's expression was totally blank, her gaze fixed unseeingly before her. Her drenched white nightgown clung to her thin body, and raindrops were running down her cheeks, but she acted as if she didn't feel them.

She turned and moved back toward the door, fumbling at the lock. "The abbey. I can do it right this time. I have to go . . ."

Jean Marc stepped in front of her and leaned against the door, blocking her way while his gaze raked her face. A chill ran through him that had nothing to do with the clamminess of his rain-soaked clothing.

Good God, she was asleep! He had heard tales of people walking and talking while asleep, but he had never believed them. Or perhaps it wasn't sleep but some disorder of the mind.

"Blood." She had the lock undone and was tugging frantically at the door. "I have to stop the blood." She was becoming agitated, her eyes glinting with tears. "Why can't I stop the blood?"

"Juliette, don't." He grasped her shoulders. "Let me—"

She screamed.

He went rigid as the raw, tormented sound tore through him.

He couldn't stand it. He shook her, hard. Harder. "*Sacre bleu*, wake up! I'll not have this, Wake—"

"Will you please stop shaking me?" Juliette asked

haughtily. "I knew you wanted to hurt me, but this is uncalled for."

"You're awake." Relief surged through him. Her eyes were not only clear but snapping with anger at him. His hands dropped from her shoulders as he stepped back. "Mother of God, you frightened me."

"You should be frightened. I'm very angry. Why did you carry me down here?"

He gazed at her in astonishment. "I didn't. You were asleep and walked downstairs and out—"

"Poppycock. No one walks while sleeping, and I certainly wouldn't."

"Have it your way." His gaze narrowed on her face. "You remember nothing?"

"What is there to remember? You obviously came to my chamber and carried me here for some purpose of your own." She frowned down at the wet gown clinging to her body. "And why did you open the door and let the rain come in? I'm all wet."

"My apologies." He studied her face. Clearly, she not only had no memory of what had transpired but was fabricating excuses to keep from remembering. "Perhaps you'd better go up and change your gown. I'll wake Marie and have her prepare tea."

"That won't be necessary. I shall have no trouble going to sleep, if you're finished with your little jest."

"Oh, I've quite finished."

She turned away, the cotton nightgown undulating with her body as she moved toward the staircase.

"Do you ever dream of the abbey, Juliette?"

She stopped but didn't turn around. "No, of course not. Don't you remember? It's Catherine who has the bad dreams. I've put all thoughts of those *canailles* behind me."

"I see." He stood at the bottom of the stairs and watched her as she climbed the stairs and disappeared down the corridor.

It's not finished.

I have to go back to the abbey.

Let me do it right this time.

Strange words for a woman who had put those memories behind her.

He blew out the candles and moved toward the stairs. He would change his wet clothes and then go back to the study and try to work. He doubted if he would succeed, but he knew he was even less likely to rest now than he had been before, when it was only his body that was frustrated.

All his life he'd had a passion for unraveling riddles, and now it was his mind that was intrigued by the puzzle Juliette had flung at him to solve.

Anne Dupree sat down gracefully on the satin couch, spreading her wide brocade skirts primly. "You appear in good health, Raoul. You haven't been to see me in over two months and if I hadn't heard how busy you've been, I'd accuse you of neglecting me."

"I couldn't get away. Marat found me irreplaceable." His mother looked as grand as a duchess in the gown of pink brocade, and the slight stoutness of her tall form made her appear all the more majestic, Raoul Dupree thought adoringly. Anne Dupree's gray-streaked hair had been dressed in the latest fashion by the maid Raoul had provided her the year before, her lips painted into a vermilion pout and a small beauty patch in the shape of a heart resting just to the left of her lips. Beauty patches enchanted her, and she often bemoaned their passing from fashion. She was gazing at him expectantly, her gray eyes bright with eagerness. Her eyes were not always kind, but they were kind that day.

"But you would have left Marat and come to me if I'd sent for you?"

He nodded, feeling the happiness flood him as he looked at her. "I've brought you a present," he said tentatively. "It belonged to a princess." He wasn't sure of the ownership of the necklace, but he knew his mother would value it more if she thought it had been worn by a royal.

His mother's gaze went eagerly to the silk-wrapped

object he had handed her. "The Princess de Lambelle? I heard you got rid of that piece of goods."

"No, another one." He watched eagerly as she unwrapped the necklace. It wasn't as easy to please his mother now as it had been before he'd showered her with this fine house and servants, but surely this trinket would earn him her pleasure. "From the Abbaye de la Reine."

"Impious whores." His mother smiled. "You did well there, Raoul."

He felt an exquisite rush of pleasure. "Marat praised me highly and Danton speaks of wishing to commandeer my services. Should I accept him?"

"I'll think about it while you're away in Spain." His mother held up the necklace. "Very nice."

Dupree was disappointed. "You don't like it?"

She smiled. "I was teasing you. It's a splendid gift." She held out her arms. "Come here."

He rushed across the room and sat down beside her. She enfolded him in a close embrace and rocked him gently back and forth. Raoul closed his eyes and let the sweet relief pour through him. She was pleased with him. *This* was what he had been waiting for through the long months away from her. It was unbearable not to be sure he was doing what she wished him to do. Sometimes the uncertainty had grown into a terrible fever and he had wanted to rush back to her and beg her to give him assurance.

Her hands stroked his hair and her voice was soft as she placed her pouty lips close to his ear. "Have you missed me?"

His arms tightened about her stout body. She knew he was never complete without her but she always made him say the words. "Yes."

"And you haven't been doing naughty things with any of those wicked women?"

"No," he lied. Mother must never know about Camille. She did not mind the anonymous rapine of the women of the abbey but would instantly condemn his relationship with Camille. "You know I always obey you, Mother."

"And hasn't it served you well? You're in the company of great men and soon it will be time for you to take their place."

He nodded contentedly, knowing he need not respond. She had been saying those words as long as he could remember. She was sure even when he was a small child he was going to be a great man and had carefully taught him what he must do. The lessons had been harsh and sometimes he hadn't understood, but she had alternated punishment and reward until he had finally come to the realization of what was required of him. He must become a rich and powerful man and make his mother the queen she deserved to be. She did not belong in this small village, married to the ignorant merchant who had fathered him. It was his duty to free her from this bourgeois prison. His father was dead now but Raoul's duty was still not done.

She pushed him away and looked down at the necklace again. "Is there a picture in the locket?"

"Locket?"

She gave him an impatient glance. "Of course it's a locket." Her nails pried at the golden circlet. "Don't be stupid."

The locket opened with a snap and his mother regarded the picture critically. "Quite lovely. Was this the princess?"

Raoul took the locket and looked down at the miniature of the girl he had seen for a fleeting moment in the bell tower. He slowly straightened. "Yes, that's her." It was an excellent likeness and could be useful. He could ride back to Paris and give it to an artist to reproduce a sketch to hang outside the Hôtel de Ville. He absently stroked the jagged scar that had formed on his throat from that black-haired bitch's teeth. The two girls had been together, and if he found the girl in the locket, there was every chance he could force her to tell him where to find Citizeness Justice. "Could I have it back for—" He had said it clumsily and could feel her stiffen with displeasure. He hurried on desperately. "Only for a little while. I'll give you—"

"Certainly, Raoul." His mother stood up. "Of course

you may have it back. You wish to give it to someone else? Someone you value more than you do me?" She smiled brilliantly. "Perhaps you'd better leave now, Raoul. I believe I shall be exceedingly busy this week."

"No, it was only a thought." He jumped to his feet, panic racing through him. He could feel the darkness closing around him, the horrid crawling, the black bile coating his tongue. "Forgive me. You know how I was looking forward to spending this time with you. I'll not be able to see you again until I return from Spain. Don't send me away."

She stared at him coldly. "You will beg my pardon for your insolence."

"I do, I do." He thrust the locket back into her hand and closed her fingers around it. He would wait until he had returned from his mission to try to persuade her to temporarily relinquish the locket. Maybe she would have grown tired of it by then.

"It's not enough."

He immediately dropped to his knees and buried his face in the skirt of her brocade gown. The material was smooth against his flesh and smelled of frangipani and the cedar lining of her armoire. "I do beg your pardon. It was very wicked of me. I'm not worthy to be your son." He waited. Sometimes the humiliation must be deeper before she rewarded him with her forgiveness. He kissed her hand. "Please, *ma mère*. I'm truly repentant."

She must not have been too upset with him. She was stroking his hair with a loving hand. "Then you must strive harder to be worthy."

"I will, Mother. May I stand?"

"Yes." She turned away. "I've been thinking about it and we must discuss the matter of this Wind Dancer more thoroughly. Possessing such a treasure could be very beneficial to me. It's far too fine a tool to give to Marat." She straightened her skirts. "But we can talk of that later. I believe we'll have goose for supper and then I'll play the viola for you. Would you like that?"

"Yes, Mother." He hated goose and she knew it. She was still angry with him. She would watch him eat a large portion of the goose, making sure he gave no sign of distaste. But the punishment might have been worse. She could have sent him away.

FOURTEEN

The front door was opening.

"Christ, not again!" Jean Marc muttered as he pushed back his chair and swiftly covered the distance between his desk and the door of the study he had deliberately left ajar. After three nights he had begun to think Juliette's sleepwalking had been only a singular occurrence not to be repeated.

The front door was standing wide open again. The blasted woman was probably halfway to the goddamned abbey. At least she'd picked a night that wasn't rainy this time.

But when Jean Marc reached the doorway, Juliette had only just reached the bottom of the stone steps. In another moment he was standing beside her.

"Juliette."

She didn't answer and, with a muttered curse, he picked her up in his arms and carried her back to the foyer.

She stiffened in his arms. "The abbey . . ."

"No." He kicked the door shut with his foot and carried her across the foyer toward the staircase. "It's over."

She shook her head, her eyes glazed, unseeing.

He started up the stairs. "You've got to stop this, you idiotic woman. I have no desire to spend my nights chasing you through the streets of Paris."

Why was he even talking to her? She obviously wasn't comprehending anything he said.

She had left the door of her chamber open and he carried her across the room, laid her on the bed, and pulled the covers over her. A crisp autumn breeze and pale moonlight poured through the open window beside the bed, illuminating Juliette's strained expression.

He stood looking down at her, his hands closing into fists at his sides, trying to crush the aching pity and tenderness raging through him. He didn't *want* to feel like this. It wasn't at all what he had planned for her. He could permit himself lust, amusement, even respect for a worthy opponent, but not this. Mother of God, he had wanted her for five long years, and he would not let this softness rob him of her.

"Let me do it again," she whispered.

He could see the shimmer of her eyes in the moonlit darkness, and he knew he couldn't leave her until those eyes closed and she fell into a normal sleep. He sat down beside her on the bed, every muscle and tendon of his body stiff and unyielding.

Merde, he didn't want this.

"I can do it right this time. I have to go to the abbey and do it again."

Her eyes were moistly brilliant now, and the agony in them woke a pain that echoed with unbearable intensity through Jean Marc.

He couldn't let it go on.

"I'm afraid you're right." He gently stroked an unruly curl back from Juliette's temple and whispered, "Very well, *ma petite*, we'll go back to the abbey and do it again."

"But I have to get to my work, Mademoiselle Juliette," Robert protested. "I've been sitting on this bench so long my bones are melting into it."

"Hush, Robert, I'm almost finished." Juliette added a little more shadow to the seamed lines fanning his eyes. "What's more important? A painting that will give you immortality or doing your chores?"

"Marie would say my chores," Robert said dryly. "Keeping the house clean and putting meals on the table with no other servants in the house are not easy tasks."

"But you've both done splendidly. I'll help you with your chores as soon as we're finished here." Juliette grinned as she looked at him over the easel. "I suppose you'll be glad to see us all gone and the house closed again."

"Of course he will," Jean Marc answered for Robert as he strolled down the path toward them. "You can escape now, Robert."

"*Merci.*" Robert scrambled to his feet and hurried away from them toward the house.

"You shouldn't have done that." Juliette stiffened with wariness, her gaze avoiding Jean Marc's. "I would have let him go soon. What are you doing here anyway? Have you nothing better to do than take strolls in the garden and interrupt my work?"

"And a pleasant good morning to you also." Jean Marc stopped before the easel and tilted his head in consideration. "You've caught his likeness. It's quite adequate."

"Adequate?" she asked, stung. "I don't do 'adequate' work. It's excellent."

"But boring."

"*Boring.*"

"There's no sweep, no daring. As I remember, you didn't used to be afraid to paint the truth."

"This *is* truth. This is Robert."

"And you obviously chose him because he's a safe subject and would cause you no difficulty." Jean Marc shrugged. "You shouldn't feel bad. Many artists prefer to paint the ordinary rather than challenge themselves."

"I'm not 'many artists'." Juliette glared at him as she set her brush down. "You don't know what you're talking about. I do challenge myself."

"Do you?" Jean Marc sat down on the marble bench across from her. "I've seen no sign of it of late. You've avoided the greatest challenge to your skill."

"You?" A sudden eagerness tempered the anger in her expression. "Will you let me paint you? If you posed for me, I might be able to—"

"Not me." He met her gaze. "The abbey. You haven't painted what happened at the abbey."

"No!" She recoiled as if he had struck her. "I don't want to paint what happened at the abbey. It was ugly."

"And you're afraid of ugliness." He nodded. "It's entirely understandable."

"No, I'm *not* afraid. I've never been afraid. I just don't want to paint it."

"Is it that you don't want to paint it or you don't know if you can? Such a subject could be done only by a master."

"I could do it!"

"But you're afraid to try."

"No, I'm not afraid. Why should I be afraid?" She drew a deep, shaky breath. "I wish you'd go away. You're making me very angry."

"Am I? You showed a great deal of promise as a youngster. It's a shame you've chosen to become only mediocre."

"I'm not afraid and I'm not mediocre. Why should I paint something no one wants to see?"

"Is that your excuse?" He leaned forward, his intent gaze holding her own. "*I* want to see what happened at the abbey, Juliette. I want to see what you saw."

Her cheeks were flushed and her eyes glittering with tears as she thrust aside the easel and snatched up the sketchbook sitting on the bench beside her. "You like to see blood? I'll show you." She picked up the pen with a shaking hand and began to sketch with feverish, reckless strokes. "You want to see rape? I'll show you. You want to see death? I'll show you. I'll show you. I'll show you . . ."

In a few minutes she finished the sketch, threw it aside, and began another. She finished that sketch and began another. The sketches flew from her pen like dead leaves drifting from a tortured, twisted branch.

Jean Marc sat quietly watching as the pile of sketches grew around her. Her face was set in terrible lines of stress and her eyes glittered wildly. Every now and then she muttered something unintelligible, but he knew she wasn't speaking to him. He doubted if she knew he was there any longer.

Late morning marched into afternoon and then faded into the first blue hours of twilight, and still the pile of sketches grew on the bench beside her.

Finally, Juliette stopped, staring numbly down at the sketch in her hands.

"Are you finished?" Jean Marc rose to his feet and walked over to the bench where she was sitting. "May I see them?"

Juliette nodded.

Jean Marc began to leaf through the sketches on the bench. She had shown him, he thought grimly. She had shown him rape and murder and unsurpassed brutality. *Dieu*, how had she survived it?

He put the pile of sketches back on the bench. "May I see that last one in your hand?"

She thrust the sketch at him and closed her eyes.

"Who's the kneeling woman?"

"Sister Mary Magdalene, the Reverend Mother."

"And the man with the revolutionary bonnet and the scythe?"

"I don't know his name." She shuddered. "Butcher. He was the butcher."

"And this is you?"

She opened her eyes. "Yes. Me. The butcher."

"You said the man with the scythe was the butcher."

"He was." She wrapped her arms around herself to still her trembling. "And I was."

He went still. "They made you kill the nuns?"

"Yes."

Jean Marc was silent a moment. "How?"

"The blood."

"What blood?"

"The blood in the chalice. I thought no one would do anything so bestial. I didn't know. I didn't know."

"Wouldn't do what, Juliette?"

"Sister Mathilde. They brought her before the tribunal table and made her kneel before me. She was so frightened. I could see how frightened she was. Dupree said I had to toast his fine Marseilles and their work at the abbey. Someone brought the chalice of the Holy Sacrament from the chapel." She stopped and moistened her dry lips. "I said no."

"And then?"

"They cut Sister Mathilde's throat." Her eyes shut again. "And they filled the chalice with her blood. Dupree said I had to drink it and I said no again.

"They brought Sister Mary Magdalene before the tribunal and told me if I didn't drink it they would kill her." Her eyes opened and she stared blindly ahead. "I drank the blood but it made me sick and I threw it up. They killed the Reverend Mother and filled the cup again. They brought another nun to kneel before the tribunal. She was crying for me to help her. I tried to help her. I tried and tried but I kept getting sick. I should have been able to do it. I should have been stronger. All I had to do was what they asked and I still couldn't do it." The tears began to run down her cheeks. "They killed them. Six. I couldn't do it and they killed them."

"No." Jean Marc scooped her up and cradled her in his arms. "Shh, it wasn't your fault. They would have killed them anyway. You know that, Juliette."

Her tears fell silently. "I know. I do know." She leaned her cheek wearily against his chest and whispered, "Sometimes."

Jean Marc rocked her back and forth, his palm pressing her face into his shirt. Mother of God, the pain she must have suppressed in these last weeks. She had cared for Catherine, managed the household, tried to manage all of them, and all the while carrying this hideous burden of horror and guilt within her.

She stayed in his arms a long time, clinging to him like a small child.

Dusk had become evening when she finally lifted her head and looked at him. "This was a very cruel thing you did to me, Jean Marc."

"Yes."

"But I don't think you did it for a cruel reason." She slipped from his lap to the bench and wiped her damp cheeks with the back of her hand. "So I shall forgive you."

A smile tugged at his lips. It was evident she was rapidly putting this period of vulnerability behind her. "I'm very grateful."

"You lie." She straightened the lace fichu of her gown. "You don't care if I forgive you or not." She gazed up at him. "But since you made me give you all these sketches, I think you owe me something in return."

"You wish to charge me for the sketches?"

"Would you give free passage on one of your ships or a loan without interest?"

This time he made no attempt to smother his smile. "I wouldn't even consider it."

"Then you must pay me." She nodded triumphantly. "You must pose for me. I'll paint you and find out all *your* secrets."

He frowned. "I'm too busy for that nonsense now."

"I'll wait for a time that's more convenient for you. You promise?"

He started to chuckle. Only Juliette would try to wrest a victory from her moment of weakness. "Very well." He hurriedly qualified his statement. "When I have time."

"Good."

He tapped the stack of sketches. "Since I've agreed to pay for them, I assume all these sketches are now my possessions?"

She avoided looking at the sketches. "Of course."

"Then I may do what I wish with them?"

"Certainly."

"Tear them up."

Her gaze flew to his face. "What?"

"I want you to tear them up."

"All of them?"

"All of them."

"Why?"

He smiled faintly. "A whim. Humor me." He handed her the first sketch. "Tear it up."

She took the sketch gingerly and tore it lengthwise.

"Again."

She tore the sketch horizontally and dropped the shredded pieces on the path.

He handed her another sketch. "Tear it up."

She ripped the sketch in half and then again.

She reached for the next sketch and ripped it in smaller pieces.

When all the sketches had been shredded she sat looking down at the bits of paper on the ground for a long moment. "You confuse me, Jean Marc."

"Because I indulge my whims?"

"No, because I think perhaps you've been very kind to me and I wonder why. Sometimes it's as if you're two different men . . ." Juliette didn't wait for a reply but jumped to her feet. "I've done as you wished me to do, and now we must go see if Marie has some supper for us. You've already made me miss dinner." She turned away and started down the path to the house.

Jean Marc rose to his feet and caught up with her in four strides. "May I remind you that I've had no meal either? I'd think you'd be a little—"

"A package, Monsieur Andreas." Robert met them as they reached the door and handed Jean Marc a small cloth-wrapped object. "A young boy brought it to the front door a few minutes ago."

"Thank you, Robert. Will you tell Marie we're ready for supper?" He slipped the cloth from around the package.

Juliette took a step closer and peered down at the object he removed from the wrapping. "What is it?"

"It appears to be a fan."

It was a cheap paper fan like the ones Nana Sarpelier had been selling at the café. Juliette took the fan and unfurled it. Painted on the coarse brownish-white surface was the exterior of a café on which a sign portraying a slyly smiling cat waved jauntily in the breeze.

"She wants us to come to the café." Juliette's eyes were shining with excitement as she turned away. "You'd better ring for Robert and tell him we won't be home for supper. I'll go change my gown and put on my wig."

"We don't have to go tonight."

"But why shouldn't we?" She looked back at him in surprise. "Why wait?"

He gazed at her in rueful astonishment. A few moments earlier she had been more fragile and vulnerable than he ever seen her, and now she was again ready to grapple with Titans. "No reason. You said you were hungry."

"Don't be foolish." The words trailed behind her as she hurried away from him. "We can do both. That Raymond person at the café said he made an excellent lamb stew."

"You mentioned two million livres." Nana Sarpelier spread several fans on the table. "We went to a great deal of trouble to accommodate you. We want the money before I give you the information."

"That's absurd. I can't give you the money until I sell the—" Juliette stopped and then continued. "The object you spoke to the queen about. That's the purpose of all this. You'll have to trust me to give you the money later."

"Trust?"

"The queen trusts me. Why shouldn't you?"

Nana Sarpelier looked gravely at Juliette for a moment before she began to gather up her fans.

"Tell us," Jean Marc said.

Nana stood up and tossed the fans back on her tray.

"The name," Juliette urged.

Nana hesitated, then picked up the tray. "Celeste de

Clement." The next moment she was weaving her way through the tables of the café.

Juliette sank back in her chair, stunned.

Jean Marc lifted the goblet to his lips. "Your mother. Interesting." He took another sip of wine. "And regrettable."

"I didn't think—" Juliette stopped and lifted her hand to her lips. "Why would she do it?"

"Steal the Wind Dancer? I'd think it would pose a temptation to almost anyone. She had the opportunity and seized it."

"No, that's not what I meant." Juliette shook her head. "Of course she'd take it. But why would she stay here in Paris and become the mistress of that merchant if she had the Wind Dancer?"

"Because she knew she wouldn't keep the Wind Dancer if anyone knew she'd stolen it. The assembly wanted it very badly at the time."

"Then she had it all along at that house on the rue de Richelieu?"

"Presumably."

"I . . . don't think so. She said something about her papers . . ." Juliette's brow knotted in thought as she tried to remember her mother's exact words on the night of the massacre. "She said to get papers to leave Paris she'd had to bargain with Marat. She said, 'That pig thinks I'll send it to him but he'll find I'm not so easily cowed—'" She leaned forward. "Don't you see? Send. Not give. She was going to send him the price of the papers when she reached her destination, and what price would be big enough to appease Marat?"

"The Wind Dancer." Jean Marc leaned forward. "Which evidently she never intended to send to him. When did she have the opportunity to take the Wind Dancer out of the country?"

Juliette tried to think. "The sisters told me they'd heard my mother had left Paris for a trip to her home in Andorra a few months after the queen was forced to leave Versailles." Juliette smiled crookedly. "They were very gentle when they told me. They thought she'd abandoned me."

"But she returned to Paris. Why?"

"She hates Andorra and thinks Paris and Versailles are the only civilized cities in Europe. Perhaps she thought the clock would turn back and the king would regain power."

"It's possible. There was a great sympathy for the royal family at that time."

"But no more." Juliette shivered as she remembered the threatening gloom of the Tower. She tried to focus her thoughts on the problem at hand. "Then she must have left the statue at Andorra and come back to Paris. If the queen did regain power, my mother could return the Wind Dancer and be showered with favor for her loyalty. If not, she could return to Andorra, pry the jewels from the statue, and discreetly sell them. Either way she'd have what she wanted. She didn't realize she'd have to bargain for her life with Marat."

"A bargain on which she obviously reneged."

Juliette wearily shook her head. "I don't understand it. She's not an honorable woman but she's really quite shrewd. She must have known Marat was a dangerous man to cheat." Her hand shook as she brushed a pale golden tendril from her temple.

Jean Marc's gaze narrowed on Juliette's face. Dark shadows smudged the delicate flesh beneath her eyes and made them appear enormous in her thin face. In spite of her protest, the knowledge her mother had betrayed the queen had jolted Juliette and reliving the events at the abbey earlier in the day was enough to try anyone's stamina.

Jean Marc threw a few francs on the table and stood up. "Come along. We're leaving."

She looked up, startled. "But we have to discuss this. I'm not giving up. Don't you want to get the Wind Dancer back?"

"I have every intention of getting it back." He pulled her to her feet, bundled her cloak about her shoulders, and propelled her toward the door. "I'll not have my appetite whetted and then leave the table hungry."

"Then we should decide what we're going to do."

"Tomorrow will do as well."

"No, I want to—"

"Juliette." Jean Marc opened the door. "I'm tired and I'm irritated and I can see a mountain of problems on the horizon for which I have no solution. If you don't need your rest, I most certainly do. We'll discuss the matter in the morning."

She gazed at him for a moment and then, to his surprise, surrendered. "Oh, very well, if you're that weary." A sudden twinkle appeared in her eyes. "I keep forgetting you've passed your thirtieth natal day." She preceded him toward the waiting carriage. "You can sleep and I'll lie in bed and plan what we're going to do."

"Thank you." Jean Marc made no attempt to veil the irony in his tone as he helped her into the carriage. He'd wager Juliette was so exhausted she'd be asleep the minute her head rested on the pillow, while he would have to remain awake and make sure the release she'd received this afternoon would be sufficient to keep her from again running barefoot through the streets of Paris. Dear God, how had he wandered so far from his original intentions? The role of seducer suited him much better than father confessor and guardian.

Well, he'd have more than enough to occupy his mind while he kept the vigil. How the devil was he going to get the statue from Celeste de Clement?

"I told her the name. I decided it would do us no good to be stubborn about it," Nana whispered as she rubbed her cheek lazily in the hollow of William's naked shoulder. "Was I wrong?"

"No. We need the other pieces of the puzzle."

"She may not act on it. The woman is her mother."

"Familial love doesn't always triumph in this world."

The bitterness in his voice startled her and she was silent a moment and then asked quietly, "What did the last message from Monsieur say?"

She could feel the muscles of his shoulder tense beneath her cheek.

"William?"

"He grows impatient."

"We're all impatient. Is that all?"

"No."

"What else?"

William turned over on his side. "Go to sleep, Nana."

"I've decided we must leave immediately for Andorra," Juliette announced as she came into the breakfast room to find Jean Marc at the table the next morning. "If we wait, my mother will start to sell off the jewels."

Jean Marc took a bite of croissant. "And have you also decided how it's to be done? Perhaps you've forgotten that we could go to war with Spain at any moment. As Andorra lies just over the border, we may have both the Spaniards *and* the French with which to contend."

"That's why we must involve François and Danton again." She frowned. "They may be reluctant to help us, you know. François wasn't pleased about my going to the Temple. However, we must think of some way to persuade them to our way of thinking."

"*Our* way of thinking?" Jean Marc lifted a brow. "You seem to have made all the decisions without my participation."

"Well, someone had to do something. Why are you just sitting there? I've told you what we have to do. Let's go to see Danton."

"Sit down and have your breakfast." Jean Marc took another bite of croissant. "I have no intention of going anywhere this morning."

"But, Jean Marc, we have to—"

"Pardon, Monsieur Andreas." Robert stood in the doorway. "Monsieur Etchelet and Monsieur Danton have arrived and I've shown them into the Gold Salon as you instructed."

"Thank you, Robert." Jean Marc patted his lips with his napkin, placed it on the table, and rose to his feet.

"Please tell Marie to begin packing Mademoiselle's clothing."

"Everything?"

"Everything." Jean Marc came around the table and took Juliette's arm. "She won't be returning."

Juliette was gazing at him in bewilderment. "Why are they here?"

"Because I sent for them." Jean Marc propelled her toward the arched doorway. "Come along. It's impolite to keep them waiting, and I'm sure an important man like Danton isn't accustomed to being sent for before breakfast."

"But why did you send for them?"

"Because last night I made a few decisions myself." He threw open the doors of the Gold Salon. "*Bonjour,* gentlemen. Thank you for coming."

Both men turned to face them.

"You knew we'd come," Danton said. "Besides the lure of curiosity at the urgency of your invitation, you held out the welcome news we're at last about to bid farewell to Citizeness de Clement. We've obtained two passes for the lady. I'm almost afraid to hope our third attempt will bear fruit."

"Her valises are being packed even as we speak." Jean Marc smiled. "But please be seated. There's no use your being uncomfortable while—"

"You pick our pockets?" François finished dryly. "You want something, Andreas."

"Of course, but I'm not going to pick your pockets." Jean Marc paused. "I want to put something in them."

"You've already put a great deal of money in my pockets," François said. "I don't require more."

"I've included you in the discussion only as a matter of courtesy." Jean Marc turned toward Danton. "It's you I wish to tempt, Danton."

"Indeed?"

"You're a reasonable man who knows most things in this life have a price."

"Are you trying to bribe me?"

"Yes," Jean Marc admitted calmly. "But not in any

way that would compromise your moral position as a member of the convention. I'm not fool enough to try that again. However, you're extremely worried about the Jacobin domination in the convention. How would you like me to buy enough votes from the uncommitted members to give you the balance you need?"

Danton's gaze narrowed on Jean Marc's face. "It would be expensive. You must want a great deal in return."

"I want papers that will get Juliette and me through the barriers to Vasaro." Jean Marc paused. "And I want another document designating me as a special agent of the republic with powers *extraordinaire*. I want to have no trouble either getting one of my ships cleared out of Cannes or with any army units I might encounter along the border."

"Border?"

"I'm making a trip into Spain."

"For what purpose?"

"It's private in nature and offers no threat to the security of the republic."

"Where in Spain?"

"Andorra. I'll probably be there no more than a week or two and then return to Cannes."

"Providing you can escape Spain without getting a musket ball in your gut," Danton said grimly.

"I'd leave instructions with my man of business, Bardot, to give you the required assistance. Then my demise would not affect you one way or the other."

"You won't tell me why you're going to Andorra?"

"Why should I?"

A thoughtful frown creased Danton's forehead as he looked at Jean Marc. He turned abruptly and walked toward the door. "I'll let you know."

"When? My business has a certain urgency."

"Later today."

François paused before following Danton out the door to gaze at Jean Marc and Juliette. "You go first to Vasaro?"

"Yes." Jean Marc cast a sly glance at Juliette. "I have some baggage to drop off."

"I'm not baggage," she said indignantly. "And I'll not be—"

"Just keep her out of Paris," François said. "This has gone on too long." He didn't wait for a reply but left the room.

Juliette turned to Jean Marc, and to his surprise did not continue her harangue. "You did that very well. Do you think Danton will give you what you need?"

"It depends on how badly he wants a balanced convention."

"He let himself be known as one of the butchers of the September massacres to assure it." She gazed at him curiously. "What will you do if he doesn't agree?"

"Think of something else." Jean Marc smiled sardonically. "Though you perceive me as ancient, my maturity does give me some advantages. It allows me to draw upon experience and make certain choices."

"Why didn't you tell me you'd summoned them here?"

"Did you give me an opportunity? As I remember, you were too busy telling me what to do to listen to me."

"Oh, you should have just told me to be quiet. Catherine always does." She gazed at him speculatively. "I believe you may be very clever, Jean Marc."

"I'm honored by your praise."

"Well, I must go." She turned and moved toward the door. "If we're to leave for Spain shortly, I must finish Robert's painting today." A smile suddenly lit her face. "And, if we're to stop at Vasaro, I wish to have him go purchase a present for me to take to Catherine."

"Perhaps you didn't understand me. You'll be staying at Vasaro with Catherine. The trip to Spain may be dangerous and I won't have you along."

"We have a bargain. I must get the Wind Dancer for you." She studied him thoughtfully. The morning sunlight pouring into the room touched his black hair with a dark luster and illuminated his bold features with stark clarity, but she could read nothing in his expression save mockery and cool determination. "You're . . . different. You've changed since that first night we went to the Café du Chat." Color flooded her cheeks. "I told you that you'd change your mind about me."

"You're quite correct, I have changed my mind. You've been wounded and I find I can't stomach the thought of risking hurt to you again. Believe me, that discovery astounds me far more than it does you." His lips twisted as he looked at her. "Which is the reason you'll not accompany me to Spain. You have far more chance of being hurt by me than by the Spanish border guards."

"It's because of what I told you about the abbey? I'm not really wounded. I wouldn't let Dupree hurt me." She stared at him defiantly. "And I wouldn't let you hurt me."

"I don't think we'll allow that opportunity to arise. You're going to stay at Vasaro with Catherine."

"Hmm, we'll see." She hurried from the salon.

"What do you think he's after, Georges Jacques?" François asked as he gazed thoughtfully out the window of the carriage at the passing scene.

"I have a few ideas and I think you do too."

François nodded. "It's well known Andreas tried desperately to purchase the Wind Dancer several years ago. I even noticed a portrait of the statue in his salon. Juliette goes to the Temple to speak to the queen. Andreas leaves for Spain." His gaze shifted to Danton's face. "As Andreas doesn't meddle in politics except to benefit himself, I doubt if he's on a mission for the royalists. I'd say he's going after the Wind Dancer."

"And it's a peculiar coincidence that Dupree was also sent on a mission to Andorra at virtually the same time."

"You think Marat knows where the Wind Dancer's to be found?"

Danton shrugged. "I wouldn't want to take the chance of it falling into Marat's hands. He has power and stature enough without being known as the hero who returned the Wind Dancer to the republic."

"And?"

"I *need* those Jacobins curbed."

"You're going to give Andreas what he wants."

"Oh, there was no question about that. But I'm also going to give him something he doesn't want." He grinned. "You."

François gaze flew to Danton's face. "Me?"

"I believe it's my responsibility to keep Andreas safe on this dangerous journey. And who could better assure his safety than you? You're not only equipped for the task by your professional talents, but you're Basque and know the Pyrenees well."

"You wish me to go with him?"

Danton nodded. "And, at the proper time, confiscate the Wind Dancer in the name of the republic and return it to me."

"And you'll reap the benefit of the bounty of prestige Marat's seeking."

"Certainly. Who deserves it more?"

"No one." François gazed unseeingly out the window again. "I may be gone for months. Can you do without my services?"

"Obtaining the Wind Dancer would be worth doing without them for a decade. And I may be leaving for the front shortly anyway. Will you go?"

François was silent for a long time before he finally said, "Yes, I'll go with Andreas."

FIFTEEN

Vasaro!

A curving driveway fringed with lemon and lime trees and paved with stone and cork chips led up the hill to the large two-story stone manor house. Immediately behind the mansion Catherine could glimpse a stable and carriage house and several hundred yards beyond several long stone buildings. For the first time since they had left Paris she felt a tiny stirring of excitement beneath the numb bewilderment that had enveloped her on the long trip to Vasaro.

She leaned forward to look out the window of the carriage and inhaled sharply at the sheer beauty of the scene. Sloping fields surrounded the house on all sides and in those fields grew flowers of seemingly every hue and description. Blossoms of misty blue lavender, golden jasmine, creamy tuberoses, and vivid orange-scarlet geraniums waved gently in the breeze, and still farther away she could see other fields of flowers she couldn't even identify.

Philippe nodded at the lush scarlet flowers they were passing. "The geraniums are ready for harvesting. They're very rare, you know. Vasaro is the only place in France that grows them. Jean Marc's father had them imported from Algiers as a favor to your mother."

She glanced at him beneath her lashes and then quickly looked away.

"No," he said quietly. "Look at me. It can't go on, Catherine. We've been friends too long for you to hold me in such aversion."

"I . . . don't hold you in aversion." She slowly turned her gaze to meet his own. Straight and golden and bronze, in his way he was as beautiful as the fields of flowers beyond the window. So beautiful. The color flew to her cheeks. "I don't remember any of it," she whispered. "You'd think I'd never be able to forget a place as beautiful as Vasaro, wouldn't you? Those fields of flowers are—"

"Catherine, you've been avoiding speaking to me for the entire journey. Will you not let me beg your forgiveness? I know what I did was unpardonable."

"Please, I don't want to talk about it."

"Then we'll speak no more but will you let me help—show you Vasaro? It belongs to you now, but I love it too."

All this beauty belonged to her. She gazed out of the window and felt again that stirring of excitement mixed with something else too evanescent to define.

This was her property, her land. Her mother had been the mistress of Vasaro and her mother's mother before her. They had beheld this glory, wandered in those fields, and spent their years helping it to flourish. Now she was there to take her place in caring for the blossoms of Vasaro.

"Catherine?"

She gazed at him absently. "If it's time to harvest, why are there no pickers in the fields?"

A slow smile broke over his face. "They've gone back to their village. It's over that far hill." He gestured toward a rolling hill to the west of the manor. "It's late in the afternoon and it's always best to pick flowers early in the morning, when the scent is the strongest. They usually start picking at dawn and continue until just after noon."

"Oh." She looked out into the fields again. "Everything is blooming. In Paris the flowers will die soon."

"Here, the climate is such that there are always blossoms. Not the same ones, of course. There's a season for every variety."

"And we grow them all?"

"Almost. Vasaro has the most fertile ground on the coast, and it extends for miles."

"I see." Catherine leaned back in the carriage and breathed deeply. Fresh-turned earth and the heady scent of geraniums and lavender drifted to her in an intoxicating cloud. "I don't see how the scent can be any stronger than this."

"At dawn. You should smell it at dawn."

"Should I?" She gazed out the window again and the stirring came again, stronger this time. Her land. Vasaro.

The carriage stopped at the house.

"This is Manon, Catherine." Philippe gave his hat and gloves to the plump, smiling woman who met them in the flagstoned hall. "We also have three other maids and two cooks besides the stable workers, but Manon has been here supervising the running of the house ever since I first came to Vasaro."

Manon murmured a low greeting and curtsied to Catherine.

"She'll show you to your chamber." Philippe took Catherine's hand and raised it to his lips. "Until supper."

Catherine nodded and followed the servant up the stairs and down the hall. She had no memory at all of this house, and yet she was beginning to feel a growing serenity, a sense of coming home.

Manon opened the door and preceded her into the bedchamber. The room was filled with sunshine, not only the light pouring through the long casement windows across the room but in color. The Aubusson rug spilling across the shining oak floor was patterned with delicate ivory flowers on a green background and the bed and wall hangings were also ivory with a lemon-yellow border. Yellow cushions graced both the window seat and the armchair at the elegant rosewood desk across the room.

"I'll unpack as soon as your bags are brought up, Mademoiselle." Manon strode briskly across the room and threw open the casement windows.

Scent again. Overpowering fragrance swept into the room.

"Monsieur Philippe always dresses for dinner whether he has guests or not," Manon said. "Shall I send Bettine to help you with your bath and dress your hair?"

"Yes, if you please." Catherine moved slowly across the room to stand before the window. The breeze blew gently, lifting the tendrils of hair that had escaped the confinement of her bun. Stretched before her were fields of flowers, groves of lime and lemon trees, a vineyard nestled beneath a far hill, and in the distance a glimpse of steep, jagged mountains.

"Is the scent too strong?" Manon asked anxiously. "We who live here hardly notice it, but visitors claim it makes their heads ache. I could close the window."

"No, don't close it." As she looked down at the fields of flowers that seemed to stretch into forever, Catherine again had the strong feeling of homecoming. "I'm not a visitor. I belong here. I . . . like the scent."

"No!"

Catherine sat bolt upright in the darkness.

She was trembling, sweating. The tomb. No faces. She was alone.

Dear God, where was Juliette? Juliette had left her alone with the nightmares. Alone with the fear that swelled her heart until she thought it would choke her and churned the black bile into her throat.

She wrapped her arms around herself, panting, trying to shut out the sounds of the tomb. The men's guttural laughter, the tear of fabric, the sound of her own moans.

Bells.

No, that was wrong. There weren't any bells in the tomb.

But there were bells here, fragile silvery threads of sound coming from beyond the open window across the room.

She slowly swung her feet to the floor, stood up, and crossed to look out the window.

A column of men, women, and children straggled down the road, coming from the direction Philippe had indicated as the workers' village.

The first light of dawn broke over the distant field, torching the orange-red blossoms with fire as she threw the casement window open wider and knelt on the cushioned window seat. She gazed curiously at the small throng of people walking down the road. Men and women dressed in coarse clothing and wooden shoes, the women with braided hair or heads covered with shawls or scarves.

Catherine hadn't expected to see the children. Children of all ages staggered sleepily in the wake of the grown-ups, the smallest clinging to their mothers' skirts or carried in their arms.

The pickers followed a cart drawn by two shaggy horses, and as the animals tossed their heads, Catherine heard again those silvery bells fixed to their harnesses. The driver of the cart stopped before a field of geraniums and the throng following him grabbed their large woven baskets from the cart and flowed leisurely into the field. She could catch the sound of laughter and chatter carried on the clear morning air, the scent of the flowers beckoned with irresistible allure.

Catherine turned dreamily away from the window and began to dress.

A short time later she was standing on the small hill overlooking the geranium field. The scent was almost dizzying. She watched the pickers pluck the dew-covered blossoms and toss them into their baskets. Babies were now tottering among the rows of flowers or lying in their own baskets while the older children picked the blossoms with the same amazing speed as their parents.

All except one child. A small boy slightly apart from the rest of the pickers had paused and was staring at her as intently as she was staring at the field below. The boy was no more than nine or ten, with tousled curly black hair, and winged black brows, dressed in a coarse blue shirt and ragged trousers.

She glanced away from him and drew her shawl closer about her as she sat down on the dew-wet grass of the hillock. She was soon absorbed in watching them pick and then throw, pick and throw. Why, there was a curious rhythm to their movements, as if they were moving to the beat of a drum only they could hear. She found herself unconsciously straining to hear the—

"Hello. I'm Michel. Who are you?"

She turned her head to see the curly-haired boy who had been watching her from the field. His face was too thin to qualify him as a beautiful child. His skin was browned to the color of sandstone, and his eyes were the clearest blue she had ever seen. He gazed at her with a gravity that was curiously unchildlike.

"My name is Catherine."

"You're new here." His face lit with a smile of unusual sweetness. "Would you like to pick with me today?"

She was startled. "I wasn't thinking of picking the flowers. I'm here to watch."

"You should come down to the field. It will help you. The rhythm is very good today."

Her gaze flew to his face. Rhythm? It was almost as if he had read her mind. "What do you mean?"

He knelt beside her and dug his hand into the earth. "Here, feel it. Put your hand here."

Bemusedly, she put her palm on the earth.

"Do you feel it?"

"What am I supposed to feel?"

"The earth sighing, trembling, giving up its soul."

"Soul?"

"The flowers. Everything has a soul, you know."

"No, I didn't know. Is that what the priests told you?"

He shook his head. "But I know. Can you feel it?"

She did feel a stirring beneath her palm, but it surely must have come from the breeze disturbing the grasses, their roots slightly moving in the soil. "I don't think so."

He frowned in disappointment. "I thought you might be one of the ones who felt it right away. Don't worry, you'll feel it later."

He was so earnest she found herself smiling at him. "You're so sure that—"

"Run away, Michel."

She looked around to see Philippe dismounting from a chestnut horse a few yards away. She had never seen him dressed so simply in worn brown knee-boots, dark trousers, and a linen shirt unbuttoned at the top to reveal his strong brown throat.

Michel nodded in acknowledgment, but his gaze never left Catherine's face. "You should come with me now. We can pick together."

Philippe smiled indulgently at the child. "This is the mistress of Vasaro, Michel. She won't be picking the blossoms."

Michel turned to Catherine. "Are you sure? I think you'd like it."

"She's sure. Go back to the field, Michel."

The child hesitated, smiled again, and then was running down the hill. As he reached the field, he was met by smiles and laughing remarks, drawn lovingly into the crowd of pickers.

"I was worried when Manon told me you'd left the house so early," Philippe said. "You should have told me you wanted to come to the fields this morning."

"I didn't know I did. I was standing at the window this morning and saw the workers going down the road. . . ." Her gaze was on Michel, who was picking the blossoms with a dexterity that astonished her. "Is he the son of one of those women?"

"Michel?" Philippe shook his head. "He belongs to no one. He was found almost dead by the overseer in one of the rose fields when he was only a day or so old. Evidently, his mother was a picker who gave birth to him in the field and just left him there."

"But how could she do such a thing?" Catherine asked, shocked. "A baby . . ."

"Babies aren't always wanted. The woman probably had no husband." Philippe glanced back at the field. "We think the mother was one of the pickers from Italy. There was a woman big with child who disappeared about the time the baby was found."

"And she never came back?"

He shook his head. "Never."

"Poor boy." Her gaze went back to Michel. "But he seems very happy."

"Why shouldn't he be happy? He has everything he needs. He chooses which family he'll live with every season and I give the picker an extra allowance for his food and lodging."

"That's kind of you."

"Part of managing Vasaro is providing for its workers. It doesn't cost the property a great deal and Michel works as hard as the other pickers."

"Shouldn't he be given schooling?"

"I sent him to the priest to learn his letters, but he refused to go back after a few lessons. He's happier in the fields anyway. He's a little simple."

Her eyes widened. "Nothing seemed wrong with him to me."

Philippe shrugged. "He's not like the other children. Perhaps he was damaged from lying in the field exposed to the weather those two days. You'll see, if you get to know him. He doesn't think like anyone else."

"Working in the fields seems a hard life for a child."

"All the children work. Besides, Michel likes it and doesn't work only in the fields. Sometimes I let him work with the pomades and the essences. Someday he may be of real use to us. I think he has a nose."

"Of course he does."

Philippe chuckled. "No, I mean a nose for scents. Very few people can distinguish precise ingredients in a perfume and how they should be blended to make new scents. It takes a sensitive nose and a certain instinct." He grimaced. "Unfortunately, I have neither. Thank God, a gentleman has no need for them."

"But the boy has this talent?"

"Augustine thinks he does. Augustine's our master perfumer here at Vasaro."

"We make perfumes as well as grow the flowers?"

"Recently we started to create our own scents. Why should the perfumers in Paris reap all the fattest profits?"

She turned to look at him. His expression was more enthusiastic than she had ever seen it. "That was very enterprising of you."

"I love Vasaro," he said simply. "I want it to continue to prosper." He swung up on the horse. "So I'd better be checking on the pickers in the south field. May I escort you back to the house first? You should have your breakfast."

She shook her head. Her gaze returned to the pickers. "I want to stay and watch a little while longer."

He hesitated. "You're sure that—" He stopped, his gaze on her absorbed face. "*Eh bien,* I'll come back and fetch you after the morning's work." He turned the horse and trotted down the hill toward the road.

Catherine scarcely realized he was gone as she watched the rhythm of the pickers as they plucked the blossoms and tossed them into the baskets. Some of the baskets were full now, and the men were carrying them to the waiting cart and dumping them in large casks on the bed of the cart. Then they returned to the field and the rhythm resumed.

"Catherine!"

It was the child, Michel, waving at her from the field, his tanned face alight with laughter, his eyes squinting against the sunlight. She lifted her hand and waved in return.

He was motioning to her. He wanted her to come down to the field.

She hesitated and then shook her head.

Disappointment clouded his face and Catherine felt

a sudden twinge of remorse. What difference did it make if she was the mistress of Vasaro? She jumped to her feet and was halfway down the hill before she had realized she was heading toward the boy. She reached the road, crossed it, and started winding her way through the plants, smiling shyly at the workers who stared at her with an uncertainty equal to her own. She came to the row where Michel was standing.

"You wished to speak to me?"

He smiled and shook his head. "Watch, I'll show you how it's done and then you can do it." He bent down and started to pluck the geraniums again.

"I don't want to—" She *did* want to pick the flowers, she suddenly realized. She wanted to be a part of the rhythm that united the pickers with the plants, to know how the dew-wet blossoms felt in her fingers. She wanted to be a part of Vasaro.

That was why she had been drawn from the house to the field that morning. She had not realized her purpose, but somehow the child had known.

"Tomorrow you must wear a hat. You're not as brown as the other women, so you'll burn." Michel didn't look at her as he quickly plucked the blossoms. "And wooden shoes are best. There's much mud from the dew in the morning. You'll remember?"

"I'll remember." She watched him closely and then began to clumsily pluck the blossoms and toss them into his basket. She was slow at first, but she found the occupation ambivalently both soothing and exhilarating. The work itself was mindless labor and yet the scent of the earth and flowers, the sun warming her skin, the rush of blood through her veins, and the unaccustomed exercise turned her warm and breathless. She didn't know how long she worked beside Michel, but the basket was filled to overflowing with the orange-red geraniums, emptied into the cart and filled again, emptied and filled.

Michel worked in companionable silence beside her, his fingers like the beaks of small birds biting the blossoms from the stems.

She moved down the row to another plant and reached out to find the first flower.

"No." Michel's calloused hand abruptly covered her own. "It's enough. It's time for you to leave now."

She looked at him in surprise.

"The sun's high now and you're beginning to grow very weary."

"No, I feel fine."

"It's time for you to go." His smile touched his face with a special radiance. "You can come back tomorrow. It's a big field and we won't finish today."

"But I want to stay."

"You've already taken what you need from them."

Her brow furrowed in puzzlement. "What?"

"You needed the flowers but you're at peace now. You mustn't take too much or the healing will go away. There's a . . ." He frowned, searching for a word. "Balance."

"Healing?"

He started to pick the geraniums. "Come back tomorrow, Catherine."

She stood staring at him for a moment, uncertain what to do. His words were strange, but they struck a note of rightness deep within her. She turned and walked down the row of denuded plants and then up the hill toward the manor house.

Catherine returned to the geranium field the next day and the day after that. On the fourth day the pickers moved to the field of pink bois de roses and Catherine moved with them. With every day she grew stronger, the rhythm of the work became clearer to her, more serene and better defined. On the fifth day Michel let her stay with the pickers until their workday was ended in the mid-afternoon. Pride and contentment filled her as she and Michel followed the pickers from the field.

"Where do you go when we finish in the fields, Michel?"

"Sometimes I go for walks. If you go past that hill and over two fields you can see the sea." He picked up a rose that had fallen unheeded from one of the baskets, held it to his nose, and breathed in the fragrance. "And sometimes I go to see Monsieur Augustine and he lets me help while he experiments with the essences. Today I go to the shed to help with the maceration."

"Maceration?"

"Taking the scents from the flowers."

"May I go with you?"

"No." Michel started up the road after the other pickers. "Not yet."

"Why not?"

"It would make you sad. It's better that you just pick the flowers for now."

"I could have Monsieur Philippe show me."

He stopped and gave her a troubled glance. "It would make you sad," he repeated. "You don't realize how much they've given to you. Perhaps next week I'll take you. Will you not wait for me?"

Catherine started to object, thought, and finally nodded. "I'll wait." She added firmly, "Until next week, no longer."

The corners of his eyes crinkled as he smiled widely at her. "You're beginning to fight. See how much the flowers have given you?"

She smiled back at him. "And tomorrow I want you to take me to see the sea."

He nodded as he started off at a trot after the straggling column of pickers. "Tomorrow, Catherine." He waved at a tall, gangling boy. "Ho, Donato, wait for me."

She gazed after him affectionately as he caught up with the older boy. At times Michel was a child brimming with mischief and at others he seemed to possess uncanny wisdom. She wasn't sure which Michel she liked better.

"Catherine."

She turned to see Philippe sitting his horse a few yards away. She flushed, her hand rising involuntarily to her perspiring forehead. She was suddenly conscious of the dirt and grass stains soiling her gown and the fact that her single brown braid had pulled free of its binding. "Good afternoon, Philippe. The field will be done tomorrow. Aren't the roses—"

"Don't you think it's enough, Catherine?" he interrupted. "I didn't want to interfere because you seemed so content, but you'll be mistress here someday. You don't want the pickers to remember you as working at their sides, do you?"

"Why not?" She nervously wiped her dirty palms on the skirt of her gown.

"They must have respect for you. Believe me, for them to regard you with such familiarity isn't good for your future position."

"I do believe you, but—" She gazed at him helplessly. "I *want* to do this, Philippe."

He smiled ruefully. His classic features showed fresh beauty. "Then you must do it, of course. Beautiful ladies must always do what they want to do." He bowed. "And does it please you to go back to the house for dinner, Mademoiselle?"

She nodded shyly, drinking in the sight of him, his sweet smile, the sun glinting on his hair, turning it into an aureole of gold. "I'm . . . not beautiful."

"But you are. I have both excellent vision and judgment and can assure you of that truth." He held out his arms. "Come, beautiful lady, I'll give you a ride back to the house."

She was dirty, sweat-stained, and weary and yet, as he looked at her, she suddenly did feel beautiful. Beautiful and clean and as young as the day they had ridden together in that coach to Versailles. She took a step toward him and then another; the next step put her beside the chestnut horse. He bent down, scooped her up in his arms, and set her carefully before him on the horse. He gathered up the reins. "Lean back. You won't fall. I'll hold you."

She sat stiff and unyielding as the horse started to trot down the road. He was holding her gently but a shiver of apprehension went through her. There was nothing to fear, she assured herself. This was Philippe, who was gentle and kind and all that was knightly. Why was she so afraid? She had not been nearly so tense when she had been naked in bed with François Etchelet.

But François Etchelet was gone from her life. Vasaro was her world now. Vasaro and the flowers and the boy Michel and Philippe, who was everything a man should be.

Slowly, tentatively, she leaned back against Philippe's broad chest and forced herself to relax as he urged the horse to a faster pace.

"Who lives in that pretty little house?" Catherine asked idly as she pointed down the steep hill to the right of the cliff.

Michel glanced with disinterest at the small thatched cottage nestled beneath the overhanging cypress trees. "No one. It's only the Maisonette des Fleurs."

"The cottage of flowers?"

"It belongs to Monsieur Philippe. He goes there often." Michel drew her close to the edge of the cliff and pointed in the other direction. "There's the sea. You can just see it today. I'll have to bring you back someday when it's clearer."

Catherine turned immediately in the direction he was pointing, her hand shielding her eyes. It was true the haze misting the mountains and the town of Cannes softened and muted the view of the coastline, but the blinding sunlight on the sea was breathtaking, turning the cobalt blue of the Mediterranean to a shade closer to polished steel. "It's still beautiful. How Juliette would love to paint it." She realized suddenly that whenever she had thought of Juliette of late, the memories had come gently, lovingly, not with the urgency of need but with the pang for the absence of a dear companion. "I wish she'd come to Vasaro. There's so much we could show her, Michel."

"Juliette is your friend?" Michel picked up a branch and tossed it like a javelin over the cliff. "I have many friends."

"I know you do. I have only one."

He smiled. "You have me."

She smiled back at him. "That's true. I have two friends."

"And the rest of the pickers would be your friends, only they know Monsieur Philippe wouldn't like it."

Catherine knew that was true. "It's not that he doesn't want me to be friends with them. He thinks it's not proper for me to work in the fields."

"He doesn't understand the flowers."

"He's a good man," she protested. "And he loves Vasaro."

Michel nodded. "I didn't say he wasn't a good man. All the pickers think he's a kind and just man. I only said he enjoys the flowers but he doesn't understand them." He grabbed Catherine's hand. "Come on, I want to *run*."

She started to laugh helplessly as she let him pull her down the other side of the hill toward the manor house at a dizzying speed. Somewhere along the way he released her hand but she kept on running, enjoying the exhilaration of the warm sun on her face, the wind tearing through her hair, the scent of bergamot in her nostrils.

She hadn't run like this since that night at the abbey when she'd— Her pace faltered as the memories of that last night came back to her. The muscles of her stomach clenched, knotted, and then suddenly eased. That night of horror was gone. Nothing could be more different from this lovely afternoon on Vasaro. That hideousness could never touch Vasaro and its people.

And if it did, she would deal with it. She would destroy it.

The fierce emotion accompanying that last thought startled her.

"Catherine, you're falling behind," Michel called, glancing mischievously over his shoulder.

"No, I'm not. You're wrong. I'm forging ahead." She sprinted toward him feeling young and strong enough to run to Paris and back. "I'll race you to the geranium fields!"

"I told you that you'd be sad." Michel's anxious gaze searched Catherine's stricken face as she watched the man empty the basket of bois de roses into the soupy mixture in the large caldron. "There's nothing to be sad about. You don't understand."

"They're dying."

"It's the maceration," Michel said gently. "They're giving up their souls. Don't you see that it's better this way? If the flowers had died naturally in the fields, they would have returned to the earth immediately, but this way they live longer. The perfume can survive a long time. Not always, of course, but Monsieur Augustine says some Egyptian perfumes have lasted for a thousand years and I myself have seen perfumed leather treated forty years ago that still has a strong scent. The blossoms die but their souls live on."

The delicate pink blossoms lay quivering on the gray-white surface of the mixture in the pot and then lost all color immediately as the brawny woman minding the caldron stirred them beneath the surface with her long wooden spatula. Catherine had never really thought of the picking of the flowers as killing them, but here the destruction was clear.

Michel tugged at her hand. "I'll show you." He led her across the long shed to a table where a row of stoneware crocks brimming with the thick mixture had been set. "This is the pomade. Smell."

Catherine bent her head and breathed deeply. Bois de roses, alive again, fragrant with the same scent they had borne in the fields.

"You see?"

He seemed so full of anxiety that Catherine quickly nodded and smiled. "I see."

He looked relieved. "Now, you can sit over there and watch me work. You don't want to do this, do you?"

She shook her head as she sat down on a low stool by the window. She could accept the need for the maceration but she had no desire to change those fresh, lovely blossoms into bleached, wilted corpses.

All the windows were thrown wide, but it was still suffocatingly hot in the long work shed. Four separate caldrons steamed over wood fires in the room. Beside every caldron lay a huge pile of blossoms, and each pot was attended by a man or a woman with a wooden spatula.

"What is that soupy mixture?" she asked Michel as he shoveled more blossoms into the caldron.

"Melted beef tallow and pork lard. Monsieur Philippe buys only the finest quality fat."

In spite of her initial repulsion, she found she soon became fascinated by the process. This work, too, had its own rhythm, and the more blossoms poured into the creamy oil, the more fragrant the oil became. When the soupy oil became too thick, it was strained swiftly through a sieve, freeing it of the blossoms that had already yielded their perfume and making room for the fresh blossoms. The refuse was then steeped in boiling water and put through a screw press to wring out the last drops and then a new flood of blossoms fluttered down into the greasy soup in the caldron.

"How long does this go on?"

"Days sometimes. Until the oil can absorb no more scent." Michel poured more rose blossoms into the caldron. "Then it's strained one more time and goes into the stoneware crocks. They're sealed and put down in the cellar."

"Is the pomade what Monsieur Augustine works with to make his perfume?"

He shook his head. "No, that's an *essence absolue.*"

"What's the difference?"

"I'll show you later." His brow furrowed with concentration as he looked down into the fat in the caldron. "It has to go through the sieve again."

Michel was always showing her something, she thought with tender amusement. The way to the sea, how to pluck the blossoms , the rhythm of the pickers in the fields. He never spoke when he could demonstrate. He never told her anything she could learn by herself.

But in future this maceration was one part of the duties of governing Vasaro she would gladly leave to Philippe.

"I'm worried about Juliette, Philippe." Catherine lifted her goblet of wine to her lips. "Haven't you heard anything from Paris?"

"I sent word to Jean Marc when we first arrived, but I haven't received a reply. You shouldn't be anxious about Juliette. You know Jean Marc will keep her safe."

But Catherine had thought the Abbaye de la Reine was impregnable from harm too. She shivered and set the crystal goblet down on the table. "We should never have left her in Paris. I should have made her come with us."

Philippe chuckled. "Force Juliette?"

"She's not entirely immovable." Catherine wrinkled her nose. "One must be very stubborn and keep at her. I don't know why I didn't go after her when she jumped out of the carriage."

"You weren't well yourself."

Catherine looked down into the depths of her wine. It was difficult to realize she was the same hurt, shattered woman who had left Paris almost a month earlier. She was not that woman now, nor was she the uncertain girl who had been ravished at the abbey. Vasaro had changed her into someone else entirely. "Yes, I remember." She looked up with a smile. "But now I'm quite well and we must think of Juliette. Will you write to Jean Marc and tell him he must send Juliette to us at once?"

"And what if she refuses to come?"

"Then I'll have to return to Paris to fetch her," Catherine said quietly. "Juliette's in danger in Paris. I won't have that, Philippe."

He smiled and raised his glass in a silent toast. "I'll write to Jean Marc tomorrow. I refuse to do without your presence at Vasaro now that I've become accustomed to it."

A familiar warmth fluttered within her as he smiled at her across the table. His blue eyes shimmered in the candlelight, reflecting all that sung of sweetness, gaiety, and beauty. She had become accustomed to him, too, her worship gradually deepening into something more comfortable, yet that tremulous uncertainty remained whenever he smiled at her.

She swiftly lowered her gaze to veil her eyes but her hand shook as she once more lifted the goblet to her lips. "I've been thinking about asking the priest to come to Vasaro one day a week and teach some of the pickers' children their letters."

"He won't come. He says teaching the peasants makes them discontent with their lot," Philippe said. "And I agree, Catherine. What use will they have for it?"

"There's always use for knowledge."

He shook his head. "It's a mistake."

"Then it's one I intend to make." Catherine saw him frown and went on quickly. "I do value your opinion, Philippe. I'm sorry if I distressed you."

Philippe's expression softened. "The priest will refuse to come. You'll have to find someone else to teach them."

"It doesn't have to be right away. We'll find someone."

"As long as you don't give the task to me." Philippe grimaced. "I have no head for learning, much less for teaching."

All was well between them again, Catherine thought, relieved. "One cannot do everything perfectly. You manage Vasaro superbly."

"Because I love it here." His gaze met hers. "As you do, Catherine. I never knew how much I missed sharing how I felt about Vasaro until you came."

She nodded, glowing with warmth. Vasaro and Philippe. She was learning new and wonderful things about both of them every day.

"Essence absolue." Michel smiled triumphantly at Catherine across Monsieur Augustine's small laboratory.

At Monsieur Augustine's request Michel had fetched a jar of jasmine pomade from the cellar, warmed it in a covered dish, diluted it with recycled spirits, and stirred and washed the pomade. Then he had returned it to the cellar to cool, and when the alcohol separated from the oil of the pomade, he drained it into a tiny bottle. "Smell." He thrust the bottle under her nose. "Perfume!"

The fragrance was pungent, acrid, no longer sweet. "That's not perfume."

"It's the essence. Like Vasaro is the essence." He filtered the perfumed alcohol through a gauze, then distilled it in a copper alembic over a slow flame. What remained was an even tinier quantity of light-colored liquid whose odor was even more incredibly strong and unpleasant.

"Terrible," Catherine said, making a face.

"Ah, but wait." Michel carefully poured a single drop into a crock containing a quart of alcohol and gently stirred it.

"Jasmine!" Suddenly the entire room was swimming with the scent of jasmine. Not just one flower, but an entire field of jasmine.

"You see, it's a circle. The scent of the earth, the blossoms, the scent of the blossoms, the essence, the scent again."

"With Vasaro as the *essence absolue*."

Michel nodded. "And you don't feel so sad about the maceration now that you know the scent is born again? The hurt only made it stronger than ever." His worried gaze was on her face. "You understand, Catherine?"

She smiled. "I understand, Michel. Stronger than ever." She affectionately watched him as he sealed the tiny vial and carried it carefully over to Monsieur Augustine's long table to set it beside the other similar vials in readiness for the master perfumer.

The sea was deep blue today and the mountains looked so close Catherine felt she could reach out and scoop up a handful of the snow crowning them. She leaned back against a huge rock on the cliff and sighed with contentment. Beauty like this was also *essence absolue*, spreading in magical circles to touch everyone who gazed at it.

"Why did you stop going to the priest for lessons, Michel?"

He shrugged. "I didn't like him."

"Learning is good. You should have kept going to him anyway as long as Monsieur Philippe was willing to pay."

"He kept saying I was a child of sin and my mother was a whore."

Catherine felt a surge of anger. "You didn't believe him?"

"No, I knew my mother was a flower picker and I have no more sin than anyone else. But it made me unhappy."

She said impulsively, "Will you let me teach you? I'm not as wise as a priest but—"

"You're much wiser, because you understand the flowers." Michel thought for a moment before an eager smile lit his face. "It would help me to know how to write. Then I could put down the mixes for the perfumes and not have to rely on Monsieur Augustine. He's a kind man but he thinks only of his own perfumes."

"Tomorrow night come to the manor and we'll begin."

A flush of pleasure tinted Michel's tanned cheeks. "You're sure Monsieur Philippe will let you?"

"Why should he mind? He told me himself your nose would someday be valuable to Vasaro."

He glanced away from her and said in a low voice, "He doesn't like you to spend time with me, you know."

"Nonsense."

He shook his head. "He doesn't like—" He was silent a moment and then continued. "I think he finds me . . . unpleasant."

She stared at him in astonishment. "You're mistaken." Yet she had a sudden memory of Philippe's expression of uneasiness that first morning he'd been discussing Michel. "Perhaps he needs to get to know you. Come to the house at six tomorrow evening."

A radiant smile banished Michel's frown. "Will you teach me to read the books on perfume in Monsieur Augustine's cabinet?"

"Of course, and any I can find at the manor. I'm sure your interest will help—" She broke off as her gaze fell on the small thatched cottage under the lime trees. "Look, that's Philippe's horse!" The chestnut was tied to the tree beside the door of the cottage Michel had called the Maisonette des Fleurs. "He must be inside. Let's go see him." She started running down the steep hill toward the cottage. "Come along, Michel, we'll just wish him a good day."

"No!" Michel's voice was sharp, but she paid no attention. Michel was always worried about offending Philippe, but even if he was busy he wouldn't mind them stopping by for a moment.

"Catherine, no! He won't like it!"

She knocked and then threw open the door. "Philippe, why didn't you tell me you were—"

She stopped in shock.

Naked. Philippe was crouching naked on a flower-strewn pallet, his hips moving in a sickeningly familiar manner.

She heard Philippe mutter a curse as he looked up and saw her.

The young woman beneath him cried out, her hips surging upward. Lenore. The woman's name was Lenore. Catherine had often seen her picking in the fields and thought what pretty brown hair she had. Now Philippe's hands were wound in Lenore's hair, his legs around her naked body.

"Philippe," Catherine whispered.

The tomb!

The thrust of hips. Pain. Shame.

"No!" She turned and bolted from the room.

"Catherine, come back!" Philippe shouted.

She scarcely saw Michel as she ran past him and up the hill. The tears were running unheeded down her cheeks. Philippe. The tomb. No faces.

Not here. Not at Vasaro.

She heard Michel calling her name, but she didn't stop. Sobs shuddered through her and she could no longer see where she was going.

The tomb!

She was falling.
Pain sliced through her temple!
Michel was screaming.
Or was she the one who was screaming?
Warm liquid trickled down her thighs.
Blood.
Blackness.

SIXTEEN

Green eyes, glittering fiercely.

Catherine knew those eyes, she knew that fierceness, knew the arms holding her.

She stirred and a fiery pain jolted through her head.

"Lie still," François said, looking down at her.

"You're angry with me again."

"Not with you," he said thickly. "Not this time. Try to rest. Jean Marc's ridden to Grasse for a physician."

"Jean Marc . . ." But Jean Marc was in Paris, wasn't he? He was in Paris protecting Juliette. He mustn't leave Juliette.

"No, François, he mustn't—"

The thought slipped away from her as blackness returned.

Catherine's lids slowly rose to see sparkling brown eyes, blessedly familiar.

"Juliette?" she whispered.

"Of course." Juliette smiled down at Catherine as she dipped a cloth in a basin resting on the table beside the bed and gently bathed Catherine's temple with cool water. "It's about time you woke up. It's been two days and we were beginning to worry."

"You're here." Catherine reached out to clasp Juliette's hand. She frowned in puzzlement as she looked up at her. "Something's different. Your hair . . . have you had the fever?"

"No, it just got in my way so I cut it off. You're the one who has been ill."

"Have I? I'm so glad you're here. It's beautiful here. You can paint the sea. . . ."

"Presently. First, I have to get you well."

"That's right, you said I'd been ill." Catherine was suddenly aware of an excruciating soreness in the small of her back and shoulders and memory flooded back to her. "I was bleeding. . . ."

Juliette's lips tightened. "You slipped on the stones and rolled down the hill." She paused. "You lost the child."

Catherine froze. "Child?"

"You hadn't realized yet?" Juliette paused. "You were with child, Catherine."

Catherine closed her eyes as shock rolled over her. The tomb. A child from that tomb tearing itself from her body as those men had torn into it. "I . . . suppose I should have guessed. I didn't think about it," she whispered. "Or perhaps I didn't want to acknowledge it could happen to me." Her eyes opened. "You knew, Juliette? That's why you made me marry François?"

Juliette nodded.

"You all knew. I should have been told."

"You were ill. We did what we thought was best for you."

"It was my body, my life. I should have had a choice." She paused. "Philippe knew too . . ."

Juliette muttered an oath. "I wanted to kill Philippe when we saw you on that wagon."

"Wagon?"

"Philippe was afraid to move you on his horse so he came back to the manor and got a wagon to carry you back to the house. Jean Marc, François, and I had arrived only moments before he drove the wagon up to the front door of the house."

Green eyes glittering with anger staring down at her.

"I remember François."

"He carried you upstairs while Jean Marc and Philippe rode for the doctor."

"But why is François here?"

"It's a long tale." Juliette grimaced. "And one with which Jean Marc isn't at all pleased. We'll discuss it later."

"Very well." Anything that displeased Jean Marc was too much for Catherine to cope with at the moment. Her strength seemed to be ebbing away with each word. "Where's Jean Marc now?"

"He and François went to Cannes to see if Jean Marc's ship had arrived from Marseilles. He sent a message to his shipping agent before we left Paris telling him to send . . ." Juliette trailed off and shook her head. "You're falling asleep again. The doctor said you might want to sleep a great deal in the next few days. I'll go and let you rest." She hesitated. "Philippe wants to see you, Catherine.

Catherine stiffened. "Not now."

Juliette nodded with satisfaction. "Good, the rutting idiot doesn't deserve to see you anyway."

"You know?"

"Oh, yes, Philippe was blubbering like a child when he brought you back to the house. He may be a womanizing peacock, but he's an honest one." Juliette squeezed her hand. "But there's a child you'd best see as soon as you wake. He's been curled up outside in the hall and Philippe seems upset about tripping over him all the time."

"Michel." A surge of warmth chased out a bit of the cold from within Catherine. "Yes, I do want to see Michel."

Her eyes fluttered closed and she fell deeply asleep again.

She slept unstirring until the pearl-gray hour before dawn, but as soon as she woke she was aware that someone was in the room. She tensed, her gaze searching the darkness. "Juliette?"

"Me." Michel was sitting cross-legged on the Aubusson carpet in the middle of the room. "She let me come in to wait when I told her I wouldn't go away." He stared at her accusingly. "You frightened me. I thought you were dying."

"I'm sorry. I have no intention of dying." She smiled. "I'm very glad to see you, but you should be sleeping now."

He crept closer to the bed, folded his arms on the counterpane, and laid his chin on top of them. "I shouldn't have taken you there. I just wanted you to see the sea when it was beautiful."

"And it was beautiful." Her hand reached out to stroke his black curls. "It wasn't your fault I had the accident. I saw something that—" She paused. "That upset me."

"Monsieur Philippe and Lenore fornicating."

Catherine's gaze flew to his face. "You knew they'd be doing . . ." She shivered with distaste. "That?"

"Monsieur always takes the women to the Maisonette des Fleurs when he wishes to fornicate."

"This isn't the first time? He forces the women pickers to let him—"

"No," Michel said quickly. "The women want to go with him. He pleases them and they let him use their bodies with great joy."

"Joy." Catherine swallowed. "That's not joy."

Michel frowned in puzzlement. "Most of the men

and women in the fields find it so." His small hand closed over hers. "It makes me sad that you lost the babe. I know you would have loved your child."

Would she have loved a child born of that horror? She would never know now, and that realization brought a strange hollow sadness. Any child coming into the world deserved to be loved.

"My mother didn't love me," Michel whispered. "She wanted me to die."

"No," Catherine protested softly. "Perhaps she was only frightened and didn't know what was best to do."

Michel shook his head. "She didn't want me. She never came back. I think she was afraid Monsieur Philippe would be angry."

"Because she left you in the fields?"

He shook his head, his sweeping black lashes lowered, veiling his eyes. "Because she didn't take me with her. All the women have to take their babes with them. He pays them a fat sum but everyone knows they have to take the babes. My mother cheated him."

Catherine's hand tightened on the child's. "I don't understand, Michel."

He looked at her in surprise. "My mother was one of the women who went with Monsieur Philippe to the Maisonette des Fleurs."

"Dear God," she whispered. Philippe's child. Michel was Philippe's child. "How do you know?"

Michel shrugged. "Everyone in the field knows. Many of the women were here before I was born. They know my mother cheated Monsieur Philippe."

"Cheated? What about you? She left a newborn child in the field to die and he didn't even acknowledge—" She broke off as she realized Michel was staring at her in bewilderment. "It wasn't your father who was cheated."

"My father." He repeated the word as if it were totally foreign to him. "You mean Monsieur Philippe."

"He's your father."

Michel shook his head. "He's Monsieur Philippe."

How could she fault him for his attitude? From infancy he had been raised with people who had told him Philippe was the master who had every right to impregnate a woman and then be praised for sending her on her way with money in her pocket. A man who could let his child become a worker in the fields and give him no more affection than he did any other worker's child. A man who could let that priest call Michel a child of sin and his mother a whore and never admit his own guilt.

She began to feel a ferocious anger kindle within her and she leaned forward and brushed her lips over Michel's dark curls. "Yes, you're right, he's Monsieur Philippe. He's not your father. You don't need him."

"I know. I have the flowers."

She felt the tears sting her eyes. Michel had his flowers. She had Vasaro. Juliette had her painting. Passions to comfort and heal the pain and loneliness of life, but shouldn't there be something else? "And you'll continue to have them and more besides."

"I don't need more."

"Well, you're *going* to have more." She ruffled his hair. "Now go to your bed and let me sleep. I have things to do tomorrow."

He frowned. "I heard the doctor tell Mademoiselle that you should rest in bed for a fortnight."

"I'm tired of people telling me what's best for me to do. I'm sure it's meant with the utmost kindness, but it must end. Will you come back this afternoon?"

He nodded. "After I finish in the fields."

"No, don't go to the fields. You needn't—" She stopped. Michel loved the picking of the blossoms as he did everything else to do with the flowers. Because she was indignant, for his sake she mustn't impose her will on him. After all, she had chosen to go to work in the fields herself. But, by all that was holy, it had been her own choice. Michel had never had a choice. "Come after you finish then."

He smiled and rose to his feet. "I'll bring you flowers for this room. Every room should have flowers."

"Yes, please."

She watched him move across the room toward the door, small, jaunty, vulnerable, and yet with a strength

unusual in such a young child. He would have been a
son any father would have been proud to claim, and
Philippe had rejected and thrown him away as had his
own mother.

As the door closed she nestled deeper under the
covers, the hollow sadness returning more intensely than
before. Now that sadness was not for the death of the
child who had lived for such a short time in her body
but for something precious and golden that had warmed
her since she was a small child. Had the Philippe she
had adored ever really existed, or had he changed as the
world changed?

She felt the tears run down her cheeks but made no
attempt to halt them.

A woman had the right to weep when a dream died.

"What are you doing?" Juliette gazed at Catherine
in astonishment as she watched Catherine coming slowly
down the steps. "Go right back to bed. The doctor
said—"

"I feel fine," Catherine interrupted and then grimaced. "No, not fine. I was so sore it took me almost an
hour to dress myself."

"You should have called me."

Catherine looked at her in surprise. "Why? I knew
I could do it. I had only to persevere."

"But you're too ill to—" Juliette stopped and sighed.
"I'm doing it again. I swore I wouldn't smother you with
attention and immediately I break my promise to myself."
She winked. "But it's all your fault. What can you expect
when the first thing I see is you looking as if a carriage
had run over you?"

Catherine smiled. "It's the way I feel. A very heavy
carriage like that berlin Cecile de Montard left the
abbey in that—" She stopped and drew a deep breath
and went on quickly to another subject. "Where's Philippe? I wish to see him."

"He left to go to the fields."

"Which one?"

Juliette shrugged and shook her head.

"Probably the north field. There was a good deal left there to pick a few days ago." Catherine started for the door. "I'll see you in a little while, Juliette."

"Wait. I'll order a wagon."

"A wagon?" Catherine laughed. "To take me to the field? It's only a little over a mile away. Two days ago I worked from dawn until late afternoon in that same field."

"Philippe told us." Juliette regarded her with an odd hint of sadness as her glance traveled from Catherine's golden-brown face and down her slim, strong body. "You look . . . different."

"I'm stronger. Vasaro has been good to me."

"I see that it has." Juliette turned abruptly away. "Well, if I can't convince you to be sensible, I'll go and get my sketchbook. You're right, this is a splendid place to paint."

Catherine had a distinct impression she had hurt Juliette in some fashion. "Juliette, what did—"

"Run along. But don't expect me to care for you if you collapse on the way home." Juliette quickly climbed the steps. "I'll be too busy sketching."

"I won't expect it." Catherine gazed after her, troubled. "I'll be back soon, Juliette."

Juliette nodded and glanced back over her shoulder. "Why are you just standing there? You know I'll worry until you get back."

It was the sort of roughly affectionate thing Juliette had said a hundred times to her at the abbey and Catherine felt a sudden rush of nostalgia for those days of shared childhood. No, not shared. She had been the child. Juliette had always been the one who saw life as it was. "Don't worry, I'm really quite strong now."

"I know." For an instant Catherine thought she saw the glitter of tears in Juliette's eyes. "I know you are." She hurried up the steps and out of sight.

Catherine stood looking after her. Should she follow Juliette and learn why she was so upset? She decided against it. Juliette had been near tears and wouldn't welcome anyone seeing her so vulnerable. She could talk to her later.

She slowly turned, opened the door, and left the manor to seek out Philippe.

Philippe jumped down from his horse as soon as he saw Catherine approach and rushed forward, a smile lighting his face. "Catherine, you're looking wonderfully well. I was afraid that you would . . ." He trailed off lamely. "I know you were shocked at what you saw, but you didn't understand. Lenore is a sweet woman but she means nothing to me. A man must have amusements."

"Must he?" Catherine's gaze searched his face. He was genuinely upset for her sake and not because he had been caught in a situation that could prove awkward for him. Philippe was no monster, but he also was not the golden young god she had worshiped. He was a man with faults like any other man, but one of those faults she could not tolerate. "I don't know what you 'must' do with women, Philippe, but I do know a man must take responsibility when what he does results in a child."

"Lenore's not with child. Where did you hear that?" He stiffened, his gaze wandering to the field below. "Michel."

"Michel."

"I didn't think he knew." Philippe frowned thoughtfully. "I suppose one of the pickers must have told him about his mother."

"Michel is your child. How can you treat him as if he were nothing to you?"

Philippe kept his gaze averted. "I've not been ungenerous."

"Not if he were some other man's child, but he's yours."

"Listen to me, Catherine. You know my branch of the family has no money, and when Jean Marc gave me the post here it was a gift from heaven. I couldn't have a parcel of bastards running around the estate," Philippe said desperately. "Jean Marc would never have stood for it. I knew when he put me in charge of Vasaro I'd have to act with some circumspection."

"So every time you got a woman with child you gave her money and sent her away."

"Or married her to one of the other pickers. Mother of God, there weren't that many of them." Philippe's face was white, but there was no guilt in his expression. "Catherine, you're too innocent to know about these matters. This is the way these things are done. I hurt no one. The women were glad to take the money and go."

"And what about Michel?"

"Michel is well taken care of by everyone at Vasaro."

"Everyone but you."

"I told you. I give a sum to whichever family Michel chooses—"

"Stop it," she interrupted. "It's not enough."

Philippe was silent, gazing at her miserably. "I tried once or twice to talk to Michel, but he made me uncomfortable. He's . . ."

"Not like other children?" she finished, gazing at him incredulously. "How could he be?"

"I don't understand him."

Michel's words suddenly came back to her. *Monsieur Philippe enjoys the flowers but he doesn't understand them.* "That's a pity. I think he understands you very well."

"What are you going to do?" He tried to smile. "I suppose you'll tell Jean Marc? He'll send me away from Vasaro, you know."

"No, I'm not going to tell Jean Marc."

An expression of relief brightened Philippe's features. "That's kind of you."

"I won't tell anyone. You love Vasaro and you serve it well." She met his gaze. "But I can't look at you right now. I want you to go away for a time."

"Where?"

"Anywhere. Go visit your mother and sisters for six months. Leave today."

"But you'll need me at Vasaro. You don't know a tenth of the things you should about running the property."

"Then I'll learn them from Monsieur Augustine and the pickers and Michel." She paused. "And when you return you'll find Michel has moved up to the manor and will be raised as a gentleman."

"But the son of a common picker wouldn't be comfortable at—" Philippe saw the hardening of her expression and hurried on. "I can't acknowledge him. Jean Marc would be angered and send me away."

"Jean Marc doesn't own Vasaro. I decide whether you go or stay," Catherine said. "But I have no desire for you to acknowledge Michel. It's too late."

"Yes." Philippe nodded quickly. "I'm glad you see I meant no harm. If you like, I'll try to become better acquainted with him."

"Oh, no." Her tone held irony. "Not when he makes you uncomfortable."

She turned and walked away from him.

"The Wind Dancer," Catherine murmured as she crossed the bedchamber toward the window seat where Juliette sat sketching. "But won't it be dangerous going into Spain at this time?"

"I don't see why." Juliette's pen moved with lightning strokes over the pad on her lap. Her gaze was on the pickers in the field below. "After all, I speak the language and we're not at war with Spain yet. After he lands at La Escala, Jean Marc will buy horses and travel overland just below the Pyrenees to Andorra. If I'm questioned by guards, we can always say I'm fleeing France for my grandfather's home. God knows, there are enough émigrés these days to make that appear true. No, I shall do splendidly." She grimaced. "And we have François to protect Jean Marc."

Catherine looked startled. "François is supposed to protect Jean Marc?"

"Danton says that is François's purpose in accompanying us." A smile tugged at Juliette's lips. "I find it amusing too. It's like a panther protecting a tiger, n'est-ce pas?"

"And what does Jean Marc say?"

"He thinks Danton sent François to see what he's doing in Spain. Which is probably correct."

"I'm confused. You keep saying Jean Marc, yet you tell me you also are going."

"I am." Juliette sketched in a plump baby kicking joyfully in a straw basket next to one of the pickers. "But Jean Marc says I'm to stay here at Vasaro and has convinced everyone he'll have his way."

"He usually does," Catherine said. "I wish you would stay here. I don't like the thought of you leaving again."

"I told you why I must go. How can I expect Jean Marc to give me the money for the Wind Dancer if he finds it himself?"

"He said he'd still give it to you."

"We made a bargain." Juliette's jaw set stubbornly. "A bargain must be kept."

Catherine sat down on the window seat and leaned back against the wall of the alcove, her gaze on Juliette's face. "I believe you've changed too."

Juliette shook her head. "I'm always the same."

"No, there's something . . . softer."

"You're looking at me with clearer eyes. I was never as bold and strong as you thought I was." Juliette kept her gaze on the sketch. "François once told me it was I who needed you. He must have been right, for you don't need me at all now." She smiled with an effort. "You've grown beyond me. How did it happen?"

"Vasaro."

"And Philippe's little boy?"

Catherine's eyes widened. "You know about Michel? How?"

Juliette shrugged. "The eyes are the same and the shape of the mouth."

Catherine should have known Juliette would notice what she hadn't seen. The eyes of the artist. "I'm bringing Michel to the manor to live as soon as I can persuade him to come."

Juliette became still. "You're going to marry the peacock?"

"No."

Juliette relaxed. "That's good. I've noticed some women are very foolish about men." She began sketching in the mountains in the background. "You're better off with the child than the man. I'd like to paint Michel. His face has much more character than the peacock's."

"Will you stay at Vasaro when you come back from Spain?"

Juliette shook her head. "I have something to do in Paris."

"The queen?"

"Yes, Jean Marc and I have a bargain."

"It's not safe. Dupree will—"

"Safe enough." Juliette's lashes lowered to veil her eyes. "Dupree has left Paris and I won't be recognized. I have a perfectly splendid wig in which I look quite unlike myself."

Catherine shook her head skeptically.

"Stop fretting. I'm being very good about allowing you to get along without me." Juliette's eyes twinkled. "I couldn't bear to have *you* start smothering *me*."

"You'll, at least, return to Vasaro before you go back to Paris?"

"Of course. I told you I wanted to paint Michel."

Catherine smiled and ruefully shook her head. Juliette had not really changed. She was still afraid to admit or show affection. "Then I'll marshal all my arguments and we'll discuss it when you return." She rose to her feet. "I'll leave you to your sketching and order supper."

"Wait." Juliette scrambled to her feet and tossed the sketch on the window seat. "I have a gift for you." She crossed the room to the lacquer and rosewood desk and opened the middle drawer. "I want you to promise me you'll use it."

"Gift?" Catherine had a sudden memory of the day Juliette had given her the locket with the miniature. How long ago that seemed.

Juliette was drawing a large volume bound in crimson morocco leather from the drawer. "It's a journal and you must write in it every single day. I've dated every page." She paused. "Starting on the second of September 1792."

Catherine's smile faded. "The abbey."

"It's for no one's eyes but your own." Juliette crossed the room and placed the volume in Catherine's hands. "It will help you, Catherine."

"No . . ."

"It helped me. Jean Marc made me draw what happened and it . . . I hated him all the time I was drawing those *canailles*." She met Catherine's gaze. "But it freed me. And I don't want you to stay a prisoner while I go free."

Catherine smiled shakily. "I cannot draw."

"But you can paint pictures with words. You're much more clever than I am with books. Promise you'll do it."

"I can't do it now."

Juliette nodded. "Leave the first pages blank and go back to them. But you'll do it someday?"

"Someday."

"Soon?"

Catherine hugged Juliette quickly and said huskily, "Soon." She released her friend and turned away. "Now let me leave before I start to weep and you accuse me of blubbering." She paused at the door to ask, "Will Jean Marc and François be back tonight?"

Juliette shrugged. "Jean Marc didn't tell me. I think if he could do so he'd sail away without returning. But he'll want to know you're entirely well before he leaves."

"Then it may be just the three of us for supper."

"Three? I thought you said the child would be here?"

"I've sent Philippe away for a while. It's been a long time since he visited his family." Catherine moved toward the door. "Vasaro doesn't need him at present."

"And neither does the mistress of Vasaro," Juliette added softly.

"No, she doesn't need him either." Catherine experienced a strange weightlessness, as if something caged within her had been set free, and her hands tightened on the journal. "Not at all."

Jean Marc didn't arrive back at Vasaro until after midnight and François did not come with him.

Juliette jumped out of bed when she heard the soft thud of hoofbeats on the cork and stones of the driveway and was downstairs and throwing open the door by the time Jean Marc began climbing the steps. "Do we have a ship?"

"*I* have a ship," Jean Marc said. "The *Bonne Chance* is waiting in the harbor. François stayed in Cannes to see a port representative and smooth the way to make sure we'll be able to sail tomorrow night."

"It's good that he's making himself useful." Juliette's tone was abstracted as she gazed at Jean Marc. Sharp lines of weariness slashed both sides of his mouth, and it was clear he was not in a gentle temper. "Have you supped?"

"Before I left Cannes." His gaze traveled over her. "Don't you ever wear anything to bed but that disreputable garment?"

Juliette looked down at the full white nightgown. "Why? It was very kind of Marie to give it to me, and it's warm and comfortable. The nights here aren't as cool as in Paris, but there's still—"

"Never mind." Jean Marc shut the door and crossed the hall toward the stairs. "Good night, Juliette."

"I'm going with you to Spain, you know."

He stopped but didn't turn around. "No."

"I speak the language. She's my mother. You need me."

"I don't intend to argue with you. I'm tired. All day I've been dealing with greedy officials I'd rather drown than bribe, and I still have to find a way of getting rid of François before I sail."

"But you *need* me."

He turned and looked at her, and she went still as she saw his expression. "The only way in which I'd need you on this journey is to provide me with the most basic carnal comforts and, if you choose to come, that will be your function. Do you understand?"

She suddenly couldn't breathe, and it was a moment before she could speak. "You're threatening me?"

"No, I'm warning you. A last warning." He smiled lopsidedly. "Only God knows why. I haven't had a woman since I left Marseilles, and at the moment I'm every bit as hot as your lecherous Duc de Gramont."

"He wasn't mine. He was my mother's."

"For which I find I'm exceedingly grateful. But, if you'd occupied every nobleman's bed at Versailles, I'd still invite you into mine."

"I would think that would be most unwise. A good many of them had the French pox."

"In my present state I assure you it would make not a whit of difference to me."

"That would be unreasonable of you. A moment of pleasure and then a most—" She stopped and drew a deep breath. She knew her words had been flowing with a total irrationality, for she was aware only of the tingling starting between her thighs and the flush burning her cheeks.

Jean Marc's gaze was fixed soberly on her face. "Don't do it, Juliette. I find myself in the odd position of respecting you, which is not at all common for me. For once in my life I'm trying to forget about what I want and let you go free. It's no mean sacrifice on my part." He paused. "You were right. I've never loved a woman and never intend to do so. It's all a game to me and, once I start it, I have to win. I never give up until I do. Take my advice and escape. Unless you want our relationship to culminate in the usual pleasurable manner, you'll stay at Vasaro." He started up the stairs. "And if you do decide to come, I wouldn't advise you to bring that abominable nightgown for which you have such a fondness. The very first thing, I'd throw it over the side."

"Who is he?" Michel asked.

Catherine tossed two more roses into the basket before she looked at the crest of the hill where Michel was pointing.

François Etchelet stood watching them, his gaze focused intently on Catherine. "François Etchelet, one of the visitors from Paris."

"I know that. He was there at the house the day you were hurt, but who is he to you?"

"I told you."

"He was angry with Monsieur Philippe," Michel said. "I think he wanted to kill him because he hurt you."

"You're mistaken, he cares nothing for me." Yet this man was her husband, she remembered with a sense of shock. If not in the eyes of God, in the eyes of the republic of France. The memory of that day had faded and become as dreamlike as everything else that had happened before she had looked out the carriage window the first day and seen the flowers. Vasaro was now the only reality.

"He's waiting for you. He wants you to come to him," Michel said. "I think he'll stand there until you do."

Catherine smiled. "Well, we wouldn't want him to take root on the hill. It might prove very inconvenient to have to work around him if we decide we need to plant it someday." She started down the row. "I'll be back soon, Michel."

He didn't answer, and when she glanced back it was to see Michel still gazing thoughtfully at François.

"Juliette told me you were here. I didn't expect to see you looking so well," François said as she reached the crest of the hill. His gaze went slowly over her from her thick single braid to the wooden shoes on her feet. "I thought you'd still be —"

"Lying frail and sickly in my bed?" Catherine finished. "I'm quite well again."

François nodded slowly. "I see you are." His gaze suddenly swooped to her face. "Do you still dream?"

She tensed. "I forgot you knew about that stupidity. I regret I was such a bother to everyone during that time." She paused. "I'm happy you, at least, were well paid for your efforts on my behalf."

"Very well paid," he agreed impassively. "You didn't answer me. Do you still dream?"

"Occasionally, but it's to be expected. It's been over a week since I had the last one." She was beginning to be uncomfortable beneath the intensity of his stare and rushed on. "Juliette tells me you'll be leaving tonight for Spain."

François nodded. "We sail at midnight."

"You'll wish to leave Vasaro early. I'll order supper for five o'clock."

He suddenly smiled. "A hardy laborer in the field and now gracious mistress of the household? I find myself wondering what other sides to your character I'll discover."

"I wonder myself." She turned and started back down the hill toward the fields and said over her shoulder, "You'll like the wine of Vasaro. It flows sweetly but has a delicious bite."

"An interesting description." There was a thickness in his voice that made her gaze fly back to him in surprise. His face was without expression as he said, "I look forward to trying it."

A shiver went through her like that brought by a sudden hot wind on fields wet with rain. She felt a tightening of the muscles of her stomach and suddenly her breasts felt . . . different. Fear?

She looked away from him, her pace quickening as she fled down the hill and through the field until she reached Michel. She began to feverishly pick the blossoms and toss them into the basket.

"You've lost the rhythm," Michel told her, his gaze on the hill. "He's still watching you."

Catherine slowed and began to take more care. "Why are you so interested in him?"

"He's gone now." Michel began to pick the blossoms again.

"Why?" she persisted.

"I think he's one of the ones who could understand the flowers."

Catherine laughed and shook her head. "He's not at all a gentle man, Michel."

"It doesn't take gentleness, it takes . . ." He paused, trying to put it into words. "A knowing. A feeling."

"And he has it?"

"I think so." Michel frowned. "I knew you would understand them, but he's not like you."

No, they had nothing at all in common, Catherine thought, and François was evidently capable of making her feel most uneasy. It was an excellent thing he was leaving Vasaro that night. The serenity she now possessed had been hard won, and she did not wish it to be endangered.

Catherine's uneasiness became even more acute when she walked into the salon that evening and met François's gaze. He rose to his feet and bowed politely but his stare was as intent as it had been that afternoon.

She suddenly became aware of the bareness of her shoulders gleaming in the late afternoon sunlight, the swelling of her breasts above the ivory satin of her gown. "Please, be seated." She hurriedly sat down in an armchair and looked at Jean Marc. He was dressed for the journey in boots and dark clothing and she tardily realized François was similarly garbed. "Supper will be served in a quarter hour. I hope that will be all right?"

"Perfectly all right. Wine, Catherine?" Jean Marc was at the cabinet across the room, pouring wine into glasses. "You look in splendid health."

"Splendid," François echoed softly as he resumed his seat. The warmth of his smile embraced her across the room.

Catherine tore her gaze from François. "Wine? Yes, please. Where's Juliette?"

"She hasn't come down to supper yet." Jean Marc turned and handed a glass to Catherine and then moved across the room and gave the other to François. "I haven't seen her since last night."

"I saw her this morning before I left for the fields. She's probably sketching and forgotten the time again." Catherine took a sip of wine. "If she's not down in a few minutes, I'll look for her."

"There's no hurry." Jean Marc sat down and stretched his booted legs out before him. "Juliette's seldom on time. Drink your wine."

Catherine shot him a curious glance. "You've discovered that?"

"'I've discovered a good many things about Juliette." Jean Marc glanced idly at François. "You're not drinking your wine."

Catherine smiled. "It's the Vasaro wine I told you about. You remember?"

"I remember." François quickly raised the glass to his lips and drank deeply.

"Do you like it?" Catherine asked. "This is a good vintage."

François nodded, his gaze meeting Catherine's. "I find the bite more obvious than the sweetness, but sometimes that's what a man needs."

"Is it?" Heat began to tingle through her and she hastily averted her eyes. "Philippe said this year's grapes would be excellent. I hope he's right. The vineyards are—"

A sharp clatter interrupted her words.

She looked back at François, startled. He was slumped sidewise in his chair and his glass had shattered on the floor, the red wine splashed across the oaken tiles.

Catherine jumped up and rushed toward François in alarm. "Jean Marc, he's ill!"

"No." Jean Marc stood up and moved swiftly across the room. He pushed François's head back and examined his face. He straightened and added with satisfaction, "But he's very definitely asleep. He didn't drink it all, but it should keep him out of the way until the ship is under sail."

"You *drugged* him?"

"I thought it kinder than hitting him on the head," Jean Marc said, then shrugged. "I respect the man. I didn't want to hurt him." He opened the top buttons of François's shirt and spread back the stiff collar. "Now he should be comfortable enough. I have a horse saddled and waiting in the stable. By the time he begins to stir, the *Bonne Chance* will be out of the harbor."

"This is not well done, Jean Marc," Catherine said coldly. "He is a guest in my house."

"My dear Catherine, would you have preferred I

waited until I got to Cannes and left him lying in the gutter for the thieves to pick?"

"No, but it is not right—"

"Danton set him to spy on me. I *won't* find the statue only to have him take it away from me and give it to the republic. *Au revoir*, Catherine, tell Juliette I—" He stopped. "You probably won't get a chance to tell her anything when she finds out I've left without her. She can be very voluble when she's displeased."

He left the salon and a moment later Catherine heard the front door slam behind him.

SEVENTEEN

The *Bonne Chance* sailed out of Cannes harbor in late evening.

"I see no reason for all this hurry. I hope you know we left half of the trade cargo in the warehouse, Jean Marc," Simon De Laux, Jean Marc's captain of the *Bonne Chance*, said as he looked grimly back at the shore. "Mind, this journey won't pay for itself."

"Yes, it will." Jean Marc slanted Simon a smile. "It may be the most profitable trip of our long association together."

"I don't see it."

"Just put me ashore at La Escala as soon as possible and I promise I'll be more than content."

Simon shrugged as he turned away from the rail. "If that's what you wish." He started to climb the steps to the bridge. "By the way, I sent the woman to your cabin."

Jean Marc froze. "Woman?"

"Mademoiselle de Clement. She came on board early this afternoon." He grimaced. "She's been sitting on deck all day sketching the men as they loaded cargo. If you must bring along a woman, I wish you'd choose one who doesn't order my sailors to stop their work and pose for her. I might have been able to load all the cargo if—" He stopped as he saw Jean Marc's expression. "You didn't expect her?"

Juliette. Jean Marc's hands tightened on the rail as he felt the sudden thickening in his groin. The surge of lust tearing through him was so violent it took him off guard and he couldn't speak for a moment. "Yes." Buried within him had been the knowledge Juliette would not give up. That she was on board filled him with a wild mixture of emotions he was half afraid to examine. He could accept the lust and excitement of the challenge to come, but for an instant there had also been joy and that must be banished. "Yes, I suppose I did expect her."

"I was surprised." Simon's bushy gray-black brows furrowed. "She's not your usual type of woman, Jean Marc."

"No." Jean Marc turned and strode down the deck toward the master cabin. "She's not usual in any way."

Juliette was sketching, curled comfortably on the bunk. Comfort fled and every muscle stiffened as Jean Marc walked into the cabin. His usual shuttered expression was firmly in place, but she could sense the volatility hidden beneath his quizzical smile. She swiftly lowered her gaze to the sketch she was finishing of the sailor lifting a cask of wine onto the deck. "Good evening, Jean Marc, I expected you much later. Did you rid yourself of François?"

"Yes, it proved simple enough. A bit of laudanum in his wine." He closed the door and leaned back against it. "But it's not such an easy matter to get rid of you evidently."

"Are you surprised to see me?"

"No."

"I like your Captain De Laux. He's very gruff but he knows what he wants and isn't afraid to speak his mind. Do you know he told me if I didn't stop interfering he'd have me carried to the cabin and locked in? Very intelligent of him, don't you think?"

"You've made a mistake. It took more strength than you know for me to let you go, and I have no intention of doing it again. I meant every word I said, Juliette."

She forced herself to look at him and then wished she hadn't. It was difficult to pretend to be casual when she saw the way he was staring at her. This wasn't the Jean Marc who had held her and soothed her pain in the garden at the house on the Place Royale. This man was blade-sharp, blatantly sensual. "I know you did. Why do you think I told the captain I was to occupy your cabin? I thought it would save time to make things clear in the beginning." She paused and whispered, "I *have* to go on this journey, Jean Marc."

"At the price of your virtue? I assume you *are* a virgin, since de Gramont failed to seduce you?"

She tried to shrug carelessly. "That's not so high a price. I thought about it a long time and decided none of the women I admire are virgins. Madame Vigée Le Brun and Madame de Staël have intelligence and wit and they're both reputed to have lovers. I shall have a salon and paint many famous people." She put the sketch on the mattress beside her. "Shall we proceed? I'm a little nervous and I'd like to get it over with."

"Oh, no." Jean Marc straightened away from the door. "I have no intention of hurrying. That's not the way it's done, Juliette. The consummation of the game always comes last. We have several days at sea to allow me ample time to obtain the satisfaction I want from you."

She studied him, trying to see beyond the smiling cynicism. "You don't wish to fornicate with me now?"

"My dear Juliette, I wish that so much I'm hurting with it." Jean Marc moved toward her. "A man is far more vulnerable than a woman in this kind of battle, but I've learned to control my body's reactions over the years. I can wait."

Juliette blinked. "Wait for what?"

He smiled. "Until you say, *s'il vous plaît,* Jean Marc."

She felt as if he'd struck her. "You do want to hurt me."

"I want only to win the game."

"It's the same thing." She shook her head. "I won't let you do that to me."

"Yes, you will. Because you want it as much as I do. It's been there between us since those days at the inn."

"No, I never thought of—I wanted only to paint you."

"You wanted to break the mirror," Jean Marc said softly. "Did it never occur to you that's what would happen if we came together? Destruction and then renewal."

Juliette's hands clenched into fists at her sides. Could he be right? It was true Jean Marc had dominated her thoughts since she had first met him, and when he had returned to her life she had not been able to be in the same room with him without a sense of excitement and anticipation.

No, she couldn't accept that he could be so important to her. It was much too dangerous. "I wanted only to paint you," she repeated.

He uncorked a bottle of wine at the sideboard, brought it and a glass to the table, and sat down. "It doesn't really matter now. Undress, please."

Her heart leapt in her throat. "I thought you said—"

"Oh, I did, but there are other forms of gratification besides a final consummation. While you undress I'll tell you what I'll expect of you on this journey." He poured a glass of wine and leaned against the high back of the chair. "As my mistress, naturally you'll be obedient to my wishes in all things carnal. You agree that's reasonable?"

"Yes," she said warily.

"Well, first I want to see you entirely unclothed." He raised the glass, a brilliant smile lighting his dark face. "Oblige me, *s'il vous plaît.* You see, I'm not afraid to say the words. Polite requests are natural between lovers."

"We're not lovers." Juliette began to unfasten her gown. "It's only another bargain."

"Yes, and you've placed yourself in a position where I set the terms. Shall I tell you what they are?"

Juliette's dark red gown slipped to form a pool of color at her feet. She stepped out of it. "Why do you ask me? You're going to do it anyway."

"You have the most superb skin." His gaze caressed the flesh of her shoulders. "Do you know how many times I've wanted to reach out and stroke it? To put my palm on your cheek or run my fingertips over your throat?"

Juliette tensed under his gaze and she hurriedly looked away. "You've touched me before."

"Oh, but not enough. I want to be able to touch you at will. Whenever we're in this cabin I want you available to me."

"I'll be spending a good deal of time on the deck sketching."

"Will you? I have no objection as long as you go to the cabin when you're sent."

"Is that supposed to make me angry?" Juliette sat down on the bunk and began to take off her stockings. "I'm not at all pretty and I have no idea how to please a man. You'll probably become bored quite soon and let me do as I will."

He chuckled and shook his head. "No, Juliette, it will take me a long time to become bored with you. I haven't been able to think of anything but you since I first set eyes on you." His hand tightened on the stem of the glass. "You have only a few garments left, and I find I'm becoming impatient. Shall I help you?"

"No." She stood up and with trembling hands discarded the last petticoats and stood there completely unclothed. "I need no help."

"I do." His voice was thick. "Come here."

Her gaze flew to his face and for a moment she couldn't move. He looked . . . she didn't know how to interpret how he was looking at her, but it was having a most strange effect on her. A tingling seemed to be spreading from the palms of her hands and the bare soles of her feet to every nerve and muscle in her body. She walked slowly across the room and stopped before his chair.

"Closer."

"I'm nearly on top of you now."

"What a delightful thought." His gaze moved from her breasts down her body to narrow on the tight curls surrounding her womanhood. "Dark as the other. I wondered . . ."

The blood seemed to scorch beneath her skin and then center heavily where his gaze was resting.

A flush tinted his cheeks, and his nostrils flared slightly as his breathing quickened. "Part your thighs."

She hesitated and then obeyed.

"Wider." His gaze never left her lower body. "Do you know how exquisite you are? Your breasts are quite perfect and your limbs remind me of one of the nymphs in a painting by—"

"You don't have to lie to me. I know I'm not—" She inhaled sharply as his hard, warm palm suddenly covered the curls he'd been studying so closely. He started to pet her, slowly, sensuously. The muscles in her stomach clenched helplessly as his fingers tangled and pulled at the short curls.

"You like that?" His gaze lifted to her breasts. "Yes, I see you do. You're very responsive, Juliette." He leaned forward and his tongue caressed the pointed nipple of her left breast. "Sometimes I wake in the night and remember how you looked lying on the stairs with these pretty things ruby-red and glistening, how you tasted . . ." His teeth closed gently on the distended pink tip, and he shook his head teasingly back and forth. Then his mouth opened wide and he enveloped almost her entire breast as if he wanted to devour her, his warm tongue exploring even as he drew strongly.

She was beginning to tremble, the heat between her thighs increasing until it was nearly painful, and yet she didn't want to move away from him. She could feel the pull of his mouth with every breath she drew, and for one wild instant she felt as if he were absorbing her, becoming part of her.

His eyes closed, his face flushed with sensual enjoyment. "Sweet Juliette." His mouth released her and his eyes opened. He leaned back in the chair, gazing at her engorged breasts with so much pleasure shining in his eyes that another wave of heat seared her. "Who could have known you'd prove this sweet?"

His hand closed on her narrow waist and brought her closer. He rubbed his cheek back and forth on her breasts, his dark hair brushed her nipples in soft abrasion, and the faint bristle on his hard cheek trailed fire against her softness. He slipped his palms down to cup her buttocks and squeezed gently. "You like this?"

She swallowed. "You know I do. I wouldn't be standing here like a ninny if I didn't."

"I could please you more."

Yes, she thought, if she pleaded with him to pleasure her, if she gave him dominance with her words. It was a price she wasn't willing to pay. "No." She shook her head. "No, I won't say it."

"I didn't think you would." He placed a last regretful kiss on her breast. "But I truly hoped this small exhibition would be sufficient to convince you." He pushed her gently away. "Go to bed." He rose to his feet. "I'm going to walk on deck. Sleep well."

He knew she wouldn't sleep. He had allowed her only the briefest glimpse of sensual pleasure and seen to it that she was aching with frustration. "I will." She turned and tried to walk nonchalantly away from him toward the bunk. It was no mean feat when she could feel his gaze on her every step of the way. "Though I may sketch a little first."

"By all means." She turned to see a flicker of admiration mixed with the amusement in his face. "It may be as effective a soporific as my walk on the deck." He turned and moved toward the door. "Which I'm sure will have absolutely no effect whatever."

The door closed behind him.

Juliette was still awake when he came back to the cabin hours later. She quickly closed her eyes and kept them firmly shut and her breathing steady as she heard him begin to undress.

"Oh, no, *ma petite,* if I can't sleep, neither can you. Open your eyes. I want you to see how much I want you."

She opened her eyes. Jean Marc was naked.

He was quite splendid in his bold male dominance. His body had the same golden-olive hue as his face and possessed a lean, sinewy elegance. He stood tall with well-muscled shoulders, powerful thighs and calves. A triangle of dark hair thatched his chest and another springy growth encircled his erect manhood. She stared, fascinated. "The duke was not nearly so—"

"I have no desire to hear about the duke's physical dimensions." Jean Marc climbed beneath the covers and drew her gently into his arms. She stiffened and then forced herself to relax as his warm male body pressed against her. His fingers moved up to tangle in her hair as he kissed her temple. "We'd both be much happier if you'd give in now, you know." He moved against her, and she felt the hard strength of his arousal. "You see how much I want you?" He gently stroked her hair. "And you're feeling the fever, too, aren't you?" He began pressing gossamer kisses on her face and throat. Everything he did was done lovingly, gently, handling her with the greatest care, as if she were very precious. She found herself flowing against him, arching her face to receive his kisses.

He looked down at her. "You like to be kissed?"

"Yes. I don't ever remember being kissed before. It feels very . . . sweet."

He went still. "Is that supposed to remind me of what a lonely, neglected child you were growing up at Versailles?"

"Oh, no," she said quickly. "I wasn't lonely. I had my paints."

He muttered an oath and then fell back on the bunk, laughing helplessly. "I'm beginning to think you may win the game after all, Juliette. Dear God, your instinct is infallible." He released her and rolled to the other side of the bunk. "Go to sleep before I strangle you."

Jean Marc was not in the cabin when she woke the next morning. She was fully dressed by the time he strode in and threw a white lace morning robe on the bed. "Whenever you're in the cabin, you'll wear this."

Juliette looked at the garment critically. "It's lovely. My mother had a gown like this when I was a child." She held up the sheer lace to the light. "The workmanship is quite magnificent. Where did you get it?"

"I rummaged in one of the trunks in the cargo hold. It's probably meant to grace the mistress of a Spanish grandee, but I think it will look much better on you." He gazed at her with narrowed eyes. "You don't object to wearing it?"

"No. Of course, I realize you wish to weaken me by having me consent to wear this." She tossed the robe aside. "But I think it will also weaken you. You seem to be a very passionate man, even with me."

"Particularly with you."

"Truly?" She looked at him in surprise. "Why?"

"One of the sublime tricks of fate."

"Well, I can't stay in this cabin all day and play your silly game." She avoided his gaze as she stood up. "And neither can you. We must go on deck."

"Oh, must we?"

"Yes." She took up her sketchbook and pens. "Come along, I want to catch the morning light. I think we'll put you at that huge wheel on the bridge. You'll not be able to wreck us now that we're so far from the shore, will you?"

"For your information, I would not wreck this vessel even if we were in the harbor. I've taken my turn at the wheel many times over the years." He paused. "You intend to paint me?"

She avoided looking at him. "You promised you'd pose when you had time. Now you have the time."

He lifted a brow. "I was planning on being quite busy on this journey."

"But then you'd have to break your promise and I don't think you'd do that." She started for the door. "I believe you're a man who keeps his promises even when it proves inconvenient."

"Inconvenient? I *ache,* my dear."

She flushed. "Well, it's your own fault. I made no objections to our original agreement. If it was enough for you to fornicate with me instead of trying to humble me, you would be much more comfortable now." She opened the door. "I'll see you on the bridge."

After the door closed behind her, he stood looking at the cobweb lace of the robe on the bed. Once more she was trying to snatch victory from defeat and her valor touched him even as it frustrated him.

He turned and slowly followed Juliette from the cabin.

She could do nothing with Jean Marc, Juliette thought with frustration. She had captured the wild carelessness of the wind lifting Jean Marc's dark hair and molding his white shirt to his lean body, the grace of his beautiful fingers grasping the polished oak of the wheel, but his face . . . His face was shuttered and without expression, that same glittering mirror mocking her. She had to have *more.*

"You really do know how to guide this monstrous ship." Juliette sketched the night-black sweep of hair from Jean Marc's temple. "I thought you were only a banker."

"There's no 'only' about being a banker. It requires a good deal more skill in avoiding dangerous shoals than captaining a ship. In truth, I grew up on ships. My father had no feeling for the sea, but I did. From the time I was seven I was allowed to go on short journeys along the coast from Marseilles to Nice to Toulon." Jean Marc looked past her shoulder out to sea. "It was never enough. I tried to persuade my father to let me go on a long voyage, but he refused."

"Why?"

"The usual reason. A father wishes to protect his son. He loved me."

"Did you love him?"

His face softened miraculously. "Oh, yes. I loved him."

Her pen froze in mid-stroke. She had never seen him look so vulnerable. Her pen raced across the page, trying desperately to catch the expression before it fled. "I'd think he would let you have what you wanted if he loved you."

"He was a gentle man and he knew the life at sea was a rough one. He didn't understand why I wanted to do anything so barbaric as sail. When I was fourteen I took passage as a cabin boy on the *Albatross*."

"I thought you said he wouldn't let you do it."

"He didn't. My father's mistress, Charlotte d'Abois, arranged it with Paul Basteau, the captain of the *Albatross*. I just got on the ship one day and sailed out of the harbor."

"But if your father refused you, would he not be angry with her?"

He didn't answer, and for a moment she thought she'd lost him. "Charlotte ruled him. She had a strong will and she used it." He looked hard at her. "As you do, Juliette."

The vulnerable expression was gone, but he was still open to her. Her pen moved quickly across the sheet. "Yet she gave you what you wanted when your father refused you."

"She gave me eighteen months on a slave ship." His face hardened. "I was beginning to fight her and she wanted me out of the way. Basteau was the only captain she could persuade to take me."

"A slave ship? Your company deals in slaves?"

"All shippers dealt in slaves. The slave trade was profitable and I thought nothing of it. I'd heard of the slave ships all my life, and even my father took it for granted." His eyes glittered coldly. "However, I thought about it a good deal in those months on the *Albatross*. We boarded five hundred sixty-two slaves in Africa and we landed three hundred and three in Jamaica. The slavers chained them side by side, some on top of each other." He looked blindly at the horizon. "I tried to tell Basteau to let them go, but he wouldn't listen to me. He knew his duty. I was only a boy, and Charlotte had made it quite clear to him that slaves meant gold. The loss of two hundred and fifty-nine lives was acceptable on such a long journey."

Juliette stared at him in horror as his gaze shifted to her face.

"Why are you looking at me like that?" he asked bitterly. "I didn't *know*. I tried to help them. I tried to get better food to them. I nursed some of the sick. I even tried to help them keep clean. The stench . . . It did no good. They kept dying. . . ." He drew a deep breath. "I left the ship in Jamaica. It took me seven months to get passage back to Marseilles."

She waited for him to continue, but he didn't speak again and she looked down with stinging eyes at her sketch of him. The picture she had drawn was of a man she didn't know. There was nothing hidden or cynical about this face; it held only pain, disillusionment, and an unutterable weariness. The Jean Marc she knew was a hard man, but that boy had not been hard. He had sought freedom and adventure and found only horror. "What did you do when you returned to Marseilles?"

His abstraction vanished as his gaze focused on her face and then dropped to the sketch. "You always told me you'd learn me. Is that what you've been doing by this probing?"

Her hand was trembling and she had to steady it as she deepened the planes of the face on the sketch. "I was curious and thought only to ask." Then she looked up at him and shook her head impatiently. "No, I wasn't being honest. Sometimes it helps me to get a true picture if I encourage the subject to talk. But you didn't have to answer me. Why did you?"

"God only knows," he said wearily. "Show me the sketch."

She hesitated before handing it to him.

He looked at the sketch for a long time and then smiled. "Very clever."

She had hurt him. For the first time she realized the man in that sketch needed his hard, mirrored exterior to armor him. "I could tear it up," she offered impulsively.

"Why should you do that? It's what you wanted. People should do what they wish to do. Take what they want to take." He returned the sketch and motioned to the helmsman to come and take the wheel. "It's time for you to go back to the cabin."

"Soon."

"Now, Juliette." His soft voice was veined with iron. "I have a desire to see that exquisite skin veiled only in the sheerest lace. Since that's the only flesh this particular Andreas deals in these days, I wish to be obliged." He turned away. "I'll have a glass of wine with Simon and join you shortly."

Juliette stared numbly at the filmy white lace robe spilled across the bunk. Jean Marc was clearly angry and wanted to subdue her. Angry . . . or hurt? And why couldn't she rouse herself to feel resentment? She had battled against submission all her life, fighting small battles as well as major to show everyone she could not be conquered. Yet, if she fought Jean Marc now, it would not be because she wanted to win but because she would lose pride if she lost. She had always hated the lies and pettiness in those around her, and yet was she not behaving in a muddled and petty fashion?

Oh, she just didn't *know.* Since the moment she had discovered that unknowingly she was hurting Catherine she had not been certain of her reactions to any situation, but instinct told her there was something very wrong here.

Frowning, she slowly sat down on the bunk. It was time she stopped acting on impulse and gave some thought to her relationship with Jean Marc.

She was wearing the lace robe when he walked into the cabin. Kneeling with both legs tucked under her, the luxuriant folds of the robe flowing back from her shoulders in lacy wings, she felt a queer sensation in the pit of her stomach as he looked at her. He *did* lust after her.

"Exquisite," he said, and moved toward her. "I wondered if you'd—"

"*S'il vous plaît,*" she said abruptly. "There, it's done. Does it please you?"

He stopped, regarding her warily.

"Shall I say it again? *S'il vous plaît,* Jean Marc. If you please." She met his gaze steadily. "Are there other words you wish me to speak? Tell me, and I'll say them."

"I'll think on it." He moved forward and sat down on the side of the bunk. His hands were trembling slightly as he parted the lacy robe. "You have lovely breasts." He reached out to cup those breasts, weighing them in his palms. Her breasts were swelling in his hands as his thumb nails gently brushed back and forth across the aroused nipples.

"Why?" he asked abruptly.

"What difference does it make? I've spoken the words you wanted me—" His thumbs and forefingers plucked teasingly at her nipples and she lost track of what she was saying. Heat. A tingling ache between her thighs.

"It's too sudden." His head lowered and his mouth closed on her left breast.

She gasped as she felt the strong suction of his mouth pulling, drawing, his teeth gnawing on the pointed nipple. She swayed forward and grasped his shoulders, her throat arching back. Dear heaven, his mouth . . .

His head rose. "Why?" He didn't wait for a reply as his lips closed hungrily on her other nipple. His hand continued to stimulate the breast he'd just abandoned, pumping, squeezing, his fingers plucking at the hard rosette.

She could see the pulse beating wildly in his temple, and his breath was coming faster, harsher.

He lifted his head again and his eyes were glazed, unseeing. "Never mind." His voice was guttural. "Later." He pushed her back on the bunk and stood up. He was stripping quickly, his gaze first on her swollen breasts, then on the curls surrounding her womanhood.

"Spread your legs, *chérie*. I want to see how lovely you are down there."

She obeyed him dreamily. He was the one who was beautiful. All bronze masculinity and alluring textures, the dark curling hair on his chest, the powerful sinews cording his thighs, the smooth tight musculature of his buttocks.

"Yes," he whispered, his gaze on the apex of her womanhood. "Oh, yes. You want me?"

She nodded. She couldn't force the word past the tightness of her throat. She had never wanted anything more in her life than she wanted him to come back to her, to stop the aching between her thighs.

He was naked, boldly, magnificently aroused, and she stared at him in fascination. He stood over her, his dark eyes wild in his flushed face, his mouth heavy with sensuality. He moved her thighs farther apart and stood looking at her.

She clenched, exposed, heavy, burning.

He was breathing harshly, his muscles locked with tension—yet he stood there unmoving, his gaze fixed on her.

She started to close her thighs, but he stopped her. "No." He got on the bed and moved between her legs. His fingers began caressing her, tugging at the short curls, massaging, petting.

Her back arched up from the bed as she gave a low cry.

"Soon," he said softly. "Don't be impatient. I'm trying not to hurt you."

His finger suddenly plunged into the heart of her. She gasped, her gaze flying to his face.

He was looking down at her, his face intent as his long, hard finger began moving rhythmically in and out of her body. "Do you feel yourself clinging to me? *Dieu* . . ." Another finger joined the first, and she bit her lips to keep from crying out. "I'm not hurting you?"

She shook her head, her eyes staring dazedly up at him.

He moved deeply, twisting, rotating, jabbing, while his other hand moved to press and pet her.

Pleasure so intense it took her breath rocked through her.

He bent forward and she caught the scent of warm flesh and lemon. "Open your mouth. You have such a sweet tongue. . . ."

He kissed her deeply, his tongue moving wildly as his fingers pursued their own wild rhythm. "I . . . can't wait any longer," he said between his teeth. She could feel the hard roundness of his manhood pressing into her. His eyes closed tightly, his cheeks hollowing as if he were in pain. "You're so tight. I can't . . ."

He plunged forward.

Pain, sharp and lightning-swift, lanced through her and then was gone. His fullness stretched her, filling the emptiness, and yet she wasn't satisfied. His chest was moving in and out with the force of his breathing, but he was lying huge and immobile within her body. He shifted and Juliette's nails dug into his shoulders. The sensation was odd, a hot, hard club filling her and yet not filling her, joining her to Jean Marc.

"Are you . . . all right?" His voice was low and thick and she could feel it vibrate through even that most intimate part of her.

"Yes, it's most—" She broke off as he started to move.

He plunged and thrust. Short, long, gentle, hard, not letting her become accustomed to any stroke before he changed the tempo.

Her head thrashed back and forth on the pillow as she felt a terrible tension building.

"Jean Marc, it's not—"

"Hush. Soon, *ma petite,*" Jean Marc muttered. He reached around and cupped her buttocks in his palms, lifting her up to his every thrust. He plunged deep, deeper, driving to the quick.

"Look at us," he urged thickly. "Watch us together."

She didn't know what he meant until he cradled her head in his palm and lifted it so that she could see him driving in and out of her body, drawing almost out and then plunging back, again and again.

She bit her lip to keep from screaming. It was as if watching him multiplied the sensation tenfold. His gaze darkly intent, nostrils flaring, he looked down at their joining. He held her head steady so that she could continue to watch and with the other hand closed her around himself, petting, playing, squeezing while his thrusting hips grew more forceful with every movement.

The tears were running down Juliette's cheeks as she clutched desperately at his shoulders. "Jean Marc, I can't bear . . ."

The tension flared and then broke and she surged upward convulsively.

Jean Marc cried out and clutched her to him.

Her breasts were lifting and falling as she tried to get her breath. She was shaking uncontrollably, weak, dizzy with pleasure, a heavy languor attacking every limb.

"Juliette . . ." Jean Marc's lips were on her own, his tongue warm and lazy, sweet, soft, all violence gone. Yet he was not gone. She felt him within her, still joined. He pulled back, his hands moving across her belly, stroking, pressing, soothing, possessing. "I was rougher than I meant to be. You have no pain?"

She was aware of a faint aching sensation, but she didn't want to lose his delicious fullness so she shook her head.

He was leaving her anyway, she realized with disappointment.

He moved off her and beside her, lying on his back with his arm beneath his head, his breath still coming harsh and quick, his black hair tousled.

He looked tough, overpoweringly male, and yet at the same time oddly boyish, Juliette thought. This was another kind of vulnerability than the one she had sketched on the bridge. She had a sudden desire to hold him close, smooth his hair, and stroke him tenderly.

"Why?" His lids had lifted and he was gazing at her with the same wariness he had shown when he had come into the cabin.

Juliette felt a pang of sadness. He was no longer vulnerable but armored again. "Because I suddenly realized I was being very foolish. Words don't really matter, but you were making them matter to me. You were making me play this silly game with you even though I didn't want to do it." She met his gaze composedly. "So I decided to put an end to it. You can't fight me if I won't fight back."

He gazed at her for a long time before his eyes closed once more. "Mother of God, you've done it again."

She raised herself on one elbow to look down at him. "What have I done?"

"I said you had an instinct for the game."

She frowned. "But I told you that—"

"I know what you told me. You're going to make me battle with shadows."

"I'm not battling at all. I find I very much like what you did to me. It would be very stupid of me to deny myself pleasure just to oblige you." She continued politely. "Now, may I touch you?"

His eyes opened and he looked up at her. "What?"

"Your body pleases me. You're very beautiful, you know." She moved closer, her gaze on the corded muscles of his belly pulled taut by his supine position. "I've often thought I'd like to paint a nude male. Men are so much more beautiful than women. The lines are cleaner." Her hands were running over the springy thatch on his chest, savoring the soft tickle on her palms. "But a woman never has the opportunity to study musculature. Michelangelo and da Vinci studied the dead to examine the way a man is made—" Her palm rested on his stomach and she felt the muscles contract and ripple beneath her palm. "Oh, that felt very interesting. Can you do it again?"

He was laughing softly, and her gaze flew back to his face. The mirror had vanished again and his expression was alive with humor and mischief. "I assure you it felt very interesting to me too. And yes, I'd say with your cooperation I could give you any needed response. Now, if you'd just move your hand a little farther down . . ."

He was boldly aroused again, and she felt a thrill of

heat even as she tried to look at the phenomena with a calm objectivity. How had it happened again so soon? Her hand curved around him and she felt him jerk beneath her touch. "That response is quite glorious, isn't it?" She squeezed gently and heard him gasp. "Will you let me paint you without clothing?"

"I think not. I don't believe I'd be fond of seeing my masculine attributes in a gallery." He pushed her gently back down on the bed and moved over her. "But I'll be delighted to provide you with a demonstration."

"You're very quiet. What are you thinking about?" Jean Marc idly unwound one springy ringlet at Juliette's temple and then released it. Immediately, the ringlet wound itself back into its original curl. The curl was as stubborn and true to its nature as Juliette herself, he thought in amusement. "If you're lying there planning on how next to approach me on the subject of posing without clothing, you needn't waste your time. I'm not going to do it, Juliette."

Juliette shook her head and the curly wisps brushed softly across his naked shoulder. "I wasn't thinking of the painting." She fell silent again and it was another moment before she asked, "Do you have children, Jean Marc?"

He stiffened. "No."

"How can you be certain?" She raised herself on one elbow to look down at him. "I imagine you've had a good many mistresses."

"I'm certain."

"But how?"

"I have made quite sure I've left no bastards. A child gives a woman certain powers over a man."

She nodded gravely. "And I know you'd never permit that. It would interfere with your silly game. But how can you be sure?"

He drew an exasperated breath. "I used a preventive machine made of sheep's bladder."

"What is that? It sounds quite disgusting."

"It's not at all. . . . Why are you asking these questions?"

"Because it occurred to me I could have conceived your child. One does not indulge in this sort of pleasure without the risk of a child, *n'est-ce pas?*"

Passionate possessiveness surged through him, stunning and bewildering him with its intensity. His hand moved down to gently rub back and forth across Juliette's belly. "I suppose there's a possibility."

"Why did you not use this . . . this . . . machine with me?"

"I wasn't prepared. I warned you not to come on this journey."

"But you said you were not surprised. So why did you not protect me . . . and yourself?"

She was right. Why hadn't he done it? It was not like him to be careless and yet the thought had not even occurred to him. His hand moved slowly across her belly again, and once more he felt possessiveness ripple through him. "Perhaps I decided it was time I had a child." He added dryly, "As you're so fond of telling me, I'm over thirty and no longer in my first youth."

She looked at him in astonishment. "You want a child by me?"

"I didn't say that, but it's not impossible. I hadn't thought about it until this moment. You do have certain qualities I admire."

She shook her head. "It would not suit me at all to have a babe." Her brow wrinkled in thought. "It's strange that I didn't consider the possibility before of having a child. I think I must have wanted you to do this to me very much to have ignored the danger."

"It's an act that has a way of banishing good sense." He moved down on the bed and laid his cheek on her abdomen. He slowly brushed it back and forth, savoring the smoothness of her flesh before lifting his head to look at her. "But you wanted it no more than I did."

"Having a child without being wed wouldn't destroy me as it would have Catherine, but it isn't a good thing. A woman may have lovers as long as she's discreet. A child would have to be hidden away." She met his gaze soberly. "I would love my child. I couldn't hide him away in some village with strangers as if I were ashamed of him."

"Do you think I'd abandon my child or his mother?" Jean Marc asked harshly. "I'd make it safe for—*sacre bleu*, why are we discussing this? It is quite unlikely that you would conceive these first few times with me."

She lay back and her fingers tangled in his hair. "It's done now and too late to worry, but once we reach Spain and leave the *Bonne Chance* we mustn't do this again, Jean Marc. It was quite splendid, but it would not be fair to beget a child."

"Nonsense, didn't it occur to you I could just as easily prevent getting you with child as I did the women who—"

"But I could not trust you," she said haltingly. "You said yourself you might want my child. I must guard myself from the harm you might do me. No more, Jean Marc."

"No?" The intensity of his response to her rejection startled him. He should have known she would react in this fashion. All her life she had been forced to trust herself alone for protection. Still, in some outlandish way he felt as if the child they had spoken of was already a reality and she was stealing both it and herself from him. His hand slid down her stomach to cup her womanhood, his thumb finding, pressing, rotating the sensitive nub.

She gasped and a shudder of pleasure quivered through her.

He moved over her and entered her with one deep thrust. "Then I must obviously take advantage of our time together now, *ma petite*."

Dupree leaned back against the brick wall of the house across the road from the Marquise de Clement's casa and smiled with satisfaction. It was an adequate but not a grand house, and since the marquise was not a woman who would stint herself if she had the funds to indulge her fancies, the woman must not have sold the Wind Dancer.

The small stone casa stood high above Andorra on one of the twisting streets overlooking the town on one side and a rock-strewn ravine on the other. Scarlet bougainvillea splashed over the whitewashed walls of the house and ivy climbed the high stone walls surrounding both the house and the enclosed courtyard. The house had no near neighbors and the location was isolated enough to provide him with the privacy he would need in which to do his work. The woman had only the one female servant and a cook who would be easy enough to frighten away when the time came.

Of course, there were still problems to overcome. He had made extensive inquiries since he had arrived in Andorra a few days before, and though the marquise had the reputation of being aloof and contemptuous of her bourgeois neighbors, she was spreading her shapely legs for one Colonel Miguel de Gandoria, who paid her almost nightly visits. An officer in the Spanish Army could prove very awkward to his plans, Dupree thought. He had encountered considerable difficulty with the local *policia*, who didn't appreciate either his nationality or his position in the French government. Extreme care would have to be taken to avoid landing in a Spanish prison after he'd accomplished his mission.

Oh, well, he had plenty of time to concoct a ploy in which to draw the Spanish colonel away from Andorra for the few days he needed to wrest the Wind Dancer from Celeste de Clement. He smiled as he savored that pleasant prospect in store for him. Marat had been very annoyed at the bitch's perfidy, and his orders had been both explicit and entirely satisfactory to Dupree. Yes, he must have at least three days with the enchanting marquise to make her realize she could not trifle with his employer without suffering the full consequences.

He straightened away from the wall, frowning as he flicked a trace of dust from his gray brocade coat and started back down the winding street toward the inn where he'd taken rooms. Andorra was proving a fiendishly uncivilized and inconvenient town, he thought peevishly. It was dusty, the wine was atrocious, and the steepness of the cobblestoned streets caught at the high heels of his silver-buckled shoes. If he had to endure this annoyance longer than he'd planned, he would see that the marquise suffered for it.

EIGHTEEN

François slowly opened his eyes and focused on Catherine sitting across the length of the salon.

Catherine tensed, straightening in her chair. "How do you feel?"

François raised himself gingerly on one elbow on the brocade-cushioned sofa and lifted a hand to his forehead. "As if I'd been bludgeoned." His words were slurred. "*Merde*, my head's exploding."

"I'm sure you'll be fine tomorrow." She rose to her feet. "I've had a chamber prepared for you. Let me help you up the stairs."

"I believe you've helped me quite enough." François swung his feet to the floor and struggled to a sitting position. "It was the wine. I didn't expect the wine." His gaze met hers. "And I didn't expect you. It was very clever of Jean Marc to use you."

"He didn't use me. I knew nothing about it." Her lips tightened. "You were a guest in my house and he had no right to do this to you."

François studied her a moment. "Mother of God, I believe you really didn't know."

"Of course I didn't." She added quickly, "But that doesn't mean I believe Jean Marc to be totally in the wrong in trying to rid himself of you if you were spying on him. You should not—"

"Neither do I."

"What?"

"I don't blame him for trying to get rid of me. I would have done the same. In truth, all during the journey from Paris I expected him to make an attempt." He grimaced, and rubbed his temple again. "I only wish he'd chosen a way that wouldn't have given me this hellish headache."

"He told me it was a choice between a blow on the head or the wine," she said slowly. "You're not angry with him?"

"Why should I be? As I said, I'd have done the same thing in his place." He glanced at the clock on the mantel. "It's after three in the morning. That means Andreas is well out to sea."

She nodded. "He left immediately after you fell asleep."

"And Juliette?"

"I found a note in her chamber saying she was going with him." She added hastily, "But I'm sure she didn't know of his plan to drug you."

"Perhaps not." He smiled. "But I wager she wouldn't be nearly as upset as you are that he decided on this method or place."

"Perhaps not." A smile suddenly lit her face. "But she'd no doubt lean more toward the blow on the head. She has little subtlety." Her smile faded. "What are you going to do?"

He shrugged. "What can I do? Jean Marc has obviously won. By the time I journeyed to Spain, he would have found the Wind Dancer and hidden it away. And, if I confront him, he would say I must be quite mad and that he was in Spain on business. After all, I have no proof he went after the Wind Dancer. Though I see you don't deny it."

"Nor do I affirm it."

"I'm not trying to coerce you into betraying him. I respect loyalty." He cautiously got to his feet and stood upright but swaying. "And now I believe I'll let you show me to that chamber you mentioned. I'm still so groggy I can think only of sleep."

"Let me help you." She picked up a silver candelabrum from the table beside her and moved quickly toward him. She handed him the candelabrum and placed his arm around her shoulder and her arm around his waist. "Lean on me. I'm quite strong."

He stiffened and then looked down at her in amusement. "I see you are."

She was helping him toward the door of the salon. "If you're not going to go after them, what will you do?"

"Return to Paris."

"You're not leaning on me. That's most foolish. We have all those stairs and you'll never be able to make it by yourself."

"I'm sorry." He allowed her a bit of his weight as they crossed the foyer and started up the staircase. "I'm not accustomed to leaning."

"That's quite evident. You're very wary, aren't you?"

"Yes." He took two more steps. "You smell of lilacs."

"It's a new perfume Monsieur Augustine's creating. Michel says it needs more cinnamon."

"Does it? I didn't notice."

They had reached the landing and Catherine helped him down the hall. "Will Danton be angry with you?"

"He won't be pleased, but he'd rather Jean Marc have the Wind Dancer than Marat have it. At least the balance of power will remain the same."

They stopped at the second door down the corridor and Catherine reached for the porcelain knob. "You must sleep all day and, if you're not better, I'll send for a physician from Grasse."

"I'm not ill. I have a bad head, that's all."

"This injury was done you at Vasaro. I won't let you leave here ill." She opened the door and stepped aside. "Will you need the candles?"

"No." He handed her the candelabrum. "Go to bed. You look exhausted."

"I can't go to bed. It will be dawn soon. The pickers will be going to the fields."

He frowned. "You're tired. You should rest."

"I won't work in the fields today. I'll go to all the different fields and oversee the work." She shook her head wearily. "There's so much to do and I still don't know enough."

"Isn't that Philippe's responsibility? Let him do it."

"I sent Philippe away to visit his family."

"Really?" His gaze narrowed on her face. "Now, I wonder why you did that?"

"Because I wished to." She turned away and then whirled back to face him. "You're sure you need no more help?"

One corner of his lips lifted in a half smile. "I'm sure. You've done your duty as the lady of Vasaro."

Her hand tightened on the candelabrum. His green eyes shimmered in the flickering light of the candles, and she felt again the odd tension that had afflicted her before. "If you need me, call out. I'll leave my door ajar."

"I'll certainly keep that in mind." He stepped into the bedchamber. "And, if anything could keep me from sleep in my present state, that knowledge will."

She frowned at him in puzzlement. "But sleep will be good for your headache."

"Never mind. My tongue is as clumsy as my thinking tonight. I'll see you when I wake. *Bonne nuit.*"

"*Bonne nuit.*" The frown remained on Catherine's face as she moved toward her own chamber down the hall. François Etchelet was a complex man. He had been more than a little cryptic, but she was too weary for puzzles.

She entered her room and set the candelabrum on

the table by the door before wandering over to stand in front of the open window. The darkness was already lightening, and as she had told François, it was no use trying to sleep. Soon she would change from her silk gown to her worn woolen one and go to the fields. She sat down on the window seat and leaned back against the wall of the alcove.

Journeys. Juliette and Jean Marc were out there somewhere in the darkness sailing toward Spain. Philippe had probably halted at an inn for the night on his way to Marseilles. Tomorrow François would return to Paris. She did not envy them their journeys. She wanted only to stay at Vasaro, where she belonged, and tend the earth and watch the constant struggle for birth and renewal Michel had shown her.

She looked at the desk across the room where the journal Juliette had given her lay. She knew Juliette had wanted to set her free, but the method was one she couldn't accept yet. Vasaro had healed the gaping wound but the scar tissue was still too sensitive to trust. Still, she had promised Juliette she would use the journal and she could not break her word.

Catherine suddenly rose to her feet and moved toward the desk. She had an hour or two before she had to go to the fields. She sat down at the desk and opened the journal. She would ignore those first pages and start the journal on the first day she had arrived at Vasaro, the time her life had really begun.

She paused, looking blindly down at the page and remembering how Philippe had smiled at her on that day. She had thought he was as beautiful as the flowers, but that had not turned out to be the case. His beauty bloomed only on the surface, and there was no substance beneath it to take root. If she could be fooled by Philippe for so many years, how could she trust her judgment?

She was baffled by François's behavior tonight. He should have been angrier. Why had he decided to go meekly back to Paris in defeat? He was a strong, determined man and it wasn't reasonable he should give up so easily.

Catherine shook her head as she dipped her pen in the inkwell again. Why was she worrying about Etchelet's reasons? She should be grateful he wasn't pursuing Jean Marc, and she was certainly happy he was leaving Vasaro and returning to Paris. She had no time to try to fathom why he did not react in the way she had thought he would or to worry about her own reactions to him.

Flowers were much easier to understand than people.

François mounted his horse and sent him galloping out of the stable yard toward the golden field of broom, where he could see Catherine's familiar figure standing near the flower cart.

Christ, it was nearly noon and she must have gotten no rest since early yesterday morning. As he approached she turned to look at him and he could see the lines of weariness beside her mouth, the dark circles beneath her eyes. Her gray-blue woolen gown was darkened with sweat, and the contrast between this woman and the silk-clad lady of Vasaro was nearly unbelievable to him. Yet they both possessed strength and dignity and a beauty that sent a surge of pure lust through him. Lust and a frustration that led him to pull up the horse before her and say roughly, "Go back to the house and lie down."

"I beg your pardon?"

"I said go to bed. You're exhausted and won't admit it." He glanced at the workers picking the broom fields. "I'll stay and do what's necessary. What has to be done here? They seem to be working quickly enough."

"They're good workers and they know their tasks. Philippe said all that was needed was a presence, the knowledge that someone was overseeing the—" She stopped and shook her head. "I can't let you help. This is my work."

He smiled as he looked down at her. "I'm not trying to take away your work. I'm merely attempting to make myself useful while I'm a guest at Vasaro. I'm afraid I'll have to impose on you for a little longer. I don't feel as fit as I thought I would today."

Her gaze flew to his face. "You're ill?"

He shook his head. "Just unable to contemplate a long, jarring ride to Paris. No doubt I'll be fine in a few days."

"You're welcome, of course."

"Then let me act as the presence of authority and you go get some rest. Tell the driver of the cart you've put me in charge for the next few days." He smiled coaxingly. "I assure you it would save me from excruciating boredom. I don't function at all well away from the bustle of Paris."

"No?"

"No, and it will give you a chance to discuss the running of Vasaro with your Monsieur Augustine and try to form some kind of plan for proceeding. You wouldn't want Vasaro to suffer while you learn what's needed of you."

"That's true." She hesitated. "You're sure this is your wish?"

He nodded. "If you'd so favor me."

She started for the cart and then halted. "You won't tell anyone we were wed?"

"Why should I? The bond doesn't exist now that it's not needed."

She gave him a dazzling smile and hurried over to the driver of the cart.

What the devil was he doing? François wondered. He'd had no intention of lingering at Vasaro. When he'd mounted his horse he'd intended to say his adieus and then start immediately for Paris. He had other things to do beside loll in this garden of paradise.

"You're Monsieur Etchelet, are you not?"

François turned to see a small, ragged boy who looked vaguely familiar. "Yes."

The blue eyes of the boy gazing at him were grave, his expression intent as if he were weighing François. Then, suddenly, he smiled radiantly. "Hello, my name's Michel. Would you like to pick the flowers with me today?"

"You're sure of the information?" Dupree asked.

Pedro Famiro nodded. "In two days' time the colonel will leave for San Isadoro to examine the fortifications. He'll be gone for at least a fortnight."

A fortnight was even more than Dupree had hoped for.

The soldier asked, "It's what you wanted?"

Dupree nodded and handed him a gold piece. "You've done well. Tell me when the colonel leaves Andorra and there will be another one for you."

Famiro grinned with sly lasciviousness. "You wish not to be caught with Gandoria's woman? I don't blame you. He's said to be jealous of his property and I can vouch for his skill with a sword."

"A man must be cautious." Dupree sipped his wine. "The enjoyment of a woman's body is worth much but not a sword thrust through the heart."

Famiro rose to his feet. "True. Trust me, I'll see that you keep your skin in one piece and your manhood rutting in the marquise."

Dupree smiled blandly. "Oh, I do trust you, my friend."

A moment later he watched Famiro walk out the door of the café and saunter down the street. Famiro would have to die but not immediately, he thought idly. He could attend to that small detail directly before he left Andorra. He wouldn't want any hint of suspicion to fall on him until he'd completed his mission.

He looked at the casa on the hill. In the past weeks it had become his custom to sit by this window of the café every evening to view the marquise's pretty casa. He enjoyed imagining her going about her life unknowing how insecure the walls of her casa were.

Two more days. He had been three weeks in this hellhole of a town and now he was finally to be rewarded for his patience. He'd wait until the day Gandoria left Andorra to kill the cook, he decided. A theft and murder in a street not too close to the casa would not cause undue suspicion.

His gaze on the casa became almost caressing as he felt excitement harden his groin.

Two more days.

Vasaro

The rain fell, a fine mist washing the grass on the hills to verdant brightness and pearling the blossoms in the fields.

The pickers moved down the road, returning to the village to wait for the rain to end.

Catherine glanced at François as they walked slowly back to the manor and laughed ruefully. "I know it's very foolish of me to be glad we can't pick today, but I do love it when it rains here at Vasaro."

"I can see you do."

Rain pearled her skin as it did the flowers, and her eyes shone soft, luminous.

"You're Basque, aren't you? Do you have rains like this in the mountains?"

"The rains aren't this gentle. They're usually hard and bitter and cause torrents to rush down to the valleys."

"But you liked it there?"

"There's a beauty and wildness . . . Yes, I liked the mountains."

"You like Vasaro better?" she asked quickly.

He smothered a smile. In the past week he had found Catherine passionately jealous of her Vasaro. Everyone must love it as she did. "I like Vasaro much better," he said gravely.

She nodded with satisfaction. "Anyone would prefer Vasaro to those harsh mountains." She paused. "Why do you never talk of yourself?"

"I fear to bore you. I'm not at all interesting."

She didn't look at him. "I . . . find you interesting."

His heart leapt in his breast. She meant nothing by it, he told himself. "You're very kind."

She slanted him a suddenly mischievous smile. "I'm not kind, I'm curious."

"What do you wish to know?"

"If you like the mountains, why did you choose to leave them and go to Paris?"

"The revolution."

Her smile faded. "I keep forgetting the revolution."

"I keep forgetting it myself. I think Vasaro must be like the waters of Lethe."

"You've been a great help to me in this past week," she said haltingly. "But I suppose you must be eager to return to Paris now that your health has improved."

He should be eager to return. He knew he had already been there too long. The ties were becoming stronger with each passing day and soon would become impossible to sever.

Catherine turned to look at him, clean, glowing, her luminous eyes questioning.

He tore his gaze away from her. "Next week will do as well," he said gruffly. "If you'll permit me to stay."

A brilliant smile lit her face. "Oh, yes, I'll permit you to stay."

Andorra

The marquise screamed.

"Don't do that!" Dupree flinched as he pressed the barrel of the pistol to the woman's throat. "You hurt my ears. Screams are for later. Get up, we have work to do."

He set the candlestick on the night table beside her bed and gazed at her appraisingly. Even tousled from sleep Celeste de Clement was amazingly beautiful with her violet eyes wide with fright, the flesh of her shoulders and upper breasts gleaming with the texture of fine Lyon silk.

"Who *are* you?" The marquise's voice shook with

anger and fear. "How dare you break into my house in the middle of the night and threaten me with a pistol. Do you know who I am?"

"I know." Dupree frowned. "You're wasting my time, Citizeness. Please get out of bed."

"Marguerite!" the marquise screamed.

"Is that the woman who looks like a black crow?" Dupree shook his head. "I'm afraid she won't be coming. I dislike an audience when I work. It robs the situation of a certain intimacy." He took two steps back away from the bed. "Now, please get up or I'll have to shoot you. I wouldn't kill you, but I assure you the wound would be most painful."

Celeste de Clement hesitated and then slowly swung her bare feet to the floor and stood up. "What is this all about?"

"The Wind Dancer. You failed to fulfill your promise and Citizen Marat is most annoyed with you."

"You can't take it from me."

"Oh, but I can. Where is it?"

"I won't tell you. Soon you'll be skewered like a chicken for the roasting." She smiled confidently. "This is Spain and I have protection in high places."

"A colonel is not so high and his protection will not help you in San Isadoro."

Her smile faltered. "You're well informed." She shrugged. "He will soon return."

"But not in time." Dupree stepped aside and motioned for her to precede him. "I think we'll go down to the dining salon. I saw an item of furniture there that might prove useful."

She glared at him and then turned and strode from the room.

Dupree followed close behind, his eyes on the straight, proud line of her spine. The marquise had courage, he thought with satisfaction. A woman with courage was always a more interesting challenge.

"I'll not tell you where it is," she repeated over her shoulder. "You might as well go back to that *canaille* and tell him you failed."

"I won't fail." Dupree moved down the hall after her. "You'll tell me. You'll beg me to let you tell me."

She gazed at him incredulously. "You jest."

He shook his head. "Oh, no." He smiled. "I never jest."

The woman was weeping again.

Begging him to let her tell him where she had hidden the Wind Dancer.

Begging to be released from darkness.

Dupree smiled as he lifted the glass of wine to his lips and leaned back in the chair he'd taken from the dining salon to loll in comfort on the adjoining veranda. Here he could enjoy the fresh air and look down at the city below and still hear the sounds coming from the dining salon.

"Please, I can't . . ." She began sobbing. "*Merde*, I can't bear it."

Soon he'd let her give him the information he desired. He was growing bored with the task. The woman had been broken for over two days and her courage had not given her the stamina he'd hoped. She had been as easy as all the rest, and he owed this victory as he did all those others to his mother. She had shown him the secret of the mastery of a soul.

The whip was crude, the burning brand jarring, but the darkness . . .

Ah, the darkness was the very monarch of discipline.

No candles burned in the lanterns hung beside the wrought iron gate. No light flickered beyond the arched windows of the casa.

Juliette felt a mixture of dread and anticipation as she reined in before the iron gate of the pretty little house. It would be over soon. She would see her mother and take back the treasure Celeste had stolen. Her mother would be angry with her and say words that would cut and sting. *Dieu*, why did that knowledge still bother her after all these years?

Jean Marc glanced at her as he dismounted. "We could go to an inn and wait until tomorrow—"

"I want to do it now," she interrupted. "I want to be done with it."

"The house looks deserted." Jean Marc lifted Juliette down from her mare and tied both horses to the trunk of the cork tree growing to the right of the courtyard gate. He tried the gate and it swung open. "It's odd, the gate's unlocked."

Juliette followed him into the courtyard. The casa did look deserted, she thought. Yet, though it was too dark to see very much, the courtyard didn't appear unkempt and the green and white mosaic fountain in its center still sprayed a gentle cascade of water into the deep basin below. She went to the fountain, looking up at the dark windows of the house. Her hand dipped into the water, idly scooped up a handful, and let the drops run through her fingers. "What if she's gone?"

"Then we'll go after her." He lit the lantern he was carrying. "But to do so we'd have to find out where she was headed. Let's see if there are any servants—Christ, what's wrong?"

Juliette was staring in horror into the waters of the basin of the fountain. "Marguerite!" She thought she had screamed it but it came out as a hoarse croak. "I almost touched her. Marguerite . . ."

Jean Marc took a step closer and the light of the lantern played on the clear water.

Marguerite Duclos sat upright in the fountain, only her dark hair floating above the surface of the water like ropes of seaweed. She sat not four inches from where Juliette had dipped her hand, her open eyes stared blindly forward, her black gown water-puffed about her rigid body.

"I almost touched her," Juliette repeated numbly.

Jean Marc drew Juliette away. "I think you'd better go back to the street and wait for me there."

"Why?" Her gaze flew to his face and she answered her own question. "You think she's been murdered."

"A fountain isn't the most ordinary place for a woman to die." He turned toward the door.

"I'm going with you." Juliette glanced back at the hair floating on the water and shuddered.

"No." He lifted his arm and the light of the lantern stabbed into the shadows of the courtyard. "Where do the walks on either side of the house lead?"

"To the veranda at the rear of the house that overlooks the mountains and town. My grandfather liked to sup out there on occasion."

Jean Marc tried the knob and the front door swung open. "If you won't go back to the street, stay here. I don't know what I'm going to discover."

Her mother. He was afraid they'd find her mother dead, Juliette realized.

Jean Marc slipped quietly into the house and silently closed the door.

Juliette stared at the fountain. She couldn't comprehend her sense of loss. She had disliked Marguerite intensely and yet the woman had been such an integral part of her childhood, it was as if a portion of her past had been stolen.

"Dear me, I can't credit my good fortune."

Juliette whirled to face the west side of the courtyard.

Dupree.

She couldn't believe it. As fastidiously elegant as when she'd last seen him at the abbey, he was standing at the mouth of the walk and had clearly just come from the rear of the house. In one hand he carried a lantern and in the other a pistol. It was leveled at her heart.

He took a step forward and smiled at her. "Life is truly extraordinary, is it not? And here I thought my pleasure was at an end. Would you like to tell me how I come to find you here?"

Juliette didn't answer.

"No, I'll not stand for disobedience from you again, Citizeness Justice."

"The marquise is my mother."

"And you believe your loving mother wished to share her treasure with you?" He shook his head. "I'm afraid she changed her mind and gave the Wind Dancer to me instead." He nodded at the oak chest in the shadows. "Indeed, she entreated me to rid her of it."

"You lie."

"Oh, no. She knelt on the floor at my feet and kissed my hand and begged me to take the Wind Dancer. She offered me her body and any service I wished her to perform if only I would take it. Naturally, I could not refuse her." He smiled reminiscently. "I let her pleasure me many times."

"You killed Marguerite."

"Four days ago. I had no use for her." He tilted his head. "Tell me, are you alone?"

"Yes."

"I would not believe another woman would journey here unattended, but then you possess a boldness I've not found in other females. Your mother, too, showed unusual courage. Would you like to see her? She's in the dining salon off the veranda."

"Have I a choice?"

"No." He motioned with the pistol. "Into the house."

She gazed at him a moment, then turned and walked to the brass-bracketed front door and opened it. If she could keep Dupree talking, perhaps Jean Marc would hear and be warned.

"Why did you put Marguerite into the fountain?"

Dupree followed her into the spacious foyer. "The stench. I realized I'd be here for a few days. There was no sense despoiling the air and making my stay unpleasant. You know, I've thought a good deal about you since we parted company. I truly valued our acquaintance."

"I understood you set a price on it."

Dupree chuckled as he nudged her with the pistol in the direction of the large salon to the left of the foyer. "What a clever child you are. Yes, I couldn't bear to part company without attempting to have you returned to me. Tell me, what was the name of the chit who escaped with you?"

Juliette didn't answer.

"Loyalty. What a splendid virtue. But I shall find

her, you know. She left a trinket behind with an excellent likeness."

Juliette stiffened. "The locket?"

"I only recently discovered the miniature, but on my return I shall find good use for it."

They entered the dining salon and Juliette paused just inside the door. She scarcely remembered this room. They had been there only a few months, and she had always been fed her meals upstairs in the nursery. The long, gleaming mahogany table was intricately carved in a floral design and the twenty mahogany chairs cushioned in crimson brocade. A handsome mahogany sideboard occupied one side of the room and a chest carved with the same artistry as the long table rested beside the two long doors opening onto the veranda.

"Isn't it a splendid room?" Dupree nudged her toward the doors at the far end of the room. "I've spent many happy hours here." He set the lantern on the table and threw open the doors. "Come. Let's look at this magnificent view of the town." He pulled her out to stand before the low stone balustrade and Juliette stared down the steep, stony hill at the lights of Andorra some two hundred feet below.

"Where is my mother?"

He smiled at her. "Don't you hear her? I do. Listen."

She heard nothing but the rustle of the wind through the pine trees marching down the hill.

No, the rustle wasn't coming from the trees but from the dining salon.

She slowly turned her head and looked back toward the French doors.

"Yes," Dupree said softly. "She's waiting for you." His hand closed on her arm and he pushed her back toward the dining salon, stopping inside the doors. "Now, let your ears guide you."

The rustle came again, louder, closer.

From the elaborately carved chest to the left of the veranda doors.

The mahogany chest measured five feet long by

four feet high and gleamed with dark beauty in the flickering light of the candle.

The rustle came again, like autumn leaves blown by the wind.

"Open it." Dupree's eyes fixed eagerly on her face. "She's waiting."

Juliette swallowed and moved leadenly to stand before the chest.

The rustle came again.

Dupree motioned with the pistol.

She slowly reached down and raised the lid.

She screamed.

She slammed the lid down.

"What the—" Dupree's strangled shout behind her jarred her out of the stupor of horror into which she had been hurled by what she had just seen. She whirled as Jean Marc, his arm around Dupree's neck, dragged the man through the open doorway out onto the veranda.

Dupree's eyes bulged from his head as he attempted to get his breath. He tried to lift the pistol, but Jean Marc's hand tightened around him and then jerked the pistol from his hand as he dragged him toward the stone balustrade.

Dupree turned his head and glared at Jean Marc. "I've seen you before at the convention. You're Andreas. I'll remember you. I won't forget—"

"Remember me in hell." Jean Marc pressed the gun to Dupree's side and pulled the trigger.

Dupree howled.

Juliette shuddered. She had never heard anything like that cry, high, keening, an animalistic mixture of rage, fury, and frustration.

Jean Marc lifted Dupree's slight body onto the balustrade and rolled him over the edge.

Juliette walked slowly to the balustrade and looked over the side. Dupree lay still and silent on the rocky hillside some thirty feet below.

"Is he dead?" she asked haltingly.

"If he's not, he soon will be. He was bleeding like a slaughtered pig and that fall is enough to kill a man."

"He's not a man, he's a monster." She closed her eyes. "I knew it at the abbey . . ."

"The abbey?"

"It was Dupree."

Jean Marc nodded jerkily. "I thought I recognized him. Marat must have sent him."

She nodded and opened her eyes. "My mother's in that chest."

"I was afraid she was. I was on the veranda when I heard the two of you come into the salon and hid on the walk beside the house when he dragged you here." His arms suddenly enfolded her and held her tightly. "I was afraid to try to overpower him while he had the gun pressed to your side. I had to wait until he was distracted."

Juliette's arms hung limply at her sides, but they suddenly slid around Jean Marc to cling fiercely. "He wanted me to see her."

Jean Marc's hands gently caressed her back. "Shh."

"She was always so beautiful. She's not beautiful now . . ." Juliette shivered uncontrollably. "She's lying there in that chest. She's naked and there are snakes and roaches crawling all over her. In her hair, in her mouth . . ."

"Mother of God!" Jean Marc held her tightly, then gently pushed her away. "Will you be all right if I leave you for a little while?"

Juliette's eyes opened. "Where are you going?"

"Your mother." He turned and left the veranda.

Juliette's palms clutched at the rough stone balustrade as she heard the chest open again. She heard Jean Marc's muttered oath and then the sound of movement.

Ten minutes later Jean Marc came back to the veranda. "Come with me."

She gazed at him numbly for a moment and then let him lead her through the house and up the stairs. "Where are we going?"

He opened the door at the head of the stairs. "I want you to look at your mother."

"No!" She tried to pull away. "Not again. I don't—"

"Look at her!" He jerked her into the room and

grasped her shoulders from behind. "Dammit, I don't want you remembering her the other way for the rest of your life. You have enough hellish memories now."

Her mother lay on the bed covered by a white silk sheet. Her lids and mouth were closed and though her face was gaunt it held a peaceful expression. She must certainly have yearned for death these last days, Juliette thought dully.

"How did she die? The snakes?"

"The snakes were harmless," Jean Marc said. "He stabbed her."

"Oh." She should do something but she couldn't think what it was. "Burial. I'll have to go to the priest and arrange for—"

"No." Jean Marc shook his head. "We can't be found here. Just the fact that we're French would encourage them to use any excuse to throw us into prison. We'll stop at the church and leave a note and money for the priest with full instructions."

Juliette cast one more glance at her mother before turning away. "Whatever you think best. Can we go now?"

Jean Marc hesitated. "In a little while. Just give me time to look for the statue."

"It's in a chest in the courtyard," Juliette said. "He was about to leave when we came. I think he'd just finished . . ." She had to stop and steady her voice. "I'd really like to go now, please."

Jean Marc took her arm and led her from the room, down the stairs, and out of the casa. "Go to the horses," he said gently. "I'll just check to make sure the statue's in the chest and join you in a moment."

She nodded and crossed the courtyard, careful to avoid glancing at the fountain. Jean Marc joined her only a few minutes later and tied the chest containing the Wind Dancer on the back of the stallion.

His gaze was concerned as he lifted her on the back of the mare.

"Dupree's dead."

Juliette shuddered. "Can evil like that ever die?"

"Don't think about him." Jean Marc slapped her

mare's haunches with his reins and kicked his own stallion into a trot. "Don't think about anything."

They rode half the night toward the coast.

"We'll rest here until daybreak." Jean Marc lifted her down from her horse. "*Merde*, you're cold. Why didn't you tell me?" He wrapped her cloak more closely about her and then enfolded her in a blanket. "Sit here while I find wood for a fire."

"I didn't feel cold." Juliette huddled in the blanket still only vaguely aware of the cold wind cutting through her. It was nothing compared to her inward chill.

The ground was stony, barren of vegetation, the night starless and bitter. She could hear the howling of the wind through the passes of the jagged blue-black mountains to the north.

Dupree had howled like that when Jean Marc had shot him.

"Come here."

She looked up to see Jean Marc standing before her. He opened his cloak and, for an instant, the wind caught it, forming flaring, hawklike wings.

Black Velvet.

He had looked like this the first time she saw him, she thought hazily. Then he was kneeling, taking her in his arms and enfolding her in the security of those wings.

A little of the ice clawing at her eased and then melted away. "The fire . . ."

"I'll make the fire after you go to sleep. I think you need this now."

She buried her face in his shoulder. "She didn't love me, you know. I was always in her way. When I was very tiny, every night before I'd go to sleep I'd say to myself 'Tomorrow she'll love me. Tomorrow . . .'" She shook her head. "The only reason she bore me was that she hoped to give my father a son."

Jean Marc tightened his arms about her.

"I didn't think she mattered to me any longer." She fell silent, thinking about it. "But she must have meant something or I wouldn't feel so . . . empty. I can remember her at court. She was so beautiful that everyone wanted to reach out and touch her. The queen kissed her hand and called her enchanting. I used to stare at her and wonder . . ."

"Wonder what?"

"Why they couldn't see that there was nothing inside her." She frowned. "But perhaps there was something there for everyone else. Maybe she just couldn't feel anything for me. I was never a sweet child."

"You were *her* child." Jean Marc rocked her back and forth with rough tenderness. "That should have been enough."

"I used to be so certain about everything. I used to think I didn't need anything or anyone but my painting. I used to think I could close everyone out and live in my own world. I'm not sure of anything any longer."

"Tomorrow you'll be yourself again."

"Will I? I feel very strange. Alone. I have no one now but Catherine, and she's growing away from me."

"Nonsense. She still loves you."

"She's found something . . ." She closed her eyes.

Jean Marc gently pressed her cheek into the curve of his shoulder. "I should never have taken you there. Dupree could have killed you."

"You couldn't have stopped me. She was my mother and I couldn't let her steal from the queen. The queen was the only person at Versailles who was kind to me. She was all I had during those years. I . . . think I must love her, Jean Marc." She laughed shakily. "I've never admitted I loved anyone before. I was always too frightened."

"Frightened?"

"Love hurts . . ." She wished the wind would stop its howling. The sound made her feel hollow inside. "I don't want to love her. Isn't it queer you can love someone who doesn't really love you? You'd think life would be more fair than to let that happen. And it's all my fault. Even as a little girl I knew I shouldn't love a butterfly."

"Sometimes you can't help loving the wrong people."

She scarcely heard him. "And you said a butterfly shouldn't be allowed to rule the greatest country in Europe. Well, she's not ruling it now, is she?" The tears were running down her cheeks again and she impatiently wiped them on his shirt. "I don't know why I'm crying. I suppose I keep getting my mother and the queen mixed up in my thoughts. It's foolish to weep. There's no reason. I couldn't expect the queen to love me, and my mother didn't even like me. Don't you see how stupid I'm being?"

Jean Marc didn't answer, he merely held her and gently stroked her curls until she finally drifted off to sleep.

Dupree heard a scurrying among the rocks, and panic shook him wide awake. The roaches. The roaches would get him.

He turned over on the rock and then screamed with agony.

Bone jutted out of his shoulder, gleaming white in the moonlight.

Blood gushed from the wound in his side.

He was dying.

He heard the scurrying again.

No, he couldn't die. If he was still, they'd be all over him. In his mouth, in his hair . . .

He wadded the tail of his shirt and stuck it in the wound.

Pain again.

He opened his mouth and howled.

Agony shot through his face, something was smashed in his jaw.

He began to crawl toward the softer earth beneath the trees, away from the roaches beneath the rocks.

His left leg was broken; dragging it over the rough ground made him dizzy with pain.

He couldn't stop.

He reached the trees and lay whimpering with anger and pain. Why had his mother done this to him when he had wanted only to please her?

No, it wasn't his mother this time. It was the others.

He heard the scurrying again. Were they really there or was it his imagination? It didn't matter. He couldn't take the chance. He started to inch up the hill. Light. He had to get to the light. They wouldn't follow him into the light.

He couldn't die there in the darkness.

He knew well the creatures of the night.

If he lay still, they would seek him out and devour him.

NINETEEN

I thought we were going back to Cannes, Jean Marc." Juliette's hands closed on the rail as she gazed at the tall, round turrets of the splendid château set like a jewel on the island off the *Bonne Chance*'s bow. "I told Catherine we'd come back to Vasaro before we went to Paris. Why are we here at the Ile du Lion?"

Jean Marc turned to watch the sailors lower the longboat into the turbulent sea. "There are things I must have packed and taken away from here. The furnishings, the journals, my father's paintings."

"Why?"

"Because I won't risk leaving them to the looters when they decide to take the château away from me."

Her gaze shifted to his face. "You're so sure it will happen?"

He nodded. "It will come. There's a

madness in the land and it's growing worse every day."

"Then why do you remain?"

"It's the country of my birth. I keep hoping . . ." He shook his head. "But I won't blind myself to realities because I want to remain here. The family must survive if all else perishes."

She studied his expression. "The family. That's why you would like a child by me. You want a child to help the Andreas family survive."

"Perhaps."

"It wouldn't help. The child wouldn't have the Andreas name."

Jean Marc's gaze met her own. "That's true. Certain adjustments would have to be made."

"And, besides, we both know I'm not with child."

He smiled faintly. "Yes, we do. However, one can never know what tomorrow will bring." He gazed once more at the château. "Do you wish to go ashore with me? The château has been closed since my father died and there are no servants to make you comfortable."

She was surprised at the abrupt change of subject. "How long will we be anchored here?"

"Several hours. I want to supervise the loading to make sure they've missed nothing of importance to me."

"Yes," she said slowly. "I do want to go ashore."

The rose garden they passed through on the way to the chateau in which Jean Marc had grown up was a wild tangle of thorn-laden shrubbery.

Juliette asked, "Why did you close the house after your father died?"

"I was seldom here. It was more convenient for me to buy a house in Marseilles and conduct my business from there."

"But it's so beautiful here." She gazed out over the myriad paths and graceful fountains of the garden that stretched as far as the shimmering blue-green waters of the Golfe du Lion. "This garden must have been lovely at one time."

He nodded. "One of the most beautiful in France.

The garden's actually older than the château. It was designed by Sanchia Andreas in 1511 when the island was first purchased. The château was built later." He climbed the stone steps and inserted the large brass key he carried into the lock before calling back to Captain De Laux over his shoulder. "The Jade Salon, first, Simon. It's on your right. Have the men pack everything very carefully."

"You want the furniture loaded on the ship too?" Simon asked.

"Everything. Nothing's to be left behind that can be transported."

"So that's why you wouldn't let me negotiate a return cargo at La Escala. The furniture will fill the entire hold." Simon turned and began giving the orders to the sailors straggling through the garden behind him.

Juliette followed Jean Marc into the château, gazing curiously around the huge foyer.

Dust and cobwebs had claimed the hall. Sheer lacy webs surrounded the candles in the chandelier and clouded the Venetian mirror on the wall. Grime dimmed the glory of the stained glass windows that formed an arched cupola over the entire foyer and cast rainbow prisms of color on the teak tiles of the floor.

Jean Marc opened a handsomely carved oak door. "This was my father's study. There are a few journals I want to pack myself."

Juliette followed him into the room and closed the door. Dust and cobwebs again, though all the cushioned pieces of furniture in the room were covered with sheets of linen.

Jean Marc was gazing at the painting over the fireplace.

The woman in the portrait wore a blue satin gown with wide skirts. Her classical features were flawless, her form slim yet voluptuous. Long dark lashes veiled deep blue eyes and her long golden hair was styled in a coiffure that had been popular when Juliette's mother had first taken her to Versailles. "She couldn't be that beautiful," Juliette stated positively. "The artist flattered her. My teacher, Madame Vigée Le Brun did that all the time with her subjects. Did she paint this portrait?"

"No."

"Who is she?"

"Charlotte." Jean Marc's gaze never left the painting. "It was painted by one of her lovers, a man named Pierre Kevoir."

"No wonder he flattered her."

"It was no flattery. She was far more beautiful than this."

"Truly?" She moved forward to stand before the painting. "Then she was even more lovely than my mother. Your father didn't know this artist was her lover?"

"He knew. He knew about all of them. She made little attempt to hide her affairs." Jean Marc finally tore his gaze away from the painting and walked to the desk across the room. "The journals are in this drawer . . ."

"Why did he keep the painting here?"

"He loved her. He said she was the most beautiful thing he possessed and wanted to have her likeness before him always. My mother died when I was five and my father met Charlotte d'Abois two years later. He begged her to marry him but she was never like other women. She had no use for the strictures of marriage and enjoyed the freedom of her life as a courtesan." His lips twisted. "However, she also enjoyed the power money gave her and consented to be his mistress." Jean Marc's words became jerky as he drew four large journals from the top drawer of the desk. "He didn't care that she slept with Kevoir."

"Most peculiar," Juliette said. "He must not have been at all like you. I think you'd care very much if a woman you loved cuckolded you."

"How perceptive." His voice was without intonation as he went to the bookshelves and took down two volumes. He carried them back to the desk. "But, since that circumstance is not likely to occur, we need not consider it. I have no intention of either sharing you or falling into the trap of loving you, Juliette."

Juliette felt a sudden pang and she quickly nodded.

"Of course, it was only an observation." She gazed back at the painting. "She has no expression. Was she a cold woman?"

"Not in bed. She cuckolded my father with half the men in Marseilles."

"But other than in bed?"

"Yes." Jean Marc went to the pedestal by the window, brought the crystal swan to the desk, and set it carefully with the journals. "Very cold."

"What happened when you returned from Jamaica?"

"Why are you asking these questions?" He smiled crookedly. "You have no sketchbook and pen in your hands."

"I want to know."

He suddenly slammed the drawer of the desk. "When I returned I found that two months before she had run away to Greece with her current lover, Jacques Leton. She'd been stealing funds from the company for some time and giving them to Leton. Everyone knew but my father. That was the reason she'd arranged for me to go with Basteau on the slaver." His voice harshened. "She made my father look the fool. I went after them."

Juliette's gaze remained riveted to his face. "To Greece?"

"Yes. I challenged and killed Leton. But Charlotte hadn't grown tired of him yet and felt cheated. She decided to punish me."

"How?"

"She returned to my father and begged his forgiveness."

Juliette gazed at him incredulously. "And he took her back?"

"Without even a harsh word." He smiled bitterly. "I told you she ruled my father. Four months after she returned here, she married him. She tried to make him disinherit me, but he consented only to sending me away. He told me I didn't understand Charlotte and we'd all be happier if I went to Italy to the University of Padua. She died two years later and I returned home."

He looked at Juliette. "Satisfied? You've finally stripped me of all my secrets. Does it please you?"

"No." She wanted to reach out and comfort him but he had once again retreated behind his glittering barrier. "Did you . . . have affection for her?"

"When I was a child I thought she was a magical being just as my father did. I learned quickly, however."

He had learned pain and betrayal and the knowledge that he was helpless in the wake of the power wielded by Charlotte d'Abois. Even now, after all these years, she could see those emotions burning still within him.

"I can't understand how he could take her back."

"I can. He was a dreamer. He saw her only as he wanted to see her." Jean Marc drew a deep breath. "My father always said I couldn't understand him because I was too practical to dream. Well, God save me from the dreamers of this world."

"He didn't understand you," Juliette said quietly. "I think you, too, have dreams, but you rule them instead of letting them rule you."

"Nonsense. I'm no dreamer. You're right, my father and I were not at all alike." He moved across the salon toward the door. "I believe only what I can see and touch." He locked the door. "And I want very badly to see and touch you at this moment, Juliette. Will you please unfasten your gown?"

She gazed at him in surprise. "Now?"

He smiled recklessly. "Why not? I have a fancy to take you in a place that's not moving and shifting with every wave." He took off his coat and tossed it on the desk, half covering the crystal swan. "Indulge my whim."

She had begun to realize he seldom acted on impulse. There was some reason he wanted to make love to her in this room. Something to do with the rawness of the pain she sensed within him.

Jean Marc was moving toward her. "You have no objection?"

She slowly shook her head, her gaze clinging to his. "No," she whispered. "I've no objection, Jean Marc."

She could feel the tension flowing from him, enveloping her in its power. She disrobed, every motion steady and unhurried. In a few moments she stood naked before him. "Is this what you want?" she asked quietly.

"Yes." His gaze went over her slowly. Whatever his purpose, she knew he wanted her. She could see the thick column of his manhood thrusting against the smooth snugness of his trousers, the slight flare of his nostrils, the flush darkening the high planes of his cheekbones. She knew and that knowledge was igniting an answering response.

"Yes, that's exactly what I want." He didn't touch her with anything but his eyes. Yet it was enough to send a hot shiver through her. "And more. Go over and lie down on that lovely Savonnerie carpet in front of the fireplace. I have a fancy to see you framed against those exquisite colors."

She moved slowly across the study to stand before the mantel. She stood with her back to him, looking up at the portrait of Charlotte d'Abois. "Is she the reason you hated my wig? You said you detested fair hair."

"I don't want to talk about Charlotte." He was standing behind her, his hands sliding around to cup her breasts in his hands.

She inhaled sharply as she felt the hardness of his arousal pressing against her naked buttocks. She looked down to see the tan of his hands in startling contrast against her paler flesh. His hands left her breasts and slowly slid down her rib cage to rest on her hips.

"I don't want to talk at all." He held her quite still while he rubbed slowly back and forth against her. "Since you don't seem to wish to indulge me by lying down, why don't you bend over and hold on to the mantel?"

His hands left her to make adjustments to his clothing and then he moved closer. "Yes, that's right. Now your legs, just a little wider . . ."

He sheathed himself within her in one swift plunge.

She cried out, her fingers digging at the cold Pyrenees marble of the mantel.

He froze. "Did I hurt you?"

"No." She closed her eyes, trying to steady her breathing. "It's just . . . different." His hot hardness inside her, the coldness of the marble under her hands, the feel of his clothed body against her nakedness. Different and darkly exciting.

He began to move, thrusting slowly, deeply, letting her feel every inch of him. "Don't cry out again," he said thickly. "They'll hear you in the salon." His fingers slid around and found the sensitive nub of her womanhood. His breath was hot in her ear as he began to lightly pluck with a thumb and forefinger. "You wouldn't want them to know what I'm doing to you, would you?"

She bit her lower lip to keep from screaming. The sensations he was provoking were indescribable. She could feel Jean Marc's chest rising and falling against her naked back, the crispness of his linen shirt a sensual abrasion as he plunged wildly.

"You wouldn't want them to know how much you like it." His teeth pulled at her earlobe. "How you're pushing back against me to take and take and take . . ."

Her breath was sobbing in her throat as she felt Jean Marc striking against her womb.

"You do want this, don't you?"

She didn't speak. She couldn't speak.

His finger pressed, rotated slowly. "Don't you?"

"Yes." It was an almost inaudible gasp.

"Then let me give you more." He pushed her to her knees on the Savonnerie carpet so that she was supporting herself on her hands and followed her down. His hands cupped her breasts, kneading, squeezing, pulling at them while he thrust deep. "While you tell me"—he pulled out and sank deep again—"how much you want it."

He was moving strongly, roughly, in a fever of hunger and need. "Tell me, dammit."

"How . . . can I tell . . . you?" She gasped in exasperation. "When you're giving me . . . so much pleasure I can't even breathe."

He stopped in mid-stroke and was still. "Mother of God, I should have known you'd do this to me."

He flipped her over on the carpet and she saw his

expression for the first time. Torment, pleasure, frustration, resignation.

He thrust hard, again, then a flurry of heated power.

She cried out, her fingernails digging into the carpet, not caring whether Simon's men heard her or not.

He crushed her to him, burying his face in her shoulder while the spasms of release shuddered through both of them.

"Why?" Jean Marc's voice was low as he adjusted his clothing and then moved to help her with the fastening of her gown. "Why did you say yes?"

"I don't know." Juliette didn't look at him. "It seemed a good idea at the time."

"To let me treat you like a tart I'd picked up on the docks of Marseilles?" Jean Marc's tone was suddenly savage.

"Is that how they're treated? It must not be such a terrible life. I really found it quite exhilarating."

Jean Marc put his fingers beneath her chin and turned her face up to look in her eyes. "Why?"

"Because you were kind to me in Andorra," she said simply. "And kindness should be returned. I wasn't sure at first why you needed to do this but I knew the need was there."

His expression was suddenly wary. "But you think you know now?"

"You were losing sight of the woman you were fighting and seeing me as myself." She gazed up at the woman in the picture. "You wanted to see me as the enemy again. You thought you might be able to do that here." Her gaze shifted to his face. "But you were wrong, weren't you? You found you couldn't see me in that way any longer."

"Yes." He released her chin and his hands dropped away from her. "Yes, I was wrong. It didn't work."

She rose to her feet. "You don't like me to understand you, do you?" She smoothed her curls with trembling hands. "I don't like it either. It disturbs me. *You* disturb me. I find myself thinking about you when I should be thinking of my work. I will no longer let you do this to me, Jean Marc."

"No?" His gaze narrowed on her face. "And what will you do to prevent it?"

"Once we're back in Paris there's no reason for us to have . . . a close association. We shall follow our own paths." She met his gaze. "And I shall no longer let you have my body. There will be no child and you will not be allowed in my bed."

"You intend to occupy my house but not my bed?"

"That was our agreement. The shelter of your house and protection as long as I wanted it and two million livres for the Wind Dancer. You have the Wind Dancer. As soon as we return to Paris I'll go to the Café du Chat and give them the money. I'm sure they can arrange for your writ of sale from Marie Antoinette. Then you can attend to your business and I'll attend to mine."

"Painting?"

Her lashes quickly lowered to veil her eyes. "Yes."

"And we're to live together, pure of all carnal thought?" He shook his head and the wicked smile she knew so well lit his face. "It won't do, Juliette. Your temperament is too hot and the desire between us too strong. You'll yield before a week has gone by."

"No. And you won't attempt me, for to do so would sever our bargain."

"We shall just have to test the strength of your resolve." Jean Marc stood up and moved toward the desk. "I gave you a choice once. I'll not do so again." His voice was almost casual as he added, "I believe we shall wed in time."

She stared at him, stunned. "Wed?"

"As you pointed out, the child must have the Andreas name." He smiled. "And I fully intend to get you with child, Juliette. I've just come to that decision."

"But I told you I have no intention—" She moved toward the door. "You're quite mad."

"You give me no choice. It may be the only way I can win the game."

She unlocked the door.

"Juliette."

She glanced back at him.

The mockery was gone from his expression. "I . . . I hope I didn't hurt you."

"I would not let you hurt me." She turned away from him. "I'll be in the garden when you're ready to go back to the ship. When do we set sail for Cannes?"

"We don't."

She turned back to face him. "We're not going back to Vasaro?"

"We'll leave from Marseilles to Paris. If we go back to Cannes, there's every chance François will have persuaded the representatives to impound the *Bonne Chance* and seize the cargo." He grimaced. "I won't take that risk. I've already lost eight ships to the republic."

"Won't the ship be impounded in Marseilles?"

"The ship won't dock at Marseilles. We'll anchor off the coast and go ashore by longboat with our baggage and the statue."

"You're taking the Wind Dancer to Paris?"

"I want it with me. No one would suspect I would keep the statue with me."

"And where does the *Bonne Chance* go from here?"

"To Charleston harbor in America to rendezvous with the rest of the fleet."

She stared at him thoughtfully. "You planned all of this before you left Paris."

"One must think ahead." He smiled. "And speaking of planning ahead, what name shall we choose for my son?"

She gazed at him in bewilderment and, for the first time, uncertainty. Jean Marc was clever, relentless, and had decided on a plan of action that could sweep her from the course she had set if she weren't equally clever and determined. "Impossible."

"A strange name, but if you insist, I shan't raise any objection to your—"

The closing of the door behind her cut off the rest of his words.

The broom had been harvested and now the fields of Vasaro burst into bloom with hyacinths, cassias, and narcissus. Violets, too, came into flower but not in the fields. The deep purple blossoms loved the shade, and the beds lay beneath the trees of the orange and olive groves, where the picking had to be done many hours before dawn when the scent was the strongest.

On the second morning of the harvesting of the violets François stood by the cart watching the pickers move with their lanterns through the grove. The flames of dozens of torches lit the shadows and black smoke curled upward to wind around the green leaves of the sheltering trees.

"Isn't it wonderful?"

He turned to see Catherine coming toward him, mounted on the chestnut mare.

"Why didn't you stay in bed? Both of us needn't be here this early."

"I was too excited. I had to be in the enfleurage shed yesterday and didn't get to watch the violets being picked." Catherine's gaze searched the grove and found Michel, who waved at her. She waved back and turned to François. "Isn't it beautiful? The lanterns and the darkness and the flowers."

He smiled indulgently. "Beautiful. Enfleurage?"

"Michel didn't show you? You've been spending so much time together I thought he would have taken you there." Her face lit with eagerness. "Good. I'm glad he didn't. Now I'll get to show you. Come with me."

She kicked her horse and sent it at a gallop toward the stone sheds behind the manor house. The cool night wind tore at her hair and she felt a wild exhilaration soaring through her. She heard the sound of hooves behind her and François's low laugh. She reached the stone building behind the maceration shed, slipped from the horse, and turned to face François as he reined in. "Light the lantern," she said breathlessly as she tied her horse to the rail before the door.

François dismounted and lit the lantern hooked to

his saddle. A broad smile creased his square face and his eyes were alight with an exhilaration matching hers. "What next?"

She threw open the heavy door of the long shed and preceded him into the darkened work room. The shutters of the windows were shut, the air close, and the scent of violets immediately enveloped them with heavy clouds of fragrance. The shed was empty; it was too early for any of the workers to be sitting at the tables where wooden frames of glass plates were stacked.

"I like this way much better than maceration. It's gentler somehow." Catherine moved to the first long table. "They smear these glass plates with oil and then scatter the petals over them. Then they leave them in the cool darkness for two or three days to give up their souls and then—"

"Souls?" François asked, amused.

"That's what Michel calls the scent." She tapped the frame. "Then the wilted petals are taken off and new ones are put on the glass. It happens fifteen or twenty times before the pomade is ready to store away in crocks. The yield is very small but the scent is terribly intense. Much more powerful than the souls taken by maceration or distillation."

"You said it again." François smiled. "I think it's not only Michel who thinks of scent as a soul."

She smiled back at him. "It's not such a farfetched notion. Why shouldn't the earth and the plants have souls?" She picked up the lantern and moved toward the door. "Don't you believe in souls, François?"

"Yes." François held the door open. "I believe the revolution has a soul."

She stiffened. "I can't agree with you. I had a taste of your fine revolutionaries at the abbey."

"Those men weren't the soul. They were the thorns and the weeds that invade any garden if not plucked out." François held her gaze steadily. "The Rights of Man is the soul. But we have to make sure it's not drowned in a sea of blood."

"*You* make sure," Catherine said curtly as she closed

the door and went to her horse. "I want no more to do with your fine revolution. I'll stay here at Vasaro."

"Good." He lifted her onto her horse and then mounted his own. "I don't want you anywhere near Paris. Your place is here now."

She tilted her head to look at him curiously. "Yet at one time you condemned me for clinging to my little garden in Paris. Vasaro is a huge garden."

"That seems a long time ago." François regarded her soberly. "There's nothing wrong in not wanting to venture back among the thorns. God knows, I'm tempted to find a garden of my own."

"Stay here," she said impulsively. "You like it here. Michel says you understand the flowers. There's no need for you to leave and—"

"I have to go back. I've stayed too long as it is." He smiled ruefully. "I meant to remain only a few days and it's stretched into weeks. Your Vasaro is like a drug on the senses."

Catherine felt a sudden wrenching pang. He was leaving. No longer would there be the companionable presence working beside her or in the next field, no more laughter and discussion of the day's tasks over supper, no more walks with François as well as Michel beside her. "When do you plan on leaving?"

"Tomorrow morning."

"So soon?" Catherine tried to smile. "I suppose it has something to do with that message you received yesterday. Danton cannot do without you? You told me he was very likely out of the city anyway."

"He's returned to Paris but the message wasn't from Danton." His gaze slid away. "You don't need me here any longer. You have the reins of Vasaro fully in your control." François turned his horse and started to trot toward the olive groves. "And I am needed in Paris."

"No, I don't need you." Catherine followed him, her horse picking its way through the tufts of grass on the hillside. She didn't need him but she suddenly knew she desperately wanted him there. In the past weeks he had become as much a part of Vasaro as Michel or the flowers, and she felt as fiercely possessive of him as she did of them. Why couldn't he stay there, where he was safe? Paris was a city of madness, inhabited by men like the Marseilles.

They had reached the crest of the hill and François reined in his horse to wait for her.

Dawn was just beginning to break over the olive grove, lighting only the tops of the trees, leaving the lower branches and the soft drift of pickers gathering the fragrant violets beneath them in half darkness.

"After the sun rises I'll oversee the picking in the hyacinth field," François said quietly. "Do you go with me or have you business with Monsieur Augustine this morning?"

"The hyacinth field is large." She didn't look at him but at the grove below. "I'll go with you."

They sat in silence as the golden bands of sunlight slowly unfolded over the groves and fields of Vasaro.

She found herself dressing with particular care for supper that evening in a lemon-yellow gown trimmed at the neck with a border of pearls. She was not dressing for François, she assured herself. Still, one always wanted to be remembered with a certain pleasure.

When she came into the salon she saw that François, too, had taken pains with his attire. He wore a dark blue coat and a white brocade vest, his cravat tied with exquisite intricacy. She stopped just inside the door of the salon as she met his gaze across the room, where he stood at the sideboard pouring wine into crystal goblets. "Have you said good-bye to Michel?"

"Yes." He handed her a glass of wine. "He didn't seem surprised."

She lowered her gaze to her glass. "He knew you'd have to go back sometime, but I'm sure he was disappointed. He likes you."

"I like him."

They were both silent again and she didn't know how to break the charged stillness in the room. He was different tonight. The easy camaraderie they had known in the past weeks was gone and the tingling awareness of that first evening had returned.

The silence between them lengthened.

"Where is Michel?" he asked.

"There's a wedding at the workers' village. He decided to stay there this evening." She ruefully shook her head. "I can't persuade him to come here more than a few times a week. Sometimes I think I'm wrong to push him."

"Let him go his own way and he'll come back to you."

"You think so?"

He met her gaze. "Only a fool wouldn't come to you if you wanted him."

Hot color scorched her cheeks and her chest suddenly tightened. She found her hand was trembling as she hastily set the wineglass down on the table beside her. "Shall we go in to supper?"

"No."

"What?"

His lips lifted at one corner in a lopsided smile. "I thought I could go through with this, but I find I can't. In the past I've played many roles, but I won't play the gracious departing guest. I believe I'll say my good-bye now." He lifted her hand to his lips and kissed it. "I'll miss you, Catherine of Vasaro."

She gazed at him wordlessly as he turned her hand over and lingeringly pressed his warm lips to her palm.

Intimacy. Warmth. Tenderness.

She couldn't breathe; being close to him was like being in the enfleurage room too long, intoxicating, heady, sweet.

He raised his gaze to her face as he slowly lifted her palm to his cheek. "And I want you." He felt her stiffen and shook his head. "Oh, I know I can't have you. I've always known that since that first night at the abbey. But, if I stay here, someday I'm going to forget and try to make love to you." He held her gaze as he kissed her palm again. "And it would be love, Catherine."

He didn't allow her to answer but turned and left the salon.

She stared after him in bewilderment. Love?

She realized now that she had firmly kept herself from thinking of love as well as lust in connection with François in these past weeks. All through the years love had always meant her blind worship of Philippe. Could what she was feeling for François be love too?

And what of lust? She had never felt this deep, primitive awareness when she was with Philippe. She did not flinch from François's touch. In truth, she seemed drawn to him in a physical manner.

The tomb.

But François was different from those men. Perhaps the act that had so defiled her would be different too.

She turned and slowly walked from the salon and up the stairs. She couldn't countenance the thought of food either. She was bewildered and saddened and yet there was a tiny ember of hope burning in the darkness. She must think and sort out her emotions before morning.

Before François left Vasaro.

An early morning fog lay over Vasaro, swathing the lushness of the blooming fields in a vaporous white veil.

"François!"

François turned as Catherine hurried toward him across the stable yard. She still wore the yellow satin gown she had worn last in the salon, and wisps of brown hair escaped the confines of her braid.

She stopped before him, out of breath. "Don't go."

He went still, his gaze on her face.

She took a step nearer. "Please. I don't want you to go. I want you to stay here with Michel and me. I thought about what you said all night." She moistened her lips. "I don't know if I love you, but I do feel something . . . extraordinary when I'm with you. I want you to stay with me and we can see. . . . Would it be so terrible to give me time to get accustomed to the idea?"

"No, it wouldn't be terrible at all," he said gently. "It would be sweet and warm and all that's wonderful. But nothing could come of it, Catherine."

"Will you . . . embrace me?"

"Catherine . . ."

"It's not much of a favor to ask." She took a step nearer until she was only inches away. "I don't think I'll be afraid. I believe it will be different with you. But I won't know unless you hold me."

He pulled her gently into his arms and she lay quietly against him. His body was warm and strong and yet the strength brought not fear but a sense of security. "It's really quite nice, isn't it?" Her voice was trembling as she pressed closer to him. "Rather . . . sweet."

"Yes." His voice was muffled against her hair. "Yes, love. Sweet."

Her arms went around him and she held him tightly. "Oh, I *do* love you, François," she whispered. "Don't go back to Paris. There's nothing for you there. Will you stay with me for a little while and be patient? I'll try not to be too long about—"

"No."

She stiffened and looked up at him. His face was pale beneath the tan, his eyes glittering moistly in his taut face. "Why not?"

"I can't do it." His voice was thick. His palms cradled her cheeks, his lips slowly lowered until he was only a breath away. "Catherine. My Catherine . . ."

His warm mouth touched her lips with the most exquisite tenderness she'd ever known, clung, and then released her.

Wonder.

Then with sudden roughness he pulled her into his arms, his cold, hard cheek pressed against her own, cold and yet something warm dampened the flesh of her own cheek.

He lifted his head and drew a deep shuddering breath. He stepped back and quickly mounted his horse. "Good-bye, Catherine."

He was leaving her, she thought desperately. Raw pain moved through her, surrounded her. But it made no sense for him to leave her. Not if he loved her.

She stiffened as she realized that perhaps it did make sense.

She took a step toward him. "Is it . . . because of what those men did to me at the abbey? You said it didn't matter. Have you changed your mind?"

His gaze flew to her face.

"Because if it is, I don't want you to stay. They treated me as if I were nothing. But I have worth. I tell you, I have *worth*." She blinked back the tears. "But I have to know. Is that the reason you're leaving? Because of what they did to me at the abbey?"

"Yes."

She froze, her gaze on his face.

"Christ." He looked down at her. "Not because of what those bastards did to you. You're a thousand times the woman you were that night I found you at the abbey."

"Then why—"

"Not because of what they did. Because of what I didn't do. I could have stopped them from raping you. I had the choice and I chose to let them do it."

She stared at him in shock.

"You want to know who the other man was who raped you? It was Dupree." François's words came hard, fast. "I'd just arrived at the abbey and Dupree recognized me as Danton's man and welcomed me. He took me to the south courtyard. There was a woman being torn apart by those filthy *canailles*. I saw you run across the courtyard for the gate. You looked like a child in the moonlight. A child . . ." He closed his eyes. "Dupree and Malpan ran after you. Dupree was laughing . . ."

Shivers began to ice through Catherine.

"He called to me to come with them. I followed them to the gate and saw them chase after you up the hill to the cemetery." He opened his eyes. "I could have gone after them and killed them. My God, how I wanted to do that."

"But you didn't," she said numbly. "You let them . . . hurt me."

"I made a choice. If I'd killed Dupree, I would have marked myself as a protector of aristocrats. I couldn't do that, Catherine, but it was unforgivable."

"Yes." She crossed her arms over her chest to stop their trembling. "Unforgivable."

He flinched and gathered up the reins. "*Adieu,* Catherine. If you have need of me, send word and—"

"I'll not have need of you."

"No, I don't suppose you will." He kicked the horse into a trot but reined in just before he reached the gate of the stable yard. He looked back at her, his expression tormented. "I do love you, Catherine."

She gazed stonily at him across the stable yard.

She gave him no answer.

He didn't expect one. He turned and rode away.

Within a few yards the fog claimed him and François vanished from sight as if he had never come to Vasaro.

Catherine walked toward the house, shuffling slowly, painfully, as if she were a very old woman.

She was cold. She must change from the silk gown into her old woolen one and then go down to the fields.

Michel would be at the fields. He would smile at her and some of the pain would go away.

She would not oversee today. She would pick herself and more of the agony would ease.

Vasaro would help her as it had helped her before.

TWENTY

Juliette sat down at the same table at the Café du Chat she and Jean Marc had previously occupied and deposited the black grosgrain satchel she carried at her feet before turning to look around the café.

"You have no escort." Nana Sarpelier suddenly appeared at her side, quickly setting down her tray and spreading her fans on the table. "A woman who has no escort makes herself conspicuous." She sat down opposite Juliette. "And you also make me conspicuous."

"I wanted to talk to you without Jean Marc being here." Juliette motioned to the satchel at her feet. "Two million livres."

Nana's eyes widened. "Mother of God. And you're carrying it around Paris with no escort?"

"Well, I did hire a carriage to bring me here."

Nana stared at her blankly and then threw back her head and laughed. "I suppose I should be grateful you didn't decide to stroll here from the Place Royale."

Juliette smiled. "I thought it safe enough as long as no one knew what I carried. Jean Marc was planning on bringing me here tomorrow evening but—"

"You didn't want him here," Nana finished for her. "Why?"

"My affairs aren't his concern." Juliette clasped her hands together on the table. "In exchange for the two million livres I'll need a writ from the queen giving Jean Marc Andreas legal possession of the Wind Dancer."

"The Wind Dancer." Nana's lips pursed in a soundless whistle. "So that's the 'object.'"

"I want the writ at once. Is that possible?"

"It's more difficult to see her." Nana hesitated and then nodded. "By tomorrow. For two million livres we can make the extra effort." Her gaze narrowed on Juliette's face. "You were secretive enough before about it. Why are you being so open now?"

"I decided I have to trust you since we'll be working toward the same goal."

Nana looked down at the satchel. "The two million livres will help. You know they guillotined the king two months ago?"

"Yes, it was the first thing we heard when we arrived in Paris. You could do nothing to save him?"

"We tried, but he was too well guarded. He died with great dignity." She shook her head wearily. "Sometimes it seems hopeless." Her lips tightened with determination. "But we must free the queen and the dauphin."

"What of Marie Thérèse and the king's sister?"

"By Salic law the princess can't inherit the throne, so she's safe enough. If Madame Elizabeth can be persuaded to be a little less royal in her bearing, she should be safe too."

"But the queen isn't safe," Juliette murmured. "They hate her."

Nana nodded soberly. "And little Louis Charles is

now the king of France and a rallying point for all the royalists in Europe. Too many people are beginning to find him in the way."

Juliette had a fleeting memory of that sweet, sunny little boy she had known at Versailles. "You have a plan?"

"Not yet." Nana looked down at the fans spread on the table. "We've been waiting."

"Waiting for what?"

Nana looked up. "It doesn't matter. The waiting is over. We can start to formulate a scheme now."

"And now you're not being honest with me. Isn't two million livres surety for my loyalty?"

Nana hesitated. "Perhaps."

Juliette's folded hands tightened. "I *need* to help her. I thought the money would be enough but it's not. I don't want to look back and regret I didn't do all I could."

"I'll discuss it."

Juliette grimaced. "You can at least permit me to take over the painting of these fans. You have no talent for it."

Nana grinned. "And no inclination. I'd be glad to be rid of the task. Perhaps we can come to an agreement. I'll send the materials to the Place Royale tomorrow."

"I'll purchase my own. These materials are as atrocious as your daubs."

Nana chuckled. "You may not find fan-making as easy as you think. Come to me if you have trouble. And don't make them too elaborate or I'll have to charge more than a few francs for them."

"It would do no harm to have a few fine fans to sell to your wealthier clients." Juliette found herself smiling as she looked at the other woman. Nana Sarpelier's frankness and warmth were as engaging as she remembered. "But I promise not to make them too beautiful. You'll contact me?"

Nana nodded. "If you can help in another way, we'll let you know."

Juliette hesitated. "Jean Marc will not know of this. You understand? He's not to be implicated in any way. If there's any danger of my being discovered, you must find me another place to live. He must be safe."

"He didn't impress me as a man who could be easily deceived."

Juliette's hands nervously clutched at the opening of her cloak. "He must be kept safe," she repeated.

"I like her. She's bold," Nana said. "And I think she means what she says. She could be useful."

"Yes." William gazed thoughtfully out the window at the twisting street below.

"She could paint the fans and also act as courier." Nana had said all that was needed. She waited for his decision.

"Use her." William turned and blew out the candle on the table. "We'll use everyone we can. I want the queen and her son out of there by fall."

"I know you're upset," Nana said quietly. "We did all we could to save the king, William."

"It's not your fault. He didn't give you enough help." William came toward the bed. "I find that curious."

"Monsieur has only limited means."

"Does he?" William lay down beside her and drew her into his arms. "It won't happen again. This time we have to be certain."

"We will be." Nana's hand moved down his body and then stilled. "You don't want me?"

He held her closer. "Perhaps later."

"It doesn't matter." She nestled nearer to him. "I like this too. During the day I forget how lonely the night can be. I don't like the night."

He kissed her gently. "Then go to sleep and it will soon be over."

Silence fell between them and presently they both slept.

"You took the money to the café last night?" Jean Marc's words were measured. "I told you I'd escort you there tonight."

"I wanted to give them the livres right away and you had to go to see Monsieur Bardot yesterday." Juliette bit into her croissant. "So I decided to go by myself."

"With two million livres. In case you're unaware of the fact, Paris is teeming with thieves who'd like nothing better than to slit your throat for *ten* livres."

"All went well." Juliette sipped her hot chocolate. "I need to go out today to purchase paint and canvas and it's becoming troublesome hiring a carriage every time. Now that we don't have Dupree to worry about, will you purchase a carriage and hire a coachman?"

"You're changing the subject. Are you trying to distract me?" Jean Marc asked.

"Yes," she said bluntly. "And I've already told Robert to hire whatever help we need for the house."

A faint smile touched Jean Marc's lips. "You'll not be scrubbing any more floors?"

"I'll be too busy." She pushed back her chair and stood up. "Now I must go upstairs and get the letter I wrote to Catherine last night. I want you to send a messenger with it today."

"I sent a message to Vasaro the day we arrived to tell her we'd arrived safely," Jean Marc said.

"You didn't tell me."

"We don't seem to be communicating in any fashion these days. It can't last, Juliette."

"Yes, it can." She tried to keep the desperation from her voice. "It must." The late-morning sunshine streaming into the breakfast salon gilded the night-black of Jean Marc's hair with indigo highlights and revealed the beautiful shape of his lips. She wanted to keep staring at him, but then, she always wanted to do that these days. It was as if, since she'd forbidden herself his touch, she couldn't get enough of looking at him. She forced her gaze away from him and started for the door.

"I'll go get my letter. Even though there's no urgency now, I'd still like it sent today."

He caught her wrist as she passed his chair. "I'll purchase a carriage for you today." He lifted her wrist to his mouth and his tongue caressed the sensitive blue-veined flesh.

Juliette inhaled sharply. The tingling in her wrist was spreading through her arm, her entire body. "Let me go, Jean Marc."

"Why? You like it." His teeth pressed against her wrist, nibbling delicately. "I like it. Do you know why I haven't touched you since we left the Ile du Lion?"

"Because I told you—"

"Because I decided to show you how hungry we'd both be if we were deprived of each other," Jean Marc said thickly. "In truth, I didn't expect the hunger to be so sharp. You said you liked the way I pleasured you on the island. Come upstairs and I'll show you a much more interesting—"

"No!" She wrenched her hand away and stepped back. "I won't do—"

"Monsieur Etchelet would like to see you, Monsieur Andreas." Robert stood in the doorway, carefully avoiding looking at Juliette's flushed face. "I've shown him to the Gold Salon." He hurriedly left the chamber.

"François." Juliette's gaze flew to Jean Marc's face. "What's he doing here? How did he know we'd returned to Paris?"

"Danton probably told him. I saw a few members of the convention when I called on Bardot yesterday." Jean Marc rose to his feet. "And I imagine he's here to express his displeasure at the way I parted company with him."

She frowned. "He's a dangerous man. I'm going with you."

"To protect me?" His brows rose. "I'm touched you're willing to lay down your life, if not your body, in my service. But I assure you, I'd far prefer the latter."

"Don't jest."

"I'm not jesting." Jean Marc turned and strolled toward the door. "Come along if you like. I don't think François will become violent."

François nodded at both of them with a cool smile when they entered the salon. "Welcome back to Paris. I trust you had a successful trip?"

Jean Marc nodded. "Quite successful. I regret you became too ill to accompany us. I hope the indisposition was only temporary?"

"An extremely bad head and a worse temper. However, I got over both in time."

"I hoped you would."

"The object you sought is safe?"

Jean Marc looked at him innocently. "What object?"

A reluctant smile touched François's lips. "Perhaps I'm in error, but Georges Jacques and I assumed you were seeking the same object after which Marat sent Dupree."

Jean Marc's expression hardened. "I could have wished you'd told me Dupree had been sent to Spain."

"Perhaps I would have told you if I hadn't been 'taken ill.' You encountered Dupree?"

"Yes."

François looked quickly at Juliette. "He recognized you?"

She nodded. "But Jean Marc killed him."

"Good." An expression of savage pleasure flashed across François's face before he turned to Jean Marc with his former composure. "Georges Jacques isn't at all pleased I failed to obtain the object for him, but he would have been even less pleased to have it fall into Marat's hands."

"Marat won't have it." Jean Marc met François's gaze. "You can assure him of that."

François turned away. "Then I'll leave you. I have to visit Georges Jacques at his home this afternoon. He hasn't been at the convention all week."

"Danton's not well?"

"No, he's not well at all," François said, troubled. "His wife died last month and he's been—" He searched for a word. "He's not been acting reasonably."

Juliette had a sudden memory of the pretty woman who had taken her to Danton's study. "How sad. She was young, Jean Marc."

François nodded. "Very young. Her death was unexpected and happened while Georges Jacques was in Belgium. When he returned, Camille Desmoulins said he went quite mad for a time. He made them dig up her coffin so that he could kiss her good-bye." François shook his head regretfully. "I should have been with him."

"You weren't in Paris?" Jean Marc regarded him curiously. "Where were you?"

François hesitated. "Vasaro."

"You didn't return immediately to Paris?"

"No."

"When did you return?" Juliette asked.

"Only a week before you arrived here."

"May I ask why?" Jean Marc inquired.

François gazed at him levelly. "No, you may not. I bid you good day." He turned on his heel and left the salon.

"Wait!" Juliette caught up with François as he reached the front door. "Then you left Catherine only a few weeks ago. Is she well?"

"Very well."

"Why don't you look at me? She's not ill?"

"I told you she was well." François reached into the pocket of his trousers and drew out a folded piece of paper. "I'm glad you followed me. This is for you."

Juliette took the folded paper. "From Catherine?"

"No." François opened the door. "Not from Catherine."

Juliette frowned in puzzlement as she watched the door close behind him. His manner had been most peculiar when she mentioned Catherine, and she was not at all certain she believed him when he said all was well at Vasaro. She absently unfolded the paper he had handed her and glanced down at it.

She stiffened in shock. She knew that handwriting well. The paper contained only one line of script.

I hereby grant in perpetuity the statue, the Wind Dancer, formerly the property of the royal house of Bourbon to Jean Marc Andreas.

Marie Antoinette

François had never seen Georges Jacques so haggard, his eyes glittering feverishly in his ugly face. It was probably the worst possible time to approach Danton, but all he could do was hope that even in deep despair, Georges Jacques hadn't lost the shrewdness that had caused him to rise to greatness. In any case, François had little choice. "I want you to arrange an appointment for me at the Temple."

Danton slowly lifted his leonine head. "The Temple? Why?"

François hesitated and then threw the dice. "Because I want to arrange the escape of Marie Antoinette and Louis XVII."

Danton stiffened and leaned back in his chair. "You joke."

"No," François said quietly. "I want the appointment, Georges Jacques. I could have lied to you and told you there was some other reason I needed to be there, but time's growing short and I'm done with lies."

Danton's eyes were suddenly cold. "Then you're a fool. A lie might have saved your life. Who bought you, François?"

"No one."

"I *know* you. You hate aristos. You hate—"

François shook his head. "I've been bribing the nobility out of the prisons and smuggling them out of France for the past two years."

Danton's fingers tightened on the pen in his hand. "You did lie to me. You used me, you bastard."

"As you used me. Did I ever refuse a task you set for me?"

Danton didn't answer, his gaze on François's face. "Why? Are you an aristocrat yourself?"

François shook his head. "My mother is Basque, my father is an English physician. My real name is William Darrell. We lived in the mountains near Bayonne before the revolution, but I persuaded my parents it was safer to go to England when I decided on this course. They live in Yorkshire now."

"You consider yourself an Englishman?"

François shook his head. "You know better."

"Then why?"

"The Rights of Man," François said simply. "They have to survive, but the bloodletting and corruption are washing them away. The Americans didn't start cutting off heads after they won their battle for independence. If they had, the British would have come swarming back across the sea and they'd have been crushed. That's what will happen to France if it doesn't stop." He met Danton's gaze. "We both know it."

"What you say is treason."

"What I speak is reason. You've always told me the guillotining of the king was madness."

"The madness has already been committed. It's over. We're already at war with both Spain and England."

"And we'll continue to be at war as long as the royal family remains in the Temple. It's become a holy crusade to free them." François urged softly, "Let *me* free them, Georges Jacques. They're less of a danger out of the country than they are in the Temple. I'll make sure no action of mine is traced back to you."

Danton was silent a moment. "You've taken a terrible risk coming to me. You've betrayed me. First Gabrielle, and now you. Betrayal . . ."

François frowned in puzzlement. "Your wife didn't betray you."

"She died. She left me alone." Danton cleared his throat and straightened in his chair. "I'll think on it. You may go."

François rose to his feet and stood looking at him. The risk was high. In his unstable frame of mind, Georges Jacques could go either way. "I'll be waiting at my lodgings for an answer."

Danton smiled crookedly. "And you're scared gutless my answer will be delivered by the National Guard."

"There's always that possibility." François bowed. "*Au revoir,* Georges Jacques."

"No." Georges Jacques coldly gazed at him. "Whatever my decision, I will not see you again."

François experienced a sharp pang of regret. Through these past two years they had been companions and, at times, even friends. Danton's had been a clear, sane voice in a mumbling chorus of madmen. François's life would be emptier and certainly lacking in color without Georges Jacques. "I understand."

He turned and left the study.

The next day a messenger delivered an envelope to François's lodgings. When he broke the seal and took out the document he found it to be a certificate of appointment for François Etchelet as special agent of the convention with orders to take up residence immediately in the Temple.

"You're alone again," Nana said disapprovingly to Juliette. "I told you—"

"But I'm not dressed at all richly," Juliette interrupted. "I have on a linen gown just like your own, and I'm far less handsome than you and therefore should attract even less attention. You must tell everyone I'm your new apprentice." She made a face. "It's the truth, for I've found these fans impossible to make. I was far too sure of myself. It's always been one of my most grievous faults. You must show me." She paused, lowering her voice. "And there are questions I would ask."

Nana stood up. "Come with me. I have my materials on a work table in the back room of the café."

The small room to which Nana took Juliette contained only four kegs of wine against the far wall and a work table on which a variety of paper, ribbons, and wooden spines were scattered.

"Sit down." Nana sat down across from her at the table and reached for the scissors. "What questions?"

"François. He's one of you?"

"His real name is William Darrell." Nana began to cut the coarse paper. "I think that should answer you."

"For how long?"

"Since the start of the revolution."

"Then when he came to the abbey he was trying to help us?"

Nana shook her head. "He was sent to the abbey by Danton. He didn't know what was going to happen there." She shrugged. "But even after he saw what was happening he could do nothing to help without revealing who he was. That would have meant his value to us would be ended. It was saving a few then or perhaps thousands later."

"I don't know if I could have made that decision."

"He's been making those choices for the last two years," Nana said. "Who will die. Who we can save."

"You admire him."

"He's a brave man." Nana's expression became shuttered. "And now I'll show you how to make these fans. What was your problem?"

The subject of François was evidently closed as far as Nana was concerned.

Juliette shrugged. "Everything. But I had most trouble gluing the two pieces together without destroying my painting."

"You're using the wrong glue. I use only a special glue made for me of boiled-down shreds of hide, skin, and bones."

Juliette made a face. "It sounds revolting."

"It smells that way too, but it has firmness yet give. You must use only a little or it will destroy either the mount or the sticks." Nana handed her a vial of glue and two wooden hoops. "Then you stretch the paper very tightly on the hoops and let it dry for two days. After that you can paint your picture."

"What about the sticks?"

"After the fan is folded." Nana gestured to a walnut mold into which were cut twenty grooves radiating out from the same spot. "You must get a machine like this and then take great care. You get no second chances when you're pleating. Then the sticks are carefully inserted between the leaves. If the leaf is to be single, the sticks are attached to the back and some decoration must be painted on the back to hide them. You must let them dry a full day. More if you use silk or kidskin for your mount. Then you put a rivet through the sticks to hold them together and thread your ribbons and decorations."

Juliette laughed and shook her head ruefully. "Great heavens, and all this to alleviate the heat of the day."

"In the time of the pharaohs the fan was used as a symbol of power." Nana's eyes twinkled. "But I think Madame Pompadour and Madame Du Barry wielded far more influence with theirs."

"How did you learn all this?" Juliette asked curiously.

"My husband's mother owned a fan shop in Lyon. My father delivered the fans to Madame Sarpelier's clients but he was never overfond of work. When I was thirteen he married me off to Jacques Sarpelier." Nana made a face. "Poor Jacques had a cleft mouth and was ugly as sin, but everyone believed it was a fine bargain for all of them. Madame Sarpelier thought I'd make a fine worker in the shop, Jacques thought I'd make a hardworking servant in his house and meekly accept him in bed, my father thought to secure his position in her employ."

"And for you?"

She grinned. "I enjoyed being in Jacques's bed, though I shocked him with my lack of meekness. I found to my delight that *le bon Dieu* had amply compensated poor Jacques for his ugly face. The rest of their plans didn't please me at all. When Jacques died I bid them all *adieu* and came to Paris to make my way in the world."

"It was a brave move for a woman alone. Have you ever regretted it?"

"No, I'm a woman who likes her freedom. If I'd stayed in Lyon, I would have been a slave to my mother-in-law for the rest of her life. Here in Paris I'm slave to no one."

"How did you come to belong to a royalist group?"

Nana chuckled. "What a lot of questions you ask. I assure you it wasn't because I have any great fondness for the aristos. I couldn't bear some of the ladies who came into the shop and looked at me as if I were a speck of dung." She shrugged. "When I first came to work at this café I had little money and our friend, Raymond Jordaneau, was not overgenerous. However, soon I found out he was involved in something besides the café that paid extremely well. He was receiving regular payments from the king's brother, the Comte de Provence, for helping aristos escape from the prisons."

"The Comte de Provence pays you?" Juliette asked, startled. She had never liked Louis Stanislas Xavier, the wily, ambitious man the court and most of France knew by the sobriquet Monsieur.

"He did pay me at first, but after a little while . . ." Nana shook her head. "I couldn't take it from him any longer. There was too much need for the money elsewhere." Her expression became shadowed. "I found out aristos were like everyone else. They loved their children, they were frightened of dying . . ." She rose to her feet. "You must go now. I have to get back to the café. I'll send word if I want a particular message on a fan."

"No." Juliette stood up. "I'll come here twice a week unless you send for me. But in the afternoons, not evenings. Jean Marc often spends the entire day away from the Place Royale."

Nana nodded in approval. "Afternoons will be safer for you."

"Oh, I'll be safe whenever I choose to come." Juliette grimaced. "Jean Marc has hired a giant of a man to drive my coach and a footman who's equally ferocious-looking. Léon could frighten a dozen footpads away just by frowning at them."

"Have them wait around the corner from the café," Nana said as she walked with Juliette toward the door. "It will do no good for you to discard your silk gowns if you arrive in a fine carriage."

"I'd already thought of that." Juliette ruefully looked down at her blue linen gown with its simple white muslin fichu. "Another disguise."

Juliette found that deceiving Jean Marc about her activities at the Café du Chat was blessedly simple. On the following Tuesday he was called away to Le Havre, where the local representatives had decided to place an exorbitant tax on the goods in the warehouses. He didn't return to Paris until the afternoon of June 23.

She was in the garden painting Léon as Samson when Jean Marc appeared suddenly behind her.

"That will be all, Léon."

Joy rippled through her. He was back.

The giant murmured in embarrassment to Jean Marc, snatched up his shirt, and almost ran down the path toward the house.

She carefully kept her gaze on the canvas and added a little more bronze to the flesh tones of the pectoral muscles of the figure in the painting. "I shall never get a canvas finished if you keep sending away my subjects."

"I find I don't like the idea of you painting that handsome behemoth without clothes."

"You exaggerate. Léon was only without his shirt. I asked him to pose entirely without clothes but he was too shy. I told him that to expose his beautiful body as Samson was not shameful but a religious—"

"You asked him—turn around and look at me, dammit."

She lifted her gaze from the canvas and turned to face him.

Jean Marc seemed exhausted. Deep lines grooved either side of his mouth and shadows rimmed his eyes. The desire to flow toward him, comfort him was almost irresistible. "You should have gone straight to bed instead of coming out here to harass me. You look terrible."

"Not like your beautiful Samson?" he asked caustically.

"No." She put down her brush and took an impulsive step forward. "You could never be a Samson. I could see you as a prince of the Renaissance or perhaps a pharaoh of Egypt, but I . . ." She shook her head. "No, I could never paint you as anyone but yourself. But why do you just stand here? Go to bed."

He gazed at her for a long moment. "I wanted to see you."

She met his stare and was caught, held. She had to force herself to look away. "Well, you've seen me. Did your business go well?"

"No. They wouldn't lower the tax."

"I'm sorry."

"I . . . thought about you while I was gone. Did you think of me?"

Juliette was silent. She could not confess how many nights she had stayed awake thinking of him.

"I believe you did." He smiled crookedly. He was silent again, simply looking at her. "I have a victory for you."

"A victory?"

"I found myself thinking not only how much I'd like to be between your thighs but also how much I would enjoy your company." He reached out and gently touched her cheek. "At times, I thought just being near you would be satisfaction enough. Do you not find that peculiar?"

She should move away from the bittersweet pleasure of his touch. She stood there, savoring it. "Only at times?"

"Be satisfied with a minor victory. I'll not give you more."

"I don't regard it as a victory at all." She turned back to the canvas and picked up her brush again. "I told you I wasn't doing battle with you. Now, go to bed before you collapse where you stand."

"Robert says you've been spending a good deal of time in your room. Have you been unwell?"

She went still. "Perfectly well. Am I not entitled to spend my time where I wish?"

"*Bon Dieu,* I only asked. Did it never occur to you that I might worry about you?"

Such a rush of warmth surged through her, she was afraid to look at him. "No, it never occurred to me. I . . . thank you."

She could feel his gaze on her back and she wanted desperately to turn around again.

"Juliette . . ." His voice was thick. "I missed you."

She couldn't answer him. If she spoke, her voice would tremble and he would know.

He stood silent another moment and then she heard his footsteps moving heavily away from her down the path.

She drew a deep breath and whirled to face him. She couldn't let him go like this.

"Jean Marc!"

He turned to look at her. "Yes."

She sought wildly for something to say that would not betray her. "I was looking at my painting of the Wind Dancer the other day and it's really not worthy to be in the salon. I intend to paint you another one. Where did you put the statue when we arrived in Paris?"

He stiffened. "The chest is in the cellar but I don't want it disturbed. It's hardly safe to bring the statue out to the garden to paint it." He smiled faintly. "Besides, I'm very fond of that painting in the salon. It brings back certain memories. I wish no other."

The painting brought back memories to her also—Versailles, the inn, the abbey, Jean Marc. "Very well."

He stood waiting, his gaze on her face. "Was that all?"

He was weary and discouraged and in need. She could not turn him away to protect herself. She could not yield but she must give him something.

"No." She turned back to her canvas and said huskily, "I'm glad you're home. I . . . missed you too."

On July 3 François sent word to Nana from the Temple that the little king had been separated from his mother by order of the Commune and mother and son must now be rescued separately.

Two days later Juliette received a message from François that the queen had requested Juliette come to see her at the Temple as soon as possible. Her Majesty would understand if Juliette found it too dangerous. . . .

The haggardness of the queen's face didn't surprise Juliette, but the strength and maturity of her bearing did.

Marie Antoinette moved into the shadows of the Tower and leaned wearily back against the stone wall. "It was good of you to come, Juliette. I won't keep you long." Her soft voice was anguished. "You know they've taken my little boy from me?"

"Yes." Juliette took a step closer to her. "Perhaps it's only temporary. Perhaps they'll let him come back to you."

"No." The queen's hands trembled as she drew her cloak closer about her. "They've given him to that cobbler Simon to teach him how to be a good republican. They want him to forget me, forget he's the true king of France."

"Will Simon be unkind to the boy?"

"I hope not." Marie Antoinette brushed back a wisp of white hair from her forehead. "I pray not. Simon did many kindnesses for us at one time. I think he's only stupid, not cruel."

"We have people watching here at the Temple. They'll know if Louis Charles is ill treated," Juliette said gently. "And you know Simon won't be permitted to hurt him."

"I miss him so," the queen whispered. "He's only eight, you know. He has such a sweet nature, always smiling, always trying to help me."

"You'll be together again."

"In heaven, perhaps."

"No," Juliette protested. "The plans are going well for your escape—"

"Forget me," the queen interrupted. "Rescue Louis Charles."

Juliette shook her head. "Louis Charles is safe at the moment. The convention can use him as a hostage. But we need to free you."

"Before they kill me as they did my husband?" Marie Antoinette's lips twisted. "I've heard they're already trying to gather their filth to besmirch my name. I understand one of the charges is against your dear mother. Thank God Celeste's safe from those *canailles*."

Juliette quickly looked away.

The queen shook her head. "You *know* my attachment for her was not unnatural, Juliette. I am of an extremely affectionate nature, but I had only one real love. Axel . . ." She pulled off a signet ring from her finger and looked down at it lovingly. "It's the Fersen coat of arms. Do you know the motto that's engraved on it? *Tutto a te mi guida.* Is that not beautiful?"

Everything leads me to you.

"Yes," Juliette said huskily. "Very beautiful."

"My dear Louis understood. We had affection and duty, but I needed something more." She lifted her chin. "So I took it. I loved Axel from the moment I saw him and I'm only sorry I wasted so much of our time together because I was afraid to go to him. It's far better to risk all than to live with eternal regret. Only memories bring comfort when the end draws near."

"It needn't be the end. We're trying to—"

"I know. I know. And I pray you succeed but I hope I will not be too afraid to die. I hear Louis died like a true monarch and I, too, must die like a queen." She turned to Juliette and said fiercely, "But my little Louis Charles must live! You must promise me he will live."

Juliette swallowed hard. "I give you my word."

Marie Antoinette smiled and for a moment her face lit with all the charm that had captured Juliette so many years earlier that night in the Hall of Mirrors. She patted Juliette's cheek. "I trust you. Go with God, *ma petite.*"

TWENTY-ONE

Tutto a te mi guida.

The words repeated over and over in Juliette's memory on the ride home from the Temple.

Everything leads me to you.

Jean Marc was not at home when Juliette arrived at the Place Royale, though it was evening. Since he had returned to Paris from Le Havre he seemed to be avoiding her as she avoided him.

Robert carefully expressed no surprise when he saw Juliette's ragged gown and soot-smudged face. "I'll send up heated water. Will you need anything else?"

I needed more and I took it.

"Yes, send a maid to help me bathe and do my hair." Juliette hurried up the steps.

It was almost midnight when she heard Jean Marc's steps on the stairs. A moment later she heard the door of his chamber close behind him.

She drew a shaky breath, stood up, and moved quickly toward the door she had left ajar leading to the corridor.

Jean Marc had already taken off his black brocade cutaway coat and was unbuttoning his white linen shirt when she opened the door of his chamber without knocking.

He glanced over his shoulder, then tensed, his gaze wandering over her in the white lace robe. "May I say that you never fail to surprise me?"

"Hello, Jean Marc." She nervously twisted her hands. "I've been waiting. You were gone a long time."

"I didn't know I had a reason to come home." He paused warily. "Am I to assume I was mistaken?"

She nodded and closed the door. "This isn't easy . . . I can't . . . I'm not sure what to say to—"

"That seems clear."

She moved to stand before him. "I've been thinking and I've decided—" She stopped. "This is more difficult than I believed it would be."

"Shall I help you? You've decided it's foolish to fight against what we both want."

"No." She looked up into his dark eyes. Such beautiful, wary eyes. "I've decided to tell you that I love you."

He froze.

She hurried on. "Oh, I don't expect you to say you love me. Though I do think you care for me more than you know." Her voice lowered to a whisper. "You may never love me. I'm not sure you can love any woman."

"Then why are you being so generous as to give me such a weapon?"

"Weapon?" She smiled sadly. "You see, you're still armed against me. You may never—" She stopped, and it was a moment before she could speak again. "Yes, I'll give you all the weapons you could wish, Jean Marc." Her fingers rose to trace gently the plane of his left cheek. "I love you, not only with my body, but with my heart and my mind. I'll stay with you in your bed or by your side as long as you care to have me. I hope that may be for a long time for I'll probably love you for the rest of my life. Are those enough weapons for you?"

"Yes," he said hoarsely. "May I ask what prompted this capitulation?"

"*Tutto a te mi guida.*"

"'Everything leads me to you'?"

"Those are the words the queen has engraved on her signet ring. She said that from the first she'd known there was no choice and that love should be seized before it slips away." She smiled tremulously. "I suddenly realized I couldn't escape either. Everything did lead me to you from that very first day I saw you— Catherine, my painting, the Wind Dancer, the abbey, even the revolution. If I left tomorrow, something would happen to pull me back because that's where all roads lead. Don't you see? There's too much death and destruction in the world. I *won't* be cheated of what I can have with you." She laid her head on his chest, wrapped her arms about him, and whispered, "Everything does lead me to you, Jean Marc."

"I believe I'm . . . overwhelmed." He stood unmoving; his hands rose, hovered over her shoulders, and then closed on them with the most exquisite care. "But, if you expect me to refuse your offer, you're terribly mistaken. I'd be a fool to deny myself what I want. And I'm not a fool."

"I know you aren't."

"I'm a practical man." His lips caressed her temple. "If a victory is given, I accept it."

"Yes."

He lifted her in his arms and carried her toward the bed. "And what if there's a child?"

She stiffened and then relaxed against him. "I expect nothing of you. If it happens, I'll safeguard him."

He looked down at her. "You yield all?"

"Not yield," she whispered. "Offer."

He laid her on the silken coverlet and lay beside her, braced on his elbows on the bed, looking down into her face. In his expression she saw bewilderment, lust, and, oddly, regret. "It's the same thing, is it not?"

"No." She tangled her fingers in the thickness of his hair as his lips slowly descended toward her. "It's different. You'll see."

"You protected me," Juliette whispered drowsily. "I didn't expect it."

"Is it too much to believe I can meet generosity with generosity?" He held her close, his hand moving gently over her curls. "I found myself quite moved. It's probably only a temporary weakness, but until I can overcome it I couldn't place you in a position so vulnerable to me. You can see that—are you falling asleep?"

"Yes." She nestled closer. "I'd like to stay awake but I'm very tired." She yawned. "It was a very wearing day and you were late coming."

"I guarantee I'll be earlier tomorrow. In fact, we may not get out of bed."

"That will be pleasant." She was obviously struggling to stay awake. "We haven't done that since the *Bonne Chance.*" She drifted off to sleep.

Jean Marc's arms tightened about her, his cheek pressing against the top her head. She felt small, fine-boned, and utterly breakable in his arms. She had made herself totally vulnerable to him, and yet there was no weakness in her surrender. She was stronger now than she was at her most defiant, and he had the strange feeling that at his moment of triumph he had been defeated.

He gently kissed the top of her head and closed his eyes against the hot wetness stinging his lids.

Tutto a te mi guida.

True words. No wonder they had struck a note of recognition when the queen had—

The queen.

Jean Marc's eyes flew open and he stiffened against Juliette's lax body.

He had assumed Juliette had been quoting the queen from a moment in their past in Versailles, but Juliette had always refused to dwell on the past and lived only for the moment. Why should those words trigger such a strong reaction now?

Unless the words had been spoken much more recently.

Unless she had gone to see Marie Antoinette again at the Temple . . .

He carefully slid his arm from beneath Juliette's head and drew the silk coverlet over her. He got out of bed, shrugged into his brocade robe, and glided toward the door, stopping to pick up the candelabrum on the table.

A moment later he opened the door to Juliette's chamber. What did he expect to find? Juliette would already have sent the soot-stained gown of her disguise downstairs to be cleaned if she had gone to the Temple as he suspected. Perhaps he was hoping to be wrong and find nothing at all.

A white linen sheet draped the desk across the room and on it rested a fan, a vial, and an oak machine of some sort. On the floor beside the desk lay a straw basket of paper fans.

Jean Marc moved slowly across the room toward the desk. When he reached the desk he set the candelabrum down on the cloth-covered surface.

The white silk fan lying open on the desk was exquisite. Fine lace edged the delicate silk, carved ivory sticks were polished to a glowing patina, and the picture painted on the silk was of a graceful Pegasus with eyes of tiny almond-shaped emeralds.

Jean Marc stared down at the fan, panic icing down his spine.

"What are you doing here?" Juliette stood in the doorway behind him, wearing the lace robe, her hair tousled. "I didn't tell you that you could come in here, Jean Marc. You had no right to—"

"What is this?" Jean Marc picked up the silk fan on the desk and held it up. "For God's sake, what have you done?"

"You know what it is. It's the Wind Dancer. I did it for my own pleasure. I have no intention of using it in public." She pulled her robe closer about her as she hurried forward. "You shouldn't have touched it. I'm not sure the glue is dry." She took it from him and carefully laid it back on the linen-draped desk. "It's very good, isn't it?"

"Exquisite." He motioned to the box of paper fans on the floor beside the desk. "And you did those for your own pleasure as well, I suppose."

She didn't look at him as she repeated, "You shouldn't have come in here."

His hands grasped her shoulders, his fingers digging into her flesh. "The Café du Chat. The queen. It's been going on for months, hasn't it?"

She raised her gaze to his. "Yes, but I'm very careful. There's absolutely no danger to you, Jean Marc. If I were caught, I'd never—"

"Do you think I don't know that?" His voice was harsh. "Christ, do you think I don't know you by now?"

"It won't be for much longer. She'll be free soon. But you mustn't interfere now."

"You saw her today, didn't you?"

She nodded. "She wanted me to promise that I'd find a way to free her son. Oh, Jean Marc, she's so sad. I've *got* to help her."

"For God's sake, everyone in Paris knows the National Convention is gathering evidence for her trial."

"François says the escape plan is almost in place. He's already bribed the guards at the Temple and we've only to wait until we have a way for her to safely pass the barriers."

"François!"

"He's not really Danton's man. He's head of the group that's trying to free the royal family. His real name is William Darrell."

"Surprise upon surprise," Jean Marc said grimly. "And what other information should I be privy to?"

"None."

"And when does this escape take place?"

"Two weeks from now, the twenty-third of July." She looked up at him. "This doesn't concern you. Pretend you never saw the fans, Jean Marc. Go about your business."

"Pretend . . ." His laugh was mirthless. "Do you think I can ignore the fact you're involved in a plot that can send you to the guillotine? I'm getting you out of Paris tomorrow."

"No, Jean Marc," she said quietly. "Not until she's safe. However, if you like, I'll have Nana find lodgings for me elsewhere. I knew it might come to this if—"

"No! *Why* are you doing this?"

She smiled tremulously. "Because I've changed. What happened in Andorra changed me and I think you've changed me too, Jean Marc. When I was a child I was afraid to love anyone because I was sure they wouldn't return my love. But now I know it's the loving, not the being loved that matters. And, when you love someone, you have to help them." Her eyes glittered with unshed tears. "I assure you, I'd much rather go back to the way I was before. I was ever so much more comfortable. You're fortunate to be able to hold yourself aloof."

"Am I?" His tone was weary. He didn't feel aloof, he merely felt alone and terribly frightened for her. "I can't convince you to stop this idiocy?"

She shook her head. "But I'm really quite safe, Jean Marc. I only paint the fans and carry an occasional message."

"Only?" His lips tightened. "Very well. Whenever you go on one of these missions for Etchelet, tell me, and I'll go with you."

"No!" She tried to temper the alarm in her voice. "I'll not involve you."

"Then, if you don't want me in danger, you'll have to be very careful of yourself, won't you?" His hands left her shoulders and fell to his sides. "Don't worry, I have no intention of entering into this conspiracy. My only aim is to prevent you from losing your head. I find I've become inordinately fond of it as well as other delectable portions of your person." He moved toward the door. "And, my dear Juliette, I became involved that first morning I saw you running through the woods. It's far too late to go back and try to change that now."

Their attempt to free the queen failed.

Juliette couldn't believe it. "But we were so sure," she said in bewilderment when Nana told her that evening at the Café du Chat. "Everything was in place. What could have happened?"

"The guards were changed at the last moment," Nana said grimly. "Every single guard we'd bribed was mysteriously reassigned yesterday outside the Temple."

Juliette shook her head dazedly. "It doesn't seem possible. What do we do now?"

"Keep trying. Conceive another plan." Nana shook her head. "Though, God knows, there's not much time. William says they're talking about moving her out of the Temple to the Conciergerie. We'd have little chance of success if that happened."

Juliette shivered. The Conciergerie, a grim horror of a prison, squatting only a stone's throw from the glory of Notre Dame, was the last stop before the trip to the guillotine. "You have no one in the Conciergerie?"

"We have two guards in our pay, but we'd need more than that. We'll have to keep trying."

On the twenty-ninth of July another attempt was made to free the queen from the Temple and it failed as dismally as the first.

Another attempt was planned for the tenth of August. Early on August third the queen was roused from her bed at two o'clock in the morning and moved to the Conciergerie.

One more attempt was made while the queen was awaiting trial in the Conciergerie, this time in cooperation with another group of royalists led by Baron de Batz. It also failed.

On October 14, 1793, the queen went before her accusers and stood trial. Though only thirty-seven, the queen was going through change of life and suffered terrible menstrual cramps. In spite of her pain, she defended herself valiantly against the most infamous charges a woman could face, ranging from lesbianism to incest. Her efforts were doomed from the outset and Marie Antoinette was condemned to die by the guillotine on October 16.

"For God's sake, don't go." Jean Marc watched in helpless frustration as Juliette came down the stairs. Juliette's dark blue gown hung loosely on her and her eyes looked enormous in her thin face. During the past three months he had watched the pounds drop from her slender figure and the vitality illuminating her gradually drain away. Today she appeared as wax-pale and fragile as one of the lilies of Vasaro. "You can't help her and there's no sense in you putting yourself through any more."

"It's almost over." Juliette's back was very straight as she went to the mirror in the foyer and tied the ribbons of her bonnet beneath her chin. "She has to see me. She has to know I haven't forgotten my promise. She's so alone now." She looked up to meet his gaze in the mirror. "But it would help if you'd come with me. I know it's an imposition and I'll understand if you don't wise to—"

"Of course I'll come." His voice was rough. "Why not? Someone has to be there to catch you when you swoon. Death by the guillotine isn't pretty."

"I know," she whispered. "It's ugly. She always hated ugliness. She wanted everything beautiful and—" She caught her lower lip with her teeth. "I must get very close to the platform. She must see me. I promise I won't faint."

Jean Marc moved behind her and his hands gently encircled her throat. "She'll see you. We'll make sure she does," he said huskily. "Come along."

He quietly held her hand during the long carriage ride to the Place de la Révolution. When they arrived at the square he pushed ruthlessly through the huge, excited crowd, making a place for them directly before the guillotine.

He took Juliette's hand again as the throng roared

with delight when the cart bearing the queen arrived at the platform.

Marie Antoinette was dressed in a white piqué gown, white bonnet, black stockings, and red prunella high-heeled shoes, the finery in poignant contrast to her shorn head, sunken cheeks, and frightened eyes.

Juliette swallowed to keep back the bile threatening to choke her. She must not faint.

The queen must see her.

Fight the dizziness, fight the despair. She would be better soon. She had promised Jean Marc she wouldn't swoon.

The queen climbed the steps, stumbling as she reached the platform and trod on the foot of Sanson, the executioner. "Pardon, Monsieur," she stammered. "I did not mean it."

Juliette could barely see through the veil of tears. The crowd was yelling, the queen desperately looked at those in the crowd, as if searching for help which would not come.

She *must* see her.

Juliette fumbled at the ribbons beneath her chin and tore off her bonnet, at the same time stepping closer to the platform.

At last, Marie Antoinette's frightened gaze fell on Juliette. For an instant, the faintest flicker lightened the terror in her face.

Then the executioner pushed her toward the guillotine.

A moment later Sanson triumphantly held up the queen's head for the approval of the crowd.

But Juliette was not there to see it. Jean Marc was already pushing through the crowd, propelling Juliette forcefully across the square toward the side street where the carriage waited.

"I've lost my bonnet," Juliette said woodenly. "I must have dropped it on the ground by the platform."

"Yes." As they broke free from the crowd Jean Marc's arm encircled Juliette's waist and hurried her toward the carriage

"She saw me. Did you see her expression? Just for a moment, she saw me."

"Yes, she knew you were there." Jean Marc opened the door and lifted her into the carriage. "Home," he called to the coachman before he climbed into the coach after her.

He pulled Juliette into his arms and rocked her in an agony of sympathy as the carriage rolled down the cobblestoned streets away from the Place de la Révolution.

"I didn't swoon. I promised you I wouldn't—"

She slumped against him in a dead faint.

When she awoke she was in Jean Marc's bed, unclothed except for a white satin robe. Jean Marc lay naked beside her, his arms holding her with the same gentle strength as they had in the carriage. The velvet drapes at the window were drawn, and tall white candles burned in the candelabrum across the room.

"I'm sorry," she whispered. "I broke my promise. I didn't mean to be so much trouble to you."

"Be quiet." Jean Marc's gentle kiss on her temple belied the roughness of his words.

"Will it ever stop?" she asked in wonder. "So much blood . . ." She was silent a moment. "They were glad to see her die. Did you hear them cheering?"

Jean Marc didn't answer.

"Why should they be so happy? Didn't they understand? She wasn't brilliant like Madame de Staël, she was only an ordinary woman. She made mistakes but she never truly meant to be cruel."

Jean Marc reached over and took a goblet from the table by the bed. "Fruit juice. You've eaten nothing all day. Drink it."

She obediently swallowed the tart drink and he put the goblet back on the table. He drew her closer, cradling her cheek in the hollow of his naked shoulder.

"I'm so tired, Jean Marc."

"I know." His fingers tangled in her curls. "Rest."

"I want to see Catherine. I'd like to go to Vasaro and see Catherine. Do you suppose I could do that?"

"Yes, I'll arrange it in the morning."

"Catherine . . . François loves her."

"Does he?"

"Yes, he does, Jean Marc. Every time he mentioned her name I could see . . . I knew something was wrong. I had to pull it out of him."

"I'm surprised you succeeded."

"I just kept at him."

"Now that doesn't surprise me at all."

"The dauphin. I have to help Louis Charles. I promised her . . ."

"You have time. Go to Vasaro and rest first."

"I'm so sleepy . . . How peculiar. I just woke up." She forced her lids to open. "The fruit juice. Did you put something in it?"

"Yes."

"As you did to François at Vasaro."

"Only enough to give you a sound sleep."

"With no dreams?"

He kissed her forehead. "No dreams."

Jean Marc entered the salon an hour later. "I'm sorry to have kept you waiting. But I do thank you for coming."

François didn't bother to rise from his chair or look up from his goblet of wine. "I didn't miss you. Robert kept me very well supplied from your excellent cellar."

"Juliette insisted on going to the Place de la Révolution. You weren't there?"

François took another drink of wine. "My business is to get them out of prison, not to watch them die when I fail. I decided to get drunk instead. Unfortunately I have a very good head. However, I'll arrive there eventually."

"Why the hell did you fail? You had money, the time—"

"And Monsieur working against me."

"Monsieur?"

"The good Comte de Provence, the king's brother. He originally organized our group two years ago. Everything went very well while we were freeing only the nobles. What would a king be without a court?" François lifted his glass to his lips. "It was only when it became urgent to free the royal family he suddenly discovered a lack of funds. It seems the good Monsieur wished to become king of France . . . He has to have spies in both our group and in the convention. Every time we were ready to move, he blocked us. Oh, not in any obvious way. He didn't reveal my identity or sacrifice the rest of us."

"And you don't know who the spy is in your group?"

"I have an excellent idea. I've initiated a plan to make certain."

"The count wants the boy to die too?"

"Of course, he's in the way. Louis Charles is now king of France. But I *will* get him out of the Temple."

"I *will* get him out of the Temple. But I'll have to do it alone."

Jean Marc smiled. "Do you think Juliette would let you try to free him without her help? Which places me in the unenviable position of trying to stop her or making sure she accomplishes your common goal with all speed."

François slowly lifted his head. "And which is it to be?"

"I'll not stand by and see her suffer a second time like this. I'm sending Juliette to Vasaro tomorrow. Is it possible we could get the boy out before she returns?"

"Nothing can be done at once. The convention is expecting the royalists to be stirred up by the queen's death into making some sort of rescue attempt. They've increased the guards at the Temple."

"How long do we have to wait?"

"Perhaps a month or two." François rose and swayed. "I feel . . . Perhaps I've succeeded in getting drunk after all."

Jean Marc stepped forward and put an arm around François's shoulders. "*Merde*, I seem to be doing nothing this night but acting as a prop." He sighed resignedly. "You'd best spend the night here. I'll take you upstairs and put you to bed."

"How kind of you." François's tone was scrupulously polite even as his knees gave way. "Too kind . . ."

"I agree," Jean Marc said dryly. "It seems to me I was a good deal better off when I wasn't so kind."

"She'll see Catherine. . . . Catherine . . ."

The geraniums were in full bloom, burnishing the fields with flame and heady fragrance when Juliette arrived at Vasaro.

Catherine was waiting on the front steps and threw herself at Juliette who'd just emerged from the carriage. Then she held her at arm's length, gazing into her face. Jean Marc had sent a letter by messenger on the day Juliette left Paris, warning Catherine of her dear friend's condition. Indeed she did appear to be drained, sapped of her characteristic energy and vivacity. But there was more. Much more. When Juliette had left Vasaro she had retained remnants of the impatient, impulsive child Catherine had grown up with at the abbey. Now Catherine could catch only the faintest glimpse of that child in the woman who had taken her place. Catherine experienced an instant of poignant regret. They were both changing and being changed, but not together as she had once hoped. "It's terrible what they did to Her Majesty."

"Terrible things happen everywhere." Juliette put her arm around Catherine's waist. "But perhaps not here. I needed to be reminded that there are still places like this in the world."

Catherine smiled and took off Juliette's bonnet, affectionately tousling her friend's dark curls. "You must change your gown and come down to the fields with me right away. For the next two days you'll do nothing but work with Michel and me."

Juliette looked at her quizzically. "I must labor for my bed and board?"

Catherine nodded. "Of course, everyone works at Vasaro." She smiled serenely. "You must pick the flowers, Juliette."

TWENTY-TWO

Y ou've not only failed, you've become a monster," Anne Dupree said coldly. "How do you expect to be accepted by the gentlemen of the convention?"

"I couldn't help it," Dupree whimpered. "I had to hide from the *policia* and almost died. By the time it was safe for me to go to a surgeon, my bones had healed wrong."

"Better you had died than come back to me like this. What use are you to me? Do you expect me to care for you when it's your duty to care for me?"

"No," Dupree said quickly. "Everything will be as you wish. I can still get the Wind Dancer for you. I know who has it."

"Jean Marc Andreas," Anne Dupree said caustically. "And how do you intend to wrest it from him? While you've been away Marat has been murdered and you have no patron, no power. Are you to go begging Danton or Robespierre for a place?"

"I went to Danton at his home and he refused me," Dupree admitted. "He said he had no use for murderers."

"Yet he had use for you before you went to Spain. I told you no one would be able to bear the sight of you with your twisted bones."

"But there's still hope. When I managed to escape from Spain I went first to Marseilles and asked questions." Dupree's words tumbled one after the other in his effort to convince her. "Andreas has a cousin, Catherine Vasaro, for whom he has a fondness. She may even be the girl in the locket. There has to be some connection between Juliette de Clement and Andreas."

"You told me the girl in the locket was a princess."

He had forgotten he had told her that falsehood. "I thought she was a princess but perhaps—"

"You lied to me."

"No," he said desperately. "I thought she was a princess. I only said—"

"Never mind." His mother's gaze narrowed on his face. "How will you use the Vasaro girl?"

"I'll send her a message that I have Jean Marc Andreas captive and she must come herself to ransom him."

"What if she ignores the message?"

"She won't." Dupree tried to sound confident. "She'll come. And then I'll have her."

"And you'll use her to make Andreas give you the Wind Dancer?"

Dupree nodded quickly.

"I don't like it." She frowned. "It's a plan based on sentiment."

She had identified Dupree's own worst fears, but he had to persuade her he could be successful. "She's only a foolish girl. Sentiment is common in women of—" He stopped as she turned her cold gray eyes on him. "Not you. But some women don't realize how stupid it is to let sentiment rule them."

"And Andreas? From what you've told me, I'd say he's not a man of sentiment."

"I tell you he has a fondness for her."

"You have no cunning." Anne Dupree rose to her feet with a swish of lavender taffeta. "I thought I'd taught you better. Forget this plan and go to Paris and set watch over Andreas. All men have secrets—and there might be something we can learn about this one that will profit us. It's better than trusting to sentiment. You'll leave at once."

"I thought to stay here for a few days and rest," Dupree stammered. "I'm not well. The bullet is still lodged in my body and at night I get the fever." It was the truth but not the reason he wished to stay. It had been too long since he had seen her.

"You wish to rest? Certainly." She smiled at him. "But you cannot expect to sleep in any of my nice clean beds. You've been very naughty. You failed me, Raoul. You didn't bring me the Wind Dancer and you lied to me about the princess. You know the place for naughty little boys."

"No!" Dupree got up as quickly as possible. "I'll go at once to Paris. You're right, I should watch Andreas."

"I doubt you need worry that anyone will recognize you." Anne Dupree made a delicate moue. "But be cautious, nevertheless. This is your last chance, Raoul. I shall not be so indulgent again."

He grabbed his hat from the table. "I'll not fail you." He moved awkwardly toward the door, dragging his left leg behind him. "I'll get it. I'll give you the Wind Dancer."

Anne Dupree walked to the mirror and patted the heart-shaped patch at the corner of her mouth. "That's a good boy," she said absently. "Oh, and take the locket from the jewel case in my chamber. You might have use for it, if you decide to involve the Vasaro girl in some way."

"You wouldn't mind?"

"The locket has no value now." She inclined her head to stare at her son. "Because it's not worthy of me, is it?"

She was not going to forgive him, he thought in

panic. She might never forgive him again unless he brought her the Wind Dancer. The Wind Dancer had the power to give his mother everything she had always wanted. It would make her a queen greater than the Bourbon bitch they'd beheaded last week.

"No, it's not worthy," he mumbled as he opened the door. "I'm sorry, Mother. Please . . . I'll bring you the Wind Dancer. I'll bring it . . ."

He limped from the room, pausing just outside the door to try to suppress waves of nausea. Close. It had been so close. What if she had discarded him? He was nothing without his duty to her.

A sudden thought chilled him. If he gave his mother the Wind Dancer, she would no longer need him. No, he must not let such a thing happen.

The hunger raked at his soul. She had sent him away again. The hunger must be fed.

Camille. He would go to Camille and she would feed the hunger.

"The eyes are difficult." Juliette added a little more blue to her brush. "He has such expressive eyes, doesn't he? So much wonder . . ."

Catherine looked over her shoulder at the portrait of Michel standing in a field of flowers. "But I think you've caught it." She sat down on the grass and linked her arms about her legs as she gazed thoughtfully at the pickers working at the bottom of the hill. "You've made good progress on it."

"It's truly a wonder. I can't persuade the little Gypsy to pose for me for more than five minutes at a time." She tilted her head. "It's one of the best things I've ever done. It's worthy of a gallery showing." Her lips twisted. "Not that I'll ever know that pleasure."

"Why not?"

"Even in this splendid new republic, women's artistic efforts aren't considered worthy of public display."

Catherine shook her head. "But it's wonderful."

"That makes no difference. I could have the talent of a Fragonard or Jacques-Louis David and still not be allowed to be hung next to the most amateurish of male daubers. It's not fair, but that's the way of life." She shrugged. "Oh, well, *I* know it's good."

"Are you almost finished?"

"Just a few more touches and the signature." Juliette wiped her perspiring brow with her sleeve. "I notice Michel's been spending a good deal of time with Philippe."

Catherine nodded as she picked a blade of grass and chewed on it. "Philippe's tried very hard to become friends with Michel since he returned from Marseilles."

"Have you forgiven him?"

"Forgiven him for being Philippe?" She shrugged. "It isn't my place to forgive him. It's Michel's. And Michel sees nothing to forgive."

"But you can't view him in the same fashion?"

"No, but we both love Vasaro."

"I don't like it," Juliette said flatly. "If you keep on in this vein, you'll end up by marrying the peacock."

Catherine looked down at the ground. "It's . . . a possibility." Catherine added, "Not soon. But I must have a daughter for Vasaro at some time."

Juliette shook her head. "You deserve more."

"Philippe is a cheerful companion, he works hard—"

"And he's certainly proven he can father any number of progeny."

Catherine smothered a smile. "Only you would say something so outrageous." Her smile faded. "I need someone besides Michel. I'm . . . lonely, Juliette."

Juliette was silent for a moment before glancing over the top of her easel at Catherine. "Then send for François."

Catherine stiffened. "François?"

"Why won't you talk about François, Catherine? I've told you what forced him to make the decision at the abbey and I think you understand."

"I don't wish to speak of François. I know you have a great admiration for him but—"

"You refuse to forgive him when you've obviously forgiven Philippe. Even after I told you why it was necessary he withhold his help at the abbey, you still won't talk about him." Juliette looked down at the painting. "I've been thinking about it and I believe I know why you can't forgive him."

"Juliette, I don't wish—"

"Because you love him. You don't love Philippe, so it's easy to forgive his faults." She shook her head. "Mother of God, at the abbey François didn't even know you. How could he betray you?"

Catherine stood up and jerkily brushed the grass from her gown. "You know nothing of how I feel."

"Who could know you better? I don't understand why . . ." Juliette frowned as she stared thoughtfully at Catherine. "Or perhaps it's not really a question of forgiveness at all. Did he refuse to stay with you here at Vasaro? Couldn't you hold him here in your Eden?"

"He wanted to stay! He said so. I—" Catherine broke off and gazed at Juliette defiantly. "And he said there was nothing wrong with my wanting to stay at Vasaro."

"But you knew he was wrong, didn't you?" Juliette put her brush down and regretfully shook her head. "Dear heaven, we were all so happy you'd found peace and contentment here at Vasaro we were afraid to probe beneath the surface."

"I love Vasaro."

"Who wouldn't love it? But he still left you, didn't he? And you know he would leave you again."

"Yes!" Catherine exploded, driven. "He won't stay here. He'll go back to that horrible place and I'll have to—" Her eyes widened in shock as she realized what she had said. "Mother of God . . ."

"And you know to admit you love François is to be forced to leave Vasaro. Tell me, have you ever written in the journal I gave you?"

"I write in it every day."

"But you've never written on the first page."

Catherine gazed at her, eyes bright with tears. "Dear God, you're cruel. Why are you doing this?"

"Because I love you," Juliette said wearily. "And because François loves you. He broke down and confessed to me in Paris. He *loves* you. Do you know how fortunate that makes you? I may go through my entire life without love and you have it and won't reach out and take it."

Catherine didn't speak for a moment. "Jean Marc?"

"Of course it's Jean Marc. Why are you so surprised? It's always been Jean Marc." Juliette stood up. "Catherine, admit it to yourself. You're afraid to go to François because it would mean leaving your garden. You've learned to live without fear here but you're afraid of the world he lives in." She took two steps forward and grasped Catherine's shoulders. "And, by the saints, you should be afraid. François is in danger all the time in the Temple. If he doesn't betray himself in some manner, then Danton could decide at any time to hand him over to the Committee of Public Safety. He says there are even spies in our own group. Wherever he turns there's the shadow of the guillotine."

"No!" The tears were running down Catherine's cheeks. "Why do you let him do it?"

"Because the rest of us don't live in a sheltered garden. We all must take our own risks."

Catherine pulled away from Juliette's grasp and stared at her wordlessly. Her lips formed words that refused to fall from her lips. Then she turned and ran toward the manor.

Sweet Mary, was it true? Catherine asked herself. Had she been afraid to give up the safety of Vasaro even for François? She had thought she had grown strong and independent. Was that false?

She threw open the front door and ran up the stairs into her chamber and locked the door. She leaned back against it, panting, her heart pounding. Safe. She was safe here from Juliette's words, safe from Juliette. . . .

Dieu, she loved Juliette and yet now she was shutting Juliette away, too, because she had become a threat to the serenity she had found at Vasaro.

Catherine threw herself on the bed and stared sightlessly at the window across the room. She lay there while the afternoon became evening and then darkened into night. She heard the knob turn once and another time Philippe knocked on her door and called softly. He went away when she didn't answer.

The moon had risen and was flooding the room with silver light when she got up from the bed and walked slowly to the desk. Her fingers trembled as she lit the candles in the candelabrum. She sat down and drew the journal from the drawer. She sat looking at the smooth leather cover for a long time.

Then, slowly, she opened the journal to the first page.

The date leapt out at her.

September 2, 1792.

Dear God, she couldn't . . .

She drew a deep breath and reached for the white feather quill. She quickly dipped the quill in the onyx inkwell and began to write.

The bells were ringing.

"Catherine." Juliette knocked on the door again. "If you don't answer, I'm just going to stay here until you do. It's almost midnight and I don't see—"

"Come in," Catherine called. "I've unlocked the door."

Juliette padded barefoot into the room, her white cotton nightgown drifting about her. "I feel very foolish. I tried the door before, and it was locked so I—" Her gaze fell on the ledger on the desk, then rose swiftly to Catherine's weary face. "You did it?"

Catherine nodded. "Though I didn't have very pleasant feelings toward you while I was."

"I know. I felt the same way toward Jean Marc. But it's better now?"

"It's better now. It's not over, but it did help. I've been a dreadful coward, haven't I?"

"Oh, no." Juliette knelt before Catherine's chair, her arms sliding lovingly around her friend's waist. "We all want a garden to go to when the pain becomes too great. Look at me, I ran to you and Vasaro."

"But you'll go back soon?"

"In a few days. I must get back to Paris. I have no reason to stay now. Your Vasaro has healed me."

"Vasaro . . ." Catherine shook her head. "No, we heal ourselves. There's no real magic in Vasaro."

"Isn't there?" Juliette smiled. "Don't be willing to give up every belief so easily."

Catherine's palm gently touched Juliette's curls. "You scoffed at magic a year ago."

"Perhaps I've learned the wisdom of being foolish." Juliette sat back on her heels. "And you the foolishness of being wise." She grinned, her brown eyes twinkling in the candlelight. "Doesn't that sound odiously profound? Now we can set ourselves to finding how to combine the two in some harmonious manner."

Catherine felt a sudden lifting of spirit. "Stay in my room tonight," she said impulsively. "Do you remember how sometimes I'd slip into your cell at the abbey and we'd talk and laugh until just before time for matins?"

Juliette nodded, her face lighting with eagerness. She jumped to her feet and ran over to the bed. "Get into your nightgown." She pulled down the coverlet and slipped between the sheets.

Catherine laughed and went to the bureau to get her nightgown. She suddenly felt young and carefree and filled with the joy of being alive.

Juliette began to chatter about the painting of Michel, skipped to a less than complimentary assessment of Philippe's character, and then went on to the art of making fans.

Catherine slipped into bed beside Juliette and contentedly leaned over to blow out the candles.

Juliette fell silent.

Catherine turned to her. "Juliette?"

"It's not the same. We can't bring it back, can we?"

"What do you mean?"

"The time before . . . I thought we could bring it back just for a little while— But we're not those people anymore. We can't talk and giggle until dawn. We can't be children any longer."

"No." Catherine thought about it. "But perhaps this is better." She reached out and took Juliette's hand.

"I think our friendship is stronger now. You said you loved me this afternoon. You couldn't have said that then."

Juliette's fingers threaded through Catherine's. "I do love you. If I loved you less, I'd have let you stay safe in your garden where I wouldn't have had to worry about you." She tried to laugh. "You know how selfish I am. Next week I'll probably be telling you to forget everything I said and— No, that's not true. I want your life to be full and rich. I won't have you cheated."

Silence fell between them.

"I want your life to be full and rich too, Juliette." Catherine hesitated before asking tentatively, "Why Jean Marc? You know he's—"

"I know. It doesn't make any difference."

They lay there, their hands joined companionably, staring at the silver-edged shadows of the room.

A long time later Catherine said quietly, "When you go back to Paris, I'm going with you."

Philippe helped Juliette into the carriage and then hesitated, looking at Catherine. "I don't approve of this. Your place is here."

"My place is where I choose it to be." Catherine smiled and held out her hand. "Take care of my Vasaro, Philippe. And take care of Michel. Make sure he does his lessons every evening."

"I will." He added gravely as he lifted her hand to his lips, "I'm trying, Catherine."

"I know you are." She let him help her into the carriage and sat down by Juliette.

Philippe stepped back, motioned to Léon, and the carriage started with a jerk.

The coach rumbled down the driveway, past the lemon and lime trees toward the road. Philippe stood looking after them, and when they turned toward Cannes he lifted his hand in farewell. A ray of early morning sun burnished his golden hair with radiance as he smiled at them.

"What are you thinking?" Juliette asked curiously, her gaze on Catherine's face.

"How beautiful he is." Catherine's tone was detached. "If the abbey had never happened, I probably would have married him and been happy. It would never have occurred to me to want more than I saw in him because I had no more depth than he."

"You were more than you think you were."

"I was an insufferable prig."

"A prig." Juliette's eyes sparkled with mischief. "Not insufferable. I suffered you, didn't I?"

"We suffered each other." Catherine chuckled. "Good God, why I ever let you make me chase after you to that tomb—" Her laughter faded and then she determinedly smiled, blocking out the other memories and keeping only the ones to cherish. "You were perfectly abominable to me on occasion."

Juliette had noticed the hesitation and reached out to take Catherine's hand with careful casualness. "It was good for your character. Now François will seem a saint to you in comparison."

François. Catherine leaned back in the carriage, excitement and fear equally mixed within her. How did she know François even wanted her any longer? Juliette said he did but she could be mistaken. Six months was a long time. Perhaps there was even someone else.

Well, if it was too late, she would face it without shirking.

She could no longer hide in Eden.

"Mademoiselle Catherine, it's good to see you looking so well." Robert smiled warmly as he held open the front door. His gaze went beyond Catherine's shoulder to the street where Juliette was supervising the unloading of her paints and canvas. She suddenly turned and ran up the steps.

"*Bonjour,* Mademoiselle." Robert beamed at her. "Monsieur Andreas will be very happy you've returned. The house has seemed very empty since you've been gone."

She made a face. "I'm sure it's been a good deal quieter anyway." She untied the ribbons of her bonnet. "But why are you opening the door? Where are the servants?"

"Gone. All the servants are gone except Marie and me. Monsieur Andreas dismissed them a few days after you left Paris."

"How peculiar." Juliette frowned. "I'll speak to him about it. Where is he?"

"He's not yet arisen."

"Good Lord, it's almost noon. He always rises early." Her eyes widened in alarm. "Is he ill?" She started across the foyer toward the stairs at a run. "I must go see, Catherine. Make sure they don't damage my portrait of Michel when they unload it."

She burst into Jean Marc's darkened chamber a moment later. "What's wrong? Are you ill? I knew I should never have gone away." She saw a stirring in the bed and hurried over to the window and ripped back the drapes to let in the light. "Look what happened. There are no servants in the house and you've become ill and—"

"Juliette." Jean Marc's voice was husky with sleep and surprise as he sat up in bed. "What the devil are you doing here?"

"It's time I came back." She ran over to the bed and threw herself into his arms. Before he could move she had covered his face with kisses. "Oh, Jean Marc, I've missed you. Please don't be ill. All the time I was running up the stairs I was thinking. 'What if he's truly ill? What if he dies?' I can't bear it if you're—"

"Hush!" His arms went around her and held her close. "I'm not at all ill."

"Then why are you still in bed?"

"For the very good reason that I didn't get to bed until nearly dawn."

His heart throbbed strongly beneath her ear and she cuddled contentedly closer, nestling her cheek in the dark hair that thatched his chest. Life. "Well, it was most unkind of you to frighten me like that."

"May I call it to your attention that I didn't know

you were returning? Why didn't you send a message and— Never mind." He tugged her head back and his lips covered hers with sudden passion.

Her arms tightened about him as joy soared through her. He was well and strong and they were together again.

Jean Marc lifted his head. His breath had quickened. "One of us is overdressed, and I believe it's you. Take off your clothes, Juliette. *Dieu,* I've missed you."

"Have you? I wanted you to miss me." She looked up at him wistfully. "Truly, Jean Marc?"

"Truly." He sent her bonnet sailing across the room. "As I mean to demonstrate immediately if you'll please remove—"

"I can't." She reluctantly pushed him away and stood up. "If you're not ill, then you must dress and come downstairs. Catherine is here."

"Catherine." Jean Marc frowned. "Why has she come to Paris? She shouldn't have left Vasaro. Neither of you should have come back."

"You knew I'd come back," she said quietly. "I couldn't leave you here alone, and I have something I must do."

Jean Marc threw back the covers and got out of bed, reaching for his brocade robe on the chair. "*Merde,* haven't you heard what's going on here? The Jacobins have gone mad. They're arresting and killing everyone in sight. They've executed every Girondin and aristocrat they can lay hands on and anyone else they have a quarrel against. The guillotine's been working day and night since the queen's death. Dammit, it's not safe for you here."

"The guillotine." She shuddered as she remembered that day at the Place de la Révolution. The queen in her pretty red prunella slippers . . ."More deaths?"

Jean Marc buttoned his robe as he turned to face her. "Go back to Vasaro. When there's so many deaths, it becomes commonplace. I'd have little chance of saving you if you went before the tribunal."

She tried to smile. "And would you mind if I went

to the guillotine? I hope you would. It would be very sad to have no one mourn me."

"I'd mind," he said slowly. "I'd mind so much that I'd probably be forced to find a way to destroy both that damn guillotine and the nation who ordered it used on you."

Her eyes widened and she felt a sudden breathlessness. "How . . . extravagant. You *would* mourn me."

"Good God, did I not say—" He broke off and turned his head away so that she couldn't see his face. "However, François would be most upset if I also brought down his precious Rights of Man which would probably follow. So let's avoid it by all means. Go back to Vasaro."

She shook her head. "Even if I'd go, Catherine would not. She's going to join François at the Temple."

"No!" Jean Marc whirled back to face her. "Why?"

"She loves him," she said simply. "It's her place to be with him now."

"Not at the Temple. If she won't go back to Vasaro, let her stay here where I can try to protect—"

"She's not a child any longer, Jean Marc. You can't protect her. We must both do what we have to do."

"The devil I can't," Jean Marc said harshly. "I should order Léon to bind and gag both of you and force you to go back to Vasaro."

"We'd only come back." She smiled. "I know you care about Catherine but she's no longer your concern. She's François's wife now." She turned and moved toward the door. "I'll leave you to dress. Shall I send water up with Léon?" She frowned. "It's not his duty and he'll be quite upset. Really, Jean Marc, it's not sensible to have only Robert and Marie in the household. Why did you send the rest of the servants away?"

"I thought it best. I've had a number of visitors of late that I wanted no gossip about."

"Who?" She gazed at him curiously before pain suddenly tore through her. "A . . . woman? I suppose I should have expected it. You've always had many mistresses and I've been gone—"

"Seven weeks and three days," Jean Marc said softly.

"I'm not sure how many hours, but I'm certain I would have been able to tell you if you hadn't exploded into my chamber and roused me from a sound sleep."

"Truly?" The breathlessness came again and with it the faintest stirring of hope. "Bankers are always good at numbers, aren't they?"

"If they wish to make a success of their profession." He shook his head. "No other women, Juliette. I found myself quite uninterested in replacing you in my bed. Another victory for you."

"Then where were you last night?"

"At one of those tiresomely clandestine meetings necessary for dire plots and conspiracies. Tell me, is there some rule that they always have to take place in the middle of the night?"

"Plots?"

He smiled slowly. "I'd hoped to have your Louis Charles safely out of the Temple before you returned but, as usual, you've done the unpredictable."

"Louis Charles." She gazed at him in amazement. "You're helping us?"

"My dear Juliette, I do not help. If I become involved, I must seize control of a project."

"Why?"

"Because I have a certain amount of self-love, I suppose."

"No, I mean why are you doing this?"

"Do you expect me to say I'm doing it for the memory of the queen or the good of the country?" He shook his head. "I'm no idealist."

"Helping Louis Charles to escape could destroy you."

"Not if it's done correctly."

"But why take the risk?"

"A whim."

She shook her head. "Tell me, Jean Marc."

He was silent a moment. "Because I don't like the idea of a child being made the pawn of nations merely because of his birth." He gazed intently at her. "And because I never again want to see you hurt and broken the way you were the day Marie Antoinette was guillotined."

Hope spiraled into joy. "I wasn't broken."

His lips twitched. "No, not broken but certainly radically bent." He made a gesture as if to sweep her from the room. "Now, go order my bath. I shall feel better able to cope with you and Catherine once I have the sleep washed out of my eyes."

Jean Marc descended the stairs an hour later to find Juliette coming in the front door.

"It's too late," Juliette said cheerfully. "Catherine's gone. I just sent her to the Temple in my carriage. You must go there if you wish to argue with her, but that would be very foolish."

Jean Marc didn't seem overly upset at the news. "What a clever move on your part," he said calmly. "Then I'll argue with you instead. Come join me for breakfast."

"I've eaten already." She followed him into the breakfast chamber. "It's after noon. You should be having dinner instead of breakfast."

"That's not what we're supposed to be arguing about. Let's consider what good your presence can do here in Paris."

"I can paint the fans. I can act as courier."

"We've formed another network. You don't know these people and they don't know you."

"That was intelligent. François said he suspected the Comte de Provence had an agent in the royalist group at the Café du Chat." She frowned. "But you must not let the count know you're aware of his agent or he'll take other steps to block your attempts."

"François hasn't cut his ties with the group and goes to the Café du Chat frequently." Jean Marc sat down at the table and put his napkin on his lap. "I know you'll find it incredible but we did think of that possibility even without you."

"No one knows?"

"Nana Sarpelier." Jean Marc buttered a croissant. "I trust that meets with your approval?"

"Oh, yes." Juliette's brow knit in thought. "When do you plan on freeing Louis Charles?"

"As soon as possible. But we have to have help from inside the Temple. François has been trying to influence the couple who care for the boy."

"The Simons. The queen said she thought he was only stupid, not cruel. Do you think there's a possibility they might help?"

He shrugged. "Bribery wouldn't be a factor. François says they're fiercely loyal to the republic but seem fond of the boy." Jean Marc took a bite of croissant and chewed it thoughtfully before he added, "There are a number of problems as I see it. First, getting the boy out of the prison. Second, out of Paris and past the barriers. Then, where does he go from there? Perhaps to Vasaro for an interim period, but he won't be safe there for long. If we take the boy to his relatives in Austria, he'll probably have a fatal accident before he's free a year. If he goes to another monarchy, they'll use him as a pawn."

"No!" Juliette sat down across from him. "Both the king and queen told Louis Charles before they died that he mustn't strive to get the throne back."

"As I said, there are problems." Jean Marc finished his croissant and reached for his cup of chocolate. "We haven't formulated a firm plan to resolve any of them, but I've been working on a way to get the boy out of Paris that has a certain flamboyant appeal you might appreciate. That's where I was last night."

"Indeed?" she asked, intrigued. "How are you going to do it?"

"I think I'll wait until Monsieur Radon's finished before I divulge this particular plan." He finished his chocolate, set down his cup, and patted his mouth with his napkin. "But you can see we're working diligently on the little king's behalf. Why don't you go back to Vasaro and let us get on with it?"

She shook her head.

"I didn't believe you'd agree." Jean Marc stood up.

"I suppose I must make the best of the situation. Come along."

"Where?"

"Seven weeks, three days, *and* six hours," he said softly. "It came to me while I was in the bath. It's been a long time, Juliette."

Too long. She could feel her heart start to pound just looking at him, at the high sheen of his dark hair, at the slightly wicked curve to his lips as he smiled at her. "Yes."

"Let's see, I've argued with you to no avail. You've robbed me of Catherine to try to persuade to reason. I see no way to impose my will upon you except the one you accept most readily." He held out his hand to her. "Come to bed, *ma petite.*"

Her heart was now beating so hard she could feel its thunder in every part of her body. He had said he missed her and what she saw in his eyes must be affection at the very least. She smiled brilliantly as she placed her hand in his and said meekly, "As you wish, Jean Marc."

"As I wish? When have you ever done as I wished?"

The sound of their laughter echoed from the high-arched ceilings as they ran up the stairs, down the hall, and into his chamber.

Jean Marc's laughter vanished as soon as the door shut behind them.

At first Juliette didn't notice his sudden sobering as she started toward the bed, her fingers fumbling at the fastenings of her gown.

"No."

She glanced at him over her shoulder and saw him taking off his pearl-gray satin coat.

"Don't undress, Juliette." His voice was soft, his gaze night-dark. "Not yet."

She gazed at him uncertainly. "But you're undressing."

"Oh, yes." He strolled forward and draped his coat carefully over the back of the blue and ivory tapestry-cushioned chair. "As quickly and expediently as possible." He began to unfasten his white linen shirt. "But

I've decided I don't want you to do it." He gestured to the chair where he had laid his coat. "Will you sit down?"

She crossed the room and dropped down on the chair he'd indicated, staring at him in bewilderment. "Jean Marc, you're behaving very oddly."

"Am I?" He stripped off the shirt and threw it aside. "Bear with me. It all has a purpose."

She didn't care a whit about his purpose. She wanted to *touch* him. She wanted to close her fingers on the dark, springy thatch on his chest, rub her palms on the smooth, hard musculature of his shoulders. "It's been *seven* weeks, Jean Marc."

He nodded. "Too long. I had a good deal of time to think." He sat down on the bed, pulled off his left boot, and then tugged at his right boot. "About you, Juliette."

Her hands closed tightly on the cushioned arms of the chair. Sweet heaven, he was beautiful. The sunlight streaming into the room bathed him in a golden glow, delineating each feature of his face, the tough, sinewy grace of his chest and shoulders.

"Aren't you going to ask what I thought?" He tossed the other boot aside before he stood up again and quickly resumed stripping.

"Could we speak of this later?"

Jean Marc was naked now and she could feel heat suffuse her body as she looked at him.

He stood in the middle of the room, standing with legs slightly astride, lean buttocks tight, every muscle tense, his manhood boldly aroused.

She couldn't breathe, the air in the room seemed heavy, vibrating with the same arousal she saw in him. She started to stand up and go to him.

"No." He moved forward and pushed her gently back down in the chair. He dropped to his knees beside her chair, took her hands, and held them tightly. "Tell me what you want me to do."

"What?" He knew what she wanted of him, and it had nothing to do with him kneeling before her like a beautiful naked God come down from Olympus to seduce a mortal.

His gaze fastened intently on her face. "I want to give you something. I've always been the one who has taken. Now I want you to take." His hands tightened on her own. "Use me, Juliette."

Shocked, she merely stared at him.

He lifted her hand and placed it on his naked chest. She could feel the springy hair brush her flesh and the thunder of his heart beneath her palm. "I want you," he said quietly. "I don't think I've ever wanted you more. It's important that you know that."

"Then, by all that's holy, *take* me," she said in exasperation.

The faintest smile tugged at his lips as he shook his head. "Tell me what you want. Do you want me to undress you?"

She nodded jerkily. "It would be an excellent start."

He rose to his feet and pulled her up from the chair, his hands deftly undoing the fastenings at her neck. As his fingers brushed her flesh she inhaled sharply. Her gaze flew to his face, and what she saw there caused her heart to start to pound harder.

The golden olive of his skin was pulled taut with strain over his cheekbones, and his dark eyes glowed as they held hers. "Do you remember that first day in the cabin on the *Bonne Chance*?"

"Of course I do."

Her gown fell into a pool of green silk about her feet.

His head lowered slowly and he placed his lips with the greatest gentleness on the exact place where her shoulder met her arm. "*S'il vous plaît*, Juliette."

She shivered as his hands moved to the tie of her petticoat. She knew he was trying to tell her something, but the fever of need was rising and she couldn't think.

The petticoats fell to the floor and his hands moved up to caress her breasts through the thin linen of her chemise, squeezing and releasing rhythmically. She made a sound low in her throat and closed her eyes as sensation after sensation rippled through her.

"I've been thinking about how you looked lying on the bunk on the ship, how brave you were at the Place de la Révolution. And I recalled the child I first knew at the inn at Versailles. I thought about how you told me you felt when you painted. Swathed in moonlight and sunlight . . ." As the last of her undergarments fluttered to the floor he whispered, "Drunk on rainbows . . ."

"Did I say that?" Dear heaven, that had been over five years before at the inn when she had first met him. "That was a long time ago. I'm surprised you remember."

"I probably remember every word you've ever said to me." His fingers moved down to pet and caress the curls surrounding her womanhood. "I've decided I'm jealous of your painting. I want to be the one to show you rainbows."

"I don't know what you're talking about."

He lifted her in his arms and carried her to the bed. "Pleasure. Pleasure so intense it's close to pain. The way you feel when you're painting." He laid her on the black velvet spread, then followed her down and gently parted her thighs. He entered her slowly, carefully, until he filled her entirely. Her nails dug into the velvet coverlet. His very slowness and deliberateness was unbearably erotic and sensual. "*Your* pleasure, Juliette."

And in the fevered hours that followed she came to realize that it was her pleasure alone of which he was speaking. He used his knowledge of her body and responses to arouse and sustain her pleasure at heights they'd never before reached in their months together. Time after time he roused her to a frenzy of passion and then gave her an equally fiery release.

But he never once allowed himself release, never permitted himself that final climax of passion.

Afternoon became evening and their coming together became less frantic but still urgent.

"Jean Marc . . ." She could scarcely speak through the hot haze of pleasure still surrounding her as she held him tightly within her body. "Why . . . ?"

He looked down and his warm smile embraced her.

"I told you once I'd learned to control my responses over the years of playing the game." He leaned down and kissed her lingeringly. "I saw no reason why I shouldn't use that control to bring you pleasure."

And then, finally, she understood. He would probably never say the words, but this self-imposed restraint was an apology for all his past attempts to dominate and subjugate her. The tears stung her eyes as she looked up at him. Jean Marc truly must care for her if he would give up his blasted battleground and yield so much to her.

"Was it enough?" Jean Marc whispered.

She nodded. "Rainbows . . ."

"Then"—his voice was almost inaudible—"*s'il vous plaît*, may I take my own pleasure?"

Her fingers tightened on his shoulders. "Please, Jean Marc."

He moved swiftly, strongly, the expression on his face harshly contorted as if he were in pain. Perhaps he was in pain. The past hours of restraint must have been incredibly difficult for him.

Only a moment later he stiffened, throwing his head back, the cords of his neck distended, as shudder after shudder of release convulsed his body.

He collapsed on top of her, his breath coming in gasps. "Mother of God, I didn't think I'd be able to do it."

She didn't see how he *had* done it. She gently stroked back a dark lock of his hair that had fallen down on his forehead. "Jean Marc, I believe you must be as idiotically noble as that crazy old Don Quixote in the Cervantes book. You didn't have to—"

"Noble? Nonsense. Pleasure has nothing to do with nobility of the soul." He moved off Juliette and lay down beside her. He drew her into his arms and held her close. He was trembling, shivering, as if he had been through a terrible ordeal.

"You think not?" Her arms slid around him and she held him possessively, protectively.

The room was silent except for the sound of their breathing.

"You're sure it was enough?" Jean Marc asked when his breathing had steadied. "I wanted it to be another 'something beautiful' for you to remember."

She nodded as she drew closer to his long, strong body. How could it not be enough? she wondered as she blinked back the tears. This surrender had been no easy thing for him. He had made himself vulnerable to her and at the same time given her his trust. "Oh, yes, it was, Jean Marc." She pressed a loving kiss in the hollow of his throat. "Something very, very beautiful."

The bitch was back.

Dupree felt the joy rise within him as he moved out of the shadows of the house across the square from the Andreas residence. His mother had been right as usual. Everyone was coming to him. The de Clement bitch had returned to her lover, Andreas. Even the Vasaro girl had arrived on the scene. If he wished, he could go to Robespierre and denounce both women—and Andreas for harboring them.

The power was sweet, heady, and he enjoyed toying with it for a moment before putting it reluctantly aside. Not yet. It had come to his attention in these weeks of watching the Andreas house that there was far greater power to be gained by holding his hand for a while.

He wiped the fluid running from his broken nose with a lace-trimmed handkerchief and limped down the street to the waiting carriage. His hip ached badly, as it always did after standing all day. Well, it wouldn't go on much longer. He had found out all he needed to know to get both the Wind Dancer and the power he needed to maintain his position in his mother's life.

The letter he had placed in the pocket of his coat that morning seemed to spread a glowing, comforting warmth while whispering of safety, riches, and revenge.

He opened the door of the carriage and carefully, painfully, pulled himself up the step and into the coach. "The Café du Chat," he called to the man on the box. He didn't bother to give the direction. The man had taken him to the café many times before.

Nana Sarpelier sat at a long table in the back room of the Café du Chat gluing sticks onto the painted rendering of the guillotining of Charlotte Corday, the murderess of Marat.

She looked up when Dupree came into the room. She involuntarily recoiled, but recovered quickly. "Pardon, Monsieur. This is a work room. Customers are not served here."

"I'm allowed here." Dupree limped forward and dropped into the chair across the table from her. "I'm allowed to do anything I wish to do. Your friend Raymond Jordaneau sent me back here to see you. You're Nana Sarpelier?"

"Yes." She gazed at him warily. "Who are you?"

"Your new master." His smile only twisted the left side of his face. "Raoul Dupree. Ah, I see you've heard of me."

"Who hasn't, Monsieur? Your fame during the massacres—"

"Don't bother to pretend," Dupree interrupted. "I'm well aware you're an agent for the Comte de Provence." He smiled as he saw her stiffen. "That frightens you, doesn't it? Good, I enjoy fear in a woman."

"You're going to turn me over to the tribunal?"

"If I were, I'd not be here now."

Nana gathered her composure. "That's just as well. For naturally your accusation is entirely false."

He shook his head. "I've been watching this café for many weeks. I knew almost at once that all of you here were royalists."

Nana remained silent, gazing at him with no expression.

"You see, I followed François Etchelet here from Andreas's house one night." He tapped his temple with his index finger. "And I asked myself what could be the connection between an official of the Temple and Jean Marc Andreas. You do know Andreas has the Wind Dancer?"

"Has he?" Nana placed another stick on the fan.

"I think you know. Then I asked myself another question. Who could have told Andreas that Celeste de Clemente had the Wind Dancer?" He smiled. "The queen, of course. My former employer, Marat, had always suspected the Comte de Provence had a group of royalist sympathizers here in Paris whose duty was to free the noblesse and the royal family. Pursuing that suspicion was going to be my next task after I returned from Spain." He leaned back in the chair. "You can see how all the pieces fit together?"

"Very clever."

"So I watched for a few days and saw the members of your little group coming and going. I have names and I have addresses. I could send every one of you to the guillotine."

Nana's eyes were cold as she looked up from the fan. "Then you're a fool to come here. We'd be stupid to let you leave alive."

He laughed. "Why do you think Jordaneau allowed me to come back here to see you?" He reached into his coat and brought out an envelope. "Because I showed him this letter from the Comte de Provence. It's very carefully worded, of course, but it places me in complete control of the actions of both you and your friend Raymond Jordaneau."

She froze. "Indeed?"

He nodded with satisfaction. "After I realized who your master was, I immediately wrote and offered my services. I no longer have a secure position in the government now that Marat is dead."

"So you now serve the Bourbons."

"Why not? There's a certain glory in royalty. My mother will be pleased to be honored at the court of Vienna." He dabbed at his nose with his handkerchief. "The count said he had heard of my work and would be pleased to have my help in a certain awkward matter. So he gave me authority over the two of you."

"Why not the entire group?"

"You know the answer to that." He smiled. "Because only you and Raymond Jordaneau are totally his creatures. You do the count's bidding, not Etchelet's."

He tapped the letter with his forefinger. "The count made it quite clear whom I can trust in this delicate matter."

"And we're to obey you?"

"Without question or he'll be forced to do without your services. He's very concerned about the possibility the little king might be freed and taken, not to his own loving arms, but to England. He believes Etchelet is working toward that aim without informing him."

Nana was silent a moment. "It's true. Etchelet only recently told me about it. I would have sent word to Monsieur in my next report."

"But you don't have to report to him now. You report to me," Dupree said. "Much more convenient. We can't allow Etchelet to succeed, of course. The count has made that perfectly clear."

"What are we to do?"

"Kill the boy."

Nana nodded. It was the answer she had expected. "It's the sensible thing to do. If Etchelet didn't free the boy, then one of the other groups might. The Baron de Batz almost managed to free the queen days before she was guillotined. How will you kill the child?"

"I haven't decided. I'll let you know. The count wants the death blamed on Robespierre in order to disrupt the convention." He shrugged. "That may take some manipulation."

"You have access to the boy?"

"Of course. You forget who I am. I may no longer have my former power, but all the guards know of Raoul Dupree." He rose to his feet. "Find out all you can from Etchelet regarding their plans. We must strike before them."

She nodded. "Where do I reach you?"

He gave her the address of his lodgings. "You'll come to me tonight."

She looked at him in surprise. "I may not know anything for a few days."

"You will come to me anyway. I require certain services."

"What—" She broke off as she realized his meaning and couldn't keep the distaste from her expression.

"You find me less than pleasing?" He laughed harshly. "So does the entire world. Andreas made me into this monster. Andreas and his bitch. We shall have to find a way to include them in our plans." He turned away. "In the meantime, if you don't wish me to send a report to the count that I found you unobliging, you'll come to me tonight."

He limped from the room.

TWENTY-THREE

François's lodgings in the Temple looked more like a cell than living quarters for a municipal official, Catherine thought with a shiver as the officer stepped aside for her to enter. The stone walls seemed to breathe a damp chill and the furnishings were almost nonexistent: a simply crafted table with three chairs, a small chest, a narrow bed with only a shabby linen coverlet.

"I'll have to wait here with you until Citizen Etchelet comes," Captain Ardlaine told her apologetically as he pulled out a chair for her. "No one is allowed alone in the Tower without the proper papers."

"I told you my husband didn't know I was coming. He would have arranged to have me admitted if he'd—" She frowned. "Is it always this cold?" Catherine drew her crimson cloak more closely around her. The December cold seemed to pierce the thick stone walls. "Why is there no fire in the stove?"

"I'll light one." He moved toward the porcelain stove. "The citizen's duties keep him away for most of the day, and it's not practical to keep a fire—"

"Catherine!" François stood in the doorway.

He appeared harder, thinner, wearier than he had at Vasaro, she thought, but still he looked wonderful. She jumped to her feet. "This gentleman believes I don't belong here, François. Please tell him I'm your wife."

"My . . . wife," François repeated slowly. He turned to the soldier. "Yes, of course, Paul, this is my wife, Catherine. God in heaven, what are you doing here, Catherine?"

She came toward him. "Why should I live in comfort at Vasaro when you choose to serve the republic by existing in this hovel? I decided I should be by your side." She turned and smiled at the captain. "Thank you for being so kind, Captain. Will you have my boxes brought up from the courtyard now?"

The captain nodded. "You're a lucky man, Citizen. But remember to get proper papers for her."

"I'll remember." François's gaze never left Catherine. "If she stays. My wife's spirit is stronger than her constitution. I'm not sure living here would be the best thing for her."

Catherine smiled at him. "I should know what's best for me. Everyone knows a woman's place is with her husband."

As soon as the heavy oak door closed behind the captain, François demanded, "What's this about, Catherine? Why are you here?"

She drew a deep breath. "This isn't easy for me."

"You have a message from Jean Marc?"

"No, I arrived only this morning. I haven't seen Jean Marc yet." She smiled ruefully. "Juliette knew he wouldn't approve of my coming here, so she whisked me off before I could even—"

"Why?"

"Because you're my husband," she said simply.

He shook his head. "Nonsense. You never regarded that ceremony as anything but expedient."

"It's true that I'd like to be married again by a priest. Could we please do that, François?"

He went still. "What are you saying?"

"That . . . I love you." She rushed on. "And I know you may not love me any longer, but I had to tell you. I had to try to—"

"Mother of God." He swept her into his arms and buried his face in her hair. "Of course I love you," he said thickly. "Always. But the abbey . . ."

Relief poured through her as her arms went around him to hold him tightly. "You persist in acting as if you'd raped me yourself. You should have explained why you couldn't help me instead of letting Juliette tell me of William Darrell. Did you think me so shallow I would put my violation over the lives you've saved since then?"

"You forgive me?"

Her expression was sober as she stepped back and looked up at him. "The question is, do you forgive *me*? I was afraid to share your life even though I loved you. I don't even know how you could still love me."

"Don't you?" His lips pressed her temple. "Perhaps because you have strength and gentleness . . . and truth."

"Not truth. I seem to have told myself a good many lies in the past." She smiled tremulously. "But I'll try to give you truth from now on."

His hands cupped her cheeks as he looked down into her eyes. "Catherine, I . . ." He kissed her gently, sweetly, with exquisite tenderness. He lifted his head and the expression on his face was as beautiful as the dawn rising over the fields of Vasaro. "My love."

The joy became too strong to bear, and she closed her eyes for a moment. He was still looking at her with the same expression when she opened them and she knew she had to do something to lighten the moment or she would start to weep. She took a step back and laughed shakily. "Then it's settled." She looked around the apartment. "I must do something to improve this place. I don't know how you can live in such discomfort. If we're to stay here for any length of time, we must have blankets and carpets and a curtain for the window. And perhaps a comfortable chair by the stove for—"

"We?" He shook his head. "You can't stay here."

"Oh, but I can." She gazed at him steadily. "I intend to stay here as long as you do, François. Make up your mind to the fact that I won't return to Vasaro until you can return with me."

"Catherine, I *can't* come with you. There is much I have to do here."

"I know, Juliette told me." She reached up and touched his lips with her fingers. He belonged to her, she thought wonderingly. She had the right to reach out and touch him whenever she liked. "Then I'll help you do them. We worked very well together at Vasaro. I'm sure we'll do equally well here."

"No." His jaw set stubbornly. "You can't stay at the Temple. For God's sake, it's a prison, Catherine."

"That's another reason we must make our surroundings as comfortable as possible." Catherine brushed a kiss on his cheekbone before moving toward the door. "They're bringing my boxes now. Will you see if that nice captain can find me an armoire in this vast place? I must go back to Jean Marc's house and beg linens and blankets."

"Stay there."

"And we must keep a fire burning in the stove all the time. These stone walls are dreadfully damp."

"Catherine, I have no intention of arranging a pass for you. The guards will refuse to let you back through the gates."

"No, they won't." She paused at the door, her smile infinitely loving as she looked back at him. "Because, if they do, I'll sit at the gate and weep and wail until they let me come to you. And that would cause a good deal of attention, don't you think?"

"Yes, but you still—"

"And attention shouldn't be focused on you at the present time. Besides, didn't you marry me to protect me from the eye of the republic? Would you want word of François's poor, rejected bride to be bandied among the soldiers and come to the ears of the Commune?"

A slow smile lit his face. "You'd really do it, wouldn't you?"

She smiled serenely. "Certainly. I thought I'd made clear my position. If you wish me to be gone from here, you must accomplish your task quickly so that we may both leave."

He shook his head ruefully as he bowed with a flourish. "I'll do all within my power to oblige you, Madame."

"And I'll do all to oblige you," she said softly, her gaze clinging to his a moment longer before she turned away and opened the door. "Remember the armoire."

A Savonnerie carpet patterned in beige and ivory now covered the cold stone floor and heavy rose-colored-velvet drapes hung at the window. A scarlet velvet coverlet had replaced the linen blanket, and a massive cream-covered cushioned chair with a matching footrest occupied the area next to the porcelain stove.

"It's not too bad." Catherine tilted her head critically as she looked around the room. "I like the yellow curtains in my room at Vasaro better, but these are heavier and will do more to shut out the cold."

"Did you leave Jean Marc any furniture?" François asked as he leaned back and rested his head on the cushioned back of the chair. "As I recall, he had a fondness for this chair. He always sat in it when we met in the Gold Salon."

"Because it's large enough for a big man. You need it more than he does." Catherine smiled. "Don't worry, he didn't argue with me when I took it. Jean Marc has many chairs and he can spare us this one." She shivered. "It's still chilly here. We can't seem to get rid of the cold. Is the little boy's apartment this cold?"

François nodded. "But he's not uncomfortable. The Simons treat him very well, by their own standards. Of late they've let him live a normal life." His lips twisted. "Though, God knows, at first they did everything to turn him into what the republic wanted."

"What do you mean?"

"Simon had orders to coarsen him, educate him in the ways of the common man."

She frowned, puzzled. "What did they do?"

"Brought in whores, taught him to drink wine as if it were water. He was in a drunken haze during most of the period before they guillotined his mother."

Catherine looked at him in horror. "But he's only a little boy. How could they do that to him?"

"It's Simon's idea of heaven for the common man," François said dryly. "Whores, wine, and time to enjoy both. In his eyes he was only doing his duty and showing the boy a fine time."

Catherine shook her head. "How is Louis Charles now?"

"Old for his years. When I look at him and remember Michel . . ." His gaze met her own. "They've robbed him of his childhood. I want to give it back to him, Catherine, but I don't know if anyone can."

Tears welled in Catherine's eyes as she heard the weariness and discouragement in his tone. He had struggled long and hard against tremendous odds and had lost as often as he had won. Pray God he did not lose this time. "When can I meet him?"

"Tomorrow. I have supper with the Simons twice a week and then play cards with Simon and a few of the officers. You're sure you want to do this? They're crude, bawdy people."

"The field workers at Vasaro are certainly not genteel." She smiled. "And I liked them very much indeed." Her smile faded. "Though I don't believe I'll like these people. To bring whores to an eight-year-old boy . . ."

He held out his hand and she came to stand before him. He took her hand and pressed it to his lips. "You could always go back to your garden."

"No, I couldn't," she whispered. "Not without you. Never again without you, François."

He pulled her down on his lap and cradled her in his arms. He sat holding her, carefully, lovingly, for a long time without speaking. At first she was aware only of the delicious pleasure of being close and held as if she were a treasure infinitely precious to him. However, gradually she became aware the muscles of his body were hardening against her own. Her heart leapt and then began to pound harder as his lips pressed to her throat.

"You do know how much I want you?" he whispered.

She stiffened and then forced herself to relax against him. She had known this moment would come, and she had thought she'd prepared herself for it. She laughed shakily. "That night we were wed you said you didn't like skinny women."

"I lied."

"When I thought about it later, I suspected you had."

"I wanted you so much I was hurting."

They were silent a long time.

His voice was muffled against her hair. "It doesn't have to be tonight. I can wait."

She was frightened. She could tell him to wait and he would do it. She wouldn't have to face the fear tonight.

But if she told him to wait, she would be hiding again.

"No." Her voice was trembling. "Now. Though I may not be able to please you."

"You'll please me." His fingers sought and found the pins holding her bun, plucking them out one by one and dropping them on the floor. "If you only let me hold you close, you'll please me. It pleases me to look at you, to hear you laugh." He threaded his fingers through her long hair. "That's the difference between love and lust, Catherine."

His green eyes were so intent, his smile so tender, she felt her fear melting away. "How . . . do we start?"

He lifted a long silken strand and rubbed it on his lips. "Anywhere we choose. We can do anything we like. There are no rules." Suddenly his smile widened mischievously. "I know. Why don't I brush your hair, my sweet?"

The pounding of her heart was starting to steady as she looked up at François. "Is . . . it over?"

A shudder went through François's body as he moved off her and lay down beside her. "Yes." His chest was moving in and out with the unevenness of his breathing. He turned her over and cradled her spoon fashion. "For now."

"You were quite . . . intense." She thought about it. "Does it always bring you that much pleasure?"

"It always brings pleasure but this"—he kissed her ear—"this is extraordinary, my love."

"Why?"

"Do you suppose it's because I love you? I can't think of any other reason."

"I like to know I brought you pleasure. It . . . warms me."

He went still. "But you felt no pleasure yourself, did you?"

"I don't know what you mean. I told you I—"

"Were you frightened?"

"At first, but not later." She kissed the arm binding her to him. "You were so kind to me. I was afraid I'd see . . . but there was only you."

"That's good." His voice was husky in her ear. "But I want more for you. Tell me what you felt, Catherine. I need to know."

"Warmth, comfort, love." She nestled against him. "It was really quite pleasant."

"Nothing else?"

"Toward the end a kind of . . . tingling." She rushed to assure him. "But you didn't hurt me. I know you were being very careful."

"Not careful enough. I should have taken more time. I tried but . . ." His lips brushed her ear and his voice was suddenly hoarse. "I've loved you for too long, Catherine."

"Why do you feel so bad? I told you that I thought you—"

"Kind and gentle." His arms tightened about her. "I believe I'm too impatient."

"There's something wrong? I was supposed to do something else?"

"No, I just thank God you're not afraid of me." He kissed her gently. "Never mind, another time. This is enough for now."

"You came." Dupree felt a fierce burst of pleasure as he gazed at Nana Sarpelier. He hadn't been sure she would obey him even though it meant displeasing the count. He had watched her closely these past weeks and knew she wasn't hesitant about jumping into the bed of any man who took her fancy. Still, she seemed to be of a deplorably independent nature. "Come in." He stepped aside as she came into the room. "I expected you, of course. You have seen Etchelet?"

She shook her head. "I told you I wouldn't be able to contact him so quickly."

"Tomorrow will do as well." He closed the door, his gaze running over her. "Take off your cloak."

She took off her coat and draped it over a chair. "I don't like this, Dupree."

"But you do like the extra livres the count gives you."

"A woman must eat."

"There are other needs that must be met as well." He sat down in a cushioned chair and leaned his arm on the table beside him. "And you can imagine that in my present state I have great difficulty persuading a woman to pleasure me."

"I understand the strumpets on the Palais Royal care little how a man looks as long as he has money in his pockets."

"But they can't give me what I need. I used to have a choice mistress who was quite wonderful. She was an actress at the Comédie Française. Camille Cadeaux. Perhaps you've heard of her?"

Nana shook her head.

"She looked a little like you. A tall, strapping, full-figured woman. She suited my purpose admirably."

"Then I suggest you return to her."

"Oh, I can't. While I was in Spain she took another lover, and when I tried to get her to change her mind, she refused to accommodate me."

"Perhaps you can persuade her to see how mistaken she'd be to discard a truly admirable gentleman such as yourself."

"Sarcasm isn't permitted," Dupree said. "It's clear I'll have to train you as I did her."

"It hardly seems worth your time when your Camille is already—"

"Camille is dead." Dupree smiled as he saw the shock on her face. "I really couldn't permit her to live and continue to go to another man's bed. It would have desecrated the role she played."

"Role?"

"I told you she was an actress." He nodded to a large armoire against the wall. "You'll find a gown and a wig in there. They were Camille's, but I'm sure they'll fit you just as well. Put them on."

She simply stared at him. What was his game?

"Now, you know you would never have come here unless you intended to do as I wished."

She went to the armoire. "Have you decided how you're going to dispose of the king?"

"Poison, I think. I know an apothecary on the rue Marat who will oblige me with what I need. Poison would seem a safe, reasonable method for Robespierre to choose, and I no longer have the strength for a physical struggle."

"The king is only eight. He wouldn't struggle hard enough to—"

"I don't want to speak of the king. Put on the gown."

Twenty minutes later she stood before him in the pink brocade gown, tucking her own brown hair beneath the stylishly coiffed gray wig.

Dupree could feel the excitement rise within as he looked at her. "Magnificent," he said breathily. "You have a strength Camille never possessed." He reached into his pocket and pulled out a small silver snuff box. "Bend down. There's one last touch."

She bent close to him, her expression wooden.

He opened the snuff box, carefully extracted the heart-shaped beauty mark, and put it just to the left of her mouth. "There, you're quite perfect now." His hands were shaking as he closed the snuff box and replaced it in his pocket. "Kneel before me."

Nana hesitated and then sank to her knees before his chair.

"Very good. Now the words. You must say them very sincerely or I'll be displeased."

"What words?"

His voice took on a high, simpering note. "Raoul, promise me we'll be together always. You're mother's own sweet boy. I'll never punish you again."

She repeated the words.

His hand cracked against her cheek. "Sincerely. Again."

Nana opened her mouth to speak, her eyes glittering with anger, then she drew a deep breath. A moment later she repeated the words.

"Better. Now say 'I was so wicked to put you in the wood box with all those nasty creatures.'"

"I was so wicked to put you in the wood box with all those nasty creatures."

He bent forward, his breath coming in short, hard gasps. "I beg you to forgive me."

"I beg you to forgive me." Nana looked up to see his face convulsed with pleasure.

"Say it again."

"I beg you to forgive me." Nana was silent for a moment. "Is that all?"

"Oh, no." Dupree smiled, his eyes glazed with pleasure. "There's much more. You may kiss my hand."

The next evening Catherine carefully avoided speaking directly to Louis Charles during supper, concentrating instead on making herself agreeable to the Simons.

She found to her surprise that it wasn't such a difficult task. As François had said, they were rough, obscene, and not overly intelligent, but they appeared good-natured. Of the two, she preferred the woman to her husband. Madame Simon was a squat, tubby little woman with heavy masculine features and a pimpled face, but she had a warm smile and appeared genuinely fond of the child.

It wasn't until the men had settled down to their card game and Madame Simon to her knitting by the stove that Catherine dared wander casually over to where Louis Charles was reading by the window.

"It's overwarm by the stove," she said. "May I sit here beside you?"

"As you like, Citizeness." His gaze was wary and returned at once to his book.

A wave of pity swept through Catherine. François had said that Louis Charles was too old for his years and now she saw what he meant. His air of grave maturity was not so much quaint as saddening. She sat down in the chair across from him and studied the little boy from beneath her lashes. He was truly a beautiful child, though he bore only a faint resemblance to Marie Antoinette. He possessed the same fair hair and wide-set blue eyes, but his features were far handsomer than his mother's.

"I don't like people to stare at me," he said without lifting his gaze from the book. "I wish you would not do it."

"I was thinking you look a little like your mother."

He looked up quickly. "You've seen my mother?"

"A long time ago when you were a baby. She was very kind to me."

He nodded eagerly. "She's always kind." He lowered his voice. "But we must not talk of her here. They don't like it."

"Very wise. What are you reading?"

"A book by Rousseau. Citizen Robespierre thinks he's a fine man. They took away all the books Papa gave me but they let me have these." He nodded to the four books stacked on the table beside him.

She reached for a volume bound in dark blue leather.

Louis Charles swiftly put his hand on the book to keep her from taking it. "No."

She looked at him in surprise.

His gaze met her own. "It's not a book you should look at, Citizeness."

"Why not?"

"There are pictures of unclothed men and women doing . . ." He stopped and shrugged. "It's not a proper book for a lady who knows my *maman*."

"But it's proper for you?"

He shook his head. "I don't know." He nodded across the room at Simon. "He says it's the only kind of book a man should read."

"Do you believe him?"

"I don't know," he repeated. "How can I know what's true and what's false if everyone tells me something different?"

"Do you like Citizen Simon and his wife?"

"They're very jolly most of the time." For an instant his air of maturity slipped as he said wistfully, "But I wish they'd let me see my *maman* sometimes."

"But she's—" Catherine stopped when she realized with shock that he had been referring to his mother in the present tense. Louis Charles thought his mother was still alive! She was silent a moment before asking, "Where is your *maman*?"

"In the apartment on the floor above us with my sister and aunt." His hand tightened on the book. "They say she's a wicked woman and I must not talk about her."

Catherine felt a sense of poignant sympathy. "I didn't find her wicked. I think you must make up your own mind about that, Louis Charles."

"Charles. They call me Charles here."

She smiled. "I'll try to remember."

"Yes, it's hard to remember everything they want of you." His gaze was as bleak and world-weary as a very old man's. "*Maman* says one must do one's best."

Catherine knew she had lingered too long and must

return to the group by the stove, but she found herself reluctant to leave him. Louis Charles was so terribly alone. More alone than he knew. "Do you like flowers?" she asked impulsively.

He nodded. "At Versailles we had beautiful gardens and even at the Tuileries . . ." He trailed off and then his gaze focused on her face. "My *maman* loves flowers. She wears a perfume that smells of violets."

"My cousin has a garden in the city where the most beautiful violets grow. Would you like me to bring you a box? You could care for them and watch them grow."

He frowned uncertainly. "I know nothing of growing flowers."

"Then I'll teach you. I have a garden even bigger than the one at Versailles. It's called Vasaro and I'll tell you all about it."

Eagerness illuminated his features. "I think I'd like that."

"I know you will." She stood up. "And I'll tell you all about my friend Michel. You'd also like Michel. He's only a little older than you and knows all about flowers and perfume and—"

"Could he come and see me? We could talk and play ball in—" The enthusiasm faded from his expression. "I forgot. No one can come to the Temple."

"But I can come here," she said gently. "And at the least I can tell you about Michel. I have another friend who knew your mother much better than I did and you as well. Her name's Juliette and we'll talk about her too."

He nodded, smiling tentatively. "That's very kind of you. I know I mustn't ask too much."

Catherine felt the sting of tears. "I'll come to see you day after tomorrow, Louis Charles."

"Charles," he corrected her gravely. "Only Charles."

Catherine turned away and moved toward the group gathered by the stove.

She sat down by Madame Simon, who casually glanced up from her knitting. "You were talking a long time to Charles."

Catherine stiffened. Had her absorption in the boy appeared suspicious? "He's a sweet-natured lad."

Madame Simon nodded. "Everyone always wants to stare at him and touch him. The baker's wife even offered me an extra loaf if I'd cut a lock of his hair for her."

Catherine relaxed and leaned back in her chair. "Did you give it to her?"

"Would I do that?" She shook her head. "The poor lad would be bald in a week if I gave a lock of hair to everyone who wanted it. Besides, they want the hair of a king, and Charles isn't a king any longer. He's only a good republican." Pride and affection shone in the woman's face as she glanced at the boy in the corner. "We've done a fine piece of work with the boy, if I do say so myself."

Catherine avoided looking at her. "I see he's reading Rousseau."

"A republican book. I can't read a word myself, but what Citizen Robespierre likes is good enough for me."

"He doesn't know his mother is dead."

Madame Simon glanced at her anxiously. "You didn't tell him?"

Catherine shook her head.

The woman looked relieved. "My husband wanted to tell him but I said there was no sense in making the lad unhappy."

"I promised to bring the boy a box of violets. Would that be all right?"

She shrugged. "Why not? As long as he cares for them himself. I'm too busy to bother and my husband's in his cups most of the time." She smiled tentatively at Catherine. "I'm glad you've come to join François. A man needs a wife, even if he thinks he doesn't." She cast a sour glance at her husband. "It will be right pleasant to have another woman to talk to."

Catherine smiled. "I hope we can become friends." She carefully kept her gaze from straying to the boy across the room. "Very close friends."

"I want to *do* something, François." Catherine nestled closer to him, her eyes staring blindly into the darkness. "That poor child."

"We're doing all we can."

"I want him away from here. Children are so helpless. First Michel and now Louis Charles. But at least Michel is happy and free. I want Louis Charles to be free too."

François stroked her hair. "Soon."

"How soon?"

"I have a few ideas. I need to talk to Jean Marc tomorrow and then go to the Café du Chat. Perhaps before the end of next month we might have him free."

"Dear God, I hope so."

"So do I, love." François closed his eyes. "Now go to sleep."

"Now?"

His eyes opened again. "You don't want to go to sleep?"

"I thought we might . . . I know you weren't happy last night." She drew a deep breath. "I thought we might try again."

He lay still, his hand stroking her hair stopped in mid-motion. "You don't have to do this."

"It was pleasant. I like being close to you."

He slowly drew her to him. "Then I believe we'll make a valiant attempt to get very, very close indeed, my love."

"It's like a flower releasing its perfume, isn't it?" Catherine asked dreamily. "This is what you wanted me to feel?"

François chuckled. "Trust you to find a comparison that would bring us back to Vasaro."

"Is it like that for you too?" She raised herself on one elbow to look down at him. "Is that what you feel?"

"Yes." He kissed her shoulder, his voice husky. "An entire field of flowers releasing their perfume, sunlight shining and soft rain falling."

"Is it always like this?"

"No, sometimes it's only pleasant, a way to ward off the loneliness."

She stared at him thoughtfully. He must often have

been lonely in the years when he had lived two lives and never been able to trust anyone. "Did you—" She stopped. She didn't have the right to question his past, yet she desperately wanted to know about those secret years. She wanted to know *him*. All of him. He had told her once that he was many people and she knew only Danton's angry François, the François of Vasaro, and François, the lover. Now she wanted to know William Darrell. "Was there someone who helped you to—" She didn't know exactly how to put the question into words.

He stiffened. "What is it, Catherine?" When she didn't answer, his gaze intently searched her face. "There's never been anyone but you since Vasaro. Not like this."

"But there was someone?"

He nodded. "Someone."

"Who?"

"Nana Sarpelier."

"The woman you told me about who works at the Café du Chat. Juliette says she's a fine woman." Catherine was silent a moment. "You . . . cared for her?"

"I cared for her as a friend, as a comrade, Catherine. She helped me. There were dark days and sometimes she made life brighter."

"I see."

"What are you thinking?" François's hands cradled her face in his hands and forced her to look into his eyes. "You're my love. She's my friend. There's a difference. Please believe me."

"I believe you." A thoughtful frown wrinkled her brow. "I'd like to meet her, François. Will you take me to the Café du Chat?"

"I told you—"

Her fingers on his lips stopped his words as she smiled suddenly. "I'm not angry. I may be jealous of her. I'm not sure about that yet. But I'm grateful she helped you and I think I should become acquainted with her."

He chuckled. "You do realize your attitude is extremely unwifely?"

She settled down beside him and cuddled close to his naked strength. "I love you. I trust you. I want all that's best for you. How can that be unwifely?"

The box measured approximately two feet by two feet and was filled to overflowing with deep green leaves and white violets just starting to bloom.

Louis Charles gently touched one fragile blossom. "It feels like velvet, like the skirt of one of *maman*'s gowns . . . only cooler."

Catherine sat down at the small table. "Robert, my cousin's gardener, says you must not water these more than every four days or they may die."

"I'll be careful." He sat down beside her. "But there's not much sunlight in here."

"Violets like the shade. At home at Vasaro we plant them in great beds beneath the trees. Their scent is greatest in the middle of the night when it's darkest." Catherine drew closer. "You'll see what I mean if you wake some night and smell the fragrance. Michel says the fragrance is the soul of the flower."

Louis Charles's solemn gaze was fixed in fascination on her face. "What a peculiar idea. Is he mad?"

Catherine laughed and reached out and gave him a quick hug as she might have done with Michel. "Not in the least. He just doesn't think like anyone else."

Louis Charles frowned thoughtfully. "You mean he doesn't believe what people tell him to believe?"

"No."

"It must be pleasant to be able to make up one's own mind," he said wistfully. He touched the blossom again. "Tell me more about this Michel."

"Shall I tell you how I first met him? I was most unhappy about something that had happened to me and I awoke one morning and went down to the geranium field . . ."

It was dinnertime and Pierre Barshal was a man who had infinite respect for the joys of the palate, as was evidenced by the rolls of fat straining against his linen shirt and the rosy paunchiness of his cheeks. He sat at the counter of his apothecary shop devouring a full loaf of bread and a quarter pound of cheese, and washing it down with a bottle of wine. He looked with disfavor at Dupree as he walked in the front door.

"You have it?" Dupree asked eagerly, drawing nearer to the counter, his gaze on Barshal's plump face.

Barshal reached under the counter and drew out a small green bottle.

"How fast?"

"Half a minute, perhaps." Barshal shrugged. "But it takes effect immediately. He won't be able to scream, if that's what's worrying you."

"Excellent." Dupree handed him the money. "You're sure it's stoppered tightly?"

Barshal nodded. "You won't lose a drop."

"How much do I need to use?"

"Only a few drops. I don't know why you ordered so much."

"I always like to be prepared for any eventuality." Dupree smiled with satisfaction. "You've done well, Citizen."

"The poison is not without pain."

"No matter, as long as it's quick. That was the most import—" Dupree broke off, collapsing against the counter, flinching with pain. "Mother of God!"

Barshal looked at him with no expression. "What's wrong?"

"My leg," he gasped. "I've been walking too long on it today. Laudanum. Prepare a potion . . ."

"It will cost you extra."

Dupree's face contorted. "I don't care. The pain . . ."

Barshal shrugged and went into the preparation room in the back of the shop. He came back a few minutes later with a glass of milky fluid.

Dupree grabbed it quickly and drained the glass. "*Merci*, Citizen." He lowered his head and took several long breaths. "It's already helping."

"Four francs."

Dupree lifted his head. "You overcharge me."

Barshal lifted one shoulder. "You said you'd pay."

Dupree reluctantly handed over the francs. "I'll

take care not to fall ill in your shop again." He turned and limped toward the door. "*Bonjour*, Citizen."

Barshal grinned at his departing back before putting the money away in the cash box. Served the ugly bastard proper, he thought with satisfaction. The man's face turned his stomach and put him off his food. He reached for his bread and cheese and took a sizable bite of each before reaching for the bottle of wine and finishing it with three swallows.

Dupree's hand closed caressingly on the bottle Barshal had given him as he hurried down the street. It was a pity he'd had to dispose of the apothecary. An amoral man of his profession was very useful, but Barshal was known to others in the city beside himself. The comte must be made aware how sharp was his new tool and how ruthlessly it cut.

He hefted the tiny bottle, such a light, lethal weight. Yet, even with the drops of poison he had put in Barshal's wine, he was sure he would still have more than enough for his purpose.

"You can't see him today," Madame Simon told Catherine when she came to the door of the cell three days later. "The boy just lies there in bed and stares."

Catherine's eyes widened in alarm. "Is he ill?"

"No." Madame Simon's lips tightened as she glared at her husband nursing a mug of wine by the fire. "It was that stupid husband of mine. He got drunk and told Charles about old Sanson choppin' his mother."

"He had to know sometime," Simon said with a surly look. "Everyone else does."

"You didn't have to dance around singing and pretending you were holding the bitch's head," Madame Simon said crossly. "He wasn't ready to hear it like that."

White hot anger surged through Catherine, and she had to turn away so they wouldn't see it in her expression. "I'll come back tomorrow."

"You won't see me," Simon said bitterly. "I'm leaving the Tower. They tricked me."

Catherine's gaze flew to Madame Simon. "What happened?"

She shrugged. "The Commune promised him a better position and he resigned as guardian for the boy."

"But they didn't give me the other position and now they won't let me take back my resignation." Simon drained his cup. "They'll be sorry. No one was ever better to that boy than I was."

"What are they going to do with Charles?"

"Do you think I'd give up four thousand a year just because my stupid husband leaves the Tower?" Madame Simon frowned. "I'm staying with the boy as long as they'll let me, of course."

So now, if they worked quickly, they would have only Madame Simon to contend with in freeing Louis Charles. François should know about this at once. Catherine turned away and started for the door.

"Catherine!"

She turned to see Louis Charles raised up on one elbow. "Don't go, Catherine."

Catherine glanced pleadingly at Madame Simon.

The woman shrugged and turned back to her seat by the stove. "See if you can get him to eat."

Catherine moved across the room toward the small bed.

Louis Charles's ghastly pallor made his blue eyes look enormous as he gazed at her in desperation. "They cut off her head, Catherine," he whispered. "Like they did Papa's."

Catherine sat down beside him on the bed. "Yes."

"You knew?"

She swallowed hard and nodded.

"She wasn't wicked," he said with sudden fierceness. "They shouldn't have done it."

"Shh." Catherine glanced over her shoulder at the couple by the fire but they didn't appear to have heard. "You must be careful, Louis Charles."

"Why? They're only going to cut my head off too."

"No, not you."

"I'm the king. No one likes kings anymore." Tears were running down his face. "But they didn't have to cut off her head. She was only the queen. They should have killed me instead."

Catherine's hands gently stroked the fair hair from his face. "I know it's hard to understand why bad things happen. I can't understand it myself."

"He said they didn't give her proper burial. They just threw her body into a pit with lots of other traitors and poured lime into it so that no one would ever know she lived. He said since she didn't have the proper rites she couldn't ever go to heaven." His eyes were wide with panic. "She's *lost*, Catherine."

Catherine cursed Simon beneath her breath. It wasn't enough that he'd told the child his mother was dead, he had to condemn her soul as well. What could she say? she wondered frantically.

"Listen, Louis Charles, do you remember what I told you about some fragrances living for thousands of years? Perhaps souls are like fragrances. Perhaps they don't really need a body or rites or hallowed ground to live on."

Louis Charles's gaze clung desperately to her face. "She's not lost?"

She shook her head. She was silent a moment and then spoke hesitantly, feeling her way. "I think memory must be the fragrance of the soul. As long as we remember your *maman*, she'll linger with us. She won't be lost."

"I'll remember her," Louis Charles whispered, his thin fingers nervously clutching the coverlet. "I'll remember her every day so she'll never be lost."

"It doesn't have to be every day." Catherine took out her handkerchief and gently wiped his damp cheeks. "Sometimes at Vasaro we barely notice the perfume of the flowers because it's always with us. But then suddenly something happens to remind us. It rains and the scent becomes more powerful or there's a strong breeze after a long stillness. You don't have to try to remember what's already a part of your life, Louis Charles. Do you understand?"

"I think so." He shook his head. "I don't know. I wish I had something to remember her by. I'm afraid she'll slip away if I don't have anything to remind me of her. They keep telling me things and sometimes I believe them. I'm not like your friend Michel."

"You don't have to be like Michel. You're fine just as you are." She kissed his forehead. The nuns would have probably condemned every word Catherine had spoken, but she had been desperate to help him and they had seemed somehow right. "Will you eat something now?"

He shook his head. "Will you bring me my violets?"

She got up and went to the cabinet and brought back the box of violets. "I see you have some new blossoms."

He nodded, his gaze on the violets. "If they don't cut off my head, I'll have an entire garden of violets someday."

"They won't do—" She stopped in mid-sentence. How could she assure him this world would not take his life when it had taken both his parents? If they didn't manage to get Louis Charles out of this prison soon, he could well lose his head. "I'll bring you another box of violets the next time I go to see my cousin."

She wasn't sure he had heard her. His head was bent forward over the violets and he breathed deeply, taking in the fragrance. He murmured something, but she couldn't quite catch the word.

It might have been *merci.*

Or it could have been *maman* . . .

TWENTY-FOUR

You're surprised I sent for you?" Danton leaned back in his chair and regarded Jean Marc wearily. "I'm a little surprised myself. I was very annoyed with you at one time. I didn't like losing a pawn of the magnitude of the Wind Dancer."

"One cannot lose what one has never possessed." Jean Marc seated himself in the chair across from Danton's desk. "Though, of course, I have not the faintest idea as to your meaning."

"Of course." Danton smiled sardonically. "However, you should know I was so annoyed that I failed to inform you I was paid a call by a mutual acquaintance of ours several weeks ago."

"Indeed?"

"Raoul Dupree."

Jean Marc froze.

"You did good work on the bastard. His

body is crippled and his face would do justice to a nightmare."

"Not good enough, evidently. I meant to kill him."

"I know. He told me. He was frothing with plans for vengeance. He said he'd take the statue from you and the two of us would share the glory of the Wind Dancer." He smiled faintly. "Naturally, his plans called for your very painful demise."

"How surprising, and I thought he was so fond of me."

"He also mentioned your cousin, Mademoiselle Catherine, and Juliette de Clement."

"And?"

Danton shrugged. "I told him I wasn't interested in obtaining his services. I was quite busy at the time trying to keep Robespierre from chopping off half the heads in Paris and certainly wasn't interested in having yours served up to me."

"I suppose I should be grateful you were otherwise occupied."

"Dupree swore he'd go to Robespierre when I refused him." Danton frowned. "But since you're still alive I doubt he did as he threatened."

"May I ask why you're suddenly concerned for my continued well-being?"

"Oh, I'm not. You must take your chances with the rest of us," Danton said bitterly.

"Then why are you warning me?"

"It's come to my ears that your cousin now occupies the quarters of François Etchelet in the Temple. A romantic, foolish gesture on her part."

"I agree. I couldn't persuade her to do otherwise."

"If I know she's in Paris, then it's reasonable to assume Dupree knows also. He has many contacts in the city and Pirard, his former lieutenant, is now serving in the Temple. It would be wise of you to safeguard her."

"I'll endeavor to do so." Jean Marc stood up. "Thank you for your warning. May I ask why you bothered to give it?"

"I remembered her face that night at the abbey . . ." Danton shook his head wearily. "She's suffered enough.

So many innocents dying . . . Did you hear about my wife Gabrielle?"

"Yes, my deepest sympathy, Citizen."

"I'm married again now. Lucille is Gabrielle's cousin, a fine woman. After I married her we went away to the country for a number of months. We were very happy there." He sighed. "I didn't want to come back."

"But you did."

"I have to try to halt it," Danton said. "The tumbrils keep rolling to the guillotine. Robespierre thinks terror is the only way the revolution will survive."

"Good luck," Jean Marc said gravely. "I'd not like to wager on your chances of stopping that madman."

"I'm not sure I would either. God, I'm weary of it all." Danton stood up. "Good day, Andreas. Guard your cousin well."

"François will guard her."

"François." For an instant an expression of sadness crossed Danton's face before it hardened. "I hope he gives her more loyalty than he showed me."

"Good day, Danton." Jean Marc turned away.

"Juliette de Clement."

Jean Marc glanced over his shoulder.

"He mentioned your cousin only in passing, but he was quite venomous on the score of Mademoiselle de Clement. I think he'd go out of his way to hurt her badly. If he doesn't dispose of her himself, I'm quite sure he'll find a way to send her to the guillotine."

"He said that?"

Danton nodded. "If she has value to you, I'd send her out of harm's way."

"She has value to me."

Jean Marc opened the door and left the study.

"Set a date," Jean Marc told François tersely. "I want it over."

"Even if I set a date, we may have to change it," François said with a frown. "We can't be sure—"

"I told you what Danton said." Jean Marc whirled away from the window to face him. "It's *Dupree*, for

God's sake. You know what he's like. Who knows when he'll decide to move against all of us?"

"He's held his hand this far."

"Set a date. I want Juliette safely away from all this."

François nodded, staring absently at the portrait of the Wind Dancer on the wall in the corner of the room. "Very well, we'll take the boy from the Temple on January nineteenth."

"January nineteenth." Nana pulled the gray wig on her hand and began tucking her hair beneath it. "They're going to tell Simon and his wife there's a threat of rescue by William Darrell. They've bribed four of the guards to act as escort and Juliette de Clemente is going to forge Robespierre's signature to a writ to have the boy released to Etchelet's custody and removed to a place of safety." She went to the mirror and took the heart-shaped beauty patch from the silver snuff box. "Once away from the Simons, the boy will be escorted by the guards through the front gates and taken out of Paris to Le Havre."

"Very clever. That beauty patch is too close to your mouth. Move it a little to the left." Dupree looked thoughtful. "The de Clement bitch will have to practice the signature in order to get it right. I want one of the papers she discards, but it must contain only the signature. Nothing else. You understand?"

"I'm not stupid."

"You have a saucy tongue. You're fortunate I've been pleased with you in other ways. I told you what I did to Barshal." Dupree gazed at her critically. "Stop fussing. You look fine now. Come here."

Nana stiffened and then turned and moved slowly toward him. "We move on January nineteenth, then?"

"Why not? It would be amusing to use their plans to augment my own. I spoke to Pirard today and he's eager to earn a generous stipend for a day's work. Kneel down."

She knelt before him. "You've told Pirard about the count?"

"I've told him nothing beyond his duties in the enterprise. Men like Pirard are only tools. You hate kneeling to me, don't you?"

"Yes."

"But you do it anyway." His index finger touched the beauty patch on her cheek. "Camille rather liked it. I think I prefer your attitude. It's more satisfying."

"Shall I begin?"

"In a moment." His hand stroked the fullness at the sides of the wig. "Someday I'll take off all your clothes and put you in that armoire across the room. That's what you did to me, remember? It was a chest in the cellar and you said I must learn—"

"I didn't say that to you."

He slapped her, hard. "Of course that was you. Say it."

"It was . . . me."

"And then you put the roaches in with me. I couldn't have done anything so naughty as to deserve that, could I?"

"No."

"But don't worry. After I take you out of the chest, I'll hold you and stroke you and tell you what you must do to be a good girl and please me."

Her voice shook with a terror that was no pretense. "Don't . . . put me in the armoire."

"Not now," he agreed. "One must savor such discipline." He leaned back in the chair. "You may begin."

Nana's voice still trembled as she altered her tone to the high, pleading pitch he preferred. "Promise me we'll always be together. You're my own sweet boy, Raoul. . . .

"The forgery is quite good." Nana handed Dupree the blank paper with Robespierre's signature at the bottom of the page. "It was the best of the lot, but I told her they were all only adequate. I slipped this one beneath the fans in my basket when she wasn't looking."

Dupree critically scanned the signature. "Very good.

She's really quite gifted. I couldn't tell the difference myself."

"Shall I put on the gown?"

"What?" He glanced at her impatiently. "No, I have no time for it tonight. I have to see Pirard and arrange a few matters. You may go."

Nana looked at him in surprise.

"Go." Dupree turned away. "I told you, I have some arrangements to make with Pirard."

"I cannot help?"

"They don't concern you." He was limping toward the desk across the room "Come back tomorrow."

"Tomorrow is the seventeenth of January. We should be preparing for—"

"You dare try to tell me what I should do? Perhaps you *should* put on the gown."

"No." She hurried to the door. "I'll come back tomorrow."

The hammering assaulted Juliette's ears as she came down the stairs.

"What's going on here?" Juliette hurried into the Gold Salon. "Dear heaven! What on earth are you doing, Robert?"

"Packing."

"So I see." She looked around the room in bewilderment. All the paintings had been stripped from the walls and several boxes and trunks set around the room.

Robert looked up from the painting he was boxing. "Monsieur Andreas said we must pack all of these for travel." He went back to his work.

Juliette wandered around the room, looking at the vacant walls. All the Fragonards, Bouchers, even the portrait of the Wind Dancer were gone. "Where is Monsieur Andreas now?" she shouted above the hammering.

"He went to see Monsieur Bardot," Robert said. "He left directly after breakfast."

Juliette paused beside a familiar brass-bound oak

chest. The Wind Dancer itself. "He had you bring this up from the cellar?"

Robert nodded. "He asked particularly for that chest. Everything of value must be readied to leave. You're going on a journey, Mademoiselle?"

"I . . . don't know." For an instant she felt panic surge through her. Perhaps Jean Marc was tired of her and sending her away. No, he wouldn't pack up the entire household just to rid himself of a mistress.

"Make sure you pack all of Mademoiselle's paintings in her room, Robert." Jean Marc stood in the doorway of the salon. "And tell Marie she'd better start packing Mademoiselle's clothing as well."

Her clothes. No mention of his. The panic came again and Juliette tried desperately to keep it from showing. "We're going somewhere?"

"Yes." He turned to Robert. "We'll be in my study, sorting out the papers in my desk." He pulled Juliette along by the wrist.

She hurried to keep up with him as he crossed the foyer.

"I'm sending Robert and Marie to Vasaro tomorrow with the paintings and the statue. I'm not sure they'll be safe in Paris after we've gone. If everything goes well, Catherine and François's part in this may not be discovered and Vasaro will be a safe haven for all of them."

"Them? We're not going to Vasaro, Jean Marc?"

He shook his head. "Charleston. I've just come from Bardot's offices to make final arrangements for the channeling of money to François to help free some of those poor devils headed for the guillotine and to pick up the Andreas jewels. I hadn't seen some of them for years. I think you'll look quite fetching in the rubies." He pulled her into the study and slammed the door behind them. "Do you wish to see them?"

"No." She gazed at him in bewilderment. "Charleston? Is that what all the packing is about? Why Charleston?"

"It seemed a good idea. America has hordes of savages, but their government doesn't cut heads off and has the greatest respect for bourgeois businessmen such as myself." He released her wrist and crossed the study to the desk stacked high with ledgers and papers. "*Merde,* I don't know where to start." He frowned down at the ledger on top of the stack. "And the boy will be safe there."

She went still. "Boy?"

He looked up and smiled at her. "Vasaro's hardly a safe place for Louis Charles. If we stayed anywhere on the Continent, they'd find him eventually. He'll be much safer in Charleston with us."

"You're going to . . . keep him?"

"My dear Juliette, I have no intention of undergoing any more of these tiresome plots ever again. I know very well that if the boy were recaptured, you'd insist on going to his rescue. I'll be much more comfortable having him under my eye."

"And under your protection." Juliette added huskily, "You know that as soon as you leave the country, the National Convention will seize everything you own."

"Everything they can lay hands on," he agreed. "I've tried to modify their seizures in the past few weeks by discreetly liquidating and sending everything I could to my agents in Switzerland. But the losses will still be enormous."

"Yet you're willing to accept them?"

"Oh, I fully intend to be recompensed." His dark eyes were suddenly twinkling. "After all, I wouldn't be a good man of business if I didn't demand my price." He paused. "I want a son, Juliette."

She stared at him silently.

"And a wife. Do you think you can bring yourself to oblige me?"

"Why?" she whispered.

The laughter disappeared from his face. "Because I'm not at all sure I could live without you. You should be happy. You've won the game, Juliette."

"There is no game." She took a step toward him, her gaze desperately searching his face. "Don't hide from me. I need you to say it."

"I don't want to say the words. They will strip me naked."

"I enjoy you very much without clothing." Juliette took another step. "And I've been naked for months."

"To my infinite delight. You won't spare me?"

"No, I *can't* spare you."

He gazed at her silently for a moment. "I . . . love you." He paused. "I love you as completely and foolishly as my father did Charlotte d'Abois."

Joy surged through her, filling her with light. "Not foolishly." Juliette smiled radiantly. "We're quite different. She was not a nice woman and I'm well worth loving." She launched herself into his arms and hugged him with all her strength. "And I'll give you so much love that you won't— When did you know? It was very wicked of you not to tell me before this."

His arms went around her and his dark eyes glittered with a suspicious moisture as he looked down at her. "That shouldn't surprise you. I've never been overly kind to you."

"Yes, you have." Her smile faded and her expression became grave. "Even when you didn't want to be kind, you couldn't stop yourself. You have a great heart, Jean Marc. You gave me understanding and compassion and— Now, tell me when."

He cradled her cheeks in his hands. "You never give up, do you? It didn't come with a crash of thunder. It just . . . came. I suppose I always knew. Since the time you cared for me at the inn at Versailles. You walked into a room and it became your room. You left a room and it became . . . empty. You moved me and tormented me yet gave me peace." He kissed her tenderly on the lips. "And if I had the great heart you mistakenly think I have, I would have been able to force myself to say these words long before this."

"It doesn't matter. You've said them now." She slipped back into his arms and laid her head contentedly on his shoulder. "I can't believe it. You truly care for me? You're not toying with me? Truly, Jean Marc?"

His arms tightened around her and he didn't answer for a moment. When he did, the words were soft and muffled in her hair.

"*Tutto a te mi guida.*"

"You're a very enigmatic man, you know. It's just like you not to tell me we're going to America until the day before we leave." Juliette glanced at him as they strolled through the garden a few hours later. "I wonder if I'm ever going to learn all your secrets."

"Do you want to know all my secrets?"

Juliette had a sudden memory of the vulnerability of his expression when he'd looked down at the revealing sketch she'd made on the *Bonne Chance*. Let him keep his secrets. She had no desire to learn anything that would hurt him to disclose. "Only if you wish to tell them. I imagine I'll find out everything about you in the next fifty years or so. It might even make life more interesting if you surprised me occasionally."

Jean Marc threaded his fingers through her own. "I shall endeavor to do so. I'd hate you to become bored with me."

"I don't mind your secretiveness as much as I do your stubbornness. I don't know how I could come to love such a stubborn man. You made me very unhappy with all your dawdling."

"You didn't show it."

"I have pride. I gave you my love, and I had no intention of letting you know I wasn't happy with the little you gave me." She walked in silence for a moment. "I've been thinking about it and I think perhaps you should have shot Charlotte d'Abois instead of her lover. We would all have been much happier if you hadn't let her scar you."

Jean Marc chuckled. "Could I challenge the woman to a duel?"

"Why not? If you hadn't been so honorable, I'm sure your father would—"

"I wasn't honorable." The laughter had disappeared from Jean Marc's face. "I betrayed him."

Juliette stopped and turned to look at him.

"Secrets? Here's one I've never told anyone." Jean Marc's lips twisted in a bitter smile. "Charlotte d'Abois came to my bed when I was fourteen. I didn't turn her away."

Juliette's eyes widened in shock. "You loved her?"

"Mother of God, no!" he said violently. "By that time I knew what she was and I didn't even like her. It didn't matter. I knew she didn't really want me. She was amused by my antagonism and wanted to show me how helpless I was. She knew exactly what to do to me to make it not matter. During that summer she came to me several times and I couldn't send her away." His expression was tormented. "She belonged to my father and I cuckolded him."

"Did he know?"

"No, but *I* knew. I loved him, I respected him, and still I betrayed him."

"You said she was very beautiful."

"What difference does that make?" he said fiercely. "I should have sent her away. I tried, but she was too strong for me. She was like a fever."

Strength. He had been defeated by Charlotte d'Abois and suffered the most painful torment possible. Was it any wonder he had been fighting to prove over and over he could never be so subdued again?

"You were only a boy." Juliette frowned. "And I think she must have been even worse than I thought. Is that why you wanted to leave your home and go away on a voyage?"

"Partly. I couldn't look at my father without wanting to go out and jump into the sea. I finally told her no more." One corner of his lips rose in a twisted smile. "She wasn't pleased."

"And she arranged to send you away on the slave ship."

"The fault wasn't entirely hers. I betrayed him."

She gazed at him in astonishment. "Mother of God, your father was a grown man and he was helpless before her and you were only a boy. Your father brought his mistress into your home and let her hurt you. If anyone was to blame, besides that pig of a woman, it was your father. Where is your good sense?"

He looked at her in surprise. "I never thought

of—" A slow smile lit his face. "You're so angry you're trembling. I didn't mean to upset you."

"Well, I am upset. I don't like what that woman did to you and I don't like the idea of her in your bed. It makes me angry and frightened."

"Frightened? Why should you be frightened?"

Juliette tried to control her voice. "Because she had the power to hurt you and I'm afraid you cared more for her than you've told me."

"You have nothing to be frightened about." His hands gently encircled her throat, his thumbs rubbing the hollow where she pulsed with life. "She was only a boy's first passion. I've never loved any woman but you."

"Nor shall you ever," she said with sudden fierceness. "I think I'd be very angry if you decided to play that stupid game with another woman."

He kissed her gently. "You've forgotten. The game is over and you've won it."

"No." She met his gaze directly. "If there ever was a game, *we've* won it."

He smiled and the last shadow vanished from his expression. "I would never dare to disagree with you in your present uncivilized mood. Very well, we've won it, *ma petite.*"

TWENTY-FIVE

January 19, 1794
6:34 A.M.

The morning dawned cold, bright, and clear. Juliette slipped out of bed and padded barefoot across the bedchamber to throw open the casement window. Her face was alight with eagerness as she called back over her shoulder. "There's a strong west wind, Jean Marc. That's a good sign, isn't it?"

"It's a sign you'll catch a chill if you don't come back to bed."

"It's blowing toward Charleston." Juliette stood there another moment, looking down into the garden and then beyond the wall to the steep slate rooftops of Paris. "It's blowing toward America."

"Come to bed, *ma petite.*"

Juliette reluctantly closed the window, turned, and walked across the room toward him. "I still think it's a good sign."

7:30 A.M.

"I'm frightened," Catherine whispered as she drew closer to François. The fire had gone out in the porcelain stove and the room looked cold and dreary in the pale morning light. "I didn't think I'd be afraid, but I am. So many things could go wrong."

"Nothing's going to go wrong," François said as he tucked the covers around her. "We've planned everything down to the last detail. The boy will be freed."

"You and Juliette made plans before and the queen still died."

"We were betrayed. It will be different this time."

"I hope so." She closed her eyes and moved still nearer into the security of his arms. "I pray it will."

8:37 A.M.

Dupree shivered as he pushed the coverlet aside and swung his feet to the floor. As always, he was bathed in sweat from the fever that attacked him every night. He knew he was growing weaker with every passing day.

He wondered if he was slowly dying.

No, he couldn't die. Death would mean he could never be near his mother again. He had only to get through today and all would be well. He had realized he hadn't the strength for extensive or elaborate schemes and had planned everything to explode in one splendid burst of violence and consummate vengeance. Mother would be pleased with him, the Comte de Provence would be pleased with him.

And Juliette de Clement, and Jean Marc Andreas, and the queen's whelp would be vanquished . . . forever.

"Jean Marc is being very generous," Nana said. "The money will help us free many prisoners. I somehow didn't expect him to remain involved after the boy was freed."

"Jean Marc seldom does what one expects him to do, and he's not nearly as hard as people think." Juliette rummaged through the basket of fans she'd set on the table. "I've brought you a gift." She handed Nana the white lace fan on which she'd painted the Pegasus. Her eyes twinkled as she unfurled it with a flourish. "I thought it only proper you should have the best fan I've ever made, since it was you who taught me the art."

"It's lovely." Nana took the fan and wafted it gently back and forth before her face. "But it's much too fine for me. I certainly can't use it here at the Café du Chat."

"A gift doesn't always have to be used, but only brought out now and then as a remembrance. I thoroughly approve of gifts." Juliette reached across the table to clasp Nana's hand affectionately. "And I just wanted to give you something as a farewell present. You've been a good friend to me during this last year." Her face became shadowed. "It hasn't been a happy time for either of us, has it? The queen . . ." She smiled with an effort. "Jean Marc and I are leaving France tonight. I hope we won't be gone forever, but who knows what life will bring?"

Nana looked down at Juliette's hand gripping her own. "Yes, it's best that you leave Paris." She squeezed Juliette's hand and quickly released it. "And I thank you for the fan. You'd better go now. We all have things to do today."

Nana actually looked shaken, Juliette thought with sudden anxiety. How strange, when she was usually fully in control of herself and any situation. "You are quite right, I must return to the Place Royale." She pushed her chair back and stood up. "You're a brave woman, Nana, and I admire you very much. *Au revoir*." She started to turn away.

"Juliette!"

She glanced back at Nana and saw again that uncharacteristic expression of nervousness. "Yes?"

Nana gazed at her a moment and then shook her head. "Nothing. I just wanted to say I admire you, too . . . very much." Nana met her gaze. "I hope all goes well for you." She looked down at the silk fan. "And . . . be careful."

Juliette nodded, then made her way out of the café. While she'd been inside the sun had disappeared and fog had descended on the city.

Her hired carriage waited at the curb a few yards down the street, but the coachman was nowhere to be seen. Puzzled, she stopped short. She shrugged and crossed the short distance to the door of the coach. Many cafés lined the Pont Neuf, and it was likely the coachman had only stepped inside one of them to refresh himself.

She opened the door of the carriage.

"*Bonjour*, Citizeness."

At first she didn't recognize the man sitting on the seat of the carriage. The entire left side of his jawbone was crushed inward and his nose smashed and twisted until it bore little resemblance to the original orifice.

Then his pouty lips smiled with catlike pleasure and she knew who he was.

"Dupree," she whispered.

"Certainly. And, of course, you do remember my old friend Pirard from the abbey? He's standing right behind you."

She started to turn her head.

Blinding pain crashed through her left temple.

12:30 P.M.

Jean Marc opened the envelope, drew out the paper, and read the note.

He paled as panic engulfed him.

"Monsieur Andreas?" Robert gazed at Jean Marc in concern. "Is all well?"

"No." Jean Marc's voice was hoarse. "I'll need a carriage." His hand clenched, crushing the note. "Immediately."

1:47 P.M.

"Splendid, Andreas. You were very prompt." Dupree's gaze fastened eagerly on the oak chest Jean Marc carried. "You can put the chest down there by the bed. You won't mind if I make sure the Wind Dancer is inside, will you?"

"Where is she?" Jean Marc strode into the room, kicked the door shut with his boot, and dropped the chest on the floor. "You said she'd be here."

"She is here." Dupree nodded to the armoire as he limped toward the chest. "A bargain is a bargain. I promised you the woman for the Wind Dancer, and there she is. Just open the door of the armoire."

Jean Marc went rigid as he remembered the sight of Juliette's mother in the chest in the casa at Andorra. "You promised she'd be alive, you bastard."

"Perhaps she is alive." Dupree smiled maliciously. "Why don't you go and see?" He glanced casually into the dark interior of the chest as he lifted the lid. "Ah, those emerald eyes of the statue are quite magnificent, aren't they?"

Jean Marc moved slowly toward the armoire, his stomach churning with fear.

Dupree closed the chest. "You don't seem to be overeager to see your *petite amie.*"

"If she's dead, I'll kill you."

"You tried to kill me once." Dupree sat down on the chair. "I admit that sometimes while I lay in pain all those months I wished you'd succeeded. Go on, open the door of the armoire. I want to see your face."

Jean Marc drew a deep breath and opened the door.

Juliette lay bound and gagged, huddled up in one corner of the huge wardrobe. Her eyes were closed and her muscles lax. Dead?

"Juliette . . ."

Her lids slowly opened and she made a sound behind the gag.

Dizzying relief poured through Jean Marc. He lifted Juliette out of the armoire onto the floor and quickly jerked the gag down from her mouth. "For God's sake, she can't breathe, you *canaille*."

Dupree leaned back in the chair. "You may leave the gag off for a while if you like."

Jean Marc's hands trembled as he gently smoothed Juliette's hair back from her face. "Did he hurt you?"

"My head . . ." Juliette's voice shook. "He surprised me. We didn't expect this, did we?"

"No." Jean Marc glared over his shoulder at Dupree. "You have me and you have the Wind Dancer. Now let her go."

"Oh, I couldn't do that," Dupree said. "Not after I spent so much time planning the events of the day. Did you really think I'd let her go free to get in my way this afternoon?"

Jean Marc's gaze shifted back to Juliette's face. "I don't know what you mean."

"Of course you do. The queen's whelp. You were going to try to take him from the Temple at six o'clock this evening. I shall arrive at the Simons' quarters at five o'clock instead. Actually, you had quite an interesting plan, but I've improved on it. Shall I tell you how?"

Jean Marc didn't answer.

"The armed guard to take the boy out of the Temple would never have worked. They would certainly have been challenged. I've arranged to have the boy taken out in a laundry cart driven by myself and I've made sure my old friend Pirard is at the gate to pass it through. Instead of the writ stating simply that the boy be removed from the Temple, I've substituted one that says the boy be drugged and given into my custody." He shook his head disapprovingly. "That's another fault with your plan. Citeness Simon is a stubborn woman and would have balked at giving Etchelet the child. But she's always had a healthy fear of me and I expect no such problem. I shall even instruct her to give the boy the drink herself."

"What drink?" Juliette asked.

"Why, one very similar to this." He plucked a napkin off a goblet on the table beside him. "The one I've prepared especially for you, Andreas."

"You can't make him drink that," Juliette said hoarsely.

"I believe I can." Dupree struggled to his feet. Picking up the goblet in one hand and carrying the pistol in the other, he limped across the room toward them. "My mother was wrong. It seems Andreas is a man of sentiment. Of course I couldn't be sure until he actually brought the Wind Dancer to ransom your life."

He knelt beside them, carefully extending his bad leg to one side, and held out the goblet to Jean Marc. "Drink it." He pressed the barrel of the pistol to Juliette's head. "Or I'll shoot and splatter her brains from here to kingdom come."

Juliette inhaled sharply. "Don't do it, Jean Marc. He'll kill me anyway."

"But not right away," Dupree said. "I have a plan to school you in the same stimulating way I did your mother, the marquise."

"Then kill me now."

Dupree shook his head. "Think about it, Andreas. There are always possibilities. While she's alive, she has a chance of being rescued. Etchelet might be able to save her from me. Or the potion I put in the goblet may be a drug and not a poison." He smiled. "Of course, the chances of both are slim."

"Don't drink it." Juliette pleaded, her gaze clinging to Jean Marc's. "Please don't drink it."

"I have to drink it." Jean Marc took the goblet and smiled into her eyes. "You see, the bastard's right. I am a man of sentiment when it comes to you, *ma petite.*"

"No," she whispered.

"It will all come to the same thing. If I don't drink it, he'll shoot me." He lifted the goblet. "And this will give you a chance."

"I don't want a chance. Not if it means— Don't!"

He paused with the goblet at his lips and smiled lovingly at her. "It's all right, Juliette. It's only for a little while. Remember? Everything leads me to you. Even this."

He drained the goblet.

"*Jean Marc!*"

His face contorted with agony and the goblet fell from his hand. Both hands clutched his throat. He tried to speak, but only a ghastly croak emerged. He slumped sidewise to the floor.

Juliette screamed and hurled herself across his body. "He's dead. You've killed him!"

"I certainly hope so. That was the purpose."

Tears ran down Juliette's cheeks as she tried to creep nearer Jean Marc's still body, hampered by the ropes that bound her. "Poison. It wasn't a drug. It was a poison."

"And very efficient too." Dupree pocketed the pistol and pulled the gag back into her mouth. "You'll forgive me if I don't stay to mourn him, but I have business at the Temple." He stood up and gazed at Jean Marc's dark head cradled half against, half beneath Juliette's breast. "What a touching picture. I really can't bear to part the two of you by putting you back in the armoire." He limped across the room and picked up the chest.

"I'll return tomorrow after I take this lovely thing to my mother and we'll get rid of Andreas and begin your lessons."

Juliette's shoulders shook with silent sobs as she huddled closer to Jean Marc's body.

Dupree limped to the door, set the chest down until he opened it, and then struggled to pick it up again. "Good day, Citizeness. Until tomorrow."

5:10 P.M.

Louis Charles grabbed at his throat, his blue eyes pleading desperately as he tried to speak.

"What is it?" Madame Simon jerked the goblet away. "What is it, Charles?"

The little boy slumped to the floor.

"You said the drug wouldn't hurt him." Madame Simon whirled on Dupree. "You said it would just put him to sleep." She sidled toward the fallen child.

Dupree stepped between her and the boy. "He is asleep."

The woman tried to peer over Dupree's shoulder at Louis Charles. "Then why is he so still?"

"He's not hurt." Curious bitch. Dupree moved around her and threw the sheet he carried over the boy's body. "The drug works quickly." He turned to the woman. "Roll the boy up in the sheet and then in another blanket and carry him down to the cart in the courtyard."

She hesitated.

"Do it," Dupree ordered. "Or do you want me to report to Citizen Robespierre that you're not loyal to the republic."

"Citizen Robespierre knows we're loyal." Madame Simon took a step closer to the shrouded body of the little boy. "Take the sheet off him. I want to see if he's—"

"There's no time. Are you going to stand there while even now Darrell may be on his way to rescue the boy?" He frowned. "Perhaps there's a reason for your disobedience. Perhaps you've been bribed by Darrell to help the boy escape and don't wish Citizen Robespierre to keep him safe for the republic."

"No!" Madame Simon hurried forward and began to carefully roll the boy up in the sheet. "I just wanted to make sure he wasn't hurt. It will take only a moment. I must make sure Charles can breathe through this sheet."

"I have no objection to waiting . . . a moment," Dupree said blandly, watching her throw the blanket over the limp body of the boy. "Citizen Robespierre would be most upset if you hurt the child."

6:15 P.M.

Dark had fallen by the time Dupree halted the laundry cart in the alley behind Robespierre's lodgings and the thick fog made the gardens, alcoves, and even the houses themselves barely visible for more than a few feet. He could hear the scampering of the rats in the garbage piled on the cobblestones but could catch only a faint glimpse of their eyes as they darted to escape the wheels of the cart.

Happiness surged through him as he clumsily got down from the wagon, tied the horse's reins to the iron railings of a garden gate, and limped to the back of the wagon. The bed of the wagon was piled high with blankets and linens, and he was forced to burrow for a minute before he found the chest with the Wind Dancer he had placed in the wagon before he'd gone to the Temple. As he lifted the chest out of the cart, one of the sheets shrouding the boy pulled free, revealing Louis Charles's silky fair hair.

Dupree swore with annoyance beneath his breath. He was tempted not to bother to recover the child. The thick, cold fog and the foul smell of garbage belching from the cobblestones of the alley made it doubtful anyone would venture out of their warm houses and discover the wagon. Yet it was essential no one find the whelp's body until Nana brought Danton and the soldiers to confront Robespierre. He set the chest down on the cobblestones and carefully tucked the sheet back over Louis Charles's head before pulling a blanket and several sheets on top of him.

Then he picked up the chest and limped down the alley to the street. Going up and down the stairs of the Temple had been a hideous strain, and his hip and bad leg throbbed with agony.

Yet what did the pain matter when his soul soared with exhilaration? He had done it! He had triumphed over all his enemies, he had carved himself a place in the court of Comte de Provence and perhaps history itself by killing the boy, and he had the Wind Dancer safe in his hands to give to his mother.

He reached the street and painfully made his way to the hired carriage he'd arranged to have waiting for him a few houses from Robespierre's residence.

"Clairemont. It's just outside the barriers. I'll give

you the direction once we reach the village," he said as he opened the door of the carriage and set the oak chest inside before levering himself inside and onto the seat. He leaned wearily back in the coach and sighed with contentment as it started to roll down the street.

He had been good. No one could say he had not been very good indeed. Now he could go home to his mother for his reward.

"Quick, Catherine." François moved swiftly out of the shadows of the alcove of the back door of the house across the alley from Robespierre's residence. He ran toward the wagon and in another moment he had unwrapped Louis Charles from his shroud of linens and blankets.

"Is he all right?" Catherine appeared beside him, her gaze fixed worriedly on the boy's still body. "Oh, dear, how pale he is."

Louis Charles opened his eyes and drew a deep breath. "Stinks."

Catherine laughed shakily in relief as she helped the boy to an upright position in the cart. "You're in an alley. Of course it stinks."

"No, all these dirty sheets stink." Louis Charles wrinkled his nose in distaste. "It was most unpleasant lying here covered with all this dirty linen all the way from the Temple. No more laundry wagons, Catherine."

"No more laundry wagons," Catherine agreed as she reached over and hugged him. "We have a carriage waiting two streets from here." She helped him down from the wagon. "Can you walk?"

"Of course. I wish you'd been there to see how well I did. It was just like one of *Maman's* theatricals." Louis Charles clutched his throat and croaked melodramatically. "I remembered everything you told me to do. I was so good, Citizeness Simon thought I was really ill. You should have been there to see me."

"No, I shouldn't. I was terribly afraid just knowing what was happening." She draped the cloak she was carrying about the boy's shoulders. "You did wonderfully well without us, Louis Charles."

"The stuff didn't taste good." Louis Charles grimaced. "What was it?"

"Olive oil and bitters. Jean Marc had a taste of it earlier today and he was in complete agreement with you." François put a tricorned hat on the child's head. "Keep your head down and the hat shadowing your face."

Louis Charles nodded as he fell into step with them.

"I saw Dupree get into a carriage. He's going to Clairemont just as I told you he would." Nana joined them as they reached the end of the alley, her gaze anxiously searching Louis Charles's face. "He looks well enough."

"This is Nana Sarpelier, Louis Charles," François said. "You owe her a great debt. She substituted the olive oil for the poison Dupree had planned on giving you and tricked him into helping us."

"*Merci*, Mademoiselle," Louis Charles said gravely. "Though I wish you'd put honey instead of bitters in the olive oil."

Nana laughed. "I thought it better if it tasted bitter in case Dupree became suspicious and tasted it. You're very welcome, Your Majesty. It was a great pleasure helping you." Nana's face hardened. "Anything I could do to harm that *canaille* was a pleasure."

François stared into Nana's eyes. "Such vehemence. I wonder if you've been entirely honest with us regarding the ease of your task in dealing with Dupree these last weeks."

Nana forced a smile. "I told you he did me no harm. I just don't like the *canaille*." She pulled up the hood to shadow her face. "Now take the boy to Monsieur Radon's house and let me get on with my task."

"You'll join us at Monsieur Radon's?" Catherine asked as she took Louis Charles by the hand and started down the street.

"If I can. If not, I'll meet you at the Café du Chat tomorrow."

François shook his head. "I want you at Monsieur n's by midnight, Nana."

Oh, very well." Nana watched them until they

disappeared around the corner and then briskly proceeded to Robespierre's lodgings.

She deliberately tousled her hair before pounding with both hands on the door. "Open the door!" She pounded again, her voice sounding frantic. "Citizen Robespierre! You must hear me."

The door jerked open and icy green eyes glared into her own. "What is this? Is a man not entitled to peace at his evening meal?"

"Citizen Robespierre?" Nana's gaze desperately searched his face. "Thank God I've found you. All of Paris knows of you, Citizen, but no one knows where you live. I've been sent from place to place until I'm nearly mad."

Robespierre drew his small frame up like a bristling porcupine. "There are reasons why I can't be bothered by all and sundry. If you have a relative condemned to the guillotine, then he must be guilty. The tribunal is always just."

"I know. That is why I have come to you. You are an admirer of virtue and justice and I could not bear to see you made a victim." She gazed into his eyes. "I'm Nana Sarpelier and I've come to tell you of a terrible plot threatening not only the republic but yourself. You must hear me out."

Robespierre gazed at her without expression for a moment. He stepped aside. "Come in, Citizeness."

8:10 P.M.

Anne Dupree lifted the golden Pegasus from the chest and set it on the table. "You've done very well, Raoul." She stepped back and tilted her head to gaze at it appraisingly. "It's magnificent."

Dupree sipped his wine and basked in her pleasure.

She said, "But it doesn't fit in this room. It belongs in an elegant salon."

"I thought in a few days we'd leave for Vienna and take it to the Comte de Provence."

She shook her head. "He'd claim it for the Bourbons. I have no intention of handing it over to him."

"Very well, we won't tell him we have it."

"We?"

"*You* have it," he amended quickly. "It's yours, Mother."

She turned back to the statue and smiled with pleasure. "Yes, it's mine."

"But you'll come to Vienna with me?" Dupree pleaded. "The count will wish to honor me, and I want to share that glory with you. Now that the boy is dead, the count is heir to the throne. You could reign in his court."

"I could have my own court here in Paris. I don't need the Comte de Provence." She touched the golden filigree cloud on which the Pegasus ran. "Everyone will want to come to my salon and see the Wind Dancer. They'll fight for invitations. Of course, I'll have to seek a means to pacify the National Convention, but I'll find a way."

Panic rose in him. "Very well, if you don't want to go to Vienna, we'll stay here."

"No." She turned to look at him. "I'll stay here. You'll go to Vienna."

She was sending him away. His worst nightmare was staring at him from her implacable face.

For an instant, terror held him speechless. "Please," he stammered. "You know I can't go without you. I want to be with you, Mother. Always."

"Look at you. You'd be an embarrassment, not a help to me."

"No." He fell to his knees, scarcely noticing the jolt of pain in his leg. "Vienna's too far away. You know I can't bear to be away from you. I beg you to reconsider."

His mother turned away. "I'll expect you gone by morning." She moved to the archway leading to the stairs. "Good-bye, Raoul."

He scrambled to his feet again. He wasn't going to be able to persuade her. She was sending him away and this time she would not let him come back.

"*Mother!*" The word was a howl of agony.

She looked back over her shoulder with a frown. "Don't be difficult, Raoul. You know what happens when you become—"

The front door burst open.

"Citizen Dupree?" An officer in the uniform of the National Guard strode into the room, followed by four soldiers. "You're to come with us. You're under arrest."

"By whose order?" Dupree gazed at him numbly, scarcely able to comprehend the man's words.

She was sending him away.

"How dare you barge into my home?" Anne Dupree asked coldly. "Whatever my son has done, I'm a loyal citizen of the republic."

"That will be decided by Citizen Robespierre. He's waiting in the carriage outside."

She would never permit him near her again.

"I'll not go," Anne Dupree said. "Raoul, tell him he's not to force me to—"

But Dupree was being hustled through the front doorway by two soldiers. She reluctantly followed him out of the cottage to the waiting carriage.

Icy rage froze Robespierre's delicate features into a menacing mask as he stepped down onto the cobblestones from the carriage. "I'm a just man. Because of your past service to the republic I give you one chance to defend yourself before I condemn you. You're Raoul Dupree, Marat's former agent?"

"Yes," Raoul said dully.

He would never see her again.

"And you conspired to free Louis Charles Capet and lay the blame at my door?"

"Free? No, I killed him."

"Lies. We know you smuggled him from the city and even now he's on his way to Le Havre." Robespierre pulled out a familiar-looking paper. "Do you deny you gave this writ to Citizeness Simon with my name forged upon it giving custody of the boy to you?"

"I killed him. He's in the laundry wagon in the alley behind your lodgings."

"I was told by your whore how you smuggled the

boy out of the Temple but no body was found in the wagon." Robespierre's hand tightened on the writ. "Where is the boy?"

"Dead."

"You're thinking to destroy me by linking me with the monarchists who want to free the boy, but you'll not succeed." Robespierre's voice rose shrilly. "Do you hear me? You won't succeed. I'll send you to the guillotine tonight." He pointed to a horse-drawn tumbril rumbling out of the fog. "That cart will take you to the guillotine. Why do you not speak? Do you think I lack the power to deny you a trial before the tribunal?"

Why was Robespierre shouting? Didn't he know that none of it mattered any longer? "No, I know you have the power."

"I'll cut off your head and have you tossed in a common grave with the other traitors who seek to destroy me."

"Citizen Robespierre, may I go back in the house?" Anne Dupree asked politely. "It's quite cold tonight and none of this concerns me. I'm only Raoul's mother. I've scarcely seen him for years until he came to me tonight begging me to hide him. Naturally, I was about to refuse when your soldier—"

"You're his mother?" Robespierre interrupted, his gaze shifting to her face. "Yes, Dupree's whore mentioned your name as well. I find it strange that he'd run to you after this treason if you had no part in it."

"I told you, he wished me to hide him. In spite of his faults, I've always been a loving mother."

Death.

"Is that right, Dupree?"

A common grave.

She nervously cleared her throat. "Tell him the truth, Raoul."

Together.

She was frightened. He must save her. It was his duty to serve her, to save her.

Then it came to him, the solution bursting upon him with an effulgence that filled the entire world.

His mother took a step closer to him. "Why don't you speak? Tell Citizen Robespierre I'm innocent."

Why hadn't he understood before? Dupree wondered. She had told him over and over through the years. She had knelt at his feet and told him what she wanted, what they both wanted.

And now, at last, he could give it to her.

"I can't tell him that, Mother. It's not true."

Her eyes bulged. "Raoul!"

He turned to Robespierre. "Of course my mother knew. She guides me in everything I do."

"*Raoul!*"

Dupree turned to his mother and smiled lovingly. "It's going to be fine, Mother. Don't be afraid. Don't you see? Remember what you begged of me?" His voice suddenly became high and simpering. "'Promise me we'll always be together, Raoul.' That's what you've always asked of me. Now it can be true. Now we'll be together. Always."

He could vaguely hear her screaming as the soldiers led them away toward the tumbril that had drawn up behind Robespierre's carriage. Poor Mother. She didn't understand yet, but she would afterward.

A smile still on his lips, he stepped into the tumbril and waited for them to bring his mother to join him.

10:47 P.M.

Nana turned away from the guillotine and made her way quickly through the sparse crowd in the Place de la Révolution. With the guillotine working day and night these last months, beheadings had become too common to draw large crowds. Unless the victim was someone of fame or high noble rank, the executioner's work went virtually unnoticed except by a small group of the morbid and fanatic.

She moved quickly down the street, drawing her cloak closely about her, the guillotine and its few acolytes disappearing into the fog behind her. She had come to witness the execution of Dupree so that she might be free of the ugliness he had brought into her life. But the fear and ugliness seemed to corrode her soul—and what she had just witnessed had only added to her sense of horror.

She doubted she would ever forget Dupree's joyful loving smile as they had decapitated Anne Dupree.

11:55 P.M

"Dupree?" François asked Nana as soon as she entered Monsieur Radon's small house on the right bank of the Seine.

"Guillotined," she said succinctly.

"You're sure?"

"I watched it. I had to be sure." Nana turned to the little boy who sat on the sofa next to Catherine. "Are you ready for your journey, Louis Charles?"

"Oh, yes, this is all most interesting." The child's blue eyes blazed with excitement as he leaned his head against Catherine's shoulder. "Catherine says I'm to go to America, but she's not sure if they still have savages in Charleston."

"Well, if they don't, I'm sure Juliette will find something of equal interest for you to see. She may even go searching for savages herself to paint." Catherine smiled gently at him. "You'll have a good life there, Louis Charles."

"I wish you were going with me," the boy whispered. "I'll miss you, Catherine."

"Perhaps you'll be able to come back someday." Catherine pressed a kiss on his forehead. "Or maybe we'll come to Charleston to visit you."

"But not now?"

"There are many people François still needs to help. Our place is here, Louis Charles." Catherine felt an aching sympathy for the little boy. He no sooner formed an attachment than it was severed. "Believe me, you'll learn to love Juliette and Jean Marc."

Louis Charles was silent for a long time. "I wanted to meet Michel."

"Someday." Catherine thought a moment. "You could write to him. Michel would love to get letters from across the sea."

"Would he correspond with me?"

"I'm sure he would. But you'll have to be very careful what you say."

"I'm used to that." Louis Charles expression brightened. "Letters . . ."

Jean Marc came in the front door, his gaze going at once to François. "All safe?"

François nodded at the boy. "All safe."

Jean Marc smiled at Louis Charles. "I'm Jean Marc Andreas, and I'm delighted to meet you."

"Monsieur Andreas." Louis Charles stiffly inclined his head. "It's very kind of you to help me."

Jean Marc lifted a brow at the child's formality and turned to Nana. His amusement was replaced by seriousness. "Dupree didn't give you any hint what he intended for Juliette?"

She stiffened. "Of course not. Do you think I'd let her walk into a trap? What kind of—"

"Wait." Jean Marc held up his hand. "I'm not accusing you. I think you've done splendidly. We simply didn't expect him to strike at us today. We thought he'd wait until after the business at the Temple." He paused. "Juliette is outside saying good-bye to Robert and Marie. They're taking a wagon with some of our belongings to Vasaro. I understand you're to go with them."

"What?" Nana's eyes widened in surprise. "I'm not going anywhere. No, absolutely not. I don't wish to leave Paris."

"It's not safe for you here now," François said quietly. "Robespierre is going to be in a panic when he doesn't find the boy at Le Havre. He may have let you go tonight, but tomorrow he'll start with a vengeance to rout out all who might have had a part in the boy's escape. I'm sure he's already sent men to the Temple to pick up Pirard, and the National Guard may be at the Café du Chat waiting for you."

"Good, then they'll pick up that bastard Raymond. I could scarcely tolerate him these last weeks." Nana scowled. "*Dieu,* I hate the country. Can't I go to Marseilles? It's not Paris, but at least there will be people."

"It's only for a little while," Catherine said. "And you may like Vasaro better than you think. When it's safe for you to come back, we'll send for you immediately."

Nana hesitated, then shrugged wearily and turned. "Very well. I suppose it doesn't matter." She walked out the front door.

"She didn't argue as much as I thought she would." François frowned. "And she doesn't look well."

"How do you expect her to look? She's borne the brunt of Dupree's malice for the last few weeks," Jean Marc said.

François nodded. "But she said he did nothing to hurt her."

"We shouldn't have believed her," Catherine said. Nana had done so much for them. François had told her how Nana had suspected Raymond Jordaneau of being the traitor in the group and had contacted the Comte de Provence supposedly to ally herself with him in order to verify Raymond's guilt. When Dupree had appeared on the scene she had insisted it was her place to turn Dupree's plan against himself. Well, she had done it. But at what cost to herself they would probably never know. "Dupree managed to hurt all of us. Why should she have been different?"

"Dupree's dead, Jean Marc," François said quietly. "Nana saw him guillotined."

"Thank God." Jean Marc's lips tightened. "I wanted to slice him into pieces myself this afternoon when I saw Juliette in that armoire."

"You know you couldn't do that. We would never have been able to get the boy out of the Temple without Dupree's help," François said. "Nana's sent a message to the Comte de Provence saying the boy is dead. The count's assassins won't be searching for him. Robespierre won't be able to make an overt search because he'll not be sure if there's any other evidence linking him to the escape. It was the best possible plan and you were right to play dead until Dupree left the lodgings."

"You can say that now." Juliette came into the room and smiled ruefully at Jean Marc. "But Jean Marc nearly frightened me to death. How could I be sure Dupree had used the same potion that Nana had switched? You were entirely too convincing, Jean Marc." She turned to Louis Charles. "How do you do? My name is Juliette."

"Hello." Louis Charles drew closer to Catherine. "Catherine says you knew my *maman*."

"Very well." Juliette smiled. "And you too. You liked me very much at one time. Of course, you were too young to have very good taste, but I'm sure I've improved since then. Did Catherine tell you how we're going to get past the barriers and out of Paris?"

"Yes." His expression was suddenly eager. "What a splendid idea."

"I think so too. You'll find Jean Marc is always very clever." She turned to Jean Marc. "Why don't you take him out in the garden and show it to him?"

Jean Marc looked inquiringly at the child.

Louis Charles straightened away from Catherine. "I'd like very much to see it, please."

"I believe I'll go too," François said. "It's time we lit the fire."

Catherine nodded, her gaze fixed on Juliette. A moment later the two men and the little boy hurried out the back door.

Silence settled on the room. The two women looked at each other.

"Jean Marc says it may not be safe for us to return for a very long time," Juliette finally said. "I wish you were going with us."

Catherine shook her head. "You know that's not possible."

"I know." Juliette blinked back the tears. "François wishes to save all of France. I don't know why I encouraged you to love such a paragon of virtue. A man of ideals is much harder to live with than a roué like Philippe."

Catherine laughed. "François is no paragon of virtue."

"What is he, then?"

"Joy, strength," Catherine said softly. "Gentleness."

Juliette averted her gaze. "When will you return to Vasaro?"

"When there are no more battles to fight. When we've earned our garden."

"I've changed my mind. It's you who have become the paragon of virtue." Juliette came toward her across the room. "Now I know I shouldn't leave you. You and François will probably become martyrs." She grimaced. "Or the most pompous of prigs. Either way, you clearly need me at hand to prick your consequence."

Catherine rose to her feet. "Juliette, stop talking nonsense and let me tell you how much I shall miss you."

"You always were overly sentimental. I refuse to turn this into a tearful parting. It's not forever, you know. What's an ocean between friends? I'm sure we will see—" Juliette suddenly rushed forward and hugged Catherine with all her strength. Her voice was thick with tears when she continued. "Send for me if you have need. I'll come. I'll always come to you."

"And I'll always come to you." Catherine's throat tightened painfully as she hugged Juliette. So many years together, so much laughter, so many tears. "Go with God."

Juliette laughed shakily as she stepped back. "I go with Jean Marc, who is not at all godlike, but I hope *le bon Dieu* will be there with us too. And with you, Catherine. *Au revoir.*" She turned and walked quickly across the room and out the door leading to the back garden.

The huge black balloon was beginning to inflate and the wire brazier in the basket burned brightly as Juliette stepped out of the house. Jean Marc strode toward her across the clearing. "We should leave now."

His gaze searched her strained face. "It may not be forever, Juliette."

"And, then again, it may." She smiled tremulously as she took his hand. "One never knows, so we must make the most of every moment. Where's Louis Charles?"

"He's sitting on the bale of straw in the basket." He smiled. "He can hardly wait to get under way."

"Then we mustn't disappoint him. I have to say good-bye to François. Where— Oh, I see him." François was on the other side of the basket, waiting to release the lead ropes.

Juliette marched up to him and into his arms. "*Au revoir.*" She whispered fiercely, "You are *not* to let either Catherine's or your own head be cut off. Do you understand?"

"I understand." He solemnly kissed her on the forehead. "I'll endeavor to do all possible to obey you."

She stepped back. "And you must do one other thing for me. Jean Marc was forced to give that *canaille* Dupree the Wind Dancer to save my life, and we had no time to retrieve it from his mother's home. I don't want you to endanger yourself, but the statue has great value to Jean Marc."

"I'll find a way of getting it for him," François said. "Though it may take time."

She stood on tiptoe and kissed his cheek. "*Merci.*" She turned and moved toward the straw basket in which Louis Charles stood, his hands clutching the edge, his eyes wide with eagerness. "We're going now, Louis Charles. Did Jean Marc tell you what we're going to do? He had Monsieur Radon, who was a pupil of Montgolfier, build this fine machine for us. This is a balloon like the one I saw at Versailles when I was a little girl. It's black so that it can't be seen easily against the night sky and we'll soar up and up—"

"And over the barriers," Louis Charles said. "And then when we're safely out of the city we'll come down to earth and Jean Marc has arranged to have a carriage with fast horses to speed us to the sea." He frowned. "But what if we land in the wrong place?"

"We have lanterns to light after we cross the barriers. The carriage will see the lights and follow our passage until we reach a landing place," Jean Marc said as he came to stand beside them. "Our ship's docked at Dieppe, and Robespierre's men are searching at Le Havre, which is over a hundred miles distant. So we should be well out to sea before they begin to consider other ports."

"Won't the fire that propels the balloon be seen from the ground?" Louis Charles asked.

"Possibly." Jean Marc grinned. "But how often do soldiers on guard duty contemplate the heavens at one o'clock in the morning? If they do see it, they'll probably think it's a shooting star."

"A shooting star," Louis Charles repeated, his gaze on the night sky. "We'll be a shooting star."

Juliette saw Catherine come out of the house and walk toward François. The light from the lantern she carried lit Catherine's face with a soft glow that made her look as young as the day Juliette had first met her at the inn at Versailles.

Juliette could feel the tears sting her eyes again and determinedly looked away from Catherine and down at Louis Charles. Those times at Versailles and the abbey were in the past; they must both think of the future.

Jean Marc lifted Juliette into the basket before climbing in after her. "Release the ropes, François." He poured more straw and chopped wood on the flames in the brazier and the balloon billowed, tugging at the ropes even as François freed them.

Jean Marc turned to Juliette, a broad smile on his face. "The fog's beginning to clear and there's a strong west wind. Someone once told me that was a good sign."

"That someone must have been very intelligent." Juliette clutched desperately at Jean Marc's hand as the balloon began to rise from the ground. She could see François and Catherine standing together, waving to them. Their images blurred and then became lost to view as the balloon soared high above the rooftops of Paris. "It's a very good sign."

TWENTY-SIX

The golden Pegasus shone in the candle-light, its beauty pure and terrible as virtue itself.

"This was found in the Dupree woman's cottage?" Robespierre tried to smother the wild burst of eagerness exploding within him. The Wind Dancer. This statue had to be the Wind Dancer. All his life he'd heard tales of the Wind Dancer, and now it was before him.

The lieutenant nodded. "We searched but found no papers or information regarding the dauphin." He glanced casually at the statue he'd set on the table before Robespierre. "But finding a statue so valuable appeared suspicious, so I brought it to you instead of taking it directly to the offices of the National Convention, as we usually do with confiscated property."

"You behaved correctly. No doubt the traitors were given this prize to pay for their perfidy." Robespierre wished desperately to reach out and touch the statue, but he carefully restrained the impulse. The lieutenant clearly had no inkling of how great was the treasure he had brought. On no account must he find out. "Naturally, this discovery must remain as secret as every other aspect of tonight's happenings. The safety of the republic depends on it."

"Of course, Citizen Robespierre." The lieutenant hesitated. "But should we not tell the convention that the child has escaped the Temple?"

"No!" Robespierre tried to temper the sharpness of his tone as he continued. "I've no doubt we'll recapture the boy very soon, and it would do damage to the honor of the republic if it was learned the Capet boy couldn't be held by the entire National Guard."

The lieutenant frowned in puzzlement. "But everyone will know he's no longer in the Temple."

"I've already sent a delegation to the Temple supposedly to take over custody of the boy from the Simons. We'll issue a statement that the boy's now in solitary confinement and no one will be permitted to see him."

"Won't the Simons—"

"You think the Simons will not obey me?"

The lieutenant suppressed a shiver as he met Robespierre's cold eyes. "I'm sure they'll obey you, sir." He started backing toward the door. "If you'll excuse me, I'll go and see if there's any report from my men who are searching Le Havre."

"You're excused." Robespierre waved his hand, his gaze still on the statue. "Just remember that no one is to know of this on pain of execution."

"You can trust in me, Citizen." The lieutenant inclined his head, turned on his heel, and hurriedly left the room.

As soon as the door shut behind him, Robespierre reached out with a trembling hand and touched the Wind Dancer, symbol of a power that was the ultimate virtue.

Throughout all Robespierre's years he had sought to teach the ignorant world the power of virtue and the terror that was its protector and friend. Now it was as if some higher entity had looked down and seen the light he'd brought to those around him and rewarded him with this glorious gift.

But there would be those who wouldn't understand that he was the only rightful guardian of the virtue embodied in the statue, he thought with a frown. They would call it theft from the coffers of the republic. The mere idea filled him with outrage. He, Maximilien Robespierre, a thief? He, the man who had sent thousands of traitors to the guillotine to keep intact the virtue of the republic? It only showed how wise he was to keep this symbol from the hands of those who would not know how to care for it.

But he must be very cautious and make sure no one knew the Wind Dancer had come into his guardianship. He would put it on a pedestal in his bedchamber so that his eyes only would fall upon its beauty and draw inspiration for the work in the days ahead.

He knew the enemies of virtue would delight in any excuse to send his head rolling from his body.

The wagon moved slowly up the winding driveway of lemon and lime trees toward the front door of the manor house.

Nana's legs dangled from the back of the wagon as she lifted her head and gazed out over the fields of golden broom just beginning to bloom. No houses or cafés anywhere in sight, she thought gloomily. No music. No boats floating down the Seine, no cheerful chatter of tradesmen. Just wind and flowers and sunlight. Why had she ever consented to leave Paris for this wilderness?

But she knew why she had agreed to come to Vasaro. Even Paris had seemed drab and ugly after those weeks in the dark, twisted world of Dupree. This place was as good as any other.

Robert stopped the wagon before the front door and looked back to grin at her. "Did you ever see such flowers, Nana?"

She would far rather have seen them on a flower cart on the Pont Neuf, she thought. But the old man seemed so happy, she forced herself to smile. "Well, there are certainly a great many of them."

Marie jumped down from the wagon, her slim, wiry body brimming with energy. "Why are we sitting here? It's growing late and this wagon must be unpacked before dark. I'll go see if I can find you some help, Robert." She marched up the steps and knocked briskly on the door.

Nana stayed where she was on the bed of the wagon. It would be time enough to move when they all began the laborious task of unpacking the paintings and furniture Jean Marc had sent to Vasaro for safekeeping.

"Hello."

She looked down to see a small boy with curly black hair and eyes as clear and blue as the Seine on a sunny day standing a few feet away from the wagon.

"You must be Nana." The little boy smiled at her and Nana had the odd feeling the darkness inside her had suddenly been touched by sunlight. "Catherine sent a message ahead to tell me you were coming. My name is Michel."

Juliette, Jean Marc, and Louis Charles arrived in Charleston on March 3, 1794. On March 7 Juliette and Jean Marc were joined in marriage by Father John Bardonet and took up temporary residence in a pleasant red brick house on Delaney Street.

On May 21, 1794, Juliette received her first communication from Catherine.

Dear Juliette,

Let me tell you the good news first. No one knows the boy has escaped. Robespierre has thrown a cloak of silence around the Temple and it's assumed the child is in solitary confinement.

There is no other news that is in the least hopeful. On April fifth Danton was guillotined. François was stricken and said that the last sane voice in France has been silenced. It appears to be true, for Paris is in a frenzy of terror of Robespierre. We have left the Temple and gone into hiding, for everyone connected with Danton is suspect.

We still manage to continue our work, but only le bon Dieu knows how long we can go on. Still, we cannot leave Paris for Vasaro while Robespierre lives and the Terror goes on. François has a plan he hopes may turn the convention against Robespierre. When trying to locate the Wind Dancer for Jean Marc, it came to his ears that Robespierre may have possession of the statue without knowledge of the convention. If that's true, a few whispers to influential members might turn the tide against Robespierre.

You mustn't worry if you don't hear from me for a long while. François says we must be cautious lest any message fall into the wrong hands. I only dared write so frankly this time because we found a messenger who was absolutely safe.

I think of you constantly and hope all is well with all of you. Pray for us as we pray for you.

> *Always,*
>
> *Catherine*

"Jean Marc, I'm so frightened." Juliette put down the letter, her eyes bright with tears. "Perhaps we shouldn't have left them. Is there nothing we can do?"

Jean Marc drew her into his arms and held her tightly. "Pray for them, *ma petite*. Just pray for them."

The second letter arrived on September 3, 1794.

Dear Juliette,

Forgive me for writing so short a message, but we have just arrived and I'm so weary I can scarce keep my eyes open to put pen to paper. I promise I'll write in detail at a later time, but this letter must be sent off tomorrow or you'll scold me. Dear God, I wish I could hear your voice railing at me again.

I will tell you only what is of most importance.

Robespierre was guillotined on the twenty-eighth of July.

The Terror is over.

I am with child.

We have come home to Vasaro.

> *Always,*
>
> *Catherine*

"It's beautiful, Jean Marc," Juliette said.

The white-columned brick mansion stood on a bluff several miles north of the city of Charleston. To the east it overlooked the sea and, to the west, miles of untamed forest.

"There's a natural harbor a mile from the house," Jean Marc said as he pointed out the window of the carriage at a path leading down to the shore. "You can have your own boat, Louis Charles."

"Thank you," Louis Charles said politely. "But I wouldn't know how to sail it."

"I'll teach you," Jean Marc said. "And when you're a little older, I'll let you go with me on short runs along the coast in a larger vessel."

"That would be very kind of you."

Juliette sighed as she exchanged a look with Jean Marc over the little boy's head. In more than seven months they had made little headway in breaching the distance Louis Charles kept between them. She could understand the child had undergone too many partings and tragedies to want to form new attachments, but it was still discouraging.

The coachman reined in the horses and a moment later Jean Marc lifted Juliette from the carriage and then swung Louis Charles down to the ground. "There's a stable in back of the house with twelve fine horses," he told the boy gravely. "And I wouldn't be at all surprised if you found one that was small enough for you to ride."

"Truly?" Louis Charles's face lit up. "May I go see them?"

Jean Marc nodded and Louis Charles bolted across the lawn and around the house.

"I've not seen him so enthusiastic about anything since our ride in the balloon." Juliette started up the four wooden steps leading to the wide porch. "I've been worried about him. He's wonderfully polite but he's always so guarded. For heaven's sake, what more can we do, Jean Marc? Have you noticed how he still flinches when either of us touches him?"

"You can understand his being cautious." Jean Marc unlocked the front door and let her precede him into the spacious foyer. "And neither of us trusts easily ourselves. It will just take time." He closed the door behind him and smiled at her. "Now, stop worrying and show a little appreciation for our new home. I've hired stable help but no servants. I thought you'd prefer to select them yourself." He paused. "Slaves are used extensively in both Charleston and the surrounding plantations, but we will have no slaves."

"Of course not." Juliette had caught sight of something glittering on a cabinet on the far side of the foyer and was moving toward it. "The crystal swan. I remember it from your father's study at the Ile du Lion."

He nodded. "All the furnishings from the Ile du Lion were brought to Charleston and stored in one of the warehouses on the dock. I had them all transported here last week when the house was finished. Of course, you may rearrange everything as you see fit once you have time to see whether or not it suits you."

"Where are the paintings by Titian and Fragonard?" Juliette asked. "I hope they found a suitable place to hang them."

"The library. Would you like to see them now?"

She nodded and then frowned in puzzlement. Jean Marc appeared curiously tense. "Now, what could you have done with them, Jean Marc?"

He led her toward two tall double doors. "Why don't you see for yourself?"

She moved slowly forward into the library and nodded approvingly. "Yes, you've hung them in fine places."

"And does everything else meet with your approval?"

She glanced around the room. "It seems quite—" Her eyes widened in shock. "The Wind Dancer!"

On a white marble pedestal by a tall French door the statue shimmered with golden splendor in the sunlight.

"But how could—" Juliette whirled to face him. "We left the Wind Dancer in France. Dupree's mother . . ." She shook her head in bewilderment. "I don't understand."

"There are two Wind Dancers," Jean Marc said quietly. "The real Wind Dancer and the copy I ordered from Desedero to try to deceive my father. Unfortunately, my father instantly knew Desedero's was a copy and I thought it useless to me." He shrugged. "So I ordered it melted down and the jewels sold off."

"But it was never done." Juliette looked back at the statue on the pedestal, her mind working quickly. "And when we went back to the Ile du Lion from Andorra you substituted the real statue you'd gotten from my mother for Desedero's statue which was still on the island. Then you sent the real statue to Charleston with the captain and took the false one to Paris."

Jean Marc smiled. "Yes and no."

"What do you mean? That's what you must have done."

"Yes, I sent the real statue to Charleston and took Desedero's to Paris." He paused. "But I didn't substitute the statue your mother took from the queen. You see, your mother never had the Wind Dancer, Juliette. I stole the Wind Dancer from the Hall of Mirrors myself in 1787 and substituted Desedero's statue for it."

She froze. "What?"

"I didn't want to do it." His smile faded. "I'd have

offered the queen everything I owned if I could have persuaded her to sell."

"I remember . . ." Juliette shook her head dazedly. "She refused you."

"My father *needed* the Wind Dancer. It was the great dream of his life and he was dying. Marie Antoinette thought of it only as a bauble, a good-luck piece," Jean Marc said. "I was desperate in those weeks before I left for Versailles. That's why I went back and told Desedero not to destroy the statue. I knew I had to have the Wind Dancer—one way or the other." His lips twisted. "When the queen refused to sell, I realized I had to steal it. I went back to Versailles three days later and substituted the statue. To soothe my conscience I gave the king his loan and the queen the two jewels." His voice was suddenly urgent. "Don't you see? She couldn't tell the difference. The statue remained at Versailles for *two* years and no one at court realized the Wind Dancer had been substituted." His gaze shifted to the statue. "And my father had his dream throughout the six months before his death. I'm not sorry. I'd do it again, Juliette."

Juliette nodded slowly. She could see how desperate Jean Marc must have been with the father he loved dying and he unable to give him what he wished more than anything in the world. "You took a great chance. If you'd been caught, you'd have been stripped of everything you owned, and very likely thrown into prison or executed."

"I loved him," he said simply.

And this was the man who was convinced he was incapable of dreams, Juliette thought. "But why did you go to Andorra after the false statue? Why would you even want it?"

"I didn't want Desedero's statue," Jean Marc said. "I only wanted the queen to issue me the writ giving me legal right to the Wind Dancer. She would never have given me the writ if she'd known I'd stolen the statue from her. I had to reclaim the statue she thought was the Wind Dancer before I could gain legal documentation for the real one."

Juliette started to laugh helplessly. "Jean Marc,

you're truly impossible. You make me dizzy. Only you would become involved in such convoluted maneuvering to get what you want."

"Some things are worth a great deal of trouble." He took a step nearer, his gaze searching her face. "You are, Juliette, and so is my Wind Dancer."

"Why didn't you tell me? I was worried because we had to leave the Wind Dancer in France."

"I suppose I was afraid to tell you. I stole the statue from the queen and she was your friend."

"You stole because of love, not greed," she said softly. "And, God knows, you tried to repay her in every way you could. I can't condemn you for that." A frown suddenly furrowed her brow. "But wait, there's something that does bother me. When you arranged to have me sent to the abbey, was it because you thought I might be able to tell the difference in the statues?"

He grinned teasingly. "Well, Desedero did warn me that an artist would be able to tell the difference." His smile faded and he slowly shook his head. "No, Juliette, even then I knew I had to find some way to keep you in my life."

She turned toward the pedestal and leaned her head back on his shoulder as she stared dreamily at the Wind Dancer.

Everything leads me to you.

The words she had spoken to Jean Marc in love came suddenly back to her. She had the odd feeling they applied also to this statue that had drawn them, shaped all their lives, inexorably interwoven their paths, even leading Jean Marc and her to this new land. "That's because you have excellent good sense and knew I would love and protect you for—"

"The groom says I must ask you if I can ride my horse now."

They turned to see Louis Charles, his eyes glowing with eagerness, standing in the doorway behind them. "Please, Jean Marc, may I ride—" He stopped, his gaze on the statue on the pedestal across the room. "What is that?" He moved slowly across the library until he stood before the pedestal. "I've seen this before. I *know* him."

Juliette and Jean Marc moved across the room so that they stood on either side of the little boy before the pedestal.

"He's called the Wind Dancer and he once belonged to your mother." Juliette watched the little boy's face. "Isn't he beautiful?"

Louis Charles nodded, his eyes curiously intent as he stared directly into the shimmering emerald eyes of the Wind Dancer. "I remember, this statue was at Versailles. But he seems *more* now."

Louis Charles had been too young to recall any but Desedero's statue, Juliette realized. "You're older now. Perhaps you view it differently."

"Yes." Louis Charles's gaze never left the statue. "May I come here to see it every day?"

"Of course, if you like," Jean Marc said.

"Oh, yes, please," Louis Charles whispered. "It belonged to *Maman*. You see, I don't have anything else that belonged to her. I must see it every day and remember . . . You understand?"

Juliette felt the tears sting her eyes as she recalled what Catherine had told her about Louis Charles's desperate unhappiness regarding his mother's burial.

Another link. Another path merged by the Wind Dancer.

"Yes, we do understand, Louis Charles."

The three of them stood there for a long time, looking at the Wind Dancer, remembering.

Then, slowly, tentatively, his gaze never leaving the emerald eyes of the Wind Dancer, Louis Charles reached out and took first Juliette's hand and then Jean Marc's.

AUTHOR'S AFTERWORD

All facts regarding Marie Antoinette—her life at Versailles and imprisonment at the Temple—are as accurate as my research could make them. As for her character, a good deal had to come from my imagination, inferences I made from the huge, conflicting body of writing on this tragic queen. In an age abounding with larger-than-life figures, she seemed quite ordinary. Not particularly clever, she was undoubtedly selfish and flighty in her youth, yet she was also sentimental, generous, a very good mother, and brave at the last in the face of adversity and death.

Danton's brilliance and earthy love of life are well documented and in sharp contrast to the rabid fanaticism of some of the other leaders of the revolution. Many historians believe that if he hadn't grown weary of the insanity taking place around him and absented himself from the political scene at a crucial period, he might have been able to guide the country through the turmoil and spare France the worst of the Terror under Robespierre.

The Comte de Provence declared himself King of France on the announcement of the death of Louis XVII and later did ascend the throne after the return of the Bourbons. No evidence exists he had anything to do directly with the death of the royal family but he was known to be ambitious, jealous, and manipulative with no liking for his royal brother.

Did Louis Charles escape the Temple?

Opinion is divided. According to record, a child named by the government as Louis XVII died in the Temple on June 8, 1795. No doubt exists of the child's death, only that the child was Louis XVII. At the time rumors were rife that there had been an escape and a substitution and in later years at least forty claimants came forth asserting they were Louis XVII. Their stories regarding aid received, dates, and methods of escape are as varied as the claimants themselves.

The reason I chose January 19, 1794, for the child's escape was that in the historical record that date appears to have been a mysterious turning point for the boy in the tower.

After that night the child was totally isolated and never seen alive again by any disinterested witness who had previously known and could identify him. During the next six months no sound was heard from the child by his sister, who occupied the upstairs apartment. This was an unusual circumstance since the boy had cried for two days when separated from his mother and had been clearly heard by Marie Thérèse. There were tales of his apartment being walled up, of the child being fed through a hole, but records of masonry work being done are curiously absent from the Temple accounts. There are only accounts of cleaning of stovepipes and the insertion of a glass window above the boy's stove.

Madame Simon spent her last years as a charity inmate of the Home for Incurable Diseases and was described by the sisters as a clean, well-behaved, decent old woman and perfectly sound mentally. Yet she stated to the sisters that Louis Charles had been spirited out of the Temple in a cart of dirty linen and a dumb child with rickets taken from a Paris hospital had been substituted. She still swore to this fact on her deathbed in 1819 while taking the last sacrament.

Suppositions abound that there were two substitutions during the period between January 19, 1794, and June 5, 1795. It seems strange that after the child in the Tower died, his sister, who was on the premises, was not called down to identify the body.

Of course, there are many historians who claim there was no possibility of escape, that tales of Louis Charles's survival are just that—tales.

But I find it intolerable to think of that desolate child dying in his grim, lonely Tower. I choose to think he escaped, that there was one beam of light and hope for him during the period of his darkness.

And, if I believe, and you also believe . . . then it must be so.

Iris Johansen, who has more than twenty-seven million copies of her books in print, has won many awards for her achievements in writing. The bestselling author of *Killer Dreams*, *Blind Alley*, *Firestorm*, *Fatal Tide*, *Dead Aim*, *Body of Lies*, *The Search*, and many other novels, she lives near Atlanta, Georgia, where she is currently at work on a new novel.